Edge o

Five classic scien...
complete in ... .

Robert Silverberg was born in New York in 1935. He sold his first novel while still a student at Columbia University, and has been a full-time writer since graduation. He has published more than fifty novels as well as serious works of history and archaeology, and has been nominated for more awards for his fiction than any other science fiction writer, alive or dead. He and his wife now live in San Francisco.

BY THE SAME AUTHOR

The Face Of The Waters
Kingdoms Of The Wall
Hot Sky at Midnight
Starborne
The Alien Years

The Collected Stories Of Robert Silverberg

Volume 1: Pluto In The Morning Light
Volume 2: The Secret Sharer
Volume 3: Beyond the Safe Zone
Volume 4: Nightfall
Volume 5: Ringing the Changes

Voyager

ROBERT SILVERBERG

Edge of Light

A Time Of Changes
Downward to the Earth
The Second Trip
Dying Inside
Nightwings

HarperCollinsPublishers

Voyager
An Imprint of HarperCollins*Publishers*
77–85 Fulham Palace Road,
Hammersmith, London W6 8JB

The *Voyager* World Wide Web site address is
http://www.harpercollins.co.uk/voyager

Published by *Voyager* 1998
1 3 5 7 9 8 6 4 2

A catalogue record for this book
is available from the British Library

ISBN 0 00 648 0381

Typeset in Meridien by
Palimpsest Book Production Limited,
Polmont, Stirlingshire

Printed and bound in Great Britain by
Caledonian International Book Manufacturing Ltd, Glasgow

CONTENTS

A Time Of Changes   1

Downward to the Earth   213

The Second Trip   393

Dying Inside   593

Nightwings   791

A Time of Changes

For Terry and Carol Carr

ONE

I am Kinnall Darival and I mean to tell you all about myself.

That statement is so strange to me that it screams in my eyes. I look at it on the page, and I recognize the hand as my own – narrow upright red letters on the coarse gray sheet – and I see my name, and I hear in my mind the echoes of the brain impulse that hatched those words. *I am Kinnall Darival and I mean to tell you all about myself.* Incredible.

This is to be what the Earthman Schweiz would call an autobiography. Which means an account of one's self and deeds, written by one's self. It is not a literary form that we understand on our world – I must invent my own method of narrative, for I have no precedents to guide me. But this is as it should be. On this my planet I stand alone, now. In a sense, I have invented a new way of life; I can surely invent a new sort of literature. They have always told me I have a gift for words.

So I find myself in a clapboard shack in the Burnt Lowlands, writing obscenities as I wait for death, and praising myself for my literary gifts.

I am Kinnall Darival.

Obscene! Obscene! Already on this one sheet I have used the pronoun 'I' close to twenty times, it seems. While also casually dropping such words as 'my', 'me', 'myself', more often than I care to count. A torrent of shamelessness. I I I I I. If I exposed my manhood in the Stone Chapel of Manneran on Naming Day, I would be doing nothing so foul as I am doing here. I could almost laugh. Kinnall Darival practising a solitary vice. In this miserable lonely place he massages his stinking ego and shrieks offensive pronouns into the hot wind, hoping they will sail on the gusts and soil his fellow men. He sets down sentence after sentence in the naked syntax of madness. He would, if he could, seize you by the wrist and pour cascades of filth into your unwilling ear. And why? Is proud Darival in fact insane? Has his sturdy spirit entirely collapsed under the gnawing of mindsnakes? Is nothing left but the shell of him, sitting in this dreary hut, obsessively titillating himself with disreputable language, muttering 'I' and 'me' and 'my' and 'myself', blearily threatening to reveal the intimacies of his soul?

No. It is Darival who is sane and all of you who are sick, and though I know how mad that sounds, I will let it stand. I am no lunatic muttering filth to wring a feeble pleasure from a chilly universe. I have passed through a time of changes, and I have been healed of the sickness that affects those who inhabit my world, and in writing what I intend to write I hope to heal you as well, though I know you are on your way into the Burnt Lowlands to slay me for my hopes.

So be it.

I am Kinnall Darival and I mean to tell you all about myself.

TWO

Lingering vestiges of the customs against which I rebel still plague me. Perhaps you can begin to comprehend what an effort it is for me to frame my sentences in this style, to twist my verbs around in order to fit the first-person construction. I have been writing ten minutes and my body is covered with sweat, not the hot sweat of the burning air about me but the dank, clammy sweat of mental struggle. I know the style I must use, but the muscles of my arm rebel against me, and fight to put down the words in the old fashion, saying, *One has been writing for ten minutes and one's body is covered with sweat*, saying, *One has passed through a time of changes, and he has been healed of the sickness that affects those who inhabit his world.* I suppose that much of what I have written could have been phrased in the old way, and no harm done; but I do battle against the self-effacing grammar of my world, and if I must, I will joust with my own muscles for the right to arrange my words according to my present manner of philosophy.

In any case, however my former habits trick me into misconstructing my sentences, my meaning will blaze through the screen of words. I may say, 'I am Kinnal Darival and I mean to tell you all about myself,' or I may say, 'One's name is Kinnall Darival and he means to tell you all about himself,' but there is no real difference. Either way, the content of Kinnal Darival's statement is – by your standards, by the standards I would destroy – disgusting, contemptible, obscene.

THREE

Also I am troubled, at least in these early pages, by the identity of my audience. I assume, because I must, that I will have readers. But who are they? Who are you? Men and women of my native planet, perhaps, furtively turning my pages by torchlight, dreading the knock at the door. Or maybe otherworlders, reading for amusement, scanning my book for the insight it may give into an alien and repellent society. I have no idea. I can establish no easy relationship with you, my unknown reader. When I first conceived my plan of setting down my soul on paper, I thought it would be simple, a mere confessional, nothing but an extended session with an imaginary drainer who would listen endlessly and at last give me absolution. But now I realize I must take another approach. If you are not of my world, or if you are of my world but not of my time, you may find much here that is incomprehensible.

Therefore I must explain. Possibly I will explain too much, and drive you off by pounding you with the obvious. Forgive

me if I instruct you in what you already know. Forgive me if
my tone and mode of attack show lapses of consistency and
I seem to be addressing myself to someone else. For you will
not hold still for me, my unknown reader. You wear many
faces for me. Now I see the crooked nose of Jidd the drainer,
and now the suave smile of my bondbrother Noim Condorit,
and now the silkiness of my bondsister Halum, and now you
become the tempter Schweiz of pitiful Earth, and now you are
my son's son's son's son's son, not to be born for a cluster of
years and eager to know what manner of man your ancestor
was, and now you are some stranger of a different planet, to
whom we of Borthan are grotesque, mysterious, and baffling.
I do not know you, and so I will be clumsy in my attempts to
talk to you.

But, by Salla's Gate, before I am done you will know me, as
no man of Borthan has ever been known by others before!

FOUR

I am a man of middle years. Thirty times since the day of my
birth has Borthan travelled around our golden green sun, and
on our world a man is considered old if he has lived through
fifty such circuits, while the most ancient man of whom I ever
heard died just short of his eightieth. From this you may be
able to calculate our spans in terms of yours, if otherworlder
you happen to be. The Earthman Schweiz claimed an age of
forty-three years by his planet's reckoning, yet he seemed no
older than I.

My body is strong. Here I shall commit a double sin, for not
only shall I speak of myself without shame, but I shall show
pride and pleasure in my physical self. I am tall: a woman of
normal height reaches barely to the lower vault of my chest.
My hair is dark and long, falling to my shoulders. Lately streaks
of gray have appeared in it, and likewise in my beard, which is

full and thick, covering much of my face. My nose is prominent and straight, with a wide bridge and large nostrils; my lips are fleshy and give me, so it is said, a look of sensuality; my eyes are deep brown and are set somewhat far apart in my skull. They have, I am given to understand, the appearance of the eyes of one who has been accustomed all his life to commanding other men.

My back is broad and my chest is deep. A dense mat of coarse dark hair grows nearly everywhere on me. My arms are long. My hands are large. My muscles are well developed and stand out prominently beneath my skin. I move gracefully for a man my size, with smooth co-ordination; I excel in sports, and when I was younger I hurled the feathered shaft the entire length of Manneran Stadium, a feat that had never been achieved until then.

Most women find me attractive – all but those who prefer a flimsier, more scholarly looking sort of man and are frightened of strength and size and virility. Certainly the political power I have held in my time has helped to bring many partners to my couch, but no doubt they were drawn to me as much by the look of my body as by anything more subtle. Most of them have been disappointed in me. Bulging muscles and a hairy hide do not a skilled lover make, nor is a massive genital member such as mine any guarantee of ecstasy. I am no champion of copulation. See: I hide nothing from you. There is in me a certain constitutional impatience that expresses itself outwardly only during the carnal act; when I enter a woman I find myself swiftly swept away, and rarely can I sustain the deed until her pleasure comes. To no one, not even a drainer, have I confessed this failing before, nor did I ever expect that I would. But a good many women of Borthan have learned of this my great flaw in the most immediate possible way, to their cost, and doubtless some of them, embittered, have circulated the news in order that they might enjoy a scratchy joke at my expense. So I place it on the record here, for perspective's sake. I would not have you think of me as a hairy mighty giant without also your knowing how often my flesh has betrayed

my lusts. Possibly this failing of mine was among the forces that
shaped my destinies towards this day in the Burnt Lowlands,
and you should know of that.

FIVE

My father was hereditary septarch of the province of Salla on
our eastern coast. My mother was daughter to a septarch of
Glin; he met her on a diplomatic mission, and their mating
was, it was said, ordained from the moment they beheld one
another. The first child born to them was my brother Stirron,
now septarch in Salla in our father's place. I followed two years
later; there were three more after me, all of them girls. Two
of these still live. My youngest sister was slain by raiders from
Glin some twenty moontimes ago.

I knew my father poorly. On Borthan everyone is a stranger
to everyone, but one's father is customarily less remote from
one than others; not so with the old septarch. Between us lay
an impenetrable wall of formality. In addressing him we used
the same formulas of respect that subjects employed. His smiles
were so infrequent that I think I can recall each one. Once,
and it was unforgettable, he took me up beside him on his
rough-hewn blackwood throne, and let me touch the ancient
yellow cushion, and called me fondly by my child-name; it
was the day my mother died. Otherwise he ignored me. I
feared and loved him, and crouched trembling behind pillars
in his court to watch him dispense justice, thinking that
if he saw me there he would have me destroyed, and yet
unable to deprive myself of the sight of my father in his
majesty.

He was, oddly, a man of slender body and modest height,
over whom my brother and I towered even when we were
boys. But there was a terrible strength of will in him that
led him to surmount every challenge. Once in my childhood

there came some ambassador to the septarchy, a hulking sun-blackened westerner who stands in my memory no smaller than Kongoroi Mountain; probably he was as tall and broad as I am now. At feasting-time the ambassador let too much blue wine down his throat, and said, before my father and his courtiers and his family, 'One would show his strength to the men of Salla, to whom he may be able to teach something of wrestling.'

'There is one here,' my father replied in sudden fury, 'to whom, perhaps, nothing need be taught.'

'Let him be produced,' the huge westerner said, rising and peeling back his cloak. But my father, smiling – and the sight of that smile made his courtiers quake – told the boastful stranger it would not be fair to make him compete while his mind was fogged with wine, and this of course maddened the ambassador beyond words. The musicians came in then to ease the tension, but the anger of our visitor did not subside, and, after an hour, when the drunkenness had lifted somewhat from him, he demanded again to meet my father's champion. No man of Salla, said our guest, would be able to withstand his might.

Whereupon the septarch said, 'I will wrestle you myself.'

That night my brother and I were sitting at the far end of the long table, among the women. Down from the throne-end came the stunning word 'I' in my father's voice, and an instant later came 'myself'. These were obscenities that Stirron and I had often whispered, sniggering, in the darkness of our bedchamber, but we had never imagined we would hear them hurled forth in the feasting-hall from the septarch's own lips. In our shock we reacted differently, Stirron jerking convulsively and knocking over his goblet, myself letting loose a half-suppressed shrill giggle of embarrassment and delight that earned me an instant slap from a lady-in-waiting. My laughter was merely the mask for my inner horror. I could barely believe that my father knew those words, let alone that he would say them before this august company. *I will wrestle you myself*. And while the reverberations of the forbidden forms of speech still dizzied me, my father swiftly stepped forward, dropping his

cloak, and faced the great hulk of an ambassador, and closed
with him, and caught him by one elbow and one haunch in
a deft Sallan hold, and sent him almost immediately toppling
to the polished floor of grey stone. The ambassador uttered a
terrible cry, for one of his legs was sticking strangely out at a
frightening angle from his hip, and in pain and humiliation he
pounded the flat of his hand again and again against the floor.
Perhaps diplomacy is practised in more sophisticated ways now
in the palace of my brother Stirron.

The septarch died when I was twelve and just coming into
the first rush of my manhood. I was near his side when death
took him. To escape the time of rains in Salla he would go each
year to hunt the hornfowl in the Burnt Lowlands, in the very
district where now I hide and wait. I had never gone with him,
but on this occasion I was permitted to accompany the hunting
party, for now I was a young prince and must learn the skills
of my class. Stirron, as a future septarch, had other skills to
master; he remained behind as regent in our father's absence
from the capital. Under a bleak and heavy sky bowed with
rainclouds the expedition of some twenty groundcars rolled
westward out of Salla City and through the flat, sodden,
winter-bare countryside. The rains were merciless that year,
knifing away the precious sparse topsoil and laying bare the
rocky bones of our province. Everywhere the farmers were
repairing their dikes, but to no avail; I could see the swollen
rivers running yellow-brown with Salla's lost wealth, and I
nearly wept to think of such treasure being carried into the
sea. As we came into West Salla, the narrow road began to
climb the foothills of the Huishtor range, and soon we were
in drier, colder country, where the skies gave snow and not
rain, and the trees were mere bundles of sticks against the
blinding whiteness. Up we went into the Huishtors, following
the Kongoroi road. The countryfolk came out to chant welcomes to the septarch as he passed. Now the naked mountains
stood like purple teeth ripping the grey sky, and even in our
sealed groundcars we shivered, although the beauty of this
tempestuous place took my mind from my discomforts. Here

great flat shields of striated tawny rock flanked the rugged road, and there was scarcely any soil at all, nor did trees or shrubs grow except in sheltered places. We could look back and see all of Salla like its own map below us, the whiteness of the western districts, the dark clutter of the populous eastern shore, everything diminished, unreal. I had never been this far from home before. Though we were now deep into the uplands, midway, as it were, between sea and sky, the inner peaks of the Huishtors still lay before us, and to my eye they formed an unbroken wall of stone spanning the continent from north to south. Their snow-covered summits jutted raggedly from that continuous lofty breastwork of bare rock: were we supposed to go over the top, or would there be some way through? I knew of Salla's Gate, and that our route lay towards it, but somehow the gate seemed mere myth to me at that moment.

Up and up and up we rode, until the generators of our groundcars were gasping in the frosty air, and we were compelled to pause frequently to defrost the power conduits, and our heads whirled from shortness of oxygen. Each night we rested at one of the camps maintained for the use of travelling septarchs, but the accommodations were far from regal, and at one, where the entire staff of servants had perished some weeks before in a snow-slide, it was necessary for us to dig our way through mounds of ice in order to enter. We were all of us in the party men of the nobility, and all of us wielded shovels except the septarch himself, for whom manual labor would have been sinful. Because I was one of the biggest and strongest of the men, I dug more vigorously than anyone, and because I was young and rash, I strained myself beyond my strength, collapsing over my shovel and lying half dead in the snow for an hour until I was noticed. My father came to me while they were treating me, and smiled one of his rare smiles; just then I believed it was a gesture of affection, and it greatly sped my recovery, but afterwards I came to see it was more likely a sign of his contempt.

That smile buoyed me through the remainder of our ascent of the Huishtors. No longer did I fret about getting over the mountains, for I knew that I would, and on the far side my father and I would hunt the hornfowl in the Burnt Lowlands, going out together, guarding one another from peril, collaborating ultimately on the tracking and on the kill, knowing a closeness that had never existed between us in my childhood. I talked of that one night to my bondbrother Noim Condorit, who rode with me in my groundcar, and who was the only person in the universe to whom I could say such things. 'One hopes to be chosen for the septarch's own hunt-group,' I said. 'One has reason to think that one will be asked. And an end made to the distance between father and son.'

'You dream,' said Noim Condorit. 'You live in fantasies.'

'One could wish,' I replied, 'for warmer encouragement from one's bondbrother.'

Noim was ever a pessimist; I took his dourness in stride, and counted the days to Salla's Gate. When we reached it, I was unprepared for the splendor of the place. All morning and half an afternoon we had been following a thirty-degree grade up the broad breast of Kongoroi Mountain, shrouded in the shadow of the great double summit. It seemed to me we would climb forever and still have Kongoroi looming over us. Then our caravan swung around to the left, car after car disappearing behind a snowy pylon on the flank of the road, and our car's turn came, and when we had turned the corner, I beheld an astonishing sight: a wide break in the mountain wall, as if some cosmic hand had pried away one corner of Kongoroi. Through the gap came daylight in a glittering burst. This was Salla's Gate, the miraculous pass across which our ancestors came when first they entered our province, so many hundreds of years back, after their wanderings in the Burnt Lowlands. We plunged joyously into it, riding two and even three cars abreast over the hard-packed snow, and before we made camp for the night we were able to see the strange splendor of the Burnt Lowlands spread out astonishingly below us.

All the next day and the one that followed we rode the switchbacks down Kongoroi's western slope, creeping at a comical pace along a road that had little room to spare for us: a careless twitch of the stick and one's car would tumble into an infinite abyss. There was no snow on this face of the Huishtors, and the raw sun-pounded rock had a numbing, oppressive look. Ahead everything was red soil. Down into the desert we went, quitting winter and entering a stifling world where every breath tingled in the lungs, where dry winds lifted the ground in clouds, where odd twisted-looking beasts scampered in terror from our oncoming cavalcade. On the sixth day we reached the hunting-grounds, a place of ragged escarpments far below sea level. I am no more than an hour's ride from that place now. Here the hornfowl have their nests; all day long they range the baking plains, seeking meat, and at twilight they return, collapsing groundward in weird spiralling flight to enter their all but inaccessible burrows.

In the dividing of personnel I was one of thirteen chosen for the septarch's companions. 'One shares your joy,' Noim told me solemnly, and there were tears in his eyes as well as in mine, for he knew what pain my father's coldness had brought me. At daybreak the hunt-groups set out, nine of them, in nine directions.

To take a hornfowl near its nest is deemed shameful. The bird returning is usually laden with meat for its young, and it therefore is clumsy and vulnerable, shorn of all its grace and power. Killing one as it plummets is no great task, but only a craven selfbarer would attempt it. (*Selfbarer!* See how my own pen mocks me! I, who have bared more self than any ten men of Borthan, still unconsciously use the term as a word of abuse! But let it stand.) I mean to say that the virtue in hunting lies in the perils and difficulties of the chase, not in the taking of the trophy, and we hunt the hornfowl as a challenge to our skills, not for its dismal flesh.

Thus hunters go into the open Lowlands, where even in winter the sun is devastating, where there are no trees to give shade or streams to ease the thirst. They spread out, one man here, two men there, taking up stations in that trackless expanse of barren red soil, offering themselves as the hornfowl's prey. The bird cruises at inconceivable heights, soaring so far overhead that it can be seen only as a black scratch in the brilliant dome of the sky; it takes the keenest vision to detect one, though a hornfowl's wingspread is twice the length of a man's body. From its lofty place the hornfowl scans the desert for incautious beasts. Nothing, no matter how small, escapes its glossy eyes; and when it detects good quarry, it comes down through the turbulent air until it hovers house-high above the ground. Now it commences its killing-flight, flying low, launching itself on a series of savage circles, spinning a death-knot around its still unsuspecting victim. The first swing may sweep over the equivalent of half a province's area, but each successive circuit is tighter and tighter, while acceleration mounts, until ultimately the hornfowl has made itself a frightful engine of death that comes roaring in from the horizon at nightmarish velocity. Now the quarry learns the truth, but it is knowledge not held for long: the rustle of mighty wings, the hiss of a slim powerful form cleaving the hot sluggish air, and then the single long deadly spear sprouting from the bird's bony forehead finds its mark, and the victim falls, enfolded in the black fluttering wings. The hunter hopes to bring down his hornfowl while it cruises, almost at the limits of human sight; he carries a weapon designed for long-range shooting, and the test is in the aim, whether he can calculate the interplay of trajectories at such vast distances. The peril of hunting hornfowl is this, that one never knows if one is the hunter or the hunted, for a hornfowl on its killing-flight cannot be seen until it strikes its stroke.

So I went forth. So I stood from dawn to midday. The sun worked its will on my winter-pale skin, such of it as I dared to expose; most of me was swaddled in hunting clothes of soft crimson leather, within which I boiled. I sipped from my canteen no more often than survival demanded, for I imagined that the eyes of my comrades were upon me and I would reveal no weaknesses to them. We were arrayed in a double hexagon with my father alone between the two groups. Chance had it that I drew the point of my hexagon closest to him, but it was more than a feathered shaft's toss from his place to mine, and all the morning long the septarch and I exchanged not a syllable. He stood with feet planted firm, watching the skies, his weapon at ready. If he drank at all as he waited, I did not see him do it. I too studied the skies, until my eyes ached for it, until I felt twin strands of hot light drilling my brain and hammering against the back wall of my skull. More than once I imagined I saw the dark splinter of a hornfowl's shape drifting into view up there, and once in sweaty haste I came to the verge of raising my gun to it, which would have brought me shame, for one must not shoot until one has established priority of sighting by crying one's claim. I did not fire, and when I blinked and opened my eyes, I saw nothing in the sky. The hornfowl seemed to be elsewhere that morning.

At noon my father gave a signal, and we spread farther apart over the plain, maintaining our formation. Perhaps the hornfowl found us too closely clustered, and were staying away. My new position lay on top of a low earthen mound, in the form almost of a woman's breast, and fear took hold of me as I took up my place on it. I supposed myself to be terribly exposed and in imminent peril of hornfowl attack. As fright crept through my spirit, I became convinced that a hornfowl was even now flying its fatal circuits around my hummock, and that at any moment its lance would pierce my kidneys while I gazed stupidly at the metallic sky. The premonition grew so strong that I had to struggle to hold my ground; I shivered, I stole wary peeks over my shoulders, I clenched the stock of my gun for comfort, I strained my ears for the sound of my enemy's approach, hoping to whirl and fire before I was speared. For this cowardice I reproached myself severely, even offering thanks that Stirron had been born before me, since obviously I was unfit to succeed to the septarchy. I reminded myself that not in three years had a hunter been killed in this way. I asked myself if it was plausible that I should die so young, on my first hunt, when there were others like my father who had hunted for thirty seasons and gone unscathed. I demanded to know why I felt this overwhelming fear, when all my tutors had labored to teach me that the self is a void and concern for one's person a wicked sin. Was not my father in equal jeopardy, far across the sun-smitten plain? And had he not much more than I to lose, being a septarch and a prime septarch at that, while I was only a boy? In this way I cudgelled the fear from my damp soul, and studied the sky without regard for the spear that might be aimed at my back, and in minutes my former fretting seemed an absurdity to me. I would stand here for days, if need be, unafraid. At once I had the reward of this triumph over self: against the shimmering fierceness of the sky I made out a dark floating form, a notch in the heavens, and this time it was no illusion, for my youthful eyes spied wings and horn. Did the others see it? Was the bird mine to attempt? If I made the kill, would the septarch pound my back and call me his best son? All was silence from the other hunters.

'One cries claim!' I shouted jubilantly, and lifted my weapon, and eyed the sight, remembering what I had been taught, to let the inner mind make the calculations, to aim and fire in one swift impulse before the intellect, by quibbling, could spoil the intuition's command.

And in the instant before I sent my bolt aloft there came a ghastly outcry from my left, and I fired without aiming at all, turning in the same instant towards my father's place, and seeing him half hidden beneath the madly flapping form of another hornfowl that had gored him from spine to belly. The air about them was clouded with red sand as the monster's wings furiously slapped the ground; the bird was struggling to take off, but a hornfowl cannot lift a man's weight, though this does not prevent them from attacking us. I ran to aid the septarch. He still was shouting, and I saw his hands clutching for the hornfowl's scrawny throat, but now there was a liquid quality about his cries, a bubbling tone, and when I reached the scene – I was the first one there – he lay sprawled and quiet, with the bird still rammed through him and covering his body like a black cloak. My blade was out; I slashed the hornfowl's neck as if it were a length of hose, kicked the carcass aside, began to wrench desperately at the demonic head mounted so hideously upon the septarch's upturned back. Now the others came; they pulled me away; someone seized me by the shoulders and shook me until my fit was past. When I turned to them again, they closed their ranks, to keep me from seeing my father's corpse, and then, to my dismay, they dropped to their knees before me to do homage.

But of course it was Stirron and not I who became septarch in Salla. His crowning was a grand event, for, young though he was, he would be the prime septarch of the province. Salla's six other septarchs came to the capital – only on such an occasion were they ever to be found at once in the same city – and for a time everything was feasting and banners and the blare of trumpets. Stirron was at the centre of it all, and I on the margins, which was as it should be, though it left me feeling more like a stableboy than a prince. Once he was enthroned, Stirron offered me titles and land and power, but he did not really expect me to accept, and I did not. Unless a septarch is a weakling, his younger brothers had best not stay nearby to help him rule, for such help is not desired often. I had had no living uncles on my father's side of the family, and I did not care to have Stirron's sons be able to make the same statement; therefore I took myself quickly from Salla once the time of mourning was ended.

I went to Glin, my mother's land. There, however, things were unsatisfactory for me, and after a few years I moved on to the steamy province of Manneran, where I won my wife and sired my sons and became a prince in more than name, and lived happily and sturdily until my time of changes began.

SIX

Perhaps I should set down some words concerning my world's geography.

There are five continents on our planet of Borthan. In

this hemisphere there are two, Velada Borthan and Sumara Borthan, which is to say, the Northern World and the Southern World. It is a long sea journey from any shore of these continents to the continents of the opposite hemisphere, which have been named merely Umbis, Dabis, Tibis, that is, One, Two, Three.

Of those three distant lands I can tell you very little. They first were explored some seven hundred years ago by a septarch of Glin, who laid down his life for his curiosity, and there have not been five seeking-parties to them in all the time since. No human folk dwell in that hemisphere. Umbis is said to be largely like the Burnt Lowlands, but worse, with golden flames bursting from the tormented land in many places. Dabis is jungles and fever-ridden swamps, and someday will be full of our people hoping to prove manhood, for I understand it is thick with dangerous beasts. Tibis is covered with ice.

We are not a race afflicted with the wanderlust. I myself was never a voyager until circumstances made me one. Though the blood of the ancient Earthmen flows in our veins, and they were wanderers whose demons drove them out to prowl the stars, we of Borthan stay close to home. Even I who am somewhat different from my comrades in my way of thinking never hungered to see the snowfields of Tibis or the marshes of Dabis, except perhaps when I was a child and eager to gobble all the universe. Among us it is considered a great thing merely to journey from Salla to Glin, and rare indeed is the man who has crossed the continent, let alone ventured to Sumara Borthan, as I have done.

As I have done.

Velada Borthan is the home of our civilization. The mapmakers' art reveals it to be a large squarish land-mass with rounded corners. Two great V-shaped indentations puncture its periphery: along the northern coast, midway between the eastern and western corners, there is the Polar Gulf, and, due south on the opposite coast, there is the Gulf of Sumar. Between those two bodies of water lie the Lowlands, a trough that spans the entire continent from north to south. No point in the Lowlands rises higher above sea level than the height of five men, and there are many places, notably in the Burnt Lowlands, that are far below sea level.

There is a folktale we tell our children concerning the shape of Velada Borthan. We say that the great iceworm Hrungir, born in the waters of the North Polar Sea, stirred and woke one day in sudden appetite, and began to nibble at the northern shore of Velada Borthan. The worm chewed for a thousand thousand years, until it had eaten out the Polar Gulf. Then, its voracity having made it somewhat ill, it crawled up on the land to rest and digest what it had devoured. Uneasy at the stomach, Hrungir wriggled southward, causing the land to sink beneath its vast weight and the mountains to rise, in compensation, to the east and west of its resting-place. The worm rested longest in the Burnt Lowlands, which accordingly were depressed more deeply than any other region. In time the worm's appetite revived, and it resumed its southward crawl, coming at last to a place where a range of mountains running from east to west barred its advance. Then it chewed the mountains, creating Stroin Gap, and proceeded towards our southern coast. In another fit of hunger the worm bit out the Gulf of Sumar. The waters of the Strait of Sumar rushed in to fill the place where the land had been, and the rising tide carried Hrungir to the continent of Sumara Borthan, where now the iceworm lives, coiled beneath the volcano Vashnir and emitting poisonous fumes. So the fable goes.

The long narrow basin that we think of as Hrungir's track is divided into three districts. At the northern end we have the Frozen Lowlands, a place of perpetual ice where no man is ever seen. Legend has it that the air is so dry and cold that a single breath will turn a man's lungs to leather. The polar influence reaches only a short distance into our continent, however. South of the Frozen Lowlands lie the immense Burnt Lowlands, which are almost totally without water, and on which the full fury of our sun constantly falls. Our two towering north-south mountain ranges prevent a drop of rain from entering the Burnt Lowlands, nor do any rivers or streams reach it. The soil is bright red, with occasional yellow streaks, and this we blame on the heat of Hrungir's belly, though our geologists tell another tale. Small plants live in the Burnt Lowlands, taking their nourishment from I know not where, and there are many kinds of beasts, all of them strange, deformed and unpleasant. At the southern end of the Burnt Lowlands there is a deep east-west valley, several days' journey in breadth, and on its far side lies the small district known as the Wet Lowlands. Northerly breezes coming off the Gulf of Sumar carry moisture through Stroin Gap; these winds meet the fierce hot blasts out of the Burnt Lowlands and are forced to drop their burden not far above the Gap, creating a land of dense, lush vegetation. Never do the water-laden breezes from the south succeed in getting north of the Wet Lowlands to bathe the zone of red soil. The Frozen Lowlands, as I have said, go forever unvisited, and the Burnt Lowlands are entered only by hunters and those who must travel between the eastern and western coasts, but the Wet Lowlands are populated by several thousand farmers, who raise exotic fruits for the city folk. I am told that the constant rain rots their souls, that they have no form of government, and that our customs of self-denial are imperfectly observed. I would be among them now, to discover their nature at first hand, if only I could slip through the cordon that my enemies have set up to the south of this place.

The Lowlands are flanked by two immense mountain ranges: the Huishtors in the east, the Threishtors in the west. These mountains begin on Velada Borthan's northern coast, virtually at the shores of the North Polar Sea, and march southward, gradually curving inland; the two ranges would join not far from the Gulf of Sumar if they were not separated by Stroin Gap. They are so high that they intercept all winds. Therefore their inland slopes are barren, but the slopes facing the oceans enjoy fertility.

Mankind in Velada Borthan has carved out its domain in the two coastal strips, between the oceans and the mountains. In most places the land is at best marginal, so that we are hard put to have all the food we need, and life is constant struggle against hunger. Often one wonders why our ancestors, when they came to this planet so many generations ago, chose Velada Borthan as their settling-place; the farming would have been far easier in the neighboring continent of Sumara Borthan, and even swampy Dabis might have offered more cheer. The explanation we are given is that our forefathers were stern, diligent folk who relished challenge, and feared to let their children dwell in a place where life might be insufficiently harsh. Velada Borthan's coasts were neither uninhabitable nor unduly comfortable; therefore they suited the purposes. I believe this to be true, for certainly the chief heritage we have from those ancient ones is the notion that comfort is sin and ease is wickedness. My bondbrother Noim, though, once remarked that the first settlers chose Velada Borthan because that was where their starship happened to come down, and, having hauled themselves across all the immensities of space, they lacked the energy to travel onward even one more continent in quest of a better home. I doubt it, but the slyness of the idea is characteristic of my bondbrother's taste for irony.

The firstcomers planted their initial settlement on the western coast, at the place we call Threish, that is, the place of the Covenant. They multiplied rapidly, and, because they were a stubborn and quarrelsome tribe, they splintered early, this group and that going off to live apart. Thus the nine western provinces came into being. To this day there are bitter border disputes among them.

In time the limited resources of the west were exhausted, and emigrants sought the eastern coast. We had no air transport then, not that we have a great deal now; we are not a mechanically minded people, and we lack natural resources to serve as fuel. Thus they went east by groundcar, or whatever served as groundcars then. The three Threishtor passes were discovered, and the bold ones bravely entered the Burnt Lowlands. We sing long mythic epics of the hardships of these crossings. Getting over the Threishtors into the Lowlands was difficult, but getting out on the far side was close to impossible, for there is only one route over the Huishtors out of the red-soil country fit for humans, and that is by way of Salla's Gate, the finding of which was no small task. But they found it and poured through, and established my land of Salla. When the quarrelling came, a good many went north and founded Glin, and later others went south to settle in holy Manneran. For a thousand years it was sufficient to have but three provinces in the east, until in a new quarrel the small but prosperous maritime kingdom of Krell carved itself out of a corner of Glin and a corner of Salla.

There also were some folk who could not abide life in Velada Borthan at all, and put to sea from Manneran, sailing off to settle in Sumara Borthan. But one need not speak of them in a geography lesson; I will have much to say of Sumara Borthan and its people when I have begun to explain the changes that entered my life.

SEVEN

This cabin where I hide myself now is a shabby thing. Its clapboard walls were indifferently put together to begin with, and now are crazed, so that gaps yawn at the joins and no angle is true. The desert wind passes through here unhindered; my page bears a light coating of red soil, my clothes are caked with it, even my hair has a red tinge. Lowlands creatures crawl freely in with me: I see two of them moving about the earthen floor now, a many-legged gray thing the size of my thumb and a sluggish two-tailed serpent not so long as my foot. For hours they have circled one another idly, as though they wish to be mortal foes but cannot decide which of them is to eat the other. Dry companions for a parched time.

I should not mock this place, though. Someone troubled to drag its makings here, in order that weary hunters might

have shelter in this inhospitable land. Someone put it together,
doubtless with more love than skill, and left it here for me, and
it serves me well. Perhaps it is no fit home for a septarch's son,
but I have known my share of palaces, and I no longer need
stone walls and groined ceilings. It is peaceful here. I am far
from the fishmongers and the drainers and the wine-peddlers
and all those others whose songs of commerce clang in the
streets of cities. A man can think; a man can look within his
soul, and find those things that have been the shaping of him,
and draw them forth, and examine them, and come to know
himself. In this our world we are forbidden by custom to make
our souls known to others, yes, but why has no one before me
observed that that same custom, without intending it, keeps
us from coming to know ourselves? For nearly all my life I
kept the proper social walls between myself and others, and
not till the walls were down did I see I had walled myself
away from myself as well. But here in the Burnt Lowlands I
have had time to contemplate these matters and to arrive at
understanding. This is not the place I would have chosen for
myself, but I am not unhappy here.

I do not think they will find me for some while yet.

Now it is too dark in here to write. I will stand by the cabin
door and watch the night come rolling across the Lowlands
towards the Huishtors. Perhaps there will be hornfowl drifting
through the dusk, heading home from an empty hunt. The
stars will blaze. Schweiz once tried to show me the sun of
Earth from a mountaintop in Sumara Borthan, and insisted
he could see it, and begged me to squint along the line of his
pointing hand, but I think he was playing a game with me. I
think that that sun may not be seen at all from our sector of
the galaxy. Schweiz played many a game with me when we
travelled together, and perhaps he will play more such games
one day, if ever we meet again, if still he lives.

EIGHT

Last night in a dream my bondsister Halum Helalam came to me.

With her there can never be more games, and only through the slippery-walled tunnel of dreams is she apt to reach me. Therefore while I slept she glowed in my mind more brightly than any star that lights this desert, but waking brought me sadness and shame, and the memory of my loss of her who is irreplaceable.

Halum of my dream wore only a light filmy veil through which her small rosy-tipped breasts showed, and her slim thighs, and her flat belly, the belly of an unchilded woman. It was not the way she often dressed in life, especially when paying a call on her bondbrother, but this was the Halum of my dream, made wanton by my lonely and troubled soul. Her smile was warm and tender and her dark shining eyes glistened with love.

In dreams one's mind lives on many levels. On one level of mine I was a detached observer, floating in a haze of moonlight somewhere near the roof of my hut, looking down upon my own sleeping body. On another level I lay asleep. The dream-self that slept did not perceive Halum's presence, but the dream-self that watched was aware of her, and I, the true dreamer, was aware of them both, and also aware that all I saw was coming to me in a vision. But inevitably there was some mingling of these levels of reality, so that I could not be sure who was the dreamer and who the dreamed, nor was I certain that the Halum who stood before me in such radiance was a creature of my fantasy rather than the living Halum I once had known.

'Kinnall,' she whispered, and in my dream I imagined that my sleeping dream-self awoke, propping himself upon his elbows, with Halum kneeling close beside his cot. She leaned forward until her breasts brushed the shaggy chest of that man who was I, and touched her lips to mine in a flick of a caress, and said, 'You look so weary, Kinnall.'

'You should not have come here.'

'One was needed. One came.'

'It is not right. To enter the Burnt Lowlands alone, to seek out one who has brought you only harm –'

'The bond that links one to you is sacred.'

'You've suffered enough for that bond Halum.'

'One has not suffered at all,' she said, and kissed my sweaty forehead. 'How *you* must suffer, hiding in this dismal oven!'

'It is no more than one has earned,' I said.

Even in my dream I spoke to Halum in the polite grammatical form. I had never found it easy to use the first person with her; certainly I never used it before my changes, and afterwards, when no reason remained for me to be so chaste with her, I still could not. My soul and my heart had yearned to say 'I' to Halum, and my tongue and lips were padlocked by propriety.

She said, 'You deserve so much more than this place. You must come forth from exile. You must guide us, Kinnall, towards a new Covenant, a Covenant of love, of trust in one another.'

'One fears he has been a failure as a prophet. One doubts the value of continuing such efforts.'

'It was all so strange to you, so new!' she said. 'But you were able to change, Kinnall, and to bring changes to others –'

'To bring grief to others and to oneself.'

'No. No. What you tried to do was right. How can you give up now? How can you resign yourself to death? There's a world out there in need of being freed, Kinnall!'

'One is trapped in this place. One's capture is inevitable.'

'The desert is wide. You can slip away from them.'

'The desert is wide, but the gates are few, and all of them are watched. There's no escape.'

She shook her head, and smiled, and pressed her hands urgently against my hips, and said, in a voice thick with hope, 'I will lead you to safety. Come with me, Kinnall.'

The sound of that *I* and the *me* that followed it, out of

Halum's imagined mouth, fell upon my dreaming soul like a rainfall of rusted spikes, and the shock of hearing those obscenities in her sweet voice nearly awakened me. This thing I tell you to make it clear that I am not fully converted to my own changed way of life, that the reflexes of my upbringing still govern me in the deepest corners of my soul. In dreams we reveal our true selves, and my reaction of numb dismay to the words that I had placed (for who else could have done it?) in the dream-Halum's mouth told me a great deal about my innermost attitudes. What happened next was also revealing, though far less subtle. To urge me from my cot Halum's hands slipped over my body, working their way through the tangled thatch over my gut, and her cool fingers seized the stiffened rod of my sex. Instantly my heart thundered and my seed spurted, and the ground heaved as though the Lowlands were splitting apart, and Halum uttered a little cry of fear. I reached for her, but she was growing indistinct and insubstantial, and in one terrible convulsion of the planet I lost sight of her and she was gone. And there was so much I had wanted to say to her, so many things I had meant to ask. I woke, coming up through the levels of my dream. I found myself alone in the hut, of course, sticky-skinned with my outpourings and sickened by the villainies that my shameful mind, allowed to roam the night unfettered, had concocted.

'*Halum!*' I cried. 'Halum, Halum, Halum!'

My voice made the cabin quiver, but she did not return. And slowly my sleep-fogged mind grasped the truth, that the Halum who had visited me had been unreal.

We of Borthan do not take such visions lightly, however. I rose, and went from my cabin into the darkness outside, and walked about, scuffing at the warm sand with my bare toes as I struggled to excuse my inventions to myself. Slowly I calmed. Slowly I came to equilibrium. Yet I sat by my doorstep unsleeping for hours, until dawn's first green fingers crept upon me.

Beyond doubt you will agree with me that a man who has been apart from women some time, living under the tensions

I have known since my flight into the Burnt Lowlands, will occasionally experience such sexual eruptions in his sleep, nor is there anything unnatural about them. I must maintain also, though I have little enough evidence to prove it, that many men of Borthan find themselves giving way in slumber to expressions of desire for their bondsisters, simply because such desires are so rigidly repressed in the waking time. And further, although Halum and I enjoyed intimacies of soul far beyond those which men customarily enjoy with their bondsisters, never once did I seek her physically, nor did such a union ever occur. Take this on faith, if you will: in these pages I tell you so much that is discreditable to me, making no attempt to conceal that which is shameful, that if I had violated Halum's bond I would tell you that as well. So you must believe that it was not a deed I did. You may not hold me guilty of sins committed in dreams.

Nevertheless I held myself guilty through the waning of the night and into this morning, and only as I purge myself now by putting the incident on paper does the darkness lift from my spirit. I think what has really troubled me these past few hours is not so much my sordid little sexual fantasy, for which even my enemies would probably forgive me, as it is my belief that I am responsible for Halum's death, for which I am unable to forgive myself.

NINE

Possibly I should say that every man of Borthan, and by the same token every woman, is sworn at birth or soon thereafter to a bondsister and bondbrother. No member of any such tripling may be blood-kin to any other. The bondings are arranged soon after a child is conceived, and often are the subject of intricate negotiation, since one's bondbrother and bondsister are customarily closer to one than one's own family-by-blood; hence a father owes it to his child to make the bondings with care.

Because I was to be a septarch's second son, arranging my bondings was a matter of high circumstance. It might have been good democracy, but poor sense, to bond me to a peasant's child, for one must be reared on the same social plane as one's bond-kin if any profit is to come from the relationship. On the other hand I could not be bonded to the kin of some other septarch, since fate might one day elevate me to my father's throne, and a septarch must not be tangled in ties of bonding to the royal house of another district lest he find his freedom of decision circumscribed. Thus it was necessary to make bondings for me with the children of nobility but not of royalty.

The project was handled by my father's bondbrother, Ulman Kotril; it was the last aid he ever gave my father, for he was slain by bandits from Krell not long after my birth. To find a bondsister for me, Ulman Kotril went down into Manneran and obtained bonding with the unborn child of Segvord Helalam, High Justice of the Port. It had been determined that Helalam's child was to be female; hence my father's bondbrother returned to Salla and completed the tripling by compacting with Luinn Condorit, a general of the northern patrol, for his coming son.

Noim, Halum, and I were born all the same week, and my father himself performed the service of bonding. (We were known by our child-names then, of course, but I ignore that here to simplify things.) The ceremony took place in the septarch's palace, with proxies standing in for Noim and Halum; later, when we were old enough to travel, we repledged our bonds in each other's presence, I going to Manneran to be bonded to Halum. Thereafter we were only infrequently apart. Segvord Helalam had no objection to letting his daughter be raised in Salla, for he hoped she would strike a glittering marriage with some prince at my father's court. In this he was to be disappointed, for Halum went unmarried, and, for all I know, virgin, to her grave.

This scheme of bondings allows us a small escape from the constricting solitude in which we of Borthan are expected to live. You must know by now – even if you who read this be a stranger to our planet – that it has long been forbidden by custom for us to open our souls to others. To talk excessively of oneself, so our forefathers believed, leads inevitably to self-indulgence, self-pity, and self-corruption; therefore we are trained to keep ourselves to ourselves, and, so that the prisoning bands of custom may be all the more steely, we are prohibited even from using such words as 'I' or 'me' in polite discourse. If we have problems, we settle them in silence; if we have ambitions, we fulfill them without advertising our hopes; if we have desires, we pursue them in a selfless and impersonal way. To these harsh rules only two exceptions are made. We may speak our hearts freely to our drainers, who are religious functionaries and mere hirelings; and we may, within limits, open ourselves to our bond-kin. These are the rules of the Covenant.

It is permissible to confide almost anything to a bondsister or a bondbrother, but we are taught to observe etiquette in going about it. For example, proper people consider it improper to speak in the first person even to one's bond-kin. It is not done, ever. No matter how intimate a confession we make, we must couch it in acceptable grammar, not in the vulgarities of a common selfbarer.

(In our idiom a *selfbarer* is one who exposes himself to others, by which is meant that he exposes his soul, not his flesh. It is deemed a coarse act and is punished by social ostracism, or worse. Selfbarers use the censured pronouns of the gutter vocabulary, as I have done throughout what you now read. Although one is allowed to *bare* one's *self* to one's bond-kin, one is not a *selfbarer* unless one does it in tawdry blurtings of 'I' and 'me'.)

Also we are taught to observe reciprocity in our dealings with bond-kin. That is, we may not overload them with our woes, while failing to ease them of their own burdens. This is plain civility: the relationship depends on mutuality, and we may make use of them only if we are careful to let them make use of us. Children are often one-sided in their dealings with bond-kin; one may dominate his bondbrother, and chatter endlessly at him without pausing to heed the other's woes. But such things usually come into balance early. It is an unpardonable breach of propriety to show insufficient concern for one's bond-kin; I know no one, not even the weakest and most slovenly among us, who is guilty of that sin.

Of all the prohibitions having to do with bonding the most severe is the one against physical relationships with our bondkin. In sexual matters we are generally quite free, only we dare not do this one thing. This struck at me most painfully. Not that I yearned for Noim, for that has never been my path, nor is it a common one among us; but Halum was my soul's desire, and neither as wife nor as mistress could she ever comfort me. Long hours we sat up together, her hand in mine, telling one another things we could tell no one else, and how easy it would have been for me to draw her close, and part her garments, and slip my throbbing flesh inside hers. I would not attempt it. My conditioning held firm; and, as I hope to survive long enough to tell you, even after Schweiz and his potion had changed my soul, still did I respect the sanctity of Halum's body, although I was able to enter her in other ways. But I will not deny my desire for her. Nor can I forget the shock I felt when I learned in boyhood that of all Borthan's women only Halum, my beloved Halum, was denied to me.

I was extraordinarily close to Halum in every but the physical way, and she was for me the ideal bondsister: open, giving, loving, serene, radiant, adaptable. Not only was she beautiful – creamy-skinned, dark-eyed and dark of hair, slender and graceful – but also she was remarkable within herself, for her soul was gentle and sleek and supple, a wondrous mixture of purity and wisdom. Thinking of her, I see the image of a forest glade in the mountains, with black-needled evergreen trees rising close together like shadowy swords springing from a bed of newly fallen snow, and a sparkling stream dancing between sun-spattered boulders, everything clean and untainted and self-contained. Sometimes when I was with her I felt impossibly thick and clumsy, a hulking lumbering mountain of dull meat, with an ugly hairy body and stupid ponderous muscles; but Halum had the skill of showing me, with a word, with a laugh, with a wink, that I was being unjust to myself when I let the sight of her lightness and gaiety lead me to wish I was woman-soft and woman-airy.

On the other side I was equally close to Noim. He was my foil in many ways: slender where I am burly, crafty where I am direct, cautious and calculating where I am rash, bleak of outlook where I am sunny. With him as with Halum I frequently felt awkward, not really in any bodily sense (for, as I have told you, I move well for a man my size) but in my inward nature. Noim, more mercurial than I, livelier, quicker of wit, seemed to leap and cavort where I merely plodded, and yet the prevailing pessimism of his spirit made him appear deeper than I as well as more buoyant. To give myself credit, Noim looked with envy on me just as I did on him. He was jealous of my great strength, and furthermore he confessed that he felt mean-souled and petty when he peered into my eyes. 'One sees simplicity and power there,' he admitted, 'and one is aware that one often cheats, that one is lazy, that one breaks faith, that one does a dozen wicked things daily, and none of these things is any more natural to you than dining on your own flesh.'

You must understand that Halum and Noim were no bond-kin to one another, and were linked only by way of their common relationship to me. Noim had a bondsister of his own, a certain Thirga, and Halum was bonded to a girl of Manneran, Nald by name. Through such ties the Covenant creates a chain that clasps our society together, for Thirga had a bondsister too, and Nald a bondbrother, and each of them was bonded in turn on the other side, and so on and so on to form a vast if not infinite series. Obviously one comes in contact often with the bond-kin of his own bond-kin, though one is not free to assume with them the same privileges one has with those of his own bonding; I frequently saw Noim's Thirga and Halum's Nald, just

as Halum saw my Noim and Noim saw my Halum, but there
was never anything more than nodding friendship between
me and Thirga or me and Nald, while Noim and Halum took
to each other with immediate warmth. Indeed I suspected for
a time that they might marry one another, which would have
been uncommon but not illegal. Noim, though, perceived that
it would disturb me if my bondbrother shared my bondsister's
bed, and took care not to let the friendship ripen into love of
that sort.

Halum now sleeps forever under a stone in Manneran, and
Noim has become a stranger to me, perhaps even an enemy
to me, and the red sand of the Burnt Lowlands blows in my
face as I set down these lines.

TEN

After my brother Stirron became septarch in Salla, I went, as
you know, to the province of Glin. I will not say that I *fled*
to Glin, for no one openly compelled me to leave my native
land; but call my departure a deed of tact. I left in order to
spare Stirron the eventual embarrassment of putting me to
death, which would have weighed badly upon his soul. One
province cannot hold safely the two sons of a late septarch.

Glin was my choice because it is customary for exiles from
Salla to go to Glin, and also because my mother's family held
wealth and power there. I thought, wrongly as it turned out,
that I might gain some advantage from that connection.

I was about three moontimes short of the age of thirteen
when I took my leave of Salla. Among us that is the threshold
of manhood; I had reached almost my present height, though
I was much more slender and far less strong than I would
soon become, and my beard had only lately begun to grow
full. I knew something of history and government, something
of the arts of warfare, something of the skills of hunting, and

I had had some training in the practice of the law. Already I had bedded at least a dozen girls, and three times I had known, briefly, the tempests of unhappy love. I had kept the Covenant all my life; my soul was clean and I was at peace with our gods and with my forefathers. In my own eyes at that time I must have seemed hearty, adventurous, capable, honorable, and resilient, with all the world spread before me like a shining highway, and the future mine for the shaping. The perspective of thirty years tells me that that young man who left Salla then was also naïve, gullible, romantic, over-earnest, and conventional and clumsy of mind: quite an ordinary youth, in fact, who might have been skinning seapups in some fishing village had he not had the great good fortune to be born a prince.

The season of my going was early autumn, after a spring-time when all Salla had mourned my father and a summer when all Salla had hailed my brother. The harvest had been poor – nothing odd in Salla, where the fields yield pebbles and stones more graciously than they do crops – and Salla City was choked with bankrupt husbandmen, hoping to catch some largess from the new septarch. A dull hot haze hung over the capital day after day, and above it lay the first of autumn's heavy clouds, floating in on schedule from the eastern sea. The streets were dusty; the trees had begun to drop their leaves early, even the majestic firethorns outside the septarch's palace; the dung of the farmers' beasts clogged the gutters. These were poor omens for Salla at the beginning of a septarch's reign, and to me it seemed like a wise season for getting out. Even this early Stirron's temper was fraying and unlucky councilors of state were going off to dungeons. I was still cherished at court, coddled and complimented, plied with fur cloaks and promises of baronies in the mountains, but for how long, how long? Just now Stirron was troubled with guilt that he had inherited the throne and I had nothing, and so he treated me softly, but let the dry summer give way to a bitter winter of famine and the scales might shift; envying me my freedom from responsibility, he might well turn on me. I had studied the annals of royal houses well. Such things had happened before.

Therefore I readied myself for a hasty exit. Only Noim and Halum knew of my plans. I gathered those few of my possessions that I had no wish to abandon, such things as a ring of ceremony bequeathed by my father, a favorite hunting jerkin of yellow leather, and a double-cameo amulet bearing the portraits of my bondsister and bondbrother; all my books I relinquished, for one can get more books wherever one goes, and I did not even take the hornfowl spear, my trophy of my father's death-day, that hung in my palace bedchamber. There was to my name a fairly large amount of money, and this I handled in what I believed was a shrewd manner. It was all on deposit in the Royal Salla Bank. First I transferred the bulk of my funds to the six lesser provincial banks, over the course of many days. These new accounts were held jointly with Halum and Noim. Halum then proceeded to make withdrawals, asking that the money be paid into the Commerical and Seafarers Bank of Manneran, for the account of her father Segvord Helalam. If we were detected in this transfer, Halum was to declare that her father had undergone financial reverses and had requested a loan of short duration. Once my assets were safely on deposit in Manneran, Halum asked her father to transfer the money again, this time to an account in my name in the Covenant Bank of Glin. In this zigzag way I got my cash from Salla to Glin without arousing the suspicions of our Treasury officials, who might wonder why a prince of the realm was shipping his patrimony to our rival province of the north. The fatal flaw in all this was that if the Treasury became disturbed about the flow of capital to Manneran, questioned Halum, and then made inquiries of her father, the truth would emerge that Segvord prospered and had had no need of the 'loan', which would have led to further questions and, probably, to my exposure. But my maneuvers went unnoticed.

Lastly I went before my brother to ask his permission to leave the capital, as courtly etiquette required.

This was a tense affair, for honour would not let me lie to
Stirron, yet I dared not tell him the truth. Long hours I spent
with Noim, first, rehearsing my deceptions. I was a slow pupil
in chicanery; Noim spat, he cursed, he wept, he slapped his
hands together, as time and again he slipped through my guard
with a probing question. 'You were not meant to be a liar,' he
told me in despair.

'No,' I agreed, 'this one never was meant to be a liar.'

Stirron received me in the northern robing chamber, a dark
and somber room of rough stone walls and narrow windows,
used mainly for audiences with village chieftains. He meant
no offence by it, I think; it was merely where he happened
to be when I sent in my equerry with word that I wished a
meeting. It was late afternoon; a thin greasy rain was falling
outside; in some far tower of the palace a carillonneur was
instructing apprentices, and leaden bell-tones, scandalously
awry, came humming through the draughty walls. Stirron was
formally dressed: a bulky gray robe of stormshield furs, tight red
woollen leggings, high boots of green leather. The sword of the
Covenant was at his side, the heavy glittering pendant of office
pressed against his breast, rings of title cluttered his fingers,
and if memory does not deceive me, he wore yet another
token of power around his right forearm. Only the crown
itself was missing from his regalia. I had seen Stirron garbed
this way often enough of late, at ceremonies and meetings of
state, but to find him so enveloped in insignia on an ordinary
afternoon struck me as almost comical. Was he so insecure
that he needed to load himself with such stuff constantly,
to reassure himself that he was indeed septarch? Did he feel
that he had to impress his own younger brother? Or did he,
childlike, take pleasure in these ornaments for pleasure's own
sake? No matter which, some flaw in Stirron's character was
revealed, some inner foolishness. It astounded me that I could
find him amusing rather than awesome. Perhaps the genesis
of my ultimate rebellion lies in that moment when I walked
in on Stirron in all his splendor and had to fight to hold my
laughter back.

Half a year in the septarchy had left its mark on him. His face was gray and his left eyelid drooped, I suppose from exhaustion. He held his lips tightly compressed and stood in a rigid way with one shoulder higher than the other. Though only two years separated us in age, I felt myself a boy beside him, and marveled how the cares of office can etch a young man's visage. It seemed centuries since Stirron and I had laughed together in our bedchambers, and whispered all the forbidden words, and bared our ripening bodies to one another to make the edgy comparisons of adolescence. Now I offered formal obeisance to my weary royal brother, crossing my arms over my breast and flexing my knees and bowing my head as I murmured, 'Lord Septarch, long life be yours.'

Stirron was man enough to deflect my formality with a brotherly grin. He gave me a proper acknowledgement of my greeting, yes, arms raised and palms turned out, but then he turned it into an embrace, swiftly crossing the room and seizing me. Yet there was something artificial about his gesture, as though he had been studying how to show warmth to his brother, and quickly I was released. He wandered away from me, eyeing a nearby window, and his first words to me were, 'A beastly day. A brutal year.'

'The crown lies heavy, lord septarch?'

'You have leave to call your brother by his name.'

'The strains show in you, Stirron. Perhaps you take Salla's problems too closely to heart.'

'The people starve,' he said. 'Shall one pretend that is a trifling thing?'

'The people have always starved, year upon year,' I said. 'But if the septarch drains his soul in worry over them —'

'Enough, Kinnall. You presume.' Nothing brotherly about the tone now; he was hard put to hide his irritation with me. He was plainly angered that I had so much as noticed his fatigue, though it was he who had begun our talk with lamenting. The conversation had veered too far towards the intimate. The condition of Stirron's nerves was no affair of mine: it was not my place to comfort him, he had a bondbrother for that.

My attempted kindness had been improper and inappropriate. 'What do you seek here?' he asked roughly.

'The lord septarch's leave to go from the capital.'

He whirled away from the window and glared at me. His eyes, dull and sluggish until this moment, grew bright and harsh, and flickered disturbingly from side to side. 'To go? To go where?'

'One wishes to accompany one's bondbrother Noim to the northern frontier,' I said as smoothly as I could manage. 'Noim pays a call on the headquarters of his father, General Luinn Condorit, whom he has not seen this year since your lordship's coronation, and one is asked to travel northward with him, for bondlove and friendship.'

'When would you go?'

'Three days hence, if it please the septarch.'

'And for how long a stay?' Stirron was virtually barking these questions at me.

'Until the first snow of winter falls.'

'Too long. Too long.'

'One might be absent then a shorter span,' I said.

'Must you go at all, though?'

My right leg quivered shamefully at the knee. I struggled to be calm. 'Stirron, consider that one has not left Salla City for so much as an entire day since you assumed the throne. Consider that one cannot justly ask one's bondbrother to journey uncomforted through the northern hills.'

'Consider that you are the heir to the prime septarchy of Salla,' Stirron said, 'and that if misfortune comes to your brother while you are in the north, our dynasty is lost.'

The coldness of his voice, and the ferocity with which he had questioned me a moment earlier, threw me into panic. Would he oppose my going? My fevered mind invented a dozen reasons for his hostility. He knew of my transfers of funds, and had concluded I was about to defect to Glin; or he imagined that Noim and I, and Noim's father with his troops, would stir up an insurrection in the north, the aim being to place me on the throne; or he had already resolved to arrest and destroy me, but the time was not yet ripe for it, and he wished not to let me get far before he could pounce; or – but I need not multiply hypotheses. We are a suspicious people on Borthan, and no one is less trusting than one who wears a crown. If Stirron would not release me from the capital, and it appeared that he would not, then I must sneak away, and I might not succeed at that.

I said, 'No misfortunes are probable, Stirron, and even so, it would be no large task to return from the north if something befell you. Do you fear usurpation so seriously?'

'One fears everything, Kinnall, and leaves little to chance.'

He proceeded then to lecture me on necessary caution, and on the ambitions of those who surrounded the throne, naming a few lords as possible traitors whom I would have placed among the pillars of the realm. As he spoke, going far beyond the strictures of the Covenant in exposing his uncertainties to me, I saw with amazement what a tortured, terrified man my brother had become in this short time of septarchy; and I realized, too, that I was not going to be granted my leave. He went on and on, fidgeting as he spoke, rubbing his talismans of authority, several times picking up his scepter from where it lay on an ancient wood-topped table, walking to the window and coming back from it, pitching his voice now low and now high as though searching for the best septarchical resonances. I was frightened for him. He was a man of my own considerable size, and at that time much thicker in body and greater in strength than I, and all my life I had worshiped him and modeled myself upon him; and here he was corroded with terror and committing the sin of *telling me about it*. Had just these few moontimes of supreme power brought Stirron to this collapse? Was the loneliness of the septarchy that awful for him? On Borthan we are born lonely, and lonely we live, and lonely we die; why should wearing a crown be so much more difficult than bearing the burdens we inflict upon ourselves each day? Stirron told me of assassins' plots and of revolution brewing among the farmers who thronged the town, and even hinted that our father's death had been no accident. I tried to persuade

myself that hornfowl could be trained to slay a particular man
in a group of thirteen men, and would not swallow the notion.
It appeared that royal responsibilities had driven Stirron mad.
I was reminded of a duke some years back who displeased my
father, and was sent for half a year to a dungeon, and tortured
each day that the sun could be seen. He had entered prison a
sturdy and vigorous figure, and when he emerged he was so
ruined that he befouled his own clothes with his dung, and
did not know it. How soon would Stirron be brought to that?
Perhaps it was just as well, I thought, that he was refusing me
permission to go away, for it might be better that I remain at the
capital, ready to take his place if he crumbled beyond repair.

But he amazed me at the finish of his rambling oration; for
it had taken him clear across the room, to an alcove hung with
dangling silver chains, and at the end, suddenly bunching the
chains and yanking a dozen of them from their mountings, he
swung round to face me and cried hoarsely, 'Give your pledge,
Kinnall, that you will come back from the north in time to
attend the royal wedding!'

I was doubly pronged. For the last several minutes I had
begun to make plans on the basis of staying in Salla City; now
I found I could depart after all, and was not sure I should, in
view of Stirron's deterioration. And then too he demanded
from me a promise of swift return, and how could I give the
septarch such a promise without lying to him, a sin I was not
prepared to commit? So far all that I had told him was the
truth, though only part of the truth; I *did* plan to travel north
with Noim to visit his father, I *would* remain in northern Salla
until winter's first snow. How though could I set a date for my
coming back to the capital?

My brother was due to marry, forty days hence, the youngest
daughter of Bryggil, septarch of Salla's south-eastern district. It
was a cunning match. So far as the traditional order of primacy
went, Bryggil stood seventh and lowest in the hierarchy of
Salla's septarchs, but he was the oldest, the cleverest, and
the most respected of the seven, now that my father was
gone. To combine Bryggil's shrewdness and stature with the

prestige that accrued to Stirron by virtue of his rank as prime septarch would be to cement the dynasty of our family to the throne. And no doubt sons would shortly come marching out of Bryggil's daughter's loins, relieving me of my position as heir apparent: her fertility must have passed the necessary tests, and of Stirron's there could be no question, since he had already scattered a litter of bastards all over Salla. I would have certain ceremonial roles to play at the wedding as brother to the septarch.

I had wholly forgotten the wedding. If I skipped out of Salla before it came about, I would wound my brother in a way that saddened me. But if I stayed here, with Stirron in this unstable state, I had no guarantee of being a free man when the nuptial day arrived, or even of still owning my head. Nor was there any sense in going north with Noim if I bound myself to return in forty days. It was a hard choice: to postpone my departure and run the risks of my brother's royal whims, or to leave now, knowing I was taking on myself the stain of breaking a pledge to my septarch.

The Covenant teaches us that we should welcome dilemmas, for it toughens character to grapple with the insoluble and find a solution. In this instance events made a mockery of the Covenant's lofty moral teachings. As I hesitated in anguish, Stirron's telephone summoned him; he snatched its handpiece, jabbed at the scrambler, and listened to five minutes of gibberish, his face darkening and his eyes growing fiery. At length he broke the contact and peered up at me as though I were a stranger to him. 'They are eating the flesh of the newly dead in Spoksa,' he muttered. 'On the slopes of the Kongoroi they dance to demons in hopes of finding food. Insanity! Insanity!' He clenched his fists and strode to the window, and thrust his face to it, and closed his eyes, and I think forgot my presence for a time. Again the telephone asked for him. Stirron jerked back like one who has been stabbed, and started towards the machine. Noticing me standing frozen near the door, he fluttered his hands impatiently at me and said, 'Go, will you? Off with your bondbrother, wherever you go.

This province! This famine! Father, father, father!' He seized the handpiece. I started to offer a genuflection of parting, and Stirron furiously waved me from the room, sending me unpledged and unchecked towards the borders of his realm.

ELEVEN

Noim and I set forth three days afterwards, just the two of us and a small contingent of servants. The weather was bad, for summer's dryness had given way not merely to the thick dreary gray clouds of autumn but to a foresampling of winter's heavy rains. 'You'll be dead of the mildew before you see Glin,' Halum told us cheerfully. 'If you don't drown in the mud of the Grand Salla Highway.'

She stayed with us, at Noim's house, on the eve of our departure, sleeping chastely apart in the little chamber just under the roof, and joined us for breakfast as we made ready to go. I had never seen her looking lovelier; that morning she wore a bloom of shimmering beauty that cut through the murk of the drizzly dawn like a torch in a cave. Perhaps what enhanced her so greatly then was that she was about to pass from my life for an unknown length of time, and, conscious of my self-inflicted loss, I magnified her attractiveness. She was clad in a gown of delicate golden chainmesh, beneath which only a gossamer wrap concealed her naked form, and her body, shifting this way and that under its flimsy coverings, aroused in me thoughts that left me drenched in shame. Halum then was in the ripeness of early womanhood, and had been for several years; it had already begun to puzzle me that she remained unwed. Though she and Noim and I were of the same age, she had leaped free of childhood before us, as girls will do, and I had come to think of her as older than the two of us, because for a year she had had breasts and the monthly flow, while Noim and I were still without hair on cheek or body. And while we had caught up to her in physical maturity, she was still more adult in her bearing than my bondbrother or I, her voice more smoothly modulated, her manner more poised, and it was impossible for me to shake off that notion that she was senior sister to us. Who soon must accept some suitor, lest she become over-ripe and sour in her maidenhood; I was suddenly certain that Halum would marry while I was off hiding in Glin, and the thought of some sweaty stranger planting babies between her thighs so sickened me that I turned away from her at the table, and lurched to the window to gulp the humid air into my throbbing lungs.

'Are you unwell?' Halum asked.

'One feels a certain tension, bondsister.'

'Surely there's no danger. The septarch's permission has been granted for you to go north.'

'There is no document to show it,' Noim pointed out.

'You are a septarch's son!' Halum cried. 'What guardian of the roads would dare to trifle with you?'

'Exactly,' I said. 'There is no cause for fear. One feels only a sense of uncertainty. One is beginning a new life, Halum.' I forced a faint smile. 'The time of going must be here.'

'Stay a while longer,' Halum begged.

But we did not. The servants waited in the street. The groundcars were ready. Halum embraced us, clasping Noim first, then me, for I was the one who would not be returning, and that called for a longer farewell. When she came into my arms I was stunned by the intensity with which she offered herself: her lips to my lips, her belly to my belly, her breasts crushed against my chest. On tiptoes she strained to press her body into mine, and for a moment I felt her trembling, until I began myself to tremble. It was not a sisterly kiss and certainly not a bondsisterly kiss; it was the passionate kiss of a bride sending her young husband off to a war from which she knows there is no coming back. I was singed by Halum's sudden fire. I felt as though a veil had been ripped away and some Halum I had not known before had flung herself against me, one who burned with the needs of the flesh, one who did not mind revealing her forbidden hunger for a bondbrother's body. Or did I imagine those things in her? It seemed to me that for a single protracted instant Halum repressed nothing and allowed her arms and lips to tell me the truth about her feelings; but I could not respond in kind – I had trained myself too well in the proper attitudes towards one's bondsister – and I was distant and cool as I clasped her. I may even have thrust her back a little, shocked by her forwardness. And, as I say, there may have been no forwardness at all except in my overwrought mind, but only legitimate grief at a parting. In any event the intensity went quickly from Halum; her embrace slackened and she released me, and she appeared downcast and chilled, as if I had rebuffed her cruelly by being so prim when she was giving so much.

'Come, now,' Noim said impatiently, and, trying somehow to rescue the situation, I lifted Halum's hand and touched my palm lightly to her cool palm, and smiled an awkward smile, and she smiled even more awkwardly, and perhaps we would have said a stumbling word or two, but Noim caught me by the elbow and stolidly led me outside to begin my journey away from my homeland.

TWELVE

I insisted on opening myself to a drainer before leaving Salla City. I had not planned on doing so, and it irritated Noim that I took the time for it; but an uncontrollable yearning for the comforts of religion rose up in me as we neared the outskirts of the capital.

We had been travelling almost an hour. The rain had thickened, and gusty winds slammed it against the windscreens of our groundcars, so that cautious driving was in order. The cobbled streets were slippery. Noim drove one of the cars, I sitting sullenly beside him; the other, with our servants, followed close behind. The morning was young and the city still slept. Each passing street was a surgery to me, for a segment of my life was ripped off by it: there goes the palace compound, there go the spires of the House of Justice, there the university's great gray blocky buildings, there the godhouse where my royal father brought me into the Covenant, there the Museum of Mankind that I visited so often with my mother to stare at the treasures from the stars. Circling through the fine residential district that borders the Skangen Canal, I even spied the ornate townhouse of the Duke of Kongoroi, on whose handsome daughter's silken bedsheets I had left my virginity in a clammy puddle, not too many years before. In this city I had lived all my life, and I might never see it again; my yesterdays were washing away, like the topsoil of Salla's sad farms under the knives of the winter rains. Since boyhood I had known that one day my brother would be septarch and this city would cease to have a place for me, but yet I had denied that to myself, saying, 'It will not happen soon, perhaps it will not happen at all.' And my father lay dead in his firethorn coffin, and my brother crouched beneath the awful weight of his crown, and I was fleeing from Salla before my life had fairly begun, and such a mood of self-pity came over me that I did not dare even to speak to Noim, though what is a bondbrother for if not to ease one's soul? And when we were driving through the ramshackle streets of Salla Old Town, not far from the city walls, I spied a dilapidated godhouse and said to Noim, 'Pull up at the corner here. One must go within to empty himself.'

Noim, fretful, did not want to spare the time, and made as if to drive on. 'Would you deny one the god-right?' I asked him hotly, and only then, simmering and cross, did he halt the car and back it up to let me out by the godhouse.

Its façade was worn and peeling. An inscription beside the door was illegible. The pavement before it was cracked and tilted. Salla Old Town has a pedigree of more than a thousand years; some of its buildings have been continuously inhabited since the founding of the city, though most are in ruins, for the life of that district ended, in effect, when one of the medieval septarchs chose to move his court to our present palace on top of Skangen Hill, much to the south. At night Salla Old Town comes alive with pleasure-seekers, who guzzle the blue wine in cellar cabarets, but at this misty hour it was a grim place. Blank stone walls faced me from every building: we have a fashion of making mere slits serve for windows in Salla, but here they carried it to an extreme. I wondered if the godhouse could have a scanning machine in working order to watch my approach. Yes, as it happened. When I neared the godhouse door, it swung partly open, and a scrawny man in drainer's robes looked out. He was ugly, of course. Who ever saw a handsome drainer? It is a profession for the ill-favoured. This one had greenish skin, heavily pocked, and a rubbery snout of a nose, and a dimness in one eye: standard for his trade. He gave me a fishy stare and, by his wariness, seemed to be regretting having opened the door.

'The peace of all gods be on you,' I said. 'Here is one in need of your craft.'

He eyed my costly costume, my leather jerkin and my heavy jewelry, and studied the size and swagger of me, and evidently concluded I was some young bully of the aristocracy out to stir trouble in the slums. 'It is too early in the day,' he said uneasily. 'You come too soon for comfort.'

'You would not refuse a sufferer!'

'It is too early.'

'Come, come, let one in. A troubled soul stands here.'

He yielded, as I knew he must, and with many a twitch of his long-nosed face he admitted me. Within there was the reek of rot. The old woodwork was impregnated with the damp, the draperies were mouldering, the furniture had been gnawed by insects. The lighting was dim. The drainer's wife, as ugly as the drainer himself, skulked about. He led me to his chapel, a small sweaty room off the living-quarters, and left me kneeling by the cracked and yellowing mirror while he lit the candles. He robed himself and finally came to me where I knelt.

He named his fee. I gasped.

'Too much by half,' I said.

He reduced it by a fifth. When I still refused, he told me to find my priesting elsewhere, but I would not rise, and, grudgingly, he brought the price of his services down another notch. Still it was probably five times what he charged the folk of Salla Old Town for the same benefit, but he knew I had money, and, thinking of Noim fuming in the car, I could not bring myself to haggle.

'Done,' I said.

Next he brought me the contract. I have said that we of Borthan are suspicious people; have I indicated how we rely on contracts? A man's word is merely bad air. Before a soldier beds a whore they come to the terms of their bargain and scrawl it on paper. The drainer gave me a standard form, promising me that all I said would be held in strictest confidence, the drainer merely acting as intermediary between me and the god of my choice, and I for my part pledging that I would hold the drainer to no liability for the knowledge he would have of me, that I would not call him as witness in a lawsuit or make him my alibi in some prosecution, et cetera, et cetera. I signed. He signed. We exchanged copies and I gave him his money.

'Which god would you have preside here?' he asked.

'The god who protects travelers,' I told him. We do not call our gods aloud by their names.

He lit a candle of the appropriate color – pink – and put it beside the mirror. By that it was understood that the chosen god would accept my words.

'Behold your face,' the drainer said. 'Put your eyes to your eyes.'

I stared at the mirror. Since we shun vanity, it is not usual to examine one's face except on these occasions of religion.

'Open now your soul,' the drainer commanded. 'Let your griefs and dreams and hungers and sorrows emerge.'

'A septarch's son it is who flees his homeland,' I began, and at once the drainer jerked to attention, impaled by my news. Though I did not take my eyes from the mirror, I guessed that he was scrabbling around to look at the contract and see who it was that had signed it. 'Fear of his brother,' I continued, 'leads him to go abroad, but yet he is sore of soul as he departs.'

I went on in that vein for some while. The drainer made the usual interjections every time I faltered, prying words out of me in his craft's cunning way, and shortly there was no need for such midwifery, for the words gushed freely. I told him of my desire for my bondsister and how her embrace had unsettled me; I told him how close I had come to lying to Stirron; I confessed that I would miss the royal wedding and give my brother injury thereby; I admitted several small sins of self-esteem, such as anyone commits daily.

The drainer listened.

We pay them to listen and to do nothing but listen, until we are drained and healed. Such is our holy communion, that we lift these toads from the mud, and set them up in their god-houses, and buy their patience with our money. It is permitted under the Covenant to say anything to a drainer, even if it is drivel, even if it is a shameful catalog of throttled lusts and hidden filth. We may bore a drainer as we have no right to bore our bond-kin, for it is the drainer's obligation by contract to sit with the patience of the hills as we speak of ourselves. We need not worry what the drainer's problems may be, nor what he thinks of us, nor whether he would be happier doing something else. He has his calling and he takes his fee, and he must serve those who have need of him. There was a time when I felt it was a miraculously fine scheme, to give us drainers in order that we might rid our hearts of pain. Too much of my life was gone before I realized that to open oneself to a drainer is no more comforting than to make love to one's own hand: there are better ways of loving, there are happier ways of opening.

But I did not know that then, and I squatted by the mirror, getting the best healing that money could buy. Whatever residue of wrongness was in my soul came forth, syllable smoothly following syllable, the way sweet liquor will flow when one taps the thorny flanks of the gnarled and repellent-looking flesh-trees that grow by the Gulf of Sumar. As I spoke the candles caught me in their spell, and by the flickering of them I was drawn into the curved surface of the mirror so that I was drawn out of myself; the drainer was a mere blur in the darkness, unreal, unimportant, and I spoke now directly to the god of travelers, who would heal me and send me on my way. And I believed that this was so. I will not say that I imagined a literal god-place where our deities sit on call to serve us, but I had then an abstract and metaphorical understanding of our religion by which it seemed to me, in its way, as real as my right arm.

My flow of words halted and the drainer made no attempt to renew the outpour. He murmured the phrases of absolution. I was done. He snuffed the god-candle between two fingers and rose to doff his robes. Still I knelt, weak and quivering from my draining, lost in reveries. I felt cleansed and purified, stripped of my soul's grit and debris, and, in the music of that moment, was only dimly aware of the squalor about me. The chapel was a place of magic and the drainer was aflame with divine beauty.

'Up,' he said, nudging me with the tip of his sandal. 'Out. Off about your journeys.'

The sound of his splintery voice doused all the wonder. I stood up, shaking my head to cure it of its new lightness, while the drainer half pushed me into the corridor. He was no longer afraid of me, that ugly little man, even though I might be a septarch's son and could kill him with one wad of my spittle, for I had told him of my cowardice, of my forbidden hunger for Halum, of all the cheapnesses of my spirit, and that knowledge reduced me in his eyes: no man newly drained can awe his drainer.

The rain was even worse when I left the building. Noim sat scowling in the car, his forehead pressed to the steering-stick. He looked up and tapped his wrist to tell me I had dallied too long at the godhouse.

'Feel better now that your bladder's empty?' he asked.

'What?'

'That is, did you have a good soul-pissing in there?'

'A foul phrase, Noim.'

'One grows blasphemous when his patience is extended too far.'

He kicked the starter and we rolled forward. Shortly we were at the ancient walls of Salla City, by the noble tower-bedecked opening known as Glin Door, which was guarded by four sourfaced and sleepy warriors in dripping uniforms. They paid no heed to us. Noim drove through the gate and past a sign welcoming us to the Grand Salla Highway. Salla City dwindled swiftly behind us; northward we rushed towards Glin.

THIRTEEN

The grand Salla highway passes through one of our best farming districts, the rich and fertile Plain of Nand, which each spring receives a gift of topsoil stripped from the skin of West Salla by our busy streams. At that time the septarch of the Nand district was a notorious coinclutcher, and thanks to his penury the highway was in poor repair there, so, as Halum had predicted in jest, we were hard put to wallow through the mud that clogged the road. It was good to finish with Nand and enter North Salla, where the land is a mixture of rock and sand and the people live on weeds and on scuttling things that they take from the sea. Groundcars are unusual sights in North Salla, and twice we were stoned by hungry and sullen townsfolk, who found our mere passage through their unhappy place an insult. But at least the road was free of mud.

Noim's father's troops were stationed in extreme North Salla, on the lower bank of the River Huish. This is the grandest of Velada Borthan's rivers. It begins as a hundred trifling brooks trickling down the eastern slopes of the Huishtors in the northern part of West Salla; these brooks merge in the foot-hills to become a swift stream, gray and turbulent, that rushes through a narrow granite canyon marked by six great step-like plunges. Emerging from those wild cascades on to its alluvial plain, the Huish proceeds more serenely on a north-eastern course towards the sea, growing wider and wider in the flatlands, and splitting ultimately so that, at its broad delta, it gives itself to the ocean through eight mouths. In its rapid western reaches the Huish forms the boundary between Salla and Glin; at its placid easternmost end it divides Glin from Krell.

For all its length the great river is unbridged, and one might think little need exists to fortify its banks against invaders from the far side. But many times in Salla's history have the men of Glin crossed the Huish by boat to make war, and just as many times have we of Salla gone to ravage Glin; nor is the record of neighborlines between Glin and Krell any happier. So all along the Huish sprout military outposts, and generals like Luinn Condorit consume their lives studying the riverfogs for glimpses of the enemy.

I stayed a short while at Noim's father's camp. The general was not much like Noim, being a large-featured, heavy man whose face, eroded by time and frustration, was like a contour map of bouldery North Salla. Not once in fifteen years had there been any significant clash along the border he guarded, and I think that idleness had chilled his soul: he said little, scowled often, turned every statement into a bitter grumble, and retreated speedily from conversation into private dreams. They must have been dreams of war; no doubt he could not glance at the river without wishing that it swarmed with the landing-craft of Glin. Since men like him surely patrol the Glin side of the river as well, it is a wonder that the border guards do not trespass on one another out of sheer boredom, every few years, and embroil our provinces in pointless conflict.

A dull time we had of it there. Noim was bound by filial ties to call upon his father, but they had nothing to say to one another, and the general was a stranger to me. I had told Stirron I would stay with Noim's father until the first snow of winter fell, and I was true to that, yet luckily it was no lengthy visit I made; winter comes early in the north. On my fifth day there white sprinkles fluttered down and I was released from my self-imposed pledge.

Ferries, shuttling between terminals in three places, link Salla to Glin except when there is war. Noim drove me to the nearest terminal one black dawn, and solemnly we embraced and made our farewells. I said I would send my address, when I had one in Glin, so that he could keep me informed of doings in Salla. He promised to look after Halum. We talked vaguely of when he and she and I would meet again; perhaps they would visit me in Glin next year, perhaps we would all three go on holiday in Manneran. We made these plans with little conviction in our voices.

'This day of parting should never have come,' Noim said.

'Partings lead only to reunions,' I told him jauntily.

'Perhaps you could have come to some understanding with your brother, Kinnall –'

'There was never hope of that.'

'Stirron has spoken warmly of you. Is he then insincere?'

'He means his warmth, just now. But it would not be long before it became inconvenient for him to have a brother dwelling by his side, and then embarrassing, and then impossible. A septarch sleeps best when there is no potential rival of the royal blood close at hand.'

The ferry beckoned me with a bellow of its horn.

I clasped Noim's arm and we made farewells again, hurriedly. The last thing I said to him was, 'When you see the septarch, tell him that his brother loves him.' Then I went aboard.

The crossing was too quick. Less than an hour and I found myself on the alien soil of Glin. The immigration officials examined me brusquely, but they thawed at the sight of my passport, bright red to denote my place in the nobility, with a golden stripe to show that I was of the septarch's family. At once I had my visa, good for an indefinite stay. Such officials are a gossipy sort; beyond question they were on the telephone the instant I left them, sending word to their government that a prince of Salla was in the land, and I suppose that not much later that bit of information was in the hands of

Salla's diplomatic representatives in Glin, who would relay it to my brother for his displeasure.

Across the way from the customs shed I came upon a branch of the Covenant Bank of Glin, and changed my Salla money for the currency of the northerners. With my new funds I hired a driver to take me to the capital city, which they call Glain, half a day's journey north of the border.

The road was narrow and winding, and traversed a bleak countryside where winter's touch had long ago pulled the leaves from the trees. Dirty snow was banked high. Glin is a frosty province. It was settled by men of a puritan nature, who found the living too easy in Salla, and felt that if they remained there, they might be tempted away from the Covenant; failing to reform our forefathers into great piety, they left, crossing the Huish by rafts to hack out a livelihood in the north. Hard folk for a hard land; however poor the farming is in Salla, it is twice as unrewarding in Glin, and they live there mainly by fishing, by manufacturing, by the jugglements of commercial dealings, and by piracy. But that my mother had sprung from Glin, I would never have chosen it for my place of exile. Not that I gained anything from my family ties.

FOURTEEN

Nightfall saw me in Glain. A walled city it is, like Salla's capital, but otherwise not much like it. Salla City has grace and power; its buildings are made of great blocks of substantial stone, black basalt and rosy granite quarried in the mountains, and its streets are wide and sweeping, affording noble vistas and splendid promenades. Apart from our custom of letting narrow slits stand in place of true windows, Salla City is an open, inviting place, the architecture of which announces to the world the boldness and self-sufficiency of its citizens. But that dismal Glain! Oh!

Glain is fashioned of scruffy yellow brick, here and there trimmed with miserable poor pink sandstone that rubs to particles at a finger's nudge. It has no streets, only alleyways; the houses jostle one another as if afraid that some interloper may try to slip between them if they relax their guard. An avenue in Glain would not impress a gutter in Salla. And the architects of Glain have created a city fit only for a nation of drainers, since everything is lopsided, awry, uneven, and coarse. My brother, who had once been to Glain on a diplomatic errand, had described the place to me, but I put his harsh words off to mere patriotic prejudice; now I saw that Stirron had been too kind.

Nor were the folk of Glain more lovely than their city. On a world where suspicion and secrecy are godly virtues, one expects to find charm in short supply; yet I found the Glainish virtuous beyond all necessity. Dark clothes, dark frowns, dark souls, closed and shrunken hearts. Their speech itself displays their constipation of spirit. The language of Glin is the same as that of Salla, though the northerners have pronounced accents, clipping their syllables and shifting their vowels. That did not disturb me, but their syntax of self-effacement did. My driver, who was not a city man and therefore seemed almost friendly, left me at a hostelry where he thought I would have kind treatment, and I entered and said, 'One would have a room for tonight, and for some days beyond this one, perhaps.' The innkeeper stared balefully at me as if I had said, 'I would have a room,' or something equally filthy. Later I discovered that even our usual polite circumlocution seems too vain for a northerner; I should not have said, 'One would have a room,' but rather, 'Is there a room to be had?' At a restaurant it is wrong to say, 'One will dine on thus and thus,' but rather, 'These are the dishes that have been chosen.' And so on and so on, twisting everything into a cumbersome passive form to avoid the sin of acknowledging one's own existence.

For my ignorance the innkeeper gave me his meanest room, and charged me twice the usual tariff. By my speech I had branded myself a man of Salla; why should he be courteous?

But in signing the contract for my night's lodgings I had to show him my passport, which made him gasp when he saw that he was host to a visiting prince; he softened more than a little, asking me if I would have wine sent to my room, or maybe a buxom Glainish wench. I took the wine but declined the wench, for I was very young and overly frightened of the diseases that might lurk in foreign loins. That night I sat alone in my room, watching snowflakes drowning in a murky canal below my window, and feeling more isolated from humanity than ever before, ever since.

FIFTEEN

Over a week passed before I found the courage to call upon my mother's kin. I strolled the city for hours every day, keeping my cloak wrapped close against the winds and marveling at the ugliness of all I beheld, people and structures. I located the embassy of Salla, and lurked outside it, not wishing to go in but merely cherishing the link to my homeland that the squat grim building provided. I bought heaps of cheaply printed books and read far into the night to learn something of my adopted province: there was a history of Glin, and a guidebook to the city of Glain, and an interminable epic poem dealing with the founding of the first settlements north of the Huish, and much else. I dissolved my loneliness in wine – not the wine of Glin, for none is made there, but rather the good sweet golden wine of Manneran, that they import in giant casks. I slept poorly. One night I dreamed that Stirron had died of a fit and a search was being made for me. Several times in my sleep I saw the hornfowl strike my father dead; this is a dream that still haunts me, coming twice or thrice a year. I wrote long letters to Halum and Noim, and tore them up, for they stank of self-pity. I wrote one to Stirron, begging him to forgive me for fleeing, and tore that up too. When all else failed, I asked the innkeeper for a wench. He sent me a skinny girl a year or two older than I, with odd large breasts that dangled like inflated rubber bags. 'It is said you are a prince of Salla,' she declared coyly, lying down and parting her thighs. Without replying I covered her and thrust myself into her, and the size of my organ made her squeal with fear and pleasure both, and she wriggled her hips so fiercely that my seed burst from me within half a moment. I was angered at myself for that, and turned my wrath on her, pulling free and shouting, 'Who told you to start moving? I wasn't ready to have you move! I didn't want you to!' She ran from my room still naked, terrified more, I think, by my obscenities than by my wrath. I had never said 'I' in front of a woman before. But she was only a whore, after all. I soaped myself for an hour afterwards. In my naïveté I feared that the innkeeper would evict me for speaking so vulgarly to her, but he said nothing. Even in Glin, one need not be polite to whores.

I realized that there had been a strange pleasure in shouting those words at her. I yielded to curious reveries of fantasy, in which I imagined the big-breasted slut naked on my bed, while I stood over her crying, 'I! I! I! I! I!' Such daydreams had the power to make my maleness stand tall. I considered going to a drainer to get rid of the dirty notion, but instead, two nights later, I asked the innkeeper for another wench, and with each jab of my body I silently cried, 'I! Me! I! Me!'

Thus I spent my patrimony in the capital of puritan Glin, wenching and drinking and loitering. When the stench of my own idleness offended me, I put down my timidity and went to see my Glainish relatives.

My mother had been a daughter of a prime septarch of Glin; he was dead, as was his son and successor; now his son's son, Truis, my mother's nephew, held the throne. It seemed too forward to me to go seeking preferment from my royal cousin directly. Truis of Glin would have to weigh matters of state as well as matters of kinship, and might not want to aid the runaway brother of Salla's prime septarch, lest it lead him into friction with Stirron. But I had an aunt, Nioll, my mother's younger sister, who had often been in Salla City in my mother's lifetime, and who had held me fondly when I was a babe; would she not help me?

She had married power to power. Her husband was the Marquis of Huish, who held great influence at the septarch's court, and also – for in Glin it is not thought unseemly for the nobility to dabble in commerce – controlled his province's wealthiest factor-house. These factor-houses are something akin to banks, but of another species; they lend money to brigands and merchants and lords of industry, only at ruinous rates, and always taking a slice of ownership in any enterprise they aid; thus they insinuate their tentacles into a hundred organizations and attain immense leverage in economic matters. In Salla the factor-houses were forbidden a century ago, but in Glin they thrive almost as a second government. I had no love for the system, but I preferred joining it to begging.

Some inquiries at the inn gained me directions to the palace of the marquis. By Glainish standards it was an imposing structure of three interlocking wings beside a mirror-smooth artificial lake, in the aristocrats' sector of the city. I made no attempt to talk my way inside; I had come prepared with a note, informing the marquise that her nephew Kinnall, the septarch's son of Salla, was in Glain and wished the favour of an audience; he could be found at such-and-such a hostelry. I returned to my lodgings and waited, and on the third day the innkeeper, popeyed with awe, came to my room to tell me I had a visitor in the livery of the Marquis of Huish. Nioll had sent a car for me; I was taken to her palace, which was far more lavish within than without, and she received me in a great hall cunningly paneled with mirrors set at angles to other mirrors to create an illusion of infinity.

She had aged greatly in the six or seven years since I had last seen her, but my amazement at her white hair and furrowed face was swallowed up in her astonishment over my transformation from tiny child to hulking man in so short a time. We embraced in the style of Glin, fingertips to fingertips; she offered condolences on the death of my father, and apologies for not having attended Stirron's coronation; then she asked me what brought me to Glin, and I explained, and she showed no surprise. Did I propose to dwell permanently here? I did, I said. And how would I support myself? By working in the factor-house of her husband, I explained, if such a position could be procured for me. She did not act as though she found my ambition unreasonable, but merely asked if I had any skills that might recommend me to the marquis. To this I replied that I had been trained in the lawcodes of Salla (not mentioning how incomplete my training was) and might be of value in the factor-house's dealings with that province; also, I said, I had connections of bonding to Segvord Helalam, High Justice of the Port of Manneran, and could serve the firm well in its Manneran business; lastly, I remarked, I was young and strong and ambitious, and would place myself wholly in the service of the factor-house's interests, for our mutual advantage. These statements seemed to sit smoothly with my aunt, and she promised to gain for me an interview with the marquis himself. I left her palace much pleased with my prospects.

Several days later came word to the hostelry that I should present myself at the offices of the factor-house. My appointment, however, was not with the Marquis of Huish; rather, I was to see one of his executives, a certain Sisgar. I should have taken that as an omen. This man was smooth to the point of oiliness, with a beardless face and no eyebrows and a bald head that looked as if it had been waxed, and a dark green robe that was at once properly austere and subtly ostentatious. He questioned me briefly about my training and experience, discovering in some ten queries that I had had little of the former and none of the latter; but he exposed my failings in a gentle and amiable way, and I assumed that despite my ignorance, my high birth and kinship to the marquise would gain me a post. Alas for complacency! I had begun to hatch a dream of climbing to great responsibilities in this factor-house when I caught with only half an ear the words of Sisgar, telling me, 'Times are hard, as surely your grace comprehends, and it is unfortunate that you come to us at a time when retrenching is necessary. The advantages of giving you employment are many, yet the problems are extreme. The marquis wishes you to know that your offer of service was greatly appreciated, and it is his hope to bring you into the firm when economic conditions permit.' With many bows and a pleasant smile of dismissal he drove me from his office, and I was on the street before I realized how thoroughly I had been destroyed. They could give me nothing, not even a fifth assistant clerkship in some village office! How was this possible? I nearly rushed back within, planning to cry, 'This is a mistake, you deal with your septarch's cousin here, you reject the nephew of the marquise!' But they knew those things, and yet they shut their doors to me. When I telephoned my aunt to express my shock, I was told she had gone abroad, to pass the winter in leafy Manneran.

SIXTEEN

Eventually what had occurred became clear to me. My aunt had spoken of me to the marquis, and the marquis had conferred with the septarch Truis, who, concluding that it might embarrass him with Stirron to allow me any kind of employ, instructed the marquis to turn me away. In my fury I thought of going straight to Truis to protest, but I saw the futility of that soon enough, and since my protector Nioll had plainly gone out of Glin to shake herself free of me, I knew there was no hope in that direction. I was alone in Glain with the winter coming on, and no position in this alien place, and my lofty birth worse than useless to me.

Harder blows followed.

Presenting myself at the Covenant Bank of Glin one morning to withdraw funds for living expenses, I learned that my account had been sequestered at the request of the Grand Treasurer of Salla, who was investigating the possibility of an illegal transfer of capital out of that province. By blustering and waving my royal passport about, I managed to break loose enough money for seven days' food and lodging, but the rest of my savings was lost to me, for I had no stomach for the kind of appeals and maneuvers that might free it.

Next I was visited at my hostelry by a diplomat of Salla, a jackal of an undersecretary who reminded me, with many a genuflection and formula of respect, that my brother's wedding would shortly take place and I was expected to return and serve as ring-linker. Knowing that I would never leave Salla City again if ever I gave myself into Stirron's hands, I explained that urgent business required me to remain in Glain during the season of the nuptials, and asked that my deep regrets be conveyed to the septarch. The undersecretary received this with professional grace, but it was not hard for me to detect the savage gleam of pleasure beneath his outer mask: I was buying me trouble, he was telling himself, and he would gladly help me close the contract.

On the fourth day thereafter my innkeeper came to tell me that I could no longer stay at the hostelry, for my passport had been revoked and I had no legal status in Glin.

This was an impossibility. A royal passport such as I carried is granted for life, and is valid in every province of Velada Borthan except in times of war, and there was no war at the moment between Salla and Glin. The innkeeper shrugged away my words; he showed me his notice from the police, ordering him to evict his illegal alien, and he suggested that if I had objections I should take the matter up with the appropriate bureau of the Glinish civil service, for it was beyond his scope. I regarded filing such an appeal as unwise. My eviction had not come about by accident, and should I appear at any government office, I was likely to find myself arrested and hustled across the Huish into Stirron's grasp forthwith.

Seeing such an arrest as the most probable next development, I wondered how to elude the government agents. Now I sorely felt the absence of my bondbrother and bondsister, for where else could I turn for help and advice? Nowhere in Glin was there anyone to whom I might say, 'One is frightened, one is in grave peril, one asks assistance of you.' Everyone's soul was walled against me by stony custom. In all the world were only two whom I could regard as confidants, and they were far away. I must find my own salvation.

I would go into hiding, I decided. The innkeeper granted me a few hours to prepare myself. I shaved my beard, traded my royal cloak for the dim rags of another lodger nearly my height, and arranged the pawn of my ring of ceremony. My remaining possessions I bundled together to serve as a hump on my back, and I hobbled out of the hostelry doubled up, with one eye sealed shut and my mouth twisted far around to one side. Whether it was a disguise that could have fooled anyone, I cannot say; but no one waited to arrest me, and thus uglified I walked out of Glain under a cold, thin rain that soon turned to snow.

SEVENTEEN

Outside the city's north-western gate (for it was there my feet had taken me) a heavy truck came rumbling by me, and its treads rolled through a pool of half-frozen slush, spraying me liberally. I halted to scrape the chilly stuff from my leggings; the truck halted too, and the driver clambered down, exclaiming, 'There is cause for apology here. It was not intended to douse you so!'

This courtesy so astounded me that I stood to my full height, and let the distortions slip from my features. Evidently the driver had thought me a feeble, bent old man; he showed amazement at my transformation, and laughed aloud. I knew not what to say. Into my gaping silence he declared, 'There is room for one to ride, if you have the need or the whim.'

Into my mind sprang a bright fantasy: he would drive me towards the coast, where I would sign on aboard a merchant vessel bound for Manneran, and in that happy tropical land I would throw myself on the mercies of my bondsister's father, escaping all this harassment.

'Where are you bound?' I asked.

'Westward, into the mountains.'

So much for Manneran. I accepted the ride all the same. He offered me no contract of defined liabilities, but I let that pass. For some minutes we did not speak; I was content to listen to the slap of the treads on the snowy road, and think of the distance growing between myself and the police of Glain.

'Outlander, are you?' he said at length.

'Indeed.' Fearing that some alarm might be out for a man of Salla, I chose belatedly to adopt the soft slurred speech of southern folk, that I had learned from Halum, hoping he would come to believe that I had not spoken first to him with Sallan accents. 'You travel with a native of Manneran, who finds your winter a strange and burdensome thing.'

'What brought you north?' he asked.

'The settlement of one's mother's estate. She was a woman of Glain.'

'Did the lawyers treat you well, then?'

'Her money melted in their hands, leaving nothing.'

'The usual story. You're short of cash, eh?'

'Destitute,' I admitted.

'Well, well, one understands your situation, for one has been there oneself. Perhaps something can be done for you.'

I realized from his phrasing, from his failure to use the Glinish passive construction, that he too must be an outlander. Swinging round to face him, I said, 'Is one right that you likewise are from elsewhere?'

'This is true.'

'Your accent is unfamiliar. Some western province?'

'Oh, no, no.'

'Not Salla, then?'

'Manneran,' he said, and burst into hearty laughter, and covered my shame and confusion by telling me, 'You do the accent well, friend. But you needn't make the effort longer.'

'One hears no Manneran in your voice,' I mumbled.

'One has lived long in Glin,' he said, 'and one's voice is a soup of inflections.'

I had not fooled him for a moment, but he made no attempt to penetrate my identity, and seemed not to care who I might be or where I came from. We talked easily a while. He told me that he owned a lumber mill in western Glin, midway up the flanks of the Huishtors where the tall yellow-needled honey-trees grow; before we had driven much farther along he was offering me a job as a logger in his camp. The pay was poor, he said, but one breathed clean air there, and government officials were never seen, and such things as passports and certificates of status did not matter.

Of course I accepted. His camp was beautifully situated, above a sparkling mountain lake which never froze, for it was fed by a warm spring whose source was said to be deep beneath the Burnt Lowlands. Tremendous ice-topped Huishtor peaks hung above us, and not far away was Glin Gate, the pass through which one goes from Glin to the Burnt Lowlands, crossing a bitter corner of the Frozen Lowlands on the way. He had a hundred men in his employ, rough and foul-mouthed, forever shouting 'I' and 'me' without shame, but they were honest and hardworking men, and I had never been close to their sort before. My plan was to stay there through the winter, saving my pay, and go off to Manneran when I had earned the price of my passage. Some news of the outer world reached the camp from time to time, though, and I learned in this way that the Glinish authorities were seeking a certain young prince of Salla, who was believed to have gone insane and was wandering somewhere in Glin; the septarch Stirron urgently wished the unhappy young man to be returned to his homeland for the medical care he so desperately needed. Suspecting that the roads and ports would be watched, I extended my stay in the mountains through the spring, and, my caution deepening, I stayed the summer also. In the end I spent something more than a year there.

It was a year that changed me greatly. We worked hard,

felling the huge trees in all weathers, stripping them of boughs, feeding them to the mill, a long tiring day and a chilly one, but plenty of hot wine at night, and every tenth day a platoon of women brought in from a nearby town to amuse us. My weight increased by half again, all of it hard muscle, and I grew taller until I surpassed the tallest logger in the camp, and they made jokes about my size. My beard came in full and the planes of my face changed as the plumpness of youth went from me. The loggers I found more likeable than the courtiers among whom all my prior days had been passed. Few of them were able even to read, and of polite etiquette they knew nothing, but they were cheerful and easy-spirited men, at home in their own bodies. I would not have you think that because they talked in 'I' and 'me' they were open-hearted and given to sharing of confidences; they kept the Covenant in that respect, and might even have been more secretive than educated folk about certain things. Yet they seemed more sunny of soul than those who speak in passives and impersonal pronouns, and perhaps my stay among them planted in me that seed of subversion, that understanding of the Covenant's basic wrongness, which the Earthman Schweiz later guided into full flowering.

I told them nothing of my rank and origin. They could see for themselves, by the smoothness of my skin, that I had not done much hard labor in my life, and my way of speaking marked me as an educated man, if not necessarily one of high birth. But I offered no revelations of my past, and none were sought. All I said was that I came from Salla, since my accent marked me as Sallan anyway; they granted me the privacy of my history. My employer, I think, guessed early that I must be the fugitive prince whom Stirron sought, but he never queried me about that. For the first time in my life, then, I had an identity apart from my royal status. I ceased to be Lord Kinnall, the septarch's second son, and was only Darival, the big logger from Salla.

From that transformation I learned much. I had never played one of your swaggering, bullying young nobles; being a second son instills a certain humility even in an aristocrat. Yet I could not help feeling set apart from ordinary men. I was waited on, bowed to, served, and pampered; men spoke softly to me and made formal gestures of respect, even when I was a child. I was, after all, the son of a septarch, that is to say a king, for septarchs are hereditary rulers and thus are part of mankind's procession of kings, a line that goes back to the dawn of human settlement on Borthan and beyond, back across the stars to Earth itself, to the lost and forgotten dynasties of her ancient nations, ultimately to the masked and painted chieftains enthroned in prehistoric caves. And I was part of that line, a man of royal blood, somehow superior by circumstance of birth. But in this logging camp in the mountains I came to understand that kings are nothing but men set high. The gods do not anoint them, but rather the will of men, and men can strip them of their lofty rank; if Stirron were to be cast down by insurrection, and in his place that loathsome drainer from Salla Old Town became septarch, would not the drainer then enter that mystic procession of kings, and Stirron be relegated to the dust? And would not that drainer's sons become blood-proud, even as I had been, although their father had been nothing for most of his life, and their grandfather less than that? I know, I know, the sages would say that the kiss of the gods had fallen upon that drainer, elevating him and all his progeny and making them forever sacred, yet as I felled trees on the slopes of the Huishtors I saw kingship with clearer eyes, and, having been cast down by events myself, I realized that I was no more than a man among men, and always had been. What I would make of myself depended on my natural gifts and ambitions, not upon the accident of rank.

So rewarding was that knowledge, and the altered sense of self it brought me, that my stay in the mountains ceased to seem like an exile, but more like a vocation. My dreams of fleeing to a soft life in Manneran left me, and, even after I had saved more than enough to pay my passage to that land, I found myself with no impulse to move onward. It was not entirely fear of arrest that kept me among the loggers, but also a love of the crisp clear cold Huishtor air, and of my arduous new craft, and of the rough but genuine men among whom

I dwelled. Therefore I stayed on, through summer and into autumn, and welcomed the coming of a new winter, and gave no thought to going.

I might be there yet, only I was forced into flight. One woeful winter afternoon, with the sky like iron and the threat of a blizzard over us like a fist, they brought the whores up from town for our regularly appointed night of frolic, and this time there was among them a newcomer whose voice announced her place of birth to be Salla. I heard her instantly as the women came cavorting into our hall of sport, and would have crept away, but she spied me and gasped and cried out on the spot: 'Look you there! For sure that is our vanished prince!'

I laughed and tried to persuade everyone that she was drunk or mad, but my scarlet cheeks gave me the lie, and the loggers peered at me in a new way. A prince? A prince? Was it so? They whispered to one another, nudging and winking. Recognizing my peril, I claimed the woman for my own use and drew her aside, and when we were alone, I insisted to her she was mistaken: I am no prince, I said, but only a common logger. She would not have it. 'The Lord Kinnall marched in the septarch's funeral procession,' she said, 'and this one beheld him, with these eyes. And you are he!' The more I protested, the more convinced she was. There was no shifting her mind. Even when I embraced her, she was so awe-smitten at opening herself to a septarch's son that her loins remained dry, and I injured her in entering her.

Late that night, when the revelry had ended, my employer came to me, solemn and uneasy. 'One of the girls has made strange talk about you this evening,' he said. 'If the talk is true, you are endangered, for when she returns to her village she'll spread the news, and the police will be here soon enough.'

'Must one flee, then?' I asked.

'The choice is yours. Alarms still are out for this prince; if you are he, no one here can protect you against the authorities.'

'Then one must flee. At daybreak –'

'Now,' he said. 'While the girl still lies here asleep.'

He pressed money of Glin into my hand, over and beyond

what he owed me in current wages; I gathered my few belongings, and we went outside together. The night was moonless
and the winter wind was savage. By starlight I saw the glitter of
lightly falling snow. My employer silently drove me down the
slope, past the foothills village from which the whores came,
and out along a back-country road which we followed for some
hours. When dawn met us we were in south-central Glin, not
overly far from the River Huish. He halted, at last, in a village
that proclaimed itself to be Klaek, a winter-bound place of
small stone cottages bordering on broad snowy fields. Leaving
me in the truck, he entered the first of the cottages, emerging
after a moment accompanied by a wizened man who poured
forth a torrent of instructions and gesticulations; with the aid
of this guidance we found our way to the place my employer
was seeking, the cottage of a certain farmer named Stumwil.
This Stumwil was a fair-haired man of about my own height,
with washed-out blue eyes and an apologetic smile. Maybe he
was some kinsman of my employer's, or, more probably, he
owed him a debt – I never asked. In any case the farmer
readily agreed to my employer's request, and accepted me
as a lodger. My employer embraced me and drove off into
the gathering snow; I saw him never again. I hope the gods
were kind to him, as he was to me.

EIGHTEEN

The cottage was one large room, divided by flimsy curtains into
areas. Stumwil put up a new curtain, gave me straw for my
mattress, and I had my living quarters. There were seven of
us under that roof: Stumwil and myself, and Stumwil's wife,
a weary wench who I could have been persuaded was his
mother, and three of their children – two boys some years
short of manhood and a girl in mid-adolescence – and the
bondsister of the girl, who was lodging with them that year.

They were sunny, innocent, trusting folk. Though they knew nothing about me, they all instantly adopted me as a member of the family, some unknown uncle unexpectedly returned from far voyaging. I was not prepared for the easy way they accepted me, and credited it at first to some net of obligation in which my former employer had bound them to me, but no: they were kindly by nature, unquestioning, unsuspicious. I took my meals at their table; I sat among them by their fire; I joined in their games. Every fifth night Stumwil filled a huge dented tub with hot water for the entire family, and I bathed with them, two or three of us in the tub at once, though it disturbed me inwardly to rub up against the plump bare bodies of Stumwil's daughter and her friend. I suppose I could have had the daughter or the bondsister if I had cared to, but I kept back from them, thinking such a seduction would be a breach of hospitality. Later, when I understood more about peasants, I realized that it was my abstinence that had been a breach of hospitality, for the girls were of age and surely willing, and I had disdained them. But I saw that only after I had left Stumwil's place. Those girls now have adult children of their own. I suppose by this time they have forgiven me for my lack of gallantry.

I paid a fee for my lodging, and I helped also with the chores, though in winter there was little to do except shovel snow and feed the fire. None of them showed curiosity about my identity or history. They asked me no questions, and I believe that no questions ever passed through their minds. Nor did the other townspeople pry, though they gave me the scrutiny any stranger would receive.

Newspapers occasionally reached this village, and those that did went from hand to hand until all had read them, when they were placed on deposit at the wineshop at the head of the main village thoroughfare. I consulted them there, a file of stained and tattered scraps, and learned what I could of the events of the past year. I found that my brother Stirron's wedding had taken place on schedule, with appropriate regal pomp; his lean troubled face looked up out of a blurry, grease-splotched bit of

old paper, and beside him was his radiant bride, but I could not
make out her features. There was tension between Glin and
Krell over fishing rights in a disputed coastal area, and men
had died in border skirmishes. I pitied General Condorit, whose
patrol sector was at the opposite end of the boundary, almost,
from the Krell-Glin line, and who therefore must have missed
the fun of somehow involving Salla in the shooting. A sea
monster, golden-scaled and sinuous, more than ten times the
length of a man's body, had been sighted in the Gulf of Sumar
by a party of Mannerangi fishermen, who had sworn a mighty
oath in the Stone Chapel as to the authenticity of their vision.
The prime septarch of Threish, a bloody old brigand if the tales
they tell of him are true, had abdicated, and was dwelling in a
godhouse in the western mountains not far from Stroin Gap,
serving as a drainer for pilgrims bound to Manneran. Such was
the news. I found no mention of myself. Perhaps Stirron had
lost interest in having me seized and returned to Salla.

It might therefore be safe for me to try to leave Glin.

Eager as I was to get out of that frosty province, where my
own kin rebuffed me and only strangers showed me love, two
things held me back. For one, I meant to stay with Stumwil
until I could help him with his spring planting, in return for his
kindness to me. For another, I would not set forth undrained
on so dangerous a journey, lest in some mishap my spirit go
to the gods still full of poisons. This village of Klaek had no
drainer of its own, but depended for its solace on itinerant
drainers who passed now and then through the countryside.
In the winter these wanderers rarely came by, and so perforce I
had gone undrained since the late summer, when a member of
that profession had visited the logging camp. I felt the need.

There came a late-winter snow, a storm of wonders that
coated every branch with a fiery skin of ice, and immediately
thereafter there came a thaw. The world melted. Klaek was
surrounded by oceans of mud. A drainer driving a battered
and ancient groundcar came to us through this slippery sea
and set up shop in an old shack, doing fine business among
the villagers. I went to him on the fifth day of his visit, when

the lines were shorter, and unburdened myself for two hours, sparing him nothing, neither the truth about my identity nor my subversive new philosophy of kingship nor the usual grimy little repressed lusts and prides. It was more of a dose, evidently, than a country drainer expected to receive, and he seemed to puff and swell as I poured out my words; at the end he was shaking as much as I, and could barely speak. I wondered where it was that drainers went to unload all the sins and sorrows they absorbed from their clients. They are forbidden to talk to ordinary men of anything they have learned in the confessional; did they therefore have drainer-drainers, servants of the servants, to whom they might deliver that which they could not mention to anyone else? I did not see how a drainer could carry such a bundle of sadnesses for long unaided, as he got from any dozen of his customers in a day's listening.

With my soul cleansed, I had only to wait for planting-time, and it was not long in coming. The growing season in Glin is short; they get their seeds into the ground before winter's grip has fully slipped, so that they can catch every ray of spring sunlight. Stumwil waited until he felt certain that the thaw would not be followed by one last tumult of snow, and then, with the land still a sucking quagmire, he and his family went out into the fields to plant breadseed and spice-flower and blueglobe.

The custom was to go naked to the planting. On the first morning I looked out of Stumwil's cottage and beheld the neighbors on all sides walking bare towards the furrows, children and parents and grandparents stripped to the skin with sacks of seed slung over their shoulders – a procession of knobby knees, sagging bellies, dried-out breasts, wrinkled buttocks, illuminated here and there by the smooth firm bodies of the young. Thinking I was in some waking dream, I looked around and saw Stumwil and his wife and their daughter already disrobed, and beckoning to me to do the same. They took their sacks and left the cottage. The two young sons scampered after them, leaving me with the bondsister of Stumwil's daughter, who had overslept and had just appeared.

She shucked her garments too; a supple saucy body she had, with small high dark-nippled breasts and slender well-muscled thighs. As I dropped my clothes I asked her, 'Why is it done to be naked outdoors in such a cold time?'

'The mud gives cause for slipping,' she explained, 'and it is easier to wash raw skin than garments.'

There was truth enough in that, for the planting was a comic show, with peasants skidding in the tricky muck every tenth step they took. Down they went, landing on hip or haunch and coming up smeared with brown; it was a matter of skill to grasp the neck of one's seed-sack as one toppled, so that no precious seeds would be scattered. I fell like the rest, learning the knack of it quickly, and indeed there was pleasure in slipping, for the mud had a voluptuous oozy feel to it. So we marched on, staggering and lurching, slapping flesh to mud again and again, laughing, singing, pressing our seeds into the cold soft soil, and not one of us but was covered from scalp to tail with muck within minutes. I shivered miserably at the outset, but soon I was warmed by laughter and tripping, and when the day's work was done, we stood around shamelessly naked in front of Stumwil's cottage and doused one another with buckets of water to clean ourselves. By then it seemed reasonable to me that they should prefer to expose their skins rather than their clothing to such a day's labour, but in fact the girl's explanation was incorrect: I learned from Stumwil later that week that the nakedness was a religious matter, a sign of humility before the gods of the crops, and nothing else.

Eight days it took to finish the planting. On the ninth, wishing Stumwil and his people a hearty harvest, I took my leave of the village of Klaek, and began my journey to the coast.

NINETEEN

A neighbor of Stumwil's took me eastward the first day in his cart. I walked most of the second, begged a ride on the third and fourth, and walked again on the fifth and sixth. The air was cool but the crackle of spring was in it, as buds unfolded and birds returned. I bypassed the city of Glain, which might have been dangerous for me, and without any events that I can clearly recall I made my way swiftly to Biumar, Glin's main seaport and second most populous city.

It was a handsomer place than Glain, though hardly beautiful: a greasy gray sprawl of an oversized town, backed up against a gray and menacing ocean. On my first day there I learned that all passenger service between Glin and the southern provinces had been suspended three moontimes before, owing to the dangerous activities of pirates operating out of Krell, for Glin and Krell were now engaged in an undeclared war. The only way I could reach Manneran, it seemed, was overland via Salla, and I hardly wished to do that. I was resourceful, though. I found myself a room in a tavern near the docks and spent a few days picking up maritime gossip. Passenger service might be suspended, but commercial seafaring, I discovered, was not, since the prosperity of Glin depended upon it; convoys of merchant vessels, heavily armed, went forth on regular schedules. A limping seaman who stayed in the same tavern told me, when blue wine of Salla had oiled him sufficiently, that a merchant convoy of this sort would leave in a week's time, and that he had a berth aboard one of the ships. I considered drugging him on the eve of sailing and borrowing his identity, as is done in pirate tales for children, but a less dramatic method suggested itself to me: I bought his shipping-papers. The sum I offered him was more than he would have earned by shipping out to Manneran and back, so he was happy to take my money and let me go in his place. We spent a long drunken night conferring about his duties on the ship, for I knew nothing, of seamanship. At the coming of dawn I still knew nothing, but I saw ways I could bluff a minimal sort of competence.

I went unchallenged on board the vessel, a low-slung air-powered craft heavily laden with Glinish goods. The checking of papers was perfunctory. I picked up my cabin assignment, installed myself, reported for duty. About half the jobs they asked me to do, over the first few days, I managed to carry out reasonably well by imitation and experiment; the other things I merely muddled with, and soon my fellow sailors recognized me for a bungler, but they kept knowledge of that from the officers. A kind of loyalty prevailed in the lower ranks. Once again I saw that my dark view of mankind had been overly colored by my boyhood among aristocrats; these sailors, like the loggers, like the farmers, had a kind of hearty good fellowship among themselves that I had never found among those more strict to the Covenant. They did for me the jobs I could not do myself, and I relieved them of dull work that was within my narrow skills, and all went well. I swabbed decks, cleaned filters, and spent endless hours manning the guns against pirate attacks. But we got past Krell's dreaded pirate coast without incident, and slipped easily down the coast of Salla, which already was green with spring.

Our first port of call was Cofalon, Salla's chief seaport, for five days of selling and buying. I was alarmed at this, for I had not known we planned to halt anywhere in my homeland. I thought at first to announce myself ill and hide belowdecks all our time in Cofalon; but then I rejected the scheme as cowardly, telling myself that a man must test himself frequently against risk, if he would keep his manhood. So I boldly went wenching and wining in town with my shipmates, trusting that time had sufficiently changed my face, and that no one would expect to find Lord Stirron's missing brother in a sailor's rough clothes in such a town as this. My gamble succeeded: I went unvexed the full five days. From newspapers and careful overhearing I learned all I could about events in Salla in the year and a half since my leaving. Stirron, I gathered, was popularly held to be a good ruler. He had brought the province through its winter of famine by purchasing surplus food from Manneran on favourable terms, and our farms had since then had better fortune. Taxes had been cut. The people were content. Stirron's wife had been delivered of a son, the Lord Dariv, who now was heir to the prime septarchy, and another son was on the way. As for the Lord Kinnall, brother to the septarch, nothing was said of him; he was forgotten as though he had never been.

We made other stops here and there down the coast, several in southern Salla, several in northern Manneran. And in good time we came to that great seaport at the south-eastern corner of our continent, the holy city of Manneran, capital of the province that bears the same name. It was in Manneran that my life would begin anew.

TWENTY

Manneran the province was favoured by the gods. The air is mild and sweet, filled all the year through with the fragrance of flowers. Winter does not reach so far south, and the Mannerangi, when they would see snow, go as tourists to the Huishtor peaks and gape at the strange cold coating of whiteness that passes for water in other lands. The warm sea that borders Manneran on east and south yields food enough to feed half the continent, and to the south-west there is the Gulf of Sumar as well, with further bounty. War has rarely touched Manneran, protected as it is by a shield of mountains and water from the peoples of the western lands, and separated from its neighbor to the north, Salla, by the immense torrent of the River Woyn. Now and again we have attempted to invade Manneran by sea, but never with any conviction that we would be successful, nor has there been any success; when Salla engages seriously in war, the foe is always Glin.

Manneran the city must also have enjoyed special divine blessings. Its site is the finest natural harbor in all Velada Borthan, a deep-cut bay framed by two opposing fingers of land, jutting towards one another in such a way that no breakwaters are needed there, and ships sit easily at anchor. This harbor is one mighty source of the province's prosperity. It constitutes the chief link between the eastern and western provinces, for there is little landborne commerce across the continent by way of the Burnt Lowlands, and since our world lacks natural fuels, so far as we know, airborne traffic is never likely to amount to much here. So ships of the nine western provinces travel eastward through the Strait of Sumar to the port of Manneran, and ships from Manneran make regular calls on the western coast. The Mannerangi then retail western goods to Salla, Glin, and Krell in their own vessels, reaping the usual profits of go-betweens. The harbor of Manneran is the only place on our world where men of all thirteen provinces mingle and where all thirteen flags may be seen at once; and this busy commerce spills an unending flow of wealth into the coffers of the Mannerangi. In addition, their inland districts are rich in fertility, even up to the Huishtor slopes, which in their latitudes are unfrozen except at the summits. The farms of Manneran have two or three harvests a year, and, by way of Stroin Gap, the Mannerangi have access to the Wet Lowlands and all the strange and valuable fruits and spices produced there. Small wonder, then, that those who love luxuries seek their fortunes in Manneran.

As if all this good fortune were not enough, the Mannerangi have persuaded the world that they live in the holiest spot on Borthan, and multiply their revenues by maintaining sacred shrines as magnets for pilgrims. One might think that Threish, on the western coast, where our ancestors first settled and the Covenant was drawn up, would put itself forward as a place of pilgrimage second to none. Indeed, there is some sort of shrine in Threish, and westerners too poor to travel to Manneran visit it. But Manneran has established itself as the holy of holies. The youngest of all our provinces, too, except only the breakaway kingdom of Krell; yet by a show of inner conviction and energetic advertisement has Manneran managed to make itself sacred. There is irony in this, for the Mannerangi hold more loosely to the Covenant than any of us in the thirteen provinces; their tropical life has softened them somewhat, and they open their souls to one another to a degree that would get them ostracized as selfbarers in Glin or Salla. Still, they have the Stone Chapel, where miracles are reliably reported to have occurred, where the gods supposedly came forth in the flesh only seven hundred years ago, and it is everyone's hope to have his child receive his adult name in the Stone Chapel on Naming Day. From all over the continent they come for that festival, to the vast profit of the Mannerangi hotelkeepers. Why, I was named in the Stone Chapel myself.

TWENTY-ONE

When we were docked in Manneran and the longshoremen were at work unloading our cargo, I collected my pay and left ship to enter town. At the foot of the pier I paused to pick up a shore pass from the Mannerangi immigration officials. 'How long will you be in town?' I was asked, and blandly I replied that I meant to stay among them for three days, although my real intent was to settle for the rest of my years in this place.

Twice before had I been in Manneran: once just out of my infancy, to be bonded to Halum, and once when I was seven, for my Naming Day. My memories of the city amounted to nothing more than vague and random patterns of colors: the pale pink and green and blue tones of the buildings, the dark green masses of the heavy vegetation, the black solemn interior of the Stone Chapel. As I walked away from the waterfront those colors bombarded me again, and glowing images out of my childhood shimmered before my dazzled eyes. Manneran is not built of stone, as our northern cities are, but rather of

a kind of artificial plaster, which they paint in light pastel
hues, so that every wall and façade sings joyfully, and billows
like a curtain in the sunlight. The day was a bright one, and
the beams of light bounced gaily about, setting the streets
ablaze and forcing me to shade my eyes. I was stunned also
by the complexity of the streets. Mannerangi architects rely
greatly on ornament; the buildings are decked with ornate
ironwork balconies, fanciful scrollings, flamboyant rooftiles,
gaudy window-draperies, so that the northern eye beholds
at first glance a monstrous baffling clutter, which resolves
itself only gradually into a vista of elegance and grace and
proportion. Everywhere, too, there are plants: trees lining
both sides of each street, vines cascading from window boxes,
flowers bursting forth in kerbside gardens, and the hint of lush
vegetation in the sheltered courtyards of the houses. The effect
is refined and sophisticated, an interplay of jungle profusion
and disciplined urban textures. Manneran is an extraordinary
city, subtle, sensuous, languorous, over-ripe.

My childhood recollections did not prepare me for the heat.
A steamy haze enveloped the streets. The air was wet and
heavy. I felt I could almost touch the heat, could seize it
and grasp it, could wring it like water from the atmosphere.
It was raining heat and I was drenched in it. I was clad in
a coarse, heavy gray uniform, the usual wintertime issue
aboard a Glinish merchant ship, and this was a sweltering
spring morning in Manneran; two dozen paces in that stifling
humidity and I was ready to rip off my chafing clothes and go
naked.

A telephone directory gave me the address of Segvord
Helalam, my bondsister's father. I hired a taxi and went
there. Helalam lived just outside the city, in a cool leafy
suburb of grand homes and glistening lakes; a high brick wall
shielded his house from the view of passers-by. I rang at the
gate and waited to be scanned. My taxi waited too, as if the
driver knew certainly that I would be turned away. A voice
within the house, some butler, no doubt, queried me over the
scanner line and I replied, 'Kinnall Darival of Salla, bondbrother

to the daughter of the High Justice Helalam, wishes to call upon the father of his bondsister.'

'The Lord Kinnall is dead,' I was informed coldly, 'and you are some impostor.'

I rang again. 'Scan this, and judge if he be dead,' I said, holding up to the machine's eye my royal passport, which I had kept so long concealed. 'This is Kinnall Darival before you, and it will not go well with you if you deny him access to the High Justice!'

'Passports may be stolen. Passports may be forged.'

'Open the gate!'

There was no reply. A third time I rang, and this time the unseen butler told me that the police would be summoned unless I departed at once. My taxi driver, parked just across the road, coughed politely. I had not reckoned on any of this. Would I have to go back to town, and take lodgings, and write Segvord Helalam for an appointment, and offer evidence that I still lived?

By good fortune I was spared those bothers. A sumptuous black groundcar drew up, of a kind used generally only by the highest aristocracy, and from it stepped Segvord Helalam, High Justice of the Port of Manneran. He was then at the height of his career, and he carried himself with kingly grace: a short man, but well constructed, with a fine head, a florid face, a noble mane of white hair, a look of strength and purpose. His eyes, an intense blue, were capable of flashing fire, and his nose was an imperial beak, but he canceled all his look of ferocity with a warm, ready smile. He was recognized in Manneran as a man of wisdom and temperance. I went immediately towards him, with a glad cry of 'Bondfather!' Swinging about, he stared at me in bewilderment, and two large young men who had been with him in his groundcar placed themselves between the High Justice and myself as though they believed me to be an assassin.

'Your bodyguard may relax,' I said. 'Are you unable to recognize Kinnall of Salla?'

'The Lord Kinnall died last year,' Segvord replied quickly.

'That comes as grievous news to Kinnall himself,' I said. I drew myself tall, resuming princely mien for the first time since my sad exit from the city of Glain, and gestured at the High Justice's protectors with such fury that they gave ground, slipping off to the side. Segvord studied me carefully. He had last seen me at my brother's coronation; two years had gone by since then, and the last softness of childhood had been stripped from me. My year of felling logs showed in the contours of my frame, and my winter among the farmers had weathered my face, and my weeks as a sailor had left me grimy and unkempt, with tangled hair and a shaggy beard. Segvord's gaze cut gradually through these transformations until he was convinced of my identity; then suddenly he rushed at me, embracing me with such fervor that I nearly lost my footing in surprise. He cried my name, and I cried his; then the gate was opening, and he was hurrying me within, and the lofty cream-colored mansion loomed before me, the goal of all my wanderings and turmoil.

TWENTY-TWO

I was conducted to a pretty chamber and told that it was to be mine, and two servant-girls came to me, plucking off my sweaty seaman's garb; they led me, giggling all the while, to a huge tiled tub, and bathed and perfumed me, and cropped my hair and beard somewhat, and let me pinch and tumble them a bit. They brought me clothes of fine fabric, of a sort I had not worn since my days as royalty, all sheer and white and flowing and cool. And they offered me jewelry, a triple ring set with – I later learned – a sliver of the Stone Chapel's floor, and also a gleaming pendant, a tree-crystal from the land of Threish, on a leather thong. At length, after several hours of polishing. I was deemed fit to present to the High Justice. Segvord received me in the room he called his study, which actually was a great hall worthy of a septarch's palace, in which he sat enthroned even as a ruler would. I recall feeling some annoyance at his pretensions, for not only was he not royal, but he was of the lower aristocracy of Manneran, who had been of no stature whatever until his appointment to high office had put him on the road to fame and wealth.

I asked at once after my bondsister Halum.

'She fares well,' he said, 'though her soul was darkened by the tidings of your supposed death.'

'Where is she now?'

'On holiday, in the Sumar Gulf, on an island where we have another home.'

I felt a chill. 'Has she married?'

'To the regret of all who love her, she has not.'

'Is there anyone, though?'

'No,' Segvord said. 'She seems to prefer chastity. Of course, she is very young. When she returns, Kinnall, perhaps you could speak to her, pointing out that she might think now about making a match, for now she might have some fair lord, while in a few years' time there will be new maidens ahead of her in line.'

'How soon will she be back from this island?'

'At any moment,' said the High Justice. 'How amazed she will be to find you here!'

I asked him concerning my death. He replied that word had come, two years earlier, that I was mad and had wandered, helpless and deluded, into Glin. Segvord smiled as though to tell me that he knew right well why I had left Salla, and that there had been nothing of insanity about my motives. 'Then,' he said, 'there were reports that the Lord Stirron had sent agents into Glin after you, so that you could be brought back for treatment. Halum feared greatly for your safety at that time. And lastly, this summer past, one of your brother's ministers gave it out that you had gone roaming in the Glinish Huishtors in the pit of winter, and had been lost in the snows, in a blizzard no man could have survived.'

'But of course the Lord Kinnall's body was not recovered in

the warm months of the year gone by, and was left to wither in the Huishtors, instead of being brought back to Salla for a proper burial.'

'There was no news of finding the body, no.'

'Then obviously,' I said, 'the Lord Kinnall's body awakened in the springtime, and trekked about on a ghostly parade, and went its way southward, and now at last has presented itself on the doorstep of the High Justice of the Port of Manneran.'

Segvord laughed. 'A healthy ghost!'

'A weary one, as well.'

'What befell you in Glin?'

'A cold time in more ways than one.' I told him of my snubbing at the hands of my mother's kin, of my stay in the mountains, and all the rest. When he had heard that, he wished to know what my plans were in Manneran; to this I replied that I had no plans other than to find some honorable enterprise, and succeed in it, and marry, and settle down, for Salla was closed to me and Glin held no temptations. Segvord nodded gravely. There was, he said, a clerkship open at this very moment in his office. The job carried little pay and less prestige, and it was absurd to ask a prince of Salla's royal line to accept it, but still it was clean work, with a fine chance of advancement, and it might serve to give me a foothold while I acclimated myself to the Mannerangi way of life. Since I had had some such opportunity in mind all along, I told him at once that I would gladly enter his employ, with no heed to my royal blood, since all that was behind me now, done with, and imaginary besides. 'What one makes of himself here,' I said soberly, 'will depend wholly on his merits, not on the circumstances of rank and influence.' Which was, of course, pure piffle: instead of trading on my high birth, I would instead here make capital out of being bondbrother to the High Justice of the Port's daughter, a connection that had come to me because of my high birth alone, and where was the effect of merit in any of that?

TWENTY-THREE

The searchers are getting closer to me all the time. Yesterday, while on a long walk through this zone of the Burnt Lowlands, I found, well south of here, the fresh track of a groundcar impressed deep in the dry and fragile crust of the red sand. And this morning, idly strolling in the place where the hornfowl gather – drawn there by some suicidal impulse, maybe? – I heard a droning in the sky, and looked up to see a plane of the Sallan military passing overhead. One does not often see sky-vehicles here. It swooped and circled, hornfowl-fashion, but I huddled under a twisted erosion-knoll, and I think I went unnoticed.

I might be mistaken about these intrusions: the groundcar just some hunting party casually passing through the region, the plane merely out on a training flight. But I think not. If there are hunters here, it is I they hunt. The net will close about me. I must try to write more quickly, and be more concise; too much of what I need to say is yet untold, and I fear being interrupted before I am done. Stirron, let me be for just a few more weeks!

TWENTY-FOUR

The High Justice of the Port is one of Manneran's supreme officials. He holds jurisdiction over all commercial affairs in the capital; if there are disputes between merchants, they are tried in his court, and by treaty he has authority over the nationals of every province, so that a sea-captain of Glin or Krell, a Sallan or a westerner, when hailed before the High Justice, is subject to his verdicts with no rights of appeal to the courts of his homeland. This is the High Justice's ancient function, but if he were nothing but an arbiter of mercantile squabbles he would hardly have the grandeur that he does. However, over the centuries other responsibilities have fallen to him. He alone regulates the flow of foreign shipping into the harbor of Manneran, granting trade permits for so many Glinish vessels a year, so many from Threish, so many from Salla. The prosperity of a dozen provinces is subject to his decisions. Therefore he is courted by septarchs, flooded with gifts, buried in kindnesses and praise, in the hope that he will allow this land or that an extra ship in the year to come. The High Justice, then, is the economic filter of Velada Borthan, opening and closing commercial outlets as he pleases; he does this not by whim but by consideration of the ebb and flow of wealth across the continent, and it is impossible to overestimate his importance in our society.

The office is not hereditary, but the appointment is for life, and a High Justice can be removed only through intricate and well-nigh impracticable impeachment procedures. Thus it comes to pass that a vigorous High Justice, such as Segvord Helalam, can become more powerful in Manneran than the prime septarch himself. The septarchy of Manneran is in decay in any case; two of the seven seats have gone unfilled for the past hundred years or more, and the occupants of the remaining five have ceded so much of their authority to civil servants that they are little more than ceremonial figures. The prime septarch still has some shreds of majesty, but he must consult with the High Justice of the Port on all matters of economic concern, and the High Justice has entangled himself so inextricably in the machinery of Manneran's government that it is difficult to say truly who is the ruler and who the civil servant.

On my third day in Manneran, Segvord took me to his courthouse to contract me into my job. I who was raised in a palace was awed to see the headquarters of the Port Justiciary; what amazed me was not its opulence (for it had none) but its great size. I beheld a broad yellow-colored brick structure, four storeys high, squat and massive, that seemed to run the entire length of the waterfront two blocks inland from the piers. Within it at worn desks in high-ceilinged offices were armies of drudging clerks, shuffling papers and stamping receipts, and my soul quivered at the thought that this was how I was to spend my days. Segvord led me on an endless march through the building, receiving the homage of the workers as he passed their dank and sweaty offices; he paused here and there to greet someone, to glance casually at some half-written report, to study a board on which, apparently, the movements of every vessel within three days' journey of Manneran were being charted. At length we entered a noble suite of rooms, far from the bustle and hurry I had just seen. Here the High Justice himself presided. Showing me a cool and splendidly furnished room adjoining his own chamber, Segvord told me that this was where I would work.

The contract I signed was like a drainer's: I pledged myself to reveal nothing of what I might learn in the course of my duties, on pain of terrible penalties. For its part the Port Justiciary promised me lifetime employment, steady increases of salary, and various other privileges of a kind princes do not normally worry about.

Quickly I discovered that I was to be no humble inkstained clerk. As Segvord had warned me, my pay was low and my rank in the bureaucracy almost non-existent, but my responsibilities proved to be great ones; in effect, I was his private secretary. All confidential reports intended for the High Justice's eyes would cross my desk first. My task was to discard those that were of no importance and to prepare abridgements of the others, all but those I deemed to be of the highest pertinence, which went to him complete. If the High Justice is the economic filter of Velada Borthan, I was to be the filter's filter, for he would read only what I wished him to read, and make his decisions on the basis of what I gave him. Once this was clear to me I knew that Segvord had placed me on the path to great power in Manneran.

TWENTY-FIVE

Impatiently I awaited Halum's return from her isle in the Gulf of Sumar. Neither bondsister nor bondbrother had I had for over two years, and drainers could not take their place; I ached to sit up late at night with Halum or Noim, as in the old days, opening self to self. Noim was somewhere in Salla, I supposed, but I knew not where, and Halum, though she was said to be due back imminently from holidaying, did not appear in my first week in Manneran, nor the second. During the third, I left the Justiciary office early one day, feeling ill from the humidity and the tensions of mastering my new role, and was driven to Segvord's estate. Entering the central courtyard on my way to my room, I caught sight of a tall, slender girl at the far end, plucking from a vine a golden flower for her dark glossy hair. I could not see her face, but from her figure and bearing I had no doubt of her, and joyfully I cried, 'Halum!' and rushed across the courtyard. She turned frowning to me, halting me in mid-rush. Her brow was furrowed and her lips were tight together; her gaze was chilly and remote. What did that cold glance mean? Her face was Halum's face – dark eyes, fine slim proud nose, firm chin, bold cheekbones – and yet her face was strange to me. Could two years have changed my bondsister so greatly? The main differences between the Halum I remembered and the woman I saw were subtle ones, differences of expression, a tilt of the eyebrows, a flicker of the nostrils, a quirking of the mouth, as though the whole soul itself within her had altered. Also there were some minor differences of feature, I saw as I drew nearer, but these could be ascribed to the passing of time or to the faults of my memory. My heart sped and my fingers trembled and an odd heat of confusion spread across my shoulders and back. I would have gone to her and embraced her, but suddenly I feared her in her transformations.

'Halum?' I said uncertainly, hoarse-voiced, dry-throated.

'She is not yet here.' A voice like falling snow, deeper than Halum's, more resonant, colder.

I was stunned. Like enough to Halum to be her twin! I knew of only one sister to Halum, then still a child, not yet sprouting her breasts. It was not possible for her to have concealed from me all her life a twin, or a sister somewhat older. But the resemblance was extraordinary and disturbing. I have read that on old Earth they had ways of making artificial beings out of chemicals, that could deceive even a mother or a lover with the likeness to some real person, and I could well have been persuaded that moment that the process had come down to us, across the centuries, across the gulf of night, and that this false Halum before me was a devilishly clever synthetic image of my true bondsister.

I said, 'Forgive this foolish error. One mistook you for Halum.'

'It happens often.'

'Are you some kin of hers?'

'Daughter to the brother of the High Justice Segvord.'

She gave her name as Loimel Helalam. Never had Halum spoken to me of this cousin, or if she had, I had no recollection of it. How odd that she had hidden from me the existence of this mirror-Halum in Manneran! I told her my name, and Loimel recognized it as that of Halum's bondbrother, of whom she had evidently heard a good deal; she softened her stance a little, and some of the chill that was about her now thawed. For my part I was over the shock of finding the supposed Halum to be another, and I was beginning to warm to Loimel, for she was beautiful and desirable, and – unlike Halum herself! – available. I could by looking at her out of one eye pretend to myself that she was indeed Halum, and I even managed to deceive myself into accepting her voice as my bondsister's. Together we strolled the courtyard, talking. I learned that Halum would come home this evening and that Loimel was here to arrange a hearty reception for her; I learned also some things about Loimel, for, in the injudicious fashion

of many Mannerangi, she guarded her privacy less sternly than
a northerner would. She told me her age: a year older than
Halum (and I also). She told me she was unmarried, having
recently terminated an unpromising engagement to a prince of
an old but unfortunately impoverished family of Mannerangi
nobility. She explained her resemblance to Halum by saying
that her mother and Halum's were cousins, as well as her
father being brother to Halum's, and five minutes later, when
we walked arm in arm, she hinted scandalously that in fact the
High Justice had invaded his elder brother's bridal couch long
ago, so that she was properly half-sister to Halum, not cousin.
And she told me much more.

   I could think only of Halum, Halum, Halum, Halum. This
Loimel existed for me solely as a reflection of my bondsister.
An hour after we first met, Loimel and I were together in
my bedroom, and when her gown had dropped from her I
told myself that Halum's skin must be creamy as this, that
Halum's breasts must be much like these, that Halum's thighs
could be no less smooth, that Halum's nipples would also turn
to turrets when a man's thumbs brushed their tips. Then I
lay naked beside Loimel and made her ready for taking with
many cunning caresses; soon she gasped and pumped her hips
and cried out, and I covered her with my body, but an instant
before I would have thrust myself into her the thought came
coldly to me, *Why, this is forbidden, to have one's bond-sister,*
and my weapon went limp as a length of rope. It was only
a momentary embarrassment: looking down at her face, I
told myself brusquely that this was Loimel and not Halum
who waited for my thrust, and my manhood revived, and
our bodies joined. But another humiliation awaited me. In
the moment of entering her my traitor mind said to me, *You
cleave Halum's flesh,* and my traitor body responded with an
instantaneous explosion of my passions. How intricately our
loins are linked to our minds, and how tricky a thing it is
when we embrace a woman while pretending she is another!
I sank down on Loimel in shame and disgust, hiding my face
in the pillow; but she, gripped by urgent needs thrashed about

against me until I found new vigor, and this time I carried her to the ecstasy she sought.

That evening my bondsister Halum at last returned from her holiday in the Gulf of Sumar, and wept with happy surprise to see me alive and in Manneran. When she stood beside Loimel I was all the more amazed by their near twinship: Halum's waist was more slender, Loimel's bosom deeper, but one finds these variations even in true sisters, and in most ways of the body Halum and her cousin seemed to have been stamped from the same mould. Yet I was struck by a profound and subtle difference also, most visible in the eyes, through which, as the poem says, there shines the inner light of the soul. The radiance that came from Halum was tender and gentle and mild, like the first soft beams of sunlight drifting through a summer morning's mist; Loimel's eyes gave a colder, harsher glow, that of a sullen winter afternoon. As I looked from one girl to the other, I formed a quick intuitive judgement: *Halum is pure love, and Loimel is pure self.* But I recoiled from that verdict the instant it was born. I did not know Loimel; I had not found her thus far to be anything but open and giving; I had no right to disparage her in that way.

The two years had not aged Halum so much as burnished her, and she had come to the full radiance of her beauty. She was deeply tanned, and in her short white sheath she seemed like a bronzed statue of herself; the planes of her face were more angular than they had been, giving her a delicate look of almost boyish charm; she moved with floating grace. The house was full of strangers for this her homecoming party, and after our first embrace she was swept away from me, and I was left with Loimel. But towards the end of the evening I claimed my bondright and took Halum away to my chamber, saying, 'There is two years' talking to do.' Thoughts tumbled chaotically in my mind: how could I tell her all that had happened to me, how could I learn from her what she had done, all in the first rush of words? I could not arrange my thinking. We sat down facing one another at a prim distance, Halum on the couch where only a few hours before I had coupled with her cousin, pretending then to myself that she was Halum. A tense smile passed between us. 'Where can one begin?' I said, and Halum, at the same instant, said the same words. That made us laugh and dissolved the tension. And then I heard my own voice asking, without preamble, whether Halum thought that Loimel would accept me as her husband.

TWENTY-SIX

Loimel and I were married by Segvord Helalam in the Stone Chapel at the crest of the summer, after months of preparatory rituals and purifications. We made these observances by request of Loimel's father, a man of great devoutness. For his sake we undertook a rigorous series of drainings, and day after day I knelt and yielded up the full contents of my soul to a certain Jidd, the best-known and most costly drainer in Manneran. When this was done Loimel and I went on pilgrimage to the nine shrines of Manneran, and I squandered my slender salary on candles and incense. We even performed the archaic ceremony known as the Showing, in which she and I stepped out on a secluded beach one dawn, chaperoned by Halum and Segvord, and, screened from their eyes by an elaborate canopy, formally disclosed our nakedness to one another, so that neither of us could say afterwards that we had gone into marriage concealing defects from the other.

The rite of union was a grand event, with musicians and singers. My bondbrother Noim, summoned from Salla, stood up as pledgeman for me, and did the ring-linking. Manneran's prime septarch, a waxen old man, attended the wedding, as did most of the local nobility. The gifts we received were of immense value. Among them was a golden bowl inlaid with strange gems, manufactured on some other world, and sent to us by my brother Stirron, along with a cordial message expressing regret that affairs of state required him to remain in Salla. Since I had snubbed his wedding, it was no surprise for him to snub mine. What did surprise me was the friendly tone of his letter. Making no reference to the circumstances of my disappearance from Salla, but offering thanks that the rumor of my death had proven false, Stirron gave me his blessing and asked me to come with my bride for a ceremonial visit to his capital as soon as we were able. Apparently he had learned that I meant to settle permanently in Manneran, and so would be no rival for his throne; therefore he could think of me warmly again.

I often wondered, and after all these years still do wonder, why Loimel accepted me. She had just turned down a prince of her own realm because he was poor: here was I, also a prince, but an exiled one, and even poorer. Why take me? For my charm in wooing? I had little of that; I was still young and thick-tongued. For my prospects of wealth and power? At that time those prospects seemed feeble indeed. For my physical appeal? Certainly I had some of that, but Loimel was too shrewd to marry just for broad shoulders and powerful muscles; besides, in our very first embrace I had shown her my inadequacies as a lover, and rarely did I improve on that bungled performance in the couplings that followed. I concluded, finally, that there were two reasons why Loimel took me. First, that she was lonely and troubled after the breakup of her other trothing, and, seeking the first harbor that presented itself, went to me, since I was strong and attractive and of royal blood. Second, that Loimel envied Halum in all things, and knew that by marrying me she would gain possession of the one thing Halum could never have.

My own motive for seeking Loimel's hand needs no deep probing to uncover. It was Halum I loved; Loimel was Halum's image; Halum was denied me, therefore I took Loimel. Beholding Loimel, I was free to think I beheld Halum. Embracing Loimel, I might tell myself I embraced Halum. When I offered myself to Loimel as husband, I felt no particular love for her, and had reason to think I might not even like her; yet I was driven to her as the nearest proxy to my true desire.

Marriages contracted for such reasons as Loimel's and mine do not often fare well. Ours thrived poorly; we began as strangers and grew ever more distant the longer we shared a bed. In truth I had married a secret fantasy, not a woman. But we must conduct our marriages in the world of reality, and in that world my wife was Loimel.

TWENTY-SEVEN

Meanwhile in my office at the Port Justiciary I struggled to do the job my bondfather had given me. Each day a formidable stack of reports and memoranda reached my desk; each day I tried to decide which must go before the High Justice and which were to be ignored. At first, naturally, I had no grounds for judgement. Segvord helped me, though, as did several of the senior officials of the Justiciary, who rightly saw that they had more to gain by serving me than by trying to block my inevitable rise. I took readily to the nature of my work, and before the full heat of summer was upon Manneran I was operating confidently, as if I had spent the last twenty years at this task.

Most of the material submitted for the guidance of the High Justice was nonsense. I learned swiftly to detect that sort by a quick scanning, often by looking at just a single page. The style in which it was written told me much: I found that a man who cannot phrase his thoughts cleanly on paper probably has no thoughts worth notice. The style is the man. If the prose is heavy-footed and sluggish, so too, in all likelihood, is the mind of its author, and then what are his insights into the operations of the Port Justiciary worth? A coarse and common mind offers coarse and common perceptions. I had to do a great deal of writing myself, summarizing and condensing the reports of middling value, and whatever I have learned of the literary art may be traced to my years in the service of the High Justice.

My style too reflects the man, for I know myself to be earnest, solemn, fond of courtly gestures, and given to communicating more perhaps than others really want to know; all these traits I find in my own prose. It has its faults, yet am I pleased with it: I have my faults, yet am I pleased with me.

Before long I realized that the most powerful man in Manneran was a puppet whose strings I controlled. I decided which cases the High Justice should handle, I chose the applications for special favor that he would read, I gave him the capsuled commentaries on which his verdicts were based. Segvord had not accidentally allowed me to attain such power. It was necessary for someone to perform the screening duties I now handled, and until my coming to Manneran the job had been done by a committee of three, all ambitious to hold Segvord's title some day. Fearing those men, Segvord had arranged to promote them to positions of greater splendor but lesser responsibilities. Then he slid me into their place. His only son had died in boyhood; all his patronage therefore fell upon me. Out of love of Halum he had coolly chosen to make a homeless Sallan prince one of the dominant figures of Manneran.

It was widely understood, by others long before by me, how important I was going to be. Those princes at my wedding had not been there out of respect for Loimel's family, but to curry favor with me. The soft words from Stirron were meant to ensure I would show no hostility to Salla in my decision-making. Doubtless my royal cousin Truis of Glin now was wondering uneasily if I knew that it was his doing that the doors of his province had closed in my face; he too sent a fine gift for my marriage-day. Nor did the flow of gifts cease with the nuptial ceremony. Constantly there came to me handsome things from those whose interests were bound up in the doings of the Port Justiciary. In Salla we would call such gifts by their rightful name, which is *bribes*; but Segvord assured me that in Manneran there was no harm in accepting them, so long as I did not let them interfere with my objectivity of judgement. Now I realized how, on the modest salary of a judge, Segvord had come to live in such princely style. In truth I did try to put all this bribery from my mind while at my official duties, and weigh each case on its merits alone.

So I found my place in Manneran. I mastered the secrets of the Port Justiciary, developed a feel for the rhythms of maritime commerce, and served the High Justice ably. I moved among princes and judges and men of wealth. I purchased a small but sumptuous house close by Segvord's, and soon had the builders out to increase its size. I worshiped, as only the mighty do, at the Stone Chapel itself, and went to the celebrated Jidd for my drainings. I was taken into a select athletic society, and displayed my skills with the feathered shaft in Manneran Stadium. When I visited Salla with my bride the springtime after our wedding, Stirron received me as if I were a Mannerangi septarch, parading me through the capital before a cheering multitude and feasting me royally at the palace. He said not a word to me about my flight from Salla, but was wholly amiable in a reserved and distant fashion. My first son, who was born that autumn, I named for him.

Two other sons followed, Noim and Kinnall, and daughters named Halum and Loimel. The boys were straight-bodied and strong; the girls promised to show the beauty of their namesakes. I took great pleasure in heading a family. I longed for the time when I could have my sons with me hunting in the Burnt Lowlands, or shooting the rapids of the River Woyn; meanwhile I went hunting without them, and the spears of many hornfowl came to decorate my home.

Loimel, as I have said, remained a stranger to me. One does not expect to penetrate the soul of one's wife as deeply as that of one's bondsister, but nevertheless, despite the customs of self-containment we observe, one expects to develop a certain communion with someone one lives with. I never penetrated anything of Loimel's except her body. The warmth and openness she had shown me at our first meeting vanished swiftly, and she became as aloof as any coldbelly wife of Glin. Once in the heat of lovemaking I used 'I' to her, as I sometimes did with whores, and she slapped me and twisted her hips to cast me from her loins. We drifted apart. She had her life, I mine; after a time we made no attempt to reach across the gulf to one another. She spent her time at music, bathing, sunsleeping, and piety, and I at hunting, gaming, rearing my sons, and doing my work. She took lovers and I took mistresses. It was a frosty marriage. We scarcely ever quarreled; we were not close enough even for that.

Noim and Halum were with me much of the time. They were great comforts to me.

At the Justiciary my authority and responsibility grew year by year. I was not promoted from my position as clerk to the High Justice, nor did my salary increase by any large extent; yet all of Manneran knew that I was the one who governed Segvord's decisions, and I enjoyed a lordly income of 'gifts'. Gradually Segvord withdrew from most of his duties, leaving them to me. He spent weeks at a time on his island retreat in the Gulf of Sumar, while I initialed and stamped documents in his name. In my twenty-fourth year, which was his fiftieth, he gave up his office altogether. Since I was not a Mannerangi by birth, it was impossible for me to become High Justice in his place; but Segvord arranged for the appointment of an amiable nonentity as his successor, one Noldo Kalimol, with the understanding that Kalimol would retain me in my place of power.

You would be right to assume that my life in Manneran was one of ease and security, of wealth and authority. Week flowed serenely into week, and, though perfect happiness is given to no man, I had few reasons for discontent. The failings of my marriage I accepted placidly, since deep love between man and wife is not often encountered in our kind of society; as for my other sorrow, my hopeless love for Halum, I kept it buried deep within me, and when it rose painfully close to the surface of my soul I soothed myself by a visit to the drainer Jidd. I might have gone on uneventfully in that fashion to the end of my days, but for the arrival in my life of Schweiz the Earthman.

TWENTY-EIGHT

Earthmen come rarely to Borthan. Before Schweiz, I had seen only two, both in the days when my father held the septarchy. The first was a tall redbearded man who visited Salla when I was about five years old; he was a traveler who wandered from world to world for his own amusement, and had just crossed the Burnt Lowlands alone and on foot. I remember studying his face with intense concentration, searching for the marks of his otherwordly origin – an extra eye, perhaps, horns, tendrils, fangs.

He had none of these, of course, and so I openly doubted his story of having come from Earth. Stirron, with the benefit of two years' more schooling than I, was the one who told me, in a jeering tone, that all the worlds of the heavens, including our own, had been settled by people from Earth, which was why an Earthman looked just like any of us. Nevertheless, when a second Earthman showed up at court a few years later, I still searched for fangs and tendrils. This one was a husky, cheerful man with light brown skin, a scientist making a collection of our native wildlife for some university in a far part of the galaxy. My father took him out into the Burnt Lowlands to get hornfowl; I begged to go along, and was whipped for my nagging.

I dreamed of Earth. I looked it up in books and saw a picture of a blue planet with many continents, and a huge pockmarked moon going around it, and I thought, This is where we all came from. This is the beginning of everything. I read of the kingdoms and nations of old Earth, the wars and devastation, the monuments, the tragedies. The going-forth into space, the attainment of the stars. There was a time when I even imagined I was an Earthman myself, born on that ancient planet of wonders, and brought to Borthan in babyhood to be exchanged for a septarch's true son. I told myself that when I grew up I would travel to Earth and walk through cities ten thousand years old, retracing the line of migration that had led my forefathers' forefathers from Earth to Borthan. I wanted to own a piece of Earth, too, some potsherd, some bit of stone, some battered coin, as a tangible link to the world at the heart of man's wanderings. And I longed for some other Earthman to come to Borthan, so that I could ask him ten thousand thousand questions, so that I could beg a slice of Earth for myself, but none came, and I grew up, and my obsession with the first of man's planets faded.

Then Schweiz crossed my way.

Schweiz was a man of commerce. Many Earthmen are. At the time I met him he had been on Borthan a couple of years as representative of an exporting firm based in a solar system not far from our own; he dealt in manufactured goods and sought our furs and spices in return. During his stay in Manneran, he had become entangled in controversy with a local importer over a cargo of stormshield furs from the north-western coast; the man tried to give Schweiz poor quality at a higher-than-contracted price, Schweiz sued, and the case went to the Port Justiciary. This was about three years ago, and a little more than three years after the retirement of Segvord Helalam.

The facts of the case were clear-cut and there was no doubt about the judgement. One of the lower justices approved Schweiz's plea and ordered the importer to make good on his contract with the swindled Earthman. Ordinarily I would not have become involved in the matter. But when the papers on the case came to High Justice Kalimol for routine review just prior to affirmation of verdict, I glanced at them and saw that the plaintiff was an Earthman.

Temptation speared me. My old fascination with that race – my delusion of fangs and tendrils and extra eyes – took hold of me again. I had to talk with him. What did I hope to get from him? The answers to the questions that had gone unanswered when I was a boy? Some clue to the nature of the forces that had driven mankind to the stars? Or merely amusement, a moment of diversion in an overly placid life?

I asked Schweiz to report to my office.

He came in almost on the run, a frantic, energetic figure in clothes of flamboyant style and tone. Grinning with a manic glee, he slapped my palm in greeting, dug his knuckles into my desktop, pushed himself back a few steps, and began to pace the room.

'The gods preserve you, your grace!' he cried.

I thought his odd demeanor, his coiled-spring bounciness and his wild-eyed intensity, stemmed from fear of me, for he had good reason to worry, called in by a powerful official to discuss a case that he thought he had won. But I found later that Schweiz's mannerisms were expressions of his own seething nature, not of any momentary and specific tension.

He was a man of middle height, very sparely built, not a scrap of fat on his frame. His skin was tawny and his hair was the color of dark honey; it hung down in a straight flow to his shoulders. His eyes were bright and mischievous, his smile quick and sly, and he radiated a boyish vigor, a dynamic enthusiasm, that charmed me just then, though it would eventually make him an exhausting companion for me. Yet he was no boy: his face bore the first lines of age and his hair, abundant though it was, was starting to go thin at the crown.

'Be seated,' I said, for his capering was disturbing me. I wondered how to launch the conversation. How much could I ask him before he claimed Covenant at me and sealed his lips? Would he talk about himself and his world? Had I any right to pry into a foreigner's soul in a way that I would not dare do with a man of Borthan? I would see. Curiosity drove me. I picked up the sheaf of documents on his case, for he was looking at the file unhappily, and held them towards him, saying, 'One places the first matters first. Your verdict has been affirmed. Today High Justice Kalimol gives his seal and within a moonrise you'll have your money.'

'Happy words, your grace.'

'That concludes the legal business.'

'So short a meeting? It seems hardly necessary to have paid this call to exchange only a moment's talk, your grace.'

'One must admit,' I said, 'that you were summoned here to discuss things other than your lawsuit.'

'Eh, your grace?' He looked baffled and alarmed.

'To talk of Earth,' I said. 'To gratify the idle inquisitiveness of a bored bureaucrat. Is that all right? Are you willing to talk a while, now that you've been lured here on the pretence of business? You know, Schweiz, one has always been fascinated by Earth and by Earthmen.' To win some rapport with him, for he still was frowning and mistrustful, I told him the story of the two other Earthmen I had known, and of my childhood belief that they should be alien in form. He relaxed and listened with pleasure, and before I was through he was laughing heartily. 'Fangs!' he cried. 'Tendrils!' He ran his hands over his face. 'Did you really think that, your grace? That Earthmen were such bizarre creatures? By all the gods, your grace, I wish I had some strangeness about my body, that I could give you amusement!'

I flinched each time Schweiz spoke of himself in the first person. His casual obscenities punctured the mood I had attempted to build. Though I tried to pretend nothing was amiss, Schweiz instantly realized his blunder, and, leaping to his feet in obvious distress, said, 'A thousand pardons! One tends to forget one's grammar sometimes, when one is not accustomed to –'

'No offence is taken,' I said hastily.

'You must understand, your grace, that old habits of speech die hard, and in using your language one sometimes slips into the mode most natural for himself, even though –'

'Of course, Schweiz. A forgivable lapse.' He was trembling. 'Besides,' I said, winking, 'I'm a grown man. Do you think I'm so easily shocked?' My use of the vulgarities was deliberate, to put him at his ease. The tactic worked; he subsided, calming. But he took no licence from the incident to use gutter talk with me again that morning, and in fact was careful to observe the niceties of grammatical etiquette for a long time thereafter, until such things had ceased to matter between us.

I asked him to tell me now about Earth, the mother of us all.

'A small planet,' he said. 'Far away. Choked in its own ancient wastes; the poisons of two thousand years of carelessness and overbreeding stain its skies and its seas and its land. An ugly place.'

'In truth, ugly?'

'There are still some attractive districts. Not many of them, and nothing to boast about. Some trees, here and there. A little grass. A lake. A waterfall. A valley. Mostly the planet is a dunghole. Earthmen often wish they could uncover their early ancestors, and bring them to life again, and then throttle them. For their selfishness. For their lack of concern for the generations to come. They filled the world with themselves and used everything up.'

'Is this why Earthmen built empires in the skies, then, to escape the filth of their home world?'

'Part of it is that, yes,' Schweiz said. 'There were so many billions of people. And those who had the strength to leave all went out and up. But it was more than running away, you know. It was a hunger to see strange things, a hunger to undertake journeys, a hunger to make fresh starts. To create new and better worlds of man. A string of Earths across the sky.'

'And those who did not go?' I asked. 'Earth still has those other billions of people?' I was thinking of Velada Borthan and its sparse forty or fifty millions.

'Oh, no, no. It's almost empty now, a ghost-world, ruined cities, cracking highways. Few live there any longer. Fewer are born there every year.'

'But you were born there?'

'On the continent called Europe, yes. One hasn't seen Earth for almost thirty years, though. Not since one was fourteen.'

'You don't look that old,' I said.

'One reckons time in Earthlength years,' Schweiz explained. 'By your figuring one is only approaching the age of thirty.'

'Also this one,' I said. 'And here also is one who left his

homeland before reaching manhood.' I was speaking freely, far more freely than was proper, yet I could not stop myself. I had drawn out Schweiz, and felt an impulse to offer something of my own in return. 'Going out from Salla as a boy to seek his fortune in Glin, then finding better luck in Manneran after a while. A wanderer, Schweiz, like yourself.'

'It is a bond between us, then.'

Could I presume on that bond? I asked him, 'Why did you leave Earth?'

'For the same reasons as everyone else. To go where the air is clean and a man stands some chance to become something. The only ones who spend their whole lives there are those who can't help but stay.'

'And this is the planet that all the galaxy reveres!' I said in wonder. 'The world of so many myths! The planet of boys' dreams! The centre of the universe – a pimple, a boil!'

'You put it well.'

'Yet it is revered.'

'Oh, revere it, revere it, certainly!' Schweiz cried. His eyes were aglow. 'The foundation of mankind! The grand originator of the species! Why not revere it, your grace? Revere the bold beginnings that were made there. Revere the high ambitions that sprang from its mud. And revere the terrible mistakes, too. Ancient Earth made mistake after mistake, and choked itself in error, so that you would be spared from having to pass through the same fires and torments.' Schweiz laughed harshly. 'Earth died to redeem you starfolk from sin. How's that for a religious notion? A whole liturgy could be composed around that idea. A priestcraft of Earth the redeemer.' Suddenly he leaned forward and said, 'Are you a religious man, your grace?'

I was taken aback by the thrusting intimacy of his question. But I put up no barriers.

'Certainly,' I said.

'You go to the godhouse, you talk to the drainers, the whole thing?'

I was caught. I could not help but speak.

'Yes,' I said. 'Does that surprise you?'

'Not at all. Everyone on Borthan seems to be genuinely religious. Which amazes one. You know, your grace, one isn't religious in the least, oneself. One tries, one has always tried, one has worked *so hard* to convince oneself that there are superior beings out there who guide destiny, and sometimes one almost makes it, your grace, one almost believes, one breaks through into faith, but then scepticism shuts things down every time. And one ends by saying, No, it isn't possible, it can't be, it defies logic and common sense. Logic and common sense!'

'But how can you live all your days without a closeness to something holy?'

'Most of the time, one manages fairly well. Most of the time.'

'And the rest of the time?'

'That's when one feels the impact of knowing one is entirely alone in the universe. Naked under the stars, and the starlight hitting the exposed skin, burning, a cold fire, and no one to shield one from it, no one to offer a hiding place, no one to pray to, do you see? The sky is ice and the ground is ice and the soul is ice, and who's to warm it? There isn't anyone. You've convinced yourself that no one exists who can give comfort. One wants some system of belief, one wants to submit, to get down and kneel, to be governed by metaphysics, you know? To believe, to have faith! And one can't. And that's when the terror sets in. The dry sobs. The nights of no sleeping.' Schweiz's face was flushed and wild with excitement; I wondered if he could be entirely sane. He reached across the desk, clamped his hand over mine – the gesture stunned me, but I did not pull back – and said hoarsely, 'Do you believe in gods, your grace?'

'Surely.'

'In a literal way? You think there's a god of travelers, and a god of fishermen, and a god of farmers, and one who looks after septarchs, and –'

'There is a force,' I said, 'that gives order and form to the universe. The force manifests itself in various ways, and for the sake of bridging the gap between ourselves and that force, we regard each of its manifestations as a "god", yes, and extend our souls to this manifestation or that one, as our needs demand. Those of us who are without learning accept these gods literally, as beings with faces and personalities. Others realize that they are metaphors for the aspects of the divine force, and not a tribe of potent spirits living overhead. But there is no one in Velada Borthan who denies the existence of the force itself.'

'One feels such fierce envy of that,' said Schweiz. 'To be raised in a culture that has coherence and structure, to have such assurance of ultimate verities, to feel yourself part of a divine scheme – how marvelous that must be! To enter into a system of belief – it would almost be worth putting up with this society's great flaws, to have something like that.'

'Flaws?' Suddenly I found myself on the defensive. 'What flaws?'

Schweiz narrowed his gaze and moistened his lips. Perhaps he was calculating whether I would be hurt or angered by what he meant to say. '*Flaws* was possibly too strong a word,' he replied. 'One might say instead, this society's limits, its – well, its narrowness. One speaks now of the necessity to shield one's self from one's fellow men that you impose. The taboos against reference to self, against frank discourse, against any opening of the soul –'

'Has one not opened his soul to you today in this very room?'

'Ah,' Schweiz said, 'but you've been speaking to an alien, to one who is no part of your culture, to someone you secretly suspect of having tendrils and fangs! Would you be so free with a citizen of Manneran?'

'No one else in Manneran would have asked such questions as you have been asking.'

'Maybe so. One lacks a native's training in self-repression. These questions about your philosophy of religion, then – do they intrude on your privacy of soul, your grace? Are they offensive to you?'

'One has no objections to talking of such things,' I said, without much conviction.

'But it's a taboo conversation, isn't it? We weren't using naughty words, except that once when one slipped, but we were dealing in naughty ideas, establishing a naughty relationship. You let your wall down a little way, eh? For which one is grateful. One's been here so long, years now, and one hasn't ever talked freely with a man of Borthan, not once! Until one sensed today that you were willing to open yourself a bit. This has been an extraordinary experience, your grace.' The manic smile returned. He moved jerkily about the office. 'One had no wish to speak critically of your way of life here,' he said. 'One wished in fact to praise certain aspects of it, while trying to understand others.'

'Which to praise, which to understand?'

'To understand your habit of erecting walls about yourselves. To praise the ease with which you accept divine presence. One envies you for that. As one said, one was raised in no system of belief at all, and is unable to let himself be overtaken by faith. One's head is always full of nasty sceptical questions. One is constitutionally unable to accept what one can't see or feel, and so one must always be *alone*, and one goes around the galaxy seeking for the gateway to belief, trying this, trying that, and one never finds –' Schweiz paused. He was flushed and sweaty. 'So you see, your grace, you have something precious here, this ability to let yourselves become part of a larger power. One would wish to learn it from you. Of course, it's a matter of cultural conditioning. Borthan still knows the gods, and Earth has outlived them. Civilization is young on this planet. It takes thousands of years for the religious impulse to erode.'

'And,' I said, 'this planet was settled by men who had strong religious beliefs, who specifically came here to preserve them, and who took great pains to instill them in their descendants.'

'That too. Your Covenant. Yet that was – what, fifteen hundred, two thousand years ago? It could all have crumbled by now, but it hasn't. It's stronger than ever. Your devoutness, your humility, your denial of self –'

'Those who couldn't accept and transmit the ideals of the first settlers,' I pointed out, 'were not allowed to remain among them. That had its effect on the pattern of the culture, if you'll agree that such traits as rebelliousness and atheism can be bred out of a race. The consenters stayed; the rejecters went.'

'You're speaking of the exiles who went to Sumara Borthan?'

'You know the story, then?'

'Naturally. One picks up the history of whatever planet one happens to be assigned to. Sumara Borthan, yes. Have you ever been there, your grace?'

'Few of us visit the continent,' I said.

'Ever thought of going?'

'Never.'

'There are those who do go there,' Schweiz said, and gave me a strange smile. I meant to ask him about that, but at that moment a secretary entered with a stack of documents, and Schweiz hastily rose. 'One doesn't wish to consume too much of your grace's valuable time. Perhaps this conversation could be continued at another hour?'

'One hopes for the pleasure of it,' I told him.

TWENTY-NINE

When Schweiz was gone I sat a long while with my back to my desk, closing my eyes and replaying in my mind the things we had just said to one another. How readily he had slipped past my guard! How quickly we had begun to speak of inner matters! True, he was an otherworlder, and with him I did not feel entirely bound by our customs. Yet we had grown dangerously close so extraordinarily fast. Ten minutes more and I might have been as open as a bondbrother to him, and he to me. I was astounded and dismayed by my easy dropping of propriety, by the way he had drawn me slyly into such intimacy.

Was it wholly his doing? I had sent for him, I had been the first to ask the close questions. I had set the tone. He had sensed from that some instability in me, and he had seized upon it, quickly flipping the conversation about, so that I was the subject and he the interrogator. And I had gone along with it. Reluctantly but yet willingly, I had opened to him. I was drawn to him, and he to me. Schweiz the tempter! Schweiz the exploiter of my weakness, hidden so long, hidden even from myself! How could he have known I was ready to open?

His high-pitched rapid speech still seemed to echo in the room. Asking. Asking. Asking. And then revealing. *Are you a religious man? Do you believe in literal gods? If only I could find faith! How I envy you. But the flaws of your world. The denial of self. Would you be so free with a citizen of Manneran? Speak to me, your grace. Open to me. I have been alone here so long.*

How could he have known, when I myself did not know?

A strange friendship had been born. I asked Schweiz to dine at home with me; we feasted and we talked, and the blue wine of Salla flowed and the golden wine of Manneran, and when we were warmed by our drinking we discussed religion once more, and Schweiz's difficulties with faith, and my convictions that the gods were real. Halum came in and sat with us an hour, and afterwards remarked to me on the power of Schweiz to loosen tongues, saying, 'You seemed more drunk than you have ever been, Kinnall. And yet you shared only three bottles of wine, so it must have been something else that made your eyes shine and your words so easy.' I laughed and told her that a recklessness came over me when I was with the Earthman, that I found it hard to abide by custom with him.

At our next meeting, in a tavern by the Justiciary, Schweiz said, 'You love your bondsister, eh?'

'Of course one loves one's bondsister.'

'One means, though, you *love* her.' With a knowing snigger.

I drew back, tense. 'Was one then so thoroughly wined the other night? What did one say to you of her?'

'Nothing,' he replied. 'You said it all to her. With your eyes, with your smile. And no words passed.'

'May we talk of other things?'

'If your grace wishes.'

'This is a tender theme, and painful.'

'Pardon, then, your grace. One only meant to confirm one's guess.'

'Such love as that is forbidden among us.'

'Which is not to say that it doesn't sometimes exist, eh?' Schweiz asked, and clinked his glass against mine.

In that moment I made up my mind never to meet with him again. He looked too deep and spoke too freely of what he saw. But four days afterwards, coming upon him on a pier, I invited him to dine a second time. Loimel was displeased by the invitation. Nor would Halum come, pleading another engagement; when I pressed her, she said that Schweiz made her uncomfortable. Noim was in Manneran, though, and joined us at the table. We all drank sparingly, and the conversation was a stilted and impersonal one, until, with no perceptible shifting of tone, we found ourselves telling Schweiz of the time when I had escaped from Salla in fear of my brother's jealousies, and Schweiz was telling us of his departure from Earth; when the Earthman went home that night, Noim said to me, not altogether disapprovingly, 'There are devils in that man, Kinnall.'

THIRTY

'This taboo on self-expression,' Schweiz asked me when we were together another time. 'Can you explain it, your grace?'

'You mean the prohibition against saying "I" and "me"?'

'Not that, so much as the whole pattern of thought that would have you deny there are such things as "I" and "me",' he said: 'The commandment that you must keep your private affairs private at all times, except only with bond-kin and drainers. The custom of wall-building around oneself that affects even your grammar.'

'The Convenant, you mean?'

'The Covenant,' said Schweiz.

'You say you know our history?'

'Much of it.'

'You know that our forefathers were stern folk from a northern climate, accustomed to hardship, mistrustful of luxury and ease, who came to Borthan to avoid what they saw as the contaminating decadence of their native world?'

'Was it so? One thought only that they were refugees from religious persecution.'

'Refugees from sloth and self-indulgence,' I said. 'And, coming here, they established a code of conduct to protect their children's children against corruption.'

'The Covenant.'

'The Covenant, yes. The pledge they made each to each, the pledge that each of us makes to all his fellow men on his Naming Day. When we swear never to force our turmoils on another, when we vow to be strong-willed and hardy of spirit, so that the gods will continue to smile on us. And so on and so on. We are trained to abominate the demon that is self.'

'Demon?'

'So we regard it. A tempting demon, that urges us to make use of others instead of relying on our own strengths.'

'Where there is no love of self, there is neither friendship nor sharing,' said Schweiz.

'Perhaps so.'

'And thus there is no trust.'

'We specify areas of responsibility through contract,' I said. 'There is no need for knowledge of the souls of others, where law rules. And in Velada Borthan no one questions the rule of law.'

'You say you abominate self,' said Schweiz. 'It seems, rather, that you glorify it.'

'How so?'

'By living apart from one another, each in the castle of his skull. Proud. Unbending. Aloof. Uncaring. The reign of self indeed, and no abomination of it!'

'You put things oddly,' I said. 'You invert our customs, and think you speak wisely.'

'Has it always been like this,' Schweiz asked, 'since the beginning of settlement in Velada Borthan?'

'Yes,' I said. 'Except among those malcontents you know of, who fled to the southern continent. The rest of us abide by the Covenant. And our customs harden: thus we now may not talk of ourselves in the first person singular, since this is a raw exposure of self, but in medieval times this could be done. On the other hand, some things soften. Once we were guarded even in giving our names to strangers. We spoke to one another only when absolutely necessary. We show more trust nowadays.'

'But not a great deal.'

'But not a great deal,' I admitted.

'And is there no pain in this for you? Every man sealed against all others? Do you never say to yourselves that there must be a happier way for humans to live?'

'We abide by the Covenant.'

'With ease or with difficulty?'

'With ease,' I said. 'The pain is not so great, when you consider that we have bond-kin, with whom we are exempted from the rule of selflessness. And the same with our drainers.'

'To others, though, you may not complain, you may not unburden a sorrowful soul, you may not seek advice, you may not expose your desires and needs, you may not speak of dreams and fantasies and romance, you may not talk of anything but chilly, impersonal things.' Schweiz shuddered. 'Pardon, your grace, but one finds this a harsh way to live. One's own search has constantly been for warmth and love and human contact, for sharing, for opening, and this world here seems to elevate the opposite of what one prizes most highly.'

'Have you had much luck,' I asked, 'finding warmth and love and human contact?'

Schweiz shrugged. 'It has not always been easy.'

'For us there is never loneliness, since we have bond-kin. With Halum, with Noim, with such as these to offer comfort, why does one need a world of strangers?'

'And if your bond-kin are not close at hand? If one is wandering, say, far from them in the snows of Glin?'

'One suffers, then. And one's character grows tougher. But that is an exceptional situation. Schweiz, our system may force us into isolation, yet it also guarantees us love.'

'But not the love of husband for wife. Not the love of father for child.'

'Perhaps not.'

'And even the love of bond-kin is limited. For you yourself, eh, have admitted that you feel a longing for your bondsister Halum that cannot be –'

I cut him off, telling him sharply, 'Speak of other things!' Color flared in my cheeks; my skin grew hot.

Schweiz nodded and smiled a chastened smile. 'Pardon, your grace. The conversation became too intense; there was loss of control, but no injury meant.'

'Very well.'

'The reference was too personal. One is abashed.'

'You meant no injury,' I said, guilty over my outburst, knowing he had stung me at a vulnerable place and that I had over-reacted to the bite of truth. I poured more wine. We drank in silence for a time.

Then Schweiz said, 'May one make a proposal, your grace? May one invite you to take part in an experiment that may prove interesting and valuable to you?'

'Go on,' I said, frowning, ill at ease.

'You know,' he began, 'that one has long felt uncomfortably conscious of his solitary state in the universe, and that one has sought without success some means of comprehending his relationship to that universe. For you, the method lies in religious faith, but one has failed to reach such faith because of his unfortunate compulsion towards total rationalism. Eh? One cannot break through to that larger sense of *belonging* by words alone, by prayer alone, by ritual alone. This thing is possible for you, and one envies you for it. One finds himself trapped, isolated, sealed up in his skull, condemned to metaphysical solitude: a man apart, a man on his own. One does not find this state of godlessness enjoyable or desirable. You of Borthan can tolerate the sort of emotional isolation you impose on yourselves, since you have the consolations of your religion, you have drainers and whatever mystical mergings-with-the-gods the act of draining gives you; but the one who speaks to you now has no such advantages.'

'All this we have discussed many times,' I said. 'You spoke of a proposal, an experiment.'

'Be patient, your grace. One must explain oneself fully, step by step.'

Schweiz flashed me his most charming smile, and turned on me eyes that were bright with visionary schemes. His hands roamed the air expressively, conjuring up invisible drama, as he said, 'Perhaps your grace is aware that there are certain chemical substances – drugs, yes, call them drugs – that allow one to make an opening into the infinite, or at least to have the illusion that one has made such an opening – to attain a brief and tentative glimpse into the mystic realms of the intangible. Eh? Known for thousands of years, these drugs, used in the days before Earthmen ever went to the stars. Employed in ancient religious rites. Employed by others as a substitute for religion, as a secular means of finding faith, the gateway to the infinite for such as this one, who can get there no other way.'

'Such drugs are forbidden in Velada Borthan,' I said.

'Of course, of course! For you they offer a means of side-stepping the processes of formal religion. Why waste time at a drainer's if you can expand your soul with a pill? Your law is wise on this point. Your Covenant could not survive if you allowed these chemicals to be used here.'

'Your proposal, Schweiz,' I said.

'One first must tell you that he has used these drugs himself, and found them not entirely satisfactory. True, they open the infinite. True, they let one merge with the Godhead. But only for moments: a few hours at best. And at the end of it, one is as alone as before. It is the illusion of the soul's opening, not the opening itself. Whereas this planet produces a drug that can provide the real thing.'

'What?'

'In Sumara Borthan,' said Schweiz, 'dwell those who fled the rule of the Covenant. One is told that they are savages, going naked and living on roots and seeds and fish; the cloak of civilization has dropped away from them and they have slipped back into barbarism. So one learned from a traveler who had visited that continent not long ago. One also learned that in Sumara Borthan they use a drug made from a certain powdered root, which has the capacity of opening mind to mind, so that each can read the inmost thoughts of the other. It is the very opposite of your Covenant, do you see? They know one another from the soul out, by way of this drug they eat.'

'One has heard stories of the savagery of those folk,' I said.

Schweiz put his face close to mine. 'One confesses himself tempted by the Sumaran drug. One hopes that if he could ever get inside another mind, he could find that community of soul for which he has searched so long. It might be the bridge to the infinite that he seeks, the spiritual transformation. Eh? In quest of revelations he has tried many substances. Why not this?'

'If it exists.'

'It exists, your grace. This traveler who came from Sumara Borthan brought some of it with him to Manneran, and sold some of it to the curious Earthman.' Schweiz drew forth from a pocket a small glossy envelope, and held it towards me. It contained a small quantity of some white powder; it could have been sugar. 'Here it is,' he said.

I stared at it as if he had pulled out a flask of poison.

'Your proposal?' I demanded. 'Your experiment, Schweiz?'

'Let us share the Sumaran drug,' he said.

THIRTY-ONE

I might have slapped the powder from his hand and ordered his arrest. I might have commanded him to get away from me and never come near again. I might at the very least have cried out that it was impossible I would ever touch any such substance. But I did none of those things. I chose instead to be coolly intellectual, to show casual curiosity, to remain calm and play conversational games with him. Thus I encouraged him to lead me a little deeper into the quicksand.

I said, 'Do you think that one is so eager to contravene the Covenant?'

'One thinks that you are a man of strong will and enquiring mind, who would not miss an opportunity for enlightenment.'

'Illegal enlightenment?'

'All true enlightenment is illegal at first, within its context. Even the religion of the Covenant: were your forefathers not driven out of other worlds for practising it?'

'One mistrusts such analogy-making. We are not talking of religions now. We talk of a dangerous drug. You ask one to surrender all the training of his lifetime, and open himself to you as he has never done even to bond-kin, even to a drainer.'

'Yes.'

'And you imagine that one might be willing to do such a thing?'

'One imagines that you might well emerge transformed and cleansed, if you could bring yourself to try,' Schweiz said.

'One might also emerge scarred and twisted.'

'Doubtful. Knowledge never injures the soul. It only purges that which encrusts and saps the soul.'

'How glib you are, Schweiz! Look, though: can you believe it would be possible to give one's inner secrets to a stranger, to a foreigner, to an otherworlder?'

'Why not? Better to a stranger than to a friend. Better to an Earthman than a fellow citizen. You'd have nothing to fear: the Earthman would never try to judge you by the standards of Borthan. There'd be no criticisms, no disapprovals of what's under your skull. And the Earthman will leave this planet in a year or two, on a journey of hundreds of light-years, and what then will it matter that your mind once merged with his?'

'Why are you so eager to have this merger happen?'

'For eight moontimes,' he said, 'this drug has been in one's pocket, while one hunts for someone to share it with. It looked as though the search would be in vain. Then one met you, and saw your potential, your strength, your hidden rebelliousness –'

'One is aware of no rebelliousness, Schweiz. One accepts his world completely.'

'May one bring up the delicate matter of your attitude towards your bondsister? That seems a symptom of a fundamental discontent with the restrictions of your society.'

'Perhaps. Perhaps not.'

'You would know yourself better after sampling the Sumaran drug. You would have fewer perhapses and more certainties.'

'How can you say this, if you haven't had the drug yourself?'

'So it seems to one.'

'It is impossible,' I said.

'An experiment. A secret pact. No one would ever know.'

'Impossible.'

'Is it that you fear to share your soul?'

'One is taught that such sharing is unholy.'

'The teachings can be wrong,' he said. 'Have you never felt the temptation? Have you never tasted such ecstasy in a draining that you wished you might undergo the same experience with someone you loved, your grace?'

Again he caught me in a vulnerable place. 'One has had such feelings occasionally,' I admitted. 'Sitting before some ugly drainer, and imagining it was Noim instead, or Halum, and that the draining was a two-way flow –'

'Then you already long for this drug, and don't realize it!'

'No. No.'

'Perhaps,' Schweiz suggested, 'it is the idea of opening to a stranger that dismays you, and not the concept of opening itself. Perhaps you would take this drug with someone other than the Earthman, eh? With your bondbrother? With your bondsister?'

I considered that. Sitting down with Noim, who was to me like a second self, and reaching his mind on levels that had never been available to me before, and he reaching mine. Or with Halum – or with Halum –

Schweiz, you tempter!

He said, after letting me think a while, 'Does the idea please you? Here, then. One will surrender his chance with the drug. Take it, use it, share it with one whom you love.' He pressed the envelope into my hand. It frightened me; I let it fall to the table as if it were aflame.

I said, 'But that would deprive you of your hoped-for fulfillment.'

'No matter. One can get more of the drug. One may perhaps find another partner for the experiment. Meanwhile you would have known the ecstasy, your grace. Even an Earthman can be unselfish. Take it, your grace. Take it.'

I gave him a dark look. 'Would it be, Schweiz, that this talk of taking the drug yourself was only pretence? That what you really look for is someone to offer himself as an experimental subject, so you can be sure the drug is safe before you risk it?'

'You misunderstand, your grace.'

'Maybe not. Maybe this is what you've been driving towards.' I saw myself administering the drug to Noim, saw him falling into convulsions before my eyes as I made ready to bring my own dose to my lips. I pushed the envelope back towards Schweiz. 'No. The offer is refused. One appreciates the generosity, but one will not experiment on his loved ones, Schweiz.'

His face was very red. 'This implication is unwarranted, your grace. The offer to relinquish one's own share of the drug was made in good faith, and at no little cost to one's own plans. But since you reject it, let us return to the original proposition. The two of us will sample the drug, in secrecy, as an experiment in possibilities. Let us find out together what its powers may be and what doors it can open for us. We would have much to gain from this adventure, one is sure.'

'One sees what you would have to gain,' I said. 'But what purpose is there in it for –'

'Yourself?' Schweiz chuckled. Then he rammed me with the barbed hook. 'Your grace, by making the experiment you would learn that the drug is safe, you would discover the proper dosage, you would lose your fear of the mind-opening itself. And then, after obtaining a further supply of the drug, you would be properly prepared to use it for a purpose from which your fears now hold you back. You could take the drug together with the only person whom you truly love. You could use it to open your mind to your bondsister Halum, and to open hers to you.'

THIRTY-TWO

There is a story they tell to children who are still learning the Covenant, about the days when the gods had not yet ceased to walk the world in human form, and the first men had not yet arrived on Borthan. The gods at that time did not know they were divine, for they had no mortals about them for comparison, and so they were innocent beings, unaware of their powers, who lived in a simple way. They dwelled in Manneran (this is the source of Manneran's claim to superior holiness, the legend that it was once the home of the gods) and ate berries and leaves, and went without clothing except in the mild Mannerangi winter, when they threw shawls of animal hide loosely over their shoulders. And there was nothing godlike about them.

One day two of these ungodlike gods decided they would go off to see something of the world. The idea for making such a journey came first to the god whose secret name is Kinnall, now the god who looks after wayfarers. (Yes, he for whom I was named.) This Kinnall invited the goddess Thirga to join him, she whose responsibility now is the protection of those who are in love. Thirga shared Kinnall's restlessness and off they went.

From Manneran they walked west along the southern coast until they came to the shores of the Gulf of Sumar. Then they turned north, and passed through Stroin Gap just by the place where the Huishtor Mountains come to an end. They entered the Wet Lowlands, which they found less to their liking, and finally they ventured into the Frozen Lowlands, where they thought they would perish of the cold. So they turned south again, and this time they also walked to the west, and shortly they found themselves staring at the inland slopes of the Threishtor Mountains. There seemed no way for them to cross over this mighty range. They followed its eastern foothills south, but could not get out of the Burnt Lowlands, and they suffered great hardships, until at last they stumbled upon Threish Gate, and made their way through that difficult pass into the cool and foggy province of Threish.

On their first day in Threish the two gods discovered a place where a spring flowed out of a hillside. The opening in the hillside was nine-sided, and the rock surrounding the opening was so bright that it dazzled the eye, for it rippled and iridesced, and glowed with many colors constantly pulsing and changing, red and green and violet and ivory and turquoise and many more. And the water that came forth was of the same shimmering quality, having in it every color anyone ever had seen. The stream flowed only a short distance this way, and then was lost in the waters of a much larger brook, in which all the wondrous colors vanished.

Kinnall said, 'We have wandered a long while in the Burnt Lowlands, and our throats are dry from thirst. Shall we drink?' And Thirga said, 'Yes, let us drink,' and knelt by the opening in the hillside. She cupped her hands and filled them with the glittering water, and poured it into her mouth, and Kinnall drank also, and the taste of the water was so sweet that they thrust their faces right against the flow of the spring, gulping down all they could.

As they did this they experienced strange sensations of their bodies and minds. Kinnall looked towards Thirga and realized that he could see the thoughts within her soul, and they were thoughts of love for him. And she looked towards him, and saw his thoughts as well. 'We are different now,' Kinnall said, and he did not even need words to convey his meaning, for Thirga understood him as soon as his thought formed. And she replied, 'No, we are not different, but are merely able to understand the use of the gifts we have always had.'

And it was true. For they had many gifts, and they had never used them before. They could rise in the air and travel like birds; they could change the shape of their bodies; they could walk through the Burnt Lowlands or the Frozen Lowlands and feel no discomfort; they could live without taking in food; they could halt the ageing of their flesh and become as young as they pleased; they could speak without saying words. All these things they might have done before coming to the spring, except that they had not known how, and now they were capable of using the skills with which they had been born. They had learned, by drinking the water of the bright spring, how to go about being gods.

Even so, they did not yet know that they were gods.

After some time they remembered the others who lived in Manneran, and flew back to tell them about the spring. The journey took only an instant. All their friends crowded round as Kinnall and Thirga spoke of the miracle of the spring, and demonstrated the powers they had mastered. When they were done, everyone in Manneran resolved to go to the spring, and set out in a long procession, through Stroin Gap and the Wet Lowlands and up the eastern slopes of the Threishtors to Threish Gate. Kinnall and Thirga flew above them, guiding them from day to day. Eventually they reached the place of the spring, and one by one they drank of it and became as gods. Then they scattered, some returning to Manneran, some going to Salla, some going even to Sumara Borthan or the far continents of Umbis, Dabis, and Tibis, since, now that they were as gods, there were no limits on the speed of their travel, and they wished to see those strange places. But Kinnall and Thirga settled down beside the spring in eastern Threish and were content to explore one another's soul.

Many years passed, and then the starship of our forefathers came down in Threish, near the western shore. Men had at last reached Borthan. They built a small town and went about the task of collecting food for themselves. A certain man named Digant, who was among these settlers, ventured deep into the forest in search of meat-animals, and became lost, and roamed and roamed until finally he came to the place where Kinnall and Thirga lived. He had never seen any such as they before, nor they anyone such as he.

'What sort of creatures are you?' he asked.

Kinnall replied, 'Once we were quite ordinary, but now we do quite well, for we never grow old, and we can fly faster than any bird, and our souls are open to each other, and we can take on any shape we please.'

'Why, then, you are gods!' Digant cried.

'Gods? What are gods?'

And Digant explained that he was a man, and had no such powers as theirs, for men must use words to talk, and can neither fly nor change their shape, and grow older with each journey of the world around the sun, until the time of dying comes. Kinnall and Thirga listened with care, comparing themselves to Digant, and when he was done speaking they knew it was true, that he was a man and they were gods.

'Once we were almost like men ourselves,' Thirga admitted. 'We felt hunger and grew old and spoke only by means of words and had to put one foot in front of the other to get from place to place. We lived like men out of ignorance, for we did not know our powers. But then things changed.'

'And what changed them?' Digant asked.

'Why,' said Kinnall in his innocence, 'we drank from that glistening spring, and the water of it opened our eyes to our powers and allowed us to become as gods. That was all.'

Then Digant's soul surged with excitement, for he told himself that he too could drink from the spring, and then he would join this pair in godhood. He would keep the spring a secret afterwards, when he returned to the settlers on the coast, and they would worship him as their living god, and treat him with reverence, or he would destroy them. But Digant did not dare ask Kinnall and Thirga to let him drink from the spring, for he feared that they would refuse him, being jealous of their divinity. So he hatched a scheme to get them away from that place.

'Is it true,' he asked them, 'that you can travel so fast that you are able to visit every part of this world in a single day?'

Kinnall assured him that this was true.

'It seems difficult to believe,' said Digant.

'We will give you proof,' Thirga said, and she touched her hand to Kinnall's, and the two gods went aloft. They soared to the highest peak of the Threishtors and gathered snowflowers there; they descended into the Burnt Lowlands and scooped up a handful of the red soil; in the Wet Lowlands they collected herbs; by the Gulf of Sumar they took some liquor from a flesh-tree; on the shores of the Polar Gulf they pried out a sample of the eternal ice; then they leaped over the top of the world to frosty Tibis, and began their journey through the far continents, so that they might bring back to the doubting Digant something from every part of the world.

The moment Kinnall and Thirga had departed on this enter-prise, Digant rushed to the spring of miracles. There he hesi-tated briefly, afraid that the gods might return suddenly and strike him down for his boldness; but they did not appear, and Digant thrust his face into the flow and drank deeply, thinking, Now I too shall be as a god. He filled his gut with the glowing water and swayed and grew dizzy, and fell to the ground. Is this godhood, he wondered? He tried to fly and could not. He tried to change his shape and could not. He tried to make himself younger and could not. He failed in all these things because he had been a man to begin with, and not a god, and the spring could not change a man into a god, but could only help a god to realize his full powers.

But the spring gave Digant one gift. It enabled him to reach into the minds of the other men who had settled in Threish. As he lay on the ground, numb with disappointment, he heard a tiny tickling sound in the middle of his mind, and paid close heed to it and realized he was hearing the minds of his friends. And he found a way of amplifying the sound so that he could hear everything clearly: yes, and this was the mind of his wife, and this was the mind of his sister, and this was the mind of his sister's husband, and Digant could look into any of them and any other mind, reading the innermost thoughts. This is godhood, he told himself. And he probed their minds deeply, flushing out all their secrets. Steadily he increased the scope of his power until every mind at once was connected to his. Forth from them he drew the privacies of their souls, until, intoxicated with his new power, swollen with the pride of his godhood, he sent out a message to all those minds from his mind, saying, 'HEAR THE VOICE OF DIGANT. IT IS DIGANT THE GOD THAT YOU SHALL WORSHIP.'

When this terrible voice broke into their minds, many of the settlers in Threish fell down dead with shock, and others lost their sanity, and others ran about in wild terror, crying, 'Digant has invaded our minds! Digant has invaded our minds!' And the waves of fear and pain coming out of them were so intense that Digant himself suffered greatly, falling into a paralysis and stupor, though his dazed mind continued to roar, 'HEAR THE VOICE OF DIGANT. IT IS DIGANT THE GOD THAT YOU SHALL WORSHIP.' Each time that great cry went forth, more settlers died and more lost their reason, and Digant, responding to the mental tumults he had caused, writhed, and shook in agony, wholly unable to control the powers of his brain.

Kinnall and Thirga were in Dabis when this occurred, drawing forth from a marsh a triple-headed worm to show to Digant. The bellowings of Digant's mind sped around the world even to Dabis, and, hearing those sounds, Kinnall and Thirga left off what they were doing and hurried back to Threish. They found Digant close to death, his brain all but burned out, and they found the settlers of Threish dead or mad; and they knew at once how this had come to pass. Swiftly they brought an end to Digant's life, so that there would be silence in Threish. Then they went among the victims of the would-be god, and raised all the dead and healed all the injured. And lastly they sealed the opening in the hillside with a seal that could not be broken, for it was plain to them that men must not drink of that spring, but only gods, and all the gods had already taken their draughts of it. The people of Threish fell on their knees before those two, and asked in awe, 'Who are you?' and Kinnall and Thirga replied, 'We are gods, and you are only men.' And that was the beginning of the end of the innocence of the gods. And after that time it was forbidden among men to seek ways of speaking mind to mind, because of the harm that Digant had done, and it was written into the Covenant that one must keep one's soul apart from the souls of others, since only gods can mingle souls without destroying one another, and we are not gods.

THIRTY-THREE

Of course I found many reasons to postpone taking the Sumaran drug with Schweiz. First, High Justice Kalimol departed on a hunting trip, and I told Schweiz that the doubled pressures of my work in his absence made it impossible for me to undertake the experiment just then. Kalimol returned; Halum fell ill; I used my worry over her as the next excuse. Halum recovered; Noim invited Loimel and myself to spend a holiday at his lodge in southern Salla. We came back from Salla; war broke out between Salla and Glin, creating complex maritime problems for me at the Justiciary. And so the weeks went. Schweiz grew impatient. Did I mean to take the drug at all? I could not give him an answer. I did not truly know. I was afraid. But always there burned in me the temptation he had planted there. To reach out, godlike, and enter Halum's soul –

I went to the Stone Chapel, waited until Jidd could see me, and let myself be drained. But I kept back from Jidd all mention of Schweiz and his drug, fearing to reveal that I toyed with such dangerous amusements. Therefore the draining was a failure, since I had not fully opened my soul to the drainer; and I left the Stone Chapel with a congestion of the spirit, tense and morose. I saw clearly now that I must necessarily yield to Schweiz, that what he offered was an ordeal through which I must pass, for there was no escaping it. He had found me out. Beneath my piety I was a potential traitor to the Covenant. I went to him.

'Today,' I said. 'Now.'

THIRTY-FOUR

We needed seclusion. The Port Justiciary maintains a country lodge in the hills two hours north-west of the city of Manneran, where visiting dignitaries are entertained and treaties of trade negotiated. I knew that this lodge was not currently in use, and I reserved it for myself for a three-day span. At midday I picked Schweiz up in a Justiciary car and drove quickly out of the city. There were three servants on duty at the lodge – a cook, a chambermaid, a gardener. I warned them that extremely delicate discussions would be taking place so that they must on no account cause interruptions or offer distractions. Then Schweiz and I sealed ourselves in the inner living quarters. 'It would be best,' he said, 'to take no food this evening. Also they recommend that the body be absolutely clean.'

The lodge had an excellent steambath. We scrubbed ourselves vigorously, and when we came out we donned loose, comfortable silken robes. Schweiz's eyes had taken on the glassy glitter that came over them in moments of high excitement. I felt frightened and uneasy, and began to think that I would suffer some terrible harm out of this evening. Just then I regarded myself as one who was about to undergo surgery from which his chances of recovery were slight. My mood was sullen resignation: I was willing. I was here, I was eager to make the plunge and have done with it.

'Your last chance,' Schweiz said, grinning broadly. 'You can still back out.'

'No.'

'You understand that there are risks, though? We are equally inexperienced in this drug. There are dangers.'

'Understood,' I said.

'Is it also understood that you enter this voluntarily, and under no coercion?'

I said, 'Why this delay, Schweiz? Bring out your potion.'

'One wishes to assure himself that your grace is fully prepared to meet any consequences.'

In a tone of heavy sarcasm I said, 'Perhaps there should be a contract between us, then, in the proper fashion, relieving you of any liability in case one wishes later to press a claim for damage to the personality –'

'If you wish, your grace. One does not feel it necessary.'

'One wasn't serious.' I said. I was fidgety now. 'Can it be that you're nervous about it too, Schweiz? That you have some doubts?'

'We take a bold step.'

'Let's take it, then, before the moment goes by. Bring out the potion, Schweiz. Bring out the potion.'

'Yes,' he said, and gave me a long look, his eyes to mine and clapped his hands in childlike glee. And laughed in triumph. I saw how he had manipulated me. Now I was begging him for the drug! Oh, devil, devil!

From his traveling case he fetched the packet of white powder. He told me to get wine, and I ordered two flasks of chilled Mannerangi golden from the kitchen, and he dumped half the contents of the packet into my flask, half into his. The powder dissolved almost instantly: for a moment it left a cloudy gray wake, and then there was no trace of it. We gripped our flasks. I remember looking across the table at Schweiz and giving him a quick smile; he described it to me later as the pale, edgy smirk of a timid virgin about to open her thighs. 'It should all go down at once,' Schweiz said, and he gulped his wine and I gulped mine, and then I sat back, expecting the drug to hit me instantly. I felt a faint giddiness, but that was only the wine doing its work in my empty gut. 'How long does it take to begin?' I asked. Schweiz shrugged. 'It will be some while yet,' he replied. We waited in silence. Testing myself, I tried to force my mind to go forth and encounter his, but I felt nothing. The sounds of the room became magnified: the creak of floorboards, the rasping of insects outside the window, the tiny hum of the bright electric light. 'Can you explain,' I said hoarsely, 'the way this drug is thought to operate?' Schweiz answered, 'One can tell you only what was told to him. Which is, that the potential power to link one mind to another exists in all of us from birth, only we have evolved a chemical substance in the blood that inhibits the power. A very few are born without the inhibitor, and these have the gift of reaching minds, but most of us are forever blocked from achieving this silent communication, except when for some reason the production of the hormone ceases of its own accord and our minds open for a while. When this occurs it is often mistaken for madness. This drug of Sumara Borthan, they say, neutralizes the natural inhibitor in our blood, at least for a short time, and permits us to make contact with one another, as we would normally do if we lacked the counteracting substance in the blood. So one has heard.' To this I answered, 'We all might be supermen, then, but we are crippled by our own glands?' And Schweiz, gesturing grandly, said, 'Maybe it is that there were good biological reasons for evolving this protection against our own powers. Eh? Or maybe not.' He laughed. His face had turned very red. I asked him if he really believed this story of an inhibitory hormone and a counterinhibitory drug, and he said that he had no grounds for making judgement. 'Do you feel anything yet?' I asked. 'Only the wine,' he said. We waited. We waited. Perhaps it will do nothing, I thought, and I will be reprieved. We waited. At length Schweiz said, 'It may be beginning now.'

THIRTY-FIVE

I was at first greatly aware of the functioning of my own body: the *thud-thud* of my heart, the pounding of the blood against the walls of arteries, the movements of fluids deep within my ears, the drifting of corpuscular bodies across my field of vision. I became enormously receptive to external stimuli, currents of air brushing my cheek, a fold of my robe touching my thigh, the pressure of the floor against the sole of my foot. I heard an unfamiliar sound as of water tumbling through a distant gorge. I lost touch with my surroundings, for as my perceptions intensified the range of them also narrowed, and I found myself incapable of perceiving the shape of the room, for I saw nothing clearly except in a constricted tunnel at the other end of which was Schweiz; beyond the rim of this tunnel there was only haze. Now I was frightened, and fought to clear my mind, as one may make a conscious effort to free the brain of the muddle caused by too much wine; but the harder I struggled to return to normal perception, the more rapidly did the pace of change accelerate. I entered a state of luminous drunkenness, in which brilliant radiant rods of colored light streamed past my face, and I was certain I must have sipped from Digant's spring. I felt a rushing sensation, like that of air moving swiftly against my ears. I heard a high whining sound that was barely audible at first, but swept up in crescendo until it took on tangibility and appeared to fill the room to overflowing, yet the sound was not painful. The chair beneath me throbbed and pulsated in a steady beat that seemed tuned to some patient pulsation of our planet itself. Then, with no discernible feeling of having crossed a boundary, I realized that my perceptions had for some time been double: now I was aware of a second heartbeat, of a second spurt of blood within vessels, of a second churning of intestines. But it was not mere duplication, for these other rhythms were different, setting up complex symphonic interplays with the rhythms of my own body, creating percussive patterns that were so intricate that the fibres of my mind melted in the attempt to follow them. I began to sway in time with these beats, to clap my hands against my thighs, to snap my fingers; and, looking down my vision-tunnel, I saw Schweiz also swaying and clapping and snapping, and realized whose bodily rhythms it was I had been receiving. We were locked together. I had difficulty now distinguishing his heartbeat from my own, and sometimes, glancing across the table at him, I saw my own reddened, distorted face. I experienced a general liquefying of reality, a breaking down of walls and restraints; I was unable to maintain a sense of Kinnall Darival as an individual; I thought not in terms of *he* and *I*, but of *we*. I had lost not only my identity but the concept of self itself.

At that level I remained a long while, until I started to think that the power of the drug was receding. Colors grew less brilliant, my perception of the room became more conventional, and I could again distinguish Schweiz's body and mind from my own. Instead of feeling relief that the worst was over, though, I felt only disappointment that I had not achieved the kind of mingling of consciousness that Schweiz had promised.

But I was mistaken.

The first wild rush of the drug was over, yes, yet we were only now coming into the true communion. Schweiz and I were apart but nevertheless together. This was the real selfbaring. I saw his soul spread out before me as though on a table, and I could walk up to the table and examine those things that were on it, picking up this utensil, that vase, these ornaments, and studying them as closely as I wished.

Here was the looming face of Schweiz's mother. Here was a swollen pale breast streaked with blue veins and tipped by an enormous rigid nipple. Here were childhood furies. Here were memories of Earth. Through the eyes of Schweiz I saw the mother of worlds, maimed and shackled, disfigured and discolored. Beauty gleamed through the ugliness. This was the place of his birth, this dishevelled city; these were highways ten thousand years old; these were the stumps of ancient temples. Here was the node of first love. Here were disappointments and departures. Betrayals, here. Shared confidences, here. Growth and change. Corrosion and despair. Journeys. Failures. Seductions. Confessions. I saw the suns of a hundred worlds.

And I passed through the strata of Schweiz's soul, inspecting the gritty layers of greed and the boulders of trickery, the oily pockets of maliciousness, the decaying loam of opportunism. Here was self incarnate; here was a man who had lived solely for his own sake.

Yet I did not recoil from the darkness of Schweiz.

I saw beyond those things. I saw the yearning, the god-hunger in the man, Schweiz alone on a lunar plain, splay-footed on a black shield of rock under a purple sky, reaching up, grasping, taking hold of nothing. Sly and opportunistic he might be, yes, but also vulnerable, passionate, honest beneath all his capering. I could not judge Schweiz harshly. He was I. I was he. Tides of self engulfed us both. If I were to cast Schweiz down, I must also cast down Kinnall Darival. My soul was flooded with warmth for him.

I felt him, too, probing me. I erected no barriers about my spirit as he came to explore it. And through his own eyes I saw what he was seeing in me. My fear of my father. My awe of my brother. My love for Halum. My flight into Glin. My choosing of Loimel. My petty faults and my petty virtues. Everything, Schweiz. Look. Look. Look. And it all came back refracted through his soul, nor did I find it painful to observe. Love of others begins with love of self, I thought suddenly.

In that instant the Covenant fell and shattered within me.

Gradually Schweiz and I pulled apart, though we remained in contact some time longer, the strength of the bond ebbing steadily. When it broke at last, I felt a shivering resonance, as if a taut string had snapped. We sat in silence. My eyes were closed. I was queasy in the pit of my stomach and conscious, as I had never been conscious before, of the gulf that keeps each of us forever alone. After some long time I looked across the room at Schweiz.

He was watching me, waiting for me. He wore that demonic look of his, the wild grin, the bright-eyed gleam, only now it seemed to me less a look of madness than a reflection of inner joy. He appeared younger now. His face was still flushed.

'I love you,' he said softly.

The unexpected words were bludgeons. I crossed my wrists before my face, palms out, protecting myself.

'What upsets you so much?' he asked. 'My grammar or my meaning?'

'Both.'

'Can it be so terrible to say. *I love you?*'

'One has never – one does not know how to –'

'To react? To respond?' Schweiz laughed. 'I don't mean I love you in any physical way. As if that would be so hideous. But no. I mean what I say, Kinnall. I've been in your mind and I liked what I saw there. I love you.'

'You talk in "I",' I reminded him.

'Why not? Must I deny self even now? Come on: break free, Kinnall. I know you want to. Do you think what I just said to you is obscene?'

'There is such a strangeness about it.'

'On my world those words have a holy strangeness,' said Schweiz. 'And here they're an abomination. Never to be allowed to say "I love you", eh? A whole planet denying itself that little pleasure. Oh, no, Kinnall, no, no, no!'

'Please,' I said faintly. 'One still has not fully adjusted to the things the drug did. When you shout at one like that –'

But he would not subside.

'You were in my mind too,' he said. 'What did you find

there? Was I so loathsome? Get it out, Kinnall. You have no secrets from me now. The truth. The truth!'

'You know, then, that one found you more admirable than one had expected.'

Schweiz chuckled. 'And I the same! Why are we afraid of each other now, Kinnall? I told you: I love you! We made contact. We saw there were areas of trust. Now we have to change, Kinnall. You more than me, because you have farther to go. Come. Come. Put words to your heart. Say it.'

'One can't.'

'Say "I".'

'How difficult that is.'

'Say it. Not as an obscenity. Say it as if you love yourself.'

'Please.'

'Say it.'

'I,' I said.

'Was that so awful? Come, now. Tell me how you feel about me. The truth. From the deepest levels.'

'A feeling of warmth – of affection, of trust –'

'Of love?'

'Of love, yes,' I admitted.

'Then say it.'

'Love.'

'That isn't what I want you to say.'

'What, then?'

'Something that hasn't been said on this planet in two thousand years, Kinnall. Now say it. I –'

'I –'

'Love you.'

'Love you.'

'I love you.'

'I – love – you.'

'It's a beginning,' Schweiz said. Sweat streamed down his face and mine. 'We start by acknowledging that we can love. We start by acknowledging that we have selves *capable* of loving. Then we begin to love. Eh? We begin to love.'

THIRTY-SIX

Later I said, 'Did you get from the drug what you were looking for, Schweiz?'

'Partially.'

'How so, partially?'

'I was looking for God, Kinnall, and I didn't quite find him, but I got a better idea of where to look. What I did find was how not to be alone any more. How to open my mind fully to someone else. That's the first step on the road I want to travel.'

'One is happy for your sake, Schweiz.'

'Must you still talk to me in that third-person lingo?'

'I can't help myself,' I said. I was terribly tired. I was beginning to feel afraid of Schweiz again. The love I bore for him was still there, but now suspicion was creeping back. Was he exploiting me? Was he milking a dirty little pleasure out of our mutual exposures? He had pushed me into becoming a selfbarer. His insistence on my speaking in 'I' and 'me' to him – was that a token of my liberation, was it something beautiful and pure, as he claimed, or was it only a revelling in filth? I was too new to this. I could not sit placidly while a man said, '*I love you.*'

'Practise it,' Schweiz said. 'I.I.I.I.'

'Stop. Please.'

'Is it that painful?'

'It's new and strange to me. I need – there, you see? – I need to slide into this more gradually.'

'Take your time, then. Don't let me rush you. But don't ever stop moving forward.'

'One will try. I will try.' I said.

'Good.' After a moment he said. 'Would you try the drug again, ever?'

'With you?'

'I don't think there's any need for that. I mean with someone like your bondsister. If I offered you some, would you use it with her?'

'I don't know.'

'Are you afraid of the drug now?'

I shook my head. 'That isn't easy for me to answer. I need time to come to terms with the whole experience. Time to think about it, Schweiz, before getting involved again.'

'You've tasted the experience. You've seen that there's only good to be had from it.'

'Perhaps. Perhaps.'

'Without doubt!' His fervor was evangelical. His zeal tempted me anew.

Cautiously I said, 'If more were available, I would seriously consider trying it again. With Halum, maybe.'

'Good!'

'Not immediately. But in time. Two, three, four moontimes from now.'

'It would have to be farther from now than that.'

'Why?'

Schweiz said, 'This was my entire stock of the drug that we used this evening. I have no more.'

'But you could get some, if you tried?'

'Oh, yes. Yes, certainly.'

'Where?'

'In Sumara Borthan,' he said.

THIRTY-SEVEN

When one is new to the ways of pleasure, it is not surprising to find guilt and remorse following first indulgence. So was it with me. In the morning of our second day at the lodge I awoke after troubled sleep, feeling such shame that I prayed the ground to swallow me. What had I done? Why had I let Schweiz goad me into such foulness? Selfbaring! Selfbaring! Sitting with him all night, saying 'I' and 'me' and 'me' and 'I', and congratulating myself on my new freedom from convention's strangling hand! The mists of day brought a mood of disbelief. Could I have actually opened myself like that? Yes, I must, for within me now were memories of Schweiz's past, which I had not had access to before. And myself within him, then. I prayed for a way of undoing what I had done. I felt I had lost something of myself by surrendering my apartness. You know, to be a selfbarer is not a pretty thing among us, and those who expose themselves gain only a dirty pleasure from it, a furtive kind of ecstasy. I insisted to myself that I had done nothing of that, but had embarked rather on a spiritual quest; but even as I put the phrase to myself it sounded portentous and hypocritical, a flimsy mask for shabby motives. And I was ashamed, for my sake, for my sons' sake, for the sake of my royal father and his royal forefathers, that I had come to this. I think it was Schweiz's '*I-love you*' that drove me into such an abyss of regret, more than any other single aspect of the evening, for my old self saw those words as doubly obscene, even while the new self that was struggling to emerge insisted that the Earthman had meant nothing shameful, neither with his '*I*' nor with his '*love*'. But I rejected my own argument and let guilt engulf me. What had I become, to trade endearments with another man, an Earthborn merchant, a lunatic? How could I have given my soul to him? Where did I stand, now that I was so wholly vulnerable to him? For a moment I considered killing Schweiz, as a way of recovering my privacy. I went to him where he slept, and saw him with a smile on his face, and I could feel no hatred for him then.

That day I spent mostly alone. I went off into the forest and bathed at a cool pond; then I knelt before a firethorn tree and pretended it was a drainer, and confessed myself to it in shy whispers; afterwards I walked through a brambly wood, coming back to the lodge thorned and smudged. Schweiz asked me if I felt unwell. No, I told him, nothing is wrong. I said little that evening, but huddled in a floating-chair. The Earthman, more talkative than ever, a torrent of buoyant words, launched

himself into the details of a grand scheme for an expedition
to Sumara Borthan to bring back sacks of the drug, enough
to transform every soul in Manneran, and I listened without
commenting, for everything had become unreal to me, and
that project seemed no more strange than anything else.

I hoped the ache of my soul would ease once I was back in
Manneran and at my desk in the Justiciary. But no. I came
into my house and Halum was there with Loimel, the cousins
exchanging clothes with one another, and at the sight of them
I nearly turned and fled. They smiled warm woman-smiles at
me, secret smiles, the token of the league they had formed
between themselves all their lives, and in despair I looked
from my wife to my bondsister, from one cousin to the other,
receiving their mirrored beauty as a double sword in my belly.
Those smiles! Those knowing eyes! They needed no drug to
pull the truths from me.

Where have you been, Kinnall?

To a lodge in the forest, to play at selfbaring with the Earthman.

And did you show him your soul?

Oh, yes, and he showed his.

And then?

*Then we spoke of love. I love you, he said, and one replied, I
love you.*

What a wicked child you are, Kinnall!

Yes, Yes. Where can one hide from his shame?

This silent dialog whirled through my brain in an instant,
as I came towards them where they sat beside the courtyard
fountain. Formally I embraced Loimel, and formally I embraced
my bondsister, but I kept my eyes averted from theirs, so sharp
was my guilt. It was the same in the Justiciary office for me.
I translated the glances of the underlings into accusing glares.
*There is Kinnall Darival, who revealed all our mysteries to Schweiz
of Earth. Look at the Sallan selfbarer slink by us! How can he stand
his own reek?* I kept to myself and did my work poorly. A
document concerning some transaction of Schweiz's crossed
my desk, throwing me into dismay. The thought of facing
Schweiz ever again appalled me. It would have been no great

chore for me to revoke his residence permit in Manneran, using the authority of the High Justice; poor payment for the trust he showed me, but I came close to doing it, and checked myself only out of a deeper shame even than I already bore.

On the third day of my return, when my children too had begun to wonder what was wrong with me, I went to the Stone Chapel to seek healing from the drainer Jidd.

It was a damp day of heavy heat. The soft furry sky seemed to hang in looping folds over Manneran, and everything was coated in glistening beads of bright moisture. That day the sunlight was a strange color, almost white, and the ancient black stone blocks of the holy building gave off blinding reflections as though they were edged with prisms; but once inside the chapel, I found myself in dark, cool, quiet halls. Jidd's cell had pride of place in the chapel's apse, behind the great altar. He awaited me already robed; I had reserved his time hours in advance. The contract was ready. Quickly I signed and gave him his fee. This Jidd was no more lovely than any other of his trade, but just then I was almost pleased by his ugliness, his jagged knobby nose and thin long lips, his hooded eyes, his dangling earlobes. Why mock the man's face? He would have chosen another for himself, if he had been consulted. And I was kindly disposed to him, for I hoped he would heal me. Healers were holy men. *Give me what I need from you, Jidd, and I will bless your ugly face!* He said, 'Under whose auspices will you drain?'

'The god of forgiving.'

He touched a switch. Mere candles were too common for Jidd. The amber light of forgiveness came from some concealed gas-jet and flooded the chamber. Jidd directed my attention towards the mirror, instructing me to behold my face, put my eyes to my eyes. The eyes of a stranger looked back at me. Droplets of sweat clustered in the roots of my beard, where the flesh of my cheeks could be seen. *I love you*, I said silently to the strange face in the mirror. Love of others begins with love of self. The chapel weighed on me; I was in terror of being crushed beneath a block of the ceiling. Jidd was saying the preliminary

words. There was nothing of love in them. He commanded me
to open my soul to him.

I stammered. My tongue turned upon itself and was knotted.
I gagged; I choked; I pulled my head down and pressed it
to the cold floor. Jidd touched my shoulder and murmured
formulas of comfort until my fit softened. We began the rite
a second time. Now I traveled more smoothly through the
preliminaries, and when he asked me to speak, I said, as though
reciting lines that had been written for me by someone else,
'These days past one went to a secret place with another, and
we shared a certain drug of Sumara Borthan that unseals the
soul, and we engaged in selfbaring together, and now one feels
remorse for his sin and would have forgiveness for it.'

Jidd gasped, and it is no little task to astonish a drainer. That
gasp nearly punctured my will to confess; but Jidd artfully
recovered control, coaxing me onward with bland priestly
phrases, until in a few moments the stiffness left my jaws and
I was spilling everything out. My early discussions of the drug
with Schweiz. (I left him unnamed. Though I trusted Jidd to
maintain the secrecy of the draining, I saw no spiritual gain
for myself in revealing to anyone the name of my companion
in sin.) My taking of the drug at the lodge. My sensations as
the drug took hold. My exploration of Schweiz's soul. His
entry into mine. The kindling of deep affection between us
as our union of spirit developed. My feeling of alienation from
the Covenant while under the drug's influence. That sudden
conviction of mine that the denial of self which we practise
is a catastrophic cultural error. The intuitive realization that
we should deny our solitude instead, and seek to bridge the
gulfs between ourselves and others, rather than glorying in
isolation. Also I confessed that I had dabbled in the drug for
the sake of eventually reaching the soul of Halum; hearing
from me this admission of yearning for my bondsister was old
stuff to Jidd by now. And then I spoke of the dislocations I had
experienced since coming out of my drug-trance: the guilt, the
shame, the doubt. At last I fell silent. There before me, like
a pale globe glowing in the dimness, hung the facts of my

misdeeds, tangible and exposed, and already I felt cleaner for having revealed them. I was willing now to be brought back into the Covenant. I wanted to be purged of my aberration of selfbaring. I hungered to do penance and resume my upright life. I was eager to be healed, I was begging for absolution and restoration to my community. But I could not feel the presence of the god. Staring into the mirror, I saw only my own face, drawn and sallow, the beard in need of combing. When Jidd began to recite the formulas of absolution, they were merely words to me, nor did my soul lift. I was cut off from all faith. The irony of that distracted me: Schweiz, envying me for my beliefs, seeking through the drug to understand the mystery of submission to the supernatural, had stripped me of my access to the gods. There I knelt, stone knees on stone floor, making hollow phrases, while wishing that Jidd and I could have taken the drug together, so there might have been true communion between us. And I knew that I was lost.

'The peace of the gods be with you now,' said Jidd.

'The peace of the gods is upon one.'

'Seek no more for false succor, and keep your self to yourself, for other paths lead only to shame and corruption.'

'One will seek no other paths.'

'You have bondsister and bondbrother, you have a drainer, you have the mercies of the gods. You need no more.'

'One needs no more.'

'Go in peace, then.'

I went, but not in his kind of peace, for the draining had been a leaden thing, meaningless and trifling. Jidd had not reconciled me to the Covenant: he had simply demonstrated the degree of my separation from it. Unmoved though I had been by the draining, however, I emerged from the Stone Chapel somehow purged of guilt. I no longer repented my selfbaring. Perhaps this was some residual effect of the draining, this inversion of my purpose in going to Jidd, but I did not try deeply to analyze it. I was content to be myself and to be thinking these thoughts. My conversion at that instant was complete. Schweiz had taken my faith from me, but he had given me another in its place.

THIRTY-EIGHT

That afternoon a problem came to me concerning a ship from Threish and some false cargo manifests, and I went to a pier to verify the facts. There by chance I encountered Schweiz. Since parting from him a few days before, I had dreaded meeting him again; it would be intolerable, I thought, to look into the eyes of this man who had beheld my entire self. Only by keeping apart from him could I eventually persuade myself that I had not, in fact, done with him what I had done. But then I saw him near me on the pier. He clutched a thick sheaf of invoices in one hand and was shaking the other furiously at some watery-eyed merchant in Glinish dress. To my amazement I felt none of the embarrassment I had anticipated, but only warmth and pleasure at the sight of him. I went to him. He clapped my shoulder; I clapped his. 'You look more cheerful now,' he said.

'Much.'

'Let me finish with this scoundrel and we'll share a flask of golden, eh?'

'By all means,' I said.

An hour later, as we sat together in a dockside tavern, I said, 'How soon can we leave for Sumara Borthan?'

THIRTY-NINE

The voyage to the southern continent was conducted as though in a dream. Not once did I question the wisdom of undertaking the journey, nor did I pause to ask myself why it was necessary for me to take part in person, rather than let Schweiz make the trip alone, or send some hireling to gather the drug on our behalf. I simply set about the task of arranging for our passage.

No commercial shipping goes regularly between Velada Borthan and Sumara Borthan. Those who would travel to the southern continent must charter a vessel. This I did, through the instrumentality of the High Justiciary, using intermediaries and dummy signatories. The vessel I chose was no Mannerangi craft, for I did not care to be recognized when we sailed, but rather a ship of the western province of Velis that had been tied down in Manneran Harbour for the better part of a year by a lawsuit. It seemed there was some dispute over title to the ship going on in its home port, and the thicket of injunctions and counter-injunctions had succeeded in making it impossible for the vessel to leave Manneran after its last voyage there. The captain and crew were bitter over this enforced idleness and had already filed a protest with the Justiciary; but the High Justice had no jurisdiction over a lawsuit that was being fought entirely in the courts of Velis, and we therefore had had to continue the stay on the vessel's departure until word came from Velis that title was clear. Knowing all this, I issued a decree in the High Justice's name that would permit the unfortunate craft temporarily to accept charters for voyages to points 'between the River Woyn and the eastern shore of the Gulf of Sumar'. That usually was taken to mean any point along the coast of the province of Manneran, but I specified also that the captain might hire himself out for trips to the northern coast of Sumara Borthan. Doubtless that clause left the poor man puzzled, and it must have puzzled him even more when, a few days later, he was approached by my agents and asked to make a voyage to that very place.

Neither Loimel nor Halum nor Noim nor anyone else did I tell of my destination. I said only that the Justiciary required me to go abroad for a short while. At the Justiciary I was even less specific, applying to myself for a leave of absence, granting it at once, and informing the High Justice at the last possible moment that I was not going to be available for the immediate future.

To avoid complications with the collectors of customs, among other things, I picked as our port of departure the town of Hilminor, in south-western Manneran on the Gulf of Sumar. This is a medium-sized place that depends mainly on the fishing trade, but which serves also as a halfway stop for ships traveling between the city of Manneran and the western provinces. I arranged to meet our chartered captain in Hilminor; he then set out for that town by sea, while Schweiz and I made for it in a groundcar.

It was a two-day journey via the coastal highway, through a countryside ever more lush, ever more densely tropical, as we approached the Gulf of Sumar. Schweiz was in high spirits, as was I. We talked to one another in the first person constantly; to him it was nothing, of course, but I felt like a wicked boy sneaking off to whisper 'I' and 'me' in a playmate's ear. He and I speculated on what quantity of the Sumaran drug we would obtain, and what we would do with it. No longer was it just a question of my getting some to use with Halum: we were talking now of proselytizing everyone and bringing about a wholesale liberation of my self-stifling countrymen. That evangelical approach had crept gradually into our plans almost without my realizing it, and had swiftly become dominant.

We came to Hilminor on a day so hot the sky itself seemed to break out in blisters. A shimmering dome of heat covered everything, and the Gulf of Sumar, as it lay before us, was golden-skinned in the fierce sunlight. Hilminor is rimmed by a chain of low hills, which are thickly forested on the seaward side and desert on the landward; the highway curved through them, and we stopped at one point so that I could show Schweiz the flesh-trees that covered the parched inland slopes. A dozen of the trees were clustered in one place. We walked through crackling tinder-dry underbrush to reach them: twice the height of men they were, with twisted limbs and thick pale bark, spongy to the touch like the flesh of very old women. The trees were scarred from repeated tapping of their sap, making them look all the more repugnant. 'Can we taste the fluid?' Schweiz asked. We had no implements for making the tap, but just then a girl of the town came along, perhaps ten years old, half-naked, tanned a deep brown to hide the dirt; she was carrying an auger and a flask, and evidently had been sent out by her family to collect flesh-tree sap. She looked at us sourly. I produced a coin and said, 'One would show his companion the taste of the flesh-tree.' Still a sour look; but she jammed her auger into the nearest tree with surprising force, twisted it, withdrew, and caught the gush of clear thick fluid. Sullenly she handed her flask to Schweiz. He sniffed it, took a cautious lick, finally had a gulp. And whooped in delight. 'Why isn't this stuff sold all over Velada Borthan?' he asked.

'The whole supply comes from one little area along the Gulf,' I told him. 'Most of it's consumed locally, and a lot gets shipped to Threish, where it's almost an addiction. That doesn't leave much left over for the rest of the continent. You can buy it in Manneran, of course, but you have to know where to look.'

'You know what I'd like to do, Kinnall? I'd like to start a flesh-tree plantation, grow them by the thousands and get enough juice bottled so we not only could market it all over Velada Borthan, but could set up an export deal. I –'

'*Devil!*' the girl cried, and added something incomprehensible in the coast dialect, and snatched the flask from his hand. She ran off wildly, knees high, elbows out-thrust, several times looking back to make a finger-jabbing sign of contempt or defiance at us. Schweiz, bewildered, shook his head. 'Is she crazy?' he asked.

'You said "I" three times,' I said. 'Very careless.'

'I've slipped into bad habits, talking with you. But can it really be such a filthy thing to say?'

'Filthier than you'll ever imagine. That girl is probably on her way to tell her brothers about the dirty old man who obscened at her on the hillside. Come on: let's get into town before we're mobbed.'

'Dirty old man,' Schweiz murmured. 'Me!'

I pushed him into the groundcar and we hurried towards the port of Hilminor.

FORTY

Our ship rode at anchor, a small squat craft, twin screws, auxiliary sail, hull painted blue and gold. We presented ourselves to the captain – Khrisch was his name – and he greeted us blandly by the names we had assumed. In late afternoon we put out to sea. At no time during the voyage did Captain Khrisch question us about our purposes, nor did any of his ten crewmen. Surely they were fiercely curious about the motives of anyone who cared to go to Sumara Borthan, but they were so grateful to be out of their escrow even for this short cruise that they were chary of offending their employers by too much prying.

The coast of Velada Borthan dipped from sight behind me and ahead lay only the grand open sweep of the Strait of Sumar. No land at all could be seen, neither aft nor fore. That frightened me. In my brief career as a Glinish seaman I had never been far from the coast, and during stormy moments I had soothed myself with the comforting deceit that I might always swim to shore if we capsized. Here, though, the universe seemed all to be of water. As evening approached, a gray-blue twilight settled over us, stitching sky seamlessly to sea, and it became worse for me: now there was only our little bobbing, throbbing ship adrift and vulnerable in this directionless, dimensionless void, this shimmering antiworld

where all places melted into a single nonplace. I had not
expected the strait to be so wide. On a map I had seen in
the Justiciary only a few days before, the strait had had less
breadth than my little finger; I had assumed that the cliffs of
Sumara Borthan would be visible to us from the earliest hours
of the voyage; yet here we were amid nothingness. I stumbled
to my cabin and plunged face first on to my bunk, and lay there
shaking, calling upon the god of travelers to protect me. Bit
by bit I came to loathe myself for this weakness. I reminded
myself that I was a septarch's son and a septarch's brother and
another septarch's cousin, that in Manneran I was a man of the
highest authority, that I was the head of a house and a slayer
of hornfowl. All this did me no good. What value is lineage to
a drowning man? What use are broad shoulders and powerful
muscles and a skill at swimming, when the land itself has been
swallowed up, so that a swimmer would have no destination?
I trembled. I think I may have wept. I felt myself dissolving into
that gray-blue void. Then a hand lightly caught my shoulder.
Schweiz. 'The ship is sound,' he whispered. 'The crossing is a
short one. Easy. Easy. No harm will come.'

If it had been anyone else who had found me like that, any
other man except perhaps Noim, I might have killed him or
myself, to bury the secret of my shame.

I said, 'If this is what it is like to cross the Strait of Sumar,
how can one travel between the stars without going mad?'

'One grows accustomed to travel.'

'The fear – the emptiness –'

'Come above.' Gently. 'The night is very beautiful.'

Nor did he lie. Twilight was past and a black bowl pocked
with fiery jewels lay over us. Near cities one cannot see
the stars so well, because of the lights and the haze. I had
looked upon the full glory of the heavens while hunting in
the Burnt Lowlands, yes, but then I had not known the
names of what I saw. Now, Schweiz and Captain Khrisch
stood close alongside me on deck, taking turns calling out
the names of stars and constellations, vying with each other
to display their knowledge, each one pouring his astronomy

into my ear as though I were a terrified child who could be kept from screaming only by a constant flow of distractions. See? See? And see, there? I saw. A host of our neighboring suns, and four or five of the neighboring planets of our system, and even a vagrant comet that night. What they taught me stayed with me. I could step out of my cabin now, I believe, here in the Burnt Lowlands, and call off the stars the way Schweiz and the captain called them off to me aboard ship in the Strait of Sumar. How many more nights do I have, I wonder, on which I will be free to look at the stars?

Morning brought an end to fear. The sun was bright, the sky was lightly fleeced, the broad strait was calm, and it did not matter to me that land was beyond sight. We glided towards Sumara Borthan in an almost imperceptible way; I had to study the surface of the sea with care to remind myself we were in motion. A day, a night, a day, a night, a day, and then the horizon sprouted a green crust, for there was Sumara Borthan. It provided a fixed point for me, except that we were the fixed point, and Sumara Borthan was making for it. The southern continent slid steadily towards us, until at last I saw a rim of bare yellow-green rock stretching from east to west, and on top of those naked cliffs rose a thick cap of vegetation, lofty trees knitted together by heavy vines to form a closed canopy, stubbier shrubs clustering in the darkness below, everything cut down the side as if to reveal the jungle's edge to us in cross-section. I felt not fear but wonder at the sight of that jungle. I knew that not one of those trees and plants grew in Velada Borthan; the beasts and serpents and insects of this place were not those of the continent of my birth; what lay before us was alien and perhaps hostile, an unknown world awaiting the first footstep. In a tumble of tangled imaginings I dropped down the well of time, and saw myself as an explorer peeling the mystery from a newly found planet. Those gigantic boulders, those slender, high-crowned trees, those dangling snaky vines, all were products of a raw, elemental mystery straight out of evolution's belly, which now I was about to penetrate. That dark jungle was the gate to something strange and terrible, I thought, yet I was not frightened so much as I was stirred, deeply moved, by the vision of those sleek cliffs and tendrilled avenues. This was the world that existed before man came. This was as it was when there were no godhouses, no drainers, no Port Justiciary: only the silent leafy paths, and the surging rivers scouring the valleys, and the unplumbed ponds, and the long heavy leaves glistening with the jungle's exhalations, and the unhunted prehistoric beasts turning in the ooze, and the fluttering winged things that knew no fear, and the grassy plateaux, and the veins of precious metals, a virgin kingdom, and over everything brooding the presence of the gods, of the god, of the god, waiting for the time of worshippers. The lonely gods who did not yet know they were divine. The lonely god.

Of course the reality was nothing so romantic. There was a place where the cliffs dipped to sea level and yielded to a crescent harbour, and here a squalid settlement existed, the shacks of a few dozen Sumarnu who had taken to living here so that they might meet the needs of such ships as occasionally did come from the northern continent. I had thought that all the Sumarnu lived somewhere in the interior, naked tribesmen camping down by the volcanic peak Vashnir, and that Schweiz and I would have to hack our way through the whole apocalyptic immensity of this mysterious land, unguided and uncertain, before we found what passed for civilization and made contact with anyone who might sell us that for which we had come. Instead, Captain Khrisch brought his little ship smartly to shore by a crumbling wooden pier, and as we stepped forth a small delegation of Sumarnu came to offer us a sullen greeting.

You know my fantasy of fanged and grotesque Earthmen. So, too, I instinctively expected these people of the southern continent to look in some way alien. I knew it was irrational; they were, after all, sprung from the same stock as the citizens of Salla and Manneran and Glin. But had these centuries in the jungle not transformed them? Had their disavowal of the Covenant not laid them open to infiltration by the vapors of the forest, and turned them into unhuman things? No and no. They looked to me like peasants of any province's back country. Oh, they wore unfamiliar ornaments, odd jeweled pendants and bracelets of an un-Veladan sort, but there was nothing else about them, neither tone of skin nor shape of face nor color of hair, that set them apart from the men I had always known.

There were eight or nine of them. Two, evidently the leaders, spoke the dialect of Manneran, though with a troublesome accent. The others showed no sign of understanding northern languages, but chattered among themselves in a tongue of clicks and grunts. Schweiz found communication easier than I did, and entered into a long conversation, so difficult for me to follow that I soon ceased to pay attention. I wandered off to inspect the village, and was inspected in turn by goggle-eyed children – the girls here walked about naked even after they were of the age when their breasts had sprouted – and when I returned Schweiz said, 'It's all arranged.'

'What is?'

'Tonight we sleep here. Tomorrow they'll guide us to a village that produces the drug. They don't guarantee we'll be allowed to buy any.'

'Is it only sold at certain places?'

'Evidently. They swear there's none at all available here.'

I said, 'How long a journey will it be?'

'Five days. On foot. Do you like jungles, Kinnall?'

'I don't know the taste of them yet.'

'It's a taste you're going to learn,' said Schweiz.

He turned now to confer with Captain Khrisch, who was planning to go off on some expedition of his own along the Sumaran coast. Schweiz arranged to have our ship back at this harbor waiting for us when we returned from our trip into the jungle. Khrisch's men unloaded our baggage – chiefly trade-goods for barter, mirrors and knives and trinkets, since the Sumarnu had no use for Veladan currency – and got their ship out into the strait before night fell.

Schweiz and I had a shack for ourselves, on a lip of rock overlooking the harbor. Mattresses of leaves, blankets of

animal hide, one lopsided window, no sanitary facilities: this is
what the thousands of years of man's voyage through the stars
have brought us to. We haggled over the price of our lodgings,
finally came to an agreement in knives and heat-rods, and at
sundown were given our dinner. A surprisingly tasty stew
of spicy meats, some angular red fruits, a pot of half-cooked
vegetables, a mug of what might have been fermented milk –
we ate what was given us, and enjoyed it more than either of
us had expected, though we made edgy jokes about the diseases
we were likely to catch. I poured out a libation to the god of
travelers, more out of habit than conviction. Schweiz said, 'So
you still believe, after all?' I replied that I found no reason not
to believe in the gods, though my faith in the teachings of men
had been greatly weakened.

This close to the equator, darkness came on swiftly, a sudden
black curtain rolling down. We sat outside a little while,
Schweiz favoring me with some more astronomy, and testing
me on what I had already learned. Then we went to bed. Less
than an hour later, two figures entered our shack; I was still
awake and sat up instantly, imagining thieves or assassins,
but as I groped for a weapon a stray moonbeam showed me
the profile of one of the intruders, and I saw heavy breasts
swinging. Schweiz, out of the dark far corner, said, 'I think
they're included in tonight's price.' Another instant and warm
naked flesh pressed against me. I smelled a pungent odour, and
touched a fat haunch and found it coated in some spicy oil: a
Sumarnu cosmetic, I found out afterwards. Curiosity warred
with caution in me. As I had when a boy taking lodgings in
Glain, I feared catching a disease from the loins of a woman
of a strange race. But should I not experience the southern
kind of loving? From Schweiz's direction I heard the slap of
meat on meat, hearty laughter, liquid lip-noises. My own girl
wriggled impatiently. Parting the plump thighs, I explored,
aroused, entered. The girl squirmed into what I suppose was
the proper native position, lying on her side, facing me, one
leg flung over me and her heel jammed hard against my
buttocks. I had not had a woman since my last night in

Manneran; that and my old problem of haste undid me, and I unloaded myself in the usual premature volleys. My girl called out something, probably in derision of my manhood, to her moaning and sighing companion in Schweiz's corner, and got a giggled answer. In rage and chagrin I forced myself to revive and, pumping slowly, grimly, I ploughed her anew, though the stink of her breath nearly paralyzed me, and her sweat, mingling with her oil, formed a nauseous compound. Eventually I pushed her over the brink of pleasure, but it was cheerless work, a tiresome chore. When it was done she nipped my elbow with her teeth: a Sumarnu kiss, I think it was. Her gratitude. Her apology. I had done her good service after all. In the morning I scanned the village maidens, wondering which lass it was had honored me with her caresses. All of them gaptoothed, sagbreasted, fisheyed: let my couchmate have been none of the ones I saw. For days afterwards I kept uneasy watch on my organ, expecting it each morning to be broken out in red spots or running sores; but all I caught from her was a distaste for the Sumarnu style of passion.

FORTY-ONE

Five days. Six, actually: either Schweiz had misunderstood, or the Sumarnu chieftain was poor at counting. We had one guide and three bearers. I had never walked so much before, from dawn to sunset, the ground yielding and bouncy beneath my feet. The jungle rising, a green wall, on both sides of the narrow path. Astonishing humidity, so that we swam in the air, worse than on the worst day in Manneran. Insects with jeweled eyes and terrifying beaks. Slithering many-legged beasts rushing past us. Strugglings and horrid cries in the underbrush, just beyond sight. The sunlight falling in dappled streaks, barely making it through the canopy high above. Flowers bursting from the trunks of trees: parasites, Schweiz said. One of them a puffy yellow thing that had a human face, goggly eyes, a gaping pollen-smeared mouth. The other even more bizarre, for from the midst of its red and black petals rose a parody of genitalia, a fleshy phallus, two dangling balls. Schweiz, shrieking with amusement, seized the first of these that we found, wrapped his hand around the floral cock, bawdily flirted with it and stroked it. The Sumarnu muttered things; perhaps they were wondering if they had done right to send girls to our shack that night.

We crept up the spine of the continent, emerging from the jungle for a day and a half to climb a good-sized mountain, then more jungle on the other side. Schweiz asked our guide why we had not gone around the mountain instead of over it, and was told that this was the only route, for poison-ants infested all the surrounding lowlands: very cheering. Beyond the mountain lay a chain of lakes and streams and ponds, many of them thick with gray toothy snouts barely breaking the surface. All this seemed unreal to me. A few days' sail to the north lay Velada Borthan, with its banking houses and its groundcars, its customs collectors and its godhouses. That was a tamed continent, but for its uninhabitable interior. Man had made no impact at all, though, on this place where we marched. Its disorderly wildness oppressed me – that and the heavy air, the sounds in the night, the unintelligible conversations of our primitive companions.

On the sixth day we came to the native village. Perhaps three hundred wooden huts were scattered over a broad meadow at a place where two rivers of modest size ran together. I had the impression that there once had been a larger town here, possibly even a city, for on the borders of the settlement I saw grassy mounds and humps, quite plausibly the site of ancient ruins. Or was that only an illusion? Did I need so badly to convince myself that the Sumarnu had regressed since leaving our continent, that I had to see evidences of decline and decay wherever I looked?

The villagers surrounded us: not hostile, only curious. Northerners were uncommon sights. A few of them came close and touched me, a timid pat on the forearm, a shy squeeze of the wrist, invariably accompanied by a quick little smile. These jungle folk seemed not to have the sullen sourness of those who lived in the shacks by the harbor. They were gentler, more open, more childlike. Such little taint of Veladan civilization as had managed to stain the harbor folk had darkened their spirits; not so here, where contact with northerners was less frequent.

An interminable parley began among Schweiz, our guide, and three of the village elders. After the first few moments Schweiz was out of it: the guide, indulging in long cascades of verbal embellishments footnoted by frantic gesticulations, seemed to be explaining the same thing over and over to the villagers, who constantly made the same series of replies to him. Neither Schweiz nor I could understand a syllable of it. At last the guide, looking agitated, turned to Schweiz and poured forth a stream of Sumarnu-accented Mannerangi, which I found almost wholly opaque but which Schweiz, with his tradesman's skill at communicating with strangers, was able to penetrate. Schweiz said finally to me, 'They're willing to sell to us. Provided we can show them that we're worthy of having the drug.'

'How do we do that?'

'By taking some with them, at a love-ritual this evening. Our guide's been trying to talk them out of it, but they won't budge. No communion, no merchandise.'

'Are there risks?' I asked.

Schweiz shook his head. 'It doesn't seem that way to me. But the guide has the idea that we're only looking for profit in the drug, that we don't mean to use it ourselves but intend to go back to Manneran and sell what we get for many mirrors and many heat-rods and many knives. Since he thinks we aren't users, he's trying to protect us from exposure to it. The villagers also think we aren't users, and they're damned if they'll turn a speck of the stuff over to anyone who's merely planning to peddle it. They'll make it available only to true believers.'

'But we *are* true believers,' I said.

'I know. But I can't convince our man of that. He knows enough about northerners to know that they keep their minds closed at all times, and he wants to pamper us in our sickness of soul. But I'll try again.'

Now it was Schweiz and our guide who parleyed, while the village chiefs stood silent. Adopting the gestures and even the accent of the guide, so that both sides of the conversation became unintelligible to me, Schweiz pressed and pressed and pressed, and the guide resisted all that the Earthman was telling him, and a feeling of despair came over me so that I was ready to suggest that we give up and go empty-handed back to Manneran. Then Schweiz somehow broke through. The guide, still suspicious, clearly asked Schweiz whether he really wanted what he said he wanted, and Schweiz emphatically said he did, and the guide, looking sceptical, turned once more to the village chiefs. This time he spoke only briefly with them, and then briefly again with Schweiz. 'It's been settled,' Schweiz told me. 'We'll take the drug with them tonight.' He leaned close and touched my elbow. 'Something for you to remember. When you go under: *be loving*. If you can't love them, all is lost.'

I was offended that he had found it necessary to warn me.

FORTY-TWO

Ten of them came for us at sundown and led us into the forest east of the village. Among them were the three chieftains and two other older men, along with two young men and three women. One of the women was a handsome girl, one a plain girl, and one quite old. Our guide did not go with us; I am not sure whether he was not invited to the ceremony or simply did not feel like taking part.

We marched a considerable distance. No longer could we hear the cries of children in the village or the barking of domestic animals. Our halting-place was a secluded clearing, where hundreds of trees had been felled and the dressed logs laid out in five rows as benches, to form a pentagonal amphitheatre. In the middle of the clearing was a clay-lined fire-pit, with a great heap of firewood neatly stacked beside it; as soon as we arrived, the two young men commenced building a towering blaze. On the far side of the woodpile I saw a second clay-lined pit, about twice as wide as a large man's body; it descended diagonally into the ground and gave the appearance of being a passage of no little depth, a tunnel offering access to the depths of the world. By the glow of the firelight I tried to peer into it from where I stood, but I was unable to see anything of interest.

Through gestures the Sumarnu showed us where we should sit: at the base of the pentagon. The plain girl sat beside us. To our left, next to the tunnel entrance, sat the three chiefs. To our right, by the fire-pit, were the two young men. In the far right corner sat the old woman and one of the old men; the other old man and the handsome girl went to the far left corner. Full darkness was upon us by the time we were seated. The Sumarnu now removed what little clothing they wore, and, seeing them obviously beckoning to us to do the same, Schweiz and I stripped, piling our clothes on the benches behind us. At a signal from one of the chiefs the handsome girl rose and went to the fire, poking a bough into it until she had a torch; then, approaching the slanting mouth of the tunnel, she wriggled awkwardly feet-first into it, holding the torch high. Girl and torch disappeared entirely from view. For a little while I could see the flickering light of the firebrand coming from below, but soon it went out, sending up a gust of dark smoke. Shortly the girl emerged, without the torch. In one hand she carried a thick-rimmed red pot, in the other a long flask of green glass. The two old men – high priests? – left their benches and took these things from her. They began a tuneless chant, and one, reaching into the pot, scooped from it a handful of white powder – the drug! – and dropped it into the flask. The other solemnly shook the flask from side to side in a mixing motion. Meanwhile the old woman – a priestess? – had prostrated herself by the mouth of the tunnel and began to chant in a different intonation, a jagged gasping rhythm, while the two young men flung more wood on the fire. The chanting continued for a good many minutes. Now the girl who had descended into the tunnel – a slim high-breasted wench with long silken red-brown hair – took the flask from the old man and brought it to our side of the fire, where the plain girl, stepping forward, received it reverently with both hands. Solemnly she carried it to the three seated chieftains and held it towards them. The chieftains now joined the chanting for the first time. What I thought of as the Rite of the Presentation of the Flask went on and on; I was fascinated at first, finding delight in the strangeness of the ceremony, but soon I grew bored and had to amuse myself by trying to invent a spiritual content for what was taking place. The tunnel, I decided, symbolized the genital opening of the world-mother, the route to her womb, where the drug – made from a root, from something growing underground – could be obtained. I devised an elaborate metaphorical construct involving a mother-cult, the symbolic meaning of carrying a lighted torch into the world-mother's womb, the use of plain and handsome girls to represent the universality of womanhood, the two young fire-warders as guardians of the chieftains' sexual potency, and a great deal more, all of it nonsense, but – so I thought – an impressive enough scheme to be assembled by a bureaucrat like myself, of no great intellectual powers. My pleasure in my own musings evaporated abruptly when I realized how patronizing I was being. I was treating these Sumarnu like quaint savages, whose chants and rites were of mild aesthetic interest but could not possibly have any serious content. Who was I to take this lofty attitude? I had come to them, had I not, begging the drug of enlightenment that my soul craved; which of us then was the superior being? I assailed myself for my snobbery. *Be loving*. Put aside courtly sophistication. Share their rite if you can, and at the least show no contempt for it, feel no contempt, *have* no contempt. *Be loving*. The chieftains were drinking now, each taking a sip, handing the flask back to the plain-looking girl, who when all three had sipped began to move about the circle, bringing the flask first to the old men, then to the old woman, then to the handsome girl, then to the young fire-tenders, then to Schweiz, then to me. She smiled at me as she gave me the flask. By the fire's leaping light she seemed suddenly beautiful. The flask contained a warm gummy wine; I nearly gagged as I drank. But I drank. The drug entered my gut and journeyed thence to my soul.

FORTY-THREE

We all became one, the ten of them and the two of us. First there were the strange sensations of going up, the heightening of perception, the loss of bearings, the visions of celestial light, the hearing of eerie sounds; then came the detecting of other heartbeats and bodily rhythms about me, the doubling, the overlapping of awarenesses; then came the dissolution of self, and we became one, who had been twelve. I was plunged into a sea of souls and I perished. I was swept into the Centre of All Things. I had no way of knowing whether I was Kinnall the septarch's son, or Schweiz the man of old Earth, or the fire-tenders, or the chiefs, or the priests, or the girls, or the priestess, for they were inextricably mixed up in me and I in them. And the sea of souls was a sea of love. How could it be anything else than that? We were each other. Love of self bound us each to each, all to all. Love of self is love of others; love of others is love of self. And I loved. I knew more clearly than ever why Schweiz had said to me, *I love you*, as we were coming out of the drug the first time – that odd phrase, so obscene on Borthan, so incongruous in any case when man is speaking to man. I said to the ten Sumarnu, *I love you*, though not in words, for I had no words that they would understand, and even if I had spoken to them in my own tongue and they had understood, they would have resented the foulness of my words, for among my people *I love you* is an obscenity, and no help for it. *I love you*. And I meant it, and they accepted the gift of my love. I who was part of them. I who not long ago had patronized them as amusing primitives worshiping bonfires in the woods. Through them I sensed the sounds of the forest and the heaving of the tides, and, yes, the merciful love of the great world-mother, who lies sighing and quaking beneath our feet, and who has bestowed on us the drug-root for the healing of our sundered selves. I learned what it is to be Sumarnu and live simply at the meeting-place of two small rivers. I discovered how one can lack groundcars and banking houses and still belong to the community of civilized humanity. I found out what half-souled things the people of Velada Borthan have made of themselves in the name of holiness, and how whole it is possible to be, if one follows the way of the Sumarnu. None of this came to me in words or even in a flow of images, but rather in a rush of received knowledge, knowledge that entered and became part of me after a manner I can neither describe nor explain. I hear you saying now that I must be either lying or lazy, to offer you as little specific detail of the experience as I have done. But I reply that one cannot put into words what never *was* in words. One can deal only in approximations, and one's best effort can be nothing more than a distortion, a coarsening of the truth. For I must transform perceptions into words and set them down as my skills permit, and then you must pick my words from the page and convert them into whatever system of perceptions your mind habitually employs, and at each stage of this transmission a level of density leaches away, until you are left only with the shadow of what befell me in the clearing in Sumara Borthan. So how can I explain? We were dissolved in one another. We were dissolved in love. We who had no language in common came to total comprehension of our separate selves. When the drug at length lost its hold on us, part of me remained in them and part of them remained in me. If you would know more than that, if you would have a glimpse of what it is to be released from the prison of your

skull, if you would taste love for the first time in your life, I
say to you, Look for no explanations fashioned out of words,
but put the flask to your lips. Put the flask to your lips.

FORTY-FOUR

We had passed the test. They would give us what we wanted.
After the sharing of love came the haggling. We returned to the
village, and in the morning our bearers brought out our cases of
trade-goods, and the three chieftains brought out three squat
clay pots, with the white powder visible within them. And we
heaped up a high stack of knives and mirrors and heat-rods,
and they carefully poured quantities of powder from two of
the pots into the third. Schweiz did most of the bargaining.
The guide we had brought from the coast was of little value,
for, though he could talk these chieftains' language, he had
never talked to their souls. In fact the bargaining inverted itself
suddenly, with Schweiz happily piling still more trinkets into
the price, and the chiefs responding by adding more powder
to our bowl, everyone laughing in a sort of hysterical good
nature as the contest of generosity grew more frenzied. In the
end we gave the villagers everything we had, keeping only a
few items for gifts to our guide and bearers, and the villagers
gave us enough of the drug to snare the minds of thousands.

Captain Khrisch was waiting when we reached the harbor.
'One sees you have fared well,' he remarked.

'Is it so obvious?' I asked.

'You were worried men when you went into this place. You
are happy men coming out of it. Yes, it is obvious.'

On the first night of our voyage back to Manneran, Schweiz
called me into his cabin. He had the pot of white powder out,
and he had broken the seal. I watched as he carefully poured
the drug into little packets of the kind in which that first dose
had come. He worked in silence, scarcely glancing at me,

filling some seventy or eighty packets. When he was done,
he counted out a dozen of them and pushed them to one
side. Indicating the others, he said, 'Those are for you. Hide
them well about your luggage, or you'll need all your power
with the Port Justiciary to get them safely past the customs
collectors.'

'You've given me five times as much as you've taken,' I
protested.

'Your need is greater,' Schweiz told me.

FORTY-FIVE

I did not understand what he meant by that until we were
in Manneran again. We landed at Hilminor, paid Captain
Khrisch, went through a minimum of inspection formalities
(how trusting the port officials were, not very long ago!) and
set out in our groundcar for the capital. Entering the city of
Manneran by the Sumar Road, we passed through a crowded
district of market-places and open-air shops, where I saw
thousands of Mannerangi jostling, haggling, bickering. I saw
them driving their hard bargains and whipping out contract
forms to close the deals. I saw their faces, pinched, guarded,
the eyes bleak and unloving. And I thought of the drug I
carried and told myself, *If only I could change their frosty souls*. I
had a vision of myself going among them, accosting strangers,
drawing this one aside and that, whispering gently to each
of them, 'I am a prince of Salla and a high official of the
Port Justiciary, who has put such empty things aside to bring
happiness to mankind, and I would show you how to find
joy through selfbaring. Trust me: I love you.' No doubt some
would flee from me as soon as I began to speak, frightened by
the initial obscenity of my 'I am', and others might hear me
out and then spit in my face and call me a madman, and some
might cry for the police; but perhaps there would be a few who

would listen, and feel tempted, and come off with me to a quiet dockside room where we could share the Sumaran drug. One by one I would open souls, until there were ten in Manneran like me – twenty – a hundred – a secret society of selfbarers, knowing one another by the warmth and love in their eyes, going about the city unafraid to say 'I' or 'me' to their fellow initiates, giving up not merely the grammar of politeness but all the poisonous denials of self-love that that grammar implied. And then I would charter Captain Khrisch again for a voyage to Sumara Borthan, and return laden with packets of white powder, and continue on through Manneran, I and those who now were like me, and we would go up to this one and that, smiling, glowing, to whisper, 'I would show you how to find joy through selfbaring. Trust me: I love you.'

There was no role for Schweiz in this vision. This was not his planet; he had no stake in transforming it. All that interested him was his private spiritual need, his hunger to break through to a sense of the godhood. He had begun that breakthrough already, and could complete it on his own, apart. Schweiz had no need to skulk about the city, seducing strangers. And this was why he had given me the greater share of our Sumaran booty: I was the evangelist, I was the new prophet, I was the messiah of openness, and Schweiz realized that before I did. Until now he had been the leader – drawing me into his confidence, getting me to try the drug, luring me off to Sumara Borthan, making use of my power in the Port Justiciary, keeping me at his side for companionship and reassurance and protection. I had been in his shadow throughout. Now he would cease to eclipse me. Armed with my little packets, I alone would launch the campaign to change a world.

It was a role I welcomed. All my life I had been overshadowed by one man or another, so that for all my strength of body and ability of mind I had come to seem second-rate to myself. Perhaps that is a natural defect of being born a septarch's second son. First there had been my father, whom I could never hope to equal in authority, agility, or might; then Stirron, whose kingship brought only exile for me; then my master in the Glinish logging camp; then Segvord Helalam; then Schweiz. All of them men of determination and prestige, who knew and held their places in our world, while I wandered in frequent bewilderment. Now, in the middle of my years, I could at last emerge. I had a mission. I had purpose. The spinners of the divine design had brought me to this place, had made me who I was, had readied me for my task. In joy I accepted their command.

FORTY-SIX

There was a girl I kept for my sport, in a room on the south side of Manneran, in the tangle of old streets back of the Stone Chapel. She claimed to be a bastard of the Duke of Kongoroi, spawned when the duke was on a state visit to Manneran in the days of my father's reign. Perhaps her story was true. Certainly she believed it. I was in the habit of going to her twice or thrice each moontime for an hour of pleasure, whenever I felt too stifled by the routine of my life, whenever I felt boredom's hand at my throat. She was simple but passionate: lusty, available, undemanding. I did not hide my identity from her, but I gave her none of my inner self, and none was expected; we talked very little, and there was no question of love between us. In return for the price of her lodgings, she let me make occasional use of her body, and the transaction was no more complex than that: a touching of skins, a sneeze of the loins. She was the first to whom I gave the drug. I mixed it with golden wine. 'We will drink this,' I said, and when she asked me why I replied, 'It will bring us closer together.' She asked, in no great curiosity, what it would do to us, and I explained, 'It will open self to self, and make all walls transparent.' She offered no protests – no talk of the Covenant, no whining about privacy, no lectures of the evils of selfbaring. She did as she was told, convinced I would bring no harm to her. We took the dose, and then we lay

naked on her couch waiting for the effects to begin. I stroked
her cool thighs, kissed the tips of her breasts, playfully nibbled
her earlobes, and soon the strangeness started, the buzzing and
the rush of air, and we began to detect one another's heartbeats
and pulse. 'Oh,' she said. 'Oh, one feels so peculiar!' But it did
not frighten her. Our souls drifted together and were fused in
the clear white light coming from the Center of All Things.
And I discovered what it is like to have only a slit between
my thighs, and I learned how it is to wriggle one's shoulders
and have heavy breasts slap together, and I felt eggs throbbing
and impatient in my ovaries. At the height of our voyage we
joined our bodies. I felt my rod slide into my cavern. I felt
myself moving against myself. I felt the slow sucking oceanic
tide of ecstasy beginning to rise somewhere at my dark hot
moist core, and I felt the hot prickling tickle of impending
ecstasy dancing along my tool, and I felt the hard hairy shield
of my chest crushing against the tender globes of my breasts,
and I felt lips on my lips, tongue on my tongue, soul in my
soul. This union of our bodies endured for hours, or so it
seemed. And in that time my self was open to her, so that
she could see in it all she chose, my boyhood in Salla, my
flight to Glin, my marriage, my love for my bondsister, my
weaknesses, my self-deceptions, and I looked into her and
saw the sweetness of her, the giddiness, the moment of first
finding blood on her thighs, the other blood of a later time,
the image of Kinnall Darival as she carries it in her mind, the
vague and unformed commandments of the Covenant, and all
the rest of her soul's furniture. Then we were swept away by
the storms of our senses. I felt her orgasm and mine, mine and
mine, hers and hers, the double column of frenzy that was one,
the spasm and the spurt, the thrust and the thrust, the rise and
the fall. We lay sweaty and sticky and exhausted, the drug still
thundering through our joined minds. I opened my eyes and
saw hers, unfocused, the pupils dilated. She gave me a lopsided
smile. 'I – I – I – I – I,' she said. 'I!' The wonder of it seemed to
daze her. 'I! I! I!' I planted a kiss between her breasts and felt
the brush of my lips myself. 'I love you,' I said.

FORTY-SEVEN

There was a clerk in the Port Justiciary, a certain Ulman, half my age and clearly a man of promise, whom I had come to like. He knew my power and my ancestry and showed no awe of me over that; his respect for me was based entirely on my skills in evaluating and handling the problems of the Justiciary. I kept him late one day and called him into my office when the others were gone. 'There is this drug of Sumara Borthan,' I said, 'that allows one mind freely to enter another.' He smiled and said that he had heard of it, yes, but understood it was difficult to obtain and dangerous to use. 'There is no danger,' I answered. 'And as for the difficulty of obtaining it –' I drew forth one of my little packets. His smile did not fade, though dots of color came into his cheeks. We took the drug together in my office. Hours later, when we left for our homes, I gave him some so that he could take it with his wife.

FORTY-EIGHT

In the Stone Chapel I dared to reach out to a stranger, a short, thickbodied man in princely clothes, possibly a member of the septarch's family. He had the clear serene eyes of a man of good faith and the posie of one who has looked within himself and is not displeased by what he has seen. But when I spoke my words to him, he shoved me away and cursed me with such fury that his anger became contagious; maddened by his words, I nearly struck him in blind frenzy. *'Selfbarer! Selfbarer!'* The shout echoed through the holy building, and people emerged from rooms of meditation to stare. It was the worst shame I had known in years. My exalted mission came into another perspective: I saw it as filthy, and myself as something pitiful, a creeping slinking dog of a man driven by who knew what compulsion to expose his shabby soul to strangers. My anger drained from me and fear flowed in: I slipped into the shadows and out of a side door, dreading arrest. For a week I walked about on tiptoe, forever looking back over my shoulder. But nothing pursued me except my panging conscience.

FORTY-NINE

The moment of insecurity passed. Again I saw my mission whole, and recognized the merit of what I had pledged myself to do, and felt only sorrow for the man in the Stone Chapel who had spurned my gift. And in a single week I found three strangers who would share the drug with me. I wondered how I could ever have doubted myself. But other seasons of doubt lay ahead.

FIFTY

I tried to arrive at a theoretical basis for my use of the drug, to construct a new theology of love and openness. I studied the Covenant and many of its commentaries, attempting to discover why the first settlers of Velada Borthan had found it necessary to deify mistrust and concealment. What did they fear? What were they hoping to preserve? Dark men in a dark time, with mindsnakes creeping through their skulls. In the end I came to no real understanding of them. They were convinced of their own virtue. They had acted for the best. Thou shalt not thrust the inwardness of thy soul upon thy fellow man. Thou shalt not unduly examine the needs of thine own self. Thou shalt deny thyself the easy pleasures of intimate conversation. Thou shalt stand alone before thy gods. And so we had lived, these hundreds of years, unquestioning, obedient, keeping the Covenant. Maybe nothing keeps the Covenant alive now, for most of us, except simple politeness: we are unwilling to embarrass others by baring ourselves, and so we go locked up, our inner wounds festering, and we speak our language of third-person courtliness. Was it time to create a new Covenant? A bond of love, a testament of sharing? Hidden in my rooms at home, I struggled to write one. What could I say that would be believed? That we had done well enough following the old ways, but at grievous personal cost. That the perilous conditions of the first settling no longer obtained among us, and certain customs, having become handicaps rather than assets, could be discarded. That societies must evolve if they are not to decay. That love is better than hate and trust is better than mistrust. But little of what I wrote convinced even me. Why was I attacking the established order of things? Out of profound conviction, or merely out of the hunger for dirty pleasures? I was a man of my own time; I was embedded firmly in the rock of my upbringing even as I toiled to turn that rock to sand. Trapped in the tension between my old beliefs and my still unformed new ones, I swung a thousand times a day from pole to pole, from shame to exaltation. As I labored over the draft of my new Covenant's preamble one evening, my bondsister Halum unexpectedly entered my study. 'What are you writing?' she asked pleasantly. I covered one sheet with another. My face must have reflected my discomfort, for hers showed signs of apology for having intruded. 'Official reports,' I said. 'Foolishness. Dull bureaucratic trivia.' That night I burned all I had written, in a paroxysm of self-contempt.

FIFTY-ONE

In those weeks I took many voyages of exploration into unknown lands. Friends, strangers, casual acquaintances, a mistress: companions on strange journeys. But through all the early phase of my time of changes I said not a word to Halum about the drug. To share it with her had been my original goal, that had brought the drug to my lips in the first place. Yet I feared to approach her. It was cowardice that kept me back: what if, by coming to know me too well, she ceased to love me?

FIFTY-TWO

Several times I came close to broaching the subject with her. I held myself back. I did not dare to move towards her. If you wish you may measure my sincerity by my hesitation; how pure, you may ask, was my new creed of openness, if I felt that my bondsister would be above such a communion? But I will not pretend there was any consistency in my thinking then. My liberation from the taboos on selfbaring was a willed thing, not a natural evolution, and I had constantly to battle against the old habits of our custom. Though I talked in 'I' and 'me' with Schweiz and some of the others with whom I had shared the drug, I was never comfortable in doing so. Vestiges of my broken bonds still crept together to shackle me. I looked at Halum and knew that I loved her, and told myself that the only way to fulfill that love was through the joining of her soul and mine, and in my hand was the powder that would join us. And I did not dare. And I did not dare.

FIFTY-THREE

The twelfth person with whom I shared the Sumaran drug was my bondbrother Noim. He was in Manneran to spend a week as my guest. Winter had come, bringing snow to Glin, hard rains to Salla, and only fog to Manneran, and northerners needed little prodding to come to our warm province. I had not seen Noim since the summer before, when we had hunted together in the Huishtors. In this past year we had drifted apart somewhat; in a sense Schweiz had come to take Noim's place in my life, and I no longer had quite the same need for my bondbrother.

Noim now was a wealthy landowner in Salla, having come into the inheritance of the Condorit family as well as the lands of his wife's kin. In manhood he had become plump, though not fat; his wit and cunning were not hidden deep beneath his new layers of flesh. He had a sleek, well-oiled look, with dark unblemished skin, full, complacent lips, and round sardonic eyes. Little escaped his attention. Upon arriving at my house he surveyed me with great care, as though counting my teeth and the lines about my eyes, and, after the formal bondbrotherly greetings, after the presentation of his gift and the one he had brought from Stirron, after we had signed the contract of host and guest, Noim said unexpectedly, 'Are you in trouble, Kinnall?'

'Why do you ask that?'

'Your face is sharper. You've lost weight. Your mouth – you hold it in a quirky grin that doesn't announce a relaxed man within. Your eyes are red-rimmed and they don't want to look directly into other eyes. Is anything wrong?'

'These have been the happiest months of one's life,' I said, a shade too vehemently, perhaps.

Noim ignored my disclaimer. 'Are you having problems with Loimel?'

'She goes her way, and one goes his own.'

'Difficulties with the business of the Justiciary, then?'

'Please, Noim, won't you believe that –'

'Your face has changes inscribed in it,' he said. 'Do you deny there have been changes in your life?'

I shrugged. 'And if so?'

'Changes for the worse?'

'One does not think so.'

'You're being evasive, Kinnall. Come: what's a bondbrother for, if not to share problems?'

'There are no problems,' I insisted.

'Very well.' And he let the matter drop. But I saw him watching me that evening, and again the next day at morning's meal, studying me, probing me. I could never hide anything from him. We sat over blue wine and talked of the Sallan harvest, talked of Stirron's new programme of reforming the tax structure, talked of the renewed tensions between Salla and Glin, the bloody border raids that had lately cost me the life of a sister. And all the while Noim watched me. Halum dined with us, and we talked of our childhood, and Noim watched me. He flirted with Loimel, but his eyes did not wander from me. The depth and intensity of his concern preyed on me. He would be asking questions of others, soon, trying to get from Halum or from Loimel some notion of what might be bothering me, and he might stir up troublesome curiosities in them that way. I could not let him remain ignorant of the central experience of his bondbrother's life. Late the second night, when everyone else had retired, I took Noim to my study, and opened the secret place where I stored the white powder, and asked him if he knew anything of the Sumaran drug. He claimed not to have heard of it. Briefly I described its effects to him. His expression darkened; he seemed to draw in on himself. 'Do you use this stuff often?' he asked.

'Eleven times thus far.'

'Eleven – *why*, Kinnall?'

'To learn the nature of one's own self, through sharing that self with others.'

Noim laughed explosively: it was almost a snort. 'Selfbaring, Kinnall?'

'One takes up odd hobbies in one's middle years.'

'And with whom have you played this game?'

I said, 'Their names don't matter. No one you would know. People of Manneran, those with some adventure in their souls, those who are willing to take risks.'

'Loimel?'

Now it was my turn to snort. 'Never! She knows nothing of this at all.'

'Halum, then?'

I shook my head. 'One wishes one had the courage to approach Halum. So far one has concealed everything from her. One fears she's too virginal, too easily shocked. It's sad, isn't it, Noim, when one has to hide something as exciting as this, as wonderfully rewarding, from one's bondsister.'

'From one's bondbrother too,' he observed testily.

'You would have been told in time,' I said. 'You would have been offered your chance to experience the communion.'

His eyes flashed. 'Do you think I'd want it?'

His deliberate obscenity earned only a faint smile from me. 'One hopes one's bondbrother will share all of one's experiences. At present the drug opens a gulf between us. One has gone again and again to a place you have never visited. Do you see, Noim?'

Noim saw. He was tempted; he hovered at the edge of the abyss; he chewed his lips and tugged at his ear-lobes, and everything that passed across his mind was as transparent to me as if we had already shared the Sumaran powder. For my sake he was uneasy, knowing that I had seriously strayed from the Covenant and might soon find myself in grave spiritual and legal trouble. For his own sake he was gnawed by curiosity, aware that selfbaring with one's bondbrother was no great sin and half-eager to know the kind of communion he might have with me under the drug. Also his eyes revealed a glint of jealousy, that I had bared myself to this one and this one and that, unimportant strangers, and not to him. I tell you that I comprehended these things at that moment, though I confirmed them later when Noim's soul was open to me.

We said nothing to one another about these matters for several days. He came with me to my office, and watched in admiration as I dealt with matters of the highest national significance. He saw the clerks bowing in and out of my presence, and also the clerk Ulman, who had had the drug, and whose cool familiarity with me touched off suspicious vibrations in Noim's sensitive antennae. We visited with Schweiz, and emptied many a flask of good wine, and discussed religious topics in a hearty, earnest, drunken way. ('All my life,' said Schweiz, 'has been a quest for plausible reasons to believe in what I know to be irrational.') Noim noticed that Schweiz did not always observe the grammatical niceties. Another night we dined with a group of Mannerangi nobles in a voluptuous house in the hills overlooking the city: small birdlike men, overdressed and fidgety, and huge handsome young wives. Noim was displeased by these effete dukes and barons with their talk of commerce and jewelry, but he grew more irritable when the chatter turned to the rumor that a mind-unsealing drug from the southern continent was now procurable in the capital. To this I made only polite interjections of surprise; Noim glared at me for my hypocrisy, and even refused a dish of tender Mannerangi brandy, so tight-strung were his nerves. The day after, we went to the Stone Chapel together, not for draining but merely to view the relics of the early times, for Noim had developed antiquarian interests. The drainer Jidd happened to wander through the cloister at his devotions and smiled oddly at me: I saw Noim at once calculating whether I had drawn even the priest into my subversions. A sizzling tension was building in Noim during those days, for he clearly longed to return to the subject of our early conversation, yet could not bring himself to it. I made no move towards reopening that theme. It was Noim who made the move, finally, on the eve of his departure for his home in Salla. 'This drug of yours –' he began hoarsely.

He said he felt he could not regard himself as my true

bondbrother unless he sampled it. Those words came from him at great cost. His elegant clothes were rumpled by his restlessness, and a fine line of beaded perspiration stood out on his upper lip. We went to a room where no one could intrude, and I prepared the potion. As he took the flask, he briefly flashed at me his familiar grin, impudent and sly and bold, but his hand was shaking so badly he nearly spilled the drink. The drug took effect quickly for both of us. It was a night of thick humidity, with a dense greasy mist covering the city and its suburbs, and it seemed to me that fingers of that mist were sliding into our room through the partly opened window: I saw shimmering, pulsating strands of cloud groping at us, dancing between my bondbrother and myself. The early sensations of druggedness disturbed Noim, until I explained that everything was normal, the twinned heartbeats, the cottony head, the high whining sounds in the air. Now we were open. I looked into Noim and saw not only his self but his image of his self, encrusted with shame and self-contempt; there was in Noim a fierce and burning loathing of his imagined flaws, and the flaws were many. He held himself accused of laziness, lack of discipline and ambition, irreligiousness, a casual concern with high obligations, and physical and moral weakness. Why he saw himself in this way I could not understand, for the true Noim was there beside the image, and the true Noim was a tough-minded man, loyal to those he loved, harsh in judgement of folly, clear-sighted, passionate, energetic. The contrast between Noim's Noim and the world's was startling: it was as though he were capable of correctly evaluating everything but his own worth. I had seen such disparities before on these drug voyages; in fact they were universal in all but Schweiz, who had not been trained from childhood in self-denial; yet they were sharper in Noim than in anyone else.

Also I saw, as I had seen before, my own image refracted through Noim's sensibility: a far nobler Kinnall Darival than I recognized. How he idealized me! I was all he hoped to be, a man of action and valor, a wielder of power, an enemy of everything that was frivolous, a practitioner of the sternest inner discipline and devotion. Yet this image bore traces of a new overlay of tarnish, for was I not also now a Covenant-defiling selfbarer, who had done this and this and that and that with eleven strangers, and who now had lured his own bondbrother into criminal experimentation? And also Noim found in me the true depth of my feelings for Halum, and upon making that discovery, which confirmed old suspicions, he altered his image of me once again, not for the better. Meanwhile I showed Noim how I had always seen him – quick, clever, capable – and showed him too his own Noim and the objective Noim as well, while he gave me a view of the selves of mine he now could see beside that idealized Kinnall. These mutual explorations continued a long time. I thought the exchanges were immensely valuable, since only with Noim could I attain the necessary depth of perspective, the proper parallax of character, and he only with me; we had great advantages over a pair of strangers meeting for the first time by way of the Sumaran drug. When the spell of the potion began to lift, I felt myself exhausted by the intensity of our communion, and yet ennobled, exalted, transformed.

Not so Noim. He looked depleted and chilled. He could barely lift his eyes to mine. His mood was so frigid that I dared not break in on it, but remained still, waiting for him to recover. At length he said, 'Is it all over?'

'Yes.'

'Promise one thing, Kinnall. Will you promise?'

'Say it, Noim.'

'That you will never do this thing with Halum! Is it a promise? Will you promise it, Kinnall? Never. Never. Never.'

FIFTY-FOUR

Several days after Noim's departure some guilty impulse drove
me to the Stone Chapel. To fill the time until Jidd could see me,
I roamed the halls and byways of the dark building, pausing at
altars, bowing humbly to half-blind scholars of the Covenant
holding debate in a courtyard, brushing away ambitious minor
drainers who, recognizing me, solicited my trade. All about me
were the things of the gods, and I failed to detect the divine
presence. Perhaps Schweiz had found the godhood through
the souls of other men, but I, dabbling in selfbaring, somehow
had lost that other faith, and it did not matter to me. I knew
that in time I would find my way back to grace under this new
dispensation of love and trust that I hoped to offer. So I lurked
in the godhouse of godhouses, a mere tourist.

I went to Jidd. I had not had a draining since immediately
after Schweiz first had given me the Sumaran drug. The little
crooknosed man remarked on that as I took the contract
from him. The pressures of the Justiciary, I explained, and
he shook his head and made a chiding sound. 'You must
be full to overflowing,' Jidd said. I did not reply, but settled
down before his mirror to peer at the lean, unfamiliar face
that dwelled in it. He asked me which god I would have, and
I told him the god of the innocent. He gave me a queer look at
that. The holy lights came on. With soft words he guided me
into the half-trance of confession. What could I say? That I had
ignored my pledge, and gone on to use the selfbaring potion
with everyone who would take it from me? I sat silent. Jidd
prodded me. He did something I had never known a drainer to
do before: hearkened back to a previous draining, and asked me
to speak again of this drug whose use I had admitted earlier.
Had I used it again? I pushed my face close to the mirror,
fogging it with my breath. Yes. Yes. One is a miserable sinner
and one has been weak once more. Then Jidd asked me how
I had obtained this drug, and I said that I had taken it, the

first time, in company with one who had purchased it from a man who had been to Sumara Borthan. Yes, Jidd said, and what was the name of this companion? That was a clumsy move: immediately I was on guard. It seemed to me that Jidd's question went far beyond the needs of a draining, and certainly could have no relevance to my own condition of the moment. I refused therefore to give him Schweiz's name, which led the drainer to ask me, a little roughly, if I feared he would breach the secrecy of the ritual.

Did I fear that? On rare occasions I had held things back from drainers out of shame, but never out of fear of betrayal. Naïve I was, and I had full faith in the ethics of the godhouse. Only now, suddenly suspicious, with that suspicion having been planted by Jidd himself, did I mistrust Jidd and all his tribe. Why did he want to know? What information was he after? What could I gain, or he, by my revealing my source of the drug? I replied tautly, 'One seeks forgiveness for oneself alone, and how can telling the name of one's companion bring that? Let him do his own confessing.' But of course there was no chance that Schweiz would go to a drainer; thus I had come down to playing word-games with Jidd. All value had leaked from this draining, leaving me with an empty husk. 'If you would have peace from the gods,' Jidd said, 'you must speak your soul fully.' How could I do that? Confess the seduction of eleven people into selfbaring? I had no need of Jidd's forgiveness. I had no faith in his good will. Abruptly I stood up, a little dizzy from kneeling in the dark, swaying a bit, almost stumbling. The sound of distant hymn-singing floated past me, and a trace of the scent of the precious incense of a plant of the Wet Lowlands. 'One is not ready for draining today,' I told Jidd. 'One must examine one's soul more closely.' I lurched towards the door. He looked puzzledly at the money I had given him. 'The fee?' he called. I told him he could keep it.

FIFTY-FIVE

The days became mere vacant rooms, separating one journey with the drug from the next. I drifted idle and detached through all my responsibilities, seeing nothing of what was around me, living only for my next communion. The real world dissolved; I lost interest in sex, wine, food, the doings of the Port Justiciary, the friction between neighboring provinces of Velada Borthan, and all other such things, which to me now were only the shadows of shadows. Possibly I was using the drug too frequently. I lost weight and existed in a perpetual haze of blurred white light. I had difficulties in sleeping, and for hours found myself twisting and shifting, a blanket of muggy tropical air clamping me to my mattress, a haggard insomniac with an ache in his eyeballs and grittiness under his lids. I walked tired through my days and blinking through my evenings. Rarely did I speak with Loimel, nor did I touch her, and hardly ever did I touch any other woman. I fell asleep at midday once while lunching with Halum. I scandalized High Justice Kalimol by replying to one of his questions with the phrase 'It seems to me –' Old Segvord Helalam told me I looked ill, and suggested I go hunting with my sons in the Burnt Lowlands. Nevertheless the drug had the power of bringing me alive. I sought out new sharers, and found it ever more easy to make contact with them, for often now they were brought to me by those who had already made the inner voyage. An odd group they were: two dukes, a marquis, a whore, a keeper of the royal archives, a sea captain in from Glin, a septarch's mistress, a director of the Commercial and Seafarers Bank of Manneran, a poet, a lawyer from Velis here to confer with Captain Khrisch, and many more. The circle of selfbarers was widening. My supply of the drug was nearly consumed, but now there was talk among some of my new friends of outfitting a new expedition to Sumara Borthan. There were fifty of us by this time. Change was becoming infectious; there was an epidemic of it in Manneran.

FIFTY-SIX

Sometimes, unexpectedly, in the blank dead time between one communion and another, I underwent a strange confusion of the self. A block of borrowed experience that I had stowed in the dark depths of my mind might break loose and float up into the higher levels of consciousness, intruding itself into my own identity. I remained aware of being Kinnall Darival, the septarch's son of Salla, and yet there was suddenly among my memories a segment of the self of Noim, or Schweiz, or one of the Sumarnu, or someone else of those with whom I had shared the drug. For the length of that splicing of selves – a moment, an hour, half a day – I walked about unsure of my past, unable to determine whether some event fresh in my mind had really befallen me, or had come to me through the drug. This was disturbing but not really frightening, except the first two or three times. Eventually I learned to distinguish the quality of these unearned memories from that of my genuine past, through familiarity with the textures of each. The drug had made me many people, I realized. Was it not better to be many than to be something less than one?

FIFTY-SEVEN

In early spring a lunatic heat settled over Manneran, coupled with such frequent rains that all the city's vegetation went mad, and would have swallowed every street if not given a daily hacking. It was green, green, green, everywhere: green haze in the sky, green rain falling, green sunlight sometimes breaking through, broad glossy green leaves unfurling on every balcony and in every garden plot. A man's own soul can mildew in that. Green, too, were the awnings on the street of the spice-merchants' shops. Loimel had given me a long list of things to purchase, delicacies from Threish and Velis and the Wet Lowlands, and in a docile husbandly way I went to obtain them, since the street of spice was only a short walk from the Justiciary. She was mounting a grand feast to celebrate the Naming Day of our eldest daughter, who was at last going to come into the adult-name we had intended for her: Loimel. All the great ones of Manneran had been invited to look on as my wife acquired a namesake. Among the guests would be several who had covertly sampled the Sumaran drug with me, and I took private pleasure in that; Schweiz, though, had not been invited, since Loimel deemed him coarse, and in any event he had left Manneran on some business trip just as the weather was beginning to go berserk.

I moved through the greenness to the best of the shops. A recent rain had ended and the sky was a flat green plaque resting on the rooftops. To me came delicious fragrances, sweetnesses, pungencies, clouds of tongue-tickling flavors. Abruptly there were black bubbles coursing through my skull and for a moment I was Schweiz haggling on a pier with a skipper who had just brought a cargo of costly produce in from the Gulf of Sumar. I halted to enjoy this tangling of selves. Schweiz faded; through Noim's mind I smelled the scent of newly threshed hay on the Condorit estates, under a delicious late-summer sun; then suddenly and surprisingly I was the bank director with my hand tight on some other man's loins. I cannot convey to you the impact of that last bolt of transferred experience, brief and incandescent. I had taken the drug with the bank director not very long before, and I had seen nothing in his soul, then, of his taste for his own sex. It was not the kind of thing I would overlook. Either I had manufactured this vision gratuitously, or he had somehow shielded that part of his self from me, keeping his predilections sealed until this instant of breaking through. Was such a partial sealing possible? I had thought one's mind lay fully open. I was not upset by the nature of his lusts, only by my inability to reconcile what I had just experienced with what had come to me from him on the day of our drug-sharing. But I had little time to ponder the problem, for, as I stood gaping outside the spice-shop, a thin hand fell on mine and a guarded voice said, 'I must talk to you secretly, Kinnall.' *I*. The word jolted me from my dreaming.

Androg Mihan, keeper of the archives of Manneran's prime septarch, stood beside me. He was a small man, sharp-featured and gray, the last you would think to seek illegal pleasures; the Duke of Sumar, one of my early conquests, had led him to me. 'Where shall we go?' I asked, and Mihan indicated a disreputable-looking lower-class godhouse across the street. Its drainer lounged outside, trying to stir up business. I could not see how we could talk secretly in a godhouse, but I followed the archivist anyway; we entered the godhouse and Mihan told the drainer to fetch his contract forms. The moment the man was gone, Mihan leaned close to me and said, 'The police are on their way to your house. When you return home this evening you will be arrested and taken to prison on one of the Sumar Gulf's isles.'

'Where do you learn this?'

'The decree was verified this morning and has passed to me for filing.'

'What charge?' I asked.

'Selfbaring,' Mihan said. 'Accusation filed by agents of the Stone Chapel. There is also a secular charge: use and distribution of illegal drugs. They have you, Kinnall.'

'Who is the informer?'

'A certain Jidd, said to be a drainer in the Stone Chapel. Did you let the tale of the drug be drained from you?'

'I did. In my innocence. The sanctity of the godhouse –'

'The sanctity of the dunghouse!' Androg Mihan said vehemently. 'Now you must flee! The full force of the government is mustered against you.'

'Where shall I go?'

'The Duke of Sumar will shelter you tonight,' said Mihan. 'After that – I do not know.'

The drainer now returned, bearing a set of contracts. He gave us a proprietary smile and said, 'Well, gentlemen, which of you is to be first?'

'One has remembered another appointment,' Mihan said.

'One feels suddenly unwell,' I said.

I tossed the startled drainer a fat coin and we left the godhouse. Outside, Mihan pretended not to know me, and we went our separate ways without a word. Not for a moment did I doubt the truth of his warning. I had to take flight; Loimel would have to purchase her own spices. I hailed a car and went at once to the mansion of the Duke of Sumar.

FIFTY-EIGHT

This duke is one of the wealthiest in Manneran, with sprawling estates along the Gulf and in the Huishtor foothills, and a splendid home at the capital set amidst a park worthy of an emperor's palace. He is hereditary customs-keeper of Stroin Gap, which is the source of his family's opulence, since for centuries they have skimmed a share of all that is brought forth to market out of the Wet Lowlands. In his person this duke is a man of great ugliness or remarkable beauty, I am not sure which: he has a large flat triangular head, thin lips, a powerful nose, and strange dense tightly curled hair that clings like a carpet to his skull. His hair is entirely white, yet his face is unlined. His eyes are huge and dark and intense. His cheeks are hollow. It is an ascetic face, which to me always seemed alternately saintly and monstrous, and sometimes the both at once. I had been close with him almost since my arrival in Manneran so many years before; he had helped Segvord Helalam into power, and he had stood soulbinder to Loimel at our wedding ceremony. When I took up the use of the

Sumaran drug, he divined it as if by telepathy, and in a conversation of marvelous subtlety learned from me that I had the drug, and arranged that he should take it with me. That had been four moonrises earlier, in late winter.

Arriving at his home, I found a tense conference in progress. Present were most of the men of consequence whom I had inveigled into my circle of selfbarers. The Duke of Mannerangu Smor. The Marquis of Woyn. The bank director. The Commissioner of the Treasury and his brother, the Procurator-General of Manneran. The Master of the Border. And five or six others of similar significance. Archivist Mihan arrived shortly after I did.

'We are all here now,' the Duke of Mannerangu Smor said. 'They could sweep us up with a single stroke. Are the grounds well guarded?'

'No one will invade us,' said the Duke of Sumar, a trifle icily, clearly offended by the suggestion that common police might burst into his home. He turned his huge alien eyes on me. 'Kinnall, this will be your last night in Manneran, and no help for it. You are to be the scapegoat.'

'By whose choice?' I asked.

'Not ours,' the duke replied. He explained that something close to a *coup d'etat* had been attempted in Manneran this day, and might well yet succeed: a revolt of junior bureaucrats against their masters. The beginning, he said, lay in my having admitted my use of the Sumaran drug to the drainer Jidd. (Around the room faces darkened. The unspoken implication was that I had been a fool to trust a drainer, and now must pay the price of my folly. I had not been as sophisticated as these men.) Jidd, it seemed, had leagued himself with a cabal of disaffected minor officials, hungry for their turn at power. Since he was drainer to most of the great men of Manneran, he was in an extraordinarily good position to aid the ambitious, by betraying the secrets of the mighty. Why Jidd had chosen to contravene his oaths in this fashion was not yet known. The Duke of Sumar suspected that in Jidd familiarity had bred contempt, and after listening for years to the melancholy outpourings of his powerful clients, he had grown to loathe them: exasperated by their confessions, he found pleasure in collaborating in their destruction. (This gave me a new view of what a drainer's soul might be like.) Hence Jidd had, for some months now, been slipping useful facts to rapacious subordinates, who had threatened their masters with them, often to considerable effect. By admitting my use of the drug to him, I had made myself vulnerable, and he had sold me to certain folk of the Justiciary who wished to have me out of office.

'But this is absurd!' I cried. 'The only evidence against me is protected by the sanctity of the godhouse! How can Jidd place a complaint against me based on what I've drained to him? I'll have him up on charges for violation of contract!'

'There is other evidence,' the Marquis of Woyn said sadly.

'There is?'

'Using what he heard from your own lips,' the Marquis said, 'Jidd was able to guide your enemies into channels of investigation. They have found a certain woman who lives in the hovels behind the Stone Chapel, who has admitted to them that you gave her a strange drink that opened her mind to you –'

'The beasts.'

'They have also,' the Duke of Sumar said, 'been able to link several of us to you. Not all, but several. This morning some of us were presented, by their own subordinates, with demands to resign their offices or face exposure. We met these threats firmly, and those who made them are now under detention, but there is no telling how many allies they have in high places. It is possible that by next moonrise we will all have been cast down and new men will hold our power. However, I doubt this, since, so far as we can determine, the only solid evidence so far is the confession of the slut, who has implicated only you, Kinnall. The accusations made by Jidd will of course be inadmissible, though they can do damage anyway.'

'We can destroy her credibility,' I said. 'I'll claim I never knew her. I'll –'

'Too late,' said the Procurator-General. 'Her deposition is on record. I've had a copy from the Grand Justiciar. It will stand up. You're hopelessly implicated.'

'What will happen?' I asked.

'We will crush the ambitions of the blackmailers,' said the Duke of Sumar, 'and send them into poverty. We will break Jidd's prestige and drive him from the Stone Chapel. We will deny all of the charges of selfbaring that may be brought against us. You, however, must leave Manneran.'

'Why?' I looked at the duke in perplexity. 'I'm not without influence. If you can withstand the charges, why not I?'

'Your guilt is on record,' the Duke of Mannerangu Smor said. 'If you flee, it can be claimed that you alone, and this girl you corrupted, were the only ones involved, and the rest is merely the fabrication of self-serving underlings trying to overthrow their masters. If you stay and try to fight a hopeless case, you'll eventually bring us all down, as your interrogation proceeds.'

It was wholly plain to me now.

I was dangerous to them. My strength might be broken in court and their guilt thus exposed. Thus far I was the only one indicted, and I was the only one vulnerable to the processes of Mannerangi justice. They were vulnerable solely through me, and if I went, there was no way of getting at them. The safety of the majority required my departure. Moreover: my naïve faith in the godhouse, which had led me rashly to confess to Jidd, had led to this tempest, which otherwise might have been avoided. I had caused all this; I was the one who must go.

The Duke of Sumar said, 'You will remain with us until the dark hours of night, and then my private groundcar, escorted by bodyguards as though it were I who was traveling, will take you to the estate of the Marquis of Woyn. A riverboat will be waiting there. By dawn you will be across the Woyn and into your homeland of Salla, and may the gods journey at your side.'

FIFTY-NINE

Once more a refugee. In a single day all the power I had accumulated in fifteen years in Manneran was lost. Neither high birth nor high connections could save me: I might have ties of marriage or love or politics to half the masters of Manneran, yet they were helpless in helping me. I have made it seem as if they had forced me into exile to save their own skins, but it was not like that. My going was necessary, and it brought as much sorrow to them as to me.

I had nothing with me but the clothes I wore. My wardrobe, my weapons, my ornaments, my wealth itself, must remain behind in Manneran. As a boy-prince fleeing from Salla to Glin, I had had the prudence to transfer funds ahead of myself, but now I was cut off. My assets would be sequestered; my sons would be paupered. There had been no time for preparations.

Here at least my friends were of service. The Procurator-General, who was nearly of a size with me, had brought several changes of handsome clothing. The Commissioner of the Treasury had obtained for me a fair fortune in Sallan currency. The Duke of Mannerangu Smor pulled two rings and a pendant from his own body, so that I should not go unadorned into my native province. The Marquis of Woyn pressed on me a ceremonial dagger and his heat-rod, with a hilt worked with precious gems. Mihan promised to speak with Segvord Helalam, and tell him the details of my downfall; Segvord would be sympathetic, Mihan believed, and would protect my sons with all his influence, and keep them untainted by their father's indictment.

Lastly, the Duke of Sumar came to me at the deepest time of the night, when I sat alone sourly eating the dinner I had had no time for earlier, and handed me a small jeweled case of bright gold, of the sort one might carry medicine in. 'Open it carefully,' he said. I did, and found it brimming with white powder. In amazement I asked him where he had obtained this; he had lately sent agents secretly to Sumara Borthan, he replied, who had returned with a small supply of the drug. He claimed to have more, but I believe he gave me all he had.

'In an hour's time you will leave,' said the duke, to smother my gush of gratitude.

I asked to be allowed to make a call first.

'Segvord will explain matters to your wife,' the duke said.

'One did not mean one's wife. One meant one's bondsister.' In speaking of Halum I could not drop easily into the rough grammar we selfbarers affected. 'One has had no chance to make one's farewell to her.'

The duke understood my anguish, for he had been within my soul. But he would not grant me the call. Lines might be tapped; he could not risk having my voice go forth from his home this night. I realized then how delicate a position even he must be in, and I did not force the issue. I could call Halum tomorrow, when I had crossed the Woyn and was safe in Salla.

Shortly it was time for me to depart. My friends had already gone, some hours since; the duke alone led me from the house. His majestic groundcar waited, and a corps of body-guards on individual powercycles. The duke embraced me. I climbed into the car and settled back against the cushions. The driver opaqued the windows hiding me from view though not interfering with my own vision. The car rolled silently forward, picked up speed, plunged into the night, with my outriders, six of them, hovering about it like insects. It seemed that hours went by before we came even to the main gate of the duke's estate. Then we were on the highway. I sat like a man carved of ice, scarcely thinking of what had befallen me. Northward lay our route, and we went at such a rate that the sun was not yet up when we reached the margin of the Marquis of Woyn's estate, on the border between Manneran and Salla. The gate opened; we shot through; the road cut across a dense forest, in which, by moonlight, I could see sinister parasitic growths like hairy ropes tangling tree to tree. Suddenly we erupted into a clearing and I beheld the banks of the River Woyn. The car halted. Someone in dark robes helped me out, as though I were a dodderer, and escorted me down the spongy bank to a long narrow pier, barely visible in the thick mist rising off the breast of the river. A boat was tied up, no great craft, hardly more than a dinghy. Yet it traveled at great speed across the broad and turbulent Woyn. Still I felt no inner response to my banishment from Manneran. I was like one who has gone forth in battle and had his right leg sliced off at the thigh by a fire-bolt, and who now lies in a tumbled heap, staring calmly at his stump and sensing no pain. The pain would come, in time.

Dawn was near. I could make out the shape of the Sallan side of the river. We pulled up at a dock that jutted out of a grassy bank, plainly some nobleman's private landing. Now I felt my first alarm. In a moment I would step ashore in Salla. Where would I find myself? How would I reach some settled region? I was no boy, to beg rides from passing trucks. But all this had been settled for me hours before. As the boat bumped the shoulder of the pier, a figure emerged in the dimness and extended a hand: Noim. He drew me forth and clasped me in a tight hug. 'I know what has happened,' he said. 'You will stay with me.' In his emotion he abandoned polite usage with me for the first time since our boyhood.

SIXTY

At midday, from Noim's estate in south-western Salla, I phoned the Duke of Sumar to confirm my safe arrival – it was he, of course, who had arranged for my bondbrother to meet me at the border – and then I put through a call to Halum. Segvord had told her just a few hours earlier of the reasons for my disappearance. 'How strange this news is,' she said. 'You never spoke of the drug. Yet it was so important to you, for you risked everything to use it. How could it have had such a role in your

life, and yet be kept a secret from your bondsister?' I answered
that I had not dared to let her know of my preoccupation with
it, for fear I might be tempted to offer it to her. She said, 'Is
opening yourself then to your bondsister so terrible a sin?'

SIXTY-ONE

Noim treated me with every courtesy, indicating that I could
stay with him as long as I wished – weeks, months, even years.
Presumably my friends in Manneran would succeed eventually
in freeing some of my assets, and I would buy land in Salla and
take up the life of a country baron; or perhaps Segvord and the
Duke of Sumar and other men of influence would have my
indictment quashed, so that I could return to the southern
province. Until then, Noim told me, his home was mine. But
I detected a subtle coolness in his dealings with me, as if this
hospitality was offered only out of respect for our bonding.
Only after some days did the source of his remoteness reach
the surface. Sitting late past dinner in his great whitewashed
feasting-hall, we were talking of childhood days – our main
theme of conversation, far safer than any talk of recent events –
when Noim suddenly said, 'Is that drug of yours known to give
people nightmares?'

'One has heard of no such cases, Noim.'

'Here's a case, then. One who woke up drenched with chilly
sweat night after night, for weeks after we shared the drug in
Manneran. One thought one would lose one's mind.'

'What kind of dreams?' I asked.

'Ugly things. Monsters. Teeth. Claws. A sense of not knowing
who one is. Pieces of other minds floating through one's
own.' He gulped at his wine. 'You take the drug for *pleasure*,
Kinnall?'

'For knowledge.'

'Knowledge of what?'

'Knowledge of self, and knowledge of others.'

'One prefers ignorance, then.' He shivered. 'You know, Kinnall, one was never a particularly reverent person. One blasphemed, one stuck his tongue out at drainers, one laughed at the god-tales they told, yes? You've nearly converted one into a man of faith with that stuff. The terror of opening one's mind – of knowing that one has no defences, that you can slide right into one's soul, and are doing it – it's impossible to take.'

'Impossible for you,' I said. 'Others cherish it.'

'One leans towards the Covenant,' said Noim. 'Privacy is sacred. One's soul is one's own. There's a dirty pleasure in baring it.'

'Not baring. Sharing.'

'Does it sound prettier that way? Very well: there's a dirty pleasure in sharing it, Kinnall. Even though we are bondbrothers. One came away from you last time feeling soiled. Sand and grit in the soul. Is this what you want for everyone? To make us all feel filthy with guilt?'

'There need be no guilt, Noim. One gives, one receives, one comes forth better than one was –'

'Dirtier.'

'Enlarged. Enhanced. More compassionate. Speak to others who have tried it,' I said.

'Of course. As they come streaming out of Manneran, landless refugees, one will question them about the beauty and wonder of selfbaring. Excuse me: selfsharing.'

I saw the torment in his eyes. He wanted still to love me, but the Sumaran drug had shown him things – about himself, perhaps about me – that made him hate the one who had given the drug to him. He was one for whom walls are necessary; I had not realized that. What had I done, to turn my bondbrother into my enemy? Perhaps if we could take the drug a second time, I might make things more clear to him – but no, no hope of that. Noim was frightened by inwardness. I had transformed my blaspheming bondbrother into a man of the Covenant. There was nothing I could say to him now.

After some silence he said, 'One must make a request of you, Kinnall.'

'Anything.'

'One hesitates to place boundaries on a guest. But if you have brought any of this drug with you from Manneran, Kinnall, if you hide it somewhere in your rooms – get rid of it, is that understood? There must be none of it in this house. Get rid of it, Kinnall.'

Never in my life had I lied to my bondbrother. Never.

With the jeweled case the Duke of Sumar had given me blazing against my breastbone, I said solemnly to Noim, 'You have nothing to fear on that account.'

SIXTY-TWO

Not many days later the news of my disgrace became public in Manneran, and swiftly reached Salla. Noim showed me the accounts. I was described as the chief adviser to the High Justice of the Port, and openly labeled a man of the greatest authority in Manneran, who, moreover, had blood ties to the prime septarchs of Salla and Glin – and yet, despite these attainments and preferments, I had fallen away from the Covenant to take up unlawful selfbaring. I had violated not merely propriety and etiquette but also the laws of Manneran, through my use of a certain proscribed drug from Sumara Borthan that dissolves the god-given barriers between soul and soul. Through abuse of my high office, it was said, I had engineered a secret voyage to the southern continent (poor Captain Khrisch! Had he been arrested too?) and had returned with a large quantity of the drug, which I had devilishly forced on a lowborn woman whom I was keeping; I had also circulated the foul stuff among certain prominent members of the nobility, whose names were being withheld because of their thorough repentance. On the eve of my arrest I had escaped to Salla, and good riddance to me: if

I attempted to return to Manneran, I would immediately be apprehended. Meanwhile I would be tried in absentia, and, according to the Grand Justiciar, there could be little doubt of the verdict. By way of restitution to the state for the great injury I had done the fabric of social stability, I would be required to forfeit all my lands and property, except only a portion to be set aside for the maintenance of my innocent wife and children. (Segvord Helalam, then, had at least accomplished that.) To prevent my highborn friends from transferring my assets to me in Salla before the trial, all that I possessed was already sequestered in anticipation of the Grand Justiciar's decree of guilt. Thus spake the law. Let others who would make selfbaring monsters of themselves beware!

SIXTY-THREE

I made no secret of my whereabouts in Salla, for I had no reason now to fear the jealousy of my royal brother. Stirron as a boy newly on the throne might have been driven to eliminate me as a potential rival, but not the Stirron who had ruled for more than seventeen years. By now he was an institution in Salla, well loved and an integral part of everyone's existence, and I was a stranger, barely remembered by the older folk and unknown to the younger, who spoke with a Mannerangi accent and who had been publicly branded with the shame of selfbaring. Even if I cared to overthrow Stirron, where would I find followers?

In truth I was hungry for the sight of my brother. In times of storm one turns to one's earliest comrades; and with Noim estranged from me and Halum on the far side of the Woyn, I had only Stirron left. I had never resented having had to flee Salla on his account, for I knew that had our ages been reversed I would have caused him to flee the same way. If our relationship had grown frosty since my flight, it was a frost of his making, arising from his guilty conscience. Some years had passed, now, since my last visit to Salla City: perhaps my adversities would open his heart. I wrote Stirron a letter from Noim's place, formally begging sanctuary in Salla. Under Sallan law I had to be taken in, for I was one of Stirron's subjects and was guilty of no crime committed on Sallan soil: yet I thought it best to ask. The charges lodged against me by the Grand Justiciar of Manneran, I admitted, were true, but I offered Stirron a terse and (I think) eloquent justification of my deviation from the Covenant. I closed the letter with expressions of my unwavering love for him, and with a few reminiscences of the happy times we had had before the burdens of the septarchy had descended on him.

I expected Stirron in return to invite me to visit him at the capital, so that he could hear from my own lips an explanation of the strange things I had done in Manneran. A brotherly reunion was surely in order. But no summons to Salla City came. Each time the telephone chimed, I rushed towards it, thinking it might be Stirron calling. He did not call. Several weeks of tension and gloom passed; I hunted, I swam, I read, I tried to write my new Covenant of love. Noim remained aloof from me. His one experience at soul sharing had thrust him into so deep an embarrassment that he hardly dared to meet my eyes, for I was privy to all his innerness, and that had become a wedge between us.

At last came an envelope bearing the septarch's imposing seal. It held a letter signed by Stirron, but I pray it was some steely minister, and not my brother, who composed that pinch-souled message. In fewer lines than I have fingers, the septarch told me that my request for sanctuary in the province of Salla was granted, but only on the condition that I forswear the vices I had learned in the south. If I were caught just once spreading the use of selfbaring drugs in Salla, I would be seized and driven into exile. That was all my brother had to say. Not a syllable of kindness. Not a shred of sympathy. Not an atom of warmth.

SIXTY-FOUR

At the crest of the summer Halum came unexpectedly to visit us. The day of her arrival, I had gone riding far out across Noim's land, following the track of a male stormshield that had burst from its pen. An accursed vanity had led Noim to acquire a clutch of these vicious furbearing mammals, though they are not native to Salla and thrive poorly there: he kept twenty or thirty of them, all claws and teeth and angry yellow eyes, and hoped to breed them into a profitable herd. I chased the escaped male through woods and plain, through morning and midday, hating it more with each hour, for it left a trail of the mutilated carcasses of harmless grazing beasts. These stormshields kill for sheer love of slaughter, taking but a bite or two of flesh and abandoning the rest to scavengers. Finally I cornered it in a shadowy box-canyon. 'Stun it and bring it back whole,' Noim had instructed me, conscious of the animal's value: but when trapped it rushed at me with such ferocity that I gave it the full beam, and gladly slew it. For Noim's sake I took the trouble to strip off the precious hide. Then, weary and depressed, I rode without stopping back to the great house. A strange groundcar was parked outside, and beside it was Halum. 'You know the summers in Manneran,' she explained. 'One planned to go as usual to the island, but then one thought, it would be good to take a holiday in Salla, with Noim and Kinnall.'

She had by then entered her thirtieth year. Our women marry between fourteen and sixteen, are done bearing their children by twenty-two or twenty-four and at thirty have begun to slide into middle age, but time had left Halum untouched. Not having known the tempests of marriage and the travails of motherhood, not having spent her energies on the grapplings of the conjugal couch or the lacerations of childbed, she had the supple, pliant body of a girl: no fleshy bulges, no sagging folds, no exploded veins, no thickening of the frame. She had changed only in one respect, for in recent years her dark hair had turned silvery. This was but an enhancement, however, since it gleamed with dazzling brilliance, and offered agreeable contrast to the deep tan of her youthful face.

In her luggage was a packet of letters for me from Manneran: messages from the duke, from Segvord, from my sons Noim and Stirron and Kinnall, from my daughters Halum and Loimel, from Mihan the archivist, and several others. Those who wrote did so in tense, self-conscious style. They were the letters one might write to a dead man if one felt guilty at having survived him. Still, it was good to hear these words out of my former life. I regretted not finding a letter from Schweiz; Halum told me she had heard nothing from him since before my indictment, and thought he might well have left our planet. Nor was there any word from my wife. 'Is Loimel too busy to write a line or two?' I asked, and Halum, looking embarrassed, said softly that Loimel never spoke of me these days: 'She seems to have forgotten that she was married.'

Halum also had brought a trove of gifts for me from my friends across the Woyn. They were startling in their opulence: massy clusters of precious metals, elaborate strings of rare gems. 'Tokens of love,' Halum said, but I was not fooled. One could buy great estates with this heap of treasure. Those who loved me would not humiliate me by transferring cash to my account in Salla, but they could give me these splendors in the ordinary way of friendship, leaving me free to dispose of them according to my needs.

'Has it been very sad for you, this uprooting?' Halum asked. 'This sudden going into exile?'

'One is no stranger to exile,' I told her. 'And one still has Noim for bondlove and companionship.'

'Knowing that it would cost you what it did,' she said, 'would you play with the drug a second time, if you could turn time backwards by a year?'

'Beyond any doubt.'

'Was it worth the loss of home and family and friends?'

'It would be worth the loss of life itself,' I replied, 'if only one could be assured by that that all of Velada Borthan would come to taste the drug.'

That answer seemed to frighten her: she drew back, she touched the tips of her fingers to her lips, perhaps becoming aware for the first time of the intensity of her bondbrother's madness. In speaking those words I was not uttering mere rhetorical overstatement, and something of my conviction must have reached Halum. She saw that I believed, and, seeing the depth of my commitment, feared for me.

Noim spent many of the days that followed away from his lands, traveling to Salla City on some family business and to the Plain of Nand to inspect property he was thinking of buying. In his absence I was master of the estate, for the servants, whatever they might think of my private life, did not dare to question my authority to my face. Daily I rode out to oversee the workers in Noim's fields, and Halum rode with me. Actually little overseeing was demanded of me, since this was midway in the seasons between planting and harvest, and the crops looked after themselves. We rode for pleasure, mainly, pausing here for a swim, there for a lunch at the edge of the woods. I showed her the stormshield pens, which did not please her, and took her among the gentler animals of the grazing fields, who came up and amiably nuzzled her.

These long rides gave us hours each day to talk. I had not spent so much time with Halum since childhood, and we grew wonderfully close. We were cautious with one another at first, not wishing to get too near the bone with our questions, but soon we spoke as bond-kin should. I asked her why it was she had never married, and she answered me simply, 'One never encountered a suitable man.' Did she regret having gone without husband and children? No, she said, she regretted nothing, for her life had been tranquil and rewarding; yet there was wistfulness in her tone. I could not press her further. On her part she questioned me about the Sumaran drug, trying to learn from me what merits it had that had led me to run such risks. I was amused by the way she phrased her enquiries: trying to sound earnest and sympathetic and objective, yet nonetheless unable to hide her horror at what I had done. It was as though her bondbrother had run amok and butchered twenty people in a marketplace, and she now wished to discover, by means of patient and good-humored questioning, just what had been the philosophical basis that had led him to take up mass murder. I also tried to maintain a temperate and dispassionate manner, so that I would not sear her with my intensity as I had done in that first interchange. I avoided all evangelizing, and, as calmly and soberly as I could, I explained to her the effects of the drug, the benefits I gained from it, and my reasons for rejecting the stony isolation of self that the Covenant imposes on us. Shortly a curious metamorphosis came over both her attitude and mine. She became less the highborn lady striving with well-meant warmth to understand the criminal, and more the student attempting to grasp the mysteries revealed by an initiated master. And I became less the descriptive reporter, and more the prophet of a new dispensation. I spoke in flights of lyricism of the raptures of soul-sharing; I told her of the strange wonder of the early sensations, as one begins to open, and of the blazing moment of union with another human consciousness; I depicted the experience as something far more intimate than any meeting of souls one might have with one's bondkin, or any visit to a drainer. Our conversations became monologues. I lost myself in verbal ecstasies, and came down from them at times to see Halum, silver-haired and eternally young, with her eyes sparkling and her lips parted in total fascination. The outcome was inevitable. One scorching afternoon as we walked slowly through the aisles in a field of grain that rose chest-high on her, she said without warning, 'If the drug is available to you here, may your bondsister share it with you?' I had converted her.

SIXTY-FIVE

That night I dissolved some pinches of the powder in two flasks of wine. Halum looked uncertain as I handed one to her, and her uncertainty rebounded to me, so that I hesitated to go through with our project; but then she gave me a magical smile of tenderness and drained her flask. 'There is no flavor of it,' she said, as I drank. We sat talking in Noim's trophy-hall, decked with hornfowl spears and draped with stormshield furs, and as the drug began to take effect Halum started to shiver; I pulled a thick black hide from the wall and draped it about her shoulders, and through it I held her until the chill was past.

Would this go well? Despite all my propagandizing I was frightened. In every man's life there is something he feels driven to do, something that pricks him at the core of his soul so long as it remains undone, and yet as he approaches the doing of it he will know fear, for perhaps to fulfill the obsession will bring him more pain than pleasure. So with me and Halum and the Sumaran drug. But my fear ebbed as the drug took hold. Halum was smiling. Halum was smiling.

The wall between our souls became a membrane, through which we could slide at will. Halum was the first to cross it. I hung back, paralyzed by prudery, thinking even now that it would be an intrusion on my bondsister's maidenhood for me to enter her mind, and also a violation of the commandment against bodily intimacies between bond-kin. So I dangled in this absurd trap of contradictions, too inhibited to practise my own creed, for some moments after the last barriers had fallen; meanwhile Halum, realizing at last that nothing prevented her, slipped unhesitatingly into my spirit. My instant response was to try to shield myself: I did not want her to discover this or this or that, and particularly to learn of my physical desire for her. But after a moment of this embarrassed flurrying I ceased trying to plaster my soul with figleaves, and went across into Halum, allowing the true communion to begin, the inextricable entanglement of selves.

I found myself – it would be more accurate to say, I lost myself – in corridors with glassy floors and silvered walls, through which there played a cool sparkling light, like the crystalline brightness one sees reflected from the white sandy bottom of a shallow tropical cove. This was Halum's virginal inwardness. In niches along these corridors, neatly displayed, were the shaping factors of her life, memories, images, odors, tastes, visions, fantasies, disappointments, delights. A prevailing purity governed everything. I saw no trace of the sexual ecstasies, nothing of the fleshly passions. I cannot tell you whether Halum, out of modesty, took care to shield the area of her sexuality from my probings, or had thrust it so far from her own consciousness that I could not detect it.

She met me without fear and joined me in joy. I have no doubt of that. When our souls blended, it was a complete union, without reservation, without qualification. I swam through the glittering depths of her, and the grime of my soul dropped from me: she was healing, she was cleansing. Was I staining her even as she was refining and purifying me? I cannot say. I cannot say. We surrounded and engulfed one another, and supported one another, and interpenetrated one another; and here mingling with myself was the self of Halum, who all my life had been my staff and my courage, my ideal and my goal, this cool incorruptible perfect incarnation of beauty; and perhaps as this corruptible self of mine put on incorruption, the first corrosive plague sprouted on her shining incorruptibility. I cannot say. I came to her and she came to me. At one point in our journey through one another I encountered a zone of strangeness, where something seemed coiled and knotted: and I remembered that time in my youth, when I was setting out from Salla City on my flight into Glin, when Halum had embraced me at Noim's house, and I had thought I detected in her embrace a tremor of barely suppressed passion, a flicker of the hunger of the body. For me. For me. And I thought that I had found that zone of passion again, only when I looked more closely at it, it was gone, and I beheld the pure gleaming metallic surface of her soul. Perhaps both the first time and the second it was something I manufactured out of my own churning desires, and projected on her. I cannot say. Our souls were twined; I could not have known where I left off and Halum began.

We emerged from the trance. The night was half gone. We blinked, we shook our foggy heads, we smiled uneasily. There is always that moment, coming out of the drug's soul-intimacy, when one feels abashed, one thinks one has revealed too much, and one wants to retract what one has given. Fortunately that moment is usually brief. I looked at Halum and felt my body afire with holy love, a love that was not at all of the flesh, and I started to say to her, as Schweiz had once said to me, *I love you*. But I choked on the word. The 'I' was trapped in my teeth, like a fish in a weir. *I.I.I.I love you, Halum. I.* If I could only say it. *I. I.* It would not come. It was there, but could not get past my lips. I took her hands between mine, and she smiled a serene moonlike smile, and it would have been so easy then to hurl the words out, except that something imprisoned them. *I.* How could I speak to Halum of love, and couch my love in the syntax of the gutter? I thought then that she would not understand, that my obscenity would shatter everything. Foolishness: our souls had been one, how then could a mere phrasing of words disturb anything? Out with it! *I love you*. Faltering, I said, 'There is – such love in one – for you – such love, Halum –'

She nodded, as if to say, *Don't speak, your clumsy words break the spell*. As if to say, *Yes, there is in one such love for you also, Kinnall*. As if to say, *I love you, Kinnall*. Lightly she got to her feet, and went to the window: cold summer moonlight on the formal garden of the great house, the bushes and trees white and still. I came up behind her and touched her at the shoulders, very gently. She wriggled and made a little purring sound. I thought all was well with her. I was certain all was well with her.

We held no post-mortems on what had taken place between

us this evening. That, too, seemed to threaten a puncturing of the mood. We could discuss our trance tomorrow, and all the tomorrows beyond that. I went with her back to her room, not far down the hallway from my own, and kissed her timidly on the cheek, and had a sisterly kiss from her; she smiled again, and closed the door behind her. In my own room I sat awhile awake, reliving everything. The missionary fervor was kindled anew in me. I would become an active messiah again, I vowed, going up and down this land of Salla spreading the creed of love; no more would I hide here at my bondbrother's place, broken and adrift, a hopeless exile in my own nation. Stirron's warning meant nothing to me. How could he drive me from Salla? I would make a hundred converts in a week. A thousand, ten thousand. I would give the drug to Stirron himself, and let the septarch proclaim the new dispensation from his own throne! Halum had inspired me. In the morning I would set out, seeking disciples.

There was a sound in the courtyard. I looked out and saw a groundcar: Noim had returned from his business trip. He entered the house; I heard him in the hallway, passing my room; then there came the sound of knocking. I peered into the corridor. He stood by Halum's door, talking to her. I could not see her. What was this, that he would go to Halum, who was nothing but a friend to him, and fail to greet his own bondbrother? Unworthy suspicions woke in me – unreal accusations. I forced them away. The conversation ended; Halum's door closed; Noim, without noticing me, continued towards his own bedroom.

Sleep was impossible for me. I wrote a few pages, but they were worthless, and at dawn I went out to stroll in the gray mists. It seemed to me that I heard a distant cry. Some animal seeking its mate, I thought. Some lost beast wandering at daybreak.

SIXTY-SIX

I was alone at breakfast. That was unusual but not surprising: Noim, coming home in the middle of the night after a long drive, would have wanted to sleep late, and doubtless the drug had left Halum exhausted. My appetite was powerful, and I ate for the three of us, all the while planning my schemes for dissolving the Covenant. As I sipped my tea one of Noim's grooms burst wildly into the dining-hall. His cheeks were blazing and his nostrils were flared, as if he had run a long way and was close to collapse. 'Come,' he cried, gasping. 'The stormshields –' He tugged at my arm, half dragging me from my seat. I rushed out after him. He was already far down the unpaved road that led to the stormshield pens. I followed, wondering if the beasts had escaped in the night, wondering if I must spend the day chasing monsters again. As I neared the pens I saw no signs of a breakout, no clawed tracks, no torn fences. The groom clung to the bars of the biggest pen, which held nine or ten stormshields. I looked in. The animals were clustered, bloody-jawed, bloody-furred, around some ragged meaty haunch. They were snarling and quarreling over the last scraps of flesh; I could see traces of their feast scattered across the ground. Had some unfortunate farm beast strayed among these killers by darkness? How could such a thing have happened? And why would the groom see fit to haul me from my breakfast to show it to me? I caught his arm and asked him what was so strange about the sight of stormshields devouring their kill. He turned a terrible face to me and blurted in a strangled voice, 'The lady – the lady –'

SIXTY-SEVEN

Noim was brutal with me. 'You lied,' he said. 'You denied you were carrying the drug, but you lied. And you gave it to her last night. Yes? Yes? Yes? Don't hide anything now, Kinnall. You gave it to her!'

'You spoke with her,' I said. I could barely manage words. 'What did she tell you?'

'One stopped by her door, because one thought one heard the sound of sobbing,' Noim answered. 'One inquired if she was well. She came out: her face was strange, it was full of dreams, her eyes were as blank as pieces of polished metal, and yes, yes, she had been weeping. And one asked what was wrong, whether there had been any trouble here. No, she said, all was well. She said you and she had talked all evening. Why was she weeping, then? She shrugged and smiled and said it was a female thing, an unimportant thing – women weep all the time, she said, and need give no explanations. And she smiled again and closed the door. But that look in her eyes – it was the drug, Kinnall! Against all your vows, you gave it to her! And now – and now –'

'Please,' I said softly. But he went on shouting, loading me with accusations, and I could not reply.

The grooms had reconstructed everything. They had found the path of Halum's feet in the dew-moist sandy road. They had found the door ajar of the house that gives access to the stormshield pens. They had found marks of forcing on the inner door that leads to the feeding-gate itself. She had gone through; she had carefully opened the feeding-gate, and just as carefully closed it behind her, to loose no killers on the sleeping estate; then she had offered herself to the waiting claws. All this between darkness and dawn, perhaps even while I strolled in a different part. That cry out of the mists – Why? Why? Why? Why?

SIXTY-EIGHT

By early afternoon such few possessions as I had were packed. I asked Noim for the loan of a groundcar, and he granted it with a brusque wave of his fingers. There was no question of remaining here any longer. Not only were there echoes of Halum resonating everywhere about, but also I had to go apart, into some place where I could think undisturbed, and examine all that I had done and that I hoped to do. Nor did I wish to be here when the district police carried out their inquest into Halum's death.

Had she been unable to face me again, the morning after having given her soul away? She had gone gladly enough into the sharing of selves. But afterwards, in that rush of guilty reappraisal that often follows the first opening, she may have felt another way: old habits of reticence reasserting themselves, a sudden cascading sense of horror at what she had revealed. And the quick irreversible decision, the frozen-faced trek to the stormshield pens, the ill-considered passing of the final gate, the moment of regret-within-regret as the animals pounced and she realized she had carried her atonement too far. Was that it? I could think of no other explanation for that plunge from serenity to despair, except that it was a second thought, a reflex of shock that swept her to doom. And I was without a bondsister, and had lost bondbrother too, for Noim's eyes were merciless when he looked at me. Was this what I had intended, when I dreamed of opening souls?

'Where will you go?' Noim asked. 'They'll jail you in Manneran. Take one step into Glin with your drug and you'll be flayed. Stirron will hound you out of Salla. Where, then, Kinnall? Threish? Velis? Or maybe Umbis, eh? Dabis? No! By the gods, it will be Sumara Borthan, won't it? Yes. Among your savages, and you'll have all the selfbaring you'll need there, yes? Yes?'

Quietly I said, 'You forget the Burnt Lowlands, Noim. A

cabin in the desert – a place to think, a place of peace – there is so much one must try to understand, now –'

'The Burnt Lowlands? Yes, that's good, Kinnall. The Burnt Lowlands in high summer. A fiery purge for your soul. Go there, yes. Go.'

SIXTY-NINE

Alone, I drove northward along the flank of the Huishtors, and then westward, on the road that leads to Kongoroi and Salla's Gate. More than once I thought of swerving the car and sending it tumbling over the highway's rim, and making an end. More than once, as the first light of day touched my eyelids in some back-country hostelry, I thought of Halum and had to struggle to leave my bed, for it seemed so much easier to go on sleeping. Day and night and day and night and day, and a few days more, and I was deep into West Salla, ready to go up the mountains and through the gate. While resting one night in a town midway into the uplands I discovered that an order was out in Salla for my arrest. Kinnall Darival, the septarch's son, a man of thirty years, of this height and having these features, brother to the Lord Stirron, was wanted for monstrous crimes: selfbaring, and the use of a dangerous drug, which against the explicit orders of the septarch he was offering to the unwary. By means of this drug the fugitive Darival had driven his own bondsister insane, and in her madness she had perished in a horrible way. Therefore all citizens of Salla were enjoined to apprehend the evildoer, for whom a heavy reward would be paid.

If Stirron knew why Halum had died, then Noim had told him everything. I was lost. When I reached Salla's Gate, I would find officers of the West Sallan constabulary waiting for me, for my destination was known. Yet in that case why had the announcement not informed the populace that I was heading for the Burnt Lowlands? Possibly Noim had held back some of what he knew, so that I could make an escape.

I had no choice but to go forward. It would take me days to reach the coast, and I would find all of Salla's ports alerted for me when I got there; even if I slipped on board a vessel, where would I go? Glin? Manneran? Similarly it was hopeless thinking of getting somehow across the Huish or the Woyn, into the neighboring provinces: I was already proscribed in Manneran, and surely I would find a chilly greeting in Glin. The Burnt Lowlands it would have to be, then. I would stay there some while, and then perhaps try to make my way out via one of the Threishtor passes, to start a new life on the western coast. Perhaps.

I bought provisions in the town, at a place that serves the needs of hunters entering the Lowlands: dried food, some weapons, and condensed water, enough to last me by careful expansion for several moontimes. As I made my purchases, I thought the townsfolk were eyeing me strangely. Did they recognize me as the depraved prince whom the septarch sought? No one moved to seize me. Possibly they knew there was a cordon across Salla's Gate, and would take no risks with such a brute, when there were police in plenty to capture me on top of Kongoroi. Whatever the reason, I got out of the town unbothered, and set out now on the final stretch of the highway. In the past I had come this way only in winter, when snow lay deep; even now there were patches of dirty whiteness in shadowy corners, and as the road rose, the snow thickened, until near Kongoroi's double summit everything lay mantled in it. Timing my ascent carefully, I managed things so that I came to the great pass well after sundown, hoping that darkness would protect me in case of a roadblock. But the gate was unguarded. My car's lights were off as I drove the last distance – I half expected to go over the edge – and I made the familiar left turn, which brought me into Salla's Gate, and I saw no one there. Stirron had not had time to close the western border, or else he did not think I would be so mad as to flee that way. I went forward, and through the

pass, and slowly down the switchbacks on the western face of
Kongoroi, and when dawn overtook me I was into the Burnt
Lowlands, choking in the heat, but safe.

SEVENTY

Near the place where the hornfowl nest I found this cabin,
about where I remembered it to be. It was without plumbing,
nor were the walls even whole, yet it would do. It would
do. The awful heat of the place would be my purge. I set
up housekeeping inside, laying out my things, unpacking the
journal-paper I had bought in the town for this record of my
life and deeds, setting the jeweled case containing the last of
the drug in a corner, piling my clothing above it, sweeping
away the red sand. On my first full day of residence I busied
myself camouflaging my groundcar, so that it would not betray
my presence when searchers came: I drove it into a shallow
ravine, so that its top barely broke the level of the ground,
and collected woody ground-plants to make a covering for it,
throwing sand on top of the interwoven stems of the plants.
Only sharp eyes would see the car when I was done. I made
careful note of the place, lest I fail to find it myself when I
was ready to leave.

For some days I simply walked the desert, thinking. I went
to the place where the hornfowl struck my father down, and
had no fear of the sharp-beaked circling birds: let them have
me too. I considered the events of my time of changes, asking
myself, *Is this what you wanted, Is this what you hoped to bring
about, Does this satisfy you?* I relived each of my many soul
sharings, from that with Schweiz to that with Halum, asking,
*Was this good? Were there mistakes that could have been avoided?
Did you gain, or did you lose, by what you did?* And I concluded
that I had gained more than I had lost, although my losses
had been terrible ones. My only regrets were for poor tactics,

not for faulty principles. If I had stayed with Halum until her uncertainties had fled, she might not have given way to the shame that destroyed her. If I had been more open with Noim – if I had stayed in Manneran to confront my enemies – if – if – if – and yet, I had no regrets for having done my changing, but just that I had bungled my revolution of the soul. For I was convinced of the wrongness of the Covenant and of our way of life. Your way of life. That Halum had seen fit to kill herself after two hours of experiencing human love was the most scathing possible indictment of the Covenant.

And finally – not too many days ago – I began to write what you have been reading. My fluency surprised me; perhaps I verged even on glibness, though it was hard for me at first to use the grammar I imposed on myself. *I am Kinnall Darival and I mean to tell you all about myself.* So I began my memoir. Have I been true to that intent? Have I concealed anything? Day upon day my pen has scratched paper, and I have put myself down whole for you, with no cosmetic alterations of the record. In this sweatbox of a cabin have I laid myself bare. Meanwhile I have had no contact with the outside world, except for occasional hints, possibly irrational, that Stirron's agents are combing the Burnt Lowlands for me. I believe that guards are posted at the gates leading into Salla, Glin, and Manneran; and probably at the western passes as well; and also in Stroin Gap, in case I try to make my way to the Gulf of Sumar through the Wet Lowlands. My luck has held well, but soon they must find me. Shall I wait for them? Or shall I move on, trusting to fortune, hoping to find an unguarded exit? I have this thick manuscript. I value it now more than my life itself. If you could read it, if you could see how I have stumbled and staggered towards knowledge of self, if you could receive from it the vibrations of my mind – I have put everything down, I think, in this autobiography, in this record of self, in this document unique in the history of Velada Borthan. If I am captured here, my book will be captured with me, and Stirron will have it burned.

I must move on, then. But –

A sound? Engines?

A groundcar coming swiftly towards my cabin over the flat red land. I am found. It is done. At least I was able to write this much.

SEVENTY-ONE

Five days have passed since the last entry, and I am still here. The groundcar was Noim's. He came not to arrest me but to rescue me. Cautiously, as if expecting me to open fire on him, he crept about my cabin, calling, 'Kinnall? Kinnall?' I went outside. He tried to smile, but he was too tense to manage it. He said, 'One thought you would be somewhere near this place. The place of the hornfowl – it still haunts you, eh?'

'What do you want?'

'Stirron's patrols are searching for you, Kinnall. Your path was traced as far as Salla's Gate. They know you're in the Burnt Lowlands. If Stirron knew you as well as your bondbrother does, he'd come straight here with his troops. Instead they're searching to the south, on the theory that you mean to go into the Wet Lowlands to the Gulf of Sumar, and get a ship to Sumara Borthan. But they're bound to start hunting for you in this region once they discover you haven't been down there.'

'And then?'

'You'll be arrested. Tried. Convicted. Jailed or executed. Stirron thinks you're the most dangerous man on Velada Borthan.'

'I am,' I said.

Noim gestured towards the car. 'Get in. We'll slip through the blockade. Into West Salla, somehow, and down to the Woyn. The Duke of Sumar will meet you and put you aboard some vessel heading out. You can be in Sumara Borthan by next moonrise.'

'Why are you helping me, Noim? Why should you bother? I saw the hate in your eyes when I left you?'

'Hate? Hate? No, Kinnall, no hate, only sorrow. One is still your –' He paused. With an effort, he said, '*I'm* still your bondbrother. I'm pledged to your welfare. How can I let Stirron hunt you like a beast? Come. Come. I'll get you safely out of here.'

'No.'

'No?'

'We're certain to be caught. Stirron will have you, too, for aiding a fugitive. He'll seize your lands. He'll break your rank. Don't make a useless sacrifice for me, Noim.'

'I came all the way into the Burnt Lowlands to fetch you. If you think I'll go back without –'

'Let's not quarrel over it,' I said. 'Even if I escape, what is there for me? To spend the rest of my life hiding in the jungles of Sumara Borthan, among people whose language I can't speak and whose ways are alien to me? No. No. I'm tired of exile. Let Stirron take me.'

Persuading Noim to leave me here was no little task. We stood in the midday fire for eternal minutes, arguing vehemently. He was determined to effect this heroic rescue, despite the almost certain probability that we would both be captured. This he was doing out of a sense of duty, not out of love, for I could see that he still held Halum's death to my account. I would not have his disgrace scored against me as well, and told him so: he had done nobly to make this journey, but I could not go with him. Finally he began to yield, but only when I swore I would at least make some effort to save myself. I promised that I would set out for the western mountains, instead of sitting here where Stirron would surely find me. If I reached Velis or Threish safely, I said, I would notify Noim in some way, so that he would cease to fear my fate. And then I said, 'There is one thing you can do for me.' I brought my manuscript out of the cabin – a great heap of paper, red scribbling on grayish rough sheets. In this, I said, he would find the whole story: my entire self encapsulated, and all the

events that had brought me to the Burnt Lowlands. I asked
him to read it, and to pass no judgement on me until he had.
'You will find things in here that will horrify and disgust you,'
I warned him. 'But I think you'll also find much that will open
your eyes and your soul. Read it, Noim. Read it with care.
Think about my words.' And I asked one last vow of him, by
our oath of bonding: that he keep my book safely preserved,
even if the temptation came over him to burn it. 'These pages
hold my soul,' I told him. 'Destroy the paper and you destroy
me. If you loathe what you read, hide the book away, but do
no harm to it. What shocks you now may not shock you a few
years from now. And some day you may want to show my
book to others, so that you can explain what manner of man
your bondbrother was, and why he did what he did.' *And so
that you may change them as I hope my book will change you*, I
said silently. Noim vowed this vow. He took my sheaf of pages
and stored them in the hold of his groundcar. We embraced;
he asked me again if I would not ride away with him; again
I refused; I made him say once more that he would read my
book and preserve it; once more he swore he would; then he
entered the groundcar and drove slowly towards the east. I
entered the cabin. The place where I had kept my manuscript
was empty, and I felt a sudden hollowness, I suppose much
like that of a woman who has carried a child for the full seven
moontimes and now finds her belly flat again. I had poured
all of myself into those pages. Now I was nothing, and the
book was all. Would Noim read it? I thought so. And would
he preserve it? Very likely he would, though he might hide
it in the darkest corner of his house. And would he some
day show it to others? This I do not know. But if you have
read what I have written, it is through the kindness of Noim
Condorit; and if he has let it be read, then I have prevailed
over his soul after all, as I hope to prevail over yours.

SEVENTY-TWO

I had said to Noim that I would remain in the cabin no longer, but would set out for the west in an attempt to save myself. Yet I found myself unwilling to leave. The sweltering shack had become my home. I stayed a day, and another day, and a third, doing nothing, wandering the blazing solitude of the Burnt Lowlands, watching the hornfowl circle. On the fifth day, as you perhaps are able to see, I fell into the habit of autobiography again, and sat down at the place where I had lately spent so many hours sitting, and wrote a few new pages to describe my visit from Noim. Then I let three days more go by, telling myself that on the fourth I would dig my groundcar out of the red sand and head westward. But on the morning of that fourth day Stirron and his men found my hiding place, and now it is the evening of that day, and I have an hour or two more to write, by the grace of the Lord Stirron. And when I have done with this, I will write no more.

SEVENTY-THREE

They came in six well-armed groundcars, and surrounded my cabin, and called on me through loudspeakers to surrender. I had no hope of resisting them, nor any desire to try. Calmly – for what use was fear – I showed myself, hands upraised, at the cabin door. They got out of their cars, and I was amazed to find Stirron himself among them, drawn out of his palace into the Lowlands for an out-of-season hunting party with his brother as quarry. He wore all his finery of office. Slowly he walked towards me. I had not seen him in some years, and I was appalled by the signs of age on him: shoulders rounded, head thrust forward, hair thinning,

face deeply lined, eyes yellowed and dim. The profits of half
a lifetime of supreme power. We regarded one another in
silence, like two strangers seeking a point of contact. I tried to
find in him that boy, my playmate, my elder brother, whom I
had loved and lost so long ago, and I saw only a grim old man
with trembling lips. A septarch is trained to mask his inner
feelings, yet Stirron was able to hold nothing secret from me,
nor could he keep one consistent expression: I saw in his face,
one look tumbling across the other, tokens of imperial rage,
bewilderment, sorrow, contempt, and something that I took to
be a sort of suppressed love. At length I spoke first, inviting him
into my cabin for a conference. He hesitated, perhaps thinking
I had assassination in mind, but after a moment he accepted in
right kingly manner, waving to his bodyguard to wait outside.
When we were alone within, there was another silent spell,
which this time he broke, saying, 'One has never felt such
pain, Kinnall. One scarcely believes what one has heard about
you. That you should stain our father's memory –'

'Is it such a stain, Lord Septarch?'

'To foul the Covenant? To corrupt the innocent – your
bondsister among the victims? What have you been doing,
Kinnall? *What have you been doing?*'

A terrible fatigue came over me, and I closed my eyes, for
I scarcely knew where to begin explaining. After a moment
I found strength. I reached towards him, smiling, taking his
hand, and said, 'I love you, Stirron.'

'How sick you are!'

'To talk of love? But we came out of the same womb! Am
I not to love you?'

'Is this how you talk now, only in filth?'

'I talk as my heart commands me.'

'You are not only sick but sickening,' said Stirron. He turned
away and spat on the sandy floor. He seemed a remote
medieval figure to me, trapped behind his dour kingly face,
imprisoned in his jewels of office and his robes of state,
speaking in gruff, distant tones. How could I reach him?

I said, 'Stirron, take the Sumaran drug with me. I have a

little left. I'll mix it for us, and we'll drink it together, and in
an hour or two our souls will be one, and you'll understand.
I swear, you'll understand. Will you do it? Kill me afterwards,
if you still want to, but take the drug first.' I began to bustle
about, making ready the potion. Stirron caught my wrist and
halted me. He shook his head with the slow, heavy gesture of
one who feels an infinite sadness. 'No,' he said. 'Impossible.'

'Why?'

'You will not fuddle the mind of the prime septarch.'

'I'm interested in *reaching* the mind of my brother Stirron!'

'As your brother, one wishes only that you may be healed.
As prime septarch, one must avoid harm, for one belongs to
one's people.'

'The drug is harmless, Stirron.'

'Was it harmless for Halum Helalam?'

'Are you a frightened virgin?' I asked. 'I've given the drug
to scores of people. Halum is the only one who reacted badly –
Noim too, I suppose, but he got over it. And –'

'The two people in the world closest to you,' said Stirron,
'and the drug harmed them both. Now you offer it to your
brother?'

It was hopeless. I asked him again, several times, to risk an
experiment with the drug, but of course he would not touch
it. And if he had, would it have availed me anything? I would
have found only iron in his soul.

I said, 'What will happen to me now?'

'A fair trial, followed by an honest sentence.'

'Which will be what? Execution? Imprisonment for life?
Exile?'

Stirron shrugged. 'It is for the court to decide. Do you take
one for a tyrant?'

'Stirron, why does the drug frighten you so? Do you know
what it does? Can I make you see that it brings only love and
understanding? There's no need for us to live as strangers to
each other, with blankets around our souls. We can speak
ourselves out. We can reach forth. We can say '*I*', Stirron,
and not have to apologize for having selves. *I. I. I.* We can

tell each other what gives us pain, and help each other to escape that pain.' His face darkened; I think he was sure I was mad. I went past him, to the place where I had put down the drug, and quickly mixed it, and offered a flask to him. He shook his head. I drank, impulsively gulping it, and offered the flask again to him. 'Go on,' I said. 'Drink. Drink! It won't begin for a while. Take it now, so we'll be open at the same time. Please, Stirron!'

'I could kill you myself,' he said, 'without waiting for the court to act.'

'Yes! Say it, Stirron! I! Myself! Say it again!'

'Miserable selfbarer. My father's son! If I talk to you in "I", Kinnall, it's because you deserve no better than filth from me.'

'It doesn't need to be filth. Drink, and understand.'

'Never.'

'Why do you oppose it, Stirron? What frightens you?'

'The Covenant is sacred,' he said. 'To question the Covenant is to question the whole social order. Turn this drug of yours loose in the land and all reason collapses, all stability is lost. Do you think our forefathers were villains? Do you think they were fools? Kinnall, they understood how to create a lasting society. Where are the cities of Sumara Borthan? Why do they still live in jungle huts, while we have built what we have built? You'd put us on their road, Kinnall. You'd break down the distinctions between right and wrong, so that in a short while law itself would be washed away, and every man's hand would be lifted against his fellow, and where would be your love and universal understanding then? No, Kinnall. Keep your drug. One still prefers the Covenant.'

'Stirron –'

'Enough. The heat is intolerable. You are arrested; now let us go.'

SEVENTY-FOUR

Because the drug was in me, Stirron agreed to let me have a few hours alone, before we began the journey back to Salla, so that I would not have to travel while my soul was vulnerable to external sensations. A small mercy from the lord septarch: he posted two men as guards outside my cabin, and went off with the others to hunt hornfowl until the coming of dusk.

Never had I taken the drug without a sharer. So the strangeness came upon me and I was alone with them, to hear the throbbings and the whinings and the rushings, and then, as the walls fell away from my soul, there was no one for me to enter, and no one to enter me. Yet I could detect the souls of my guards – hard, closed, metallic – and I felt that with some effort I could reach even into them. But I did not, for as I sat by myself I was launched on a miraculous voyage, my self expanding and soaring until I encompassed this our entire planet, and all the souls of mankind were merged into mine. And a wondrous vision came upon me. I saw my bondbrother Noim making copies of my memoir, and distributing them to those he could trust, and other copies were made from those, to circulate through the provinces of Velada Borthan. And out of the southern land now came shiploads of the white powder, sought not merely by an elite, not only by the Duke of Sumar and the Marquis of Woyn, but by thousands of ordinary citizens, by people hungry for love, by those who found the Covenant turning to ashes, those who wished to reach one another's souls. And though the guardians of the old order did what they could to halt the movement, it could not be stopped, for the former Covenant had run its course, and now it was clear that love and gladness could no longer be suppressed. Until at last a network of communication existed, shining filaments of sensory perception linking one to one to one to all. Until at last even the septarchs and the justiciars were swept up in the tide of liberation, and all the world joined in joyous communion, each of us open to all, and the time of changes was complete; the new Covenant was established. I saw all this from my shabby cabin in the Burnt Lowlands. I saw the bright glow encompassing the world, shimmering, flickering, gaining power, deepening in hue. I saw walls crumbling. I saw the brilliant red blaze of universal love. I saw new faces, changed and exultant. Hands touching hands. Selves touching selves. This vision blazed in my soul for half a day, filling me with joy such as I had never experienced at any time, and my soaring spirit wandered in realms of dream. And only as the drug began to ebb from me did I realize that it was nothing but a fantasy.

Perhaps it will not always be a fantasy. Perhaps Noim will find readers for what I have written, and perhaps others will be persuaded to follow my path, until there are enough like me, and the changes become irreversible and universal. It has happened before. I will disappear, I the forerunner, I the anticipator, I the martyred prophet. But what I have written will live, and through me you will be changed. It may yet be that this is no idle dream.

This final page has been set down as twilight descends. The sun hastens towards the Huishtors. Soon, as Stirron's prisoner, I will follow it. I will take this little manuscript with me, hidden somewhere about me, and if I have good fortune I will find some way of giving it to Noim, so that it can be joined to the pages he has already had from me. I cannot say if I will succeed, nor do I know what will become of me and of my book. And you who read this are unknown to me. But I can say this: If the two parts have become one, and you read me complete, you may be sure that I have begun to prevail. Out of that joining can come only changes for Velada Borthan, changes for all of you. If you have read this far, you must be with me in soul. So I say to you, my unknown reader, that I love you and reach my hand towards you, I who was Kinnall Darival, I who have opened the way, I who promised to tell you all about myself, and who now can say that that promise has been fulfilled. Go and seek. Go and touch. Go and love. Go and be open. Go and be healed.

Downward to the Earth

Who knoweth the spirit of man that goeth upward, and the spirit of the beast that goeth downward to the earth?

Ecclesiastes iii, 21

ONE

He had come back to Holman's World after all. He was not sure why. Call it irresistible attraction; call it sentimentality; call it foolishness. Gundersen had never planned to revisit this place. Yet here he was, waiting for the landing, and there it was in the vision screen, close enough to grasp and squeeze in one hand, a world slightly larger than Earth, a world that had claimed the prime decade of his life, a world where he had learned things about himself that he had not really wanted to know. Now the signal light in the lounge was flashing red. The ship would shortly land. Despite everything, he was coming back.

He saw the shroud of mist that covered the temperate zones, and the great sprawling icecaps, and the girdling blue-black band of the scorched tropics. He remembered riding through the Sea of Dust at blazing twilight, and he remembered a silent, bleak river-journey beneath bowers of twittering dagger-pointed leaves, and he remembered golden cocktails on the veranda of a jungle station on the Night of Five Moons, with Seena close by his side and a herd of nildoror mooing in the bush. That was a long time ago. Now the nildoror were masters of Holman's World again. Gundersen had a hard time accepting that. Perhaps that was the real reason why he had come back: to see what sort of job the nildoror could do.

'Attention, passengers in lounge,' came a voice over the speaker. 'We enter landing orbit for Belzagor in fifteen minutes. Please prepare to return to cradles.'

Belzagor. That was what they called the planet now. The native name, the nildoror's own word. To Gundersen it seemed like something out of Assyrian mythology. Of course, it was a romanticized pronunciation; coming from a nildor it would really sound more like *Bllls'grr*. Belzagor it was, though. He would try to call the planet by the name it now wore; if that was what he was supposed to do. He attempted never to give needless offence to alien beings.

'Belzagor,' he said. 'It's a voluptuous sound, isn't it? Rolls nicely off the tongue.'

The tourist couple beside him in the ship's lounge nodded. They agreed readily with whatever Gundersen said. The husband, plump, pale, overdressed, said, 'They were still calling it Holman's World when you were last out here, weren't they?'

'Oh, yes,' Gundersen said. 'But that was back in the good old imperialist days, when an Earthman could call a planet whatever he damn pleased. That's all over now.'

The tourist wife's lips tightened in that thin, pinched, dysmenorrhoeal way of hers. Gundersen drew a somber pleasure from annoying her. All during the voyage he had deliberately played a role out of Kipling for these tourists – posing as the former colonial administrator going out to see what a beastly botch the natives must be making out of the task of governing themselves. It was an exaggeration, a distortion, of his real attitude, but sometimes it pleased him to wear masks. The tourists – there were eight of them – looked upon him in mingled awe and contempt as he swaggered among them, a big fair-skinned man with the mark of outworld experience stamped on his features. They disapproved of him, of the image of himself that he gave them; and yet they knew he had suffered and labored and striven under a foreign sun, and there was romance in that.

'Will you be staying at the hotel?' the tourist husband asked.

'Oh, no. I'm going right out into the bush, towards the mist country. Look – there, you see? In the northern hemisphere, that band of clouds midway up. The temperature gradient's very steep: tropic and arctic practically side by side. Mist. Fog. They'll take you on a tour of it. I have some business in there.'

'Business? I thought these new independent worlds were outside the zone of economic penetration that –'

'Not commercial business,' Gundersen said. 'Personal business. Unfinished business. Something I didn't manage to discover during my tour of duty here.' The signal light flashed again, more insistently. 'Will you excuse me? We really should cradle up now.'

He went to his cabin and readied himself for landing. Webfoam spurted from the spinnerets and enfolded him. He closed his eyes. He felt deceleration thrust, that curiously archaic sensation hearkening back to space travel's earliest days. The ship dropped planetward as Gundersen swayed, suspended, insulated from the worst of the velocity change.

Belzagor's only spaceport was the one that Earthmen had built more than a hundred years before. It was in the tropics, at the mouth of the great river flowing into Belzagor's single ocean. Madden's River, Benjamini Ocean – Gundersen didn't know the nildoror names at all. The spaceport was self-maintaining, fortunately. Automatic high-redundancy devices operated the landing beacon; homeostatic surveillance kept the pad repaved and the bordering jungle cropped back. All, all by machine; it was unrealistic to expect the nildoror to operate a spaceport, and impossible to keep a crew of Earthmen stationed here to do it. Gundersen understood that there were still perhaps a hundred Earthmen living on Belzagor, even after the general withdrawal, but they were not such as would operate a spaceport. And there was a treaty, in any case. Administrative functions were to be performed by nildoror, or not at all.

They landed. The webfoam cradle dissolved upon signal. They went out of the ship.

The air had the tropical reek: rich loam, rotting leaves, the droppings of jungle beasts, the aroma of creamy flowers. It was early evening. A couple of the moons were out. As always, the threat of rain was in the air; the humidity was 99%, probably. But that threat almost never materialized. Rainstorms were rare in this tropical belt. The water simply precipitated out of the air in droplets all the time, imperceptibly, coating you with fine wet beads. Gundersen saw lightning flicker beyond the tops of the hullygully trees at the edge of the pad. A stewardess marshaled the nine debarkees. 'This way, please,' she said crisply, and led them towards the one building.

On the left, three nildoror emerged from the bush and solemnly gazed at the newcomers. Tourists gasped and pointed. 'Look! Do you see them? Like elephants, they are! Are those nili – nildoror?'

'Nildoror, yes,' Gundersen said. The tang of the big beasts drifted across the clearing. A bull and two cows, he guessed, judging by the size of the tusks. They were all about the same height, three metres plus, with the deep green skins that marked them as western-hemisphere nildoror. Eyes as big as platters peered back at him in dim curiosity. The short-tusked cow in front lifted her tail and placidly dropped an avalanche of steaming purple dung. Gundersen heard deep blurred sounds, but at this distance he could not make out what the nildoror were saying. Imagine them running a spaceport, he thought. Imagine them running a planet. But they do. But they do.

There was no one in the spaceport building. Some robots, part of the homeostasis net, were repairing the wall at the far side, where the gray plastic sheeting had apparently succumbed to spore implantation; sooner or later the jungle rot got everything in this part of the planet. But that was the only visible activity. There was no customs desk. The nildoror did not have a bureaucracy of that sort. They did not care what you brought with you to their world. The nine passengers had undergone a customs inspection on Earth, just before setting out; Earth did care, very much, what was taken to undeveloped planets. There was also no spaceline office here, nor were there money-changing booths, nor newsstands, nor any of the other concessions one normally finds in a spaceport. There was only a big bare shed, which once had been the nexus of a bustling colonial outpost, in the days when Holman's World had been the property of Earth. It seemed to Gundersen that he saw ghosts of those days all about him: figures in tropical khaki carrying messages, supercargoes waving inventory sheets, computer technicians draped in festoons of memory beads, nildoror

bearers laden with outgoing produce. Now all was still. The
scrapings of the repair robots echoed across the emptiness.

The spaceline stewardess was telling the eight passengers,
'Your guide should be here any minute. He'll take you to the
hotel, and –'

Gundersen was supposed to go to the hotel too, just for
tonight. In the morning he hoped to arrange for transport. He
had no formal plans for his northward journey; it was going
to be largely an improvisation, a reconnaissance into his own
pockmarked past.

He said to the stewardess, 'Is the guide a nildor?'

'You mean, native? Oh, no, he's an Earthman, Mr Gundersen.'
She rummaged in a sheaf of printout slips. 'His name's Van
Beneker, and he was supposed to be here at least half an hour
before the ship landed, so I don't understand why –'

'Van Beneker was never strong on punctuality,' Gundersen
said. 'But there he is.'

A beetle, much rusted and stained by the climate, had
pulled up at the open entrance to the building, and from it
now was coming a short red-haired man, also much rusted
and stained by the climate. He wore rumpled fatigues and a
pair of knee-high jungle boots. His hair was thinning and his
tanned bald skull showed through the slicked-down strands.
He entered the building and peered around, blinking. His eyes
were light blue and faintly hyperthyroid-looking.

'Van?' Gundersen said. 'Over here, Van.'

The little man came over. In a hurried, perfunctory way he
said, while he was still far from them, 'I want to welcome all
you people to Belzagor, as Holman's World is now known.
My name's Van Beneker, and I'm going to show you as
much of this fascinating planet as is legally permissible to
show you, and –'

'Hello, Van,' Gundersen cut in.

The guide halted, obviously irritated, in mid-spiel. He blinked
again and looked closely at Gundersen. Finally he said, clearly
not believing it, 'Mr Gundersen?'

'Just Gundersen. I'm not your boss any more.'

'Jesus, Mr Gundersen. Jesus, are you here for the tour?'

'Not exactly. I'm here to take my own tour.'

Van Beneker said to the others, 'I want you to excuse me. Just for a minute.' To the spaceline stewardess he said, 'It's okay. You can officially convey them to me. I take responsibility. They all here? One, two, three – eight. That's right. Okay, the luggage goes out there, next to the beetle. Tell them all to wait. I'll be right with them.' He tugged at Gundersen's elbow. 'Come on over here, Mr Gundersen. You don't know how amazed I am. Jesus!'

'How have you been, Van?'

'Lousy. How else, on this planet? When did you leave, exactly?'

'2240. The year after relinquishment. Eight years ago.'

'Eight years. And what have you been doing?'

'The home office found work for me,' Gundersen said. 'I keep busy. Now I've got a year's accumulated leave.'

'To spend it *here?*'

'Why not?'

'What for?'

'I'm going up mist country,' Gundersen said. 'I want to visit the sulidoror.'

'You don't want to do that,' said Van Beneker. 'What do you want to do that for?'

'To satisfy a curiosity.'

'There's only trouble when a man goes up there. You know the stories, Mr Gundersen. I don't need to remind you, how many guys went up there, how many didn't come back.' Van Beneker laughed. 'You didn't come all the way to this place just to rub noses with the sulidoror. I bet you got some other reason.'

Gundersen let the point pass. 'What do you do here now, Van?'

'Tourist guide, mostly. We get nine, ten batches a year. I take them up along the ocean, then show them a bit of the mist country, then we hop across the Sea of Dust. It's a nice little tour.'

'Yes.'

'The rest of the time I relax. I talk to the nildoror a lot, and sometimes I visit friends at the bush stations. You'll know everyone, Mr Gundersen. It's all the old people, still out there.'

'What about Seena Royce?' Gundersen asked.

'She's up by Shangri-la Falls.'

'Still have her looks?'

'She thinks so,' Van Beneker said. 'You figure you'll go up that way?'

'Of course,' Gundersen said. 'I'm making a sentimental pilgrimage. I'll tour all the bush stations. See the old friends. Seena. Cullen. Kurtz. Salamone. Whoever's still there.'

'Some of them are dead.'

'Whoever's still there,' Gundersen said. He looked down at the little man and smiled. 'You'd better take care of your tourists, now. We can talk at the hotel tonight. I want you to fill me in on everything that's happened while I've been gone.'

'Easy, Mr Gundersen. I can do it right now in one word. Rot. Everything's rotting. Look at the spaceport wall over there.'

'I see.'

'Look at the repair robots, now. They don't shine much, do they? They're giving out too. If you get close, you can see the spots on their hulls.'

'But homeostasis –'

'Sure. Everything gets repaired, even the repair robots. But the system's going to break down. Sooner or later, the rot will get into the basic programs, and then there won't be any more repairs, and this world will go straight back into the stone age. I mean *all* the way back. And then the nildoror will finally be happy. I understand those big bastards as much as anybody does. I know they can't wait to see the last trace of Earthmen rot right off this planet. They pretend they're friendly, but the hate's there all the time, real sick hate, and –'

'You ought to look after your tourists, Van,' Gundersen said. 'They're getting restless.'

TWO

A caravan of nildoror was going to transport them from the spaceport to the hotel – two Earthmen per alien, with Gundersen riding alone, and Van Beneker, with the luggage, leading the way in his beetle. The three nildoror grazing at the edge of the field ambled over to enroll in the caravan, and two others emerged from the bush. Gundersen was surprised that nildoror were still willing to act as beasts of burden for Earthmen. 'They don't mind,' Van Beneker explained. 'They like to do us favors. It makes them feel superior. They can't hardly tell there's weight on them, anyhow. And they don't think there's anything shameful about letting people ride them.'

'When I was here I had the impression they resented it,' Gundersen said.

'Since relinquishment they take things like that easier. Anyway, how could you be sure what they thought? I mean, what they *really* thought.'

The tourists were a little alarmed at riding nildoror. Van Beneker tried to calm them by telling them it was an important part of the Belzagor experience. Besides, he added, machinery did not thrive on this planet and there were hardly any functioning beetles left. Gundersen demonstrated how to mount, for the benefit of the apprehensive newcomers. He tapped his nildor's left-hand tusk, and the alien knelt in its elephantine way, ponderously coming down on its front knees, then its back ones. The nildor wriggled its shoulders, in effect dislocating them to create the deep swayback valley in which a man could ride so comfortably, and Gundersen climbed aboard, seizing the short backward-thrusting horns as his pommels. The spiny crest down the middle of the alien's broad skull began to twitch. Gundersen recognized it as a gesture of welcome; the nildoror had a rich language of gesture, employing not only the spines but also their long ropy trunks and their many-pleated ears. '*Sssukh*!' Gundersen said, and the nildor arose. 'Do you sit well?' it asked him in its own language. 'Very well indeed,' Gundersen said, feeling a surge of delight as the unforgotten vocabulary came to his lips.

In their clumsy, hesitant way, the eight tourists did as he had done, and the caravan set out down the river road towards the hotel. Nightflies cast a dim glow under the canopy of trees. A third moon was in the sky, and the mingled lights came through the leaves, revealing the oily fast-moving river just to their left. Gundersen stationed himself at the rear of the procession in case one of the tourists had a mishap. There was only one uneasy moment, though, when a nildor paused and left the rank. It rammed the triple prongs of its tusks into the riverbank to grub up some morsel, and then resumed its place in line. In the old days, Gundersen knew, that would never have happened. Nildoror were not permitted then to have whims.

He enjoyed the ride. The jouncing strides were agreeable, and the pace was swift without being strenuous for the passengers. What good beasts these nildoror are, Gundersen thought. Strong, docile, intelligent. He almost reached forward to stroke his mount's spines, deciding at the last moment that it would seem patronizing. The nildoror are something other than funny-looking elephants, he reminded himself. They are intelligent beings, the dominant life-forms of their planet, *people*, and don't you forget it.

Soon Gundersen could hear the crashing of the surf. They were nearing the hotel.

The path widened to become a clearing. Up ahead, one of the tourist women pointed into the bush; her husband shrugged and shook his head. When Gundersen reached that place he saw what was bothering them. Black shapes crouched between the trees, and dark figures were moving slowly to and fro. They were barely visible in the shadows. As Gundersen's nildor went past, two of the dim forms emerged and stood by the edge of the path. They were husky bipeds, close to three metres tall, covered with thick coats of dark red hair. Massive tails swished slowly through the greenish gloom. Hooded eyes, slit-wide even in this scant light, appraised the procession. Drooping rubbery snouts, tapir-long, sniffed audibly.

A woman turned gingerly and said to Gundersen, 'What are they?'

'Sulidoror. The secondary species. They come from up mist country. These are northern ones.'

'Are they dangerous?'

'I wouldn't call them that.'

'If they're northern animals, why are they down here?' her husband wanted to know.

'I'm not sure,' Gundersen said. He questioned his mount and received an answer. 'They work at the hotel,' Gundersen called ahead. 'Bellhops. Kitchen hands.' It seemed strange to him that the nildoror would have turned the sulidoror into domestic servants at an Earthman's hotel. Not even before relinquishment had sulidoror been used as servants. But of course there had been plenty of robots here then.

The hotel lay just ahead. It was on the coast, a glistening geodesic dome that showed no external signs of decay. Before relinquishment, it had been a posh resort run exclusively for the benefit of the top-level administrators of the Company. Gundersen had spent many happy hours in it. Now he dismounted, and he and Van Beneker helped the tourists down. Three sulidoror stood at the hotel entrance. Van Beneker gestured fiercely at them and they began to take the luggage from the beetle's storage hold.

Inside, Gundersen quickly detected symptoms of decline. A carpet of tiger-moss had begun to edge out of an ornamental garden strip along the lobby wall, and was starting to reach on to the fine black slabs of the main hall's floor; he saw the toothy little mouths hopefully snapping as he walked in. No doubt the hotel's maintenance robots once had been programmed to cut the ornamental moss back to the border of the garden bed, but the programme must have subtly altered with the years so that now the moss was allowed to intrude on the interior of the building as well. Possibly the robots were gone altogether, and the sulidoror who had replaced them were lax in their pruning duties. And there were other hints that control was slipping away.

'The boys will show you to your rooms,' Van Beneker said. 'You can come down for cocktails whenever you're ready. Dinner will be served in about an hour and a half.'

A towering sulidor conducted Gundersen to a third-floor room overlooking the sea. Reflex led him to offer the huge creature a coin; but the sulidor merely looked blankly at him and did not venture to take it. It seemed to Gundersen that there was a suppressed tension about the sulidor, an inward seething, but perhaps it existed only in his own imagination. In the old days sulidoror had rarely been seen outside the zone of mist, and Gundersen did not feel at ease with them.

In nildoror words he said, 'How long have you been at the hotel?' But the sulidor did not respond. Gundersen did not know the language of the sulidoror, but he was aware that every sulidor was supposed to speak fluent nildororu as well as sulidororu. Enunciating more clearly, he repeated his question. The sulidor scratched its pelt with gleaming claws and said nothing. Moving past Gundersen, it deopaqued the window-wall, adjusted the atmospheric filters, and stalked solemnly out.

Gundersen frowned. Quickly he stripped and got under the cleanser. A quick whirr of vibration took from him the grime of his day's journey. He unpacked and donned evening clothes, a close gray tunic, polished boots, a mirror for his brow. He toned the color of his hair down the spectrum a short distance, dimming it from yellow almost to auburn.

Suddenly he felt very tired.

He was just into early middle years, only forty-eight, and travel ordinarily did not affect him. Why this fatigue, then? He realized that he had been holding himself unusually stiff these few hours he had been back on this planet. Rigid, inflexible, tense – uncertain of his motives in returning, unsure of his welcome, perhaps touched a bit by curdled guilts, and now the strain was telling. He touched a switch and made the wall a mirror. Yes, his face was drawn; the cheekbones, always prominent, now jutted like blades, and the lips were clamped and the forehead was furrowed. The thin slab of his nose was distended by tension-flared nostrils. Gundersen shut his eyes and went through one of the drills of a relaxation mode. He looked better thirty seconds later; but a drink might help, he decided. He went down to the lounge.

None of the tourists were there yet. The louvres were open, and he heard the roar and crash of the sea, smelled its saltiness. A white curdled line of accumulated salt had been allowed to form along the margin of the beach. The tide was in; only the tips of the jagged rocks that framed the bathing area were visible. Gundersen looked out over the moonlight-streaked water, staring into the blackness of the eastern horizon. Three moons had also been up on his last night here, when they gave the farewell party for him. And after the revelry was over, he and Seena had gone for a midnight swim, out to the tide-hidden shoal where they could barely stand, and when they returned to shore, naked and salt-encrusted, he had made love to her behind the rocks, embracing her for what he was sure would be the last time. And now he was back.

He felt a stab of nostalgia so powerful that he winced.

Gundersen had been thirty years old when he came out to Holman's World as an assistant station agent. He had been forty, and a sector administrator, when he left. In a sense the first thirty years of his life had been a pale prelude to that decade, and the last eight years of it had been a hollow epilog. He had lived his life on this silent continent, bounded by mist and ice to the north, mist and ice to the south, the Benjamini Ocean to the east, the Sea of Dust to the west. For a while he had ruled half a world, at least in the absence of the chief resident; and this planet had shrugged him off as though he had never been. Gundersen turned away from the louvres and sat down.

Van Beneker appeared, still in his sweaty, rumpled fatigues. He winked cordially at Gundersen and began rummaging in a cabinet. 'I'm the bartender too, Mr G. What can I get you?'

'Alcohol,' Gundersen said. 'Any form you recommend.'

'Snout or flask?'

'Flask. I like the taste.'

'As you say. But snout for me. It's the effect, sir, the *effect*.' He set an empty glass before Gundersen and handed him a flask containing three ounces of a dark red fluid. Highland rum, local product. Gundersen hadn't tasted it in eight years. The flask was equipped with its own condensation chiller; Gundersen thumbed it with a quick short push and quietly watched the flakes of ice beginning to form along the inside. When his drink was properly chilled he poured it and put it quickly to his lips.

'That's pre-relinquishment stock,' Van Beneker said. 'Not much of it left, but I knew you'd appreciate it.' He was holding an ultrasonic tube to his left forearm. *Zzz!* and the snout spurted alcohol straight into his vein. Van Beneker grinned. 'Works faster this way. The working-class man's boozer. Eh? Eh? Get you another rum, Mr G?'

'Not just yet. Better look after your tourists, Van.'

The tourist couples were beginning to enter the bar: first the Watsons, then the Mirafloreses, the Steins, finally the Christophers. Evidently they had expected to find the bar throbbing with life, full of other tourists giddily hailing one another from distant parts of the room, and red-jacketed waiters ferrying drinks. Instead there were peeling plastic walls, a sonic sculpture that no longer worked and was deeply cobwebbed, empty tables, and that unpleasant Mr Gundersen moodily peering into a glass. The tourists exchanged cheated glances. Was this what they had spanned the light-years to see? Van Beneker went to them, offering drinks, weeds, whatever else the limited resources of the hotel might be able to supply. They settled in two groups near the windows and began to talk in low voices, plainly self-conscious in front of Gundersen. Surely they felt the foolishness of their roles, these soft well-to-do people whose boredom had driven them to peer at the remote reaches of the galaxy. Stein ran a helix parlor in California, Miraflores a chain of lunar casinos, Watson was a doctor, and Christopher – Gundersen could not remember what Christopher did. Something in the financial world.

Mrs Stein said, 'There are some of those animals on the beach. The green elephants.'

Everyone looked. Gundersen signaled for another drink, and got it. Van Beneker, flushed, sweating, winked again and put a second snout to his arm. The tourists began to titter. Mrs Christopher said, 'Don't they have any shame at all?'

'Maybe they're simply playing, Ethel,' Watson said.

'*Playing?* Well, if you call that playing –'

Gundersen leaned forward, glancing out of the window without getting up. On the beach a pair of nildoror were coupling, the cow kneeling where the salt was thickest, the bull mounting her, gripping her shoulders, pressing his central tusk down firmly against the spiny crest of her skull, jockeying his hindquarters about as he made ready for the consummating thrust. The tourists, giggling, making heavy-handed comments of appreciation, seemed both shocked and titillated. To his considerable surprise, Gundersen realized he was shocked, too, although coupling nildoror were nothing new to him; and when a ferocious orgasmic bellowing rose from below he glanced away, embarrassed and not understanding why.

'You look upset,' Van Beneker said.

'They didn't have to do that *here*.'

'Why not? They do it all over the place. You know how it is.'

'They deliberately went out there,' Gundersen muttered. 'To show off for the tourists? Or to annoy the tourists? They shouldn't be reacting to the tourists at all. What are they trying to prove? That they're just animals, I suppose.'

'You don't understand the nildoror, Gundy.'

Gundersen looked up, startled as much by Van Beneker's words as by the sudden descent from 'Mr Gundersen' to 'Gundy'. Van Beneker seemed startled, too, blinking rapidly and tugging at a stray sparse lock of fading hair.

'I don't?' Gundersen asked. 'After spending ten years here?'

'Begging pardon, but I never did think you understood them,

even when you were here. I used to go around with you a lot to the villages when I was clerking for you. I watched you.'

'In what way do you think I failed to understand them, Van?'

'You despised them. You thought of them as animals.'

'That isn't so!'

'Sure it is, Gundy. You never once admitted they had any intelligence at all.'

'That's absolutely untrue,' Gundersen said. He got up and took a new flask of rum from the cabinet, and returned to the table.

'I would have got that for you,' Van Beneker said. 'You just had to ask me.'

'It's all right.' Gundersen chilled the drink and downed it fast. 'You're talking a load of nonsense, Van. I did everything possible for those people. To improve them, to lift them towards civilization. I requisitioned tapes for them, sound pods, culture by the ton. I put through new regulations about maximum labor. I insisted that my men respect their rights as the dominant indigenous culture. I –'

'You treated them like very intelligent animals. Not like intelligent alien *people*. Maybe you didn't even realize it yourself, Gundy, but I did, and God knows they did. You talked down to them. You were kind to them in the wrong way. All your interest in uplifting them, in improving them – crap, Gundy, they have their own culture. They didn't want yours!'

'It was my duty to guide them,' Gundersen said stiffly. 'Futile though it was to think that a bunch of animals who don't have a written language, who don't –' He stopped, horrified.

'Animals,' Van Beneker said.

'I'm tired. Maybe I've had too much to drink. It just slipped out.'

'Animals.'

'Stop pushing me, Van. I did the best I could, and if what I was doing was wrong, I'm sorry. I tried to do what was right.' Gundersen pushed his empty glass forward. 'Get me another, will you?'

Van Beneker fetched the drink, and one more snout for himself. Gundersen welcomed the break in the conversation, and apparently Van Beneker did, too, for they both remained silent a long moment, avoiding each other's eyes. A sulidor entered the bar and began to gather the empties, crouching to keep from grazing the Earthman-scaled ceiling. The chatter of the tourists died away as the fierce-looking creature moved through the room. Gundersen looked towards the beach. The nildoror were gone. One of the moons was setting in the east, leaving a fiery track across the surging water. He realized that he had forgotten the names of the moons. No matter; the old Earthman-given names were dead history now. He said finally to Van Beneker, 'How come you decided to stay here after relinquishment?'

'I felt at home here. I've been here twenty-five years. Why should I go anywhere else?'

'No family ties elsewhere?'

'No. And it's comfortable here. I get a company pension. I get tips from the tourists. There's a salary from the hotel. That's enough to keep me supplied with what I need. What I need, mostly, is snouts. Why should I leave?'

'Who owns the hotel?' Gundersen asked.

'The confederation of western-continent nildoror. The Company gave it to them.'

'And the nildoror pay you a salary? I thought they were outside the galactic money economy.'

'They are. They arranged something with the Company.'

'What you're saying is the Company still runs this hotel.'

'If anybody can be said to run it, the Company does, yes,' Van Beneker agreed. 'But that isn't much of a violation of the relinquishment law. There's only one employee. Me. I pocket my salary from what the tourists pay for accommodations. The rest I spend on imports from the money sphere. Don't you see, Gundy, it's all just a big joke? It's a routine designed to allow me to bring in liquor, that's all. This hotel isn't a commercial proposition. The Company is really out of this planet. Completely.'

'All right. All right. I believe you.'

Van Beneker said, 'What are you looking for up mist country?'

'You really want to know?'

'It passes the time to ask things.'

'I want to watch the rebirth ceremony. I never saw it, all the time I was here.'

The bulging blue eyes seemed to bulge even more. 'Why can't you be serious, Gundy?'

'I am.'

'It's dangerous to fool with the rebirth thing.'

'I'm prepared for the risks.'

'You ought to talk to some people here about it, first. It's not a thing for us to meddle in.'

Gundersen sighed. 'Have you seen it?'

'No. Never. Never even been interested in seeing it. Whatever the hell the sulidoror do in the mountains, let them do it without me. I'll tell you who to talk to, though. Seena.'

'She's watched the rebirth?'

'Her husband has.'

Gundersen felt a spasm of dismay. 'Who's her husband?'

'Jeff Kurtz. You didn't know?'

'I'll be damned,' Gundersen murmured.

'You wonder what she saw in him, eh?'

'I wonder that she could bring herself to live with a man like that. You talk about *my* attitude towards the natives! There's someone who treated them like his own property, and –'

'Talk to Seena, up at Shangri-la Falls. About the rebirth.' Van Beneker laughed. 'You're playing games with me, aren't you? You know I'm drunk and you're having a little fun.'

'No. Not at all.' Gundersen rose uneasily. 'I ought to get some sleep now.'

Van Beneker followed him to the door. Just as Gundersen went out, the little man leaned close to him and said, 'You know, Gundy, what the nildoror were doing on the beach before – they weren't doing that for the tourists. They were doing it for you. It's the kind of sense of humor they have. Good night, Gundy.'

THREE

Gundersen woke early. His head was surprisingly clear. It was just a little after dawn, and the green-tinged sun was low in the sky. The eastern sky, out over the ocean: a welcome touch of Earthliness. He went down to the beach for a swim. A soft south wind was blowing, pushing a few clouds into view. The hullygully trees were heavy with fruit; the humidity was as high as ever; thunder boomed back from the mountains that ran in an arc paralleling the coast a day's drive inland. Mounds of nildoror dung were all over the beach. Gundersen stepped warily, zigzagging over the crunching sand and hurling himself flat into the surf. He went under the first curling row of breakers and with quick powerful strokes headed towards the shoals. The tide was low. He crossed the exposed sandbar and swam beyond it until he felt himself tiring. When he returned to the shore area, he found two of the tourist men had also come out for a swim, Christopher and Miraflores. They smiled tentatively at him. 'Bracing,' he said. 'Nothing like salt water.'

'Why can't they keep the beach clean, though?' Miraflores asked.

A sullen sulidor served breakfast. Native fruits, native fish. Gundersen's appetite was immense. He bolted down three golden-green bitterfruits for a start, then expertly boned a whole spiderfish and forked the sweet pink flesh into himself as though engaged in a speed contest. The sulidor brought him another fish and a bowl of phallic-looking forest candles. Gundersen still was working on these when Van Beneker entered, wearing clean though frayed clothes. He looked blood-shot and chastened. Instead of joining Gundersen at the table he merely smiled a perfunctory greeting and sailed past.

'Sit with me, Van,' Gundersen said.

Uncomfortably, Van Beneker complied. 'About last night –'

'Forget it.'

'I was insufferable, Mr Gundersen.'

'You were in your cups. Forgiven. In vino veritas. You were calling me Gundy last night, too. You may as well do it this morning. Who catches the fish?'

'There's an automatic weir just north of the hotel. Catches them and pipes them right into the kitchen. God knows who'd prepare food here if we didn't have the machines.'

'And who picks the fruit? Machines?'

'The sulidoror do that,' Van Beneker said.

'When did sulidoror start working as menials on this planet?'

'About five years ago. Six, maybe. The nildoror got the idea from us, I suppose. If we could turn them into bearers and living bulldozers, they could turn the sulidoror into bellhops. After all, the sulidoror *are* the inferior species.'

'But always their own masters. Why did they agree to serve? What's in it for them?'

'I don't know,' Van Beneker said. 'When did anybody ever understand the sulidoror?'

True enough, Gundersen thought. No one yet had succeeded in making sense out of the relationship between this planet's two intelligent species. The presence of two intelligent species, in the first place, went against the general evolutionary logic of the universe. Both nildoror and sulidoror qualified for autonomous ranking, with perception levels beyond those of the higher hominoid primates; a sulidor was considerably smarter than a chimpanzee, and a nildor was a good deal more clever than that. If there had been no nildoror here at all, the presence of the sulidoror alone would have been enough to force the Company to relinquish possession of the planet when the decolonization movement reached its peak. But why two species, and why the strange unspoken accommodation between them, the bipedal carnivorous sulidoror ruling over the mist country, the quadrupedal herbivorous nildoror dominating the tropics? How had they carved this world up so neatly? And why was the division of authority breaking down, if breaking down was really what was happening? Gundersen knew that there were ancient treaties between these creatures, that a system of claims and prerogatives existed, that every nildor went back to the mist country when the time for its rebirth arrived. But he did not know what role the sulidoror really played in the life and the rebirth of the nildoror. No one did. The pull of that mystery was, he admitted, one of the things that had brought him back to Holman's World, to Belzagor, now that he had shed his administrative responsibilities and was free to risk his life indulging private curiosities. The shift in the nildoror-sulidoror relationship that seemed to be taking place around this hotel troubled him, though; it had been hard enough to comprehend that relationship when it was static. Of course, the habits of alien beings were none of his business, really. Nothing was his business, these days. When a man had no business, he had to appoint himself to some. So he was here to do research, ostensibly, which is to say to snoop and spy. Putting it that way made his return to this planet seem more like an act of will, and less like the yielding to irresistible compulsion that he feared it had been.

'– more complicated than anybody ever thought,' Van Beneker was saying.

'I'm sorry. I must have missed most of what you said.'

'It isn't important. We theorize a lot, here. The last hundred of us. How soon do you start north?'

'In a hurry to be rid of me, Van?'

'Only trying to make plans, sir,' the little man said, hurt. 'If you're staying, we need provisions for you, and –'

'I'm leaving after breakfast. If you'll tell me how to get to the nearest nildoror encampment so I can apply for my travel permit.'

'Twenty kilometers, southeast. I'd run you down there in the beetle, but you understand – the tourists –'

'Can you get me a ride with a nildor?' Gundersen suggested. 'If it's too much bother, I suppose I can hike it, but –'

'I'll arrange things,' Van Beneker said.

A young male nildor appeared an hour after breakfast to take Gundersen down to the encampment. In the old days Gundersen would simply have climbed on his back, but now he felt the necessity of making introductions. One does not ask an autonomous intelligent being to carry you twenty kilometers through the jungle, he thought, without attempting to enter into elementary courtesies. 'I am Edmund Gundersen of the first birth,' he said, 'and I wish you joy of many rebirths, friend of my journey.'

'I am Srin'gahar of the first birth,' replied the nildor evenly, 'and I thank you for your wish, friend of my journey. I serve you of free choice and await your commands.'

'I must speak with a many-born one and gain permission to travel north. The man here says you will take me to such a one.'

'So it can be done. Now?'

'Now.'

Gundersen had one suitcase. He rested it on the nildor's broad rump and Srin'gahar instantly curved his tail up and back to clamp the bag in place. Then the nildor knelt and Gundersen went through the ritual of mounting. Tons of powerful flesh rose and moved obediently towards the rim of the forest. It was almost as though nothing had ever changed.

They traveled the first kilometer in silence, through an ever-thickening series of bitterfruit glades. Gradually it occurred to Gundersen that the nildor was not going to speak unless spoken to, and he opened the conversation by remarking that he had lived for ten years on Belzagor. Srin'gahar said that he knew that; he remembered Gundersen from the era of Company rule. The nature of the nildoror vocal system drained all overtones and implications from the statement. It came out flat, a mooing nasal grunt that did not reveal whether the nildor remembered Gundersen fondly, bitterly, or indifferently. Gundersen might have drawn a hint from the movements of Srin'gahar's cranial crest, but it was impossible for someone seated on a nildor's back to detect any but the broadest such movements. The intricate nildoror system of nonverbal supplementary communication had not evolved for the convenience of passengers. In any event Gundersen had known only a few of the almost infinite number of supplementary gestures, and he had forgotten most of those. But the nildor seemed courteous enough.

Gundersen took advantage of the ride to practise his nildororu. So far he had done well, but in an interview with a many-born one he would need all the verbal skill he could muster. Again and again he said, 'I spoke that the right way, didn't I? Correct me if I didn't.'

'You speak very well,' Srin'gahar insisted.

Actually the language was not difficult. It was narrow in range, simple in grammar. Nildororu words did not inflect; they agglutinated, piling syllable atop syllable so that a complex concept like 'the former grazing-ground of my mate's clan' emerged as a long grumbled growl of sound unbroken even by a brief pause. Nildoror speech was slow and stolid, requiring broad rolling tones that an Earthman had to launch from the roots of his nostrils; when Gundersen shifted from nildororu to any Earth language, he felt sudden exhilaration, like a circus acrobat transported instantaneously from Jupiter to Mercury.

Srin'gahar was taking a nildoror path, not one of the old Company roads. Gundersen had to duck low-hanging branches now and then, and once a quivering nicalanga vine descended to catch him around the throat in a gentle, cool, quickly broken, and yet frightening embrace. When he looked back, he saw the vine tumescent with excitement, red and swollen from the thrill of caressing an Earthman's skin. Shortly the jungle humidity reached the top of the scale and the level of condensation became something close to that of rain; the air was so wet that Gundersen had trouble breathing, and streams of sweat poured down his body. The sticky moment passed. Minutes later they intersected a Company road. It was a narrow fading track in the jungle, nearly overgrown. In another year it would be gone.

The nildor's vast body demanded frequent feedings. Every half hour they halted and Gundersen dismounted while Srin'gahar munched shrubbery. The sight fed Gundersen's latent prejudices, troubling him so much that he tried not to look. In a wholly elephantine way the nildor uncoiled his trunk and ripped leafy branches from low trees; then the great mouth sagged open and in the bundle went. With his triple tusks Srin'gahar shredded slabs of bark for dessert. The big jaws moved back and forth tirelessly, grinding, milling. We are no prettier when we eat, Gundersen told himself, and the demon within him counterpointed his tolerance with a shrill insistence that his companion was a beast.

Srin'gahar was not an outgoing type. When Gundersen said nothing, the nildor said nothing; when Gundersen asked a question, the nildor replied politely but minimally. The strain of sustaining such a broken-backed conversation drained Gundersen, and he allowed long minutes to pass in silence. Caught up in the rhythm of the big creature's steady stride, he was content to be carried effortlessly along through the steamy jungle. He had no idea where he was and could not even tell if they were going in the right direction, for the trees far overhead met in a closed canopy, screening the sun. After the nildor had stopped for his third meal of the morning, though, he gave Gundersen an unexpected clue to their location. Cutting away from the path in a sudden diagonal, the nildor trotted a short distance into the most dense part of the forest, battering down the vegetation, and came to a halt in front of what once had been a Company building – a glassy dome now dimmed by time and swathed in vines.

'Do you know this house, Edmund of the first birth?' Srin'gahar asked.

'What was it?'

'The serpent station. Where you gathered the juices.'

The past abruptly loomed like a toppling cliff above Gundersen. Jagged hallucinatory images plucked at his mind. Ancient scandals, long forgotten or suppressed, sprang to new life. This the serpent station, this ruin? This the place of private sins, the scene of so many falls from grace? Gundersen felt his cheeks reddening. He slipped from the nildor's back and walked haltingly towards the building. He stood at the door a moment, looking in. Yes, there were the hanging tubes and pipes, the runnels through which the extracted venom had flowed, all the processing equipment still in place, half devoured by warmth and moisture and neglect. There was the entrance for the jungle serpents, drawn by alien music they could not resist, and there they were milked of their venom, and there – and there –

Gundersen glanced back at Srin'gahar. The spines of the nildor's crest were distended: a mark of tension, a mark perhaps of shared shame. The nildoror, too, had memories of this building. Gundersen stepped into the station, pushing back the half-open door. It split loose from its moorings as he did so, and a musical tremor ran *whang whang whang* through the whole of the spherical building, dying away to a blurred feeble tinkle. *Whang* and Gundersen heard Jeff Kurtz's guitar again, and the years fell away and he was thirty-one years old once more, a newcomer on Holman's World and about to begin his first stint at the serpent station, finally assigned to that place that was the focus of so much gossip. Yes. Out of the shroud of memory came the image of Kurtz. There he was, standing just inside the station door, impossibly tall, the tallest man Gundersen had ever seen, with a great pale domed hairless head and enormous dark eyes socketed in prehistoric-looking bony ridges, and a bright-toothed smile that ran at least a kilometer's span from cheek to cheek. The guitar went *whang* and Kurtz said, 'You'll find it interesting here, Gundy. This station is a unique experience. We buried your predecessor last week.' *Whang.* 'Of course, you must learn to establish a distance between yourself and what happens here. That's the secret of maintaining your identity on an alien world, Gundy. Comprehend the aesthetics of distance: draw a boundary line about yourself and say to the planet, thus far you can go in consuming me, and no farther. Otherwise the planet will eventually absorb you and make you part of it. Am I being clear?'

'Not at all,' said Gundersen.

'The meaning will manifest itself eventually.' *Whang.* 'Come see our serpents.'

Kurtz was five years older than Gundersen and had been on Holman's World three years longer. Gundersen had known him by reputation long before meeting him. Everyone seemed to feel awe of Kurtz, and yet he was only an assistant station agent, who had never been promoted beyond that lowly rank. After five minutes of exposure to him, Gundersen thought he knew why. Kurt gave an impression of instability – not quite a fallen angel but certainly a falling one, Lucifer on his way down, descending from morn to noon, noon to dewy eve, but now only in the morning of his drop. One could not trust a man like that with serious responsibilities until he had finished his transit and had settled into his ultimate state.

They went into the serpent station together. Kurtz reached up as he passed the distilling apparatus, lightly caressing tubing and petcocks. His fingers were like a spider's legs, and the caress was astonishingly obscene. At the far end of the room stood a short, stocky man, dark-haired, black-browed, the station supervisor, Gio' Salamone. Kurtz made the introductions. Salamone grinned. 'Lucky you,' he said. 'How did you manage to get assigned here?'

'They just sent me,' Gundersen said.

'As somebody's practical joke,' Kurtz suggested.

'I believe it,' said Gundersen. 'Everyone thought I was fibbing when I said I was sent here without applying.'

'A test of innocence,' Kurtz murmured.

Salamone said, 'Well, now that you're here, you'd better learn our basic rule. The basic rule is that when you leave this station, you never discuss what happens here with anybody else. *Capisce?* Now say to me, "I swear by the Father, Son, and Holy Ghost, and also by Abraham, Isaac, Jacob, and Moses –"'

Kurtz choked with laughter.

Bewildered, Gundersen said, 'That's an oath I've never heard before.'

'Salamone's an Italian Jew,' said Kurtz. 'He's trying to cover all possibilities. Don't bother swearing, but he's right: what happens here isn't anybody else's business. Whatever you may have heard about the serpent station is probably true, but nevertheless tell no tales when you leave here.' *Whang*. *Whang*. 'Watch us carefully, now. We're going to call up our demons. Loose the amplifiers, Gio'.'

Salamone seized a plastic sack of what looked like golden flour and hauled it towards the station's rear door. He scooped out a handful. With a quick upward heave he sent it into the air; the breeze instantly caught the tiny glittering grains and carried them aloft. Kurtz said, 'He's just scattered a thousand microamplifiers into the jungle. In ten minutes they'll cover a radius of ten kilometers. They're tuned to pick up the frequencies of my guitar and Gio's flute, and the resonances go bouncing back and forth all over the place.' Kurtz began to play, picking up a melody in mid-course. Salamone produced a short transverse flute and wove a melody of his own through the spaces in Kurtz's tune. Their playing became a stately sarabande, delicate, hypnotic, two or three figures repeated endlessly without variations in volume or pitch. For ten minutes nothing unusual occurred. Then Kurtz nodded towards the edge of the jungle. 'They're coming,' he whispered. 'We're the original and authentic snake charmers.'

Gundersen watched the serpents emerging from the forest. They were four times as long as a man, and as thick as a big man's arm. Undulating fins ran down their backs from end to end. Their skins were glossy, pale green, and evidently sticky, for the detritus of the forest floor stuck to them in places, bits of leaves and soil and crumpled petals. Instead of eyes, they had rows of platter-sized sensor spots flanking their rippling dorsal fins. Their heads were blunt; their mouths only slits, suitable merely for nibbling on gobbets of soil. Where nostrils might be, there protruded two slender quills as long as a man's thumb; these extended to five times that length in moments of stress or when the serpent was under attack, and yielded a blue fluid, a venom. Despite the size of the creatures, despite the arrival of perhaps thirty of them at once, Gundersen did not find them frightening, although he would certainly have been uneasy at the arrival of a platoon of pythons. These were not pythons. They were not even reptiles at all, but low-phylum creatures, actually giant worms. They were sluggish and of no apparent intelligence. But clearly they responded powerfully to the music. It had drawn them to the station, and now they writhed in a ghastly ballet, seeking the source of the sound. The first few were already entering the building.

'Do you play the guitar?' Kurtz asked. 'Here – just keep the sound going. The tune's not important now.' He thrust the instrument at Gundersen, who struggled with the fingerings a moment, then brought forth a lame, stumbling imitation of Kurtz's melody. Kurtz, meanwhile, was slipping a tubular pink cap over the head of the nearest serpent. When it was in place, the cap began rhythmic contractions; the serpent's writhings became momentarily more intense, its fin moved convulsively, its tail lashed the ground. Then it grew calm. Kurtz removed the cap and slid it over the head of another serpent, and another, and another.

He was milking them of venom. These creatures were deadly to native metabolic systems, so it was said; they never attacked, but when provoked they struck, and their poison was universally effective. But what was poison on Holman's World was a blessing on Earth. The venom of the jungle serpents was one of the Company's most profitable exports. Properly distilled, diluted, crystallized, purified, the juice served as a catalyst in limb-regeneration work. A dose of it softened the resistance of the human cell to change, insidiously corrupting the cytoplasm, leading it to induce the nucleus to switch on its genetic material. And so it greatly encouraged the reawakening of cell division, the replication of bodily parts, when a new arm or leg or face had to be grown. How or why it worked, Gundersen knew not, but he had seen the stuff in action during his training period, when a fellow trainee had lost both legs below the knee in a soarer accident. The drug made the flesh flow. It liberated the guardians of the body's coded pattern, easing the task of the genetic surgeons tenfold by sensitizing and stimulating the zone of regeneration. Those legs had grown back in six months.

Gundersen continued to strum the guitar, Salamone to play his flute, Kurtz to collect the venom. Mooing sounds came suddenly from the bush: a herd of nildoror evidently had been drawn by the music as well. Gundersen saw them lumber out of the underbrush and stand almost shyly by the border of the clearing, nine of them. After a moment they entered into a clumsy, lurching, ponderous dance. Their trunks waved in time to the music; their tails swung, their spiny crests revolved. 'All done,' Kurtz announced. 'Five liters – a good haul.' The serpents, milked, drifted off into the forest as soon as the music ceased. The nildoror stayed a while longer, peering intently at the men inside the station, but finally they left also. Kurtz and Salamone instructed Gundersen in the techniques of distilling the precious fluid, making it ready for shipment to Earth.

And that was all. He could see nothing scandalous in what had happened, and did not understand why there had been so much sly talk at headquarters about this place, nor why Salamone had tried to wring an oath of silence from him. He dared not ask. Three days later they again summoned the serpents, again collected their venom, and again the whole process seemed unexceptionable to Gundersen. But soon he came to realize that Kurtz and Salamone were testing his reliability before initiating him into their mysteries.

In the third week of his stint at the serpent station they finally admitted him to the inner knowledge. The collection was done; the serpents had gone; a few nildoror, out of more than a dozen that had been attracted by that day's concert, still lingered outside the building. Gundersen realized that something unusual was about to happen when he saw Kurtz, after darting a sharp glance at Salamone, unhook a container of venom before it started on its route through the distilling apparatus. He poured it into a broad bowl that held at least a liter of fluid. On Earth, that much of the drug would be worth a year of Gundersen's salary as an assistant station agent.

'Come with us,' Kurtz said.

The three men stepped outside. At once three nildoror approached, behaving oddly, their spines upraised, their ears trembling. They seemed skittish and eager. Kurtz handed the bowl of raw venom to Salamone, who sipped from it and handed it back. Kurtz also drank. He gave the bowl to Gundersen, saying, 'Take communion with us?'

Gundersen hesitated. Salamone said, 'It's safe. It can't work on your nuclei when you take it internally.'

Putting the bowl to his lips, Gundersen took a cautious swig. The venom was sweet but watery.

' –only on your brain,' Salamone added.

Kurtz gently took the bowl from him and set it down on the ground. Now the largest nildor advanced and delicately dipped his trunk into it. Then the second nildor drank, and the third. The bowl now was empty.

Gundersen said, 'If it's poisonous to native life –'

'Not when they drink it. Just when it's shot directly into the bloodstream,' Salamone said.

'What happens now?'

'Wait,' Kurtz said, 'and make your soul receptive to any suggestions that arise.'

Gundersen did not have to wait long. He felt a thickening at the base of his neck and a roughness about his face, and his arms seemed impossibly heavy. It seemed best to drop to his knees as the effect intensified. He turned towards Kurtz, seeking reassurance from those dark shining eyes, but Kurtz's eyes had already begun to flatten and expand, and his green and prehensile trunk nearly reached the ground. Salamone, too, had entered the metamorphosis, capering comically, jabbing the soil with his tusks. The thickening continued. Now Gundersen knew that he weighed several tons, and he tested his body's coordination, striding back and forth, learning how to move on four limbs. He went to the spring and sucked up water in his trunk. He rubbed his leathery hide against trees. He trumpeted bellowing sounds of joy in his hugeness. He joined with Kurtz and Salamone in a wild dance, making the ground quiver. The nildoror too were transformed; one had

become Kurtz, one had become Salamone, one had become
Gundersen, and the three former beasts moved in wild pirou-
ette, tumbling and toppling in their unfamiliarity with human
ways. But Gundersen lost interest in what the nildoror were
doing. He concentrated solely on his own experience. Somewhere at the core of his soul it terrified him to know that this
change had come over him and he was doomed forever to live
as a massive animal of the jungle, shredding bark and ripping
branches; yet it was rewarding to have shifted bodies this way
and to have access to an entirely new range of sensory data.
His eyesight now was dimmed, and everything that he saw
was engulfed in a furry halo, but there were compensations:
he was able to sort odors by their directions and by their
textures, and his hearing was immensely more sensitive. It
was the equivalent of being able to see into the ultraviolet
and the infrared. A dingy forest flower sent dizzying waves
of sleek moist sweetness at him; the click of insect-claws in
underground tunnels was like a symphony for percussion. And
the bigness of him! The ecstasy of carrying such a body! His
transformed consciousness soared, swooped, rose high again.
He trampled trees and praised himself for it in booming tones.
He grazed and gorged. Then he sat for a while, perfectly
still, and meditated on the existence of evil in the universe,
asking himself why there should be such a thing, and indeed
whether evil in fact existed as an objective phenomenon. His
answers surprised and delighted him, and he turned to Kurtz
to communicate his insights, but just then the effect of the
venom began to fade with quite startling suddenness, and
in a short while Gundersen felt altogether normal again. He
was weeping, though, and he felt an anguish of shame, as
though he had been flagrantly detected molesting a child. The
three nildoror were nowhere in sight. Salamone picked up the
bowl and went into the station. 'Come,' Kurtz said. 'Let's go
in too.'

   They would not discuss any of it with him. They had let him
share in it, but they would not explain a thing, cutting him
off sternly when he asked. The rite was hermetically private.

Gundersen was wholly unable to evaluate the experience. Had his body actually turned into that of a nildor for an hour? Hardly. Well, then, had his mind, his soul, somehow migrated into the nildor's body? And had the nildor's soul, if nildoror had souls, gone into his? What kind of sharing, what sort of union of innernesses, had occurred in that clearing?

Three days afterward, Gundersen applied for a transfer out of the serpent station. In those days he was easily upset by the unknown. Kurtz's only reaction, when Gundersen announced he was leaving, was a short brutal chuckle. The normal tour of duty at the station was eight weeks, of which Gundersen had done less than half. He never again served a stint there.

Later, he gathered what gossip he could about the doings at the serpent station. He was told vague tales of sexual abominations in the grove, of couplings between Earthman and nildor, between Earthman and Earthman; he heard murmurs that those who habitually drank the venom underwent strange and terrible and permanent changes of the body; he heard stories of how the nildoror elders in their private councils bitterly condemned the morbid practice of going to the serpent station to drink the stuff the Earthmen offered. But Gundersen did not know if any of these whispers were true. He found it difficult, in later years, to look Kurtz in the eye on the rare occasions when they met. Sometimes he found it difficult even to live with himself. In some peripheral way he had been tainted by his single hour of metamorphosis. He felt like a virgin who had stumbled into an orgy, and who had come away deflowered but yet ignorant of what had befallen her.

The phantoms faded. The sound of Kurtz's guitar diminished and was gone.

Srin'gahar said, 'Shall we leave now?'

Gundersen slowly emerged from the ruined station. 'Does anyone gather the juices of the serpents today?'

'Not here,' said the nildor. He knelt. The Earthman mounted him, and in silence Srin'gahar carried him away, back to the path they had followed earlier.

FOUR

In early afternoon they neared the nildoror encampment that
was Gundersen's immediate goal. For most of the day they
had been traveling across the broad coastal plain, but now
the back of the land dipped sharply, for this far inland there
was a long, narrow depression running from north to south,
a deep rift between the central plateau and the coast. At the
approach to this rift Gundersen saw the immense devastation
of foliage that signaled the presence of a large nildoror herd
within a few kilometers. A jagged scar ran through the forest
from ground level to a point about twice a man's height.

Even the lunatic tropical fertility of this region could not
keep up with the nildoror appetite; it took a year or more for
such zones of defoliation to restore themselves after the herd
had moved on. Yet despite the impact of the herd, the forest
on all sides of the scar was even more close-knit here than
on the coastal plain to the east. This was a jungle raised to
the next higher power, damp, steamy, dark. The temperature
was considerably higher in the valley than at the coast, and
though the atmosphere could not possibly have been any more
humid here, there was an almost tangible wetness about the
air. The vegetation was different, too. On the plain the trees
tended to have sharp, sometimes dangerously sharp, leaves.
Here the foliage was rounded and fleshy, heavy sagging discs
of dark blue that glistened voluptuously whenever stray shafts
of sunlight pierced the forest canopy overhead.

Gundersen and his mount continued to descend, following
the line of the grazing scar. Now they made their way along the
route of a stream that flowed perversely inland; the soil was
spongy and soft, and more often than not Srin'gahar walked
knee-deep in mud. They were entering a wide circular basin
at what seemed to be the lowest point in the entire region.
Streams flowed into it on three or four sides, feeding a dark
weed-covered lake at the center; and around the margin of the

lake was Srin'gahar's herd. Gundersen saw several hundred nildoror grazing, sleeping, coupling, strolling.

'Put me down,' he said, taking himself by surprise. 'I'll walk beside you.'

Wordlessly Srin'gahar allowed him to dismount.

Gundersen regretted his egalitarian impulse the moment he stepped down. The nildor's broad-padded feet were able to cope with the muddy floor, but Gundersen discovered that he had a tendency to begin to sink in if he remained in one place more than a moment. But he would not remount now. Every step was a struggle, but he struggled. He was tense and uncertain, too, of the reception he would get here, and he was hungry as well, having eaten nothing on the long journey but a few bitterfruits plucked from passing trees. The closeness of the climate made each breath a battle for him. He was greatly relieved when the footing became easier a short distance down the slope. Here, a webwork of spongy plants spreading out from the lake underwove the mud to form a firm, if not altogether reassuring, platform a few centimeters down.

Srin'gahar raised his trunk and sounded a trumpet-blast of greeting to the encampment. A few of the nildoror replied in kind. To Gundersen, Srin'gahar said, 'The many-born one stands at the edge of the lake, friend of my journey. You see him, yes, in that group? Shall I lead you now to him?'

'Please,' said Gundersen.

The lake was congested with drifting vegetation. Humped masses of it broke the surface everywhere: leaves like horns of plenty, cup-shaped spore-bodies, ropy tangled stems, everything dark blue against the lighter blue-green of the water. Through this maze of tight-packed flora there slowly moved huge semiaquatic mammals, half a dozen malidaror, whose tubular yellowish bodies were almost totally submerged. Only the rounded bulges of their backs and the jutting periscopes of their stalked eyes were in view, and now and then a pair of cavernous snorting nostrils. Gundersen could see the immense swaths that the malidaror had cut through the vegetation in this day's feeding, but at the far side of the lake the wounds were beginning to close as new growth hastened to fill the fresh gaps.

Gundersen and Srin'gahar went down towards the water. Suddenly the wind shifted, and Gundersen had a whiff of the lake's fragrance. He coughed; it was like breathing the fumes of a distillery vat. The lake was in ferment. Alcohol was a by-product of the respiration of these water-plants, and, having no outlet, the lake became one large tub of brandy. Both water and alcohol evaporated from it at a rapid pace, making the surrounding air not only steamy but potent; and during centuries when evaporation of water had exceeded the inflow from the streams, the proof of the residue had steadily risen. When the Company ruled this planet, such lakes had been the undoing of more than one agent, Gundersen knew.

The nildoror appeared to pay little heed to him as he came near them. Gundersen was aware that every member of the encampment was actually watching him closely, but they pretended to casualness and went about their business. He was puzzled to see a dozen brush shelters flanking one of the streams. Nildoror did not live in dwellings of any sort; the climate made it unnecessary, and besides they were incapable of constructing anything, having no organs of manipulation other than the three 'fingers' at the tips of their trunks. He studied the crude lean-tos in bewilderment, and after a moment it dawned on him that he had seen structures of this sort before: they were the huts of sulidoror. The puzzle deepened. Such close association between the nildoror and the carnivorous bipeds of the mist country was unknown to him. Now he saw the sulidoror themselves, perhaps twenty of them, sitting crosslegged inside their huts. Slaves? Captives? Friends of the tribe? None of those ideas made sense.

'That is our many-born,' Srin'gahar said, indicating with a wave of his trunk a seamed and venerable nildor in the midst of a group by the lakeshore.

Gundersen felt a surge of awe, inspired not only by the great age of the creature, but by the knowledge that this ancient beast, blue-gray with years, must have taken part several times in the unimaginable rites of the rebirth ceremony. The many-born one had journeyed beyond the barrier of spirit that held Earthmen back. Whatever nirvana the rebirth ceremony offered, this being had tasted it, and Gundersen had not, and that crucial distinction of experience made Gundersen's courage shrivel as he approached the leader of the herd.

A ring of courtiers surrounded the old one. They were gray-skinned and wrinkled, too: a congregation of seniors. Younger nildoror, of the generation of Srin'gahar, kept a respectful distance. There were no immature nildoror in the encampment at all. No Earthman had ever seen a young nildor. Gundersen had been told that the nildoror were always born in the mist country, in the home country of the sulidoror, and apparently they remained in close seclusion there until they had reached the nildoror equivalent of adolescence, when they migrated to the jungles of the tropics. He also had heard that every nildor hoped to go back to the mist country when its time had come to die. But he did not know if such things were true. No one did.

The ring opened, and Gundersen found himself facing the many-born one. Protocol demanded that Gundersen speak first; but he faltered, dizzied by tension perhaps, or perhaps by the fumes of the lake, and it was an endless moment before he pulled himself together.

He said at last, 'I am Edmund Gundersen of the first birth, and I wish you joy of many rebirths, O wisest one.'

Unhurriedly the nildor swung his vast head to one side, sucked up a snort of water from the lake, and squirted it into his mouth. Then he rumbled, 'You are known to us, Edmundgundersen, from days past. You kept the big house of the Company at Fire Point in the Sea of Dust.'

The nildor's sharpness of memory astonished and distressed him. If they remembered him so well, what chance did he have to win favors from these people? They owed him no kindnesses.

'I was there, yes, a long time ago,' he said tightly.

'Not so long ago. Ten turnings is not a long time.' The nildor's heavy-lidded eyes closed, and it appeared for some moments as though the many-born one had fallen asleep. Then the nildor said, eyes still closed, 'I am Vol'himyor of the seventh birth. Will you come into the water with me? I grow tired easily on the land in this present birth of mine.'

Without waiting, Vol'himyor strode into the lake, swimming slowly to a point some forty metres from shore and floating there, submerged up to the shoulders. A malidar that had been browsing on the weeds in that part of the lake went under with a bubbling murmur of discontent and reappeared far away. Gundersen knew that he had no choice but to follow the many-born one. He stripped off his clothing and walked forward.

The tepid water rose about him. Not far out, the spongy matting of fibrous stems below ground level gave way to soft warm mud beneath Gundersen's bare feet. He felt the occasional movement of small many-legged things under his soles. The roots of the water-plants swirled whip-like about his legs, and the black bubbles of alcohol that came up from the depths and burst on the surface almost stifled him with their release of vapor. He pushed plants aside, forcing his way through them with the greatest difficulty, and feeling a great relief when his feet lost contact with the mud. Quickly he paddled himself out to Vol'himyor. The surface of the water was clear there, thanks to the malidar. In the dark depths of the lake, though, unknown creatures moved to and fro, and every few moments something slippery and quick slithered along Gundersen's body. He forced himself to ignore such things.

Vol'himyor, still seemingly asleep, murmured, 'You have been gone from this world for many turnings, have you not?'

'After the Company relinquished its rights here, I returned to my own world,' said Gundersen.

Even before the nildor's eyelids parted, even before the round yellow eyes fixed coldly on him, Gundersen was aware that he had blundered.

'Your Company never had rights here to relinquish,' said the nildor in the customary flat, neutral way. 'Is this not so?'

'It is so,' Gundersen conceded. He searched for a graceful correction and finally said, 'After the Company relinquished possession of this planet, I returned to my own world.'

'Those words are more nearly true. Why, then, have you come back here?'

'Because I love this place and wish to see it again.'

'Is it possible for an Earthman to feel love for Belzagor?'

'An Earthman can, yes.'

'An Earthman can become *captured* by Belzagor,' Vol'himyor said with more than usual slowness. 'An Earthman may find that his soul has been seized by the forces of this planet and is held in thrall. But I doubt that an Earthman can feel love for this planet, as I understand your understanding of love.'

'I yield the point, many-born one. My soul has become captured by Belzagor. I could not help but return.'

'You are quick to yield such points.'

'I have no wish to give offence.'

'Commendable tact. And what will you do here on this world that has seized your soul?'

'Travel to many parts of your world,' said Gundersen. 'I wish particularly to go to the mist country.'

'Why there?'

'It is the place that captures me most deeply.'

'That is not an informative answer,' the nildor said.

'I can give no other.'

'What thing has captured you there?'

'The beauty of the mountains rising out of the mist. The sparkle of sunlight on a clear, cold, bright day. The splendor of the moons against a field of glittering snow.'

'You are quite poetic,' said Vol'himyor.

Gundersen could not tell if he were being praised or mocked.

He said, 'Under the present law, I must have the permission of a many-born one to enter the mist country. So I come to make application to you for such permission.'

'You are fastidious in your respect for our law, my once-born friend. Once it was different with you.'

Gundersen bit his lip. He felt something crawling up his calf, down in the depths of the lake, but he compelled himself to stare serenely at the many-born one. Choosing his words with care, he said, 'Sometimes we are slow to understand the nature of others, and we give offence without knowing that we do so.'

'It is so.'

'But then understanding comes,' Gundersen said, 'and one feels remorse for the deeds of the past, and one hopes that one may be forgiven for his sins.'

'Forgiveness depends on the quality of the remorse,' said Vol'himyor, 'and also on the quality of the sins.'

'I believe my failings are known to you.'

'They are not forgotten,' said the nildor.

'I believe also that in your creed the possibility of personal redemption is not unknown.'

'True. True.'

'Will you allow me to make amends for my sins of the past against your people, both known and unknown?'

'Making amends for unknown sins is meaningless,' said the nildor. 'But in any case we seek no apologies. Your redemption from sin is your own concern, not ours. Perhaps you will find that redemption here, as you hope. I sense already a welcome change in your soul, and it will count heavily in your favor.'

'I have your permission to go north, then?' Gundersen asked.

'Not so fast. Stay with us a while as our guest. We must think about this. You may go to shore, now.'

The dismissal was clear. Gundersen thanked the many-born one for his patience, not without some self-satisfaction at the way he had handled the interview. He had always displayed proper deference towards many-born ones – even a really Kiplingesque imperialist knew enough to show respect for venerable tribal leaders – but in Company days it had never been more than a charade for him, a put-on show of humility, since ultimate power resided with the Company's sector agent, not with any nildor no matter how holy. Now, of course, the old nildor really did have the power to keep him out of the mist country, and might even see some poetic justice in banning him from it. But Gundersen felt that his deferential and apologetic attitude had been reasonably sincere just now, and that some of that sincerity had been communicated to Vol'himyor. He knew that he could not deceive the many-born one into thinking that an old Company hand like himself was suddenly eager to grovel before the former victims of Earth's expansionism; but unless some show of earnestness did come through, he stood no chance at all of gaining the permission he needed.

Abruptly, when Gundersen was still a good distance from shore, something hit him a tremendous blow between the shoulders and flung him, stunned and gasping, face forward into the water.

As he went under, the thought crossed his mind that Vol'himyor had treacherously come up behind him and lashed him with his trunk. Such a blow could easily be fatal if aimed with real malice. Spluttering, his mouth full of the lake's liquor, his arms half numbed by the impact of the blow, Gundersen warily surfaced, expecting to find the old nildor looming above him ready to deliver the coup de grace.

He opened his eyes, with some momentary trouble focusing them. No, there was the many-born one far away across the water, looking in another direction. And then Gundersen felt a curious prickly premonition and got his head down just in time to avoid being decapitated by whatever it was that had hit him before. Huddling nose-deep in the water, he saw it swing by overhead, a thick yellowish rod like a boom out of control. Now he heard thunderous shrieks of pain and felt widening ripples sweeping across the lake. He glanced around.

A dozen sulidoror had entered the water and were killing a malidar. They had harpooned the colossal beast with sharpened sticks; now the malidar thrashed and coiled in its final agonies, and it was the mighty tail of the animal that had knocked Gundersen over. The hunters had fanned out in the shallows, waist-deep, their thick fur bedraggled and matted. Each group grasped the line of one harpoon, and they were gradually drawing the malidar towards shore. Gundersen was no longer in danger, but he continued to stay low in the water, catching his breath, rotating his shoulders to assure himself that no bones were broken. The malidar's tail must have given him the merest tip-flick the first time; he would surely have been destroyed the second time that tail came by, if he had not ducked. He was beginning to ache, and he felt half drowned by the water he had gulped. He wondered when he would start to get drunk.

Now the sulidoror had beached their prey. Only the malidar's tail and thick web-footed hind legs lay in the water, moving fitfully. The rest of the animal, tons of it, stretching five times the length of a man, was up on shore, and the sulidoror were methodically driving long stakes into it, one through each of the forelimbs and several into the broad wedge-shaped head. A few nildoror were watching the operation in mild curiosity. Most ignored it. The remaining malidaror continued to browse in the woods as though nothing had happened.

A final thrust of a stake severed the malidar's spinal column. The beast quivered and lay still.

Gundersen hurried from the water, swimming quickly, then wading through the unpleasantly voluptuous mud, at last stumbling out on to the beach. His knees suddenly failed him and he toppled forward, trembling, choking, puking. A thin stream of fluid burst from his lips. Afterward he rolled to one side and watched the sulidoror cutting gigantic blocks of pale pink meat from the malidar's sides and passing them around. Other sulidoror were coming from the huts to share the feast. Gundersen shivered. He was in a kind of shock, and a few minutes passed before he realized that the cause of his shock was not only the blow he had received and the water he had swallowed, but also the knowledge that an act of violence had been committed in front of a herd of nildoror, and the nildoror did not seem at all disturbed. He had imagined that these peaceful, nonbelligerent creatures would react in horror to the slaughter of a malidar. But they simply did not care. The shock Gundersen felt was the shock of disillusionment.

A sulidor approached him and stood over him. Gundersen stared up uneasily at the towering shaggy figure. The sulidor held in its forepaws a gobbet of malidar meat the size of Gundersen's head.

'For you,' said the sulidor in the nildoror language. 'You eat with us?'

It did not wait for a reply. It tossed the slab of flesh to the ground next to Gundersen and rejoined its fellows. Gundersen's stomach writhed. He had no lust for raw meat just now.

The beach was suddenly very silent.

They were all watching him, sulidoror and nildoror both.

FIVE

Shakily Gundersen got to his feet. He sucked warm air into his lungs and bought a little time by crouching at the lake's edge to wash his face. He found his discarded clothing and consumed a few minutes by getting it on. Now he felt a little better; but the problem of the raw meat remained. The sulidoror, enjoying their feast, rending and tearing flesh and gnawing on bones, nevertheless frequently looked his way to see whether he would accept their hospitality. The nildoror, who of course had not touched the meat themselves, also seemed curious about his decision. If he refused the meat, would he offend the sulidoror? If he ate it, would he stamp himself as bestial in the eyes of the nildoror? He concluded that it was best to force some of the meat into him, as a gesture of good will towards the menacing-looking bipeds. The nildoror, after all, did not seem troubled that the sulidoror were eating meat; why should it bother them if an Earthman, a known carnivore, did the same?

He would eat the meat. But he would eat it as an Earthman would.

He ripped some leaves from the water-plant and spread them out to form a mat; he placed the meat on this. From his tunic he took his fusion torch, which he adjusted for wide aperture, low intensity, and played on the meat until its outer surface was charred and bubbling. With a narrower beam he cut the cooked meat into chunks he could manage. Then, squatting cross-legged, he picked up a chunk and bit into it.

The meat was soft and cheesy, interlaced by tough string-like masses forming an intricate grid. By will alone Gundersen succeeded in getting three pieces down. When he decided he had had enough, he rose, called out his thanks to the sulidoror, and knelt by the lake to scoop up some of the water. He needed a chaser.

During all this time no one spoke to him or approached him.

The nildoror had all left the water, for night was approaching. They had settled down in several groups well back from the shore. The feast of the sulidoror continued noisily, but was nearing its end; already several small scavenger-beasts had joined the party, and were at work at the lower half of the malidar's body while the sulidoror finished the other part.

Gundersen looked about for Srin'gahar. There were things he wished to ask.

It still troubled him that the nildoror had accepted the killing in the lake so coolly. He realized that he had somehow always regarded the nildoror as more noble than the other big beasts of this planet because they did not take life except under supreme provocation, and sometimes not even then. Here was an intelligent race exempt from the sin of Cain. And Gundersen saw in that a corollary: that the nildoror, because they did not kill, would look upon killing as a detestable act. Now he knew that his reasoning was faulty and even naïve. The nildoror did not kill simply because they were not eaters of meat; but the moral superiority that he had attributed to them on that score must in fact be a product of his own guilty imagination.

The night came on with tropic swiftness. A single moon

glimmered. Gundersen saw a nildor he took to be Srin'gahar, and went to him.

'I have a question, Srin'gahar, friend of my journey,' Gundersen began. 'When the sulidoror entered the water –'

The nildor said gravely, 'You make a mistake. I am Thali'vanoom of the third birth.'

Gundersen mumbled an apology and turned away, aghast. What a typically Earthman blunder, he thought. He remembered his old sector chief making the same blunder a dozen dozen times, hopelessly confusing one nildor with another and muttering angrily, 'Can't tell one of these big bastards from the next! Why don't they wear badges?' The ultimate insult, the failure to recognize the natives as individuals. Gundersen had always made it a point of honor to avoid such gratuitous insults. And so, here, at this delicate time when he depended wholly on winning the favor of the nildoror –

He approached a second nildor, and saw just at the last moment that this one too was not Srin'gahar. He backed off as gracefully as he could. On the third attempt he finally found his traveling companion. Srin'gahar sat placidly against a narrow tree, his thick legs folded beneath his body. Gundersen put his question to him and Srin'gahar said, 'Why should the sight of violent death shock us? Malidaror have no *g'rakh*, after all. And it is obvious that sulidoror must eat.'

'No *g'rakh*?' Gundersen said. 'This is a word I do not know.'

'The quality that separates the souled from the unsouled,' Srin'gahar explained. 'Without *g'rakh* a creature is but a beast.'

'Do sulidoror have *g'rakh*?'

'Of course.'

'And nildoror also, naturally. But malidaror don't. What about Earthmen?'

'It is amply clear that Earthmen have *g'rakh*.'

'And one may freely kill a creature which lacks that quality?'

'If one has the need to do so, yes,' said Srin'gahar. 'These are elementary matters. Have you no such concepts on your own world?'

'On my world,' said Gundersen, 'there is only one species that has been granted *g'rakh*, and so perhaps we give such matters too little thought. We know that whatever is not of our own kind must be lacking in *g'rakh*.'

'And so, when you come to another world, you have difficulty in accepting the presence of *g'rakh* in other beings?' Srin'gahar asked. 'You need not answer. I understand.'

'May I ask another question?' said Gundersen. 'Why are there sulidoror here?'

'We allow them to be here.'

'In the past, in the days when the Company ruled Belzagor, the sulidoror never went outside the mist country.'

'We did not allow them to come here then.'

'But now you do. Why?'

'Because now it is easier for us to do so. Difficulties stood in the way at earlier times.'

'What kind of difficulties?' Gundersen persisted.

Softly Srin'gahar said, 'You will have to ask that of someone who has been born more often than I. I am once-born, and many things are as strange to me as they are to you. Look, another moon is in the sky! At the third moon we shall dance.'

Gundersen looked up and saw the tiny white disc moving rapidly, low in the sky, seemingly skimming the fringe of the treetops. Belzagor's five moons were a random assortment, the closest one just outside Roche's Limit, the farthest so distant it was visible only to sharp eyes on a clear night. At any given time two or three moons were in the night sky, but the fourth and fifth moons had such eccentric orbits that they could never be seen at all from vast regions of the planet, and passed over most other zones no more than three or four times a year. One night each year all five moons could be seen at once, just along a band ten kilometers wide running at an angle of about forty degrees to the equator from northeast to southwest. Gundersen had experienced the Night of Five Moons only a single time.

The nildoror were starting to move towards the lakeshore now.

The third moon appeared, spinning retrograde into view from the south.

So he was going to see them dance again. He had witnessed their ceremonies once before, early in his career, when he was stationed at Shangri-la Falls in the northern tropics. That night the nildoror had massed just upstream of the falls, on both banks of Madden's River, and for hours after dark their blurred cries could be heard even above the roar of the water. And finally Kurtz, who was also stationed at Shangri-la then, said, 'Come, let's watch the show!' and led Gundersen out into the night. This was six months before the episode at the serpent station, and Gundersen did not then realize how Kurtz was. But he realized it quickly enough after Kurtz joined the nildoror in their dance. The huge beasts were clustered in loose semicircles, stamping back and forth, trumpeting piercingly, shaking the ground, and suddenly there was Kurtz out there among them, arms upflung, bare chest beaded with sweat and shining in the moonslight, dancing as intensely as any of them, crying out in great booming roars, stamping his feet, tossing his head. And the nildoror were forming a group around him, giving him plenty of space, letting him enter fully into the frenzy, now running towards him, now backing away, a systole and diastole of ferocious power. Gundersen stood awed, and did not move when Kurtz called to him to join the dance. He watched for what seemed like hours, hypnotized by the boom boom *boom* boom of the dancing nildoror, until in the end he broke somehow from his trance, and searched for Kurtz and found him still in ceaseless motion, a gaunt bony skeletonic figure jerking puppet-like on invisible strings, looking fragile despite his extreme height as he moved within the circle of colossal nildoror. Kurtz could neither hear Gundersen's words nor take note of his presence, and finally Gundersen went back to the station alone. In the morning he found Kurtz, looking spent and worn, slumped on the bench overlooking the waterfall. Kurtz merely said, 'You should have stayed. You should have danced.'

Anthropologists had studied these rites. Gundersen had

looked up the literature, learning what little there was to learn. Evidently the dance was preceded and surrounded by drama, a spoken episode akin to Earth's medieval mystery plays, a theatrical reenactment of some supremely important nildoror myth, serving both as mode of entertainment and as ecstatic religious experience. Unfortunately the language of the drama was an obsolete liturgical tongue, not a word of which could be understood by an Earthman, and the nildoror, who had not hesitated to instruct their first Earthborn visitors in their relatively simple modern language, had never offered any clue to the nature of the other one. The anthropological observers had noted one point which Gundersen now found cheering: invariably, within a few days after the performance of this particular rite, groups of nildoror from the herd performing it would set out for the mist country, presumably to undergo rebirth.

He wondered if the rite might be some ceremony of purification, some means of entering a state of grace before undergoing rebirth.

The nildoror all had gathered, now, beside the lake. Srin'gahar was one of the last to go. Gundersen sat alone on the slope above the basin, watching the massive forms assembling. The contrary motions of the moons fragmented the shadows of the nildoror, and the cold light from above turned their smooth green hides into furrowed black cloaks. Looking over to his left, Gundersen saw the sulidoror squatting before their huts, excluded from the ceremony but apparently not forbidden to view it.

In the silence came a low, clear, forceful flow of words. He strained to hear, hoping to catch some clue to the meaning, seeking a magical gateway that would let him burst through into an understanding of that secret language. But no understanding came. Vol'himyor was the speaker, the old many-born one, reciting words clearly familiar to everyone at the lake, an invocation, an introit. Then came a long interval of silence, and then came a response from a second nildor at the opposite end of the group, who exactly duplicated the rhythms and sinuosities of Vol'himyor's utterance. Silence again; and then a reply from Vol'himyor, spoken more crisply. Back and forth the centre of the service moved, and the interplay between the two celebrants became what was for nildoror a surprisingly quick exchange of dialog. About every tenth line the herd at large repeated what a celebrant had said, sending dark reverberations through the night.

After perhaps ten minutes of this the voice of a third solo nildor was heard. Vol'himyor made reply. A fourth speaker took up the recitation. Now isolated lines were coming in rapid bursts from many members of the congregation. No cue was missed; no nildor trampled on another's lines. Each seemed intuitively to know when to speak, when to stay silent. The tempo accelerated. The ceremony had become a mosaic of brief utterances blared forth from every part of the group in a random rotation. A few of the nildoror were up and moving slowly in place, lifting their feet, putting them down.

Lightning speared through the sky. Despite the closeness of the atmosphere, Gundersen felt a chill. He saw himself as a wanderer on a prehistoric Earth, spying on some grotesque conclave of mastodons. All the things of man seemed infinitely far away now. The drama was reaching some sort of climax. The nildoror were bellowing, stamping, calling to one another with tremendous snorts. They were taking up formations, assembling in aisled rows. Still there came utterances and responses, antiphonal amplifications of words heavy with strange significance. The air grew more steamy. Gundersen could no longer hear individual words, only rich deep chords of massed grunts, ah ah *ah* ah, ah ah *ah* ah, the old rhythm that he remembered from the night at Shangri-la Falls. It was a breathy, gasping sound now, ecstatic, an endless chuffing pattern of exhalations, ah ah *ah* ah, ah ah *ah* ah, ah ah *ah* ah, with scarcely a break between each group of four beats, and the whole jungle seemed to echo with it. The nildoror had no musical instruments whatever, yet to Gundersen it appeared that vast drums were pounding out that hypnotically intense rhythm. Ah ah *ah* ah. Ah ah *ah* ah. AH AH *AH* AH! AH AH *AH* AH!

And the nildoror were dancing.

Down below on the margin of the lake moved scores of great shadowy shapes, prancing like gazelles, two running steps forward, stamp down hard on the third step, regain the balance on the fourth. The universe trembled. Boom boom *boom* boom, boom boom *boom* boom. The earlier phase of the ceremony, the dramatic dialog, which might have been some sort of subtle philosophical disquisition, had given way totally to this primeval pounding, this terrifying shuffling of gigantic elephantine bodies. Boom boom *boom* boom. Gundersen looked to his left and saw the sulidoror entranced, hairy heads switching back and forth in the rhythm of the dance; but not one of the bipeds had risen from the crosslegged posture. They were content to rock and nod, and now and then to pound their elbows on the ground.

Gundersen was cut off from his own past, even from a sense of his own kinship to his species. Disjointed memories floated up. Again he was at the serpent station, a prisoner of the hallucinatory venom, feeling himself transformed into a nildor and capering thickly in the grove. Again he stood by the bank of the great river, seeing another performance of this very dance. And also he remembered nights spent in the safety of Company stations deep in the forest, among his own kind, when they had listened to the sound of stamping feet in the distance. All those other times Gundersen had drawn back from whatever strangeness this planet was offering him; he had transferred out of the serpent station rather than taste the venom a second time, he had refused Kurtz's invitation to join the dance, he had remained within the stations when the rhythmic poundings began in the forest. But tonight he felt little allegiance to mankind. He found himself longing to join that black and incomprehensible frenzy at the lakeshore. Something monstrous was running free within him, liberated by the incessant repetition of that boom boom *boom* boom. But what right had he to caper

Kurtzlike in an alien ceremony? He did not dare intrude on their ritual.

Yet he discovered that he was walking down the spongy slope towards the place where the massed nildoror cavorted.

If he could think of them only as leaping, snorting elephants it would be all right. If he could think of them even as savages kicking up a row it would be all right. But the suspicion was unavoidable that this ceremony of words and dancing held intricate meanings for these people, and that was the worst of it. They might have thick legs and short necks and long dangling trunks, but that did not make them elephants, for their triple tusks and spiny crests and alien anatomies said otherwise; and they might be lacking in all technology, lacking even in a written language, but that did not make them savages, for the complexity of their minds said otherwise. They were creatures who possessed *g'rakh*. Gundersen remembered how he had innocently attempted to instruct the nildoror in the arts of terrestrial culture, in an effort to help them 'improve' themselves; he had wanted to humanize them, to lift their spirits upward, but nothing had come of that, and now he found his own spirit being drawn – downward? – certainly to their level, wherever that might lie. Boom boom *boom* boom. His feet hesitantly traced out the four-step as he continued down the slope towards the lake. Did he dare? Would they crush him as blasphemous?

They had let Kurtz dance. They had let Kurtz dance.

It had been in a different latitude, a long time ago, and other nildoror had been involved, but they had let Kurtz dance.

'Yes,' a nildor called to him. 'Come, dance with us!'

Was it Vol'himyor? Was it Srin'gahar? Was it Thali'vanoom of the third birth? Gundersen did not know which of them had spoken. In the darkness, in the sweaty haze, he could not see clearly, and all these giant shapes looked identical. He reached the bottom of the slope. Nildoror were everywhere about him, tracing out passages in their private journeys from point to point on the lakeshore. Their bodies emitted acrid odors, which, mixing with the fumes of the lake, choked and dizzied him. He heard several of them say to him, 'Yes, yes, dance with us!'

And he danced.

He found an open patch of marshy soil and laid claim to it, moving forward, then backward, covering and recovering his one little tract in his fervor. No nildoror trespassed on him. His head tossed; his eyes rolled; his arms dangled; his body swayed and rocked; his feet carried him untiringly. Now he sucked in the thick air. Now he cried out in strange tongues. His skin was on fire; he stripped away his clothing, but it made no difference. Boom boom *boom* boom. Even now, a shred of his old detachment was left, enough so that he could marvel at the spectacle of himself dancing naked amid a herd of giant alien beasts. Would they, in their ultimate transports of passion, sweep in over his plot and crush him into the muck? Surely it was dangerous to stay here in the heart of the herd. But he stayed. Boom boom *boom* boom, again, again, yet again. As he whirled he looked out over the lake, and by sparkling refracted moonslight he saw the malidaror placidly munching the weeds, heedless of the frenzy on land. They are without *g'rakh*, he thought. They are beasts, and when they die their leaden spirits go downward to the earth. Boom. Boom. BOOM. Boom.

He became aware that glossy shapes were moving along the ground, weaving warily between the rows of dancing nildoror. The serpents! This music of pounding feet had summoned them from the dense glades where they lived.

The nildoror seemed wholly unperturbed that these deadly worms moved among them. A single stabbing thrust of the two spiny quills would bring even a mighty nildor toppling down; but no matter. The serpents were welcome, it appeared. They glided towards Gundersen, who knew he was in no mortal danger from their venom, but who did not seek another encounter with it. He did not break the stride of his dance, though, as five of the thick pink creatures wriggled past him. They did not touch him.

The serpents passed through, and were gone. And still the

uproar continued. And still the ground shook. Gundersen's heart hammered, but he did not pause. He gave himself up fully, blending with those about him, sharing as deeply as he was able to share it the intensity of the experience.

The moons set. Early streaks of dawn stained the sky.

Gundersen became aware that he no longer could hear the thunder of stamping feet. He danced alone. About him, the nildoror had settled down, and their voices again could be heard, in that strange unintelligible litany. They spoke quietly but with great passion. He could no longer follow the patterns of their words; everything merged into an echoing rumble of tones, without definition, without shape. Unable to halt, he jerked and twisted through his obsessive gyration until the moment that he felt the first heat of the morning sun.

Then he fell exhausted, and lay still, and slipped down easily into sleep.

SIX

When he woke it was some time after midday. The normal life of the encampment had resumed; a good many of the nildoror were in the lake, a few were munching on the vegetation at the top of the slope, and most were resting in the shade. The only sign of last night's frenzy was in the spongy turf near the lakeshore, which was terribly scuffed and torn.

Gundersen felt stiff and numb. Also he was abashed, with the embarrassment of one who has thrown himself too eagerly into someone else's special amusement. He could hardly believe that he had done what he knew himself to have done. In his shame he felt an immediate impulse to leave the encampment at once, before the nildoror could show him their contempt for an Earthman capable of making himself a thrall to their festivity, capable of allowing himself to be beguiled by their incantations. But he shackled the thought, remembering that he had a purpose in coming here.

He limped down to the lake and waded out until its water came up to his breast. He soaked a while, and washed away the sweat of the night before. Emerging, he found his clothing and put it on.

A nildor came to him and said, 'Vol'himyor will speak to you now.'

The many-born one was half-way up the slope. Coming before him, Gundersen could not find the words of any of the greetings formulas, and simply stared raggedly at the old nildor until Vol'himyor said, 'You dance well, my onceborn friend. You dance with joy. You dance with love. You dance like a nildor, do you know that?'

'It is not easy for me to understand what happened to me last night,' said Gundersen.

'You proved to us that our world has captured your spirit.'

'Was it offensive to you that an Earthman danced among you?'

'If it had been offensive,' said Vol'himyor slowly, 'you would not have danced among us.' There was a long silence. Then the nildor said, 'We will make a treaty, we two. I will give you permission to go into the mist country. Stay there until you are ready to come out. But when you return, bring with you the Earthman known as Cullen, and offer him to the northernmost encampment of nildoror, the first of my people that you find. Is this agreed?'

'Cullen?' Gundersen asked. Across his mind flared the image of a short broad-faced man with fine golden hair and mild green eyes. 'Cedric Cullen, who was here when I was here?'

'The same man.'

'He worked with me when I was at the station in the Sea of Dust.'

'He lives now in the mist country,' Vol'himyor said, 'having gone there without permission. We want him.'

'What has he done?'

'He is guilty of a grave crime. Now he has taken sanctuary

among the sulidoror, where we are unable to gain access to him. It would be a violation of our covenant with them if we removed this man ourselves. But we may ask you to do it.'

Gundersen frowned. 'You won't tell me the nature of his crime?'

'Does it matter? We want him. Our reasons are not trifling ones. We request you to bring him to us.'

'You're asking one Earthman to seize another and turn him in for punishment,' said Gundersen. 'How am I to know where justice lies in this affair?'

'Under the treaty of relinquishment, are we not the arbiters of justice on this world?' asked the nildor.

Gundersen admitted that this was so.

'Then we hold the right to deal with Cullen as he deserves,' Vol'himyor said.

That did not, of course, make it proper for Gundersen to act as catspaw in handing his old comrade over to the nildoror. But Vol'himyor's implied threat was clear: do as we wish, or we grant you no favors.

Gundersen said, 'What punishment will Cullen get if he falls into your custody?'

'Punishment? Punishment? Who speaks of punishment?'

'If the man's a criminal —'

'We wish to purify him,' said the many-born one. 'We desire to cleanse his spirit. We do not regard that as punishment.'

'Will you injure him physically in any way?'

'It is not to be thought.'

'Will you end his life?'

'Can you mean such a thing? Of course not.'

'Will you imprison him?'

'We will keep him in custody,' said Vol'himyor, 'for however long the rite of purification takes. I do not think it will be long. He will swiftly be freed, and he will be grateful to us.'

'I ask you once more to tell me the nature of his crime.'

'He will tell you that himself,' the nildor said. 'It is not necessary for me to make his confession for him.'

Gundersen considered all aspects of the matter. Shortly he

said, 'I agree to our treaty, many-born one, but only if I may add several clauses.'

'Go on.'

'If Cullen will not tell me the nature of his crime, I am released from my obligation to hand him over.'

'Agreed.'

'If the sulidoror object to my taking Cullen out of the mist country, I am released from my obligation also.'

'They will not object. But agreed.'

'If Cullen must be subdued by violence in order to bring him forth, I am released.'

The nildor hesitated a moment. 'Agreed,' he said finally.

'I have no other conditions to add.'

'Then our treaty is made,' Vol'himyor said. 'You may begin your northward journey today. Five of our once-born ones must also travel to the mist country, for their time of rebirth has come, and if you wish they will accompany you and safeguard you along the way. Among them is Srin'gahar, whom you already know.'

'Will it be troublesome for them to have me with them?'

'Srin'gahar has particularly requested the privilege of serving as your guardian,' said Vol'himyor. 'But we would not compel you to accept his aid, if you would rather make your journey alone.'

'It would be an honor to have his company,' Gundersen said.

'So be it, then.'

A senior nildor summoned Srin'gahar and the four others who would be going towards rebirth. Gundersen was gratified at this confirmation of the existing data: once more the frenzied dance of the nildoror had preceded the departure of a group bound for rebirth.

It pleased him, too, to know that he would have a nildoror escort on the way north. There was only one dark aspect to the treaty, that which involved Cedric Cullen. He wished he had not sworn to barter another Earthman's freedom for his own safe-conduct pass. But perhaps Cullen had done something really loathsome, something that merited punishment – or purification, as Vol'himyor put it. Gundersen did not understand how that normally sunny man could have become a criminal and a fugitive, but Cullen had lived on this world a long time, and the strangeness of alien worlds ultimately corroded even the brightest souls. In any case, Gundersen felt that he had opened enough honorable exits for himself if he needed to escape from his treaty with Vol'himyor.

Srin'gahar and Gundersen went aside to plan their route. 'Where in the mist country do you intend to go?' the nildor asked.

'It does not matter. I just want to enter it. I suppose I'll have to go wherever Cullen is.'

'Yes. But we do not know exactly where he is, so we will have to wait until we are there to learn it. Do you have special places to visit on the way north?'

'I want to stop at the Earthman stations,' Gundersen said. 'Particularly at Shangri-la Falls. So my idea is that we'll follow Madden's River northwestward, and –'

'These names are unknown to me.'

'Sorry. I guess they've all reverted back to nildororu names. And I don't know those. But wait –' Seizing a stick, Gundersen scratched a hasty but serviceable map of Belzagor's western hemisphere in the mud. Across the waist of the disc he drew the thick swath of the the tropics. At the right side he gouged out a curving bite to indicate the ocean; on the left he outlined the Sea of Dust. Above and below the band of the tropics he drew the thinner lines representing the northern and southern mist zones, and beyond them he indicated the gigantic icecaps. He marked the spaceport and the hotel at the coast with an X, and cut a wiggly line up from there, clear across the tropics into the northern mist country, to show Madden's River. At the midway point of the river he placed a dot to mark Shangri-la Falls. 'Now,' said Gundersen, 'if you follow the tip of my stick –'

'What are those marks on the ground?' asked Srin'gahar.

A map of your planet, Gundersen wanted to say. But there

was no nildororu word in his mind for 'map.' He found that he also lacked words for 'image,' 'picture,' and similar concepts. He said lamely, 'This is your world. This is Belzagor, or at least half of it. See, this is the ocean, and the sun rises here, and –'

'How can this be my world, these marks, when my world is so large?'

'This is *like* your world. Each of these lines, here, stands for a place on your world. You see, here, the big river that runs out of the mist country and comes down to the coast, where the hotel is, yes? And this mark is the spaceport. These two lines are the top and the bottom of the northern mist country. The –'

'It takes a strong sulidor a march of many days to cross the northern mist country,' said Srin'gahar. 'I do not understand how you can point to such a small space and tell me it is the northern mist country. Forgive me, friend of my journey. I am very stupid.'

Gundersen tried again, attempting to communicate the nature of the marks on the ground. But Srin'gahar simply could not comprehend the idea of a map, nor could he see how scratched lines could represent places. Gundersen considered asking Vol'himyor to help him, but rejected that plan when he realized that Vol'himyor, too, might not understand; it would be tactless to expose the many-born one's ignorance in any area. The map was a metaphor of place, an abstraction from reality. Evidently even beings possessing *g'rakh* might not have the capacity to grasp such abstractions.

He apologized to Srin'gahar for his own inability to express concepts clearly, and rubbed out the map with his boot. Without it, planning the route was somewhat more difficult, but they found ways to communicate. Gundersen learned that the great river at whose mouth the hotel was situated was called the Seran'nee in nildororu, and that the place where the river plunged out of the mountains into the coastal plain, which Earthmen knew as Shangri-la Falls, was Du'jayukh to nildoror. Then it was simple for them to agree to follow the Seran'nee to its source, with a stop at Du'jayukh and at any other settlement of Earthmen that happened to lie conveniently on the path north.

While this was being decided, several of the sulidoror brought a late breakfast of fruit and lake fish to Gundersen, exactly as though they recognized his authority under the Company. It was a curiously anachronistic gesture, almost servile, not at all like the way in which they had tossed him a raw slab of malidar meat the day before. Then they had been testing him, even taunting him; now they were waiting upon him. He was uncomfortable about that, but he was also quite hungry, and he made a point of asking Srin'gahar to tell him the sulidororu words of thanks. There was no sign that the powerful bipeds were pleased or flattered or amused by his use of their language, though.

They began their journey in late afternoon. The five nildoror moved in single file, Srin'gahar at the back of the group with Gundersen perched on his back; the Earthman did not appear to be the slightest burden for him. Their path led due north along the rim of the great rift, with the mountains that guarded the central plateau rising on their left. By the light of the sinking sun Gundersen stared towards that plateau. Down here in the valley, his surroundings had a certain familiarity; making the necessary allowances for the native plants and animals, he might almost be in some steamy jungle of South America. But the plateau appeared truly alien. Gundersen eyed the thick tangles of spiky purplish moss that festooned and nearly choked the trees along the top of the rift wall. The way the parasitic growth drowned its hosts the trees seemed grisly to him. The wall itself, of some soapy gray-green rock, dotted with angry blotches of crimson lichen and punctuated every few hundred meters by long ropy strands of a swollen blue fungus, cried out its otherworldliness: the soft mineral had never felt the impact of raindrops, but had been gently carved and shaped by the humidity alone, taking on weird knobbinesses and hollows over the millennia. Nowhere on Earth could one see a rock wall like that, serpentine and involute and greasy.

The forest beyond the wall looked impenetrable and vaguely sinister. The silence, the heavy and sluggish air, the sense of dark strangeness, the flexible limbs of the glossy trees bowed almost to the ground by moss, the occasional distant snort of some giant beast, made the central plateau seem forbidding and hostile. Few Earthmen had ever entered it, and it had never been surveyed in detail. The Company once had had some plans for stripping away large patches of jungle up there and putting in agricultural settlements, but nothing had come of the scheme, because of relinquishment. Gundersen had been in the plateau country only once, by accident, when his pilot had had to make a forced landing en route from coastal headquarters to the Sea of Dust. Seena had been with him. They spent a night and a day in that forest, Seena terrified from the moment of landing, Gundersen comforting her in a standard manly way but finding that her terror was somehow contagious. The girl trembled as one alien happening after another presented itself, and shortly Gundersen was on the verge of trembling too. They watched, fascinated and repelled, while an army of innumerable insects with iridescent hexagonal bodies and long hairy legs strode with maniacal persistence into a sprawling glade of tiger-moss; for hours the savage mouths of the carnivorous plants bit the shining insects into pieces and devoured them, and still the horde marched on to destruction. At last the moss was so glutted that it went into sporulation, puffing up cancerously and sending milky clouds of reproductive bodies spewing into the air. By morning the whole field of moss lay deflated and helpless, and tiny green reptiles with broad rasping tongues moved in to devour every strand, laying bare the soil for a new generation of flora. And then there were the feathery jelly-like things, streaked with blue and red, that hung in billowing cascades from the tallest trees, trapping unwary flying creatures. And bulky rough-skinned beasts as big as rhinos, bearing mazes of blue antlers with interlocking tines, grubbed for roots a dozen meters from their camp, glaring sourly at the strangers from Earth. And long-necked browsers with eyes like beacons munched on high leaves, squirting barrelfuls of purple urine from openings at the bases of their taut throats. And dark fat otter-like beings ran chattering past the stranded Earthmen, stealing anything within quick grasp. Other animals visited them also. This planet, which had never known the hunter's hand, abounded in big mammals. He and Seena and the pilot had seen more grotesqueness in a day and a night than they had bargained for when they signed up for outworld service.

'Have you ever been in there?' Gundersen asked Srin'gahar, as night began to conceal the rift wall.

'Never. My people seldom enter that land.'

'Occasionally, flying low over the plateau, I used to see nildoror encampments in it. Not often, but sometimes. Do you mean that your people no longer go there?'

'No,' said Srin'gahar. 'A few of us have need to go to the plateau, but most do not. Sometimes the soul grows stale, and one must change one's surroundings. If one is not ready for rebirth, one goes to the plateau. It is easier to confront one's own soul in there, and to examine it for flaws. Can you understand what I say?'

'I think so,' Gundersen said. 'It's like a place of pilgrimage, then – a place of purification?'

'In a way.'

'But why have the nildoror never settled permanently up there? There's plenty of food – the climate is warm –'

'It is not a place where *g'rakh* rules,' the nildor replied.

'Is it dangerous to nildoror? Wild animals, poisonous plants, anything like that?'

'No, I would not say that. We have no fear of the plateau, and there is no place on this world that is dangerous to us. But the plateau does not interest us, except those who have the special need of which I spoke. As I say, *g'rakh* is foreign to it. Why should we go there? There is room enough for us in the lowlands.'

The plateau is too alien even for them, Gundersen thought. They prefer their nice little jungle. How curious!

He was not sorry when darkness hid the plateau from view.

They made camp that night beside a hissing-hot stream. Evidently its waters issued from one of the underground cauldrons that were common in this sector of the continent; Srin'gahar said that the source lay not far to the north. Clouds of steam rose from the swift flow; the water, pink with high-temperature micro-organisms, bubbled and boiled. Gundersen wondered if Srin'gahar had chosen this stopping place especially for his benefit, since nildoror had no use for hot water, but Earthmen notoriously did.

He scrubbed his face, taking extraordinary pleasure in it, and supplemented a dinner of food capsules and fresh fruit with a stew of greenberry roots – delectable when boiled, poisonous otherwise. For shelter while sleeping Gundersen used a monomolecular jungle blanket that he had stowed in his backpack, his one meager article of luggage on this journey. He draped the blanket over a tripod of boughs to keep away nightflies and other noxious insects, and crawled under it. The ground, thickly grassed, was a good enough mattress for him.

The nildoror did not seem disposed towards conversation. They left him alone. All but Srin'gahar moved several hundred meters upstream for the night. Srin'gahar settled down protectively a short distance from Gundersen and wished him a good sleep.

Gundersen said, 'Do you mind talking a while? I want to know something about the process of rebirth. How do you know, for instance, that your time is upon you? Is it something you feel within yourself, or is it just a matter of reaching a certain age? Do you –' He became aware that Srin'gahar was paying no attention. The nildor had fallen into what might have been a deep trance, and lay perfectly still.

Shrugging, Gundersen rolled over and waited for sleep, but sleep was a long time coming.

He thought a good deal about the terms under which he had been permitted to make this northward journey. Perhaps another many-born one would have allowed him to go into the mist country without attaching the condition that he bring back Cedric Cullen; perhaps he would not have been granted safe-conduct at all. Gundersen suspected that the results would have been the same no matter which encampment of nildoror he had happened to go to for his travel permission. Though the nildoror had no means of long-distance communication, no governmental structure in an Earthly sense, no more coherence as a race than a population of jungle beasts, they nevertheless were remarkably well able to keep in touch with one another and to strike common policies.

What was it that Cullen had done, Gundersen wondered, to make him so eagerly sought?

In the old days Cullen had seemed overwhelmingly normal: a cheerful, amiable ruddy man who collected insects, spoke no harsh words, and held his liquor well. When Gundersen had been the chief agent out at Fire Point, in the Sea of Dust, a dozen years before, Cullen had been his assistant. Months on end there were only the two of them in the place, and Gundersen had come to know him quite well, he imagined. Cullen had no plans for making a career with the Company; he said he had signed a six-year contract, would not renew, and intended to take up a university appointment when he had done his time on Holman's World. He was here only for seasoning, and for the prestige that accrues to anyone who has a record of outworld service. But then the political situation on Earth grew complex, and the Company was forced to agree to relinquish a great many planets that it had colonized. Gundersen, like most of the fifteen thousand Company people here, had accepted a transfer to another assignment. Cullen, to Gundersen's amazement, was among the handful who opted to stay, even though that meant severing his ties with the home world. Gundersen had not asked him why; one did not discuss such things. But it seemed odd.

He saw Cullen clearly in memory, chasing bugs through the Sea of Dust, killing bottle jouncing against his hip as he ran from one rock outcropping to the next – an over-grown boy, really. The beauty of the Sea of Dust was altogether lost on him. No sector of the planet was more truly alien, nor more spectacular: a dry ocean bed, greater in size than the

Atlantic, coated with a thick layer of fine crystalline mineral fragments as bright as mirrors when the sun was on them. From the station at Fire Point one could see the morning light advancing out of the east like a river of flame, spilling forth until the whole desert blazed. The crystals swallowed energy all day, and gave it forth all night, so that even at twilight the eerie radiance rose brightly, and after dark a throbbing purplish glow lingered for hours. In this almost lifeless but wondrously beautiful desert the Company had mined a dozen precious metals and thirty precious and semiprecious stones. The mining machines set forth from the station on far-ranging rounds, grinding up loveliness and returning with treasure; there was not much for an agent to do there except keep inventory of the mounting wealth and play host to the tourist parties that came to see the splendor of the countryside. Gundersen had grown terribly bored, and even the glories of the scenery had become tiresome to him, but Cullen, to whom the incandescent desert was merely a flashy nuisance, fell back on his hobby for entertainment, and filled bottle after bottle with his insects. Were the mining machines still standing in the Sea of Dust, Gundersen wondered, waiting for the command to resume operations? If the Company had not taken them away after relinquishment, they would surely stand there thoughout all eternity, unrusting, useless, amidst the hideous gouges they had cut. The machines had scooped down through the crystalline layer to the dull basalt below, and had spewed out vast heaps of tailings and debris as they gnawed for wealth. Probably the Company had left the things behind, too, as monuments to commerce. Machinery was cheap, interstellar transport was costly; why bother removing them? 'In another thousand years,' Gundersen once had said, 'the Sea of Dust will all be destroyed and there'll be nothing but rubble here, if these machines continue to chew up the rock at the present rate.' Cullen had shrugged and smiled. 'Well, one won't need to wear these dark glasses, then, once the infernal glare is gone,' he had said. 'Eh?' And now the rape of the desert was over and the machines were still; and now Cullen was a

fugitive in the mist country, wanted for some crime so terrible
the nildoror would not even give it a name.

SEVEN

When they took to the road in the morning it was Srin'gahar,
uncharacteristically, who opened the conversation.

'Tell me of elephants, friend of my journey. What do they
look like, and how do they live?'

'Where did you hear of elephants?'

'The Earthpeople at the hotel spoke of them. And also in the
past, I have heard the word said. They are beings of Earth that
look like nildoror, are they not?'

'There is a certain resemblance,' Gundersen conceded.

'A close one?'

'There are many similarities.' He wished Srin'gahar were able
to comprehend a sketch. 'They are long and high in the body,
like you, and they have four legs, and tails, and trunks. They
have tusks, but only two, one here, one here. Their eyes are
smaller and placed in a poor position, here, here. And here –'
He indicated Srin'gahar's skullcrest. 'Here they have nothing.
Also their bones do not move as your bones do.'

'It sounds to me,' said Srin'gahar, 'as though these elephants
look very much like nildoror.'

'I suppose they do.'

'Why is this, can you say? Do you believe that we and the
elephants can be of the same race?'

'It isn't possible,' said Gundersen. 'It's simply a – a –' He
groped for words; the nildororu vocabulary did not include the
technical terms of genetics. 'Simply a pattern in the development of life that occurs on many worlds. Certain basic designs
of living creatures recur everywhere. The elephant design – the
nildoror design – is one of them. The large body, the huge head,
the short neck, the long trunk enabling the being to pick up

objects and handle them without having to bend – these things will develop wherever the proper conditions are found.'

'You have seen elephants, then, on many other worlds?'

'On some,' Gundersen said. 'Following the same general pattern of construction, or at least some aspects of it, although the closest resemblance of all is between elephants and nildoror. I could tell you of half a dozen other creatures that seem to belong to the same group. And this is also true of many other life-forms – insects, reptiles, small mammals, and so on. There are certain niches to be filled on every world. The thoughts of the Shaping Force travel the same path everywhere.'

'Where, then, are Belzagor's equivalents of men?'

Gundersen faltered. 'I didn't say that there were exact equivalents everywhere. The closest thing to the human pattern on your planet, I guess, is the sulidoror. And they aren't very close.'

'On Earth, the men rule. Here the sulidoror are the secondary race.'

'An accident of development. Your *g'rakh* is superior to that of the sulidoror; on our world we have no other species that possesses *g'rakh* at all. But the physical resemblances between men and sulidoror are many. They walk on two legs; so do we. They eat both flesh and fruit; so do we. They have hands which can grasp things; so do we. Their eyes are in front of their heads; so are ours. I know, they're bigger, stronger, hairier, and less intelligent than human beings, but I'm trying to show you how patterns can be similar on different planets, even though there's no real blood relationship between –'

Srin'gahar said quietly, 'How do you know that elephants are without *g'rakh*?'

'We – they – it's clear that –' Gundersen stopped, uneasy. After a pause for thought he said carefully, 'They've never demonstrated any of the qualities of *g'rakh*. They have no village life, no tribal structure, no technology, no religion, no continuing culture.'

'We have no village life and no technology,' the nildor said. 'We wander through the jungles, stuffing ourselves with leaves and branches. I have heard this said of us, and it is true.'

'But you're different. You –'

'How are we different? Elephants also wander through jungles, stuffing themselves with leaves and branches, do they not? They wear no skins over their own skins. They make no machines. They have no books. Yet you admit that we have *g'rakh*, and you insist that they do not.'

'They can't communicate ideas,' said Gundersen desperately. 'They can tell each other simple things, I guess, about food and mating and danger, but that's all. If they have a true language, we can't detect it. We're aware of only a few basic sounds.'

'Perhaps their language is so complex that you are *unable* to detect it,' Srin'gahar suggested.

'I doubt that. We were able to tell as soon as we got here that the nildoror speak a language; and we were able to learn it. But in all the thousands of years that men and elephants have been sharing the same planet, we've never been able to see a sign that they can accumulate and transmit abstract concepts. And that's the essence of having *g'rakh*, isn't it?'

'I repeat my statement. What if you are so inferior to your elephants that you cannot comprehend their true depths?'

'A cleverly put point, Srin'gahar. But I won't accept it as any sort of description of the real world. If elephants have *g'rakh*, why haven't they managed to get anywhere in their whole time on Earth? Why does mankind dominate the planet, with the elephants crowded into a couple of small corners and practically wiped out?'

'You kill your elephants?'

'Not any more. But there was a time when men killed elephants for pleasure, or for food, or to use their tusks for ornaments. And there was a time when men used elephants for beasts of burden. If the elephants had *g'rakh*, they –'

He realized that he had fallen into Srin'gahar's trap.

The nildor said, 'On this planet, too, the 'elephants' let themselves be exploited by mankind. You did not eat us and you rarely killed us, but often you made us work for you. And yet you admit we are beings of *g'rakh*.'

'What we did here,' said Gundersen, 'was a gigantic mistake, and when we came to realize it, we relinquished your world and got off it. But that still doesn't mean that elephants are rational and sentient beings. They're animals, Srin'gahar, big simple animals, and nothing more.'

'Cities and machines are not the only achievements of *g'rakh*.'

'Where are their spiritual achievements, then? What does an elephant believe about the nature of the universe? What does he think about the Shaping Force? How does he regard his own place in his society?'

'I do not know,' said Srin'gahar. 'And neither do you, friend of my journey, because the language of the elephants is closed to you. But it is an error to assume the absence of *g'rakh* where you are incapable of seeing it.'

'In that case, maybe the malidaror have *g'rakh* too. And the venom-serpents. And the trees, and the vines, and –'

'No,' said Srin'gahar. 'On this planet, only nildoror and sulidoror possess *g'rakh*. This we know beyond doubt. On your world it is not necessarily the case that humans alone have the quality of reason.'

Gundersen saw the futility of pursuing the point. Was Srin'gahar a chauvinist defending the spiritual supremacy of elephants throughout the universe, or was he deliberately adopting an extreme position to expose the arrogances and moral vulnerabilities of Earth's imperialism? Gundersen did not know, but it hardly mattered. He thought of Gulliver discussing the intelligence of horses with the Houyhnhnms.

'I yield the point,' he said curtly. 'Perhaps someday I'll bring an elephant to Belzagor, and let you tell me whether or not it has *g'rakh*.'

'I would greet it as a brother.'

'You might be unhappy over the emptiness of your brother's mind,' Gundersen said. 'You would see a being fashioned in your shape, but you wouldn't succeed in reaching its soul.'

'Bring me an elephant, friend of my journey, and I will be the judge of its emptiness,' said Srin'gahar. 'But tell me one last thing, and then I will not trouble you: when your people call us elephants, it is because they think of us as mere beasts, yes? Elephants are 'big simple animals', those are your words. Is this how the visitors from Earth see us?'

'They're referring only to the resemblance in form between nildoror and elephants. It's a superficial thing. They say you are *like* elephants.'

'I wish I could believe that,' the nildor said, and fell silent, leaving Gundersen alone with his shame and guilt. In the old days it had never been his habit to argue the nature of intelligence with his mounts. It had not even occurred to him then that such a debate might be possible. Now he sensed the extent of Srin'gahar's suppressed resentment. Elephants – yes, that was how he too had seen the nildoror. Intelligent elephants, perhaps. But still elephants.

In silence they followed the boiling stream northward. Shortly before noon they came to its source, a broad bowshaped lake pinched between a double chain of steeply rising hills. Clouds of oily steam rose from the lake's surface. Thermophilic algae streaked its waters, the pink ones forming a thin scum on top and nearly screening the meshed tangles of the larger, thicker blue-gray plants a short distance underneath.

Gundersen felt some interest in stopping to examine the lake and its unusual life-forms. But he was strangely reluctant to ask Srin'gahar to halt. Srin'gahar was not only his carrier, he was his companion on a journey; and to say, tourist-fashion, 'Let's stop here a while,' might reinforce the nildor's belief that Earthmen still thought of his people merely as beasts of burden. So he resigned himself to passing up this bit of sightseeing. It was not right, he told himself, that he should delay Srin'gahar's journey towards rebirth merely to gratify a whim of idle curiosity.

But as they were nearing the lake's further curve, there came such a crashing and smashing in the underbrush to the east that the entire procession of nildoror paused to see

what was going on. To Gundersen it sounded as if some
prowling dinosaur were about to come lurching out of the
jungle, some huge clumsy tyrannosaur inexplicably displaced
in time and space. Then, emerging from a break in the row of
hills, there came slowly across the bare soil flanking the lake a
little snub-snouted vehicle, which Gundersen recognized as the
hotel's beetle, towing a crazy primitive-looking appendage of a
trailer, fashioned from raw planks and large wheels. Atop this
jouncing, clattering trailer four small tents had been pitched,
covering most of its area; alongside the tents, over the wheels,
luggage was mounted in several racks; and at the rear, clinging
to a railing and peering nervously about, were the eight tourists
whom Gundersen had last seen some days earlier in the hotel
by the coast.

Srin'gahar said, 'Here are some of your people. You will want
to talk with them.'

The tourists were, in fact, the last species whatever that
Gundersen wanted to see at this point. He would have preferred locusts, scorpions, fanged serpents, tyrannosaurs, toads,
anything at all. Here he was coming from some sort of mystical experience among the nildoror, the nature of which
he barely understood; here, insulated from his own kind,
he rode towards the land of rebirth struggling with basic
questions of right and wrong, of the nature of intelligence,
of the relationship of human to nonhuman and of himself to
his own past; only a few moments before he had been forced
into an uncomfortable, even painful confrontation with that
past by Srin'gahar's casual, artful questions about the souls of
elephants; and abruptly Gundersen found himself once more
among these empty, trivial human beings, these archetypes
of the ignorant and blind tourist, and whatever individuality
he had earned in the eyes of his nildor companion vanished
instantly as he dropped back into the undifferentiated class of
Earthmen. These tourists, some part of his mind knew, were
not nearly as vulgar and hollow as he saw them; they were
merely ordinary people, friendly, a bit foolish, overprivileged,
probably quite satisfactory human beings within the context

of their lives on Earth, and only seeming to be cardboard figurines here because they were essentially irrelevant to the planet they had chosen to visit. But he was not yet ready to have Srin'gahar lose sight of him as a person separate from all the other Earthmen who came to Belzagor, and he feared that the tide of bland chatter welling out of these people would engulf him and make him one of them.

The beetle, obviously straining to haul the trailer, came to rest a dozen meters from the edge of the lake. Out of it came Van Beneker, looking sweatier and seedier than usual. 'All right,' he called to the tourists. 'Everyone down! We're going to have a look at one of the famous hot lakes!' Gundersen, high atop Srin'gahar's broad back, considered telling the nildor to move along. The other four nildoror, having satisfied themselves about the cause of the commotion, had already done that and were nearly out of view at the far end of the lake. But he decided to stay a while; he knew that a display of snobbery towards his own species would win him no credit with Srin'gahar.

Van Beneker turned to Gundersen and called out, 'Morning, sir! Glad to see you! Having a good trip?'

The four Earth couples clambered down from their trailer. They were fully in character, behaving exactly as Gundersen's harsh image of them would have them behave: they seemed bored and glazed, surfeited with the alien wonders they had already seen. Stein, the helix-parlor proprietor, dutifully checked the aperture of his camera, mounted it in his cap, and routinely took a 360-degree hologram of the scene; but when the printout emerged from the camera's output slot a moment later he did not even bother to glance at it. The act of picture-taking, not the picture itself, was significant. Watson, the doctor, muttered a joyless joke of some sort to Christopher, the financier, who responded with a mechanical chuckle. The women, bedraggled and jungle-stained, paid no attention to the lake. Two simply leaned against the beetle and waited to be told what it was they were being shown, while the other two, as they became aware of Gundersen's presence, pulled facial masks from their backpacks and hurriedly slipped the thin plastic films over their heads so that they could present at least the illusion of properly groomed features before the handsome stranger.

'I won't stay here long,' Gundersen heard himself promising Srin'gahar, as he dismounted.

Van Beneker came up to him. 'What a trip!' the little man blurted. 'What a stinking trip! Well, I ought to be used to it by now. How's everything been going for you, Mr G?'

'No complaints.' Gundersen nodded at the trailer. 'Where'd you get that noisy contraption?'

'We built it a couple of years ago when one of the old cargo haulers broke down. Now we use it to take tourists around when we can't get any nildoror bearers.'

'It looks like something out of the eighteenth century.'

'Well, you know, sir, out here we don't have much left in the way of modern equipment. We're short of servos and hydraulic walkers and all that. But you can always find wheels and some planks around. We make do.'

'What happened to the nildoror we were riding coming from the spaceport to the hotel? I thought they were willing to work for you.'

'Sometimes yes, sometimes no,' Van Beneker said. 'They're unpredictable. We can't force them to work, and we can't hire them to work. We can only ask them politely, and if they say they're not available, that's it. Couple of days back, they decided they weren't going to be available for a while, so we had to get out the trailer.' He lowered his voice. 'If you ask me, it's on account of these eight baboons here. They think the nildoror don't understand any English, and they keep telling each other how terrible it is that we had to hand a planet as valuable as this over to a bunch of elephants.'

'On the voyage out here,' said Gundersen, 'some of them were voicing quite strong liberal views. At least two of them were big pro-relinquishment people.'

'Sure. Back on Earth they bought relinquishment as a political theory. "Give the colonized worlds back to their long-oppressed natives," and all that. Now they're out here and suddenly they've decided that the nildoror aren't "natives", just animals, just funny-looking elephants, and maybe we should have kept the place after all.' Van Beneker spat. 'And the nildoror take it all in. They pretend they don't understand the language, but they do, they do. You think they feel like hauling people like that on their backs?'

'I see,' said Gundersen. He glanced at the tourists. They were eyeing Srin'gahar, who had wandered off towards the bush and was energetically ripping soft boughs loose for his midday meal. Watson nudged Miraflores, who quirked his lips and shook his head as if in disapproval. Gundersen could not hear what they were saying, but he imagined that they were expressing scorn for Srin'gahar's enthusiastic foraging. Evidently civilized beings were not supposed to pull their meals off trees with their trunks.

Van Beneker said, 'You'll stay and have lunch with us, won't you, Mr G?'

'That's very kind of you,' Gundersen said.

He squatted in the shade while Van Beneker rounded up his charges and led them down to the rim of the steaming lake. When they were all there Gundersen rose and quietly affiliated himself with the group. He listened to the guide's spiel, but managed to train only half his attention on what was being said. 'High-temperature life-zone ... better than 70°C ... more in some places, even above boiling, yet things live in it ... special genetic adaptation ... thermophilic, we call it, that is, heat-loving ... the DNA doesn't get cooked, no, but the rate of spontaneous mutation is pretty damned high, and the species change so fast you wouldn't believe it ... enzymes resist the heat ... put the lake organisms in cool water and they'll freeze in about a minute ... life processes extraordinarily fast ... unfolded and denatured proteins can also function when circumstances are such that ... you get quite a range up to middle-phylum level ... a pocket environment, no interaction with the rest of the planet . . . thermal gradients . . . quantitative studies . . . the famous kinetic biologist, Dr Brock . . . continuous thermal destruction of sensitive molecules . . . unending resynthesis . . .'

Srin'gahar was still stuffing himself with branches. It seemed to Gundersen that he was eating far more than he normally did at this time of day. The sounds of rending and chewing clashed with the jerky drone of Van Beneker's memorized scientific patter.

Now, unhooking a biosensitive net from his belt, Van Beneker began to dredge up samples of the lake's fauna for the edification of his group. He gripped the net's handle and made vernier adjustments governing the mass and length of the desired prey; the net, mounted at the end of an almost infinitely expandable length of fine flexible metal coil, swept back and forth beneath the surface of the lake, hunting for organisms of the programmed dimensions. When its sensors told it that it was in the presence of living matter, its mouth snapped open and quickly shut again. Van Beneker retracted it, bringing to shore some unhappy prisoner trapped within a sample of its own scalding environment.

Out came one lake creature after another, red-skinned, boiled-looking, but live and angry and flapping. An armored fish emerged, concealed in shining plates, embellished with fantastic excrescences and ornaments. A lobster-like thing came forth, lashing a long spiked tail, waving ferocious eye-stalks. Up from the lake came something that was a single immense claw with a tiny vestigial body. No two of Van Beneker's grotesque catches were alike. The heat of the lake, he repeated, induces frequent mutations. He rattled off the whole genetic explanation a second time, while dumping one little monster back into the hot bath and probing for the next.

The genetic aspects of the thermophilic creatures seemed to catch the interest of only one of the tourists – Stein, who, as a helix-parlor owner specializing in the cosmetic editing of human genes, would know more than a little about mutation himself. He asked a few intelligent-sounding questions, which

Van Beneker naturally was unable to answer; the others simply stared, patiently waiting for their guide to finish showing them funny animals and take them somewhere else. Gundersen, who had never had a chance before to examine the contents of one of these high-temperature pockets, was grateful for the exhibition, although the sight of writhing captive lake-dwellers quickly palled on him. He became eager to move on.

He glanced around and discovered that Srin'gahar was nowhere in sight.

'What we've got this time,' Van Beneker was saying, 'is the most dangerous animal of the lake, what we call a razor shark. Only I've never seen one like this before. You see those little horns? Absolutely new. And that lantern sort of thing on top of the head, blinking on and off?' Squirming in the net was a slender crimson creature about a meter in length. Its entire underbelly, from snout to gut, was hinged, forming what amounted to one gigantic mouth rimmed by hundreds of needle-like teeth. As the mouth opened and closed, it seemed as if the whole animal were splitting apart and healing itself. 'This beast feeds on anything up to three times its own size,' Van Beneker said. 'As you can see, it's fierce and savage, and –'

Uneasy, Gundersen drifted away from the lake to look for Srin'gahar. He found the place where the nildor had been eating, where the lower branches of several trees were stripped bare. He saw what seemed to be the nildor's trail, leading away into the jungle. A painful white light of desolation flared in his skull at the awareness that Srin'gahar must quietly have abandoned him.

In that case his journey would have to be interrupted. He did not dare go alone and on foot into that pathless wilderness ahead. He would have to ask Van Beneker to take him back to some nildoror encampment where he might find another means of getting to the mist country.

The tour group was coming up from the lake now. Van Beneker's net was slung over his shoulder; Gundersen saw some lake creatures moving slowly about in it.

'Lunch,' he said. 'I got us some jelly-crabs. You hungry?'

Gundersen managed a thin smile. He watched, not at all hungry, as Van Beneker opened the net; a gush of hot water rushed from it, carrying along eight or ten oval purplish creatures, each different from the others in the number of legs, shell markings, and size of claws. They crawled in stumbling circles, obviously annoyed by the relative coolness of the air. Steam rose from their backs. Expertly Van Beneker pithed them with sharpened sticks, and cooked them with his fusion torch, and split open their shells to reveal the pale quivering jelly-like metabolic regulators within. Three of the women grimaced and turned away, but Mrs Miraflores took her crab and ate it with delight. The men seemed to enjoy it. Gundersen, merely nibbling at the jelly, eyed the forest and worried about Srin'gahar.

Scraps of conversation drifted towards him.

'– enormous profit potential, just wasted, altogether wasted –'

'– even so, our obligation is to encourage self-determination on every planet that –'

'– but are they *people*?'

'– look for the soul, it's the only way to tell that –'

'– elephants, and nothing but elephants. Did you see him ripping up the trees and –'

'– relinquishment was the fault of a highly vocal minority of bleeding hearts who –'

'– no soul, no relinquishment –'

'– you're being too harsh, dear. There were definite abuses on some of the planets, and –'

'– stupid political expediency, I call it. The blind leading the blind –'

'– can they write? Can they think? Even in Africa we were dealing with human beings, and even there –'

'– the soul, the inner spirit –'

'– I don't need to tell you how much I favored relinquishment. You remember, I took the petitions around and everything. But even so, I have to admit that after seeing –'

'– piles of purple crap on the beach –'

'– victims of sentimental over-reaction –'

'– I understand the annual profit was on the order of –'

'– no doubt that they have souls. No doubt at all.' Gundersen realized that his own voice had entered the conversation. The others turned to him; there was a sudden vacuum to fill. He said, 'They have a religion, and that implies the awareness of the existence of a spirit, a soul, doesn't it?'

'What kind of religion?' Miraflores asked.

'I'm not sure. One important part of it is ecstatic dancing – a kind of frenzied prancing around that leads to some sort of mystic experience. I know. I've danced with them. I've felt at least the edges of that experience. And they've got a thing called rebirth, which I suppose is central to their rituals. I don't understand it. They go north, into the mist country, and something happens to them there. They've always kept the details a secret. I think the sulidoror give them something, some drug, maybe, and it rejuvenates them in some inner way, and leads to a kind of illumination – am I at all clear?' Gundersen, as he spoke, was working his way almost unconsciously through the pile of uneaten jelly-crabs. 'All I can tell you is that rebirth is vitally important to them, and they seem to derive their tribal status from the number of rebirths they've undergone. So you see they're not just animals. They have a society, they have a cultural structure – complex, difficult for us to grasp.'

Watson asked, 'Why don't they have a civilization, then?'

'I've just told you that they do.'

'I mean cities, machines, books –'

'They're not physically equipped for writing, for building things, for any small manipulations,' Gundersen said. 'Don't you see, they have no *hands*? A race with hands makes one kind of society. A race built like elephants makes another.' He was drenched in sweat and his appetite was suddenly insatiable. The women, he noticed, were staring at him strangely. He realized why: he was cleaning up all the food in sight, compulsively stuffing it into his mouth. Abruptly his patience shattered and he felt that his skull would explode if he did not instantly drop all barriers and admit the one great guilt that by

stabbing his soul had spurred him into strange odysseys. It did
not matter that these were not the right people from whom
to seek absolution. The words rushed uncontrollably upwards
to his lips and he said, 'When I came here I was just like you.
I underestimated the nildoror. Which led me into a grievous
sin that I have to explain to you. You know, I was a sector
administrator for a while, and one of my jobs was arranging
the efficient deployment of native labor. Since we didn't
fully understand that the nildoror were intelligent autonomous beings, we *used* them, we put them to work on heavy
construction jobs, lifting girders with their trunks, anything
we thought they were capable of handling on sheer muscle
alone. We just ordered them around as if they were machines.'
Gundersen closed his eyes and felt the past roaring towards
him, inexorably, a black cloud of memory that enveloped and
overwhelmed him, 'The nildoror let us use them, God knows
why. I guess we were the crucible in which their race had to
be purged. Well, one day a dam broke, out in Monroe District
up in the north, not far from where the mist country begins,
and a whole thornbush plantation was in danger of flooding,
at a loss to the Company of who knows how many millions.
And the main power plant of the district was endangered too,
along with our station headquarters and – let's just say that
if we didn't react fast, we'd lose our entire investment in the
north. My responsibility. I began conscripting nildoror to build
a secondary line of dikes. We threw every robot we had into
the job, but we didn't have enough, so we got the nildoror too,
long lines of them plodding in from every part of the jungle,
and we worked day and night until we were all ready to fall
down dead. We were beating the flood, but I couldn't be sure of
it. And on the sixth morning I drove out to the dike site to see
if the next crest would break through, and there were seven
nildoror I hadn't ever seen before, marching along a path going
north. I told them to follow me. They refused, very gently.
They said, no, they were on their way to the mist country for
the rebirth ceremony, and they couldn't stop. Rebirth? What
did I care about rebirth? I wasn't going to take that excuse from

them, not when it looked like I might lose my whole district. Without thinking I ordered them to report for dike duty or I'd execute them on the spot. Rebirth can wait, I said. Get reborn some other time. This is serious business. They put their heads down and pushed the tips of their tusks into the ground. That's a sign of great sadness among them. Their spines drooped. Sad. Sad. We pity you one of them said to me, and I got angry and told him what he could do with his pity. Where did he get the right to pity me? Then I pulled my fusion torch. Go on, get moving, there's a work crew that needs you. Sad. Big eyes looking pity at me. Tusks in the ground. Two or three of the nildoror said they were very sorry, they couldn't do any work for me now, it was impossible for them to break their journey. But they were ready to die right there, if I insisted on it. They didn't want to hurt my prestige by defying me, but they *had* to defy me, and so they were willing to pay the price. I was about to fry one, as an example to the others, and then I stopped and said to myself, what the hell am I doing, and the nildoror waited, and my aides were watching and so were some of our other nildoror, and I lifted the fusion torch again, telling myself that I'd kill one of them, the one who said he pitied me, and hoping that then the others would come to their senses. They just waited. Calling my bluff. How could I fry seven pilgrims even if they were defying a sector chief's direct order? But my authority was at stake. So I pushed the trigger. I just gave him a slow burn, not deep, enough to scar the hide, that was all, but the nildor stood there taking it, and in another few minutes I would have burned right through to a vital organ. And so I soiled myself in front of them by using force. It was what they had been waiting for. Then a couple of the nildoror who looked older than the others said, stop it, we wish to reconsider, and I turned off the torch, and they went aside for a conference. The one I had burned was hobbling a little, and looked hurt, but he wasn't badly wounded, not nearly as badly as I was. The one who pushes the trigger can get hurt worse than his target, do you know that? And in the end the nildoror all agreed to do as I asked. So instead of going north for rebirth they went to work on the dike, even the burned one, and nine days later the flood crest subsided and the plantation and the power plant and all the rest were saved and we lived happily ever after.' Gundersen's voice trailed off. He had made his confession, and now he could not face these people any longer. He picked up the shell of the one remaining crab and explored it for some scrap of jelly, feeling depleted and drained. There was an endless span of silence.

Then Mrs Christopher said, 'So what happened then?'

Gundersen looked up, blinking. He thought he had told it all.

'Nothing happened then,' he said. 'The flood crest subsided.'

'But what was the point of the story?'

He wanted to hurl the empty crab in her tensely smiling face. 'The point?' he said. 'The point? Why –' He was dizzy, now. He said, 'Seven intelligent beings were journeying towards the holiest rite of their religion, and at gunpoint I requisitioned their services on a construction job to save property that meant nothing to them, and they came and hauled logs for me. Isn't the point obvious enough? Who was spiritually superior there? When you treat a rational autonomous creature as though he's a mere beast, what does that make you?'

'But it was an emergency,' said Watson. 'You needed all the help you could get. Surely other considerations could be laid aside at a time like that. So they were nine days late getting to their rebirth. Is that so bad?'

Gundersen said hollowly, 'A nildor goes to rebirth only when the time is ripe, and I can't tell you how they know the time is ripe, but perhaps it's astrological, something to do with the conjunction of the moons. A nildor has to get to the place of rebirth at the propitious time, and if he doesn't make it in time, he isn't reborn just then. Those seven nildoror were already late, because the heavy rains had washed out the roads in the south. The nine days more that I tacked on made them *too* late. When they were finished building dikes for me, they simply went back south to rejoin their tribe. I didn't understand why. It wasn't until much later that I found out that I had cost them their chance at rebirth and they might have to wait ten or twenty years until they could go again. Or maybe never get another chance.' Gundersen did not feel like talking any more. His throat was dry. His temples throbbed. How cleansing it would be, he thought, to dive into the steaming lake. He got stiffly to his feet, and as he did so he noticed that Srin'gahar had returned and was standing motionless a few hundred meters away, beneath a mighty swordflower tree.

He said to the tourists, 'The point is that the nildoror have religion and souls, and that they are people, and that if you can buy the concept of relinquishment at all, you can't object to relinquishing this planet. The point is also that when Earthmen collide with an alien species they usually do so with maximum misunderstanding. The point is furthermore that I'm not surprised you think of the nildoror the way you do, because I did too, and learned a little better when it was too late to matter, and even so I didn't learn enough to do me any real good, which is one of the reasons why I came back to this planet. And I'd like you to excuse me now, because this is the propitious time for me to move on, and I have to go.' He walked quickly away from them.

Approaching Srin'gahar, he said, 'I'm ready to leave now.'

The nildor knelt. Gundersen remounted.

'Where did you go?' the Earthman asked. 'I was worried when you disappeared.'

'I felt that I should leave you alone with your friends,' said Srin'gahar. 'Why did you worry? There is an obligation on me to bring you safely to the country of the mist.'

EIGHT

The quality of the land was undoubtedly changing. They were leaving the heart of the equatorial jungle behind, and starting to enter the highlands that led into the mist zone. The climate here was still tropical, but the humidity was not so intense; the atmosphere, instead of holding everything in a constant clammy embrace, released its moisture periodically in rain, and after the rain the texture of the air was clear and light until its wetness was renewed. There was different vegetation in this region: harsh-looking angular stuff, with stiff leaves sharp as blades. Many of the trees had luminous foliage that cast a cold light over the forest by night. There were fewer vines here, and the treetops no longer formed a continuous canopy shutting out most of the sunlight; splashes of brightness dappled the forest floor, in some places extending across broad open plazas and meadows. The soil, leached by the frequent rains, was a pale yellowish hue, not the rich black of the jungle. Small animals frequently sped through the under-brush. At a slower pace moved solemn slug-like creatures, blue-green with ebony mantles, which Gundersen recognized as the mobile fungoids of the highlands – plants that crawled from place to place in quest of fallen boughs or a lightning-shattered tree-trunk. Both nildoror and men considered their taste a great delicacy.

On the evening of the third day northward from the place of the boiling lake Srin'gahar and Gundersen came upon the other four nildoror, who had marched on ahead. They were camped at the foot of a jagged crescent-shaped hill, and evidently had been there at least a day, judging by the destruction they had worked upon the foliage all around their resting-place. Their trunks and faces, smeared and stained with luminous juices, glowed brightly. With them was a sulidor, by far the largest one Gundersen had ever seen, almost twice Gundersen's own height, with a pendulous snout the length of a man's forearm. The sulidor stood erect beside a boulder encrusted with blue moss, his legs spread wide and his tail, tripod fashion, bracing his mighty weight. Narrowed eyes surveyed Gundersen from beneath shadowy hoods. His long arms, tipped with terrifying curved claws, hung at rest. The fur of the sulidor was the colour of old bronze, and unusually thick.

One of the candidates for rebirth, a female nildor called Luu'khamin, said to Gundersen, 'The sulidor's name is Na-sinisul. He wishes to speak with you.'

'Let him speak, then.'

'He prefers that you know, first, that he is not a sulidor of the ordinary kind. He is one of those who administers the ceremony of rebirth, and we will see him again when we approach the mist country. He is a sulidor of rank and merit, and his words are not to be taken lightly. Will you bear that in mind as you listen to him?'

'I will. I take no one's words lightly on this world, but I will give him a careful hearing beyond any doubt. Let him speak.'

The sulidor strode a short distance forward and once again planted himself firmly, digging his great spurred feet deep into the resilient soil. When he spoke, it was in a nildororu stamped with the accent of the north: thick-tongued, slow, positive.

'I have been on a journey,' said Na-sinisul, 'to the Sea of Dust, and now I am returning to my own land to aid in the preparations for the event of rebirth in which these five travelers are to take part. My presence here is purely accidental. Do you understand that I am not in this place for any particular purpose involving you or your companions?'

'I understand,' said Gundersen, astounded by the precise and emphatic manner of the sulidor's speech. He had known the sulidoror only as dark, savage, ferocious-looking figures lurking in mysterious glades.

Na-sinisul continued, 'As I passed near here yesterday, I came by chance to the site of a former station of your Company. Again by chance, I chose to look within, though it was no business of mine to enter that place. Within I found two Earthmen whose bodies had ceased to serve them. They were

unable to move and could barely talk. They requested me to
send them from this world, but I could not do such a thing on
my own authority. Therefore I ask you to follow me to this
station and to give me instructions. My time is short here, so
it must be done at once.'

'How far is it?'

'We could be there before the rising of the third moon.'

Gundersen said to Srin'gahar, 'I don't remember a Company
station here. There should be one a couple of days north of
here, but –'

'This is the place where the food that crawls was collected
and shipped downriver,' said the nildor.

'Here?' Gundersen shrugged. 'I guess I've lost my bearings
again. All right, I'll go there.' To Na-sinisul he said, 'Lead and
I'll follow.'

The sulidor moved swiftly through the glowing forest, and
Gundersen, atop Srin'gahar, rode just to his rear. They seemed
to be descending, and the air grew warm and murky. The
landscape also changed, for the trees here had aerial roots that
looped up like immense scraggy elbows, and the fine tendrils
sprouting from the roots emitted a harsh green radiance. The
soil was loose and rocky; Gundersen could hear it crunching
under Srin'gahar's tread. Bird-like things were perched on
many of the roots. They were owlish creatures that appeared
to lack all color; some were black, some white, some a mottled
black and white. He could not tell if that was their true hue
or if the luminosity of the vegetation simply robbed them
of color. A sickly fragrance came from vast, pallid parasitic
flowers sprouting from the trunks of the trees.

By an outcropping of naked, weathered yellow rock lay
the remains of the Company station. It seemed even more
thoroughly ruined than the serpent station far to the south;
the dome of its roof had collapsed and coils of wiry-stemmed
saprophytes were clinging to its sides, perhaps feeding on
the decomposition products that the rain eroded from the
abrasions in the plastic walls. Srin'gahar allowed Gundersen
to dismount. The Earthman hesitated outside the building,

waiting for the sulidor to take the lead. A fine warm rain began to fall; the tang of the forest changed at once, becoming sweet where it had been sour. But it was the sweetness of decay.

'The Earthmen are inside,' said Na-sinisul. 'You may go in. I await your instructions.'

Gundersen entered the building. The reek of rot was far more intense here, concentrated, perhaps, by the curve of the shattered dome. The dampness was all pervasive. He wondered what sort of virulent spores he sucked into his nostrils with every breath. Something dripped in the darkness, making a loud tocking sound against the lighter patter of the rain coming through the gaping roof. To give himself light, Gundersen drew his fusion torch and kindled it at the lowest beam. The warm white glow spread through the station. At once he felt a flapping about his face as some thermotorpic creature, aroused and attracted by the heat of the torch, rose up towards it. Gundersen brushed it away; there was slime on his fingertips afterwards.

Where were the Earthmen?

Cautiously he made a circuit of the building. He remembered it vaguely, now – one of the innumerable bush stations the Company once had scattered across Holman's World. The floor was split and warped, requiring him to climb over the buckled, sundered sections. The mobile fungoids crawled everywhere, devouring the scum that covered all interior surfaces of the building and leaving narrow glistening tracks behind. Gundersen had to step carefully to avoid putting his feet on the creatures, and he was not always successful. Now he came to a place where the building widened, puckering outward; he flashed his torch around and caught sight of a blackened wharf, overlooking the bank of a swift river. Yes, he remembered. The fungoids were wrapped and baled here and sent downriver on their voyage towards the market. But the Company's barges no longer stopped here, and the tasty pale slugs now wandered unmolested over the mossy relics of furniture and equipment.

'Hello?' Gundersen called. 'Hello, hello, hello?'

He received a moan by way of answer. Stumbling and slipping in the dimness, fighting a swelling nausea, he forced his way onward through a maze of unseen obstacles. He came to the source of the loud dripping sound. Something bright red and basket-shaped and about the size of a man's chest had established itself high on the wall, perpendicular to the floor. Through large pores in its spongy surface a thick black fluid exuded, falling in a continuous greasy splash. As the light of Gundersen's torch probed it, the exudation increased, becoming almost a cataract of tallowy liquid. When he moved the light away the flow became less copious, though still heavy.

The floor sloped here so that whatever dripped from the spongy basket flowed quickly down, collecting at the far side of the room in the angle between the floor and the wall. Here Gundersen found the Earthmen. They lay side by side on a low mattress; fluid from the dripping thing had formed a dark pool around them, completely covering the mattress and welling up over their bodies. One of the Earthmen, head lolling to the side, had his face totally immersed in the stuff. From the other one came the moans.

They both were naked. One was a man, one a woman, though Gundersen had some difficulty telling that at first; both were so shrunken and emaciated that the sexual characteristics were obscured. They had no hair, not even eyebrows. Bones protruded through parchment-like skin. The eyes of both were open, but were fixed in a rigid, seemingly sightless stare, unblinking, glassy. Lips were drawn back from teeth. Grayish algae sprouted in the furrows of their skins, and the mobile fungoids roamed their bodies, feeding on this growth. With a quick automatic gesture of revulsion Gundersen plucked two of the slug-like creatures from the woman's empty breasts. She stirred; she moaned again. In the language of the nildoror she murmured, 'Is it over yet?' Her voice was like a flute played by a sullen desert breeze.

Speaking English, Gundersen said, 'Who are you? How did this happen?'

He got no response from her. A fungoid crept across her mouth, and he flicked it aside. He touched her cheek. There was a rasping sound as his hand ran across her skin; it was like caressing stiff paper. Struggling to remember her, Gundersen imagined dark hair on her bare skull, gave her light arching brows, saw her cheeks full and her lips smiling. But nothing registered; either he had forgotten her, or he had never known her, or she was unrecognizable in her present condition.

'Is it over soon?' she asked, again in nildororu.

He turned to her companion. Gently, half afraid the fragile neck would snap, Gundersen lifted the man's head out of the pool of fluid. It appeared that he had been breathing it; it trickled from his nose and lips, and after a moment he showed signs of being unable to cope with ordinary air. Gundersen let his face slip back into the pool. In that brief moment he had recognized the man as a certain Harold – or was it Henry? – Dykstra, whom he had known distantly in the old days.

The unknown woman was trying to move one arm. She lacked the strength to lift it. These two were like living ghosts, like death-in-life, mired in their sticky fluid and totally helpless. In the language of the nildoror he said, 'How long have you been this way?'

'Forever,' she whispered.

'Who are you?'

'I don't . . . remember. I'm . . . waiting.'

'For what?'

'For the end.'

'Listen,' he said, 'I'm Edmund Gundersen, who used to be sector chief. I want to help you.'

'Kill me first. Then him.'

'We'll get you out of here and back to the spaceport. We can have you on the way to Earth in a week or ten days, and then –'

'No . . . please . . .'

'What's wrong?' he asked.

'Finish it. Finish it.' She found enough strength to arch her back, lifting her body half-way out of the fluid that nearly concealed her lower half. Something rippled and briefly bulged beneath her skin. Gundersen touched the taut belly and felt movement within, and that quick inward quiver was the most frightening sensation he had ever known. He touched the body of Dykstra, too: it also rippled inwardly.

Appalled, Gundersen scrambled to his feet and backed away from them. By faint torchlight he studied their shrivelled bodies, naked but sexless, bone and ligament, shorn of flesh and spirit yet still alive. A terrible fear came over him. 'Na-sinisul!' he called. 'Come in here! Come in!'

The sulidor shortly was at his side. Gundersen said, 'Something's inside their bodies. Some kind of parasite? It moves. What is it?'

'Look there,' said Na-sinisul, indicating the spongy basket from which the dark fluid trickled. 'They carry its young. They have become hosts. A year, two years, perhaps three, and the larvae will emerge.'

'Why aren't they both dead?'

'They draw nourishment from this,' said the sulidor, swishing his tail through the black flow. 'It seeps into their skins. It feeds them, and it feeds that which is within them.'

'If we took them out of here and sent them down to the hotel on rafts –?'

'They would die,' Na-sinisul said, 'moments after they were removed from the wetness about them. There is no hope of saving them.'

'When does it end?' the woman asked.

Gundersen trembled. All his training told him never to accept the finality of death; any human in whom some shred of life remained could be saved, rebuilt from a few scraps of cells into a reasonable facsimile of the original. But there were no facilities for such things on this world. He confronted a swirl of choices. Leave them here to let alien things feed upon their guts; try to bring them back to the spaceport for shipment to the nearest tectogenetic hospital; put them out of their misery at once; seek to free their bodies himself of whatever held them in thrall. He knelt again. He forced himself to experience that inner quivering again. He touched the woman's stomach, her thighs, her bony haunches. Beneath the skin she was a mass of strangeness. Yet her mind still ticked, though she had forgotten her name and her native language. The man was luckier; though he was infested too, at least Dykstra did not have to lie here in the dark waiting for the death that could come only when the harbored larvae erupted from the enslaved human flesh. Was this what they had desired, when they refused repatriation from this world that they loved? An Earthman can become captured by Belzagor, the many-born nildor Vol'himyor had said. But this was too literal a capture.

The stink of bodily corruption made him retch.

'Kill them both,' he said to Na-sinisul. 'And be quick about it.'

'This is what you instruct me to do?'

'Kill them. And rip down that thing on the wall and kill it too.'

'It has given no offence,' said the sulidor. 'It has done only what is natural to its kind. By killing these two, I will deprive it of its young, but I am not willing to deprive it of life as well.'

'All right,' Gundersen said. 'Just the Earthmen, then. Fast.'

'I do this as an act of mercy, under your direct orders,' said Na-sinisul. He leaned forward and lifted one powerful arm. The savage curved claws emerged full from their sheath. The claw descended twice.

Gundersen compelled himself to watch. The bodies spilt like dried husks; the things within came spilling out, unformed, raw. Even now, in some inconceivable reflex, the two corpses twitched and jerked. Gundersen stared into their eroded depths. 'Do you hear me?' he asked. 'Are you alive or dead?' The woman's mouth gaped but no sound came forth, and he did not know whether this was an attempt to speak or merely a last convulsion of the ravaged nerves. He stepped his fusion torch up to high power and trained it on the dark pool. I am the resurrection and the life, he thought, reducing Dykstra to ashes, and the woman beside him, and the squirming unfinished larvae. Acrid, choking fumes rose; not even the torch could destroy the building's dampness. He turned the torch back to illumination level. 'Come,' he said to the sulidor, and they went out together.

'I feel like burning the entire building and purifying this place,' Gundersen said to Na-sinisul.

'I know.'

'But you would prevent me.'

'You are wrong. No one on this world will prevent you from doing anything.'

But what good would it do . . . Gundersen asked himself. The purification had already been accomplished. He had removed the only beings in this place that were foreign to it.

The rain had stopped. To the waiting Srin'gahar, Gundersen said, 'Will you take me away from here?'

They rejoined the other four nildoror. Then, because they had lingered too long here and the land of rebirth was still far away, they resumed the march, even though it was night. By morning Gundersen could hear the thunder of Shangri-la Falls, which the nildoror called Du'jayukh.

NINE

It was as though a white wall of water descended from the sky. Nothing on Earth could match the triple plunge of this cataract, by which Madden's River, or the Seran'nee, dropped five hundred meters, and then six hundred, and then five hundred more, falling from ledge to ledge in its tumble towards the sea. Gundersen and the five nildoror stood at the foot of the falls, where the entire violent cascade crashed into a broad rock-flanged basin out of which the serpentine river continued its south-easterly course; the sulidor had taken his leave in the night and was proceeding northward by his own route. To Gundersen's rear lay the coastal plain, behind his right shoulder, and the central plateau, behind his left. Before him, up by the head of the falls, the northern plateau began, the highlands that controlled the approach to the mist country. Just as a titanic north-south rift cut the coastal plain off from the central plateau, so did another rift running east-west separate both the central plateau and the coastal plain from the highlands ahead.

He bathed in a crystalline pool just beyond the tumult of the cataract, and then they began their ascent. The Shangri-la Station, one of the Company's most important outposts, was invisible from below; it was set back a short way from the head of the falls. Once there had been way-stations at the foot of the falls and at the head of the middle cataract, but no trace of these structures remained; the jungle had swallowed them utterly in only eight years. A winding road, with an infinity of switchbacks, led to the top. When he first had seen it, Gundersen had imagined it was the work of Company engineers, but he had learned that it was a natural ridge in the face of the plateau, which the nildoror themselves had enlarged and deepened to make their journeys towards rebirth more easy.

The swaying rhythm of his mount lulled him into a doze; he held tight to Srin'gahar's pommel-like horns and prayed that in his grogginess he would not fall off. Once he woke suddenly and found himself clinging only by his left hand, with his body half slung out over a sheer drop of at least two hundred meters. Another time, drowsy again, he felt cold spray and snapped to attention to see the entire cascade of the falling river rushing past him no more than a dozen metres away. At the head of the lowest cataract the nildoror paused to eat, and Gundersen dashed icy water in his face to shatter his sluggishness. They went on. He had less difficulty keeping awake now; the air was thinner, and the afternoon breeze was cool. In the hour before twilight they reached the head of the falls.

Shangri-la Station, seemingly unchanged, lay before him: three rectangular unequal blocks of dark shimmering plastic, a somber ziggurat rising on the western bank of the narrow gorge through which the river sped. The formal gardens of tropical plants, established by a forgotten sector chief at least forty years before, looked as though they were being carefully maintained. At each of the building's setbacks there was an outdoor veranda overlooking the river, and these, too, were bedecked with plants. Gundersen felt a dryness in his throat and a tightness in his loins. He said to Srin'gahar, 'How long may we stay here?'

'How long do you wish to stay?'

'One day, two – I don't know yet. It depends on the welcome I get.'

'We are not yet in a great hurry,' said the nildor. 'My friends and I will make camp in the bush. When it is time for you to go on, come to us.'

The nildoror moved slowly into the shadows. Gundersen approached the station. At the entrance to the garden he paused. The trees here were gnarled and bowed, with long feathery gray fronds dangling down; highland flora was different from that to the south, although perpetual summer ruled here even as in the true tropics behind him. Lights glimmered within the station. Everything out here seemed surprisingly orderly; the contrast with the shambles of the serpent station and the nightmare decay of the fungoid station was sharp. Not even the hotel garden was this well tended. Four neat rows of fleshy, obscene-looking pink forest candles bordered the walkway that ran towards the building. Slender, stately globe-flower trees, heavy with gigantic fruit, formed little groves to left and right. There were hullygully trees and bitterfruits – exotics here, imported from the steaming equatorial tropics – and mighty swordflower trees in full bloom, lifting their long shiny stamens to the sky. Elegant glitterivy and spiceburr vines writhed along the ground, but not in any random way. Gundersen took a few steps farther in, and heard the soft sad sigh of a sensifrons bush, whose gentle hairy leaves coiled and shrank as he went by, opening warily when he had gone past, shutting again when he whirled to steal a quick glance. Two more steps and he came to a low tree whose name he could not recall, with glossy red winged leaves that took flight, breaking free of their delicate stems and soaring away; instantly their replacements began to sprout. The garden was magical. Yet there were surprises here. Beyond the glitterivy he discovered a crescent patch of tiger-moss, the carnivorous ground cover native to the unfriendly central plateau. The moss had been transplanted to other parts of the planet – there was a patch of it growing out of control at the seacoast hotel – but Gundersen remembered that Seena abhorred it, as she abhorred all the productions of that forbidding plateau. Worse yet, looking upward so that he could follow the path of the gracefully gliding leaves, Gundersen saw great masses of quivering jelly, streaked with blue and red neural fibers, hanging from several of the biggest trees: more carnivores, also natives of the central plateau. What were those sinister things doing in this enchanted garden? A moment later he had a third proof that Seena's terror of the plateau had faded: across his path there ran one of the plump, thieving otter-like animals that had bedeviled them the time they had been marooned there. It halted a moment, nose twitching, cunning paws upraised, looking for something to seize. Gundersen hissed at it and it scuttled into the shrubbery.

Now a massive two-legged figure emerged from a shadowed corner and blocked his way. Gundersen thought at first it was a sulidor, but he realized it was merely a robot, probably a gardener. It said resonantly. 'Man, why are you here?'

'As a visitor. I'm a traveler seeking lodging for the night.'

'Does the woman expect you?'

'I'm sure she doesn't. But she'll be willing to see me. Tell her Edmund Gundersen is here.'

The robot scanned him carefully. 'I will tell her. Remain where you are and touch nothing.'

Gundersen waited. What seemed like an unhealthily long span of time went by. The twilight deepened, and one moon appeared. Some of the trees in the garden became luminous. A serpent, of the sort once used as a source of venom, slid silently across the path just in front of Gundersen and vanished. The wind shifted, stirring the trees and bringing him the faint sounds of a conversation of nildoror somewhere not far inland from the riverbank.

Then the robot returned and said, 'The woman will see you. Follow the path and enter the station.'

Gundersen went up the steps. On the porch he noticed unfamiliar-looking potted plants, scattered casually as though awaiting transplantation to the garden. Several of them waved tendrils at him or wistfully flashed lights intended to bring curious prey fatally close. He went in, and, seeing no one on the ground floor, caught hold of a dangling laddercoil and let himself be spun up to the first veranda. He observed that the station was as flawlessly maintained within as without, every surface clean and bright, the decorative murals unfaded, the artifacts from many worlds still mounted properly in their niches. This station had always been a showplace, but he was surprised to see it so attractive in these years of decay of Earth's presence on Belzagor.

'Seena?' he called.

He found her alone on the veranda, leaning over the rail. By the light of two moons he saw the deep cleft of her buttocks and thought she had chosen to greet him in the nude; but as she turned towards him he realized that a strange garment covered the front of her body. It was a pale, gelatinous sprawl, shapeless, purple-tinged, with the texture and sheen that he imagined an immense amoeba might have. The central mass of it embraced her belly and loins, leaving her hips and haunches bare; her left breast also was bare, but one broad pseudopod extended upward over the right one. The stuff was translucent, and Gundersen plainly could see the red eye of her covered nipple, and the narrow socket of her navel. It was also alive, to some degree, for it began to flow, apparently of its own will, sending out slow new strands that encircled her left thigh and right hip.

The eeriness of this clinging garment left him taken aback. Except for it, she appeared to be the Seena of old; she had gained some weight, and her breasts were heavier, her hips broader, yet she was still a handsome woman in the last bloom of youth. But the Seena of old would never have allowed such a bizarreness to touch her skin.

She regarded him steadily. Her lustrous black hair tumbled to her shoulders, as in the past. Her face was unlined. She faced him squarely and without shame, her feet firmly planted, her arms at ease, her head held high. 'I thought you were never coming back here, Edmund,' she said. Her voice had deepened, indicating some inner deepening as well. When he had last known her she had tended to speak too quickly, nervously pitching her tone too high, but now, calm and perfectly poised, she spoke with the resonance of a fine cello. 'Why are you back?' she asked.

'It's a long story, Seena. I can't even understand all of it myself. May I stay here tonight?'

'Of course. How needless to ask!'

'You look so good, Seena. Somehow I expected – after eight years –'

'A hag?'

'Well, not exactly.' His eyes met hers, and he was shaken abruptly by the rigidity he found there, a fixed and inflexible gaze, a beadiness that reminded him terrifyingly of the expression in the eyes of Dykstra and his woman at the last jungle station. 'I – I don't know what I expected,' he said.

'Time's been good to you also, Edmund. You have that stern, disciplined look, now – all the weakness burned away by years, only the core of manhood left. You've never looked better.'

'Thank you.'

'Won't you kiss me?' she asked.

'I understand you're a married woman.'

She winced and tightened one fist. The thing she was wearing reacted also, deepening in color and shooting a pseudopod up to encircle, though not to conceal, her bare breast. 'Where did you hear that?' she asked.

'At the coast. Van Beneker told me you married Jeff Kurtz.'

'Yes. Not long after you left, as a matter of fact.'

'I see. Is he here?'

She ignored his question. 'Don't you *want* to kiss me? Or do you have a policy about kissing other men's wives?'

He forced a laugh. Awkwardly, self-consciously, he reached for her, taking her lightly by the shoulders and drawing her towards him. She was a tall woman. He inclined his head, trying to put his lips to hers without having any part of his body come in contact with the amoeba. She pulled back before the kiss.

'What are you afraid of?' she asked.

'What you're wearing makes me nervous.'

'The slider?'

'If that's what it's called.'

'It's what the sulidoror call it,' Seena said. 'It comes from the central plateau. It clings to one of the big mammals there and lives by metabolizing perspiration. Isn't it splendid?'

'I thought you hated the plateau.'

'Oh, that was a long time ago. I've been there many times. I brought the slider back on the last trip. It's as much of a pet as it is something to wear. Look.' She touched it lightly and it went through a series of colour changes, expanding as it approached the blue end of the spectrum, contracting towards the red. At its greatest extension it formed a complete tunic covering Seena from throat to thighs. Gundersen became aware of something dark and pulsing at the heart of it, resting just above her loins, hiding the pubic triangle: its nerve-center, perhaps. 'Why do you dislike it?' she asked. 'Here. Put your hand on it.' He made no move. She took his hand in hers and touched it to her side; he felt the slider's cool dry surface and was surprised that it was not slimy. Easily Seena moved his hand upwards until it came to the heavy globe of a breast, and instantly the slider contracted, leaving the firm warm flesh bare to his fingers. He cupped it a moment, and, uneasy, withdrew his hand. Her nipples had hardened; her nostrils had flared.

He said, 'The slider's very interesting. But I don't like it on you.'

'Very well.' She touched herself at the base of her belly, just above the organism's core. It shrank inward and flowed down her leg in one swift rippling movement, gliding away and collecting itself at the far side of the veranda. 'Is that better?' Seena asked, naked, now, sweat-shiny, moist-lipped.

The coarseness of her approach startled him. Neither he nor she had ever worried much about nudity, but there was a deliberate sexual aggressiveness about this kind of self-display that seemed out of keeping with what he regarded as her character. They were old friends, yes; they had once been lovers for several years; they had been married in all but the name for many months of that time; but even so the ambiguity of their parting should have destroyed whatever intimacy once existed. And, leaving the question of her marriage to Kurtz out of it, the fact that they had not seen one another for eight years seemed to him to dictate the necessity of a more gradual return to physical closeness. He felt that by making herself pantingly available to him within minutes of his unexpected arrival she was committing a breach not of morals but of aesthetics.

'Put something on,' he said quietly. 'And not the slider. I can't have a serious conversation with you while you're waving all those jiggling temptations in my face.'

'Poor conventional Edmund. All right. Have you had dinner?'

'No.'

'I'll have it served out here. And drinks. I'll be right back.'

She entered the building. The slider remained behind on the veranda; it rolled tentatively towards Gundersen, as though offering to climb up and be worn by him for a while, but he glared at it and enough feeling got through to make the plateau creature move hurriedly away. A minute later a robot emerged, bearing a tray on which two golden cocktails sat. It offered one drink to Gundersen, set the other on the railing, and noiselessly departed. Then Seena returned, chastely clad in a soft grey shift that descended from her shoulders to her shins.

'Better?' she asked.

'For now.' They touched glasses; she smiled; they put their drink to their lips. 'You remembered that I don't like sonic snouts,' he said.

'I forget very little, Edmund.'

'What's it like, living up here?'

'Serene. I never imagined that my life could be so calm. I read a good deal; I help the robots tend the garden; occasionally there are guests; sometimes I travel. Weeks often go by without my seeing another human being.'

'What about your husband?'

'Weeks often go by without my seeing another human being,' she said.

'You're alone here? You and the robots?'

'Quite alone.'

'But the other Company people must come here fairly frequently.'

'Some do. There aren't many of us left now,' Seena said. 'Less than a hundred, I imagine. About six at the Sea of Dust. Van Beneker down by the hotel. Four or five at the old rift station. And so on – little islands of Earthmen widely scattered. There's a sort of a social circuit, but it's a sparse one.'

'Is this what you wanted when you chose to stay here?' Gundersen asked.

'I didn't know what I wanted, except that I wanted to stay. But I'd do it again. Knowing everything I know, I'd do it just the same way.'

He said, 'At the station just south of here, below the falls, I saw Harold Dykstra –'

'Henry Dykstra.'

'Henry. And a woman I didn't know.'

'Pauleen Mazor. She was one of the customs girls, in the time of the Company. Henry and Pauleen are my closest neighbours, I guess. But I haven't seen them in years. I never go south of the falls any more, and they haven't come here.'

'They're dead, Seena.'

'Oh?'

'It was like stepping into a nightmare. A sulidor led me to them. The station was a wreck, mould and fungoids every-where, and something was hatching inside them, the larvae of some kind of basket-shaped red sponge that hung on a wall and dripped black oil –'

'Things like that happen,' Seena said, not sounding disturbed. 'Sooner or later this planet catches everyone, though always in a different way.'

'Dykstra was unconscious, and the woman was begging to be put out of her misery, and –'

'You said they were dead.'

'Not when I got there. I told the sulidor to kill them. There was no hope of saving them. He split them open, and then I used my torch on them.'

'We had to do that for Gio' Salamone, too,' Seena said. 'He was staying at Fire Point, and went out into the Sea of Dust and got some kind of crystalline parasite into a cut. When Kurtz and Ced Cullen found him, he was all cubes and prisms, outcroppings of the most beautiful iridescent minerals breaking through his skin everywhere. And he was still alive. For a while. Another drink?'

'Please. Yes.'

She summoned the robot. It was quite dark, now. A third moon had appeared.

In a low voice Seena said, 'I'm so happy you came tonight, Edmund. It was such a wonderful surprise.'

'Kurtz isn't here now?'

'No,' she said. 'He's away, and I don't know when he'll be back.'

'How has it been for him, living here?'

'I think he's been quite happy, generally speaking. Of course, he's a very strange man.'

'He is,' Gundersen said.

'He's got a quality of sainthood about him, I think.'

'He would have been a dark and chilling saint, Seena.'

'Some saints are. They don't all have to be St Francis of Assisi.'

'Is cruelty one of the desirable traits of a saint?'

'Kurtz saw cruelty as a dynamic force. He made himself an artist of cruelty.'

'So did the Marquis de Sade. Nobody's canonized *him*.'

'You know what I mean,' she said. 'You once spoke of Kurtz
to me, and you called him a fallen angel. That's exactly right.
I saw him out among the nildoror, dancing with hundreds of
them, and they came to him and practically worshiped him.
There he was, talking to them, caressing them. And yet also
doing the most destructive things to them as well, but they
loved it.'

'What kind of destructive things?'

'They don't matter. I doubt that you'd approve. He – gave
them drugs, sometimes.'

'The serpent venom?'

'Sometimes.'

'Where is he now? Out playing with the nildoror?'

'He's been ill for a while.' The robot now was serving
dinner. Gundersen frowned at the strange vegetables on his
plate. 'They're perfectly safe,' Seena said. 'I grow them myself,
in back. I'm quite the farmer.'

'I don't remember any of these.'

'They're from the plateau.'

Gundersen shook his head. 'When I think of how disgusted
you were by the plateau, how strange and frightening it seemed
to you that time we had to crash-land there –'

'I was a child then. When was it, eleven years ago? Soon
after I met you. I was only twenty years old. But on Belzagor
you must defeat what frightens you, or you will be defeated.
I went back to the plateau. Again and again. It ceased to
be strange to me, and so it ceased to frighten me, and so
I came to love it. And brought many of its plants and animals back here to live with me. It's so very different from
the rest of Belzagor – cut off from everything else, almost
alien.'

'You went there with Kurtz?'

'Sometimes. And sometimes with Ced Cullen. And most
often alone.'

'Cullen,' Gundersen said. 'Do you see him often?'

'Oh, yes. He and Kurtz and I have been a kind of triumvirate.

My other husband, almost. I mean, in a spiritual way. Physical too, at times, but that's not as important.'

'Where is Cullen now?' he asked, looking intently into her harsh and glossy eyes.

Her expression darkened. 'In the north. The mist country.'

'What's he doing there?'

'Why don't you go ask him?' she suggested.

'I'd like to do just that,' Gundersen said. 'I'm on my way up mist country, actually, and this is just a sentimental stop on the way. I'm traveling with five nildoror going for rebirth. They're camped in the bush out there somewhere.'

She opened a flask of a musky gray-green wine and gave him some. 'Why do you want to go to the mist country?' she asked tautly.

'Curiosity. The same motive that sent Cullen up there, I guess.'

'I don't think his motive was curiosity.'

'Will you amplify that?'

'I'd rather not,' she said.

The conversation sputtered into silence. Talking to her led only in circles, he thought. This new serenity of hers could be maddening. She told him only what she cared to tell him, playing with him, seemingly relishing the touch of her sweet contralto voice on the night air, communicating no information at all. This was not a Seena he had ever known. The girl he had loved had been resilient and strong, but not crafty or secretive; there had been an innocence about her that seemed totally lost now. Kurtz might not be the only fallen angel on this planet.

He said suddenly, 'The fourth moon has risen!'

'Yes. Of course. Is that so amazing?'

'One rarely sees four, even in this latitude.'

'It happens at least ten times a year. Why waste your awe? In a little while the fifth one will be up, and –'

Gundersen gasped. 'Is that what tonight is?'

'The Night of Five Moons, yes.'

'No one told me!'

'Perhaps you never asked.'

'Twice I missed it because I was at Fire Point. One year I was at sea, and once I was in the southern mist country, the time that the copter went down. And so on and on. I managed to see it only once, Seena, right here, ten years ago, with you, when things were at their best for us. And now, to come in by accident and have it happen!'

'I thought you had arranged to be here deliberately. To commemorate that other time.'

'No. No. Pure coincidence.'

'Happy coincidence, then.'

'When does it rise?'

'Perhaps an hour.'

He watched the four bright dots swimming through the sky. It was so long ago that he had forgotten where the fifth moon should be coming from. Its orbit was retrograde, he thought. It was the most brilliant of the moons, too, with a high-albedo surface of ice, smooth as a mirror.

Seena filled his glass again. They had finished eating. 'Excuse me,' she said. 'I'll be back soon.'

Alone, he studied the sky and tried to comprehend this strangely altered Seena, this mysterious woman whose body had grown more voluptuous and whose soul, it seemed, had turned to stone. He saw now that the stone had been in her all along: at their breakup, for example, when he had put in for transfer to Earth, and she had absolutely refused to leave Holman's World. I love you, she had said, and I'll always love you, but this is where I stay. Why? Why? Because I want to stay, she told him. And she stayed; and he was just as stubborn, and left without her; and they slept together on the beach beneath the hotel on his last night, so that the warmth of her body was still on his skin when he boarded the ship that took him away. She loved him and he loved her, but they broke apart, for he saw no future on this world, and she saw all her future on it. And she had married Kurtz. And she had explored the unknown plateau. And she spoke in a rich deep new voice, and let alien amoebas clasp her loins, and shrugged at the news that two nearby Earthmen had died a horrible death. Was she still Seena, or some subtle counterfeit?

Nildoror sounds drifted out of the darkness. Gundersen heard another sound, too, closer by, a kind of stifled snorting grunt that was wholly unfamiliar to him. It seemed like a cry of pain, though perhaps that was his imagination. Probably it was one of Seena's plateau beasts, snuffling around searching for tasty roots in the garden. He heard it twice more, and then not again.

Time went by and Seena did not return.

Then he saw the fifth moon float placidly into the sky, the size of a large silver coin, and so bright that it dazzled the eye. About it the other four danced, two of them mere tiny dots, two of them more imposing, and the shadows of the moonslight shattered and shattered again as planes of brilliance intersected. The heavens poured light upon the land in icy cascades. He gripped the rail of the veranda and silently begged the moons to hold their pattern; like Faust he longed to cry out to the fleeting moment, stay, stay forever, stay, you are beautiful! But the moons shifted, driven by the unseen Newtonian machinery; he knew that in another hour two of them would be gone and the magic would ebb. Where was Seena?

'Edmund?' she said, from behind him.

She was bare, again, and once more the slider was on her body, covering her loins, sending a long thin projection up to encompass only the nipple of each ripe breast. The light of the five moons made her tawny skin glitter and shine. Now she did not seem coarse to him, nor overly aggressive; she was perfect in her nudity, and the moment was perfect, and unhesitatingly he went to her. Quickly he dropped his clothing. He put his hands to her hips, touching the slider, and the strange creature understood, flowing obediently from her body, a chastity belt faithless to its task. She leaned towards him, her breasts swaying like fleshy bells, and he kissed her, here, here, there, and they sank to the veranda floor, to the cold smooth stone.

Her eyes remained open, and colder than the floor, colder than the shifting light of the moons, even at the moment when he entered her.

But there was nothing cold about her embrace. Their bodies thrashed and tangled, and her skin was soft and her kiss was hungry, and the years rolled away until it was the old time again, the happy time. At the highest moment he was dimly aware of that strange grunting sound once more. He clasped her fiercely and let his eyes close.

Afterward they lay side by side, wordless in the moonslight, until the brilliant fifth moon had completed its voyage across the sky and the Night of the Five Moons had become as any other night.

TEN

He slept by himself in one of the guest rooms on the top-most level of the station. Awakening unexpectedly early, he watched the sunrise coming over the gorge, and went down to walk through the gardens, which still were glistening with dew. He strolled as far as the edge of the river, looking for his nildoror companions; but they were not to be seen. For a long time he stood beside the river watching the irresistible downward sweep of that immense volume of water. Were there fish in the river here, he wondered? How did they avoid being carried over the brink? Surely anything once caught up in that mighty flow would have no choice but to follow the route dictated for it, and be swept towards the terrible drop.

He went back finally to the station. By the light of morning Seena's garden seemed less sinister to him. Even the plants and animals of the plateau appeared merely strange, not menacing; each geographical district of this world had its own typical fauna and flora, that was all, and it was not the fault of the plateau's creatures that man had not chosen to make himself at ease among them.

A robot met him on the first veranda and offered him breakfast.

'I'll wait for the woman,' Gundersen said.

'She will not appear until much later in the morning.'

'That's odd. She never used to sleep that much.'

'She is with the man,' the robot volunteered. 'She stays with him and comforts him at this hour.'

'What man?'

'The man Kurtz, her husband.'

Gundersen said, amazed, 'Kurtz is here at the station?'

'He lies ill in his room.'

She said he was away somewhere, Gundersen thought. She didn't know when he'd be coming back.

Gundersen said, 'Was he in his room last night?'

'He was.'

'How long has he been back from his last journey away from here?'

'One year at the solstice,' the robot said. 'Perhaps you should consult the woman on these matters. She will be with you after a while. Shall I bring breakfast?'

'Yes,' Gundersen said.

But Seena was not long in arriving. Ten minutes after he had finished the juices, fruits, and fried fish that the robot had brought him, she appeared on the veranda, wearing a filmy white wrap through which the contours of her body were evident. She seemed to have slept well. Her skin was clear and glowing, her stride was vigorous, her dark hair streamed buoyantly in the morning breeze; but yet the curiously rigid and haunted expression of her eyes was unchanged, and clashed with the innocence of the new day.

He said, 'The robot told me not to wait breakfast for you. It said you wouldn't be down for a long while.'

'That's all right. I'm not usually down this early, it's true. Come for a swim?'

'In the river?'

'No, silly!' She stripped away her wrap and ran down the steps into the garden. He sat frozen a moment, caught up in the rhythms of her swinging arms, her jouncing buttocks; then he followed her. At a twist in the path that he had not noticed before she turned to the left and halted at a circular pool that appeared to have been punched out of the living rock on the river's flank. As he reached it, she launched herself in a fine arching dive, and appeared to hang suspended a moment, floating above the dark water, her breasts drawn into a startling roundness by gravity's pull. Then she went under. Before she came up for breath, Gundersen was naked and in the pool beside her. Even in this mild climate the water was bitterly cold.

'It comes from an underground spring,' she told him. 'Isn't it wonderful? Like a rite of purification.'

A gray tendril rose from the water behind her, tipped with rubbery claws. Gundersen could find no words to warn her. He pointed with short stabbing motions of two fingers and made hollow chittering noises of horror. A second tendril spiraled out of the depths and hovered over her. Smiling, Seena turned, and seemed to fondle some large creature; there was a thrashing in the water and then the tendrils slipped out of view.

'What was *that*?'

'The monster of the pool,' she said. 'Ced Cullen brought it for me as a birthday present two years ago. It's a plateau medusa. They live in lakes and sting things.'

'How big is it?'

'Oh, the size of a big octopus, I'd say. Very affectionate. I wanted Ced to catch me a mate for it, but he didn't get around to it before he went north, and I suppose I'll have to do it myself before long. The monster's lonely.' She pulled herself out of the pool and sprawled out on a slab of smooth black rock to dry in the sun. Gundersen followed her. From this side of the pool, with the light penetrating the water at just the right angle, he was able to see a massive many-limbed shape far below. Seena's birthday present.

He said, 'Can you tell me where I can find Ced now?'

'In the mist country.'

'I know. That's a big place. Any particular part?'

She rolled over on to her back and flexed her knees. Sunlight made prisms of the droplets of water on her breasts. After a long silence she said, 'Why do you want to find him so badly?'

'I'm making a sentimental journey to see old friends. Ced and I were very close, once. Isn't that reason enough for me to go looking for him?'

'It's no reason to betray him, is it?'

He stared at her. The fierce eyes now were closed; the heavy mounds of her breasts rose and fell slowly, serenely. 'What do you mean by that?' he asked.

'Didn't the nildoror put you up to going after him?'

'What kind of crazy talk is that?' he blurted, not sounding convincingly indignant even to himself.

'Why must you pretend?' she said, still speaking from within that impregnable core of total assurance. 'The nildoror want him brought back from there. By treaty they're prevented from going up there and getting him themselves. The sulidoror don't feel like extraditing him. Certainly none of the Earthmen living on this planet will fetch him. Now, as an outsider you need nildoror permission to enter the mist country, and since you're a stickler for the rules you probably applied for such permission, and there's no special reason why the nildoror should grant favors to you unless you agree to do something for them in return. Eh? Q.E.D.'

'Who told you all this?'

'Believe me, I worked it all out for myself.'

He propped his head on his hand and reached out admiringly with the other hand to touch her thigh. Her skin was dry and warm now. He let his hand rest lightly, and then not so lightly, on the firm flesh. Seena showed no reaction. Softly he said, 'Is it too late for us to make a treaty?'

'What kind?'

'A nonaggression pact. We've been fencing since I got here. Let's end the hostilities. I've been hiding things from you, and you've been hiding things from me, and what good is it? Why can't we simply help one another? We're two human beings on a world that's much stranger and more dangerous than most people suspect, and if we can't supply a little mutual aid and comfort, what are the ties of humanity worth?'

She said quietly,

> 'Ah, love, let us be true
> To one another: for the world, which seems
> To lie before us like a land of dreams,
> So various, so beautiful, so new –'

The words of the old poem flowed up from the well of his memory. His voice cut in:

> ' – Hath really neither joy, nor love, nor light,
> Nor certitude, nor peace, nor help for pain;
> And we are here as on a darkling plain
> Swept with confused alarms of struggle and flight
> Where – where –'

'"Where ignorant armies clash by night,"' she finished for him. 'Yes. How like you it is, Edmund, to fumble your lines just at the crucial moment, just at the final climax.'

'Then there's to be no nonaggression pact?'

'I'm sorry. I shouldn't have said that.' She turned towards him, took his hand from her thigh, pressed it tenderly between her breasts, brushed her lips against it. 'All right, we've been playing little games. They're over, and now we'll speak only truth, but you go first. Did the nildoror ask you to bring Ced Cullen out of the mist country?'

'Yes,' Gundersen said. 'It was the condition of my entry.'

'And you promised you'd do it?'

'I made certain reservations and qualifications, Seena. If he won't go willingly, I'm not bound by honor to force him. But I do have to find him, at least. That much I've pledged. So I ask you again to tell me where I should look.'

'I don't know,' she said. 'I have no idea. He could be anywhere at all up there.'

'Is this the truth?'

'The truth,' she said, and for a moment the harshness was gone from her eyes, and her voice was the voice of a woman and not that of a cello.

'Can you tell me, at least, why he fled, why they want him so eagerly?'

She was slow in replying. Finally she said, 'About a year ago, he went down into the central plateau on one of his regular collecting trips. He was planning to get me another medusa, he said. Most of the time I went with him into the plateau, but this time Kurtz was ill and I had to stay behind. Ced went to a part of the plateau we had never visited before, and there he found a group of nildoror taking part in some kind of religious ceremony. He stumbled right into them and evidently he profaned the ritual.'

'Rebirth?' Gundersen asked.

'No, they do rebirth only in the mist country. This was something else, something almost as serious, it seems. The nildoror were furious. Ced barely escaped alive. He came back here and said he was in great trouble, that the nildoror wanted him, that he had committed some sort of sacrilege and had to take sanctuary. Then he went north, with a posse of nildoror chasing him right to the border. I haven't heard anything since. I have no contact with the mist country. And that's all I can tell you.'

'You haven't told me what sort of sacrilege he committed,' Gundersen pointed out.

'I don't know it. I don't know what kind of ritual it was, or what he did to interrupt it. I've told you only as much as he told me. Will you believe that?'

'I'll believe it,' he said. He smiled. 'Now let's play another game, and this time I'll take the lead. Last night you told me that Kurtz was off on a trip, that you hadn't seen him for a long time and didn't know when he'd be back. You also said he'd been sick, but you brushed over that pretty quickly. This morning, the robot who brought me breakfast said that you'd be late coming down, because Kurtz was ill and you were with him in his room, as you were every morning at this time. Robots don't ordinarily lie.'

'The robot wasn't lying. I was.'

'Why?'

'To shield him from you,' Seena said. 'He's in very bad shape, and I don't want him to be disturbed. And I knew that if I told you he was here, you'd want to see him. He isn't strong enough for visitors. It was an innocent lie, Edmund.'

'What's wrong with him?'

'We aren't sure. You know, there isn't much of a medical service left on this planet. I've got a diagnostat, but it gave me no useful data when I put him through it. I suppose I could describe his disease as a kind of cancer. Only cancer isn't what he has.'

'Can you describe the symptoms?'

'What's the use? His body began to change. He became something strange and ugly and frightening, and you don't need to know the details. If you thought that what had happened to Dykstra and Pauleen was horrible, you'd be rocked to your roots by Kurtz. But I won't let you see him. It's as much to shield you from him as the other way around. You'll be better off not seeing him.' Seena sat up, cross-legged on the rock, and began to untangle the wet snarled strands of her hair. Gundersen thought he had never seen her looking as beautiful as she looked right at this moment, clothed only in alien sunlight, her flesh taut and ripe and glowing, her body supple, full-blown, mature. And the fierceness of her eyes, the one jarring discordancy? Had that come from viewing, each morning, the horror that Kurtz now was? She said after a long while, 'Kurtz is being punished for his sins.'

'Do you really believe that?'

'I do,' she said. 'I believe that there are such things as sins, and that there is retribution for sin.'

'And that an old man with a white beard is up there in the sky, keeping score on everyone, running the show, tallying up an adultery here, a lie there, a spot of gluttony, a little pride?'

'I have no idea who runs the show,' said Seena. 'I'm not even sure that anyone does. Don't mislead yourself, Edmund: I'm not trying to import medieval theology to Belzagor. I won't give you the Father, the Son, and the Holy Ghost, and say that all over the universe certain fundamental principles hold true. I simply say that here on Belzagor we live in the presence of certain moral absolutes, native to this planet, and if a stranger comes to Belzagor and transgresses against those absolutes, he'll regret it. This world is not ours, never was, never will be, and we who live here are in a constant state of peril, because we don't understand the basic rules.'

'What sins did Kurtz commit?'

'It would take me all morning to name them,' she said. 'Some were sins against the nildoror, and some were sins against his own spirit.'

'We all committed sins against the nildoror,' Gundersen said.

'In a sense, yes. We were proud and foolish, and we failed to see them for what they were, and we used them unkindly. That's a sin, yes, of course, a sin that our ancestors committed all over Earth long before we went into space. But Kurtz had a greater capacity for sin than the rest of us, because he was a greater man. Angels have farther to fall, once they fall.'

'What did Kurtz do to the nildoror? Kill them? Dissect them? Whip them?'

'Those are sins against their bodies,' said Seena. 'He did worse.'

'Tell me.'

'Do you know what used to go on at the serpent station, south of the spaceport?'

'I was there for a few weeks with Kurtz and Salamone,' Gundersen said. 'Long ago, when I was very new here, when you were still a child on Earth. I watched the two of them call serpents out of the jungle, and milk the raw venom from them, and give the venom to nildoror to drink. And drink the venom themselves.'

'And what happened then?'

He shook his head. 'I've never been able to understand it. When I tried it with them, I had the illusion that the three of us were turning into nildoror. And that three nildoror had turned into *us*. I had a trunk, four legs, tusks, spines. Everything looked different; I was seeing through nildoror eyes. Then it ended, and I was in my own body again, and I felt a terrible rush of guilt, of shame. I had no way of knowing whether it had been a real bodily metamorphosis or just hallucination.'

'It was hallucination,' Seena told him. 'The venom opened your mind, your soul, and enabled you to enter the nildor consciousness, at the same time that the nildor was entering yours. For a little while that nildor thought he was Edmund Gundersen. Such a dream is great ecstasy to a nildor.'

'Is this Kurtz's sin, then? To give ecstasy to nildoror?'

'The serpent venom,' Seena said, 'is also used in the rebirth ceremony. What you and Kurtz and Salamone were doing down there in the jungle was going through a very mild – *very* mild – version of rebirth. And so were the nildoror. But it was blasphemous rebirth for them, for many reasons. First, because it was held in the wrong place. Second, because it was done without the proper rituals. Third, because the celebrants who guided the nildoror were men, not sulidoror, and so the entire thing became a wicked parody of the most sacred act this planet has. By giving those nildoror the venom, Kurtz was tempting them to dabble in something diabolical, literally diabolical. Few nildoror can resist that temptation. He found pleasure in the act – both in the hallucinations that the venom gave him, and in the tempting of the nildoror. I think that he enjoyed the tempting even more than the hallucinations, and that was his worst sin, for through it he led innocent nildoror into what passes for damnation on this planet. In twenty years on Belzagor he inveigled hundreds, perhaps thousands, of nildoror into sharing a bowl of venom with him. Finally his presence became intolerable, and his own hunger for evil became the source of his destruction. And now he lies upstairs, neither living nor dead, no longer a danger to anything on Belzagor.'

'You think that staging the local equivalent of a Black Mass is what brought Kurtz to whatever destiny it is that you're hiding from me?'

'I know it,' Seena replied. She got to her feet, stretched voluptuously, and beckoned to him. 'Let's go back to the station now.'

As though this were time's first dawn they walked naked through the garden, close together, the warmth of the sun and the warmth of her body stirring him and raising a fever in him. Twice he considered pulling her to the ground and taking her amidst these alien shrubs, and twice he held back, not knowing why. When they were a dozen meters from the house he felt desire climb again, and he turned to her and put his hand on her breast. But she said, 'Tell me one more thing, first.'

'If I can.'

'Why have you come back to Belzagor? Really. What draws you to the mist country?'

He said, 'If you believe in sin, you must believe in the possibility of redemption from sin.'

'Yes.'

'Well, then, I have a sin on my conscience, too. Perhaps not as grave a sin as the sins of Kurtz, but enough to trouble me, and I've come back here as an act of expiation.'

'How have you sinned?' she asked.

'I sinned against the nildoror in the ordinary Earthman way, by collaborating in their enslavement, by patronizing them, by failing to credit their intelligence and their complexity. In particular I sinned by preventing seven nildoror from reaching rebirth on time. Do you remember, when the Monroe dam broke, and I commandeered those pilgrims for a labor detail? I used a fusion torch to make them obey, and on my account they missed rebirth. I didn't know that if they were late for rebirth they'd lose their turn, and if I had known I wouldn't have thought it mattered. Sin within sin within sin. I left here feeling stained. Those seven nildoror bothered me in my dreams. I realized that I had to come back and try to cleanse my soul.'

'What kind of expiation do you have in mind?' she asked.

His eyes had difficulty meeting hers. He lowered them, but that was worse, for the nakedness of her unnerved him even more, as they stood together in the sunlight outside the station. He forced his glance upwards again.

He said, 'I've determined to find out what rebirth is, and to take part in it. I'm going to offer myself to the sulidoror as a candidate.'

'No.'

'Seena, what's wrong? You –'

She trembled. Her cheeks were blazing, and the rush of scarlet spread even to her breasts. She bit her lip, spun away from him, and turned back. 'It's insanity,' she said. 'Rebirth isn't something for Earthmen. Why do you think you can possibly expiate anything by getting yourself mixed up in an alien religion, by surrendering yourself to a process none of us knows anything about, by –'

'I have to, Seena.'

'Don't be crazy.'

'It's an obsession. You're the first person I've ever spoken to about it. The nildoror I'm traveling with aren't aware of it. I can't stop. I owe this planet a life, and I'm here to pay. I have to go, regardless of the consequences.'

She said, 'Come inside the station with me.' Her voice was flat, mechanical, empty.

'Why?'

'Come inside.'

He followed her silently in. She led him to the middle level of the building, and into a corridor blocked by one of her robot guardians. At a nod from her the robot stepped aside. Outside a room at the rear she paused and put her hand to the door's scanner. The door rolled back. Seena gestured to him to walk in with her.

He heard the grunting, snorting sound that he had heard the night before, and now there was no doubt in his mind that it had been a cry of terrible throttled pain.

'This is the room where Kurtz spends his time,' Seena said.

She drew a curtain that had divided the room. 'And this is Kurtz,' she said.

'It isn't possible,' Gundersen murmured. 'How – how –'

'How did he get that way?'

'Yes.'

'As he grew older he began to feel remorse for the crimes he had committed. He suffered greatly in his guilt, and last year he resolved to undertake an act of expiation. He decided to travel to the mist country and undergo rebirth. This is what they brought back to me. This is what a human being looks like, Edmund, when he's undergone rebirth.'

ELEVEN

What Gundersen beheld was apparently human, and probably it had once even been Jeff Kurtz. The absurd length of the body was surely Kurtzlike, for the figure in the bed seemed to be a man and a half long, as if an extra section of vertebrae and perhaps a second pair of femurs had been spliced in. The skull was plainly Kurtz's too: mighty white dome, jutting brow-ridges. The ridges were even more prominent than Gundersen remembered. They rose above Kurtz's closed eyes like barricades guarding against some invasion from the north. But the thick black brows that had covered those ridges were gone. So were the lush, almost feminine eyelashes.

Below the forehead the face was unrecognizable.

It was as if everything had been heated in a crucible and allowed to melt and run. Kurtz's fine high-bridged nose was now a rubbery smear, so snoutlike that Gundersen was jolted by its resemblance to a sulidor's. His wide mouth now had slack, pendulous lips that drooped open, revealing toothless gums. His chin sloped backward in pithecanthropoid style. Kurtz's cheekbones were flat and broad, wholly altering the planes of his face.

Seena drew the coverlet down to display the rest. The body in the bed was utterly hairless, a long boiled-looking pink thing like a giant slug. All superfluous flesh was gone, and the skin lay like a shroud over plainly visible ribs and muscles. The proportions of the body were wrong. Kurtz's waist was an impossibly great distance from his chest, and his legs, though long, were not nearly as long as they should have been; his ankles seemed to crowd his knees. His toes had fused, so that his feet terminated in bestial pads. Perhaps by compensation, his fingers had added extra joints and were great spidery things that flexed and clenched in irregular rhythms. The attachment of his arms to his torso appeared strange, though it was not until Gundersen saw Kurtz slowly rotate his left arm through a 360-degree twist that he realized the armpit must have been reconstructed into some kind of versatile ball-and-socket arrangement.

Kurtz struggled desperately to speak, blurting words in a language Gundersen had never heard. His eyeballs visibly stirred beneath his lids. His tongue slipped forth to moisten his lips. Something like a three-lobed Adam's apple bobbed in his throat. Briefly he humped his body, drawing the skin tight over curiously broadened bones. He continued to speak. Occasionally an intelligible word in English or nildororu emerged, embedded in a flow of gibberish: 'River . . . death . . . lost . . . horror . . . river . . . cave . . . warm . . . lost . . . warm . . . smash . . . black . . . go . . . god . . . horror . . . born . . . lost . . . born . . .'

'What is he saying?' Gundersen asked.

'No one knows. Even when we can understand the words, he doesn't make sense. And mostly we can't even understand the words. He speaks the language of the world where he must live now. It's a very private language.'

'Has he been conscious at all since he's been here?'

'Not really,' Seena said. 'Sometimes his eyes are open, but he never responds to anything around him. Come. Look.' She went to the bed and drew Kurtz's eyelids open. Gundersen saw eyes that had no whites at all. From rim to rim their shining surfaces were a deep, lustrous black, dappled by random spots of light blue. He held three fingers up before those eyes and waved his hand from side to side. Kurtz took no notice. Seena released the lids, and the eyes remained open, even when the tips of Gundersen's fingers approached quite closely. But as Gundersen withdrew his hand, Kurtz lifted his right hand and seized Gundersen's wrist. The grotesquely elongated fingers encircled the wrist completely, met, and coiled half-way around it again. Slowly and with tremendous strength Kurtz pulled Gundersen down until he was kneeling beside the bed.

Now Kurtz spoke only in English. As before he seemed to be in desperate anguish, forcing the words out of some nightmare recess, with no perceptible accenting or punctuation: 'Water sleep death save sleep sleep fire love water dream cold sleep plan rise fall rise fall rise rise rise.' After a moment he added, 'Fall.' Then the flow of nonsense syllables returned and the fingers relinquished their fierce grip on Gundersen's wrist.

Seena said, 'He seemed to be telling us something. I never heard him speak so many consecutive intelligible words.'

'But what was he saying?'

'I can't tell you that. But a meaning was there.'

Gundersen nodded. The tormented Kurtz had delivered his testament, his blessing: *Sleep plan rise fall rise fall rise rise rise. Fall.* Perhaps it even made sense.

'And he reacted to your presence,' Seena went on. 'He saw you, he took your arm! Say something to him. See if you can get his attention again.'

'Jeff?' Gundersen whispered, kneeling. 'Jeff, do you remember me? Edmund Gundersen. I've come back, Jeff. Can you hear anything I'm saying? If you understand me, Jeff, raise your right hand again.'

Kurtz did not raise his hand. He uttered a strangled moan, low and appalling; then his eyes slowly closed and he lapsed into a rigid silence. Muscles rippled beneath his altered skin. Beads of acrid sweat broke from his pores. Gundersen got to his feet shortly and walked away.

'How long was he up there?' he asked.

'Close to half a year. I thought he was dead. Then two sulidoror brought him back, on a kind of stretcher.'

'Changed like this?'

'Changed. And here he lies. He's changed much more than you imagine,' Seena said. 'Inside, everything's new and different. He's got almost no digestive tract at all. Solid food is impossible for him; I give him fruit juices. His heart has extra chambers. His lungs are twice as big as they should be. The diagnostat couldn't tell me a thing, because he didn't correspond to any of the parameters for a human body.'

'And this happened to him in rebirth?'

'In rebirth, yes. They take a drug, and it changes them. And it works on humans too. It's the same drug they use on Earth for organ regeneration, the venom, but here they use a stronger dose and the body runs wild. If you go up there, Edmund, this is what'll happen to you.'

'How do you *know* it was rebirth that did this to him?'

'I know.'

'How?'

'That's what he said he was going up there for. And the sulidoror who brought him back said he had undergone rebirth.'

'Maybe they were lying. Maybe rebirth is one thing, a beneficial thing, and there's another thing, a harmful thing, which they gave to Kurtz because he had been so evil.'

'You're deceiving yourself,' Seena said. 'There's only one process, and this is its result.'

'Possibly different people respond differently to the process, then. If there is only one process. But I still say you can't be sure that it was rebirth that actually did this to him.'

'Don't talk nonsense!'

'I mean it. Maybe something within Kurtz made him turn out like this, and I'd turn out another way. A better way.'

'Do you *want* to be changed, Edmund?'

'I'd risk it.'

'You'd cease to be human!'

'I've tried being human for quite a while. Maybe it's time to try something else.'

'I won't let you go,' Seena said.

'You won't? What claim do you have on me?'

'I've already lost Jeff to them. If you go up there too –'

'Yes?'

She faltered. 'All right. I've got no way to threaten you. But don't go.'

'I have to.'

'You're just like him! Puffed up with the importance of your own supposed sins. Imagining the need for some kind of ghastly redemption. It's sick, don't you see? You just want to hurt yourself, in the worst possible way.' Her eyes glittered even more brightly. 'Listen to me. If you need to suffer, I'll help you. You want me to whip you? Stamp on you? If you've got to play masochist, I'll play sadist for you. I'll give you all the torment you want. You can wallow in it. But don't go up mist country. That's carrying a game too far, Edmund.'

'You don't understand, Seena.'

'Do you?'

'Perhaps I will, when I come back from there.'

'You'll come back like *him*!' she screamed. She rushed towards Kurtz's bed. 'Look at him! Look at those feet! Look at his eyes! His mouth, his nose, his fingers, his everything! He isn't human any more. Do you want to lie there like him – muttering nonsense, living in some weird dream all day and all night?'

Gundersen wavered. Kurtz *was* appalling; was the obsession so strong on him that he wanted to undergo the same transformation?

'I have to go,' he said, less firmly than before.

'He's living in hell,' Seena said. 'You'll be there too.'

She came to Gundersen and pressed herself against him. He felt the hot tips of her breasts grazing his skin; her hands clawed his back desperately; her thighs touched his. A great sadness came over him, for all that Seena once had meant to him, for all that she had been, for what she had become, for what her life must be like with this monster to care for. He was shaken by a vision of the lost and irrecoverable past, of the dark and uncertain present, of the bleak, frightening future. Again he wavered. Then he gently pushed her away from him. 'I'm sorry,' he said. 'I'm going.'

'Why? Why? What a *waste*!' Tears trickled down her cheeks. 'If you need a religion,' she said, 'pick an Earth religion. There's no reason why you have to –'

'There is a reason,' Gundersen said. He drew her close to him again and very lightly kissed her eyelids, and then her lips. Then he kissed her between the breasts and released her. He walked over to Kurtz and stood for a moment looking down, trying to come to terms with the man's bizarre metamorphosis. Now he noticed something he had not observed earlier: the thickened texture of the skin of Kurtz's back, as if dark little plaques were sprouting on both sides of his spine. No doubt there were many other changes as well, apparent only on a close inspection. Kurtz's eyes opened once again, and the black glossy orbs moved, as if seeking to meet Gundersen's eyes. He stared down at them, at the pattern of blue speckles against the shining solid background. Kurtz said, amidst many sounds Gundersen could not comprehend, 'Dance . . . live . . . seek . . . die . . . die.'

It was time to leave.

Walking past the motionless, rigid Seena, Gundersen went out of the room. He stepped on to the veranda and saw that his five nildoror were gathered outside the station, in the garden, with a robot uneasily watching lest they begin ripping up the rarities for fodder. Gundersen called out, and Srin'gahar looked up.

'I'm ready,' Gundersen said. 'We can leave as soon as I have my things.'

He found his clothes and prepared to depart. Seena came to him again: she was dressed in a clinging black robe, and her slider was wound around her left arm. Her face was bleak. He said, 'Do you have any messages for Ced Cullen, if I find him?'

'I have no messages for anyone.'

'All right. Thanks for the hospitality, Seena. It was good to see you again.'

'The next time I see you,' she said, 'you won't know who I am. Or who you are.'

'Perhaps.'

He left her and went to the nildoror. Srin'gahar silently accepted the burden of him. Seena stood on the veranda of the station, watching them move away. She did not wave, nor did he. In a little while he could no longer see her. The procession moved out along the bank of the river, past the place where Kurtz had danced all night with the nildoror so many years ago.

Kurtz. Closing his eyes, Gundersen saw the glassy blind stare, the lofty forehead, the flattened face, the wasted flesh, the twisted legs, the deformed feet. Against that he placed his memories of the old Kurtz, that graceful and extraordinary-looking man, so tall and slender, so self-contained. What demons had driven Kurtz, in the end, to surrender his body and his soul to the priests of rebirth? How long had the reshaping of Kurtz taken, and had he felt any pain during the process, and how much awareness did he now have of his own condition? What had Kurtz said? I am Kurtz who toyed with your souls, and now I offer you my own? Gundersen had never heard Kurtz speak in any tone but that of sardonic detachment; how could Kurtz have displayed real emotion, fear, remorse, guilt? I am Kurtz the sinner, take me and deal with me as you wish. I am Kurtz the fallen. I am Kurtz the damned. I am Kurtz, and I am yours. Gundersen imagined Kurtz lying in some misty northern valley, his bones softened by the elixirs of the sulidoror, his body dissolving, becoming a pink jellied lump which now was free to seek a new form, to strive towards an altered kurtzness that would be cleansed of its old satanic impurities. Was it presumptuous to place himself in the same class as Kurtz, to claim the same spiritual shortcomings, to go forward to meet that same terrible destiny? Was Seena not right, that this was a game, that he was merely

playing at masochistic self-dramatization, electing himself the
hero of a tragic myth, burdened by the obsession to undertake
an alien pilgrimage? But the compulsion seemed real enough
to him, and not at all a pretence. I will go, Gundersen told
himself. I am not Kurtz, but I will go, because I must go. In
the distance, receding but yet powerful, the roar and throb of
the waterfall still sounded, and as the rushing water hurtled
down the face of the cliff it seemed to drum forth the words
of Kurtz, the warning, the blessing, the threat, the prophecy,
the curse: *water sleep death save sleep sleep fire love water dream
cold sleep plan rise fall rise fall rise rise rise.*

    Fall.

TWELVE

For administrative purposes, the Earthmen during their years
of occupation of Holman's World had marked off boundaries
arbitrarily here and here and here, choosing this parallel of
latitude, that meridian of longitude, to encompass a district
or sector. Since Belzagor itself knew nothing of parallels of
latitude nor of other human measures and boundaries, those
demarcations by now existed only in the archives of the Company and in the memories of the dwindling human population
of the planet. But one boundary was far from arbitrary, and
its power still held: the natural line dividing the tropics from
the mist country. On one side of that line lay the tropical
highlands, sunbathed, fertile, forming the upper limit of the
central band of lush vegetation that stretched down to the
torrid equatorial jungle. On the other side of that line, only
a few kilometers away, the clouds of the north came rolling
in, creating the white world of the mists. The transition was
sharp and, for a newcomer, even terrifying. One could explain
it prosaically enough in terms of Belzagor's axial tilt and the
effect that had on the melting of polar snows; one could speak

learnedly of the huge icecaps in which so much moisture was locked, icecaps that extended so far into the temperate zones of the planet that the warmth of the tropics was able to nibble at them, liberating great masses of water-vapor that swirled upwards, curved poleward, and returned to the icecaps as regenerating snow; one could talk of the clash of climates and of the resulting marginal zones that were neither hot nor cold, and forever shrouded in the dense clouds born of that clash. But even these explanations did not prepare one for the initial shock of crossing the divide. One had a few hints: stray tufts of fog that drifted across the boundary and blotted out broad patches of the tropical highlands until the midday sun burned them away. Yet the actual change, when it came, was so profound, so absolute, that it stunned the spirit. On other worlds one grew accustomed to an easy transition from climate to climate, or else to an unvarying global climate; one could not easily accept the swiftness of the descent from warmth and ease to chill and bleakness that came here.

Gundersen and his nildoror companions were still some kilometers short of that point of change when a party of sulidoror came out of the bush and stopped them. They were border guards, he knew. There was no formal guard system, nor any other kind of governmental or quasigovernmental organization; but sulidoror nevertheless patrolled the border and interrogated those who wished to cross it. Even in the time of the Company the jurisdiction of the sulidoror had been respected, after a fashion: it might have cost too much effort to override it, and so the few Earthmen bound for the mist-country stations obligingly halted and stated their destinations before going on.

Gundersen took no part in the discussion. The nildoror and the sulidoror drew to one side, leaving him alone to contemplate the lofty banks of white mist on the northern horizon. There seemed to be trouble. One tall, sleek young sulidor pointed several times at Gundersen and spoke at length; Srin'gahar replied in a few syllables, and the sulidor appeared to grow angry, striding back and forth and vehemently knocking bark from trees with swipes of his huge claws. Srin'gahar spoke again, and then some agreement was reached; the angry sulidor stalked off into the forest and Srin'gahar beckoned to Gundersen to remount. Guided by the two sulidoror who remained, they resumed the northward march.

'What was the argument about?' Gundersen asked.

'Nothing.'

'But he seemed very angry.'

'It did not matter,' said Srin'gahar.

'Was he trying to keep me from crossing the boundary?'

'He felt you should not go across,' Srin'gahar admitted.

'Why? I have a many-born's permission.'

'This was a personal grudge, friend of my journey. The sulidor claimed that you had offended him in time past. He knew you from the old days.'

'That's impossible,' Gundersen said. 'I had hardly any contact at all with sulidoror back then. They never came out of the mist country and I scarcely ever went into it. I doubt that I spoke a dozen words to sulidoror in eight years on this world.'

'The sulidor was not wrong in remembering that he had had contact with you,' said Srin'gahar gently. 'I must tell you that there are reliable witnesses to the event.'

'When? Where?'

'It was a long time ago,' Srin'gahar said. The nildor appeared content with that vague answer, for he offered no other details. After a few moments of silence he added, 'The sulidor had good reason to be unhappy with you, I think. But we told him that you meant to atone for all of your past deeds, and in the end he yielded. The sulidoror often are a stubborn and vindictive race.'

'What did I *do* to him?' Gundersen demanded.

'We do not need to talk of such things,' replied Srin'gahar.

Since the nildor then retreated into impermeable silence, Gundersen had ample time to ponder the grammatical ambiguities of that last sentence. On the basis of its verbal content alone, it might have meant 'It is useless to talk of such things,' or 'It would be embarrassing to me to talk of such things,' or

'It is improper to talk of such things,' or 'It is tasteless to talk of such things.' Only with the aid of the supplementary gestures, the movements of the crestspines, the trunk, the ears, could the precise meaning be fathomed, and Gundersen had neither the skill nor the right position for detecting those gestures. He was puzzled, for he had no recollection of ever having given offence to a sulidor, and could not comprehend how he might have done it even indirectly or unknowingly; but after a while he concluded that Srin'gahar was deliberately being cryptic, and might be speaking in parables too subtle or too alien for an Earthman's mind to catch. In any case the sulidor had withdrawn his mysterious objections to Gundersen's journey, and the mist country was only a short distance away. Already the foliage of the jungle trees was more sparse than it had been a kilometer or two back, and the trees themselves were smaller and more widely spaced. Pockets of heavy fog now were more frequent. In many places the sandy yellow soil was wholly exposed. Yet the air was warm and clear and the underbrush profuse, and the bright golden sun was reassuringly visible; this was still unmistakably a place of benign and even common-place climate.

Abruptly Gundersen felt a cold wind out of the north, signaling change. The path wound down a slight incline, and when it rose on the far side he looked over a hummock into a broad field of complete desolation, a nothing's-land between the jungle and the mist country. No tree, no shrub, no moss grew here; there was only the yellow soil, covered with a sprinkling of pebbles. Beyond this sterile zone Gundersen was confronted by a white palisade fiercely glittering with reflected sunlight; seemingly it was a cliff of ice hundreds of metres high that barred the way as far as he could see. In the extreme distance, behind and above this white wall, soared the tip of a high-looming mountain, pale red in color, whose rugged spires and peaks and parapets stood forth sharply and strangely against an iron-gray sky. Everything appeared larger than life, massive, monstrous, excessive.

'Here you must walk by yourself,' said Srin'gahar. 'I regret this, but it is the custom. I can carry you no farther.'

Gundersen clambered down. He was not unhappy about the change; he felt that he should go to rebirth under his own power, and he had grown abashed at sitting astride Srin'gahar for so many hundreds of kilometers. But unexpectedly he found himself panting after no more than fifty meters of walking beside the five nildoror. The pace was slow and stately, but the air here, evidently, was thinner than he knew. He forced himself to hide his distress. He would go on. He felt light-headed, oddly buoyant, and he would master the pounding in his chest and the throbbing in his temples. The new chill in the air was invigorating in its austerity. They were half-way across the zone of emptiness, and Gundersen now could clearly tell that what had appeared to be a solid white barrier stretching across the world was in fact a dense wall of mist at ground level. Outlying strands of that mist kissed his face. At its clammy touch images of death stirred in his mind, skulls and tombs and coffins and veils, but they did not dismay him. He looked towards the rose-red mountain dominating the land far to the north, and as he did so the clouds that lay over the mist country parted, permitting the sun to strike the mountain's highest peak, a snowy dome of great expanse, and it seemed to him then that the face of Kurtz, transfigured, serene, looked down at him out of that smooth rounded peak.

From the whiteness ahead emerged the figure of a giant old sulidor: Na-sinisul, keeping the promise he had made to be their guide. The sulidoror who had accompanied them this far exchanged a few words with Na-sinisul and trudged off back towards the jungle belt. Na-sinisul gestured. Walking alongside Srin'gahar, Gundersen went forward.

In a few minutes the procession entered the mist.

He did not find the mist so solid once he was within it. Much of the time he could see for twenty or thirty or even fifty meters in any direction. There were occasional inexplicable vortices of fog that were much thicker in texture, and in which he could barely make out the green bulk of Srin'gahar beside him, but these were few and quickly traversed. The sky was gray and sunless; at moments the solar ball could be discerned as a vague glow behind the clouds. The landscape was one of raw rock, bare soil, and low trees – practically a tundra, although the air was merely chilly and not really cold. Many of the trees were of species also found in the south, but here they were dwarfed and distorted, sometimes not having the form of trees at all, but running along the ground like woody vines. Those trees that stood upright were no taller than Gundersen, and gray moss draped every branch. Beads of moisture dotted their leaves, their stems, the outcroppings of rock, and everything else.

No one spoke. They marched for perhaps an hour, until Gundersen's back was bowed and his feet were numb. The ground sloped imperceptibly upwards; the air seemed to grow steadily thinner; the temperature dropped quite sharply as the day neared its end. The dreary envelope of low-lying fog, endless and all-engulfing, exacted a toll on Gundersen's spirit. When he had seen that band of mist from outside, glittering brilliantly in the sunlight, it had stirred and excited him, but now that he was inside it he felt small cheer. All color and warmth had drained from the universe. He could not even see the glorious rose-red mountain from here.

Like a mechanical man, he went onward, sometimes even forcing himself into a trot to keep up with the others. Na-sinisul set a formidable pace, which the nildoror had no difficulty in meeting, but which pushed Gundersen to his limits. He was shamed by the loudness of his own gasps and grunts, though no one else took notice of them. His breath hung before his face, fog within fog. He wanted desperately to rest. He could not bring himself to ask the others to halt a while and wait for him, though. This was their pilgrimage; he was merely the self-invited guest.

A dismal dusk began to descend. The grayness grew more gray, and the faint hint of sunlight that had been evident now diminished. Visibility lessened immensely. The air became quite cold. Gundersen, dressed for jungle country, shivered.

Something that had never seemed important to him before now suddenly perturbed him: the alienness of the atmosphere. Belzagor's air, not only in the mist country but in all regions, was not quite the Earthnorm mix, for there was a trifle too much nitrogen and just a slight deficiency in oxygen; and the residual impurities were different as well. But only a highly sensitive olfactory system would notice anything amiss. Gundersen, conditioned to Belzagor's air by his years of service here, had had no awareness of a difference. Now he did. His nostrils reported a sinister metallic tang; the back of his throat, he believed, was coated with some dark grime. He knew it was foolish illusion born of fatigue. Yet for a few minutes he found himself trying to reduce his intake of breath, as though it was safest to let as little of the dangerous stuff as possible into his lungs.

He did not stop fretting over the atmosphere and other discomforts until the moment when he realized he was alone.

The nildoror were nowhere to be seen. Neither was Nasinisul. Mist engulfed everything. Stunned, Gundersen rolled back the screen of his memory and saw that he must have been separated from his companions for several minutes, without regarding it as in any way remarkable. By now they might be far ahead of him on some other road.

He did not call out.

He yielded first to the irresistible and dropped to his knees to rest. Squatting, he pressed his hands to his face, then put his knuckles to the cold ground and let his head loll forward while he sucked in air. It would have been easy to sprawl forward altogether and lose consciousness. They might find him sleeping in the morning. Or frozen in the morning. He struggled to rise, and succeeded on the third attempt.

'Srin'gahar?' he said. He whispered it, making only a private appeal for help.

Dizzy with exhaustion, he rushed forward, stumbling, sliding, colliding with trees, catching his feet in the undergrowth. He saw what was surely a nildor to his left and ran towards it, but when he clutched its flank he found it wet and icy, and he realized that he was grasping a boulder. He flung himself away from it. Just beyond, a file of massive shapes presented themselves: the nildoror marching past him? 'Wait?' he called, and ran, and felt the shock at his ankles as he plunged blindly into a shallow frigid rivulet. He fell, landing on hands and knees in the water. Grimly he crawled to the far bank and lay there, recognizing the dark blurred shapes now as those of low, broad trees whipped by a rising wind. All right, he thought. I'm lost. I'll wait right here until morning. He huddled into himself, trying to wring the cold water from his clothes.

The night came, blackness in place of grayness. He sought moons overhead and found none. A terrible thirst consumed him, and he tried to creep back to the brook, but he could not even find that. His fingers were numb; his lips were cracking. But he discovered an island of calm within his discomfort and fear, and clung to it, telling himself that none of what was happening was truly perilous and that all of it was somehow necessary.

Unknown hours later, Srin'gahar and Na-sinisul came to him.

First Gundersen felt the soft probing touch of Srin'gahar's trunk against his cheek. He recoiled and flattened himself on the ground, relaxing slowly as he realized what it was that had brushed his skin. Far above, the nildor said, 'Here he is.'

'Alive?' Na-sinisul asked, dark voice coming from worlds away, swaddled in layers of fog.

'Alive. Wet and cold. Edmundgundersen, can you stand up?'

'Yes. I'm all right, I think.' Shame flooded his spirit. 'Have you been looking for me all this time?'

'No,' said Na-sinisul blandly. 'We continued on to the village. There we discussed your absence. We could not be sure if you were lost or had separated yourself from us with a purpose. And then Srin'gahar and I returned. Did you intend to leave us?'

'I got lost,' Gundersen said miserably.

Even now he was not permitted to ride the nildor. He staggered along between Srin'gahar and Na-sinisul, now and then clutching the sulidor's thick fur or grasping the nildor's smooth haunch, steadying himself whenever he felt his strength leaving him or whenever the unseen footing grew difficult. In time lights glimmered in the dark, a pale lantern glow coming milkily through the fogbound blackness. Dimly Gundersen saw the shabby huts of a sulidor village. Without waiting for an invitation he lurched into the nearest of the ramshackle log structures. It was steep-walled, musty-smelling, with strings of dried flowers and the bunched skins of animals suspended from the rafters. Several seated sulidoror looked at him with no show of interest. Gundersen warmed himself and dried his clothing; someone brought him a bowl of sweet, thick broth, and a little while afterward he was offered some strips of dried meat, which were difficult to bite and chew but extraordinarily well flavored. Dozens of sulidoror came and went. Once, when the flap of hide covering the door was left open, he caught sight of his nildoror sitting just outside the hut. A tiny fierce-faced animal, fog-white and wizened, skittered up to him and inspected him with disdain: some northern beast, he supposed, that the sulidoror favoured as pets. The creature plucked at Gundersen's still soggy clothing and made a cackling sound. Its tufted ears twitched; its sharp little fingers probed his sleeve; its long prehensile tail curled and uncurled. Then it leaped into Gundersen's lap, seized his arm with quick claws, and nipped his flesh. The bite was no more painful than the pricking of a mosquito, but Gundersen wondered what hideous alien infection he would now contract. He made no move to push the little animal away, however. Suddenly a great sulidor paw descended, claws retracted, and knocked the beast across the room with a sweeping swing. The massive form of Na-sinisul lowered itself into a crouch next to Gundersen; the ejected animal chattered its rage from a far corner.

Na-sinisul said, 'Did the munzor bite you?'

'Not deeply. Is it dangerous?'

'No harm will come to you,' said the sulidor. 'We will punish the animal.'

'I hope you won't. It was only playing.'

'It must learn that guests are sacred,' said Na-sinisul firmly. He leaned close. Gundersen was aware of the sulidor's fishy breath. Huge fangs gaped in the deep-muzzled mouth. Quietly Na-sinisul said, 'This village will house you until you are ready to go on. I must leave with the nildoror, and continue to the mountain of rebirth.'

'Is that the big red mountain north of here?'

'Yes. Their time is very close, and so is mine. I will see them through their rebirths, and then my turn will come.'

'Sulidoror undergo rebirth too, then?'

Na-sinisul seemed surprised. 'How else could it be?'

'I don't know. I know so little about all of this.'

'If sulidoror were not reborn,' said Na-sinisul, 'then nildoror could not be reborn. One is inseparable from the other.'

'In what way?'

'If there were no day, could there be night?'

That was too cryptic. Gundersen attempted to press for an explanation, but Na-sinisul had come to speak of other matters. Avoiding the Earthman's questions, the sulidor said, 'They tell me that you have come to our country to speak with a man of your own people, the man Cullen. Is that so?'

'It is. It's one of the reasons I'm here, anyway.'

'The man Cullen lives three villages north of here, and one village to the west. He has been informed that you have arrived, and he summons you. Sulidoror of this village will conduct you to him when you wish to leave.'

'I'll leave in the morning,' Gundersen said.

'I must declare one thing to you first. The man Cullen has taken refuge among us, and so he is sacred. There can be no hope of removing him from our country and delivering him to the nildoror.'

'I ask only to speak with him.'

'That may be done. But your treaty with the nildoror is known to us. You must remember that you can fulfill that treaty only by a breach of our hospitality.'

Gundersen made no reply. He did not see how he could promise anything of this nature to Na-sinisul without at the same time forswearing his promise to the many-born Vol'himyor. So he clung to his original inner treaty: he would speak with Cedric Cullen, and then he would decide how to act. But it disturbed him that the sulidoror were already aware of his true purpose in seeking Cullen.

Na-sinisul left him. Gundersen attempted to sleep, and for a while he achieved an uneasy doze. But the lamps flickered all night in the sulidor hut, and lofty sulidoror strode back and forth noisily around and about him, and the nildoror just outside the building engaged in a long debate of which Gundersen could catch only a few meaningless syllables. Once Gundersen awoke to find the little long-eared munzor sitting on his chest and cackling. Later in the night three sulidoror hacked up a bloody carcass just next to the place where Gundersen huddled. The sounds of the rending of flesh awakened him briefly, but he slipped back into his troubled sleep, only to wake again when a savage quarrel erupted over the division of the meat. When the bleak gray dawn came, Gundersen felt more tired than if he had not slept at all.

He was given breakfast. Two young sulidoror, Se-holomir and Yi-gartigok, announced that they had been chosen to escort him to the village where Cullen was staying. Na-sinisul and the five nildoror prepared to leave for the mountain of rebirth. Gundersen made his farewells to his traveling companions.

'I wish you joy of your rebirth,' he said, and watched as the huge shapes moved off into the mist.

Not long afterward he resumed his own journey. His new guides were taciturn and aloof: just as well, for he wanted no conversation as he struggled through this hostile country. He needed to think. He was not sure at all what he would do after he had seen Cullen; his original plan of undergoing rebirth, which had seemed so noble in the abstract, now struck him as the highest folly – not only because of what Kurtz had become, but because he saw it as a trespass, an unspontaneous and self-conscious venture into the rites of an alien species. Go to the rebirth mountain, yes. Satisfy your curiosity. But submit to rebirth? For the first time he was genuinely unsure whether he would, and more than half suspicious that in the end he would draw back, unreborn.

The tundra of the border zone was giving way now to forest country which seemed a curious inversion to him: trees growing larger here in higher latitudes. But these were different trees. The dwarfed and twisted shrubs to his rear were natives of the jungle, making an unhappy adaptation to the mist; here, deeper in the mist country, true northern trees grew. They were thick-boled and lofty, with dark corrugated bark and tiny sprays of needle-like leaves. Fog shrouded their upper branches. Through this cold and misty forest too there ran lean, straggly animals, long-nosed and bony, which erupted from holes in the ground and sped up the sides of trees, evidently in quest of bough-dwelling rodents and birds. Broad patches of ground were covered with snow here, although summer was supposedly approaching in this hemisphere. On the second night northward there came a hailstorm when a dense and tossing cloud of ice rode towards them on a thin whining wind. Mute and glum, Gundersen's companions marched on through it, and so did he, not enjoying it.

Generally now the mist was light at ground level, and often there was none at all for an hour or more, but it congealed far overhead as an unbroken veil, hiding the sky. Gundersen became accustomed to the barren soil, the angular branches of so many bare trees, the chilly penetrating dampness that was so different from the jungle's humidity. He came to find beauty in the starkness. When fleecy coils of mist drifted like ghosts across a wide gray stream, when furry beasts sprinted over glazed fields of ice, when some hoarse ragged cry broke the incredible stillness, when the marchers turned an angle in the path and came upon a white tableau of harsh wintry emptiness, Gundersen responded with a strange kind of delight. In the mist country, he thought, the hour is always the hour just after dawn, when everything is clean and new.

On the fourth day Se-holomir said, 'The village you seek lies behind the next hill.'

THIRTEEN

It was a substantial settlement, forty huts or more arranged
in two rows, flanked on one side by a grove of soaring trees
and on the other by a broad silvery-surfaced lake. Gundersen
approached the village through the trees, with the lake shining
beyond. A light fall of snowflakes wandered through the
quiet air. The mists were high just now, thickening to an
impenetrable ceiling perhaps five hundred meters overhead.

'The man Cullen –?' Gundersen asked.

Cullen lay in a hut beside the lake. Two sulidoror guarded
the entrance, stepping aside at a word from Yi-gartigok; two
sulidoror more stood at the foot of the pallet of twigs and hides
on which Cullen rested. They too stepped aside, revealing a
burned-out husk of a man, a remnant, a cinder.

'Are you here to fetch me?' Cullen asked. 'Well, Gundy,
you're too late.'

Cullen's golden hair had turned white and gone coarse; it
was a tangled snowy mat through which patches of pale
blotched scalp showed. His eyes, once a gentle liquid green,
now were muddy and dull, with angry bloodshot streaks in
the yellowed whites. His face was a mask of skin over bones,
and the skin was flaky and rough. A blanket covered him from
the chest down, but the severe emaciation of his arms indicated
that the rest of his body probably was similarly eroded. Of the
old Cullen little seemed to remain except the mild, pleasant
voice and the cheerful smile, now grotesque emerging from
the ravaged face. He looked like a man of a hundred years.

'How long have you been this way?' Gundersen demanded.

'Two months. Three, I don't know. Time melts here, Gundy.
But there's no going back for me now. This is where I stop.
Terminal. Terminal.'

Gundersen knelt by the sick man's pallet. 'Are you in pain?
Can I give you something?'

'No pain,' Cullen said. 'No drugs. Terminal.'

'What do you have?' Gundersen asked, thinking of Dykstra and his woman lying gnawed by alien larvae in a pool of muck, thinking of Kurtz anguished and transformed at Shangri-la Falls, thinking of Seena's tale of Gio' Salamone turned to crystal. 'A native disease? Something you picked up around here?'

'Nothing exotic,' said Cullen. 'I'd guess it's the old inward rot, the ancient enemy. The crab, Gundy. The crab. In the gut. The crab's pincers are in my gut.'

'Then you *are* in pain?'

'No,' Cullen said. 'The crab moves slowly. A nip here, a nip there. Each day there's a little less of me. Some days I feel that there's nothing left of me at all. This is one of the better days.'

'Listen,' Gundersen said, 'I could get you downriver to Seena's place in a week. She's bound to have a medical kit, a spare tube of anticarcin for you. You aren't so far gone that we couldn't manage a remission if we act fast, and then we could ship you to Earth for template renewal, and –'

'No. Forget it.'

'Don't be absurd! We aren't living in the Middle Ages, Ced. A case of cancer is no reason for a man to lie down in a filthy hut and wait to die. The sulidoror will set up a litter for you. I can arrange it in five minutes. And then –'

'I wouldn't ever reach Seena's, and you know it,' Cullen said softly. 'The nildoror would pick me up the moment I came out of the mist country. You know that, Gundy. You *have* to know that.'

'Well –'

'I don't have the energy to play these games. You're aware, aren't you, that I'm the most wanted man on this planet?'

'I suppose so.'

'Were you sent here to fetch me?'

'The nildoror asked me to bring you back,' Gundersen admitted. 'I had to agree to it in order to get permission to come up here.'

'Of course.' Bitterly.

'But I stipulated that I wouldn't bring you out unless you'd come willingly,' Gundersen said. 'Along with certain other stipulations. Look, Ced, I'm not here as Judas. I'm traveling for reasons of my own, and seeing you is strictly a side-venture. But I want to help you. Let me bring you down to Seena's so you can get the treatment that you have to –'

'I told you,' Cullen said, 'the nildoror would grab me as soon as they had a chance.'

'Even if they knew you were mortally ill and being taken down to the falls for medical care?'

'Especially so. They'd love to save my soul as I lay dying. I won't give them the satisfaction, Gundy. I'm going to stay here, safe, beyond their reach, and wait for the crab to finish with me. It won't be long now. Two days, three, a week, perhaps even tonight. I appreciate your desire to rescue me. But I won't go.'

'If I got a promise from the nildoror to let you alone until you were able to undergo treat –'

'I won't go. You'd have to force me. And that's outside the scope of your promise to the nildoror, isn't it?' Cullen smiled for the first time in some minutes. 'There's a flask of wine in the corner there. Be a good fellow.'

Gundersen went to get it. He had to walk around several sulidoror. His colloquy with Cullen had been so intense, so private, that he had forgotten that the hut was full of sulidoror: his two guides, Cullen's guards, and at least half a dozen others. He picked up the wine and carried it to the pallet. Cullen, his hand trembling, nevertheless managed not to spill any. When he had his fill, he offered the flask to Gundersen, asking him so insistently to drink that Gundersen could not help but accept. The wine was warm and sweet.

'Is it agreed,' Cullen said, 'that you won't make any attempt to take me out of this village? I know you wouldn't seriously consider handing me over to the nildoror. But you might decide to get me out of here for the sake of saving my life. Don't do that either, because the effect would be the same: the nildoror would get me. I stay here. Agreed?'

Gundersen was silent a while. 'Agreed,' he said finally.

Cullen looked relieved. He lay back, face towards the wall, and said, 'I wish you hadn't wasted so much of my energy on that one point. We have so much more to talk about. And now I don't have the strength.'

'I'll come back later. Rest, now.'

'No. Stay here. Talk to me. Tell me where you've been all these years, why you came back here, who you've seen, what you've done. Give me the whole story. I'll rest while I'm listening. And afterward – and afterward –'

Cullen's voice faded. It seemed to Gundersen that he had slipped into unconsciousness, or perhaps merely sleep. Cullen's eyes were closed; his breath was slow and labored. Gundersen remained silent. He paced the hut uneasily, studying the hides tacked to the walls, the crude furniture, the debris of old meals. The sulidoror ignored him. Now there were eight in the hut, keeping their distance from the dying man and yet focusing all their attention on him. Momentarily Gundersen was unnerved by the presence of these giant two-legged beasts, these nightmare creatures with fangs and claws and thick tails and drooping snouts, who came and went and moved about as though he were less than nothing to them. He gulped more wine, though he found the texture and flavor of it unpleasant.

Cullen said, eyes still shut, 'I'm waiting. Tell me things.'

Gundersen began to speak. He spoke of his eight years on Earth, collapsing them into six curt sentences. He spoke of the restlessness that had come over him on Earth, of his cloudy and mystifying compulsion to return to Belzagor, of the sense of a need to find a new structure for his life now that he had lost the scaffolding that the Company had been for him. He spoke of his journey through the forest to the lakeside encampment, and of how he had danced among the nildoror, and how they had wrung from him the qualified promise to bring them Cullen. He spoke of Dykstra and his woman in their forest ruin, editing the tale somewhat in respect for Cullen's own condition, though he suspected that such charity was unnecessary. He spoke of

being with Seena again on the Night of Five Moons. He spoke
of Kurtz and how he had been changed through rebirth. He
spoke of his pilgrimage into the mist country.

He was certain at least three times that Cullen had fallen
asleep, and once he thought that the sick man's breathing
had ceased altogether. Each time Gundersen paused, though,
Cullen gave some faint indication – a twitch of the mouth,
a flick of the fingertips – that he should go on. At the end,
when Gundersen had nothing left to say, he stood in silence
a long while waiting for some new sign from Cullen, and at
last, faintly, Cullen said, 'Then?'

'Then I came here.'

'And where do you go after here?'

'To the mountain of rebirth,' said Gundersen quietly.

Cullen's eyes opened. With a nod he asked that his pillows
be propped up, and he sat forward, locking his fingers into his
coverlet. 'Why do you want to go there?' he asked.

'To find out what kind of thing rebirth is.'

'You saw Kurtz?'

'Yes.'

'He also wanted to learn more about rebirth,' Cullen said.
'He already understood the mechanics of it, but he had to
know its inwardness as well. To try it for himself. It wasn't
just curiosity, of course. Kurtz had spiritual troubles. He was
courting self-immolation because he'd persuaded himself he
needed to atone for his whole life. Quite true, too. Quite true.
So he went for rebirth. The sulidoror obliged him. Well, behold
the man. I saw him just before I came north.'

'For a while I thought I might try rebirth also,' said Gundersen,
caught unawares by the words surfacing in his mind. 'For the
same reasons. The mixture of curiosity and guilt. But I think
I've given the idea up now. I'll go to the mountain to see what
they do, but I doubt that I'll ask them to do it to me.'

'Because of the way Kurtz looks?'

'Partly. And also because my original plan looks too – well,
too *willed*. Too unspontaneous. An intellectual choice, not an
act of faith. You can't just go up there and volunteer for rebirth

in a coldly scientific way. You have to be driven to it.'

'As Kurtz was?' Cullen asked.

'Exactly.'

'And as you aren't?'

'I don't know any longer,' Gundersen said. 'I thought I was driven, too. I told Seena I was. But somehow, now that I'm so close to the mountain, the whole quest has started to seem artificial to me.'

'You're sure you aren't just afraid to go through with it?'

Gundersen shrugged. 'Kurtz wasn't a pretty sight.'

'There are good rebirths and bad rebirths,' Cullen said. 'He had a bad rebirth. How it turns out depends on the quality of one's soul, I gather, and on a lot of other things. Give us some more wine, will you?'

Gundersen extended the flask. Cullen, who appeared to be gaining strength, drank deeply.

'Have you been through rebirth?' Gundersen asked.

'Me? Never. Never even tempted. But I know a good deal about it. Kurtz wasn't the first of us to try it, of course. At least a dozen went before him.'

'Who?'

Cullen mentioned some names. They were Company men, all of them from the list of those who had died while on field duty. Gundersen had known some of them; others were figures out of the far past, before he or Cullen had ever come to Holman's World.

Cullen said, 'And there were others. Kurtz looked them up in the records, and the nildoror gave him the rest of the story. None of them ever returned from the mist country. Four or five of them turned out like Kurtz – transformed into monsters.'

'And the others?'

'Into archangels, I suppose. The nildoror were vague about it. Some sort of transcendental merging with the universe, an evolution to the next bodily level, a sublime ascent – that kind of thing. All that's certain is that they never came back to Company territory. Kurtz was hoping on an outcome like that. But unfortunately Kurtz was Kurtz, half angel and half demon, and that's how he was reborn. And that's what Seena nurses. In a way it's a pity you've lost your urge, Gundy. You might just turn out to have one of the good rebirths. Can you call Hor-tenebor over? I think I should have some fresh air, if we're going to talk so much. He's the sulidor leaning against the wall there. The one who looks after me, who hauls my old bones around. He'll carry me outside.'

'It was snowing a little while ago, Ced.'

'So much the better. Shouldn't a dying man see some snow? This is the most beautiful place in the universe,' Cullen said. 'Right here, in front of this hut. I want to see it. Get me Hor-tenebor.'

Gundersen summoned the sulidor. At a word from Cullen, Hor-tenebor scooped the fragile, shrunken invalid into his immense arms and bore him through the door-flap of the hut, setting him down in a cradle-like framework overlooking the lake. Gundersen followed. A heavy mist had descended on the village, concealing even the huts closest at hand, but the lake itself was clearly visible under the gray sky. Fugitive wisps of mist hung just above the lake's dull surface. A bitter chill was in the air, but Cullen, wrapped only in a thin hide, showed no discomfort. He held forth his hand, palm upraised, and watched with the wonder of a child as snowflakes struck it.

At length Gundersen said, 'Will you answer a question?'

'If I can.'

'What was it you did that got the nildoror so upset?'

'They didn't tell you when they sent you after me?'

'No,' Gundersen said. 'They said that you would, and that in any case it didn't matter to them whether I knew or not. Seena didn't know either. And I can't begin to guess. You were never the kind who went in for killing or torturing intelligent species. You couldn't have been playing around with the serpent venom the way Kurtz was – he was doing that for years and they never tried to grab him. So what could you possibly have done that caused so much –'

'The sin of Actaeon,' said Cullen.

'Pardon?'

'The sin of Actaeon, which was no sin at all, but really just an accident. In Greek myth he was a huntsman who blundered upon Diana bathing, and saw what he shouldn't have seen. She changed him into a stag and he was torn to pieces by his own hounds.'

'I don't understand what that has to do with –'

Cullen drew a long breath. 'Did you ever go up on the central plateau?' he asked, his voice low but firm. 'Yes. Yes, of course you did. I remember, you crash-landed there, you and Seena, on your way back to Fire Point after a holiday on the coast, and you were stranded a little while and weird animals bothered you and that was when Seena first started to hate the plateau. Right? Then you know what a strange and somehow mysterious place it is, a place apart from the rest of this planet, where not even the nildoror like to go. All right. I started to go there, a year or two after relinquishment. It became my private retreat. The animals of the plateau interested me, the insects, the plants, everything. Even the air had a special taste – sweet, clean. Before relinquishment, you know, it would have been considered a little eccentric for anybody to visit the plateau on his free time, or at any other time. Afterward nothing mattered to anyone. The world was mine. I made a few plateau trips. I collected specimens. I brought some little oddities to Seena, and she got to be fond of them before she realized they were from the plateau, and little by little I helped her overcome her irrational fear of the plateau. Seena and I went there often together, sometimes with Kurtz also. There's a lot of flora and fauna from the plateau at Shangri-la Station; maybe you noticed it. Right? We collected all that. The plateau came to seem like any other place to me, nothing supernatural, nothing eerie, merely a neglected backwoods region. And it was my special place, where I went whenever I felt myself growing empty or bored or stale. A year ago, maybe a little less than a year, I went into the plateau. Kurtz had just come back from his rebirth, and Seena was terribly depressed by what had happened to him, and I wanted to get her a gift, some animal, to cheer her up. This time I came down a little to the southwest of my usual landing zone, over in a part of the plateau I had never seen before, where two rivers meet. One of the first things I noticed was how ripped up the shrubbery was. Nildoror! Plenty nildoror! An immense area had been grazed, and you know how nildoror graze. It made me curious. Once in a while I had seen an isolated nildor on the plateau, always at a distance, but never a whole herd. So I followed the line of devastation. On and on it went, this scar through the forest, with broken branches and trampled underbrush, all the usual signs. Night came, and I camped, and it seemed to me I heard drums in the night. Which was foolish, since nildoror don't use drums; I realized after a while that I heard them dancing, pounding the ground, and these were reverberations carried through the soil. There were other sounds, too: screams, bellows, the cries of frightened animals. I had to know what was happening. So I broke camp in the middle of the night and crept through the jungle, hearing the noise grow louder and louder, until finally I reached the edge of the trees, where the jungle gave way to a kind of broad savanna running down to the river, and there in the open were maybe five hundred nildoror. Three moons were up, and I had no trouble seeing. Gundy, would you believe that they had *painted* themselves? Like savages, like something out of a nightmare. There were three deep pits in the middle of the clearing. One of the pits was filled with a kind of wet red mud, and the other two contained branches and berries and leaves that the nildoror had trampled to release dark pigments, one black, one blue. And I watched the nildoror going down to these pits, and first they'd roll in the pit of red mud and come up plastered with it, absolutely scarlet; and then they'd go to the adjoining pits and give each other dark stripes over the red, hosing it on with their trunks. A barbaric sight: all that color, all that flesh. When they were properly decorated, they'd go running – not strolling, *running* – across the field to the place of dancing, and they'd begin that four-step routine. You know it: boom boom *boom* boom. But infinitely more fierce and frightening now, on account of the war-paint. An army of wild-looking nildoror, stamping their feet, nodding their tremendous heads, lifting their trunks, bellowing, stabbing their tusks into the ground, capering, singing, flapping their ears. Frightening, Gundy, frightening. And the moonlight on their painted bodies –

'Keeping well back in the forest, I circled around to the west to get a better view. And saw something on the far side of the dancers that was even stranger than the paint. I saw a corral with log walls, huge, three or four times the size of this village. The nildoror couldn't have built it alone; they might have uprooted trees and hauled them with their trunks, but they must have needed sulidoror to help pile them up and shape them. Inside the corral were plateau animals, hundreds of them, all sizes and shapes. The big leaf-eating ones with giraffe necks, and the kind like rhinos with antlers, and timid ones like gazelles, and dozens that I'd never even seen before, all crowded together as if in a stockyard. There must have been sulidoror hunters out beating the bush for days, driving that menagerie together. The animals were restless and scared. So was I. I crouched in the darkness, waiting, and finally all the nildoror were properly painted, and then a ritual started in the midst of the dancing group. They began to cry out, mostly in their ancient language, the one we can't understand, but they were talking in ordinary nildororu, and eventually I understood what was going on. Do you know who these painted beasts were? They were sinning nildoror, nildoror who were in disgrace! This was the place of atonement and the festival of purification. Any nildor who had been tinged with corruption in the past year had to come here and be cleansed. Gundy, do you know what sin they had committed? They had taken the venom from Kurtz. The old game, the one everybody used to play down at the serpent station, give the nildoror a swig, take one yourself, let the hallucinations come? These painted prancing nildoror here had all been led astray by Kurtz. Their souls were stained. The Earthman-devil had found their one vulnerable place, the one area of temptation they couldn't resist. So here they were, trying to cleanse themselves. The central plateau is the nildoror purgatory. They don't live there because they need it for their rites, and obviously you don't set up an ordinary encampment in a holy place.

'They danced, Gundy, for hours. But that wasn't the rite of atonement. It was only the prelude to the rite. They danced until I was dizzy from watching them, the red bodies, the dark stripes, the boom of their feet, and then, when no moons were left in the sky, when dawn was near, the real ceremony started. I watched it, and I looked right down into the darkness of the race, into the real nildoror soul. Two old nildoror approached the corral and started kicking down the gate. They broke an opening maybe ten meters wide, and stepped back, and the penned-up animals came rushing out on to the plain. The animals were terrified from all the noise and dancing, and from being imprisoned, and they ran in circles, not knowing what to do or where to go. And the rest of the nildoror charged into them. The peaceful, noble, non-violent nildoror, you know? Snorting. Trampling. Spearing with their tusks. Lifting animals with their trunks and hurling them into trees. An orgy of slaughter. I became sick, just watching. A nildor can be a terrible machine of death. All that weight, those tusks, the trunk, the big feet – everything berserk, all restraints off. Some of the animals escaped, of course. But most were trapped right in the middle of the chaos. Crushed bodies everywhere, rivers of blood, scavengers coming out of the forest to have dinner while the killing was still going on. That's how the nildoror atone: sin for sin. That's how they purge themselves. The plateau is where they loose their violence, Gundy. They put aside all their restraints and let out the beast that's within them. I've never felt such horror as when I watched how they cleansed their souls. You know how much respect I had for the nildoror. Still have. But to see a thing like that, a massacre, a vision of hell – Gundy, I was numb with despair. The nildoror didn't seem to enjoy the killing, but they weren't hesitant about it, either; they just went on and on, because it had to be done, because this was the form of the ceremony, and they thought nothing more of it than Socrates would think of sacrificing a lamb to Zeus, a cock to Aesculapius. That was the real horror, I think. I watched the nildoror destroying life for the sake of their souls, and it was like dropping through a trapdoor, entering a new world whose existence I had never even suspected, a dark new world beneath the old. Then dawn came. The sun rose, lovely, golden, light glistening on the trampled corpses, and the nildoror were sitting calmly in the midst of the devastation, resting, calm, purged, all their inner storms over. It was amazingly peaceful. They had wrestled with their demons, and they had won. They had come through all the night's horror, all the ghastliness, and – I don't know how – they really *were* purged and purified. I can't tell you how to find salvation through violence and destruction. It's alien to me and probably to you. Kurtz knew, though. He took the same road as the nildoror. He fell and fell and fell, through level after level of evil, enjoying his corruption, glorying in depravity, and then in the end he was still able to judge himself and find himself wanting, and recoil at the darkness he found inside himself, and so he went and sought rebirth, and showed that the angel within him wasn't altogether dead. This finding of purity by passing through evil – you'll have to come to terms with it by yourself, Gundy. I can't help you. All I can do is tell you of the vision I had at sunrise that morning beside the field of blood. I looked into an abyss. I peered over the edge, and saw where Kurtz had gone, where these nildoror had gone. Where perhaps you'll go. I couldn't follow.

'And then they almost caught me.

'They picked up my scent. While the frenzy was on them, I guess they hadn't noticed – especially with hundreds of animals giving off fear-smells in the corral. But they began to sniff. Trunks started to rise and move around like periscopes. The odor of sacrilege was on the air. The reek of a blaspheming spying Earthman. Five, ten minutes they sniffed, and I stood in the bushes still wrapped in my vision, not even remotely realizing they were sniffing *me*, and suddenly it dawned on me that they knew I was there, and I turned and began to slip away through the forest, and they came after me. Dozens. Can you imagine what it's like to be chased through the jungle by a herd of angry nildoror? But I could fit through places too small for them. I gave them the slip. I ran and ran and ran, until I fell down dizzy in a thicket and vomited, and I rested, and then I heard them bashing along on my trail, and I ran some more. And came to a swamp, and jumped in, hoping they'd lose my scent. And hid in the reeds and marshes, while things I couldn't see nipped at me from below. And the nildoror ringed the entire region. We know you're in there, they called to me. Come out. Come out. We forgive you and we wish to purify you. They explained it all quite reasonably to me. I had inadvertently – oh, of course, inadvertently, they were diplomatic! – seen a ceremony that no one but a nildor was allowed to see, and now it would be necessary to wipe what I had seen from my mind, which could be managed by means of a simple technique that they didn't bother to describe to me. A drug, I guess. They invited me to come have part of my mind blotted out. I didn't accept. I didn't say anything. They went right on talking, telling me that they held no malice, that they realized it obviously hadn't been my intention to watch their secret ceremony, but nevertheless since I had seen it they must now take steps, et cetera, et cetera. I began to crawl downstream, breathing through a hollow reed. When I surfaced the nildoror were still calling to me, and now they sounded more angry, as far as it's possible to tell such a thing. They seemed annoyed that I had refused to come out. They didn't blame me for spying on them, but they did object that I wouldn't let them purify me. That was my real crime: not that I hid in the bushes and watched them, but declining afterward to undergo the treatment. That's what they still want me for. I stayed in the creek all day, and when it got dark I slithered out and picked up the vector-beep of my beetle, which turned out to be about half a kilometer away. I expected to find it guarded by nildoror, but it wasn't, and I got in and cleared out fast and landed at Seena's place by midnight. I knew I didn't have much time. The nildoror would be after me from one side of the continent to the other. I told her what had happened, more or less, and I collected some supplies, and took off for the mist country. The sulidoror would give me sanctuary. They're jealous of their sovereignty; blasphemy or not, I'd be safe here. I came to this village. I explored the mist country a good bit. Then one day I felt the crab in my guts and I knew it was all over. Since then I've been waiting for the end, and the end isn't far away.'

He fell silent.

Gundersen, after a pause, said, 'But why not risk going back? Whatever the nildoror want to do to you can't be as bad as sitting on the porch of a sulidor hut and dying of cancer.'

Cullen made no reply.

'What if they give you a memory-wiping drug?' Gundersen asked. 'Isn't it better to lose a bit of your past than to lose your whole future? If you'll only come back, Ced, and let us treat your disease –'

'The trouble with you, Gundy, is that you're too logical,' Cullen said. 'Such a sensible, reasonable, rational chap! There's another flask of wine inside. Would you bring it out?'

Gundersen walked past the crouching sulidoror into the hut, and prowled the musty darkness a few moments, looking for the wine. As he searched, the solution to the Cullen situation presented itself: instead of bringing Cullen to the medicine, he would bring the medicine to Cullen. He would abandon his journey towards the rebirth mountain at least temporarily and go down to Shangri-la Falls to get a dose of anticarcin for him. It might not be too late to check the cancer. Afterward, restored to health, Cullen could face the nildoror or not, as he pleased. What happens between him and the nildoror, Gundersen told himself will not be a matter that concerns me. I regard my treaty with Vol'himyor as nullified. I said I would bring Cullen forth only with his consent, and clearly he won't go willingly. So my task now is just to save his life. Then I can go to the mountain.

He located the wine and went outside with it.

Cullen leaned backward on the cradle, his chin on his chest, his eyes closed, his breath slow, as if his lengthy monologue had exhausted him. Gundersen did not disturb him. He put the wine down and walked away, strolling for more than an hour, thinking, reaching no conclusion. Then he returned. Cullen had not moved. 'Still asleep?' Gundersen asked the sulidoror.

'It is the long sleep,' one of them replied.

FOURTEEN

The mist came in close, bringing jewels of frost that hung from every tree, every hut; and by the brink of the leaden lake Gundersen cremated Cullen's wasted body with one long fiery burst of the fusion torch, while sulidoror looked on, silent, solemn. The soil sizzled a while when he was done, and the mist whirled wildly as cold air rushed in to fill the zone of warmth his torch had made. Within the hut were a few unimportant possessions. Gundersen searched through them, hoping to find a journal, a memoir, anything with the imprint of Cedric Cullen's soul and personality. But he found only some rusted tools, and a box of dried insects and lizards, and faded clothing. He left these things where he found them.

The sulidoror brought him a cold dinner. They let him eat undisturbed, sitting on the wooden cradle outside Cullen's hut. Darkness came, and he retreated into the hut to sleep. Se-holomir and Yi-gartigok posted themselves as guards before the entrance, although he had not asked them to stay there. He said nothing to them. Early in the evening he fell asleep.

He dreamed, oddly, not of the newly dead Cullen but of the still living Kurtz. He saw Kurtz trekking through the mist country, the old Kurtz, not yet metamorphosed to his present state: infinitely tall, pale, eyes burning in the domed skull, glowing with strange intelligence. Kurtz carried a pilgrim's staff and strode tirelessly forward into the mist. Accompanying him, yet not really with him, was a procession of nildoror, their green bodies stained bright red by pigmented mud; they halted whenever Kurtz halted, and knelt beside him, and from time to time he let them drink from a tubular canteen he was carrying. Whenever Kurtz offered his canteen to the nildoror, he and not they underwent a transformation. His lips joined in a smooth sealing; his nose lengthened; his eyes, his fingers, his toes, his legs changed and changed again. Fluid, mobile, Kurtz kept no form for long. At one stage in the journey he became a sulidor in all respects but one: his own high-vaulted bald head surmounted the massive hairy body. Then the fur melted from him, the claws shrank, and he took on another form, a lean loping thing, rapacious and swift with double-jointed elbows and long spindly legs. More changes followed. The nildoror sang hymns of adoration, chanting in thick monotonous skeins of gray sound. Kurtz was gracious. He bowed, he smiled, he waved. He passed around his canteen, which never needed replenishing. He rippled through cycle upon cycle of dizzy metamorphosis. From his backpack he drew gifts that he distributed among the nildoror: torches, knives, books, message cubes, computers, statues, color organs, butterflies, flasks of wine, sensors, transport modules, musical instruments, beads, old etchings, holy medallions, baskets of flowers, bombs, flares, shoes, keys, toys, spears. Each gift fetched ecstatic sighs and snorts and moos of gratitude from the nildoror; they frolicked about him, lifting their new treasures in their trunks, excitedly displaying them to one another. 'You see?' Kurtz cried. 'I am your benefactor. I am your friend. I am the resurrection and the life.' They came now to the place of rebirth, not a mountain in Gundersen's dream but rather an abyss, dark and deep, at the rim of which the nildoror gathered and waited. And Kurtz, undergoing so many transformations that his body flickered and shifted from moment to moment, now wearing horns, now covered with scales, now clad in shimmering flame, walked forward while the nildoror cheered him, saying to him, 'This is the place, rebirth will be yours,' and he stepped into the abyss, which enfolded him in absolute night. And then from the depths of the pit came a single prolonged cry, a shrill wail of terror and dismay so awful that it awakened

Gundersen, who lay sweating and shivering for hours waiting for dawn.

In the morning he shouldered his pack and made signs of departing. Se-holomir and Yi-gartigok came to him; and one of the sulidoror said, 'Where will you go now?'

'North.'

'Shall we go with you?'

'I'll go alone,' Gundersen said.

It would be a difficult journey, perhaps a dangerous one, but not impossible. He had direction-finding equipment, food concentrates, a power supply, and other such things. He had the necessary stamina. He knew that the sulidoror villages along the way would extend hospitality to him if he needed it. But he hoped not to need it. He had been escorted long enough, first by Srin'gahar, then by various sulidoror; he felt he should finish this pilgrimage without a guide.

Two hours after sunrise he set out.

It was a good day for beginning such an endeavor. The air was crisp and cool and clear and the mist was high; he could see surprisingly far in all directions. He went through the forest back of the village and emerged on a fair-sized hill from the top of which he was able to gauge the landscape ahead. He saw rugged, heavily forested country, much broken by rivers and streams and lakes; and he succeeded in glimpsing the tip of the mountain of rebirth, a jagged sentinel in the north. That rosy peak on the horizon seemed close enough to grasp. Just reach out; just extend the fingers. And the fissures and hillocks and slopes that separated him from his goal were no challenge; they could be traversed in a few quick bounds. His body was eager for the attempt: heartbeat steady, vision exceptionally keen, legs moving smoothly and tirelessly. He sensed an inward soaring of the soul, a restrained but ecstatic upsweep towards life and power; the phantoms that had veiled him for so many years were dropping away; in this chill zone of mist and snow he felt annealed, purified, tempered, ready to accept whatever must be accepted. A strange energy surged through him. He did not mind the thinness of the air, nor the cold, nor the bleakness of the land. It was a morning of unusual clarity, with bright sunlight cascading through the lofty covering of fog and imparting a dreamlike brilliance to the trees and bare soil. He walked steadily onward.

The mist closed in at midday. Visibility dwindled until Gundersen could see only eight or ten meters ahead. The giant trees became serious obstacles; their gnarled roots and writhing buttresses now were traps for unwary feet. He picked his way with care. Then he entered a region where large flat-topped boulders jutted at shallow angles from the ground, one after another, slick mist-slippery slabs forming stepping-stones to the land beyond. He had to crawl over them, blindly feeling along, not knowing how much of a drop he was likely to encounter at the far end of each boulder. Jumping off was an act of faith; one of the drops turned out to be about four meters, and he landed hard, so that his ankles tingled for fifteen minutes afterward. Now he felt the first fatigue of the day spreading through his thighs and knees. But yet the mood of controlled ecstasy, sober and nevertheless jubilant, remained with him.

He made a late lunch beside a small, flawlessly circular pond, mirror-bright, rimmed by tall narrow-trunked trees and hemmed in by a tight band of mist. He relished the privacy, the solitude of the place; it was like a spherical room with walls of cotton, within which he was perfectly isolated from a perplexing universe. Here he could shed the tensions of his journey, after so many weeks of traveling with nildoror and sulidoror, worrying all the while that he would give offence in some unknown but unforgivable way. He was reluctant to leave.

As he was gathering his belongings, an unwelcome sound punctured his seclusion: the drone of an engine not far overhead. Shading his eyes against the glare of the mist, he looked up, and after a moment caught a glimpse of an airborne beetle flying just below the cloud-ceiling. The little snubnosed vehicle moved in a tight circle, as if looking for something. For me, he wondered? Automatically he shrank back against a tree to hide, though he knew it was impossible for the pilot to see him

here even in the open. A moment later the beetle was gone,
vanishing in a bank of fog just to the west. But the magic of the
afternoon was shattered. That ugly mechanical droning noise
in the sky still reverberated in Gundersen's mind, shattering
his newfound peace.

An hour's march onward, passing through a forest of slender
trees with red gummy-looking bark, Gundersen encountered
three sulidoror, the first he had seen since parting from Yi-
gartigok and Se-holomir that morning. Gundersen was uneasy
about the meeting. Would they permit him free access here?
These three evidently were a hunting party returning to a
nearby village; two of them carried, lashed to a pole slung
from shoulder to shoulder, the trussed-up carcass of some
large four-legged grazing animal with velvety black skin and
long recurved horns. He felt a quick instinctive jolt of fear at
the sight of the three gigantic creatures coming towards him
among the trees; but to his surprise the fear faded almost as
rapidly as it came. The sulidoror, for all their ferocious mien,
simply did not hold a threat. True, they could kill him with
a slap, but what of that? They had no more reason to attack
him that he did to burn them with his torch. And here in their
natural surroundings, they did not even seem bestial or savage.
Large, yes. Powerful. Mighty of fang and claw. But natural,
fitting, proper, and so not terrifying.

'Does the traveler journey well?' asked the lead sulidoror,
the one who bore no part of the burden of the kill. He spoke
in a soft and civil tone, using the language of the nildoror.

'The traveler journeys well,' said Gundersen. He improvised
a return salutation: 'Is the forest kind to the huntsmen?'

'As you see, the huntsmen have fared well. If your path
goes towards our village, you are welcome to share our kill
this night.'

'I go towards the mountain of rebirth.'

'Our village lies in that direction. Will you come?'

He accepted the offer, for night was coming on, and a harsh
wind was slicing through the trees now. The sulidoror village
was a small one, at the foot of a sheer cliff half an hour's walk

to the north-east. Gundersen passed a pleasant night there. The villagers were courteous though aloof, in a manner wholly free of any hostility; they gave him a corner of a hut, supplied him with food and drink, and left him alone. He had no sense of being a member of a despised race of ejected conquerors, alien and unwanted. They appeared to look upon him merely as a wayfarer in need of shelter, and showed no concern over his species. He found that refreshing. Of course, the sulidoror did not have the same reasons for resentment as the nildoror, since these forest folk had never actually been turned into slaves by the Company; but he had always imagined a seething, sizzling rage within the sulidoror, and their easy-going kindness now was an agreeable departure from that image, which Gundersen now suspected might merely have been a projection of his own guilts. In the morning they brought him fruits and fish, and then he took his leave.

The second day of his journey alone was not as rewarding as the first. The weather was bad, cold and damp and frequently snowy, with dense mist hanging low nearly all the time. He wasted much of the morning by trapping himself in a cul-de-sac, with a long ridge of hills to his right, another to his left, and, unexpectedly, a broad and uncrossable lake appearing in front of him. Swimming it was unthinkable; he might have to pass several hours in its frigid water, and he would not survive the exposure. So he had to go on a wearying westward detour over the lesser ridge of hills, which swung him about so that by midday he was in no higher a latitude than he had been the night before. The sight of the fog-wreathed rebirth mountain drew him on, though, and for two hours of the afternoon he had the illusion that he was making up for the morning's delay, only to discover that he was cut off by a swift and vast river flowing from west to east, evidently the one that fed the lake that had blocked him earlier. He did not dare to swim this, either; the current would sweep him into the distant deeps before he had reached the farther bank. Instead he consumed more than an hour following the river upstream, until he came to a place where he might ford it. It was even wider here than below, but its bed looked much more shallow, and some geological upheaval had strewn a line of boulders across it like a necklace, from bank to bank. A dozen of the boulders jutted up, with white water swirling around them; the others, though submerged, were visible just below the surface. Gundersen stared across. He was able to hop from the top of one boulder to the next, keeping dry until he had gone nearly a third of the way. Then he had to scramble in the water, wading shin-deep, slipping and groping. The mist enveloped him. He might have been alone in the universe, with nothing ahead but billows of whiteness, nothing to the rear but the same. He could see no trees, no shore, not even the boulders awaiting him. He concentrated rigidly on keeping his footing and staying to his path. Putting one foot down awry, he slid and toppled, landing in a half-crouch in the river, drenched to the armpits, buffeted by the current, and so dizzied for a moment that he could not rise. All his energy was devoted to clinging to the angular mass of rock beneath him. After a few minutes he found the strength to get to his feet again, and tottered forward, gasping, until he reached a boulder whose upper face stood half a meter above the water; he knelt on it, chilled, soaked, shivering, trying to shake himself dry. Perhaps five minutes passed. With the mist clinging close, he got no drier, but at least he had his breath again, and he resumed his crossing. Experimentally reaching out the tip of a boot, he found another dry-topped boulder just ahead. He went to it. There was still another beyond it. Then came another. It was easy, now: he would make it to the far side without another soaking. His pace quickened, and he traversed another pair of boulders. Then, through a rift in the mist, he was granted a glimpse of the shore.

Something seemed wrong.

The mist sealed itself; but Gundersen hesitated to go on without some assurance that all was as it should be. Carefully he bent low and dipped his left hand in the water. He felt the thrust of the current coming from the right and striking his open palm. Wearily, wondering if cold and fatigue had affected his mind, he worked out the topography of his situation several times and each time came to the same dismaying conclusion: if I am making a northward crossing of a river that flows from west to east, I should feel the current coming from my *left*. Somehow, he realized, he had turned himself around while scrambling for purchase in the water, and since then he had with great diligence been heading back towards the southern bank of the river.

His faith in his own judgement was destroyed. He was tempted to wait here, huddled on this rock, for the mist to clear before going on; but then it occurred to him that he might have to wait through the night, or even longer. He also realized belatedly that he was carrying gear designed to cope with just such problems. Fumbling in his backpack, he pulled out the small cool shaft of his compass and aimed it at the horizon, sweeping his arm in an arc that terminated where the compass emitted its north-indicating beep. It confirmed his conclusions about the current, and he started across the river again, shortly coming to the place of the submerged stepping-stones were he had fallen. This time he had no difficulties.

On the far shore he stripped and dried his clothing and himself with the lowest-power beam of his fusion torch. Night now was upon him. He would not have regretted another invitation to a sulidoror village, but today no hospitable sulidoror appeared. He spent an uncomfortable night huddled under a bush.

The next day was warmer and less misty. Gundersen went warily forward, forever fearing that his hours of hard hiking might be wasted when he came up against some unforeseen new obstacle, but all went well, and he was able to cope with the occasional streams or rivulets that crossed his path. The land here was ridged and folded as though giant hands, one to the north and one to the south, had pushed the globe together; but as Gundersen was going down one slope and up the next, he was also gaining altitude constantly, for the entire continent sloped upwards towards the mighty plateau upon which the rebirth mountain was reared.

In the early afternoon the prevailing pattern of east-west

folds in the land subsided; here the landscape was skewed around so that he found himself walking parallel to a series of gentle north-south furrows, which opened into a wide circular meadow, grassy but treeless. The large animals of the north, whose names Gundersen did not know, grazed here in great numbers, nuzzling in the lightly snow-covered ground. There seemed to be only four or five species – something heavy-legged and humpbacked, like a badly designed cow, and something in the style of an oversized gazelle, and several others – but there were hundreds or even thousands of each kind. Far to the east, at the very border of the plain, Gundersen saw what appeared to be a small sulidoror hunting-party rounding up some of the animals.

He heard the drone of the engine again.

The beetle he had seen the other day now returned, passing quite low overhead. Instinctively Gundersen threw himself to the ground, hoping to go unnoticed. About him the animals milled uneasily, perplexed at the noise, but they did not bolt. The beetle drifted to a landing about a thousand meters north of him. He decided that Seena must have come after him, hoping to intercept him before he could submit himself to the sulidoror of the mountain of rebirth. But he was wrong. The hatch of the beetle opened, and Van Beneker and his tourists began to emerge.

Gundersen wriggled forward until he was concealed behind a tall stand of thistle-like plants on a low hummock. He could not abide the thought of meeting that crew again, not at this stage in his pilgrimage, when he had been purged of so many vestiges of the Gundersen who had been.

He watched them.

They were walking up to the animals, photographing them, even daring to touch some of the more sluggish beasts. Gundersen heard their voices and their laughter cracking the congealed silence; isolated words drifted randomly towards him, as meaningless as Kurtz's flow of dream-fogged gibberish. He heard, too, Van Beneker's voice cutting through the chatter, describing and explaining and expounding. These nine humans before him on the meadow seemed as alien to Gundersen as the sulidoror. More so, perhaps. He was aware that these last few days of mist and chill, this solitary odyssey through a world of whiteness and quiet, had worked a change in him that he barely comprehended. He felt lean of soul, stripped of the excess baggage of the spirit, a simpler man in all respects, and yet more complex.

He waited an hour or more, still hidden, while the tourist party finished touring the meadow. Then everyone returned to the beetle. Where now? Would Van take them north to spy on the mountain of rebirth? No. No. It wasn't possible. Van Beneker himself dreaded the whole business of rebirth, like any good Earthman; he wouldn't dare to trespass on that mysterious precinct.

When the beetle took off, though, it headed towards the north.

Gundersen, in his distress, shouted to it to turn back. As though heeding him, the gleaming little vehicle veered round as it gained altitude. Van Beneker must have been trying to catch a tailwind, nothing more. Now the beetle made for the south. The tour was over, then. Gundersen saw it pass directly above him and disappear into a lofty bank of fog. Choking with relief, he rushed forward, scattering the puzzled herds with wild loud whoops.

Now all obstacles seemed to be behind him. Gundersen crossed the valley, negotiated a snowy divide without effort, forded a shallow brook, pushed his way through a forest of short, thick, tightly packed trees with narrow pointed crowns. He slipped into an easy rhythm of travel, paying no heed any longer to cold, mist, damp, altitude, or fatigue. He was tuned to his task. When he slept, he slept soundly and well; when he foraged for food to supplement his concentrates, he found that which was good; when he sought to cover distance, he covered it. The peace of the misty forest inspired him to do prodigies. He tested himself, searching for the limits of his endurance, finding them, exceeding them at the next opportunity.

Through this phase of the journey he was wholly alone.

Sometimes he saw sulidoror tracks in the thin crust of snow that covered much of the land, but he met no one. The beetle did not return. Even his dreams were empty; the Kurtz phantom that had plagued him earlier was absent now, and he dreamed only blank abstractions, forgotten by the time of awakening.

He did not know how many days had elapsed since the death of Cedric Cullen. Time had flowed and melted in upon itself. He felt no impatience, no weariness, no sense of wanting it all to be over. And so it came as a mild surprise to him when, as he began to ascend a wide, smooth, shelving ledge of stone, about thirty meters wide, bordered by a wall of icicles and decorated in places by tufts of grass and scraggly trees, he looked up and realized that he had commenced the scaling of the mountain of rebirth.

FIFTEEN

From afar, the mountain had seemed to rise dramatically from the misty plain in a single sweeping thrust. But now that Gundersen was actually upon its lower slopes, he saw that at close range the mountain dissolved into a series of ramps of pink stone, one atop another. The totality of the mountain was the sum of that series, yet from here he had no sense of a unified bulk. He could not even see the lofty peaks and turrets and domes that he knew must hover thousands of meters above him. A layer of clinging mist severed the mountain less than half-way up, allowing him to see only the broad, incomprehensible base. The rest, which had guided him across hundreds of kilometers, might well have never been.

The ascent was easy. To the right and to the left Gundersen saw sheer faces, impossible spires, fragile bridges of stone linking ledge to ledge; but there was also a switch-back path, evidently of natural origin, that gave the patient climber access to the higher reaches. The dung of innumerable nildoror littered this long stone ramp, telling him that he must be on the right route. He could not imagine the huge creatures going up the mountain any other way. Even a sulidor would be taxed by those precipices and gullies.

Chattering munzoror leaped from ledge to ledge, or walked with soft, shuffling steps across terrifying abysses spanned by strands of vines. Goat-like beasts, white with diamond-shaped black markings, capered in graveled pockets of unreachable slopes, and launched booming halloos that echoed through the afternoon. Gundersen climbed steadily. The air was cold but invigorating; the mists were wispy at this level, giving him a clear view before and behind. He looked back and saw the fog-shrouded lowlands suddenly quite far below him. He imagined that he was able to see all the way to the open meadow where the beetle had landed.

He wondered when some sulidor would intercept him.

This was, after all, the most sacred spot on this planet. Were there no guardians? No one to stop him, to question him, to turn him back?

He came to a place about two hours' climb up the mountainside where the upward slope diminished and the ramp became a long horizontal promenade, curving off to the right and vanishing beyond the mass of the mountain. As Gundersen followed it, three sulidoror appeared, coming around the bend. They glanced briefly at him and went past, taking no other notice, as though it were quite ordinary that an Earthman should be going up the mountain of rebirth.

Or, Gundersen thought strangely, as though he were *expected*.

After a while the ramp turned upwards again. Now an overhanging stone ledge formed a partial roof for the path, but it was no shelter, for the little cackling wizen-faced munzoror nested up there, dropping pebbles and bits of chaff and worse things down. Monkeys? Rodents? Whatever they were, they introduced a sacrilegious note to the solemnity of this great peak, mocking those who went up. They dangled by their prehensile tails; they twitched their long tufted ears; they spat;

they laughed. What were they saying? 'Go away, Earthman, this is no shrine of yours!' Was that it? How about, 'Abandon hope, all ye who enter here!'

He camped for the night beneath that ledge. Munzoror several times scrambled across his face. Once he woke to what sounded like the sobbing of a woman, deep and intense, in the abyss below. He went to the edge and found a bitter snowstorm raging. Soaring through the storm, rising and sinking, rising and sinking, were sleek bat-like things of the upper reaches, with tubular black bodies and great rubbery yellow wings; they went down until they were lost to his sight, and sped upwards again towards their eyries clasping chunks of raw meat in their sharp red beaks. He did not hear the sobbing again. When sleep returned, he lay as if drugged until a brilliant dawn crashed like thunder against the side of the mountain.

He bathed in an ice-rimmed stream that sped down a smooth gully and intersected the path. Then he went upwards, and in the third hour of his morning's stint he overtook a party of nildoror plodding towards rebirth. They were not green but pinkish-gray, marking them as members of the kindred race, the nildoror of the eastern hemisphere. Gundersen had never known whether these nildoror enjoyed rebirth facilities in their own continent, or came to undergo the process here. That was answered now. There were five of them, moving slowly and with extreme effort. Their hides were cracked and ridged, and their trunks – thicker and longer than those of western nildoror – drooped limply. It wearied him just to look at them. They had good reason to be tired, though: since nildoror had no way of crossing the ocean, they must have taken the land route, the terrible northeastward journey across the dry bed of the Sea of Dust. Occasionally, during his tour of duty there, Gundersen had seen eastern nildoror dragging themselves through that crystalline wasteland, and at last he understood what their destination had been.

'Joy of your rebirth!' he called to them as he passed, using the terse eastern inflection.

'Peace be on your journey,' one of the nildoror replied calmly.

They, too, saw nothing amiss in his presence here. But he did. He could not avoid thinking of himself as an intruder, an interloper. Instinctively he began to lurk and skulk, keeping to the inside of the path as though that made him less conspicuous. He anticipated his rejection at any moment by some custodian of the mountain, stepping forth suddenly to block his climb.

Above him, another two or three spirals of the path overhead, he spied a scene of activity.

Two nildoror and perhaps a dozen sulidoror were in view up there, standing at the entrance to some dark chasm in the mountainside. He could see them only by taking up a precarious position at the rim of the path. A third nildor emerged from the cavern; several sulidoror went in. Some way-station, maybe, on the road to rebirth? He craned his neck to see, but as he continued along his path he reached a point from which that upper level was no longer visible.

It took him longer than he expected to reach it. The switchback path looped out far to one side in order to encircle a narrow jutting spiky tower of rock sprouting from the great mountain's flank, and the detour proved to be lengthy. It carried Gundersen well around to the north-eastern face. By the time he was able to see the level of the chasm again, a sullen twilight was falling, and the place he sought was still somewhere above him.

Full darkness came before he was on its level. A heavy blanket of fog sat close upon things now. He was perhaps midway up the peak. Here the path spread into the mountain's face, creating a wide plaza covered with brittle flakes of pale stone, and against the vaulting wall of the mountain Gundersen saw a black slash, a huge inverted V, the opening of what must be a mighty cavern. Three nildoror lay sleeping to the left of this entrance, and five sulidoror, to its right, seemed to be conferring.

He hung back, posting himself behind a convenient boulder and allowing himself wary peeps at the mouth of the cavern. The sulidoror went within, and for more than an hour nothing happened. Then he saw them emerge, awaken one of the nildoror, and lead it inside. Another hour passed before they came back for the second. After a while they fetched the third. Now the night was well advanced. The mist, the constant companion here, approached and clung. The big-beaked bat-creatures, like marionettes on strings, swooped down from higher zones of the mountain, shrieking past and vanishing in the drifting fog below, returning moments later in equally swift ascent. Gundersen was alone. This was his moment to peer into the cavern, but he could not bring himself to make the inspection. He hesitated, shivering, unable to go forward. His lungs were choked with mist. He could see nothing in any direction now; even the bat-beasts were invisible, mere dopplering blurts of sound as they rose and fell. He struggled to recapture some of the jauntiness he had felt on that first day after Cullen's death, setting out unaccompanied through this wintry land. With a conscious effort he found a shred of that vigor at last.

He went to the mouth of the cavern.

He saw only darkness within. Neither sulidoror nor nildoror were evident at the entrance. He took a cautious step inward. The cavern was cool, but it was a dry coolness far more agreeable than the mist-sodden chill outside. Drawing his fusion torch, he risked a quick flash of light and discovered that he stood in the center of an immense chamber, the lofty ceiling of which was lost in the shadows overhead. The walls of the chamber were a baroque fantasy of folds and billows and buttresses and fringes and towers, all of stone, polished and translucent, gleaming like convoluted glass during the instant that the light was upon them. Straight ahead, flanked by two rippling wings of stone that were parted like frozen curtains, lay a passageway, wide enough for Gundersen but probably something of a trial for the bulky nildoror who had earlier come this way.

He went towards it.

Two more brief flashes from the torch got him to it. Then he proceeded by touch, gripping one side of the opening and feeling his way into its depths. The corridor bent sharply to the left and, about twenty paces farther on, angled just as sharply the other way. As Gundersen came around the second bend a dim light greeted him. Here a pale green fungoid growth lining the ceiling afforded a minimal sort of illumination. He felt relieved and yet suddenly vulnerable, for, while he now could see, he could also be seen.

The corridor was about twice a nildor's width and three times a nildor's height, rising to the peaked vault in which the fungoids dwelled. It stretched for what seemed an infinite distance into the mountain. Branching off it on both sides, Gundersen saw, were secondary chambers and passages.

He advanced and peered into the nearest of these chambers. It held something that was large and strange and apparently alive. On the floor of a bare stone cell lay a mass of pink flesh, shapeless and still. Gundersen made out short thick limbs and a tail curled tightly over broad flanks; he could not see its head, nor any distinguishing marks by which he could associate it with a species he knew. It might have been a nildor, but it did not seem quite large enough. As he watched, it swelled with the intake of a breath, and slowly subsided. Many minutes passed before it took another breath. Gundersen moved on.

In the next cell he found a similar sleeping mound of unidentifiable flesh. In the third cell lay another. The fourth cell, on the opposite side of the corridor, contained a nildor of the western species, also in deep slumber. The cell beside it was occupied by a sulidor lying oddly on its back with its limbs poking rigidly upwards. The next cell held a sulidor in the same position, but otherwise quite startlingly different, for it had shed its whole thick coat of fur and lay naked, revealing awesome muscles beneath a gray, slicklooking skin. Continuing, Gundersen came to a chamber that housed something even more bizarre: a figure that had a nildor's spines and tusks and trunk but a sulidor's powerful arms and legs and a sulidor's frame. What nightmare composite was this? Gundersen stood awed before it for a long while, trying to comprehend how the head of a nildor might have been joined to the body of a sulidor. He realized that no such joining could have occurred; the sleeper here simply partook of the characteristics of both races in a single body. A hybrid? A genetic mingling?

He did not know. But he knew now that this was no mere way-station on the road towards rebirth. This was the place of rebirth itself.

Far ahead, figures emerged from one of the subsidiary corridors and crossed the main chamber: two sulidoror and a nildor. Gundersen pressed himself against the wall and remained motionless until they were out of sight, disappearing into some distant room. Then he continued inward.

He saw nothing but miracles. He was in a garden of fantasies where no natural barriers held.

Here was a round spongy mass of soft pink flesh with just one recognizable feature sprouting from it: a sulidor's huge tail.

Here was a sulidor, bereft of fur, whose arms were foreshortened and pillar-like like the limbs of a nildor, and whose body had grown round and heavy and thick.

Here was a sulidor in full fur with a nildor's trunk and ears.

Here was raw meat that was neither nildor nor sulidor, but alive and passive, a mere thing awaiting a sculptor's shaping hand.

Here was another thing that resembled a sulidor whose bones had melted.

Here was still another thing that resembled a nildor who had never had bones.

Here were trunks, spines, tusks, fangs, claws, tails, paws. Here was fur, and here was smooth hide. Here was flesh flowing at will and seeking new shapes. Here were dark chambers, lit only by flickering fungoid-glow, in which no firm distinction of species existed.

Biology's laws seemed suspended here. This was no trifling gene-tickling that he saw, Gundersen knew. On Earth, any skilled helix-parlor technician could redesign an organism's gene-plasm with some cunning thrusts of a needle and a few short spurts of drugs; he could make a camel bring forth a hippopotamus, a cat bring forth a chipmunk, or, for that matter, a woman bring forth a sulidor. One merely enhanced the desired characteristics within sperm and ovum, and suppressed other characteristics, until one had a reasonable facsimile of the creature to be reproduced. The basic genetic building-blocks were the same for every life-form; by rearranging them, one could create any kind of strange and monstrous progeny. But that was not what was being done here.

On Earth, Gundersen knew, it was also possible to persuade any living cell to play the part of a fertilized egg, and divide, and grow, and yield a full organism. The venom from Belzagor was one catalyst for that process; there were others. And so one could induce the stump of a man's arm to regrow that arm; one could scrape a bit of skin from a frog and generate an army of frogs with it; one could even rebuild an entire human being from the shards of his own ruined body. But that was not what was being done here.

What was being done here, Gundersen realized, was a transmutation of species, a change worked not upon ova but upon adult organisms. Now he understood Na-sinisul's remark, when asked if sulidoror also underwent rebirth: 'If there were no day, could there be night?' Yes. Nildor into sulidor. Sulidor into nildor. Gundersen shivered in shock. He reeled, clutching at a wall. He was plunged into a universe without fixed points. What was real? What was enduring?

He comprehended now what had happened to Kurtz in this mountain.

Gundersen stumbled into a cell in which a creature lay midway in its metamorphosis. Smaller than a nildor, larger than a sulidor; fangs, not tusks; trunk, not snout; fur not hide; flat footpads, not claws; body shaped for walking upright.

'Who are you?' Gundersen whispered. 'What are you? What were you? Which way are you heading?'

Rebirth. Cycle upon cycle upon cycle. Nildoror bound upon a northward pilgrimage, entering these caves, becoming . . . sulidoror? Was it possible?

If this is true, Gundersen thought, then we have never really known anything about this planet. And this is true.

He ran wildly from cell to cell, no longer caring whether he might be discovered. Each cell confirmed his guess. He saw nildoror and sulidoror in every stage of metamorphosis, some almost wholly nildoror, some unmistakably sulidoror, but most of them occupying intermediate positions along that journey from pole to pole; more than half were so deep in transformation that it was impossible for him to tell which way they were heading. All slept. Before his eyes flesh flowed, but nothing moved. In these cool shadowy chambers change came as a dream.

Gundersen reached the end of the corridor. He pressed his palms against cold, unyielding stone. Breathless, sweat-drenched, he turned towards the last chamber in the series and plunged into it.

Within was a sulidor not yet asleep, standing over three of the sluggish serpents of the tropics, which moved in gentle coils about him. The sulidor was huge, age-grizzled, a being of unusual presence and dignity.

'Na-sinisul?' Gundersen asked.

'We knew that in time you must come here, Edmund-gundersen.'

'I never imagined – I didn't understand –' Gundersen paused, struggling to regain control. More quietly he said, 'Forgive me if I have intruded. Have I interrupted your rebirth's beginning?'

'I have several days yet,' the sulidor said. 'I merely prepare the chamber now.'

'And you'll come forth from it as a nildor.'

'Yes,' said Na-sinisul.

'Life goes in a cycle here, then? Sulidor to nildor to sulidor to nildor to –'

'Yes. Over and over, rebirth after rebirth.'

'All nildoror spend part of their lives as sulidoror? All sulidoror spend part of their lives as nildoror?'

'Yes. All.'

How had it begun, Gundersen wondered? How had the

destinies of these two so different races become entangled? How had an entire species consented to undergo such a metamorphosis? He could not begin to understand it. But he knew now why he had never seen an infant nildor or sulidor. He said, 'Are young ones of either race ever born on this world?'

'Only when needed as replacements for those who can be reborn no more. It is not often. Our population is stable.'

'Stable, yet constantly changing.'

'Through a predictable pattern of change,' said Na-sinisul. 'When I emerge, I will be Fi'gontor of the ninth birth. My people have waited for thirty turnings for me to rejoin them; but circumstances required me to remain this long in the forest of the mists.'

'Is nine rebirths unusual?'

'There are those among us who have been here fifteen times. There are some who wait a hundred turnings to be called once. The summons comes when the summons comes; and for those who merit it, life will have no end.'

'No – end –'

'Why should it?' Na-sinisul asked. 'In this mountain we are purged of the poisons of age, and elsewhere we purge ourselves of the poisons of sin.'

'On the central plateau, that is.'

'I see you have spoken with the man Cullen.'

'Yes,' Gundersen said. 'Just before his – death.'

'I knew also that his life was over,' said Na-sinisul. 'We learn things swiftly here.'

Gundersen said, 'Where are Srin'gahar and Luu'khamin and the others I traveled with?'

'They are here, in cells not far away.'

'Already in rebirth?'

'For some days now. They will be sulidoror soon, and will live in the north until they are summoned to assume the nildor form again. Thus we refresh our souls by undertaking new lives.'

'During the sulidor phase, you keep a memory of your past life as a nildor?'

'Certainly. How can experience be valuable if it is not retained? We accumulate wisdom. Our grasp of truth is heightened by seeing the universe now through a nildor's eyes, now through a sulidor's. Not in body alone are the two forms different. To undergo rebirth is to enter a new world, not merely a new life.'

Hesitantly Gundersen said, 'And when someone who is not of this planet undergoes rebirth? What effect is there? What kind of changes happen?'

'You saw Kurtz?'

'I saw Kurtz,' said Gundersen. 'But I have no idea what Kurtz has become.'

'Kurtz has become Kurtz,' the sulidor said. 'For your kind there can be no true transformation, because you have no complementary species. You change, yes, but you become only what you have the potential to become. You liberate such forces as already exist within you. While he slept, Kurtz chose his new form himself. No one else designed it for him. It is not easy to explain this with words, Edmundgundersen.'

'If I underwent rebirth, then, I wouldn't necessarily turn into something like Kurtz?'

'Not unless your soul is as Kurtz's soul, and that is not possible.'

'What *would* I become?'

'No one may know these things before the fact. If you wish to discover what rebirth will do to you, you must accept rebirth.'

'If I asked for rebirth, would I be permitted to have it?'

'I told you when we first met,' said Na-sinisul, 'that no one on this world will prevent you from doing anything. You were not stopped as you ascended the mountain of rebirth. You were not stopped when you explored these chambers. Rebirth will not be denied you if you feel you need to experience it.'

Easily, serenely, instantly, Gundersen said, 'Then I ask for rebirth.'

SIXTEEN

Silently, unsurprised, Na-sinisul leads him to a vacant cell and gestures to him to remove his clothing. Gundersen strips. His fingers fumble only slightly with the snaps and catches. At the sulidor's direction, Gundersen lies on the floor, as all other candidates for rebirth have done. The stone is so cold that he hisses when his bare skin touches it. Na-sinisul goes out. Gundersen looks up at the glowing fungoids in the distant vault of the ceiling. The chamber is large enough to hold a nildor comfortably; to Gundersen, on the floor, it seems immense.

Na-sinisul returns, bearing a bowl made from a hollow log. He offers it to Gundersen. The bowl contains a pale blue fluid. 'Drink,' says the sulidor softly.

Gundersen drinks.

The taste is sweet, like sugar-water. This is something he has tasted before, and he knows when it was: at the serpent station, years ago. It is the forbidden venom. He drains the bowl, and Na-sinisul leaves him.

Two sulidoror whom Gundersen does not know enter the cell. They kneel on either side of him and begin a low, mumbling chant, some sort of ritual. He cannot understand any of it. They knead and stroke his body; their hands, with the fearful claws retracted, are strangely soft, like the pads of a cat. He is tense, but the tension ebbs. He feels the drug taking effect now: a thickness at the back of his head, a tightness in his chest, a blurring of his vision. Na-sinisul is in the room again, although Gundersen did not see him enter. He carries a bowl.

'Drink,' he says, and Gundersen drinks.

It is another fluid entirely, or perhaps a different distillate of the venom. Its flavor is bitter, with undertastes of smoke and ash. He has to force himself to get to the bottom of the bowl, but Na-sinisul waits, silently insistent, for him to finish it. Again the old sulidor leaves. At the mouth of the cell he turns and says something to Gundersen, but the words are overgrown with heavy blue fur, and will not enter Gundersen's ears. 'What did you say?' the Earthman asks. 'What? What?' His own words sprout leaden weights, teardrop-shaped, somber. They fall at once to the floor and shatter. One of the chanting sulidoror sweeps the broken words into a corner with a quick motion of his tail.

Gundersen hears a trickling sound, a glittering spiral of noise, as of water running into his cell. His eyes are closed, but he feels the wetness swirling about him. It is not water, though. It has a more solid texture. A sort of gelatin, perhaps. Lying on his back, he is several centimeters deep in it, and the level is rising. It is cool but not cold, and it insulates him nicely from the chill rock of the floor. He is aware of the faint pink odor of the inflowing gelatin, and of its firm consistency, like the tones of a bassoon in its deepest register. The sulidoror continue to chant. He feels a tube sliding into his mouth, a sleek piccolo-shriek of a tube, and through its narrow core there drips yet another substance, thick, oily, emitting the sound of muted kettle-drums as it hits his palate. Now the gelatin has reached the lower curve of his jaw. He welcomes its advance. It laps gently at his chin. The tube is withdrawn from his mouth just as the flow of gelatin covers his lips. 'Will I be able to breathe?' he asks. A sulidor answers him in cryptic Sumerian phrases, and Gundersen is reassured.

He is wholly sealed in the gelatin. It covers the floor of the chamber to a depth of one meter. Light dimly penetrates it. Gundersen knows that its upper surface is smooth and flawless, forming a perfect seal where it touches the walls of the cell. Now he has become a chrysalis. He will be given nothing more to drink. He will lie here, and he will be reborn.

One must die in order that one may be reborn, he knows.

Death comes to him and enfolds him. Gently he slides into a dark abyss. The embrace of death is tender. Gundersen floats through a realm of trembling emptiness. He hovers suspended in the black void. Bands of scarlet and purple light transfix him, buffeting him like bars of metal. He tumbles. He spins. He soars.

He encounters death once more, and they wrestle, and he is defeated by death, and his body is shivered into splinters, and a shower of bright Gundersen-fragments scatters through space.

. The fragments seek one another. They solemnly circle one another. They dance. They unite. They take on the form of Edmund Gundersen, but this new Gundersen glows like pure, transparent glass. He is glistening, a transparent man through whom the light of the great sun at the core of the universe passes without resistance. A spectrum spreads forth from his chest. The brilliance of his body illuminates the galaxies.

Strands of color emanate from him and link him to all who possess g'rakh in the universe.

He partakes of the biological wisdom of the cosmos.

He tunes his soul to the essence of what is and what must be.

He is without limits. He can reach out and touch any soul. He reaches toward the soul of Na-sinisul, and the sulidor greets him and admits him. He reaches toward Srin'gahar, toward Vol'himyor the many-born, toward Luu'khamin, Se-holomir, Yi-gartigok, toward the nildoror and sulidoror who lie in the caves of metamorphosis, and toward the dwellers in the misty forest, and toward the dwellers in the steaming jungles, and toward those who dance and rage in the forlorn plateau, and to all others of Belzagor who share in g'rakh.

And he comes now to one that is neither nildor nor sulidor, a sleeping soul, a veiled soul, a soul of a color and a timbre and texture unlike the others. It is an Earth-born soul, the soul of Seena, and he calls softly to her, saying, Awaken, awaken, I love you, I have come for you. She does not awaken. He calls to her, I am new, I am reborn, I overflow with love. Join me. Become part of me. Seena? Seena? Seena? And she does not respond.

He sees the souls of the other Earthmen now. They have g'rakh, but rationality is not enough; their souls are blind and silent. Here is Van Beneker; here are the tourists; here are the lonely keepers of solitary outposts in the jungle. Here is the charred gray emptiness where the soul of Cedric Cullen belongs.

He cannot reach any of them.

He moves on, and a new soul gleams beyond the mist. It is the soul of Kurtz. Kurtz comes to him, or he to Kurtz, and Kurtz is not asleep.

Now you are among us, Kurtz says, and Gundersen says, Yes, here I am at last. Soul opens to soul and Gundersen looks down into the darkness that is Kurtz past the pearl-gray curtain that shrouds his spirit, into a place of terror where black figures shuttle with many legs along ridged webs. Chaotic forms cohere, expand, dissolve within Kurtz. Gundersen looks beyond this dark and dismal zone, and beyond it he finds a cold hard bright light shining whitely out of the deepest place, and then Kurtz says, See? Do you see? Am I a monster? I have goodness within me.

You are not a monster, Gundersen says.

But I have suffered, says Kurtz.

For your sins, Gundersen says.

I have paid for my sins with my suffering, and I should now be released.

You have suffered, Gundersen agrees.

When will my suffering end, then?

Gundersen replies that he does not know, that it is not he who sets the limits of such things.

Kurtz says, I knew you. Nice young fellow, a little slow. Seena speaks highly of you. Sometimes she wishes things had worked out better for you and her. Instead she got me. Here I lie. Here lie we. Why won't you release me?

What can I do, asks Gundersen?

Let me come back to the mountain. Let me finish my rebirth.

Gundersen does not know how to respond, and he seeks along the circuit of *g'rakh*, consulting Na-sinisul, consulting Vol'himyor, consulting all the many-born ones, and they join, they join, they speak with one voice, they tell Gundersen in a voice of thunder that Kurtz is finished, his rebirth is over, he may not come back to the mountain.

Gundersen repeats this to Kurtz, but Kurtz has already heard. Kurtz shrivels. Kurtz shrinks back into darkness. He becomes enmeshed in his own webs.

Pity me, he calls out to Gundersen across a vast gulf. Pity me, for this is hell, and I am in it.

Gundersen says, I pity you. I pity you. I pity you. I pity you.

The echo of his own voice diminishes to infinity. All is silent. Out of the void, suddenly, comes Kurtz's wordless reply, a shrill and deafening crescendo blast of rage and hatred and malevolence, the scream of a flawed Prometheus flailing at the beak that pierces him. The shriek reaches a climax of shattering intensity. It dies away. The shivering fabric of the universe grows still again. A soft violet light appears, absorbing the lingering disharmonies of that one terrible outcry.

Gundersen weeps for Kurtz.

The cosmos streams with shining tears, and on that salty river Gundersen floats, traveling without will, visiting this world and that, drifting among the nebulae, passing through clouds of cosmic dust, soaring over strange suns.

He is not alone. Na-sinisul is with him, and Srin'gahar, and Vol'himyor, and all the others.

He becomes aware of the harmony of all things *g'rakh*. He sees, for the first time, the bonds that bind *g'rakh* to *g'rakh*. He, who lies in rebirth, is in contact with them all, any time, at every time, every soul on the planet joined in wordless communication.

He sees the unity of all *g'rakh*, and it awes and humbles him.

He perceives the complexity of this double people, the rhythm of its existence, the unending and infinite swing of cycle upon cycle of rebirth and new creation, above all the union, the oneness. He perceives his own monstrous isolation, the walls that cut him off from other men, that cut off man from man, each a prisoner in his own skull. He sees what it is like to live among people who have learned to liberate the prisoner in the skull.

That knowledge dwindles and crushes him. He thinks, We made them slaves, we called them beasts, and all the time they were linked, they spoke in their minds without words, they transmitted the music of the soul one to one to one. We were alone, and they were not, and instead of kneeling before them and begging to share the miracle, we gave them work to do.

Gundersen weeps for Gundersen.

Na-sinisul says, This is no time for sorrow, and Srin'gahar says, The past is past, and Vol'himyor says, Through remorse you are redeemed, and all of them speak with one voice and at one time, and he understands. He understands.

Now Gundersen understands all.

He knows that nildor and sulidor are not two separate species but merely forms of the same creature, no more different than caterpillar and butterfly, though he cannot tell which is the caterpillar, which the butterfly. He is aware of how it was for the nildoror when they were still in their primeval state, when they were born as nildoror and died helplessly as nildoror, perishing when the inevitable decay of their souls came upon them. And he knows the fear and the ecstasy of those first few nildoror who accepted the serpent's temptation and drank the drug of liberation, and became things with fur and claws, misshapen, malformed, transmuted. And he knows their pain as they were driven out, even into the plateau where no being possessing g'rakh would venture.

And he knows their sufferings in that plateau.

And he knows the triumph of those first sulidoror, who, surmounting their isolation, returned from the wilderness bearing a new creed. Come and be changed, come and be changed! Give up this flesh for another! Graze no more, but hunt and eat flesh! Be reborn, and live again, and conquer the brooding body that drags the spirit to destruction!

And he sees the nildoror accepting their destiny and giving themselves up joyfully to rebirth, a few, and then more, and then more, and then whole encampments, entire populations, going forth, not to hide in the plateau of purification, but to live in the new way, in the land where mist rules. They cannot resist, because with the change of body comes the blessed liberation of soul, the unity, the bond of *g'rakh* to *g'rakh*.

He understands now how it was for these people when the Earthmen came, the eager, busy, ignorant, pitiful, short-lived Earthmen, who were beings of *g'rakh* yet who could not or would not enter into the oneness, who dabbled with the drug of liberation and did not taste it to the fullest, whose minds were sealed one against the other, whose roads and buildings and pavements spread like pockmarks over the tender land. He sees how little the Earthmen knew, and how little they were capable of learning, and how much was kept from them since they would misunderstand it, and why it was necessary for the sulidoror to hide in the mists all these years of occupation, giving no clue to the strangers that they might be related to the nildoror, that they were the sons of the nildoror and the fathers of the nildoror as well. For if the Earthmen had known even half the truth they would have recoiled in fright, since their minds are sealed one against the other, and they would not have it any other way, except for the few who dared to learn, and too many of those were dark and demon-ridden, like Kurtz.

He feels vast relief that the time of pretending is over on this world and that nothing need be hidden any longer, that sulidoror may go down into the lands of the nildoror and move freely about, without fear that the secret and the mystery of rebirth may accidentally be revealed to those who could not withstand such knowledge.

He knows joy that he has come here and survived the test and endured his liberation. His mind is open now, and he has been reborn.

He descends, rejoining his body. He is aware once more that he lies embedded in congealed gelatin on the cold floor of a dark cell abutting a lengthy corridor within a rose-red mountain wreathed in white mist on a strange world. He does not rise. His time is not yet come.

He yields to the tones and colors and odors and textures that flood the universe. He allows them to carry him back, and he floats easily along the time-line, so that now he is a child peering at the shield of night and trying to count the stars, and now he is timidly sipping raw venom with Kurtz and Salamone, and now he enrolls in the Company and tells a personnel computer that his strongest wish is to foster the expansion of the human empire, and now he grasps Seena on a tropic beach under the light of several moons, and now he meets her for the first time, and now he sifts crystals in the Sea of Dust, and now he mounts a nildor, and now he runs laughing down a childhood street, and now he turns his torch on Cedric Cullen, and now he climbs the rebirth mountain, and now he trembles as Kurtz walks into a room, and now he takes the wafer on his tongue, and now he stares at the wonder of a white breast filling his cupped hand, and now he steps forth into mottled alien sunlight, and now he crouches over Henry Dykstra's swollen body, and now, and now, and now, and now . . .

He hears the tolling of mighty bells.

He feels the planet shuddering and shifting on its axis.

He smells dancing tongues of flame.

He touches the roots of the rebirth mountain.

He feels the souls of nildoror and sulidoror all about him.

He recognizes the words of the hymn the sulidoror sing, and he sings with them.

He grows. He shrinks. He burns. He shivers. He changes.

He awakens.

'Yes,' says a thick, low voice. 'Come out of it now. The time is here. Sit up. Sit up.'

Gundersen's eyes open. Colors surge through his dazzled brain. It is a moment before he is able to see.

A sulidor stands at the entrance to his cell.

'I am Ti-munilee,' the sulidor says. 'You are born again.'

'I know you,' Gundersen says. 'But not by that name. Who are you?'

'Reach out to me and see,' says the sulidor.

Gundersen reaches out.

'I knew you as the nildor Srin'gahar,' Gundersen says.

SEVENTEEN

Leaning on the sulidor's arm, Gundersen walked unsteadily out of the chamber of rebirth. In the dark corridor he asked, 'Have I been changed?'

'Yes, very much,' Ti-munilee said.

'How? In what way?'

'You do not know?'

Gundersen held a hand before his eyes. Five fingers, yes, as before. He looked down at his naked body and saw no difference in it. Obscurely he experienced disappointment; perhaps nothing had really happened in that chamber. His legs, his feet, his loins, his belly – everything as it had been.

'I haven't changed at all,' he said.

'You have changed greatly,' the sulidor replied.

'I see myself, and I see the same body as before.'

'Look again,' advised Ti-munilee.

In the main corridor Gundersen caught sight of himself dimly reflected in the sleek glassy walls by the light of the glowing fungoids. He drew back, startled. He had changed, yes; he had outkurtzed Kurtz in his rebirth. What peered back at him from the rippling sheen of the walls was scarcely human. Gundersen stared at the mask-like face with hooded slots for eyes, at the slitted nose, the gill-pouches trailing to his shoulders, the many-jointed arms, the row of sensors on the chest, the grasping organs at the hips, the cratered skin, the glow-organs in the cheeks. He looked down again at himself and saw none of those things. Which was the illusion?

He hurried towards daylight.

'Have I changed, or have I not changed?' he asked the sulidor.

'You have changed.'

'Where?'

'The changes are within,' said the former Srin'gahar.

'And the reflection?'

'Reflections sometimes lie. Look at yourself through my eyes, and see what you are.'

Gundersen reached forth again. He saw himself, and it was his old body he saw, and then he flickered and underwent a phase shift and he beheld the being with sensors and slots, and then he was himself again.

'Are you satisfied?' Ti-munilee asked.

'Yes,' said Gundersen. He walked slowly towards the lips of the plaza outside the mouth of the cavern. The seasons had changed since he had entered that cavern; now an iron winter was on the land, and the mist was piled deep in the valley, and where it broke he saw the heavy mounds of snow and ice. He felt the presence of nildoror and sulidoror about him, though he saw only Ti-munilee. He was aware of the soul of old Na-sinisul within the mountain, passing through the final phases of a rebirth. He touched the soul of Vol'himyor far to the south. He brushed lightly over the soul of tortured Kurtz. He sensed suddenly, startlingly, other Earthborn souls, as free as his, open to him, hovering nearby.

'Who are you?' he asked.

And they answered, 'You are not the first of your kind to come through rebirth intact.'

Yes. He remembered. Cullen had said that there had been others, some transformed into monsters, others simply never heard from again.

'Where are you?' he asked them.

They told him, but he did not understand, for what they said was that they had left their bodies behind. 'Have I also left my body behind?' he asked. And they said, no, he was still wearing his flesh, for so he had chosen, and they had chosen otherwise. Then they withdrew from him.

'Do you feel the changes?' Ti-munilee asked.

'The changes are within me,' said Gundersen.

'Yes. Now you are at peace.'

And, surprised by joy, he realized that that was so. The fears, the conflicts, the tensions, were gone. Guilt was gone. Sorrow was gone. Loneliness was gone.

Ti-munilee said, 'Do you know who I was, when I was Srin'gahar? Reach towards me.'

Gundersen reached. He said, in a moment, 'You were one of those seven nildoror whom I would not allow to go to their rebirth, many years ago.'

'Yes.'

'And yet you carried me on your back all the way to the mist country.'

'My time had come again,' said Ti-munilee, 'and I was happy. I forgave you. Do you remember, when we crossed into the mist country, there was an angry sulidor at the border?'

'Yes,' Gundersen said.

'He was another of the seven. He was the one you touched with your torch. He had had his rebirth finally, and still he hated you. Now he no longer does. Tomorrow, when you are ready, reach towards him, and he will forgive you. Will you do that?'

'I will,' said Gundersen. 'But will he really forgive?'

'You are reborn. Why should he not forgive?' Ti-munilee said. Then the sulidor asked, 'Where will you go now?'

'South. To help my people. First to help Kurtz, to guide him through a new rebirth. Then the others. Those who are willing to be opened.'

'May I share your journey?'

'You know that answer.'

Far off, the dark soul of Kurtz stirred and throbbed. Wait, Gundersen told it. Wait. You will not suffer much longer.

A blast of cold wind struck the mountainside. Sparkling flakes of snow whirled into Gundersen's face. He smiled. He had never felt so free, so light, so young. A vision of a mankind transformed blazed within him. I am the emissary, he thought. I am the bridge over which they shall cross. I am the resurrection and the life. I am the light of the world: he that followeth me shall not walk in darkness, but shall have the light of life. A new commandment I give unto you, that ye love one another.

He said to Ti-munilee, 'Shall we go now?'

'I am ready when you are ready.'

'Now.'

'Now,' said the sulidor, and together they began to descend the windswept mountain.

The Second Trip

ONE

Even the street felt wrong beneath his feet. Something oddly rubbery about the pavement, too much give in it. As though they had changed the mix of the concrete during the four years of his troubles. A new futuristic stuff, the 2011-model sidewalk, bouncy and weird. But no. The sidewalk looked the same. *He* was the new stuff. As though, when they had altered him, they had altered his stride too, changing the swing of his knees, changing the pivot of his hips. Now he wasn't sure of his movements. He didn't know whether he was supposed to hit the pavement with his heel or his toe. Every step was an adventure in discovery. He felt clumsy and uncertain within his own body.

Or *was* it his own? How far did the Rehab people go, anyway, in reconstructing your existence? Maybe a total brain transplant. Scoop out the old gray mass, run a jolt of juice through it, stick it into a waiting new body. And put somebody else's rehabilitated brain in your vacated skull? The old wine in a new decanter. No. No. That isn't how they work at all. This is the body I was born with. I'm having a little difficulty in coordination, true, but that's only to be expected. The first day out on the street again. Tuesday the something of May, 2011. Clear blue sky over the towers of Manhattan North. So I'm a little clumsy at first. So? So? Didn't they say something like this would happen?

Easy, now. Get a grip. Can't you remember how you used to walk? Just be natural.

Step. Step. Step. Into the rhythm of it. Heel and toe, heel and toe. Step. *Step*. That's the way! One-and-two-and-*one*-and-two-and-*one*-and-two. This is how Paul Macy walks. Proudly down the goddam street. Shoulders square. Belly sucked in.

Thirty-nine years old. Prime of life. Strong as an – what did they say, strong as an ox? Yes. Ox. Ox. Opportunity beckons you. A second trip, a second start. The bad dream is over; now you're awake. Step. Step. What about your arms? Let them swing? Hands in pockets? Don't worry about that, just go on walking. Let the arms look after themselves. You'll get the hang of it. You're out on the street, you're free, you've been rehabilitated. On your way to pick up your job assignment. Your new career. Your new life. Step. Step.

One-and-two-and-*one*-and-two.

He couldn't avoid the feeling that everybody was looking at him. That was probably normal too, the little touch of paranoia. After all, he had the Rehab badge in his lapel, the glittering bit of yellow metal advertising his status as a reconstruct job. The image of the new shoots rising from the old stump, warning everybody who had known him in the old days to be tactful. No one was supposed to greet him by his former name. No one was supposed to acknowledge the existence of his past. The Rehab badge was intended as a mercy, as a protection against the prodding of absent memories. But of course it attracted attention too. People looked at him – absolute strangers, so far as he knew, though he couldn't be sure – people looked and wondered, Who is this guy, what did he do that got him sentenced to Rehab? The triple ax murderer. Raped a nine-year-old with pinking shears. Embezzled ten million. Poisoned six old ladies for their heirlooms. Dynamited the Chartres Cathedral. All those eyes on him, speculating. Imagining his sins. The badge warned them he was something special.

There was no place to hide from those eyes. Macy moved all the way over to the curb and walked just along the edge. Right inside the strip of gleaming red metal ribbon that was embedded in the pavement, the stuff that flashed the magnetic pulses that kept autos from going out of control and jumping up on the sidewalk. It was no good here either. He imagined that the drivers zipping by were leaning out to stare at him. Crossing the pavement on an inward diagonal, he found another route for himself, hugging the sides of buildings. That's right, Macy, skulk along. Keep one shoulder higher than the other and try to fool yourself into thinking that it shields your face. Hunch your head. Jack the Ripper out for a stroll. Nobody's looking at you. This is New York, remember? You could walk down the street with your dung out of your pants and who'd notice? Not here. This city is full of Rehabs. Why should anybody care about you and your sordid eradicated past? Cut the paranoia, Paul.

Paul.

That was a hard part too. The new name. *I am Paul Macy.* A sweet compact name. Who dreamed that one up? Is there a computer down in the guts of the earth that fits syllables together and makes up new names for the Rehab boys? *Paul Macy.* Not bad. They could have told me I was Dragomir Slivovitz. Izzy Levine. Leroy Rastus Williams. But instead they came up with Paul Macy. I suppose for the holovision job. You need a name like that for the networks. *'Good evening, this is Dragomir Slivovitz, bringing you the eleven-o'clock news. Speaking from his weekend retreat at the Lunar White House, the President declared –'* No. They had coined the right kind of name for his new career. Very fucking Anglo-Saxon.

Suddenly he felt a great need to see the face he was wearing. He couldn't remember what he looked like. Coming to an abrupt stop, he turned to his left and picked his reflection off the mirror-bright pilaster beside an office building's entrance. He caught the image of a wide-cheeked, thin-lipped, standard sort of Anglo-Saxon face, with a big chin and a lot of soft windblown yellow-brown hair and deep-set pale blue eyes. No beard, no mustache. The face seemed strong, a little bland, decently proportioned, and wholly unfamiliar. He was surprised to see how relaxed he looked: no tensionlines in the forehead, no scowl, no harshness of the eyes. Macy absorbed all this in a fraction of a second; then whoever had been walking behind him, caught short by his sudden halt, crashed into his side and shoulder. He whirled. A girl. His hand went quickly to her elbow, steadying her. More her fault than his: she ought to look where she's going. Yet he felt guilty. 'I'm terribly sor –'

'Nat,' she said. 'Nat Hamlin, for God's sake!'

Someone was slipping a long cold needle into his eye. Under the lid, very very delicately done, up and up and around the top of the eyeball, past the tangled ropes of the nerves, and on into his brain. The needle had some sort of extension; it seemed to expand telescopically, sliding through the wrinkled furrowed folded mass of soft tissue, skewering him from forehead to skullcap. A tiny blaze of sparkling light wherever the tip of the needle touched. Ah, so, ve cut out dis, und den ve isolate dis, and ve chop here a little, ja, ja, ist gut! And the pain. Oh, Christ, the pain, the pain, the pain, the fire running down every neuron and jumping every synapse, the pain! Like having a thousand teeth pulled all at once. They said it absolutely wouldn't hurt at all. Those lying fuckers.

They had taught him how to handle a situation like this. He had to be polite but firm. Politely but firmly he said, 'I'm sorry, but you're mistaken. My name's Paul Macy.'

The girl had recovered from the shock of their collision. She took a couple of steps back and studied him carefully. He and she now constituted an encapsulated pocket of stasis on the busy sidewalk; people were flowing smoothly around them. She was tall and slender, with long straight red hair, troubled green eyes, fine features. A light dusting of freckles on the bridge of her nose. Full lips. No makeup. She wore a scruffy blue-checked spring coat. She looked as if she hadn't been sleeping well lately. He guessed she was in her late twenties. Very pale. Attractive in a tired, frayed way. She said, 'Don't play around with me. I know you're Nat Hamlin. You're looking good, Nat.'

Each time she said the name he felt the needles wiggle behind his eyeballs.

'Macy. Paul Macy.'

'I don't like this game. It's a cruel one, Nat. Where have you been? What is it, five years?'

'Won't you please try to understand?' he asked. He glanced meaningfully at his Rehab badge. Her eyes didn't follow his.

'I understand that you're trying to hurt me, Nat. It wouldn't be the first time.'

'I don't know you at all, miss.'

'You don't know me at all. You don't know me at all.'

'I don't know you at all. Right.'

'Lissa Moore.'

'I'm sorry.'

'What kind of trip are you on, Nat?'

'My second one,' Macy said.

'Your – second – one?'

He touched the badge. This time she saw it.

'Rehab?' she said. Blinking a couple of times: obviously adjusting her frame of reference. Color in her cheeks now. Biting her lip, abashed.

He nodded. 'I've just come out. Now do you understand? I don't know you. I never did.'

'Christ,' she said. 'We had such good times, Nat.'

'Paul.'

'How can I call you that?'

'It's my name now.'

'We had such good times,' she said. 'Before you went away. Before I came apart. I'm not working much now, you know. It's been pretty bad.'

'I'm sorry,' he told her, shifting his weight uneasily. 'It really isn't good for me to spend much time with people from my first trip. Or any time at all with them, actually.'

'You don't want to go somewhere and talk?'

'I can't. I mustn't.'

'Maybe some other time?' she asked. 'When you're a little more accustomed to things?'

'I'm afraid not,' he said. Firmly but politely. 'The whole point is that I've made a total break with the past, and I mustn't try to repair that break, or let anyone repair it for me. I'm on an entirely new trip now, can you see that?'

'I can see it,' she murmured, 'but I don't want it. I'm having a lot of trouble these days, and you can help me, Nat. If only –'

'*Paul*. And I'm not in any shape for helping anybody. I can barely help myself. Look at how my hand is shaking.'

'And you've started to sweat. Your forehead's all wet.'

'There's a tremendous strain. I'm conditioned to keep away from people out of the past.'

'It kills me when you say that. *People out of the past*. Like a guillotine coming down. You loved me. And I loved you. Love. Still. Love. So when you say –'

'Please.'

'You, please.' She was trembling, hanging onto his sleeve. Her eyes, going glassy, flitted and flickered a thousand times a second. 'Let's go somewhere for a drink, for a smoke, for a talk. I realize about the Rehab thing, but I need you too much. Please. Please.'

'I can't.'

'*Please*.' And she leaned toward him, her fingertips clutching hard into the bones of his right wrist, and he felt a baffling sensation in the top of his skull. A sort of intrusion. A tickling. A mild glow of heat. Along with it came a disturbing blurring of identity, a doubling of self, so that for a moment he was knocked free of his moorings. Paul Hamlin. Nat Macy. In the core of his mind erupted a vivid scene in garish colors: himself crouched over some sort of keyboard, and this girl standing naked on the far side of a cluttered room with her hands pressed to her cheeks. *Scream*, he was saying. *Go on, Lissa, scream. Give us a good one*. The image faded. He was back on a street in Manhattan North, but he was having trouble seeing, everything out of focus and getting more bleary each second. His legs were wobbly. A spike of pain under his breastbone. Maybe a heart attack, even. 'Please,' the girl was saying. 'Don't turn me away, Nat. Nat, what's happening? Your face is so red!'

'The conditioning –' he said, gasping.

The pressure eased. The girl backed away from him, touching the tips of her knuckles to her lips. As the distance between them increased he felt better. He clung to the side of the building with one hand and made a little shooing gesture at her with the other. Go on. Away. Out of my life. Whoever you were, there's no room now. She nodded. She continued to back away. He had a last brief glimpse of her tense, puffy-eyed face, and then she was cut off from him by a stream of people. Is this what it's going to be like every time I meet somebody from the old days? But maybe the others won't be like that. They'll respect my badge and pass silently on. Give me a chance to rebuild. It's only fair. She wasn't being fair. Neurotic bitch, putting her troubles above mine. Help me, she kept saying. Please. Please, Nat. As if I could help anybody.

Twenty minutes later he arrived at the network office. Ten minutes overdue, but that was unavoidable. He had needed some time to recover after the encounter with the girl on the street. Let the adrenalin drain out of the system, let the sweat dry. It was important for him to present an unruffled exterior; more important, in fact, than showing up on time the first day. The network people were probably prepared to be tolerant of a little unpunctuality at first, considering all that he had been through. But he had to demonstrate that he had the professional qualities the job demanded. They were hiring him as an act of grace, yes, but it wasn't pure charity: he wouldn't have been accepted if he hadn't been suitable for the job. So he needed to show that he had the surface slickness, the smoothness, that a holovision commentator had to have. Pause to catch the breath. Get the hair tidy. Adjust the collar. Give yourself that seamless, sprayed-on look. You had a nasty shock or two in the street, but now you're feeling much better. All right. Now go in. A confident stride. One-and-two-and-*one*-and-two.

The lobby was dark and cavernous. Screens everywhere, a hundred sensors mounted in the onyx walls, anti-vandal

robots poised with bland impersonality to come rolling forth
if anybody tried anything troublesome. Standing beneath the
security panel, Macy activated one of the screens and a cheery
female face appeared. Just a hint of plump bare breasts at the
bottom of the screen, cut off by the prudish camera angle.
'I have an appointment,' he said. 'Paul Macy. To see Mr
Bercovici.'

'Certainly, Mr Macy. The liftshaft to your right. Thirty-
eighth floor.'

He stepped into the shaft. It was already programmed;
serenely he floated skyward. At the top, another screen. Face
of an elegant haggard black girl, shaven eyebrows, gleaming
cheekbones, no flesh to spare. The expectable gorgeous halo of
shimmering hair. 'Please step through Access Green,' she said.
A throaty, throbbing contralto. 'Mr Fredericks is expecting you
in Gallery Nine of the Rotunda.'

'My appointment is with Mr Bercovici —'

Too late. Screen dead. Access Green, an immense oval
doorway the color of a rhododendron leaf, was opening from a
central sphincter, like the irising shutter of an antique camera.
Abandon all hope, ye who enter here. Macy stepped hastily
through, worrying about having the sphincter reverse itself
when he had one leg on each side. Beyond the doorway the
air was soft and clammy, heavy with a rain-forest warmth and
humidity, and mysterious fragrances were adrift. He saw low,
dim passages radiating in a dozen directions. The walls were
pink and rounded, no corners anywhere, and seemed to be
made of some spongy resilient substance. The whole place
was like one vast womb. Trapped in the fallopian tubes. Macy
tried to persuade himself not to start sweating again. There
was a popping sound, of the sort one could make by pushing
a fingertip against the inside of one's cheek and sliding it swiftly
out of one's mouth, and the black girl emerged from a gash
in the wall that promptly resealed itself. She was sealed too,
encased in purple plastic from throat to toes, like a chrysalis,
everything covered but nothing concealed: her tight wrap
startlingly displayed the outlines of her bony body. Superb

skeletal structure. She said, 'I'm Loftus. I'll show you to Mr Fredericks' office.'

'Mr Bercovici –'

She didn't wait. Hurrying down the hall, legs going like pistons, bare feet hitting the spongy floor, thwunk thwunk thwunk. Trim flat rump: no buttocks at all, so far as he could tell, merely a termination, like a cat's hindquarters. He was upset. Bercovici was the one who had interviewed him at the Rehab Center, all smiles and sincerity, thinning blond hair, pudgy cheeks. Don't worry, Mr Macy, I'll be looking after you personally during your difficult transition back to daily life. Bercovici was his lifeline. Without looking back, the black girl called out, 'Mr Bercovici's been transferred to the Addis Ababa office.'

'But I spoke to him only ten days ago, Miss Loftus!'

She halted. Momentary blaze of the eyes. '*Loftus* is quite sufficient,' she said. Then the expression softened. Perhaps remembering she was dealing with a convalescent. 'Sometimes transfers happen rapidly here. But Mr Fredericks has your full dossier. He's aware of the problems.'

Mr Fredericks had a long cavernous office, rounded and womby, from the sloping ceiling of which dangled hundreds of soft pink globes, breast-shaped; a tiny light was mounted in each nipple. He was a small dapper man with a moist handshake. Macy received from him a sweet sad embarrassed smile, the kind one gives a man who has had a couple of limbs or perhaps his genitals amputated to check the metastasis of some new lightning cancer. 'So glad you've come, Mr Macy. Paul, may I make it? And call me Stilton. We're all informal here. A wonderful opportunity for you in this organization.' Eyes going to Macy's Rehab badge, then away, then back, as though he couldn't refrain from staring at it. The stigmata of healing.

'Show you around,' Fredericks was saying. 'Get to know everybody. The options here are tremendous: the whole world of modern data-intake at your service. We'll start you slowly, feed you into the news in ninety-second slices, first, then, as you pick up real ease at it, we'll nudge you into the front line.'

Good evening, ladies and chentlemen, this is Pavel Nathanielovitch Macy coming to you from the Kremlin on the eve of the long-awaited summit.

The rear wall of Fredericks' office vanished as though it had been annihilated by some wandering mass of antimatter, and Macy found himself staring into an immense stupefying abyss, a dark well hundreds of feet across and perhaps infinitely deep. A great many golden specks floated freely in that bowl of nothingness. He was so awestruck by the unexpected sight that he lost a chunk of Fredericks' commentary, but picked up on it in time to hear, 'You see, we have thousands, literally thousands of free-ranging hovereye cameras posted in every spot throughout the world where news is likely to break. Their normal altitude is eighty to a hundred feet, but of course we can raise or lower them on command. You can think of them simply as passive observers hanging everywhere overhead, little self-contained self-propelled passive observers, sitting up there soaking in a full range of audio and visual information and holding it all on twenty-four-hour tap-scanning drums. Those of us here at Manhattan North Headquarters can tap in on any of these inputs as needed. For instance, if I want to get some idea of what's doing at the Sterility Day parade in Trafalgar Square –' he touched a small blue button in a broad console on his desk, and up out of the darkness one of the golden specks came zooming, halting in midair just beyond the place where the wall of Fredericks' office had been. 'What we have here,' Fredericks explained, 'is the slave-servo counterpart of the hovereye camera that's hanging above that parade right now. I simply induce an output – here, we get a visual' – Macy saw gesticulating women waving banners and setting off flares – 'and here we get the audio.' Raucous screams, the chanting of slogans.

Macy hadn't heard of Sterility Day before. The world becomes terribly strange when you spend four years out of circulation.

'If we want any of this for the next newscast, you see, we

just pump the signal into a recorder and set it up for editing – and meanwhile the hovereye is still up there, soaking it all in, relaying on demand. Gathering the news is no frigging chore at all when you have ten thousand of these lovely little motherfuckers working for you all over the place.' A nervous giggle. 'Sometimes our language gets a little rough around here. You stop noticing it after a while.' One doesn't speak crude Anglo-Saxon to a man who wears the badge of his trauma on his lapel, is that it?

Fredericks had him by the arm. 'Time to meet your new colleagues,' he was saying. 'I want to fill you in completely. You're going to love it working here.'

Out of the office. The rear wall mysteriously restoring itself as they leave, the dark well of the hovereyes vanishing once more. Down the humid fallopian passageways. Doors opening. Neat, well-groomed executives everywhere, all of them getting up to greet him. Some of them speaking exceptionally loudly and clearly, as if they thought a man who had had his troubles might find it difficult to understand what they said. Long-legged girls flashing the promise of ecstasy. Some of them looking a trifle scared; maybe they were hip to the evil deeds of his former self. Macy was aware of what crimes the previous user of his body had committed, and sometimes they scared him a little, too.

'In here,' Fredericks said. Into a bright, gaudy room, twice the size of Fredericks' office. 'I'd like you to meet the chief of daytime news, Paul. One hell of a guy. Harold Griswold, and he's some beautiful son of a bitch. Harold, here's our new man, Paul Macy. Number six on the late news. Bercovici told you the story, right? Right. He's going to fit in here perfectly.'

Griswold stood up, a slow and complex process, and smiled. Macy smiled. His facial muscles were beginning to ache from all the smiling he had done in the last hour and a half. One doesn't smile much at a Rehab Center. He shook the hand of the chief of daytime news. Griswold was implausibly tall, slabjawed, perhaps fifty years old, obviously a man of great prestige; he reminded Macy somehow of George

Washington. He wore a bright-blue tank suit, an earwatch, and an elaborate breastplate of several kinds of exotic polished woods. His office was like a museum annex, with works of art everywhere: shaped paintings, crystallines, talk-spikes, programmed resonances. A million-dollar collection. In the corner, to the right of Griswold's kidney-shaped desk, stood a striking psychosculpture, a figure of an old woman. Macy, who had been glancing from piece to piece by way of an implied compliment to Griswold, lurched forward at the sight of the last work, coughed, grabbed the edge of the desk to steady himself. He felt as though he had been clubbed at the back of the neck. Instantly friendly hands clutched at him. 'Are you all right? What's the trouble, fella?' Macy fought off dizziness. He straightened and shook himself free of the propping hands.

'I don't know what hit me,' he muttered. 'Just as I looked at that sculpture in the corner –'

'The Hamlin over there?' Griswold asked. 'One of my favorites. A gift from my first wife, ten years back, when Hamlin was still an unknown –'

'If you don't mind – some cold water –'

Two gulps. Another cup. Three gulps. Carefully averting his eyes from the figure of the old woman. The Hamlin over there. The sleek smooth networkmen frowning at him, then erasing the frowns the instant he noticed. Everyone so solicitous. 'Forgive me,' he said. 'You know, it's only my first day on the outside. The strain, the tension.'

'Of course. The tension.' Griswold.

'The strain. We understand.' Fredericks.

He forced himself to look at the psychosculpture. The Hamlin over there. An excellent piece of work. Poignance; pathos; a sense of the tragedy of aging, a sense of the heroism of defying time. A soft hum coming from its resonators, subtly coloring the mood it was designed to stimulate. The Hamlin over there. Macy said, 'That's *Nathaniel* Hamlin who did it?'

'Right,' Griswold said. 'God only knows what it's worth now. On account of Hamlin's tragic fate. Not that I have the slightest interest in selling, but of course when an artist dies young his work skyrockets amazingly in value.'

He didn't know, then. He couldn't just be pretending. And he couldn't be that dumb. Either Bercovici hadn't told him, or he'd been told and hadn't cared enough to remember. That was interesting. Macy was shaken, though, by the intensity of his reaction to the unexpected sight of the sculpture. They hadn't warned him at the Rehab Center that such things might happen. He made a mental note to ask about it when he went back next week for his first session of outpatient post-therapy therapy. And a mental note, also, to stay out of Griswold's office as much as possible.

The sculpture was still exerting an effect on him. He felt an undertow, the sucking of a subcerebral ocean in his mind. Hollow echoing sounds of surf from far below. A hammering against the threshold of consciousness. The Hamlin over there. That's *Nathaniel* Hamlin who did it? On account of his tragic fate. Jesus. Jesus. A bad attack of wobbly knees. Sweaty forehead. Paroxysms of confusion. Going to collapse, going to fall down in a screaming fit, going to vomit all over Harold Griswold's nappy green electronic carpet. Unless you regain control fast. He turned apologetically to Stilton Fredericks and said in a thick furry voice, 'It's more upsetting than I thought. You'd better get me out of here fast.'

Fredericks took his arm. A firm grasp. To Griswold: 'I'll explain afterward.' Propelling Macy urgently toward the door. Stumbling feet. Head swaying on neck. Jesus. Outside the office, finally.

The moment of intolerable *angst* ebbing.

'I feel much better now,' Macy murmured.

'Can I get you a pill?'

'No. No. Nothing.'

'Are you sure you're all right?'

'Sure.'

'You don't look all right.'

'It'll pass. It shook me up more than I expected. Listen, Fredericks – Stilton – I don't want you to think that I'm fragile, or anything, but you know I've just been released from the Rehab Center, and for the first few days –'

'It's perfectly natural,' said Fredericks. A comradely pat on the shoulder. 'We understand the problem. We can make allowances. This was my fault, anyway. I should have checked things out before I brought you in there. He's got so many works of art in his office, though –'

'Sure. How could you have known?'

'I should have checked anyway. Now that I see the difficulty, I'll check the whole building. I simply didn't realize that it would upset you so much to come face to face with one of your own sculptures.'

'Not mine,' Macy said, shaking his head emphatically. 'Not mine.'

TWO

Daytime it wasn't so bad. He built a cozy routine for himself and lived within it, just as they had advised him at the Center to do. The Rehab people had found him a little apartment near the upper tip of Old Manhattan, five minutes from the network office by short-hop tube, forty minutes if he walked; he hadn't wanted to risk exposing himself to the chaotic rush-hour environment of the tubes too soon, and so at first he went to work on foot. The exercise was good for him, and he had nothing better to do with his time anyway. But from the fourth day on he took the tube. The jostling and the screeching of wheels turned out not to bother him as much as he feared it might, and, packed belly to rump in the cars, he didn't have to worry about people staring at him or his Rehab badge.

At work he slipped easily and comfortably into the net-work's news-broadcast operation. He had had six months of vocational training at the Center, and so he came to his new career already skilled in voice projection, sincerity dynamics, makeup technique, and other such things; he needed only to learn the details of the network's daily practice, the authority levels and flow patterns and such. Everybody was kind to him, although after the first few days most of them dropped the maddening exaggerated courtesy that made him feel like such a cripple. They showed him what to do, they covered his blunders, they responded patiently and good-humoredly to his questions.

In the beginning Fredericks didn't let him do any actual broadcasting, just dummy off-the-air runs under simulated studio circumstances. Instead he was put to work reading scripts aloud for the timing, and monitoring air checks of the other broadcasters. But he did so well at the dummy runs that by the fifth day they were putting him on the late news to do ninety-second capsule reports in what they called the mosaic-texture section, in which a bunch of broadcasters offered quick bouncy segments of the news in swift succession. Fredericks told him that in another few weeks he'd be allowed to handle full-scale stories, even to select his own accompanying hovereye coverage. So all went well professionally.

The nights were something else.

Lonely, for one thing. *You'd be wisest to avoid sexual liaisons, at least at the outset*, the Center therapists had suggested. *They could be disturbing during the initial two or three weeks of adjustment.* He paid heed. He refrained from bringing any of the network girls home with him, though plenty of them made it clear that they were available. Just ask, honey. At night he sat alone in the modest apartment. Watching a lot of holovision. Pretending that it was important to his career to study how the various networks handled the news. In truth he simply wanted the companionship of the bright screen and the loud audio; he left it on even when he wasn't watching anything.

He didn't go out in the evenings. A matter of economy, he told himself. Supposedly he had been a wealthy man in his former life, or at least pretty damned prosperous. A successful artist, work in constant demand, prices going up at the gallery every year, that kind of thing. But his assets had been forfeit to the state. Most of his money had been used up by the costs of his therapy and the termination settlement awarded his wife. What little was left had gone into renting and furnishing his apartment. He was essentially a pauper until the network salary checks began coming in. But he knew that the real reason for staying home was fear. He wasn't ready yet to explore the night world of this formidable city. He couldn't go out there while his new self was still moist and malleable around the edges.

Then there were the dreams.

He hadn't had nightmares at the Rehab Center. He had them now. Traumatic identity crises punctuated his sleep. He ran breathlessly down long gleaming ropy corridors, pursued by a man who wore his face. He stood by the shore of a viscous gray-green pool that bubbled and steamed and heaved, and a gnarled hairy claw reached up from its depths and groped for him. He tiptoed across a sea of quicksand, sinking deeper and deeper, and something underneath plucked at his toes. Pulling him under with a loud plop. A coven of monsters waiting down below. Teeth and green horns and yellow eyes. Often he woke up shrieking. And then lay awake, listening to something knocking on the inside of his skull. Let me out, let me out, let me out! Great gusts of wind blew through his brain. Vast snorting snores setting the medulla atremble. A slumbering giant, restless, cranky, trapped behind his forehead. Belching and farting within his head. Knock. Knock. Knock.

Also the peculiar doubleness of self assailed him, the sensation of being enshrouded and entangled in the scraps and threads of his old identity, so that he momentarily was sucked back into it. I am Nat Hamlin. Married, successful. Psychosculptor. This is my face. These are my hands. Why am I in this unfamiliar little apartment? No. No. I am Paul Macy. I used to be. Formerly was. In another country, so to speak. And besides the stench is dead. Why does he haunt me? I am not Nat Hamlin.

Sometimes at night it was hard to be sure of that, though.

By the third night Macy dreaded going to bed. There was that man with his face, always haunting him when he crossed into dreamland. Waking in distress, he wanted to call a friend and ask for reassurance. But he had no friends. The old ones had been washed away by the therapy, and he hadn't made any new ones yet, except a few people he had come to know at the Rehab Center, fellow reconstructs, and he didn't want to bother them in the middle of the night. Maybe they had demons of their own to wrestle with. And the people from the network. Mustn't call them. You'd blow the whole pretense of your stability in one gush of panicky talk. Nor could he call any of his therapists. Dr Brewster, Dr Ianuzzi, Dr Gomez. You're on your own, they said. We're cutting the umbilicus. So. So. All alone. Sweat it out. Eventually, no matter how bad a night it was, he would sleep. Eventually.

'Is there any chance,' Macy asked, 'that the Rehab job didn't completely take? I mean, sometimes I think I can feel Hamlin trying to break through.'

A Tuesday late in May, 2011. One week after his discharge from the Rehab Center. His first session of post-therapy therapy. Dr Gomez, round-faced, swarthy, drooping black mustache, not much chin, scowling and chewing on a computer stylus. Soft buzzing voice. 'No chance of that at all, Macy.'

'But these dreams –'

'A little psychic static, is all. What gives you the idea Hamlin still exists?'

'During these nightmares I feel him pushing inside my head. Like somebody trying to get out.'

'Don't mess things up with your pretty imagery, Macy. You've been having some bad dreams. Everybody has bad dreams. You think I'm immune? I've got my share of lousy karma. Without any fancy hypotheses, tell me why you think it's Hamlin.'

'The man with my face chasing me.'

'A metaphor for your own unfocused past, maybe.'

'A sense of confusion. Not knowing who I really am.'

'Who are you, really?'

'Paul Macy. But –'

'That's who you really are. Nat Hamlin doesn't exist any more. He's been stripped out of your body, cell by cell, and extinguished. You really surprise me, Macy. I thought you were going to make one of the best adjustments I ever saw.'

'I felt that way too,' Macy said. 'But since I've been outside there have been these – these bursts of psychic static. I'm scared. What if Hamlin's still there?'

'Hamlin exists only as an abstract concept. He's a famous psychosculptor who ran into trouble with the law and was eradicated. Now he exists only through his works. Like Mozart. Like Michelangelo. He isn't in your head.'

Macy said, 'My first day at the network, I walked into the office of one of the high executives and there was a big Hamlin sculpture in the corner. I looked at it and I recognized it for what it was and I just took it in, you know, the way I'd take in a Michelangelo, and after a fraction of a second I had this sensation like somebody had banged me on the head with a mallet. I almost fell over. The impact was tremendous. How do you account for that, Dr Gomez?'

'How do *you* account for it?'

'Like it was Hamlin still inside me, standing up and yelling, "That's mine, I made that!" Such a surge of pride and identity that I felt it on the conscious level as physical pain.'

'Balls,' the doctor said. 'Hamlin's gone.'

'How can you be sure of that?'

Gomez sighed. 'Look,' he said, and jabbed an output node. On the walls of his office blossomed screened images of Macy's psychological profiles. Gomez pointed. 'Over on the left, that's the EEG of Nat Hamlin. You see those greasy waves of psychopathic tendency, those ugly nasty jiggles? You see those electrical storms going on in that man's head? That's a sick EEG. That's sick as hell. Right?

'Now look over here. We've begun the mindpick operation. We're wiping out Nat Hamlin. The waves get smoother. Sweet as a baby. Chart after chart. Look. Look. Look. As Hamlin goes, we bring in Macy. You can see the overlay here. *This* is what a double mind looks like. Vestigial Hamlin, incipient Macy. Yes? Two distinct electrical patterns, no problems at all distinguishing one from the other. And now, this side of the room, you can see Hamlin wiped out entirely. Can you find any of the typical Hamlin waveforms? By shit, can you?

'You aren't saying anything, Macy. There's your brain on the wall. Alpha, beta, the whole mess. Compare your waves and Hamlin's. Altogether different. Two separate patterns. He's him, you're you. The machine says so. It isn't a matter of opinion, it's a matter of voltage thresholds. A voltage doesn't lie. Amperes don't have opinions. Resistances don't fuck around with you for sly tactical reasons. We're dealing in objective facts, and the objective facts tell me that Nat Hamlin has been wiped out. They ought to tell you that too.'

'The dreams – the sight of that psychosculpture –'

'So you're a little unstable. A couple of surprise adjustment traumas. But Hamlin? No.'

'Another thing. My first day out, that same day, I met a girl in the street, somebody from Hamlin's life. She kept calling me Nat. Telling me she loved me.'

'Weren't you wearing your Rehab badge?'

'Of course I was.'

'And the dumb bitch still dumped all that garbage on you?'

'I suppose she's disturbed mentally herself. I don't know. Anyway,' Macy said, 'she was doing all this to me, Nat this and Nat that, paying no attention when I told her I was Paul Macy, and out of nowhere I felt, well, like hot on top of my head, and for half a second I didn't know who I was. Which one of me I was. It was like something had reached into my head and mixed everything up. I could even remember myself making a psychosculpture of the girl. You see, she was one of Hamlin's models, apparently, and I had this flickering memory of her posing, me at a sculptor's keyboard –'

'Crap,' Gomez said.

'What?'

'Crap. It wasn't a memory. You couldn't possibly remember anything out of Nat Hamlin's life.'

'What was it, then?'

'It was an episode of free-floating masochism, Macy. A normal self-injury wish. You invented this phantom image of yourself sculpting the girl because you wanted to fool yourself into thinking that Hamlin was breaking through.'

'But I don't see why –'

'Shut up and I'll explain the mechanism. You lived at this Center for four years, right, and you got constant attention. It was like being in the womb. Every need instantly attended to. Okay, it's time for Paul Macy to be born, and we toss you out into the world on your ass. Not exactly as rough as that, we find you a job first, we find you a place to live, but it's still a ballbreaker to get evicted. Out you go. Suddenly no umbilicus to feed you. Suddenly no placenta to cuddle in.

'Well, you want attention, and one way to get it is to come here yelling that your personality reconstruct didn't really take, that Hamlin is knocking around inside your head. I don't mean that this is a conscious thing. It's a mechanism. Your rational self just wants to make a decent adjustment to outside life and live happily ever after as Paul Macy, but there's this irrational side of us too. Which often operates directly counter to the needs and desires of the rational side.

'Suppose I tell somebody that his sanity depends on never calling his mother-in-law by her first name, okay? And he nods, he says, 'Yes, I understand, if I do that it'll really wreck me.' So of course every time he sees the old witch he finds that her first name is on the tip of his tongue. He'll have dreams in which he calls her by her first name. He'll fantasy it while he's sitting at his desk. Because it's the most destructive fucking thing he could possibly do, so of course the temptation to do it keeps rising out of his head, and he's constantly imagining he *has* done it.

'Now back to you. The last thing you want to have happen is for Hamlin to come back to life, so naturally you fantasy yourself making a sculpture of this girl. Which upsets you and sends you in a sweat back to me, screaming for help. The immediate result of this mechanism is to give you bad dreams and general trauma, and an incidental side-effect is to supply you with that claim on my attention that you unconsciously crave. You see how the dark side of our mind always craps us up? But don't worry about it, Macy. None of this is real, in the sense that Hamlin *is* there. Oh, sure, it's real in a psychological sense, but so what?' Gomez grinned triumphantly. 'You're a smart boy. You've been following all this, right?'

Macy said, 'Isn't it possible to run some new EEGs all the same? What if I did come up with a double wave pattern?'

'You really want me to coddle you, don't you?'

'Would it be so hard to make an empirical test?'

'I could do it in five minutes.'

'Why not, then?'

'Because I don't believe in giving in to an outpatient's weepy fantasies. You think you're my first reconstruct job? I've had a hundred of you. I know what's possible and what isn't. If I tell you Hamlin is eradicated, it's because I *know* Hamlin is eradicated. I'm not just being a bull-headed bastard.'

'All right, so I'm irrational,' Macy said. 'But if I had the evidence of the EEG in front of me –'

'I won't play that game with you. The fantasy came from inside you; let the cure for it come from in there too. Sweat it out. Convince yourself that your belief in Hamlin's continued existence is nothing but a move to get sympathy from us.'

'And if the hallucinations don't go away?'

'They have to.'

'If they don't, though?'

'You'll be here again next Tuesday,' Gomez said. 'I won't be seeing you then. Dr Ianuzzi will, and as you know she's an entirely different kind of doctor. Sweet and refined and sympathetic, whereas I'm a vulgar and hostile son of a bitch. If this stuff is still bothering you then, maybe she'll run an EEG for you, though I hope she doesn't. I won't, Macy. I can't. The top sergeant never kisses you and tucks you in, no matter how piteously you ask him, and I'm top sergeant on this team. So come back next week.'

Gomez stood up. 'I saw you on the late news last night. You weren't bad at all.'

The next morning he found a message cube addressed to him in his box at the office. Puzzled, he plugged the glossy little cassette into his desk's output slot. The face of the girl who had talked to him on the street the week before appeared on the screen. Red-rimmed eyes, hollow cheeks. Her hair straggly, unkempt. She offered the camera an uncertain lopsided grin and said, 'I saw you on holovision and so I knew where to send this. Please, Nat, don't just ignore me. I can't tell you –'

His hand shot out and killed the playback. *Please, Nat.* He couldn't take that. The use of his old name: it was like slivers of wood under his fingernails, needles probing behind his eyes. Last night the dreams had been worse than ever. Seeing himself as Siamese twins, one body ripping and clawing at its identical brother. And then the trapdoor opening in the attic floor and the shambling disemboweled thing lurching up out of it. The girl had initiated all his traumas; there hadn't been bad dreams before that miserable accidental meeting. He wasn't going to give her a second chance to screw him up. If that bastard Gomez wouldn't offer supportive therapy, he was simply going to have to defend himself against potential inner turmoil. And therefore it was necessary to avoid new sources of anguish.

Macy switched the output control to *Erase* and reached for the button. Then he saw the girl's sad, eroded face in his mind. A fellow human being. She also suffers. I could at least listen once.

He turned to *Playback* again and she reappeared, saying, 'I saw you on holovision and so I knew where to send this. Please, Nat, don't just ignore me. I can't tell you how much you still mean to me, even after everything. I know you've been through Rehab and things must be very strange to you, and you don't want to hear from people out of your old life. But finding you like that was such a miracle that I can't simply pretend you don't exist. Because I can't keep going like this much longer, Nat. I'm in bad shape. I need help. I'm sinking and somebody's got to throw me a rope.'

There was more in that vein. She said she'd wait for him Wednesday night at six o'clock on the northeast corner of 227th and Broadway, opposite the network building, and that she'd be waiting for him the same time the next two nights also, in case he wasn't free Wednesday. Or if he wanted to make other arrangements he could call her at her home, any day after eleven in the morning, such-and-such a number. With all my love. Yours truly, Lissa Moore.

I can't, he thought. I don't dare. He erased the cube. That night he left ten minutes early, going out the building's east entrance to avoid her. He did the same on Thursday and Friday.

On Monday there was a new cube from her. He carried it around for three hours, unwilling to erase it, afraid to play it, and finally slipped it into the slot. On the screen, her pale face against a black velvet backdrop. The mouth drawn into a quirky grimace. A hyperthyroid bulge to the eyes that he hadn't noticed before. The lighting in the booth where she'd recorded the message was too bright, and it struck her cheeks so fiercely that it seemed to strip them to the bone. Her voice, blurting, unmodulated: 'You didn't come. I waited, but you didn't come. All right, Nat. Paul. Maybe you don't give a damn about me. Maybe you've got your own neck to look out for and can't fool around with me. I won't bother you after today. I'll wait tonight, six o'clock, same corner, Broadway and 227th, northeast side. You aren't there by half past eight, I'll be dead by nine. I mean it. Now it's up to you.'

THREE

A few minutes past six, he was still in the central news-room, finishing his last piece of the day. A cold sullen anger still gripped him. Let the bitch kill herself. I won't be blackmailed like that. She doesn't mean anything to me except trouble.

With a sharp stabbing gesture he summoned control of the hovereye that patrolled the street outside the network office building, forever keeping watch for demonstrators, bombers, self-immolators. With newly skillful motions Macy brought the airborne camera down the block until it was scanning the streetcorner where Lissa had said she'd wait. Now the fine control, the vernier.

Yes, there she is. Pacing in a taut little circle. A self-contained zone of tension on the busy street. Damn her. She can do whatever she likes to herself. Whatever she likes. Macy signed himself out of the newsroom and, gliding on the glacial flow of his rage, drifted toward the liftshaft. Down forty stories. Sweeping quickly through the lobby. Outside. A soft spring evening. Long lines of patient homegoers wearily filing into the tubemouth. So easy to avoid her, in this crowd. Just slide on past.

He found himself walking toward her, though. One-and-two-and-*one*-and-two; he couldn't stop. She seemed to be talking to herself; eyes turned inward, she didn't notice him approaching. From twenty yards away he glowered at her. Who the hell does she think she is, trying to use me this way? Playing on my sympathies. Oh, I need you, I need you so much! With throbbing violins. And working on my sense of guilt. Meet me on the corner or I'll jump off the Palisades Bridge! Sure. What business is it of mine if you want to jump off a bridge, baby? I've got nothing to feel guilty about. Guilt? I haven't done a thing. I'm brand new in the world. Christ, I'm even a virgin. That's right: Paul Macy is a virgin. A goddamn virgin.

He was only a few feet from her, now, but she hadn't seen him yet. He started to touch her arm, but halted as a curious discomfort flitted across his skull. That sense of doubleness, again, that scrambling of identities. Disorientation. A bonging sensation like the muffled tolling of a distant bell. With it came a fast spasm of nausea, a light tightening around his adams' apple.

Then all the disturbing symptoms vanished. He nudged her elbow. 'All right,' he said gruffly. 'Wake up! Here I am. You're pulling a lousy stinking trick, but I fell for it. And here I am.'

'Nat!' Looking at him in mingled amazement and delight. Color stippling her cheeks. Eyes fluttering: she's scared of me, he realized suddenly. He experienced a second spasm of strange uneasiness, here and gone before it had any real effect. 'Oh, Nat, thank God you came!'

'No,' he said. 'Let's get this established once and for all. My name's Paul Macy. You want to have anything to do with me, you call me by that name, and no options about it. Paul Macy. Say it now.'

'P-Paul.'

'Say it all.'

'Paul Macy. Paul Macy.'

'Good.' He was starting to get a headache: two spikes of pain converging on the center of his head. This girl was no good for him. 'Nat Hamlin doesn't exist any more, and don't you forget it,' he said. 'Now: you wanted me to meet you, and I met you. What's on your mind?'

'You sound so cruel, Paul.' She stumbled on the *Paul*.

'Just annoyed. Your suicide threat – what a miserable tactic that is. I goddam well should have called your bluff.'

'I wasn't bluffing.'

'Whatever you say. I fell for it. I'm here. What do you want?'

'We can't talk here,' she said. 'Not in the middle of a crowd. Not out on the street.'

'Where, then?'

'Your place?'

He shook his head. 'Absolutely not.'

'Mine, then. We can be there in fifteen minutes. Everything's filthy, but –'

'What about a restaurant?' he suggested.

She brightened. 'That would be okay. Any place you like. One of your favorites, where you'd feel comfortable.'

He tried to think of one of his favorite restaurants.

'I don't know any restaurants,' he said. 'You pick one.'

'You don't know any? But you always ate out, practically every night. It was like a compulsion with you. You –'

'That was Nat Hamlin,' he said. 'Hamlin might have been the one who ate out a lot. If you say so. But not me. Not yet.'

He reached into his stock of memories, looking for the names of some Manhattan restaurants. Zero. They really should have given him some restaurant memories when they were constructing the Paul Macy persona at the Rehab Center. It wouldn't have been any big effort for them. They had given him all kinds of other things. Star of the high school lacrosse team. Chicken pox. A mother and a father. Breaking his leg on the slopes at Gstaad. Reading Proust and Hemingway. Putting his hand under Jeanie Grossman's polo shirt. Thirty-five years of ersatz memories. But no information about restaurants. Maybe Gomez, Ianuzzi, and Brewster didn't eat out much. Or perhaps the restaurant stuff was hidden in some cranny of his mind that he hadn't found yet. He said, 'I mean it. I've got no suggestions. You pick.'

'There's a people's restaurant two blocks from here. I've been having lunch at it a lot. You know it?'

'No.'

'We could go there,' she said.

It was a deep, narrow room with tarnishing brass walls and a bunch of sputtering defective light-loops threaded through the thatchwork ceiling. Service was cafeteria-style; you took what you wanted from servo-actuated cubbyholes along the power-counter. Then you found seats at dreary long community tables. Macy, following Lissa to the counter, whispered, 'How do you know how much anything costs?'

'It's a people's restaurant.'

'So?'

'You don't know what that is?'

'I'm new to a lot of this.'

'You pay whatever you can afford,' she said. 'If you don't have any money, you just eat, and make it up next time. Or you go around back and help wash dishes.'

'Does the system work?' he asked.

'Not very well.' She smiled bleakly and began piling food on her tray. In a few moments she had it completely crammed with dishes. Five different kinds of synthetic meats, a mound of salads and vegetables, three rolls, and other things. He was more sparing: vegetable juice, proteoid steak, fried kelp, a cup of no-caffy. At the end of the counter stood a central-credit console. Lissa walked by it without giving it a glance. Macy hesitated a moment, confused, peering into the glossy dark-green screen. In a flustered way he authorized the console to charge his credit account ten dollars. A fat flat-faced girl waiting behind him in line snorted contemptuously. He wondered if he had paid too much or too little. Lissa was already far down the aisle, heading for an empty table at the back of the restaurant. He seized his tray and hurried after her.

They sat facing each other over the bare grim plank of the tabletop. 'I've got some golds,' she said. 'Want one?'

'I'm not sure.'

'Try.' She pulled out a pack. Its brim snapped up and a cigarette popped out. He took it. She took one also, and he carefully watched her nip the ignition pod with her nail. He did the same. A deep pull. Almost at once he felt the dizziness and the acceleration of his heartbeat. She winked at him and blew smoke in his face.

Then she started to eat, stuffing the food down as if she hadn't had anything in weeks. The way she wolfed it, so unselfconscious in her gluttony, fascinated him: it was like watching a fire sweep through a dry meadow. Head forward, jaws working frantically. Sounds of chewing. White teeth flashing. He sat still, dragging on the cigarette, ineffectually trying to spear a strand of kelp with his fork. She looked up. 'Aren't you hungry?' she asked, mouth full.

'Not as hungry as you are, I guess.'

'Don't mind me.'

Her wrists were dirty and there was a film of grime visible on her neck. She was wearing the same blue coat as the other day. Again, no makeup. Her fingernails were ragged. But she wasn't merely outwardly unkempt; she conveyed a sense of inner disintegration that terrified him. Obviously she had once been a beautiful girl, perhaps extraordinarily beautiful. Traces of that beauty remained. She had a parched, ravaged look, though, as if fevers of the soul had been consuming her substance. Her eyes, large and bloodshot, never were still. Always a birdlike flickering from place to place. Cheeks hollower than they ought to be. She could use about ten pounds more, he figured. And a bath. He stubbed out his roach and cut himself a slice of steak. Filet of papier-mâché. He gagged.

Lissa said, 'God, that's better! Some food in the gut again.'

'Why were you so hungry?'

'I always am. I'm burning up.'

'Are you sick?'

She shrugged. 'Who knows?' Her eyes momentarily rested on his. 'I'm trying to think of you as Paul Macy. It isn't easy, sitting here with Nat Hamlin opposite me.'

'Nat Hamlin doesn't exist.'

'You really don't remember me?'

'Zero,' he said.

'Shit almighty! What did they *do* to you at the Rehab Center?'

He said, 'They pumped Nat Hamlin full of memory-dissolving drugs until every bit of him was flushed away. Which left a kind of zombie, you see? A healthy empty body. Society doesn't like to waste a good healthy body. So then they built me inside the zombie's head.'

'Built you? What do you mean, built?'

'Created an identity for me.' He shut his eyes a moment. There was a tightness at his collar. Choking sensation. He wasn't supposed to have to explain any of this. The world was supposed to take it all for granted. 'They built up a past, a cluster of events that I could move around in as if it had really happened. Like I grew up in Idaho Falls, Idaho, and moved to Seattle when I was twelve. My father was a propulsion engineer and my mother taught school. They're both dead now. No brothers. No sisters. I collected African stamps and I did a lot of hunting and fishing. I went to college, UCLA, class of '93, got a degree in philosophy of communication. Two years of national service, stationed in Bolivia and Ecuador, doing voice-overs for the People's Democratic Channel. Then various TV and HV jobs in Europe and the States, and now here in New York. Et cetera, et cetera.'

'God,' she said. 'And it's all phony?'

'Pretty near. It follows Nat Hamlin's biography only as closely as it has to. Like in age. Or Hamlin broke a leg when he was twenty-six and you can see that in the bone, so they've given me a skiing accident for that year.'

'What would happen if I checked the UCLA alumni records, looking for Paul Macy in the class of '93?'

'You'd find him. With a Rehab asterisk saying that this is a pro forma entry covering a retroactively established identity. Same thing if you looked up the Idaho Falls birth register. They do a very thorough job.'

'Christ,' Lissa said. And shivered. 'How creepy this is! You actually are a whole new person.'

'I don't know how whole I am. But I'm new, all right.'

'You don't have any idea who I am, then.'

'You used to pose for Nat Hamlin, didn't you?'

She looked startled. 'How come you know that? I haven't said anything about —'

'The day you stopped me in the street,' he said, 'while we were talking, I got a flash picture of you naked in a kind of studio, and I was leaning over a complicated keyboard thing and telling you to scream. Like a psychosculptor trying to get an emotional effect. I saw it maybe half a second, then it was gone.' He moistened his lips. 'It was like a piece of Nat Hamlin's blotted-out mind surfacing into mine.'

'Or a piece of my mind reaching into yours,' she said.

'Eh?'

'It happens. I can't keep it under control.' A shrill giggle. 'Wherever you got it from, it was right. I was one of Nat Hamlin's models. From January to August, '06, when he was working on his *Antigone 21*. The one the Metropolitan bought. His last big work, before his breakdown. You know about his breakdown?'

'Some. Don't talk about it.' He felt a band of fire across his forehead. Simply being close to someone out of the old existence this long was painful. 'Can I have another gold?'

She offered the cigarette and said, 'I was also his mistress, all through '05 and most of '06. He said he'd get a divorce and marry me. Like Rembrandt. Like Renoir. Falling in love with the model. Only he went out of his head instead. Doing all those crazy things.'

Macy, suddenly vulnerable, tried to stop her with an upraised hand, but there was no halting the flow of her words. 'The last time I saw him was Thanksgiving Day, 2006. At his studio. We had a fight and he threw me down the stairs.' She winced. Into his mind a searing image: an endless flight, the girl falling, falling, skirt up around her thighs, legs kicking, arms clutching, the dwindling scream, the sudden twist and impact. A sound of something cracking. 'In the hospital six weeks with a broken pelvis. When I got out they were hunting him from Connecticut to Kansas. And then –'

'*No more!*' he yelled. People turned to look.

She shrank away from him. 'I'm sorry,' she said, folding into herself, huddling, shaking. His cheeks were hot with shame and turmoil. After a moment she said softly, 'Does it hurt a lot when I talk about him?'

A nod. Silence.

'You asked me to see you because you were in trouble,' he said at length.

'Yes.'

'Would you honestly have killed yourself if I hadn't shown up?'

'Yes.'

'Why?'

'I'm all alone. I have nobody at all. And I'm going out of my mind.'

'How do you know?'

'I hear voices. Other people's minds come into mine. And mine goes into theirs. Extrasensory. Perception.'

'ESP?' he said. 'Like – what is it, mental telepathy?'

'Telepathy. That's what it is. ESP. Telepathy.'

'I didn't think that that really existed.'

A bitter laugh. 'You bet your ass. Sitting right here in front of you. The genuine article.'

'You can read minds?' he said, feeling dreamfogged and unreal.

'Not exactly read. Just touch, mind to mind. It isn't under my conscious control. Things drift in, drift out. Voices humming in my brain, a word, a phrase, an image. It's been happening since I was ten, twelve years old. Only much worse now. Much, much worse.' Trembling. 'The past two years. Hell. Absolute hell.'

'How so?'

'I don't know who I am any more a lot of the time,' she said. 'I get to be five, six people at once. This mushy noise in my head. The buzzing. The voices. Like static, only sometimes words drift in on the static. I pick up all these weird emotions, and they scare me. Not knowing if I'm imagining or not. There's somebody two tables away who wants to rape me. Wishes he dared. In his head I'm naked and bloody, spreadeagled, arms and legs tied to the furniture. And over to my left, someone else, a woman, she's transmitting the odor of shit. She sees me like some kind of giant turd sitting here. I don't know why. And then you –'

'No,' he said. 'Don't tell me.'

'It isn't really ugly. You think I'm dirty and you want to take me home and give me a bath. And fuck me afterward. That's okay. I know I'm dirty. And I'd like to go to bed with you, too. But I can't stand all this crosstalk in my head. I'm wide open, Nat, wide open to every stray thought, and –'

'Paul.'

'What?'

'I said, call me Paul. It's important to me.'

'But you're –'

'Paul Macy.'

'Just now, though, you were coming through as Nat Hamlin to me. From deep underneath.'

'No. Hamlin's gone,' he said. 'I'm Paul Macy.' A feeling of seasickness. The light-loops swaying and hissing overhead. He found himself covering her hand with his. Ragged cuticles against his fingertips. He said, 'If you're suffering so much, why don't you get some help? Maybe there's a cure for ESP. Is that what you want, a cure? I could take you to see Dr Ianuzzi, she's a very sensitive woman, she could get you into the right kind of psychiatric hospital and –'

'And they'd give me shock treatment,' Lissa said. 'Memory dislocation with drugs, like I was a criminal. They'd wash half my brain out trying to heal me. There wouldn't be anything of *me* left. I'm afraid of therapy. I haven't ever gone. I don't want to go.'

'What do you want to do?'

'I don't know.'

'Then what am I supposed to do for you?' he asked.

'I don't know that either, Paul. I'm absolutely fucked up in the head, so there's no use asking me rational questions.' Her eyes glittering eerily. Sick, sick, sick. 'What you really ought to do,' she said, 'is get the hell away from me, right now, like you've wanted to do since the first minute you saw me. Only don't. God, please, don't. Help me. Help me.'

'How?'

'Just be with me a little. I'm all alone. I've cut myself off from the whole world. Look, you know how it is with me? I don't have a job. I don't have friends any more. I look in the mirror and I see my own skeleton. I sit home and wait for the voices to go away, and they scream and scream at me until my head is coming off. I live off the welfare checks. Then I go out for a walk one day, on and on and on, way the hell uptown, and I crash into some guy on the street and he turns around and he's Nat Hamlin, he's the only man I ever really loved, only he isn't Hamlin any more, he's Paul Macy, that's what he says, and –' She caught her breath. 'All right. You don't know me at all and I guess I can't say I know you. But I know your body. Every inch. That's a familiar thing to me, a landmark, something I can anchor myself to. Let me anchor. Let me hold on. I'm going under, Paul. I'm drowning, and maybe you can hold me up, for the sake of what I used to mean to the person you used to be. Maybe. Maybe for a little while. You don't owe it to me, you don't owe me anything, you could get right up and walk out of here and you'd have every right. But don't. Because I need you.'

Sweat-soaked, numb, fists pressed together under the table, he felt a wild surge of pity for her. He felt like saying, Yes, of course, whatever I can do to help you. Come home with me, take a bath, let's blow a few golds and talk about things, this telepathy of yours, this delusion. Not because I ever knew you. Not because the things that happened between you and Nat Hamlin give you any claim on me. But only because you're a suffering human being and you've turned to me for help, and how can I refuse? An act of grace. Yes, yes, I will be your anchor.

Instead he said, 'You're asking a hell of a lot from me. I'm not the most stable individual in the world either. And I'm under doctor's orders to keep away from people out of Nat Hamlin's life. You could be big trouble for me. And me for you. I think the risks for both of us are bigger than the rewards.'

'Does that mean you don't want to get involved?'

'I'm afraid so.'

'Sorry I wasted so much of your time,' she said. In a dead

voice. No change of expression. Not really believing he means it, maybe.

'It wasn't wasted. I only wish I was in shape to do you any good. But a Rehab lives right on the edge of collapse himself, in the beginning. He's got to build a whole new life. So when you ask somebody like that to take on the additional burden –' All right, Macy. Stop explaining things, get up, walk out of here, before she starts crying and you start listening to her again. Up. You don't owe her a thing. You have your own troubles and they aren't small ones. Getting to his feet, now. The girl watching him, stricken, incredulous. Giving her a sickly smile, knowing that a smile of any kind is out of context when you're condemning somebody to death. Turning. Walking away from her, up the aisle of the people's restaurant, past the counter, the sauerkraut and the algaecakes. Another ten strides and you're out the door.

A scream from the back of the room.

'No! Come back! Paul! Paul! *Nat!*'

Her words leaped across the gulf between them like a flight of arrows. Six direct hits. Thwack thwack thwack thwack thwack *thwack!* The last one a killer, straight through from back to chest. He staggered. St Sebastian stumbling in the restaurant aisle. His brain on fire, something very strange happening in there, like the two hemispheres splitting apart and taking up independent existence. And then a voice, speaking quite distinctly from a point just above his left ear, saying:

– How could you walk out on her like that, you snotty creep?

He hit the floor hard, landing elbow-first. A stunning burst of pain. Within that cone of red agony a curious clarity of perception.

Who said that? he asked, losing consciousness. And, going under, he heard:

– I did. Nat Hamlin. Your twin brother Nat.

FOUR

He was at work in his studio again, after too long a layoff. All the sculpting equipment covered with a fine coating of dust. Maybe the delicate inner mechanisms are ruined, or at least imprecise. Try to build an armature for a man, end up with a chimp, something like that. He checked all the calibration carefully: everything in order, surprisingly. Just dusty. Ought to be, after all these years. A wonder it wasn't busted up by vandals. Fucking vandals all over the place. Goths, too. He touched the main keyboard lightly. This was going to be his chef d'oeuvre, a group composition, a contemporary equivalent of *The Burghers of Calais*. But fragmented, intense, multivalued. Call it something unpretentious, like *The Human Condition*.

A fucking headache getting all the models together at the same time. But the group interactions are important: shit, they're the whole point of the thing! There they all stand, now. The fat lady from the circus, eight hundred pounds of quivering suet. Half a ton of laughs. The kid from the student co-op, the one with the shaven head. Gomez, the skull doctor, for that little touch of hostility. The pregnant chick from the supersupermarket. Get the clothes off, baby, show that bulge. Bellybutton sticking way out like a handle. And the vice-president from the bank, very very proper, turn him on a little when we're ready to start. Also the old plaster model from art school days, Apollo Belvedere, missing his prick. A real technical stunt, trying to make psychosculpture out of a hunk of plaster. Faking in the appropriate responses: the test of a master. A cat, too, the one-eyed one from downstairs, gray and white with maybe a dozen claws on each paw, the way it looks.

Lastly, Lissa. My beloved. Stand next to the banker, honey. Turn a little to the left. The banker lifts his hand. He wants to grab your tit, but he doesn't dare, and he hangs there caught in the tension between wanting and holding back. Your nipples ought to be erect for this: you ought to be in heat, some. Wait, I'll do it. A tickle or two down here, yes, look at them standing up.

Okay! Okay! Places, everybody! Group interaction, take one! I want each of you to project the emotion we talked about before, project just that emotion, as purely as you can. And really *live* it. Don't say to yourself, I'm posing for an artist, but say, I'm so-and-so and this is my life, this is my soul, and I'm radiating it in big chunks so he can grab it with his machine and turn it into a masterpiece. Ready? Ready? Hey, you sucks, why aren't you holding the pose? Who gave you permission to dissolve? Let's have some fucking *stability* in here! Hold it! Hold it! Hold it!

He was running as fast as he could, and the effort was killing him. A band of hot metal around his chest. His eyes ready to pop out of his head. He had turned left outside the restaurant, onto Broadway, down the dark street in long loping strides, thinking at first that he was going to get away, but then he heard the footsteps precisely matching his, a clop for his clop, on and on, and knew he wouldn't escape. Don't look back. Something may be gaining on you.

Nat Hamlin running smoothly behind him, wearing the same body as his only four years younger. Shouting obscenities as he ran. What a foul mouth he has! You'd think artists were aesthetic types, more refined, and yet here comes this anthology of smut running after me. Shouting, Hey, you, Macy, you dumb cocksucker, slow down! We got a lot to talk about, you asshole!

Sure we do. The first thing we talk about is which of us dies and which of us lives, and I know right away what your position is on *that*, Nat. So I'm just going to keep on running until I drop. Maybe you'll drop first, even though you're younger. With your acid and your golds and your broads tearing you down, and I've lived a clean life in the Center all these years.

On. On. Almost at the bridge, now. The shining towers of Old Manhattan ahead of me. Hamlin still screaming garbage. Isn't that one of the network hovereyes up there? Sure it is! Following right along, taping the whole thing, just in case a nice sweet murder happens. Call the police, you dumb machine! Look, there's a lunatic on my ass, a convicted criminal making an illegal breakthrough to life after having been eradicated! See, see, he's got my face! Why don't you do something? I'm a network man, can't you tell? Paul Macy. Number six on the late news. I know, you're just a machine, an objective reporter, a self-contained self-propelled passive observer, but screw all that now. My life's at stake. If he catches up with me. And I can't hold out much longer. Fire in my guts. All that spaghetti in there going up and down with every stride. Liver and lights ajiggle. Oh, Christ, a hand on my shoulder. Tag, I'm it!

Down on the ground. His knees on the crooks of my arms. Pinned. His lips drooling. A lunatic with my face. Get off! Get off! Get off! And he laughs. And over his right shoulder I see the hovereye recording everything. Wonderful. *Now we bring you the final moments of Paul Macy, thirty-nine, tragically slain by his berserk alter ego. After this brief message from the makers of Acapulco Golds.* Going. Going. Go –

He was moving warily through a sleepy suburb, Queens or Staten Island, he wasn't sure which. They all looked the same. A biting January day. High-pressure system sitting on the city: not even a cloud in the sky, just a bright blank blue shield pressing down, no hint of oncoming snow, though some blackened heaps of the Christmas snowfall still lined the curb. In this sort of dryness it was difficult to believe it would ever snow again. The leafless trees like gaunt bundles of sticks, silently shouting, I am an oak, I am a maple, I am a tulip tree, and nobody listening because they all look the same. Squat two-story brick houses, reasonably far apart, on both sides of the street. The kiddies at school. The hubbies at work. A hot little wifey behind each picture window.

He wasn't sure how he had found his way here. Starting out from Connecticut about half past nine in the morning, the work going all wrong, a fucking nightmare in the studio finishing in a horrid botch of a week's good labors, and then driving into the city, crossing two or maybe three bridges, ending up here. And the familiar yellow haze now swathing the temples and forehead, the steamy mist of madness. He welcomed it. There comes a time when you have to surrender to the dark forces. Yes, yes, go on, take possession of me. Nat Hamlin at your service. Call me Raskolnikov Junior. Ha, that crazy Rooshian understood something about intensity! How we boil inside. And sometimes boil over.

Look at this house, now. A completely stereotyped suburban villa, maybe fifty years old, product of the buggy seventies, the creepy sixties. I shall bring some illumination into its dreary existence. By an act of will I shall intensify the life-experience of its inhabitant. See how easy it is to force the side door? Just this flimsy little latch: you insert the slicer, you waggle it, you push . . . yes.

Now we go inside. Good morning, ma'am, this is the mad rapist, the Darien cocksmith, I'm peddling ecstatic terror this happy day. No, don't scream, I'm friendly. I never do unnecessary injury. I assure you that I wouldn't be here at all except for this irresistible compulsion I have. Is it my fault I'm off my hinges? A man is entitled to have a breakdown. Especially if he's a serious important artist. You ought to be thrilled to know who's going to fuck you. You're part of one of the most significant personal disintegrations in the history of western art. Like, suppose I was Van Gogh and I cut off my fucking ear right here on your kitchen linoleum? Wouldn't that give you at least a peripheral place in his biography? Well, all right, then. He had his collapse, I'm having mine. Come here, now. Let's get this tunic off you. See what kind of merchandise you're offering. Sorry, I wouldn't have ripped it if you had been cooperating. Why fight it? This can be much more meaningful for you if you just spread and give in. There. There. See, you're creaming for me! How can you deny the activity of your own

Bartholin glands? This lubrication brands you whore, milady! Ah. In. In. In. That's the ticket. In and out, in and out. *Con amore. Allegro, allegrissimo!* Wham, bam, thank you, ma'am. Zip it up. Out the door. Mad rapist strikes again. Thus we enact the latest fascinating episode in our case of personality disruption. I look so cleancut for being a psychopath. Oops! Hey, no, officer! Put that stunner down! Don't – hey, watch it – I surrender, damn you, I surrender! I'll go peacefully! I'll – go – peacefully –

Blinking furiously, soggy-headed, disoriented, he woke up. He found himself in bed, his own bed, the covers up around his chin, the lights on in the bedroom. Darkness beyond the window. The sheets cool against his skin: somebody has undressed him. From his elbow there flowed rivulets of agony. For a moment he was totally unable to recollect his last previous period of consciousness; then the incident in the people's restaurant came back to him. Walking out on Lissa. The girl calling after him. Nat Hamlin's voice whispering snakelike in his ear. Calamity. Collapse. Chaos. 'Hello?' he said, voice breaking, ragged. 'Is anybody here? Hello? Hello?'

Out of the other room came the girl. Framed in the doorway, naked. Even more slender than he had imagined, ribcage visible, the double ridge of muscle on the flat belly, thighs lean with a gap of an inch or two between them all the way up. The breasts still full, though. Not big boobs but nicely shaped. Triangular red bush. Her skin pink, scrubbed-looking, still moist. She's had a bath. Looks about five years younger now.

'How long have you been up?' she asked him.

'Maybe half a minute. What day is this?'

'It's still the same Monday night. No, it's Tuesday morning by now. Half past one in the morning.'

'You brought me home?'

'With some help. There was this cabdriver in the people's restaurant. He carried you out. Christ, I was scared, Paul. I thought you were dead!'

'Did you try to get a doctor?'

She laughed. 'At this time of night? I just sat here and

watched you and hoped you'd snap out of it. You seemed to be having nightmares. Your eyeballs rolling around under the lids. I touched your mind just once, more or less an accident, and it was pretty scary, something about being chased through a dark alley.' Coming over to the bed, she said, 'Do you feel all right? Headache?'

'Headache, yes. Jesus.'

'After a while it looked like you were just sleeping. So I took a bath, like you said I needed. You should have seen the mud come off me. But you get to feeling so shitty sometimes that you don't even bother to wash yourself, and that's where I was at. Well, that's over, now. I couldn't figure out how to work your cassette player, so I've been inside reading a book, and –'

'What happened to me in the restaurant?' he asked.

She sat on the edge of the bed. He looked at her thighs and wanted to let his hand rest on them, but it took two tries before the quivering arm would lift itself and make the ten-inch journey. Her skin was cool and smooth. He stroked her thigh, up and down, midway between knee and crotch.

She said, 'You got up to leave, remember? I didn't think you were going to do it, but you did, and there you were, walking away from me. The one hope I had, walking away from me. And I knew I had hit bottom right there.'

'So you called out to me.'

'No,' she said. 'I *reached* out. With my mind.'

'You didn't shout my name? Yell at me to come back?'

'I didn't open my mouth. I reached. And I made contact. With both of you.'

'Both?'

'I went right into your head, and there was someone called Paul Macy there, yes, but I hit you on another level, too, and I found Nat Hamlin. Coiled up like a spring. Hiding in the dark. I'll never forget it in a million years. My mind arcing across the gap from me to you, and finding two of you. The hidden one. Or the sleeping one, I guess.'

– Sleeping is more accurate.

Hamlin's voice. Macy jumped, yanking his hand back from Lissa as though she were a stove.

'Did you hear that?' he asked.

'I didn't hear anything. But I felt a kind of twinge. A little jolt of ESP action.'

'It was Hamlin, talking inside me. He said, "Sleeping is more accurate." What the hell's going on, Lissa?'

'He's still inside you,' she said.

'No. No. That's impossible. They all said he was gone forever.'

'I guess he wasn't,' Lissa said. 'A little bit of him left, down in the bottom of your head. Maybe you can't ever fully wipe out a personality. Like you can breed a whole new frog if you've got a single cell of the old one's body, and the new one will be identical to the old. Is that right? And so you had a couple of cells of Nat Hamlin still in your head, and I brought them back to life by touching them. I'm sorry, Paul. It's all my fault.'

'It isn't possible,' he said. 'It's just some hallucination I'm having.'

– You wish, brother.

'He's really there,' Lissa said. 'I *felt* him. A presence inside you. The two of you in one head.'

'No.'

– No?

'I didn't mean to bring him back, Paul. I mean, I loved him, yes, but he was no good, he hurt people, he was a criminal. When they sentenced him to be wiped out, they did the right thing. I don't want him back. How can we get rid of him?'

'Don't worry about that,' said Macy. 'He was got rid of before. He can be got rid of again.'

– Up yours, friend.

Lissa managed a brave smile. She took his hand between hers and clamped it. She looked transformed by soap and hot water, no longer the moody, embittered, disturbed waif of the restaurant. He realized that his collapse now tied her to him. She had brought him home. She had cared for him.

He couldn't throw her out. She said, 'Can I get you anything? A drink? A gold?'

'Not right now. I'd like to see – if I can stand up –'

'You ought to rest. A nasty shock you had.'

'Nevertheless.' He swung his legs over the side of the bed and tested his feet a couple of times before putting his weight on them. Precariously rising. Wobbly. Standing there showing his nakedness to her. Then a gesture that astounded him: modestly moving his hand to cover his crotch. Immediately pulling it back; he could think of six different reasons why it was crazy to want to hide himself from her, starting with the fact that she had been this body's other owner's mistress for all those months years ago.

He took a step and another, and found himself in the middle of the room, lurching a little. His left elbow was stiff and sore, which was expectable enough, considering that all his weight had landed on it. Lucky thing it wasn't broken. But there was also a curious numbness around the right side of his face. No sensation in the cheek, and his lips felt funny in the corner of his mouth. As though he'd had an anesthetic shot at the dentist. As though he'd had a stroke, maybe.

He looked at his face in the bedroom mirror. Yes, a little lopsided, the way his father had looked after *his* stroke. The mouth pulled back, the lower eyelid drooping. Macy prodded the numb part of his cheek and tried to push the lips into their proper configuration. Everything hard, like plastic flesh.

– Hi ho.

'Are *you* doing that?'

'What's the matter, Paul?'

'My face. He's holding the muscles. I can't get him to ease off.'

'Oh, Christ, Paul!' Terrified.

A battle of wills. Her terror infected him. This was grisly, having the side of your face held captive by something in your brain. Like going swimming and coming up with a lobster pinching your cock. He fought back. Tugging at the muscles, trying to soften the flesh. Re-lax – re-lax – re-*lax*. Yes. Getting the upper hand, or whatever. Some sensation returning, now. The mouth no longer distorted. Hamlin scuttling lobsterlike into deeper recesses of his brain, letting go. Tomorrow I scoot over to the Rehab Center and have this taken care of. A complete and exhaustive burnout of whatever vestiges of the previous self still remain. Macy glanced at the mirror again. Opening and closing his mouth, practicing big grins. The first round goes to me. He stumbled back to the bed and toppled onto it, quivering.

'You're soaked with sweat!' Lissa cried.

'It was a real struggle. The muscles.'

'I watched it. Your face was writhing and grimacing. It looked like you were going crazy. Here, get back under the covers. You ought to rest. Would you like to smoke?'

'Maybe that's not such a bad idea.'

She brought two golds over. Solemnly they lit up and went through the ritual of puffing, the deep drag, suck in lots of air. As the hallucinogenic smoke wandered through his lungs he imagined it traveling swiftly to his brain and befuddling the demon that Lissa's ESP had conjured into life there. Lull him back to sleep. And then, when Hamlin's groggy, drive a silver spike through his heart. Macy couldn't feel any trace of the other's presence now. For all he knew, the pot really knocked him out.

'Turn out the light,' Macy said. 'Get into bed with me. We'll lie here and smoke.'

Her thighs cool against his. He felt feverish. The strain of the last few hours, no doubt. The tips of the golds glowing in the dark. They don't burn as fast now as they did when you had to roll your own. Time to meditate, time to contemplate. But eventually they were gone. Stubbing out the roaches. He was still unable to detect the presence of the passionate, warped soul of Nat Hamlin within him. Pot the panacea, maybe.

He reached toward Lissa.

Moving about in the bed was difficult, because of his sore elbow. Yet he managed. His right arm curling around her back and the hand coming out front on the far side to cup her distant breast. Soft firm bouncy globe, overflowing his clutching fingers. Trapping the nipple gently between index and middle, twitching his digits tenderly to excite her. Then, not easily, he pivoted upward, wriggled, touched his bad arm briefly and dismayingly against the headboard, and succeeded in wedging his right knee between her thighs without losing his grip on her breast. Her legs parted and he got the top of his knee up against the warmth of her. She made little purring sounds. The trouble was that he couldn't kiss her in this position, his neck simply wouldn't reach, but okay, this would do for now. Tentatively he flexed the stiff arm, planning to slide it across to her groin if it wasn't too painful for him.

This was the first time since he had become Paul Macy that he'd been in bed with a woman.

Oh, they'd given him a set of memories. Probably Gomez had taken care of the programming job, the little horny bastard. Dreaming up phantom lays for him. A proper heterosexual background, not even neglecting a spot of innocent pubescent homophily. Here he was with Jeanie Grossman in the cabin at Mount Rainier. Sweet sixteen, both of them, tiny boobies cold and hard in his hands, Jeanie's long black hair all disheveled, her thighs clamped tight on his probing hand. Oh, no, no, Paul, don't, please don't, she was saying, and then she was breathing hoarsely and murmuring, Be gentle, darling, just the way they said it in the dumb romantic novels Gomez most likely had stolen all this from, Oh, be gentle with me, Paul, it's my first time. On her and in her, wham and bam. Frantic hasty poking. My first time too, but he doesn't tell her that. Jeanie Grossman gasping out her inaugural orgasm with the white bulk of Mount Rainier peering over her shoulder. But of course it hadn't happened. Not to him. To Gomez, maybe, long ago; maybe Gomez programmed his own sex life into all his reconstructs, for lack of imagination. Poor Jeanie, whoever you are, a hundred different men think they've had your cherry.

And there was much more to Macy's curriculum vita. The

married woman, really old, easily past thirty, who had fallen upon him with sudden ferocity when he was seventeen years old and selling encyclopedias in the summer. Sitting next to her on the couch with all his charts outspread, saying, This is an outstanding feature, our three-dimensional visual aids presentation, and we have a choice of six bindings in beautiful decorator colors, and would you like to hear about our brand-new home videotape supplement, and while he prattles she pushes the brochures off his lap and dives for his zipper and then the amazing shattering sensation of her lips engulfing his cock.

Good old Gomez. And the nurse at Gstaad, seducing him in his huge plaster cast. And the plump German girl who liked him to use the butler's entrance. And the one with the rubber underwear and the whips. The endurance contest in Kyoto, too. The orgy on the beach at Herzlia. The dear doctor had stocked him amply with vivid and varied erotica. But what was the use? None of it was real, at least not so far as Paul Macy was concerned, and so he could no more claim it as earned experience than if he had got it all from Henry Miller and the divine marquis. He was minus any authentic lovemaking memories. So in effect he was about to lose his innocence at the age of thirty-nine. But as he fondled Lissa's slim sleek body he realized the value of having had all those imaginary episodes of the flesh implanted in him. A real virgin would be up against anatomical confusions, the mechanics of the thing, the correct angle of entry, all those problems. He at least knew where the way in was to be found. Secondhand knowledge, maybe, but useful. The Rehab Center hadn't turned him loose unable to cope.

One small problem, though. He didn't seem to be able to get it up.

Lissa was primed and ready, nicely lubricated, and his item still hung slack. Through slitwide eyes she watched him and frowned. The juices souring and curdling in her as she waited to have her vacancy filled. At last understanding the reason for the delay. Cuddling against him; her hand to the scrotum, a light tickling, very skillful. Ah. Yes. Some wind in the sails, finally. The old familiar rigidifying that he had never before experienced. Up. Up. Up. At full mast, now. Swing smoothly around, slide yourself into her. They made adjustments of their positions. She prepared herself to receive him. He was athrob, inflamed, aloft.

Then came a laugh from within and a cold devilish voice:
– Take a look at this, pal.

Blossoming on the screen of his mind the image of Lissa spread wide on another bed in another room, and himself – no, not himself but Nat Hamlin – poised above her, seizing the calves of her legs, draping them over his shoulders, now lowering himself to her with ithyphallic vitality. Nailing her. And as that inward consummation took place Macy felt his own rod lose its vehemence. Limp again; shriveled, infantile, a wee-wee instead of a cock. Wearily he sagged against the girl. Doing it was impossible for him now. Not with *him* watching. I carry my own audience in my head. Hamlin, still roaring with turbulent inner laughter, was sending up scene after scene out of his no doubt actual experience, coupling with Lissa in this position, in that one, Lissa on top, Lissa down on her knees being had dogwise, the whole copulatory biography of their long-ago liaison, and Macy, helpless, his phantom images of Jeanie Grossman and the encyclopedia woman swept away by this gushing incursion of reality, lay stunned and sobbing and impotent waiting for Hamlin to stop tormenting him.

Lissa didn't seem to understand what was happening, only that Macy had lost his hard at a critical moment and was plainly upset about it. Her long thin arms cradled him affectionately. 'It's all right,' she whispered. 'You've been under a terrible strain, and anyway that kind of thing can happen to anybody. It'll be better later. Just lie here and rest. It doesn't matter. It's all right. It's all right.' Pressing his cheek against her breast. 'Try to get some sleep,' she said. He nodded. Closing his eyes, trying to relax. Out of the darkness Hamlin's voice:
– That was just to let you know I'm still here.

FIVE

Sometime during the night there must have been a flow of strength from her to him, for he had fallen asleep being comforted by her, and he was awakened by the sounds of her sobs. The room very dark: morning some hours away, yet he felt as though he'd had enough sleep. Lissa had her back to him, her bony spine pressing into his chest; she was curled up knees to breasts, making snuffling sounds, and every thirty seconds or so a great racking open-mouthed bed-shaking sob came out of her. Before he could tend to her he had to survey the condition of his own head. All seemed well. He was rested and loose. There was a delicious sense of aloneness between his ears. When he was in contact with Hamlin he felt inwardly cluttered, as though bales of barbed wire were coming unraveled in his skull. None of that now. The alter ego was sleeping, maybe, or at any rate busy in some other realm. Macy put his hand lightly on Lissa's bare shoulder and called her name. She went on sobbing. He shook her gently.

'What?' she said, sounding foggy and far away.

'Tell me what the trouble is.'

A long silence. No reply. Had she gone back to sleep? Had she ever been awake?

'Lissa? Lissa, what's the trouble?'

'Trouble?'

'You've been crying.'

'It's all a bad dream,' she said, and he realized that she was still asleep. She pulled away from him, getting even more tightly into the fetal position. Heaving a terrible sigh. Sounds of weeping. He wrapped himself around her, thighs to her buttocks, his lips just above her ear. Her skin was cold. She was shivering. 'Chasing me,' she murmured. 'Ten arms, like some kind of octopus.'

'Wake up,' he said. 'It'll all go away if you wake up.'

'Why are you so sure?'

And she sent him her dream, nicely wrapped. Popping from her mind to his, clicking smartly into place like a cassette. Jesus. A lunar landscape of crumbling concrete, thousands of miles wide, a million cracks and furrows and fissures. Not a building, not a tree, not a shrub in sight, only this gray-white plateau of flat ruinous stony pavement covering the universe. From above a fierce white light plays on the concrete, so that the upthrust rims of the fissurelines cast long harsh shadows. A frosty wind blowing. Footsteps. Lissa appears from the right, naked, breathless, running hard, her hair streaming behind her, streaming *into* the wind. Her pale white skin is marked by dozens of circular red cicatrices, suction-marks. And now her pursuer thunders after her. Nat Hamlin, yes, wearing his bland even-featured Anglo-Saxon face, but he has eight, ten, a dozen curling tentacles coming out of his shoulders, tentacles equipped with big ridged sucker-cups. Not hard to tell where Lissa got the red marks on her body. And a dick a yard long sticking out in front of him, like a club. His feet are frog-flippers the size of snowshoes. Thromp! Thromp! Thromp! He comes flapping toward her at an incredible speed. And then there are the voices. People are saying things about her in Sanskrit, in Hungarian, in Basque, in Hopi, in Turkish. Unfavorable comments about her breasts. Snide remarks about her unshaven armpits. A cutting reference to a mole on her left hind cheek. They are laughing at her in Bengali. They are offering her perversions in Polish. She hears everything. She understands everything. Hamlin now has split in two, a double pursuer, one of him somehow coming from the other side of her, and she is trapped between them. Closer . . . closer . . . impaling her fore and aft . . . she screams . . .

I reject this dream, Macy thought. It isn't a necessary nightmare. To hell with it.

'Wake up,' he said again, loudly.

Waking her wasn't so easy. She was hovering in a peculiar borderline state, almost a hypnotic trance, in which she was able to hear him and even give him rational answers, without, however, being plugged into the waking world in any meaningful way. Lost in her hallucinatory horrors. He switched on the light. Half past four in the morning. He'd been sleeping only about two hours, then. Seemed like a full night. Pulling her to a sitting position, he opened her eyes with his thumbs.

She stared blearily at him. Eyes like mirrors, seeing nothing. 'Lissa? Jesus, Lissa, *snap out of it!*' Waves of terror rippling across her face. Her sharp little elbows digging hard into her sides, fists balled and held tight to her clavicles. Still sobbing, a quick panicky inhaling and exhaling. Macy hauled her from the bed and frogmarched her into the bathroom. His palm touching the shower control. A computerized cascade of chilly water. Get under, girl. A shriek. As though he were flaying her. But she was awake now.

'My God,' she said. 'I was on some other planet.'

'I know. I know.'

'My head's all full of it. A million square miles of cracked pavement. I still see it. And that light shining overhead, such a fucking bright light. And those tentacles.'

'They're gone now,' he said.

'No. They came out of my head, didn't they? They're still in there, the way Nat Hamlin's in you. I'm going crazy, Paul, isn't that obvious? Christ, hold tight to me. Maybe the octopus is real and this is the dream.'

Her teeth were chattering. He wrapped a towel around her and guided her back to the bedroom. Her cheeks felt hot. A high fever raging in her. 'I just want to hide somewhere,' she said. 'To disappear into my own brain, you understand what I mean? To get away into some inner world where nobody can find me. Where I can't hear the voices.'

She slithered under the covers, pulling the blankets over her head. A thick mound in the bed, a lump, like a rabbit in a snake's belly. From underneath came muffled words. 'What's going to happen to us, Paul? We're both crazy.'

Macy got in beside her, and abruptly she turned to him with such fantastic ferocious passion that the breath was knocked from him. Grappling with him, knotting her arms and legs about his. Her belly pushing at his. Her pubic bone jabbing him painfully. Lissa clutching him as if she wanted to devour him. As a boy living in Seattle in the life he hadn't lived, he had watched a starfish in a tidepool going to work on a clam, pulling its shell open with its suction cups, then turning itself inside out so that its stomach might go forth and ingest. He thought of that now as Lissa writhed against him. Waiting for something long and slimy to extrude from her slit and begin digesting him. Thank you, Dr Gomez, for that lovely image. Do you hate women too, you mindfucking bastard?

'Paul,' she murmured. 'Paul. Paul. Paul.' Rhythmic exclamations. To his surprise he found his member stiffening despite everything, and in a single swift gesture he slipped it into her. She was hot and wet. As he speared her he expected Hamlin to surface and interfere with things again, but this time he was allowed the privacy of his genitals. Lissa cried out and came almost immediately. Her spasms were still going on when his began, a million and a quarter years later.

At half past seven he woke again. Lissa seemed to be sleeping soundly. Hamlin quiescent. He showered and went into the little kitchen-cum-dinette. Picked up the phone, tapped out the delayed-message code, and instructed it to call the network at nine to say that he was sick and wouldn't be coming in. Then he called the Rehab Center and arranged for today's post-therapy session to be moved up from four in the afternoon to nine in the morning. He didn't want to lose any time getting the Hamlin problem dealt with. 'Will you hold?' the Center's computer asked him, and he held, and two or three minutes later the machine came back to him and said, 'I've checked Dr Ianuzzi's schedule, Mr Macy, and it will be possible for her to see you at nine today.' The computer's face, on telephone screen, was that of an efficient, good-looking brunette. 'Fine,' Macy said, winking at her.

He peered into the bedroom. Lissa lay face down, one arm dangling to the floor. Snoring faintly. Well, she'd had a hard night. He programmed breakfast for himself.

Macy wondered if Dr Gomez would be at the Center today. He wanted to see the look on the little Mex's face when he showed up with a supposedly obliterated identity surfacing in his brain. Macy could still hear the doctor's cocky spiel. 'If I tell you Hamlin is eradicated, it's because I *know* Hamlin is eradicated.' Sure. 'I'm not just being a bullheaded bastard.' No, of course not. 'Nat Hamlin doesn't exist any more.' You tell it, baby. 'Hamlin exists only as an abstract concept.' Right on, sweetheart. How was Gomez going to explain any of last night's events? I hope Hamlin spits right in his goddam face. With my mouth.

He thought he had a good idea what had brought Hamlin back to life. Who. Lissa was who. This telepathy business of hers had somehow managed to nudge the expelled ego out of limbo and give him at least a partial grip on his former body. Looking back over his relationship with Lissa, Macy saw the pattern clearly. That first day, two weeks ago exactly, when she'd collided with him on the street, that first moment of recognition, Lissa refusing to honor his Rehab badge and calling him by Nat Hamlin's name: right then, at the beginning, he'd felt a stabbing pain, as if he were Hamlin and back at the Center having his past uprooted. And then, a few minutes later, same incident, when Lissa had leaned close and grabbed his wrist: that feeling of heat in his brain, that sense of an intrusion. Clearly it was her ESP stirring things up in him. Producing an instant of confusion, of double identity, when he wasn't sure whether he was Hamlin or Macy. Probably that was the moment at which Hamlin's return to conscious existence was stimulated. When I got that vision of myself in Hamlin's studio, Lissa posing for me. And thought I was having a heart attack on the street.

And then? Later the same day, when he almost passed out in front of Harold Griswold's Hamlin sculpture, that must have been Hamlin giving a wild whoop and a leap inside him at the sight of something familiar. That night he had the first of his pursuit dreams. Hamlin loose in his head, and chasing him. Next? When Lissa sent the letter threatening suicide, and he met her on the street. Good Christ, was that only last night? And he walked up to her and there was that doubleness again, the nausea, the confusion. No doubt she had given Hamlin another little nudge. Lastly, when he tried to leave her in the restaurant, and she cried out for him to come back. The sheer mental voltage of that must have been the clincher, awakening Hamlin fully, giving him a chance to jump to the conscious level. He was so stunned by Lissa's telepathic scream that Hamlin was able to grab some of the cerebral centers and start talking to him. Even to seize the facial muscles on the right side, for a little while. He doesn't have solid control of anything, not for long, he holds on a while and slips away, but he's there. Lissa's fault. Of course she didn't intend to. A weird telepathic accident, is all. Or maybe not so accidental. It was Hamlin she loved, he thought; I'm just a stranger in his body. Suppose this is her way of getting rid of me and helping him come back.

No.

He didn't want to believe that. She hadn't meant to yank Hamlin into consciousness. All the same, she was responsible. Now he had to get Hamlin removed again. Anguish and turmoil, most likely. After which he'd better not fool around with Lissa. Self-preservation has to come before concern for others, right? Out she goes.

The Rehab Center was just across the Connecticut line in Greenwich. Ten minutes by long-hop gravity tube from Manhattan North. Macy took the uptown shuttle to the nearest loading point for the tube. A gray, misty morning, more like late autumn than like late spring. Taut-faced commuters running this way and that. Most of them going the other way, thank God. They kept bumping into him. Giving him funny stares and going on. For over a week now he had been free of his obsession that people were staring at him, but this morning it returned. The Rehab badge seemed like a beacon drawing all eyes. Announcing: Here walks a former sinner. Doer of dreadful deeds! Behind this bland mask lurks the purified brain of a famous criminal. Do you recognize him? Do you remember the news stories? Go up close, take a good look, enlarge your life-experience through a moment of proximity with somebody who has been a household word. Guaranteed not to harm you. Guaranteed to be regenerated and redeemed from sin. He walks, he talks, he suffers like an ordinary human being! See the former monster! See! See! See!

'Greenwich,' Macy said huskily to the ticket-scanner, and tapped out his account number. From the slot came a plastic ticket with thin golden filaments embedded in it. Clutching it tightly, Macy made his way to the loading gate. The doors of the train were open. Plenty of seats inside. He found one next to the wall. No windows in here. People drifting aboard. He sat passively, thinking as little as possible. Floating in here. Just as the train itself, within its tube, floated in a larger tube on a two-foot-deep cushion of water.

'All aboard,' the computer voice calls. The pressure-tight door sliding shut. We are sealed within. Gliding forward, through the airlock. The valve swinging open. Near-vacuum in front of the train, full pressure behind: the train goes squirting into the tube. Very clever. Little sensation of motion, because of the dynamic flotation system and the sleek roller-bearing wheels. Onward, zooming silently eastward, driven by cunning pneumatic forces, the air to the train's rear gradually becoming more tenuous, the air in front undergoing steady compression. Ultimately the air in front will be our cushion for deceleration. Meanwhile gravity also drives us as we swoop through a gently sloping tunnel. To the midpoint, where we will begin to rise and slow. How shrewd these engineers are. If I could only ride the tube all day, coasting from here to there and back again at a lovely 300 mph. The ecstasies of free fall. Or almost free.

Macy sat with eyes closed. Not a twitch out of Hamlin. Stay hidden, you murderous bastard. Stay hidden.

He didn't understand how it was possible for Hamlin to have come back. At the Center he had picked up a good working knowledge of the Rehab process, and from what he knew of it he couldn't see any chance for the spontaneous or evoked resurrection of an obliterated identity. What's identity, after all, if not just the sum of all the programming we've received since the initial obstetrical slap on the rear? They pump into us a name, a set of kinship relations, a structural outlook toward society, and a succession of life experiences. And after a while feedback mechanisms come into play, so that what we've already become directs our choice of further shaping experiences, thereby reinforcing the contours of the existing self, creating the attitudes and responses that we and others consider 'typical' of that self. Fine. And this accumulation of events and attitudes is engraved on the brain, first in the form of electrical impulses and patterns, then, as short-term memories are accepted for long-term storage, in the form of chains of complex molecules, registering in the chemical structure of the brain's cells.

And so, to undo the identity-creating process, one merely undoes the electrochemical patterns by which the identity is recorded. A little electronic scrambling, first, to inhibit synapse transmission and rearrange the way the electrons jump in the brain. Then, when defenses are down, start the chemical attack. A shot of acetylcholine terminase to interfere with short-term memory fixation. One of the puromycin derivatives to wash out the involuted chains of ribonucleic acid, brain-RNA, that keep memories permanently inscribed in the brain. Flush the system with amnesifacient drugs, and presto! The web of experiences and attitudes is wiped away, leaving the body a tabula rasa, a blank sheet, without identity, without soul, without memory. So, then: feed in a new identity, any identity you like. Building takes longer than destroying, naturally. You start with a vacant hulk that has certain basic motor reactions left and nothing else: it knows how to tie its shoelaces, how to blow its nose, how to make articulate sounds. Unless the wipeout job has been done with excessive zeal, it can even speak, read, and write, though probably on a six-year-old level. Now give it a name. Using nifty hypnagogic techniques, feed it its new biography: here is where you went to school, this is your mother, this is your father, these were your childhood friends, these were your hobbies. It doesn't have to be crystalline in its consistency; most of our memories are mush anyway, out of which a bright strand projects here and there. Stuff the reconstruct with enough of a past so he won't feel disembodied. Then train him for adult life: give him some job skills, social graces, remind him what sex is all about, et cetera, et cetera. The peripheral stuff, reading and writing and language, comes back faster than you'd imagine. But the old identity *never* comes back, because it's been hit by fifty megatons of fragmentation bombs, it's been totally smashed. Right down on the cellular level, everything making up that identity has been sluiced away by the clever drugs. It's gone.

Unless. Somehow. Skulking in the cellular recesses, traces of the old self manage to remain, like scum on a pond, a mere film of demolished identity, and from this film, given the right circumstances, the old self can rebuild itself and take command of its body. What are the right circumstances? None, if you listen to Gomez & Co. No recorded case of an identity reestablishing itself after a court-ordered eradication has been carried out. But how many reconstructs have ever been exposed to ESP? The full blast of a telepath reaching out toward old and new identities simultaneously? It's a statistical problem. There are x number of reconstructs walking around today. And y number of telepaths. X is a very small number and y is even smaller than that. So what are the odds against an x meeting a y? So big, apparently, that this is the first time it's ever happened. And now look. That psychopathic fucker Hamlin crawling around loose in my brain. Why mine?

'Greenwich,' said the voice of the computer, and the train slid placidly to a halt on its cushion of compressed air.

The Rehab Center was north of the city, in the old estate district, which through inspired and desperate zoning arrangements had managed to resist the grinding glacier of population

pressures which had devastated most of suburbia. Several acts
of reconstruction and rehabilitation had been performed on
the Center itself. The main building, a gray pseudo-Tudor
stone pile three stories high, with groined stockbroker-Gothic
ceilings and leaded-glass windows, had been a private residence in the middle twentieth century, the mansion of some
old robber baron, a speculator in energy options. In the
end the speculator had outsmarted himself and gone into
bankruptcy; the big house then had been transformed into
the headquarters of a therapy cult that relied a good deal
on year-round nudity, and it was in this era that the five
plastic geodesic domes had been erected, forming a giant
pentagram around the main building, to serve as wintertime
solaria. Recriminations and lawsuits did the cult in within five
years, and the place became an avant-garde secondary school,
where the scions of the Connecticut gentry took courses in
copulatory gymnastics, polarity traumas, and social relativity.
The various minor outbuildings, with many ingenious electronic facilities, were added at this time. The school collapsed
before it had produced its first graduating class, and the
county, taking possession of the premises for nonpayment
of realty taxes, speedily turned it into the first Rehab Center
in the western half of the state in order to qualify for the
federal matching-funds grant then being offered; the national
government, eager to get the Rehab program off to a fast
start, was throwing its meager resources around quite grandly
then.

As one rode up the thousand-yard-long driveway leading
to the main building, one could behold all the discrete strata
of construction marking the epochs of the Center's past, and,
if one were imaginatively inclined, one might envision the
old speculator placing phone calls from poolside, the health
fanatics toasting in the solaria, the youthful scholars elabo-
rately fornicating on the lawn, all at once, while through
the leafy glades wandered today's candidates for personality
rehabilitation, smiling blankly as voices out of earphones
purred their pasts to them.

Macy saw none of these things today, not even the drive-way. For, as he emerged from the tube station in downtown Greenwich and looked about for an autotaxi to take him up to the Center, he felt a sensation much like that of a hatchet landing between his shoulder blades, and toppled forward, dazed and retching, sprawling to the pavement. For some moments he lay half-conscious on the elegant blue and white terrazzo tiling of the station entrance. Then, recovering somewhat, he managed to scramble up until he crouched on hands and knees, like a tipsy sprinter awaiting the starter's gun. More than that he could not do. Rising to a standing position was beyond him now. Flushed, sweating, stricken, he waited for his strength to return and hoped someone would help him up.

No one did. The commuters obligingly parted their ranks and flowed by him to either side. A boulder in a stream. No one offers to assist a boulder. Perhaps they have a lot of epileptics in Greenwich. Can't let yourself get worked up over one of *those*. Damned troublemakers always flopping on their faces, chewing on their tongues: how's a man going to get to work on time if he stops for them every morning?

Macy listened to time tolling in his head. One minute, two, three. What had happened? This was the second time in the last eighteen hours that he'd been clubbed down from within. *Hamlin?*

– You bet your ass.

What did you do to me?

– Gave you a leetle twitch in the autonomic nervous system. I'm sitting right here looking at it. A bunch of ropes and cords, the most complicated frigging mess you could imagine. I just reached out and went *plink*.

Another shaft of pain between the shoulder blades.

Stop it, Macy said. *Jesus, why are you doing that?*

– Self preservation. Like you said a little while ago, self-preservation has to come before concern for others, right?

Can you hear all my thoughts?

– Enough of them. Enough to know when I'm being threatened.

Threatened?

– Sure. Where were you heading when I knocked you off your feet?

The Rehab Center, Macy admitted.

– That's right. And what were you going to do there?

I was going for my weekly post-therapy therapy session.

– Like shit you were. You were going to tell the doctors that I had come back to life.

And if I was?

– Don't try to play innocent. You were going to have them blot me out again, right? Right, Macy?

Well –

– Admit it!

Macy, crouching on the shining tiles, attempted to call for help. A soft mewing sound came from him. The commuters continued to stream past. A flotilla of attaché cases and portable terminals. Please. Please. Help me.

From Hamlin, a second time:

– Admit it!

Let me alone.

Macy felt a sudden explosion of agony behind his breastbone. As if a hand had clasped itself about his heart for a quick powerful squeeze. Setting the valves aflap, emptying the ventricles, pinching the aorta.

– I'm learning my way around in here, pal. I can do all kinds of things today that I couldn't swing yesterday. Like tickling your heart. Isn't that a lovely sensation? Now, suppose you tell me why you were in such a hurry to get to the Rehab Center, and it better be the right answer.

To have you obliterated again, Macy confessed miserably.

– Yes. Yes. The dirty truth will out! You were conspiring in my murder, weren't you? I never murdered anybody in my life, you understand, I merely took a few liberties with my prick, and nevertheless the state was pleased to order my death –

Your rehabilitation, said Macy.

– My death, Hamlin shot back at him, giving him a tug on the right tricep by way of emphasis. They killed me and put somebody else in my body, only I came back to life, and you were going to have them kill me again. We don't need to debate the semantics of the point. Stand up, Macy.

Macy cautiously tested his strength and found that his legs now would support him. He rose, very slowly, feeling immensely fragile. A few tottering steps. Knees shaking. Skin clammy. Dryness in the throat.

– Now, friend, we have to get something understood. You aren't going to go to the Rehab Center today. You aren't going to go there at all, ever again, because the Center is a dangerous place for me, and so in order to keep you away I'll have to make it a dangerous place for you too. Let me give you just a taste of what will happen to you if you come within five miles of a Rehab Center. Just a taste.

Again, the hand tightening around his heart. But no mere squeeze this time. A fierce gripping full-strength clench. It knocked Macy down once more. Gradually the inner grasp was relaxed, but it left him nauseated and feeble, and a terrible thunder reverberated in his chest. Cheek to the tile, he kicked his legs in a frenzy of pain. This time his anguish was too visible to be ignored, and he was seized by passersby and hoisted to his feet.

'You okay? Some kind of fit?'

'Please – if I could just sit down somewhere –'

'You need a doctor?'

'It's only a little chest spasm – I've had them before –'

They took him inside. A bench in the waiting room. Advert globes floating in the air. Blinking their messages into his face. He was numb. Impossible even to think. A constant stream of people flowing by. Trains arriving, departing. Voices. Colors. After a while, his strength returned.

– If you try to go back for reconditioning, Macy, that's what I'll do to you, and not just a little squeeze. If necessary I'll shut off your heart altogether. I can do it. I see where the nerve connections are now.

But then you'll die too, Macy said.

– That's true. If it's necessary for me to interrupt the life-processes of this body that we're sharing, we'll both die. So what? I don't expect you to commit suicide for the sake of getting rid of me. But I'm perfectly prepared to commit suicide for the sake of *keeping* you from getting rid of me, because I've got no choice. I'm a dead man anyway if you get inside a Rehab Center. So I offer you the ultimate threat. Keep away, or else. It wouldn't be smart of you to call my bluff. For both our sakes, don't.

I'm supposed to show up for weekly post-therapy therapy sessions, though.

– Skip them.

It's part of the court decree. If I don't show up, they're likely to issue a warrant for me.

– We'll worry about that when the time comes. Meanwhile forget about therapy sessions.

But we can't share a body, Macy protested. *It's insanity. There's no room for two of us.*

– Don't worry about that now, either. We'll work something out. For the time being we're sharing, and you fucking well better accept the idea. Now get yourself aboard a city-bound train. Put some distance between me and that Center.

SIX

Home again, midmorning. His head throbbing. Not a peep out of Hamlin all the way back. The apartment seemed to have undergone a strange transformation in the two hours of his absence: previously a neutral place, wholly lacking emotional connotations, and now an alien and sinister cell, cramped and repellent.

The flat's dark new tone astonished him. Its mysterious autumnal resonances. Its shadows where no shadows had been. Nothing had changed in it, really. Lissa hadn't moved any furniture around or sprayed the walls a different color. And yet. And yet, how frightening it all looked now. How out of place he felt in it. That L-shaped bedroom, low ceiling, narrow bed jammed up against flimsy wall, old-fashioned light fixture dangling, bilious green paint, cheap smeary Picasso prints, slit of a window revealing splotchy May sunshine and two scraggly trees across the street – how ugly it looked, how coarse, how constricted, how squashed! Did people really live in places like this? Tiny bathroom, slick pink tiles. Not even an ultrasonic cleanser, just archaic sink and tub and crapper. A microscopic kitchen-dinette affair, everything jammed together, table, freezer, telephone screen, disposal unit, stove. At least a tiny buzz-cleanser for the dirty dishes. A sitting-room, cheap red plastic couch, some books, cassettes, a video unit.

A prison for the soul. Our impoverished century: this is the best we can afford for human beings, after our long orgies of waste and destruction. For the last couple of weeks, this apartment had been his refuge, his harbor, his hermitage; if he thought about it at all, which he doubted, it had been in a friendly way. Why did it turn him off now? After a moment, he believed he knew. Hamlin's sensibility now underlay his own. The sculptor's sophisticated perceptions bleeding through to the Macy levels of their shared mind. Hamlin's loathing for the apartment tinged Macy's view of it. To Hamlin the proportions were wrong, the ambiance vile, the psychological texture of the place slimy and grimy, the inner environmental color a nasty one. Macy shivered. He visualized Hamlin as a kind of abscess in his brain, a pocket of pus, inaccessible, destructive.

Lissa was still in bed. That bothered him. The Protestant ethic: sleeping late equals rejection of life.

But she wasn't asleep. Stirring lazily, sitting up, knuckles to eyes. A purring yawn. 'Everything taken care of?' she asked.

'No.'

'What happened?'

He told her about the episode at the Greenwich terminal. Writhing on the blue and white terrazzo with fire in his chest. Hamlin playfully strumming the harp of his autonomic nervous system. Lissa listened, big-eyed, somber-faced, and said finally, 'What are you going to do?'

'I haven't any idea.'

'But that's hideous. Having him inside you like a parasite. A crab hiding in your head. Like a case of brain cancer. Look, maybe if I call the Rehab Center –'

A warning twinge from Hamlin, deep down.

'No,' Macy said.

'I could tell them what's happened. Maybe this has happened before. Maybe they know some way to deal with him.'

'The moment they tried anything,' he said, 'Hamlin would stop my heartbeat. I know that.'

'But if there's some drug that might knock him out – I could slip it to you somehow –'

'He's listening right now, Lissa. Don't you think he'll be on guard constantly? He may not even need to sleep. We can't take chances.'

'But how can you go on with somebody else inside your head, trying to take you over?'

Macy pondered that one. 'What makes you think he's trying to take me over?'

'Isn't it obvious? He wants his body back. He'll try to cut you down, one block of nerves at a time, until there's nothing left of you at all. He'll push you out. And then he'll be Nat Hamlin again.'

'He just said he wanted to share the body with me,' Macy muttered.

'Will he stop there? Why should he?'

'But Nat Hamlin's a proscribed criminal. Legally he doesn't even exist any more. If he tried to return to life –'

'Oh, he'd go on using the Macy identity,' Lissa said. 'Only

he'd take up sculpting again, in another country, maybe. He'd look up his old friends. He'd be the old Hamlin, except his passport would say Macy, and –' She halted. 'He'd look up his old friends,' she repeated. She seemed to be examining the idea from various angles. 'Old friends such as me.'

'Yes. You.' In a tone that he recognized as unpleasant, but which he found impossible to alter, Macy said, 'He could even marry you. As he was originally planning to do.'

'His wife is still alive, I'm sure.'

'That marriage was legally dissolved at the time he was sentenced,' Macy said. 'It's automatic. They cut all ties. Officially, he wouldn't be Hamlin even if he took over. He'd be Macy, and Macy is single. There you are, Lissa.' The edge of cruelty coming into his voice again. 'You'd finally get to be his wife. What you've always wanted.'

She shook her head. 'I don't want it any more.'

'You said you loved him.'

'I once did love him. But I told you, that's all dead now. The things he did. The crimes. The rapes.'

'The first time we met,' said Macy heavily, 'when you were still insisting on calling me Nat, you made a point of saying you were still in love with me. The old me. *Him*. You said it two or three times. Talking about how much you missed him. Refusing to believe that there was somebody new living behind his face.'

'You misunderstand,' she said. 'I felt so lonely. So fucking *lost*. And all of a sudden I was standing next to somebody I knew, somebody out of the past – I just wanted help, I had to talk to him – I mean, I crashed right into you in the street, was I supposed to walk away and not even say hello?'

'You saw my Rehab badge and you ignored it.'

'I didn't see it at all.'

'You must have blanked it out deliberately. You knew Nat Hamlin had been put away for Rehab.'

'You're shouting at me.'

'I'm sorry. I can't help it. I'm tense as hell, Lissa. Look, so you saw somebody in the street and you thought he was Nat

Hamlin, so you said hello, but did you have to tell him you were still in love with him, too?'

'I didn't mean it.'

'You said it.'

'What else could I do?' she asked. Her voice was shrill now. 'Stand there and say, Hello, you look like Nat Hamlin who I used to love, and of course I don't love him any more and in any case he's been wiped out but since you look just like him I'll fall in love with you instead, so let's go home and ball a little? How could I say that? But I couldn't let you just vanish without saying something to you. I was making a stab at the past, trying to catch it, trying to bring it back. The beautiful past, before the hellish part started. And you were my only link to that, Paul, and I was excited, and I said Nat, Nat, I talked about being in love –'

'Exactly. You called me Nat, and said you were still in love with –'

'Why are you doing this to me, Paul?'

'Doing what?'

'Chewing on me. Shouting. All these questions.'

'I'm trying to find out which one of us you're really loyal to. Hamlin or me. Which side you're going to take when the struggle for this body gets rough.'

'You aren't trying to find out any such thing. You just want to hurt me.'

'Why should I want to –'

'How would I know? Because you blame me for bringing him back to life, maybe. Because you hate me for having loved him once. Because he's sitting inside you right now forcing you to hurt me. I don't know. Christ, I don't know at all. Only why do you need to find out where my loyalty is? Didn't I tell you last night that I didn't want him coming back? Didn't I offer to call the Rehab Center just now?'

'Yes. Yes.'

'So how could I possibly be on his side? I want him to be wiped out. I want him gone forever. I want – oh, Christ –'

She halted suddenly. Leaping from the bed as though stung,

arms and legs flying stiffly out from her torso. Turning toward him. Her face contorted, the eyes bulging, the mouth a rigid hole, the muscles of her throat bunched and jutting. From her lips a bizarre clotted baritone, hoarse and unfocused, like the blunt blurtings of a deaf-mute, no words intelligible: '*Mfss. Shlrrm. Skk-kk. Vshh. Vshh. Vshh.*' A terrible gargling cry, all the more horrible because of the deep masculine tone in which it was delivered.

She lurched around the room, stumbling into things, clawing at the air. A plain case of demonic possession. What rides her?

'*Grkk. Lll. Llll. Pkd-dd.*' Eyes wild, pleading. Bare breasts heaving wildly. A sheen of sweat on her skin.

Macy rushed toward her, trying to embrace her, calm her, ease her back to the bed. She pivoted like a robot and her arm crashed across his chest, doubling him up in gasps. When he looked at her again her face was scarlet with strain and her mouth was open to the full reach of her jaws, beyond it, perhaps. The wild gargling sounds still erupted from her, and her eyes registered total horror and despair.

Once again Macy tried to seize her. This time successfully. Muscles leaping and churning and twitching all over her spare naked form. He forced her down on the bed and covered her with his body, hands gripping her wrists, knees imprisoning her thighs. A sour smell of sweat rising from her, bad sweat, fear-sweat.

Some kind of epileptic fit? Epilepsy was much on his mind this morning. In a low urgent voice he talked to her, tried to soothe her, to reach her somehow. More baritone drivel coming out of her in halting husky bleeps of thick noise. The static of the soul.

'Lissa?' he said. 'Lissa, can you hear me? Try to go limp. Let all your muscles hang loose.'

Easier said than done. She still twitched. While in the midst of this he felt a hot sensation at the base of his skull, as of an auger drilling into him. Or drilling toward the outside from the soft center of his brain. Something jumped frantically within his mouth, and it was a moment before he realized that it was his tongue, jerking itself crazily backward toward his gullet. 'Vshh. Vshh. Pkd-dd. Slrr. Msss.' The sounds not from Lissa this time. From him.

Lying there congealed and coagulated on top of Lissa, he understood perfectly what was happening. Nat Hamlin, having conserved his strength for a couple of hours, was trying to achieve a takeover of a new level of their shared brain. Specifically, Hamlin was attempting to grab Macy's speech centers.

Macy knew that that would mark the start of his own obliteration; once Hamlin had control of the voice, it would be *his* thoughts, not Macy's, that their body would express. Hamlin would have access to the external world and Macy would be shut inside. But at the moment Hamlin wasn't doing too well. He had grabbed the neural sectors governing speech, only his grasp was incomplete, and the best he could manage were these bursts of nonsense. Somehow, Macy realized, Lissa had become entangled in the battle before he himself had known it was going on. Her brain hooked into his; Hamlin speaking, or trying to, through her mouth. A microphoning effect of some kind. Now they were both doing it, the two of them bellowing like demented seals. Feeding hour at the zoo. Is this where it ends? Does Hamlin take over from me now? No. No. Fight back. Stop him here and drive him into a corner.

How, though?

The way you did last night, when he had hold of the side of your mouth. Pry him loose. Through sheer strength of concentration, break his grip.

Macy tried to visualize the interior of his brain. Telling himself, This is where Hamlin lives, this pocket of gunk, and these are the pathways he's been building to other parts of my brain, and this is the place he's attacking now. It was a purely imaginary construct, but it would serve for the moment. Try to visualize the speech centers themselves. Say, row upon row of tight-strung pink cords, a kind of piano deal, with a switchboard attached. Hamlin at the switchboard, plugging things in, looking for the right connection; and the pink cords, all ajangle, giving off weird groaning noises. Come up behind him. Grab his arms. He isn't any stronger than you are. Pull him away, knock him on his ass. Jump on him. Careful, don't smash any of the machinery. You'll need it when this is over. Just hang on to him. Stay on top. Pin him, pin him, pin him! Good! Smash his head against the floor a couple of times! Okay, the floor's spongy, it gives a little, smash him anyway. Stun him. Right. Now start hauling him the hell out of there. Heavy fucker, isn't he? One hundred ninety pounds, same as you. Heave. Heave. Heave. Into this musty corridor. A hot humid smell coming out of it. Things must be rotting in there. In with him! Down the chute! Slam the door. There. Easier than you expected, eh? All it takes is some mental energy. Perseverance. You can relax now. Catch your breath.

Hey, Jesus, what's this? He must have come to, in there. Hammering on the other side of the door. Starting to push it open. Wow, you can't let him do that. Hold it closed! Push . . . push . . . push . . . a stalemate. He can't get it open any farther, you can't close it that last crack. *Push*. He's pushing back. *Push*. *Push*. Bear down. Oh, Jesus. There! It's closed again. All right, keep your shoulder to the door, hold it tight. The bear's locked in his cave; you don't want him coming out again.

Now fasten the door. With what? Slip a bolt in place, dodo. But there isn't a bolt. Sure there is. This is your mind, your own fucking mind, can't you use a little imagination? Invent a bolt! Like that. Fine. Now ram it home. In the slot. In. In. There. Okay, step back. See if he can break out. Be ready to clobber him if he does. He's banging on the door. Throwing himself against it. But the bolt holds. It holds. Good deal. Let's check out the machinery now. Make sure he didn't screw it up. Loud and clear, let's hear it:

'My name is Paul Macy.'

Good. Nice to hear some sense out of your mouth again. Keep going.

'I was born in Idaho Falls, Idaho, on the twelfth of March, 1972. My father was a propulsion engineer and my mother was a schoolteacher.'

Voice production generally okay. A little rusty around the edges, a little froggy in the lower frequencies, but that's only to be expected, the way he was abusing your pipes. It'll clear up fast, most likely.

You win this round, Macy.

Slowly, shakily, he rose from the bed. Lissa still lay there, looking crumpled and flattened. She didn't move. Her face had resumed its normal appearance. Her eyes were open. No glow in them. A sullen, absent expression.

'Are you all right?' he asked.

No response. Off in another galaxy somewhere.

'Lissa? Are you okay?'

Staring blankly at him, she said, 'Do you give a shit if I am?' Her voice was as hoarse as his.

'What kind of question is that?'

'You were really letting me have it before all the fireworks started,' she said. 'Telling me you suspected I was on his side, and a lot of other crap. If I had any sense I'd get the hell away from you, fast. I don't need to be pushed around like that.' She stood up, huddling her arms against her sides, looking more vulnerable than ever. The blue streaks of veins visible in her breasts. Stretch marks in the skin of her hips, showing where she had lost weight lately. Quick angry motions. Snatching at her clothes, throwing things on. A blouse, a tunic. She said, 'That was him, wasn't it? Hamlin? Trying to talk through my voice?'

'And then through mine, yes.'

'Where did he go?'

'I beat him down. I made him let go.'

'Hurray for you.' Tonelessly. 'My hero. You see my sandals anywhere?'

'Where are you going?' he asked.

'This is a crazyhouse. I'm worse off here than I was alone. I'm going home.'

'No,' he said. He remembered that he had decided, only this dawn, to sever her from his life once the Rehab Center had plucked the resurgent Nat Hamlin from his brain. Telling himself then that it was too dangerous to have her around him, because of her gift, her curse, whatever it was that had awakened Hamlin. Out she goes, he had decided. Self-preservation first and always. Out she goes. How hollow that sounded to him now. He still had Hamlin inside him, and he was frightened by the thought of having to grapple with him in solitude. Lissa wasn't as dispensable now as she had seemed earlier. 'Don't go,' he said. 'Please.'

'I'll get nothing but trouble here.'

'I didn't mean to yell at you. My nerves were raw, is all. You can understand that. I didn't intend to accuse you of anything, Lissa.'

'Even so. You got me all stirred up. And then *him*, jumping into my head. The sounds I was making. I never did that before. Like I was some kind of ventriloquist's dummy, and I could feel Nat trying to move my lips, trying to push my vocal cords, trying to get his words out through me –' She seemed to gag on something. 'It was coming out of you, Paul. I thought my head would blow. I don't want to go through that again.'

'I beat him back,' Macy said. 'I shut him off.'

'And if he gets out again? Or if you start suspecting me again? Asking me if I'm really on his side? Maybe next time you'll bang me around some. You could break my arms. You could knock all my teeth out. And then you'd apologize later.'

'There's no possibility of that.'

'But you've got reason to be hostile. I'm responsible for waking him up inside you, right? Even if I wanted to stay here, you know, it wouldn't be smart for you if I did. Maybe he'll use me now to finish the takeover of your body. Play his mental energy through my ESP output, or something. He almost did that just now, didn't he? Do you want to chance it?'

'Who knows?' Macy said. He caught her by the arm as she

moved slowly toward the door. 'Do I have to beg you, Lissa? Don't leave me now.'

'First you didn't want anything to do with me. Then you screamed at me that you didn't trust me. Now you don't want me to go. I can't figure you, Paul. When somebody comes out of a Rehab Center, he's supposed to be sane, isn't he? You scare me too much. I want to get out of here.'

'Please. Stay.'

'What for?'

'To help me fight against him. I need you. And you need me. We can support each other. Separately we're both going to go under. Together –'

'Together we'll both go under too,' she said. Moving no closer to the door, though. 'Look, I thought you could help me, Paul. That's why I wrote you at the network, that's why I begged you to see me. But now I realize that your troubles are as bad as mine. Worse, maybe. I just hear voices from outside. You've got somebody else in your head. On account of me. We can only harm each other.'

'No.'

'You ought to believe it. Look what I've already done to you, bringing *him* back. And then you, bouncing him into my head for a couple of minutes. And on and on and on like that, things getting worse and worse and worse for both of us.'

He shook his head. 'I'm going to fight. I've beaten him twice in two days. Next time I'll finish him altogether. But I don't want to be alone while I'm doing it.'

Shrugging, she said, 'Don't blame me if –'

'I won't.' He looked at the time. A sudden bold idea hooking him. By their works ye shall know them. Yes. Go to the museum, see his version of Lissa. Look at her through his eyes.

An unexpectedly powerful hunger rose in him to know the real past, to find out what manner of man he had been, what he had been capable of creating. In a sense what *I* was capable of, in my other self. And the sculpture of Lissa a bridge to that hidden past. Leading him out of this shadowy unlife into the realm of authentic experience. *He* did this, *he* made it, *his* unique and irreplaceable vision was at work. And I must understand him in order to defeat him.

Macy said, 'Listen, there's no sense in my going to the office this late in the day. But we've still got the whole afternoon. You know where I want to go? The Metropolitan Museum. To see the sculpture he did of you, the *Antigone 21*.'

'Why?'

'Old maxim: Know your enemy. I want to see his interpretation of you. Find out what his mind is like. Size him up, look for the places where I can attack.'

'I don't think we should go. It could trigger anything, Paul. You said yourself, how at your office you saw one of his pieces and it almost knocked you out. Suppose at the museum —'

'I was caught by surprise that first time. This is different. I've got to take the offensive, Lissa. Carry the battle to him, do you see? And the museum's as good a place to start as any. Showing him that I can hold my own under any conditions. All right? Let's go, shall we? The museum.'

'All right,' she said distantly. 'The museum.'

SEVEN

Entering the huge building, he felt apprehensive and ill at ease. An overwhelming sense of not belonging in this vast and labyrinthine palace of culture oppressed him.

Searching his stock of synthetic memories, he couldn't find any recollection of having been here before. Or any other art museum. The Rehab people hadn't built a strong interest in the visual arts into him, it seemed. Music, yes. The theater. Even ballet. But not sculpture, not painting, not anything that was likely to impinge on the world Nat Hamlin had inhabited. A deliberate divergence from the abolished past.

Still, why was he so edgy about going in? Afraid of being recognized, maybe? People turning, whispering, pointing? Look,
that's Nathaniel Hamlin, the famous psychosculptor. He did
that naked woman we saw before. Hamlin. Hamlin. That man
looks just like Hamlin. Requiring you to say something by way
of correction. Pardon me, ma'am, you are in error. My name is
Paul Macy. Never done a sculpture in my life. Ostentatiously
rubbing your Rehab badge. Thrusting it in her eyes. I must tell
you, ma'am, that Nathaniel Hamlin has become an unperson.
And the woman fading away in embarrassment, heels clicking
on the stone floor, looking back at him over her shoulder,
sniffing a little in disdain. Maybe even reporting him to a
guard for molesting her.

Macy smiled sourly and swept the whole scenario away. Not
much chance of any of that happening. Rembrandt could walk
through this place and nobody'd recognize him. Michelangelo.
Picasso. Mommy, who's that funny little bald-headed man?
Shh, dear, I think that's some senator. Yes. Macy shook off
his apprehensions. They went inside.

Just within the main entrance they were held for a moment
in a cone of tingling blue light, some kind of scanning device
ascertaining that they carried no explosives, knives, cans of
paint, or other instruments of vandalism. Evidently there was
a lot of free-floating masterpiece-directed hostility in this
city. They passed the test and advanced into the colossal
central hall. Pink granite pharaohs to the left; bleached marble
Apollos to the right. Straight ahead, an immense dizzying
vista of receding hallway. The dry smell of the past in here:
the nineteenth century, the fourteenth, the third.

'Where is it?' he asked. 'Your statue.'

'Second floor, all the way in the back, the modern art wing,'
Lissa said. Once again she seemed remote and abstracted. She
slipped easily into that kind of withdrawal, that closed-and-
sealed surliness. 'You go, Paul. I'll wait here and do the
Egyptian stuff or something. I don't want to see it.'

'I'd like you to come with me.'

'No.'

'Jesus, why not?'

'Because it shows how beautiful I was. I don't want to be in the room with you when you see it. And when you turn and look at me afterward and see what I've become. Go on, Paul. You won't have any trouble finding it.'

He was stubborn. Refusing to leave her. Unwilling to face the Hamlin piece without her. Suppose the sight of it struck him down again; who would help him up? But she was equally firm. Not going with him, simply not going. The museum expedition was his crazy idea, not hers. She couldn't bear to see that piece. Won't you? I won't. I won't. A tense little scene in the grand hallway. Their harsh whispers echoing from alabaster arcades. People staring at them as they bickered. He half expected someone to say, any minute, Say, isn't that the sculptor Nathaniel Hamlin? Over there, the big one arguing with the redhead. Terrified by that irrational prospect. His discomfort grew so strong that he was on the verge of letting her have her way when suddenly she nipped her upper lip with her lower teeth, pressed her knuckles to her jawbone, hunched her shoulders as if trying to touch her earlobes with them, sucked in her cheeks. Began quirking her mouth from side to side. Possibly she was being skewered by invisible darts. Eyes wild. Glossy with panic. Saying to him, after some moments, in a veiled, barely audible voice: 'Okay, come on, then. I'll go with you. But hurry!'

'What's happening to you, Lissa?'

'I'm picking up voices again.' A fusillade of twitches distorting her face. 'They're bouncing off the walls, a dozen different strands of thought. Getting louder and louder. All garbled up. Christ, get me out of this room. *Get me out of this room.*'

Everybody in the museum must have heard that. She seemed about to come apart.

He took her elbow and steered her hastily into the long hallway facing them. Hardly anyone here. Without any real idea of where he was going, he hustled her along, infected by the urgency of her distress; she slipped and slid on the smooth polished floor, but he kept her upright. Mounted figures in chain mail streaming toward them and vanishing to the rear. Shimmering tapestries looming in the dusk. Swords. Lances. Engraved silver bowls. All the loot of the past, and no one around, just a couple of blank-faced robot guards.

When they had gone about a hundred yards he halted, aware that Lissa had grown more calm, and they stood for a moment in front of a case of small iridescent Roman glass flasks and vases with elaborate spiral handles. She turned to him, haggard, sweat-streaked, and clung to him, cheek to his chest. Her anxiety definitely subsiding, but she was still upset.

Finally she said, 'How awful that was. One of the worst ones yet. A dozen of them all talking at once, each one with a pipeline right into my skull. A torrent of nonsense. Swelling and swelling and swelling my head till it wants to explode.'

'Is it better now?'

'I don't hear them, anyway. But the echoes inside me . . . the noise bouncing around upstairs . . . You know, I wish I could go far away from the whole human race. To some icy planet. To one of the moons of Jupiter. And just live there in a plastic dome, all by myself. Although even there I'd probably pick up the static. Minds radiating at me right across space. Can you imagine what it's like, Paul, never to have real privacy? Never to know when your head is going to turn into a goddam two-way radio?' Then a chilly laugh from her. 'Hey, that's funny. Me asking you about privacy. And you with your own ghost sitting in your head. Worse off than I am. Paul and Lissa, Lissa and Paul. What a pair of fucking cripples we are, you and me!'

'Somehow we'll manage.'

'I bet.'

'We can get help, Lissa.'

'Sure we can. He'll kill you as soon as you go within a mile of your doctors. And nobody can fix me without chopping my brain into hamburger. But we can get help, yeah. I like your optimism, kid.' She pointed. 'We can take that staircase. Nightmare Number Sixteen is waiting for us.'

Up the stairs, through another hall full of Chinese porcelains and Assyrian palace reliefs, past a room of Persian miniatures, one of Iranian pottery, gallery after gallery of archaic treasures, and emerging ultimately in an opulent cube of clear plastic cantilevered out of the rear of the building to overhang the wilted greenery of Central Park. The modern-art wing.

Crowded, too; Macy looked nervously at Lissa, fearing she would tumble into another telepathic abyss, but she appeared to be in control of herself. Guiding him coolly down yards of gaudy paintings and sculpture and tick-tock artifacts and dancing posters and metabolic mirrors and liquespheres and all the rest.

Left turn. Deep breath. A small room, no door, just a circular entrance. Over the entrance, in raised gilded letters: ANTIGONE 21 BY NATHANIEL HAMLIN. Jesus. A private exhibition hall for it. What he had taken to be the absence of a door was in fact the presence of an invisible airseal, providing secret shelter for the masterwork within, ensuring it its own environment and psychological habitat. They stepped through. No sensation while breaching the seal: cooler on the other side, the air tingling, full of wandering ions. A faint chemical odor. A low hum.

'That's it,' Lissa said.

Ten, twelve people clustered in front of it; he couldn't see. She hung tensely against him, arm jammed through his, ribs raking his side. Her tautness leaked through to him, a mental emanation of something just short of fear. He felt the same way. The knot of onlookers parted and as though through a rift in the clouds he beheld Nathaniel Hamlin's *Antigone 21*.

Nude female figure, larger than life. Unmistakably Lissa, yet no danger that anyone in the room would turn from that radiant statue to the drab drained girl and connect the two of them. Firm, full body. The breasts higher and heavier: had the sculptor idealized them or had Lissa lost weight there too? The pose an aggressive, dynamic one, head flung back, one arm outstretched, legs apart. O Pioneers, that sort of thing. Emphasizing the strength of the woman, the resilience of her. Eyes bright and fierce. Mouth not quite smiling but almost. The entire solid figure crying out, I can take it, I can handle anything, stress and turmoil and flood and famine and revolution and assassination, I have endured, I will endure, I am the essence of endurance. The eternal feminine. And so forth.

But of course the sculpture was not merely just a sexy academic nude in a high-powered nineteenth-century mode, nor was it only a sentimentally-conceived monument to stereotyped concepts of womanhood. It was those things, yes, but it was also a psychosculpture, meaning that it approached the condition of being alive, it was a whole cosmos in itself. It did tricks. The room was rigged to heighten the effects. Imperceptible changes of lighting. That odd humming sound, coming from a battery of hidden sonic generators, controlled the mood through its pattern of modulations, hitting the onlookers at some subterranean level of their psyches.

The degree of ionization in the room was constantly changing, too. And the statue itself. Going through a cycle of transformations. Look, the nipples are erect now, the breasts are heaving (but are they, or does it just seem that they move?), the eyes are those of a woman in heat. What has become of the defiant, all-enduring woman of three minutes ago? Now we behold the essence of cuntliness. One could rush forward gladly and prong her.

And yet she changes again. Her juices going sour, her nipples softening: a woman thwarted, a woman denied. How bitter that fractional smile. She holds grudges. In the darkness of the night she would gladly castrate the unsuspecting male. But the strength of hatred ebbs from her. She is afraid; she knows that there are questions for which she has no answers; she feels the phantoms of the night fluttering against the windows, wings beating harder and harder. Terror closes its hand on her. She is alone, naked and vulnerable, not half so strong as she would have the world believe.

If they came to attack her now – but what comes is dawn. A brightening. Finding her place in the universe under a friendly sky. She seems taller. Older, though no less beautiful;

voluptuous, though cooler than before; in command of herself, beyond doubt. Venus ascendant. A totally different self each few minutes.

What machinery is at work beneath that figure's supple skin? How is this cycle of transformations propelled? Watching it, the constantly shifting play of emotions and impressions, the subtle mutations of posture and attitude, Macy feels awed and overpowered but also vaguely cheated. He had not known what to expect of the art of his former self, other than that it would be dramatic and impressive. But is this really art, this clever robot? Will all this mechanical trickery be able to stand alongside the true artistic achievements of the ages? He is no critic, in truth he knows nothing at all, yet the intense realism of the sculpture that is its outstanding characteristic makes it seem aesthetically primitive to him, a toy, a stunt, a triumph of craft, not art.

But even so. But even so. Impossible not to respond to the power of the thing. How thoroughly Lissa has been captured in those gears and cogs; not his Lissa, not the broken dazed girl he knows, but Nat Hamlin's glorious Lissa, whose caved-in shell has fallen to Hamlin's successor. What Hamlin has created here may be simpleminded next to Leonardo and Cellini and Henry Moore, but behind the superficial superficiality may lie a carefully masked profundity, Macy suspects. He could stand here studying the figure for hours. Days. As others seem to be doing. Those students muttering notes into handrecorders, and that one, holographing the work from every conceivable angle – they are trapped by it too, plainly. A masterpiece. Undoubtedly a masterpiece.

With an effort he turned away from it, feeling an almost audible snap as the sightlines of his contact with the sculpture broke, and glanced at Lissa. She was drawn back, hunched against the wall, lips parted, eyes fixed and glassy, caught by the mesmerism of her overpowering simulacrum up there. A gasp frozen on her face. What currents of identity, he wondered, were flowing from her to the sculpture, from the sculpture to her? What draining of self was going on, and what recharging? What must it be like to behold yourself made into such a work of art?

And where was Hamlin? Why wasn't he jumping and cavorting in pride before his wondrous achievement, as he had that first day in Harold Griswold's office? Hamlin was quiescent. Not absent, though. Macy became gradually aware of him glowing far below the surface, embedded deep in his brain. A thorn in his paw. A pebble in his hoof. Macy hadn't expected Hamlin to remain bolted inside his dungeon for long.

Nor did he. Rising slowly now, bubbling toward the top. Evoked into consciousness by the *Antigone 21*. That's all right, Macy thought. Let him come up. I can handle him. Bracing himself, battening down, Macy waited for his other self to finish drifting toward the surface. Not hostile, this time. Not even aggressive. A prevailing air of calmness about him. No resentment apparent over his defeat in their last battle. Perhaps a strategy of deception, though. Get me off guard, then make another quick leap for the speech centers. I'm ready, whatever he tries. But when Hamlin opened their inner conversation, his tone was easy, civil:

– What do you think of it?

Impressive. I didn't know you had it in you.

– Why? Do I seem second-rate to you, Macy?

The only aspect of you that I know is the violence, the criminality. It turns me off. I don't associate great art with that kind of personality.

– What a load of bourgeois crap that is, friend.

Is it?

– Item one, a man can be a thief, a killer, a baby-buggerer, anything, and still be a great artist. The quality of his morals has nothing to do with the quality of his perceptions, hip? You'd be surprised how much of the stuff in this museum was produced by absolute bastards. Item two, I happened to have been a pretty fair artist fifteen years before I became what they call an enemy of society. This piece you see here was entirely finished before I had my breakdown. Item three, since you never knew me, you don't have any goddam right to judge what kind of person I was.

I concede item two and maybe item one. But why should I yield on number three? I know you plenty well, Hamlin. You've knocked me down, you've played games with my heart, you've attempted to seize sections of my brain, you've threatened outright to kill me. Should I love you for that? This is the first time since you surfaced that you've seemed even halfway civilized. You come on like a thug; do you blame me for being surprised you could produce a sculpture like this?

– You really think I'm a villain?

You're a convicted criminal.

– Forget that shit. I mean my relationship to you. You think I'm acting out of evil impulses?

What else can I think?

– But I'm not, Macy. I don't dislike you, I don't want to harm you, I have no negative feelings toward you at all. It just happens that you're in the way of a man who's fighting for his life.

Meaning you.

– Exactly. I want to be myself again. I don't want to stay submerged inside you.

The court decreed –

– Fuck the court. The whole Rehab system is hysterical nonsense. Why wipe me out? Why not rehabilitate me in the real sense of the word? I wasn't hopelessly insane, Macy. Shit, yes, I did a lot of awful things, I admit that freely, I was off my head. But in the year 2007 they could have some better way of coping with insanity than the death sentence.

But –

– Let me finish. It *was* a death sentence, wasn't it? To rip me out of my own body and throw me away, and pour someone else into my head? What happened to my whole accumulation of experiences? What happened to my skills and talents? What happened to me, damn it, what happened to *me?* Killed. Killed. Nothing but a zombie body left. It's only by the merest fluke that I'm still here, even in this condition, hanging on inside you. What kind of humanitarianism is that? What are they saving, when they keep the body and throw away the soul?

I didn't make the laws.

– Agreed, Macy. But you're no fool. You can see how flagrantly unjust Rehab is. They want to separate me from society because I'm dangerous, okay, I agree, I agree, put me away, try to fix me, drain all the poison out of me. Right. But instead this. The super resources of modern science are employed to murder a great but somewhat deranged sculptor and invent a dumb holovision commentator to replace him.

Thank you.

– What else can I say? Look up there, at my *Antigone*. Could you do that? Could anybody else do that? I did it. My unique gift to mankind. And fifty others almost as good. I'm not bragging, Macy, I'm being as objective as hell. I was somebody valuable, I had a special gift, I had intensity, I had humanity. Maybe my gift drove me crazy after a while, but at least I had something to offer. And you? What are you? *Who* are you? You're nothing. You have no depth. You have no texture. You have no past. You have no reality. I've been sitting here inside you, taking an inventory. I know what you're made of, Macy, and it's all ersatz. You have no purpose in existing. You can't do anything that a robot couldn't do better. A holovision commentator? They can program a machine with pear-shaped tones, father, and it'll broadcast you off the map.

I admit all this, Macy replied. He stood stiffly, pretending to study the sculpture. He wondered how much time had elapsed during his colloquy with Hamlin. Five seconds? Five minutes? He had lost track of external things. *Granted that you were a genius and I'm a nobody, what am I supposed to do about it?*

– Vacate the premises.

Just like that.

– Yes. It wouldn't be hard. I could show you how. You relax, you lower your defenses, you let me administer the *coup de grace*. Then you disappear back into the limbo they whistled you out of, and I can function as Nat Hamlin wearing the mask of Paul Macy. I can begin to sculpt again.

Quietly. As long as I don't harm anybody, I'd get away with it.

You'd harm me.

– But you have no right to exist! You're fiction, Macy. You're not real.

I exist now. I'm here. I have feelings and ambitions and fears. When I eat a steak I taste it. When I fuck a girl I enjoy it. You know how it goes. Cut me and I bleed. I'm real, as real as anybody who ever lived.

– How can I persuade you that you aren't?

You can't. I'm as real to me as anybody else is to himself. Look, Hamlin, look, this isn't a thing for logic. I can't just say to you, Okay, you're a genius, I bow to the demands of culture, lop off my head and take my place. A far, far better thing, et cetera, et cetera. No. I'm here. I want to go on being here.

– Where does that leave me?

Up shit creek, I guess. Right now you're the one who's unreal, you know that? Officially you're dead. You're just a spook wandering around my skull. Why don't you do the noble thing? Stop fucking up a decent and inoffensive human being's life, and clear out. Vacate the premises, as you say. Lower the defenses and let me clobber you.

– Some chance.

You've given the world enough masterpieces.

– I'm still young. I'm better than you. I deserve to live.

The court said otherwise. The court sent you out of the world for God knows what kind of crimes, and –

– For rape. That's all it was, rape.

I don't care if it was for reusing old postage stamps. A verdict's a verdict. I'm not giving up my life to remedy what you consider to have been a miscarriage of justice.

– You don't *have* a life, Macy!

Sorry. I do.

A long silence. Macy peered at the sculpture, at the onlookers, at the walls. His head was spinning. Hamlin's presence remained manifest within him as a steady pressure, wordless, heavy. And then, finally:

– All right. We're getting nowhere like this. Go stroll around the museum. We'll continue the discussion some other time.

Sensation of Hamlin letting go. Dropping once more into the depths. Plop. Splash. The illusion of solitude. Solemn trombone music marking the alter ego's exit. Macy was drenched in sweat. Unsteady on his feet.

Lissa: 'Have you seen enough yet?'

'I think so. We can go. Wait, let me hold your hand.'

'Is something wrong, Paul?'

'A little wobbly.' He wasn't able to look at her. Clutching her cool fingers between his. Step. Step. Through the invisible door. In the gallery outside he found a bench and sank down on it. Lissa fluttering over him, bewildered. He said, 'While I was looking at it, I had a sort of conversation with Hamlin. Very quietly. He was almost charming.'

'What was he telling you?'

'A lot of insidious bullshit. He invited me to get out of our body so he could have it. On the grounds that he's a great artist and deserves to live more than I do.'

'That's just the sort of thing he'd say!'

'It's just the sort of thing he did say. I told him no, and he went back to his cave. And now I realize I must have put more energy into that chat than I thought.'

'Sit. Rest.'

'I'm going to.'

'How about the *Antigone?*' she asked.

'Incredible. Demolishing. I almost feel a kind of secondhand paternal pride in it. I mean, these hands here made it. This brain conceived it. Even if I wasn't there at the time. And –'

'No,' Lissa said. 'These hands made it, yes, but not this brain.' She tapped his skull lightly, affectionately, with three fingertips. 'A brain's just a globe of gray cheese. Brains don't conceive scultpures. *Minds* do. And this wasn't the mind that conceived the *Antigone.*'

'I realize that,' he told her stiffly. Somehow her quibbling upset him. A show of loyalty for Hamlin, perhaps. Arousing jealousy in him. Hard to accept the truth that she had been there while that piece was being fashioned, she posed, she was in on the white-hot hours of creation, she and Hamlin, in the days before Paul Macy was born. To think about that made him feel like an intruder in his own body. What ecstasies had Lissa and Hamlin shared, what joys and griefs, what moments of exaltation? He was shut out of all those events. Cut off by the impenetrable wall of the past. Other times, another self. But *she* could remember. Scowling, he watched the museumgoers filing by threes and fours into the Hamlin room. Hamlin is right, he thought gloomily. I'm nothing. I have no texture. I have no past. I have no reality. Abruptly standing, he said, 'Is there anything else you'd like to see, as long as we're in the museum?'

'This trip was your idea.'

'As long as we're here.'

'No, nothing,' she said. 'Not really.'

'Let's go, then.'

'Did you learn whatever you wanted to learn from the *Antigone?*' she asked.

'Yes,' he said. 'All that I wanted to learn. And more. Maybe too much more.' They hurried from the building by a side door in the Egyptian wing.

EIGHT

Emerging into the sunlight revived his vigor a bit. It was still only about four in the afternoon. At Lissa's suggestion they went uptown, to her place; there were some things she needed to get, she said. Unspoken in that was the assumption that she would be moving in with him. He didn't object. He couldn't say that he loved her, as Hamlin evidently had, or that he was even on the verge of falling in love with her; but their individually precarious circumstances demanded a mutual defense treaty, and living together was the obvious logistical arrangement. For the time being, at least.

In the tube heading north she was cheerful, even a little manic: definitely up, despite the throngs of fellow travelers pressing close. Her ESP didn't seem to operate all the time. It was something like Hamlin was for him, he imagined: coming and going, ebbing and flowing, now virtually in full possession, now weak and indetectable. When the demon was on her, she came close to disruption and collapse. At other times, such as now, she was lively, alert, buoyant. Yet there was a hard fretful edge to her gaiety. As if she were contemplating at all times the possibility that her telepathic sensitivity would switch itself on, here in the tube, and plunge her once more into frenzy.

Her apartment was grim: one shabby room in an antique building on a forgotten limb of the city. Something out of Dickens. The lame, the halt, and the blind infesting the place, dirty children everywhere, fat old women, sinister cutthroaty young men, dogs, cats, screams, shrieks, wild laughter from behind concave doors. A prevailing odor of urine and exotic spices. Not just the twentieth century surviving here; more like the nineteenth. The booming of holovision sets in the halls seemed like a grotesque anachronism.

They walked up, five flights. One didn't expect to find liftshafts in this sort of house, but one hoped it dated at least from the era of elevators. Apparently not. Why did she live here? Why not go to one of the people's cooperatives, stark but at least clean, and surely no more costly than this? She preferred this, she told him. He couldn't follow her mumbled explanation, but he thought it had to do with the construction of the walls; was she saying that in an old building like this she wasn't as bothered by her neighbors' telepathic emanations as she would be in a flimsily built co-op?

Within this dismalness she had carved an equally dismal nest. A squarish high-ceilinged room with clumsy furniture, patched draperies, simple utensils. A tiny stained powerpack to cook on, a cold-sink in lieu of real refrigeration. He didn't see toilet facilities. Everything in disarray. No housekeeper she. The bed unmade, the exposed sheets carrying half a dozen layers of yellowish stains – that bothered him, he could guess at the origin of the stains – and books scattered everywhere. On the windowsill, on the floor, even under the bed.

So she was a diligent reader. Interesting. You could judge a person's character by his reading.

Macy realized he scarcely knew Lissa at all. What could he say about her? That she seemed fairly bright but had shown no signs so far of having intellectual interests, that she was a passably good lay (so far as he was capable of telling, given the synthetic nature of his available past experience), that she once had been closely associated with an important contemporary artist. Period. Had she had an education? A career of her own, goals in life, talents, skills? A model is only a cipher, a shape, a set of curves and planes and textures; Hamlin was too complicated a man to have fallen in love with her purely as model, so there had to be something back of the exterior, she must have had some kind of interior substance, she must have done something in the world other than pose for Nat Hamlin. At least until her increasingly more turbulent inner storms had driven her to take refuge in this squalid place.

But he knew nothing. Had she traveled? Did she have a family? Dreams of becoming an artist herself? Perhaps her books might tell him something. Helplessly, he surveyed and inventoried her library while she bustled around collecting her other possessions.

Immediately he found himself in difficulties: he was no reader himself, had merely skimmed a few popular novels during his stay in the Rehab Center, and whatever Hamlin had read, if he had read anything at all, was of course gone from Macy's mind. Macy had only the *illusion* of a familiarity with literature. Dr Brewster, the literary one, had programmed him with hazy plot summaries and dislocated images and even with the physical feel of some books, so that he knew quite clearly that the *Iliad* was a tall orange volume with cream-colored paper and elegant rounded print. But what was it about? A war, long ago. A quarrel over a woman. Proud barbarian chieftains. Who was Homer? Had he lived before Hemingway? Jesus, he was an illiterate!

And so, looking through Lissa's heaps of books, he could draw no certain conclusions, except that she seemed to read (or at least to own) a lot of novels, thick serious-looking ones, and that perhaps a fifth of the books were works of biography and history, not casual light stuff by any means. So she must be a more complex person than she had revealed herself to him thus far to be. Anybody, no matter how dim, might happen to pick up a book occasionally, but Lissa had surrounded herself with them, which argued for the presence within her of psychic hungers for knowledge.

He tried to touch up his image of her, making her less waiflike and dependent, less the hapless, whining victim of circumstances, more of a self-propelled inner-guided individual with purpose and direction and a sphere of interests. But he still had difficulty seeing her as anything other than part of the furniture in Nat Hamlin's studio, or as a pitiful casualty of modern urban life. She refused to come alive for him as a genuine, fully operative human being.

Maybe it's because I don't understand people very well, being so new in the world, he thought. Or perhaps one of the doctors built his own archaic attitudes toward women in general into me – does Gomez, say, see them only as extensions and pale reflections of the men they live with? Mere bundles of foggy emotion and woolly response? But they don't just drift from event to event, letting things happen to them. They won't forget to get out of bed if nobody tells them to. Women have minds of their own. I'm sure they do. They must. They must. And interesting minds. Some commitment to something besides survival, meals, fucking, babies. Then why does she seem so hollow to me? I have to try to get to know her better.

She was filling a large battered green suitcase with her things. Clothes, knickknacks, a dozen books. Something large and flat, maybe a sketchpad. A folder of old letters and papers. She stuffed five more books in at the very last.

A tepid evening, an indifferent night. Dinner at a beanery

a few blocks from his place. Afterward, home, a couple of golds, some desultory chatter, bed. No outbursts of telepathy to plague her. No resurgences of Hamlin to bother him. They were free to pursue one another's innerness without distractions, but somehow it didn't happen; they talked all around their troubles without coming to any of the main issues. He was surprised to learn she was not quite twenty-five years old, four or five years below his guess. Born in Pittsburgh, no less. Father some kind of scientist, mother an expert on population dynamics. Good genes. They sounded like acceptable types. Lissa hadn't seen them in years. Came to New York, age seventeen, to study art. (Aha!) Thought also of writing novels. (Ahahaha!)

Turning point in life June 15, 2004, age eighteen, meets famed artist Nathaniel Hamlin. Falls wildly in love with him. He doesn't notice her at all, so she thinks (scene is a meet-the-faculty party at the Art Students' League, everybody wildly stoned, Hamlin – guest lecturer or something that semester – urbanely putting on all the pretty girls).

But a week later he calls her. Drinks? Stroll in Central Park? Of course. She is terrified. Hopes he'll accept her as a private student. Wants to bring him to her apartment (not this present uptown hovel) and show him her sketches. Doesn't dare. A nice chaste summertime stroll.

Afterward she is sure he found her too trivial, too adolescent, but no, he calls again, exactly seven days later. What a sweet time that was. Care to see my studio? Out in Darien, Connecticut. She has no idea where is Darien. He'll pick her up, never fear. Long sleek car. Driving it himself. She has brought her portfolio, just in case. He takes her to flamboyant country estate, unbelievable place: swimming pool, creek, pond full of mutated goldfish in improbable colors, big stone house, medium-big studio annex.

Turns out he isn't interested in her as an artist at all, wants her as model: has some ambitious project in mind for which she would be perfect. She is awed. Her portfolio lying neglected in the car. I need to see the body, he says. Of course. Of course.

Strips: blouse, slacks. Thoughtfully omitted to don underwear that day. He studies her carefully. Oh, God, my backside's too flat, my boobs are too big, or maybe not big enough! But no, he compliments her, good tight fanny, cute shape, will do, will do.

And suddenly his pants are open in front. Thick reddened organ sticking out. (Oh, you've seen it, Macy, you know it like your own!) She is thrown into panic. She's been laid before, yes, eight, ten fellows, not coming on as timid innocent at all, but yet this is the authentic erect cock of *Nathaniel Hamlin* that now approaches her, which is something very special. Admired his work all her life, never dreamed that one day he'd be presenting his mast to her. Can't take her eyes off it until it disappears into her box.

In and out. In and out. Nathaniel Hamlin's authentic thing knows its business. Such terrific intensity boiling within him, and he expresses it with his pecker. She comes a thousand times. Afterward they both run naked around the estate, swim, laugh, get stoned. He grabs a camera and holographs her for an hour. You and me, he says, we're going to make a masterpiece the world won't ever forget. Then they dress, he drives her to a restaurant near the Sound, such glamor that it dizzies her, and finally, late at night, deposits her, an exhausted astounded adolescent heap of much-fucked flesh, at her apartment. An unforgettable experience.

Then she doesn't hear from him for three months. Despair. At last an apologetic postcard from Morocco. Another, a month and a half later, from Baghdad. At Christmas time a card with Japanese stamps on it. Then, January '05, a phonecall. Back in town at last. See you at nine tonight, break all other engagements.

And from then on she is more or less his full-time mistress, living at Darien much of the time, naturally dropping out of art school, drifting away from old friends, who now seem naive and immature to her. New friends, exciting ones. Even becoming friendly with Hamlin's wife. (A peculiar marital relation there, Macy concluded.)

Early in '06, after nearly a year of planning, he gets down to serious work on the *Antigone 21*. Months of toil for him and for her; he is a demon when he works. Twelve, fifteen, eighteen hours a day. Finally almost finished. Almost finished with her, too. He has been talking of marrying her since the summer of '05, but their relationship grows increasingly tense. Physical violence: he slaps her, kicks her a couple of times, balls her once by main force when she doesn't want it, ultimately knocks her down the stairs and breaks her pelvis. Hospital. During which time he succumbs completely to the disintegration of personality that has, unknown to her, been going on in him for most of the year, and commits Dreadful Deeds upon the persons of a variety of women. He is arrested and tried; she sees him no more until that eerie day in May of 2011 when she crashed into Paul Macy on the streets of Manhattan North.

And your telepathy problem, Macy wants to ask? When did that start? When did it become severe? But obviously she doesn't want to talk about that. She will speak to him tonight only of old business, her romance with the defunct great artist. And now she has talked herself out. Silence. Lights out. Two red roaches in the darkness. Pungent smoke rising ceilingward. This would be the sort of moment, Macy thought, when Hamlin would appear. To append footnotes to Lissa's story. But Hamlin, missing his cue, did not appear. It began to occur to Macy that each of his encounters with Hamlin might drain the other's strength as much as it did his, possibly more; between colloquies, Hamlin had to lie doggo, recharging. Maybe not so, but a cheering possibility. Tire him out, wear him down, eventually eject him. An endurance contest.

Macy turned dutifully to Lissa, not particularly in need of her but feeling that they ought to commemorate her moving-in with some kind of celebration of passion; his hand slipped over one of her breasts, but she responded not at all, merely lying there in a passive stony haze, and an uncheering possibility struck him: When she makes love with me, is she really only

trying to recapture those moments of fire with *him?* I am Nat
Hamlin's well-endowed body minus Nat Hamlin's trouble-
somely violent nature; is that not all she seeks from me?

The thought that he might be, for her, nothing but a dead
man's reanimated penis did not amuse him. Of course she
said she enjoyed him for his own sake, but of what did his
own sake consist? Having loved a genius, could she love a
nonentity equally well? Or at all? A young, impressionable art
student would of course be drawn automatically to a magnet
such as Nat Hamlin, but Paul Macy should have no pull. Who
am I, what am I, wherein lies my texture, my density? I am
nothing. I am unreal. Hamlin's shadowy successor. His relict.
Macy attempted to check this cascade of negativisms, telling
himself that Hamlin was undoubtedly causing it by releasing
a river of poisons from his subcranial den. But he could not
coax himself just now to a higher self-esteem. Entering her,
he pushed the piston mechanically back and forth for three
or four minutes, feeling wholly detached from her except at
the point of entry, and since she gave no hint of being with
him in any way, he let himself go off and sank into the usual
bothered sleep, infested by incubi and revenants.

Many sympathetic glances at the network office the next
day. Everybody tiptoeing around him, speaking in soft tones,
grinning a lot, sidestepping every situation of potential stress
or conflict. Obviously all of them afraid he might flip at the
first jarring stimulus. It was a regression to the way they had
treated him weeks ago, when he had first come here, when
they thought a Rehab needed to be handled as carefully as a
barrel of eggs. He wondered why. Was it because he had called
in sick yesterday, and now they assumed he had been suffering
from some special affliction of Rehabs, some slippage of the
identity, that required extracautious handling? Their excessive
kindness, implying as it did that he was more vulnerable than
they, irritated him. After two and a half hours of it he cornered
Loftus, Stilton Fredericks' executive assistant, and asked her
about it.

He said, 'I want you to know that what kept me home yesterday was simply an upset stomach. A case of the runs and a lot of puking, okay?'

She looked at him blankly. 'I don't remember asking.'

'I know you didn't ask. But everybody else around this place seems to think I had some sort of nervous breakdown. At least, that's how they've been treating me today. So fucking kind it's killing me. So I thought I'd let you spread the word that I'm all right. A mere internal indisposition.'

'You don't like people to be nice to you, Macy?'

'I didn't say that. I just don't want my fellow workers making inaccurate assumptions about the state of my head.'

'Okay, so you didn't have a nervous breakdown. So why do you look so strange?'

'Strange?'

'Strange,' Loftus said.

'What way?'

'Look in the mirror.' Then, a moment of tenderness breaking through the steel: 'If anything's the matter that any of us could fix –'

'No. No. Honestly, it was only an upset stomach.'

'Uh-huh. Okay, if anybody asks, I'll tell them. Nobody's going to whisper behind your back.'

He thanked her and made a quick escape. Executive washroom: amid all the electronic gimmickry, the sonic shavers and the Klein-bottle urinals, he found a mirror, standard variety, silver-backed glass as in days of yore. A fierce, bloodshot face looking back at him. Furrowed forehead. Nostrils flaring. Lips compressed, mouth drawn off to one side. Jesus, no wonder! He was Mr Hyde and Dr Jekyll both at the same time, his features all snarled up, reflecting the most intense kind of interior agonies.

And this without a buzz from Hamlin for the past eighteen hours. This double existence, this squatter occupation of the lower reaches of his mind, was corroding his face, turning him into an ambulatory flag of distress. Of course they were all being sweet to him today; they could see the signals of imminent collapse inscribed on his brow.

Yet he felt relatively relaxed today. What must he look like when Hamlin was near the surface and prodding him? Macy ventured an exploratory sweep. *Hamlin? Hamlin, you there? My private permanent bad dream. Come up where I can see you. Let's have a chat.*

But no, all quiet on the cerebral front. Feeling snubbed, Macy set out to repair his face. Stripped to the waist. Sticking his head into the hot-air blower. Loosen the muscles, soften the scowl. A little humidity, maestro. Ah. Ah, how good that is on the tactile net. Thrust noggin now into whirlpool sink. Round and round and round, bubble bubble bubble, hold your breath and let the lovely water work its magic. Ah. Ah. Splendid. Back to the hot air to dry off. Now pop a trank. Blow a gold. Survey the map. Better, much better. The tension draining away; a lucky thing, too, they wouldn't have let you step in front of a camera looking all screwed up.

Macy was still refurbishing himself, putting his clothes back on, when Fredericks walked into the john. A hearty phony laugh out of him, ho ho ho. 'Interrupting you in a moment of relaxation, Paul?'

'No. All done relaxing now. And feeling much better.'

'We were all quite concerned when you phoned in yesterday.'

'Just a jumpy stomach, was all. Much better now. See?' Flashing his rehabilitated features at Fredericks. 'I appreciate the concern, but I'm really pretty tough. Stilton,' he added reluctantly. A hell of a name to carry through life. Fredericks addressed himself to the task of unloading his bladder. Macy went out, working hard at looking loose. The effort must have been worthwhile; people stopped pampering him.

At half past two he picked up his script for the day, ran through the visuals four or five times, rehearsed the audio. A two-minute squib on the coronation in Ethiopia, surging throngs, lions marching on chains through the streets, a herniated corner of the fifteenth century poking into the twenty-first.

Macy wondered how Mr Bercovici, he who had selected

him at the Rehab Center for this job, was making out in Addis Ababa. Was that him at the edge of the crowd, picked up by the trusty hovereye, that plump white face among the hawk-featured brown ones? Here and gone; probably the South African consul-general, or whoever. Macy carried off his voice-over nobly. '*Amid the pomp and glamor of a medieval empire, the former Prince Takla Hay-manot today became the Lion of Judan, King of the Kings of Ethiopia, His Excellency the Negus Lebna Dengel II, newest monarch in a line of royalty descended from King Solomon himself . . .*' Beautiful.

And then home to Lissa through thin rain.

She was in bed, reading, wearing a tattered green housecoat that looked old enough to be one of the Queen of Sheba's hand-me-downs, nothing at all underneath it, pinkish-brown nipples peeping through. One quick look and he knew, as if by telepathic transmission, that she had had a bad day. Her face had that sullen, pouty look; her hair was uncombed, a wild auburn tangle; the stale smell of dried sweat was sharp in the air of the bedroom. He felt strangely domesticated. Hubby coming home from hard day at office, slatternly wife about to tell him of the day's petty crises.

She tossed aside her book and sat up. 'Christ,' she said. Her favorite expletive. 'An all-day bummer, this was. Rainy weather indoors and out.'

He kicked off his shoes. 'Bad?'

'The anvil chorus in my head.' Shrugging. 'Let's not talk about it. I was going to whip up a fancy dinner, but I didn't get up the energy. I could put something together fast.'

'We'll go out. Don't bother.' He eased out of his over-clothes. Fifteen seconds of dead air. Despite her saying she didn't want to talk about today, she seemed obviously waiting for him to start questioning her. Gambit declined. He was tired and fretful himself: Hamlin beginning to clamber toward the surface again, maybe.

He looked at her. She at him. The silence continued, dragging on until it had attained a tangible presence of its own. Then Lissa appeared to tune the tension out; she disconnected something in herself and slumped back against the pillow, sinking into that brooding withdrawal that she affected about half the time.

Macy got himself a beer. When he returned to the bedroom she was still eighteen thousand light-years away. A curious notion came to him: that unless he made contact with her in some fashion this very minute, she would be wholly lost to him. Her closedness annoyed him, but he hid his pique and, going to her, pulled back the coverlet to caress the outside of her bare thigh. A friendly gesture, loving almost. She didn't seem to notice. He touched his cold beer to her skin. A hiss. 'Hey!'

'Just wanted to find out if you were still here,' he said.

'Very funny.'

'What's the matter, Lissa?' The question out of him at last.

'Nothing. Everything. This shitty rain. The air in here. I don't know.' Momentary wildness in her eyes. 'I've been picking up noise all day in my head. You and Hamlin, Hamlin and you. Like a kind of radioactive trace in the air. I shouldn't have moved in here.'

'Surely you can't pick up telepathic impulses from someone who isn't even in the room!'

'No? How do you know? Do you know anything at all about it? Maybe your ESP waves soak into the paint, into the woodwork. And radiate back at me all day. Don't try to tell me what I've been feeling. The two of you, banging at me off the walls, blam blam blam, hour after hour.' These sharp sentences were delivered in an inappropriately flat, absent tone. At the end of which she disconnected again.

'Lissa?'

Silence.

'Lissa?'

'What?'

'Remember, you came looking for *me*. I told you it wasn't good for us to be together. And you said we needed each other, right? So don't take it out on me if it doesn't work well.'

'I'm sorry.' A ten-year-old's insincere apology.

More silence.

He tried to make allowances for her mood. Cooped up all day. Raining. Hostile ions in the air. Her period coming on, maybe. A woman's entitled to be bitchy sometimes. Still, he didn't need to take it. If there was too much telepathic noise here, she could go back to the pigsty.

'I heard that,' she said.

'Oh, Jesus.'

'My period isn't due for a week. And if you want me to go to the pigsty, say it out loud and I'll pack right now.'

'Do you read my mind all the time?'

'Not like that, no. What I get, it's a general hazy fuzz that I can identify as your signal, and a different fuzz that's *his*, but not usually any sharp words. Except that time it was perfectly clear. Am I really being bitchy?'

'You aren't being much fun,' he said.

'I'm not having much fun, either.'

'How about a shower? And then a good dinner.' Trying to repair things. 'A dress-up dinner, downtown. All right?' Like humoring a cranky child. Did she hear that too? Apparently not. Getting up, shucking her housecoat. Not bothering to hold herself upright; shoulders slumped, breasts dangling, belly pushed outward. Padding across and into the shower. Well, we all have our bad days. Sound of water running. Then her head sticking into the bedroom.

She said, 'By the way, the Rehab Center phoned this morning.'

Macy looked up, and in the same instant Hamlin awoke and did something to his heartbeat, something transient and painful, that made him gasp and clap his hand to his breastbone.

'I said, the Rehab Center phoned –'

'I heard you.' Macy coughed. 'Wait a second. Hamlin acting up.' He shot a furious thought downward. *Let me be. Knock it off.* The pain subsided. Macy said, 'Who was it?'

'A woman doctor with an Italian name.'

'Ianuzzi.'

'That's the one. She wanted to know why you hadn't shown

up for your therapy yesterday. After making a special early appointment and everything.'

'What did you tell her?' he asked.

Hopes suddenly soaring. His previous identity has surfaced and is trying to take him over, Dr Ianuzzi. A terrible struggle going on inside him. Oh, is that so, Miss Moore? How unexpected. But we can handle it, of course. We'll have our mobile ego-smashing unit on the spot at seven o'clock sharp. Three quick bursts of rays from the egotron machine, beamed up from the street, and that'll be the end of Mr Nat Hamlin for once and all, oh, yes, oh, yes. Tell Mr Macy not to worry about a thing. Thank you for giving me the details, Miss Moore.

Lissa very far away. Dreamy. Macy said again, more sharply, 'What did you tell her?'

'I didn't tell her anything.'

'What?'

'She called at a bad time for me. I don't even know why I answered. I couldn't make much sense out of what she was asking me until afterward.'

'So you just hung up?'

'No, I talked, more or less. I said I didn't know much about why you missed your appointment. Or where you were at the moment.' A distant shrug. 'I guess I was pretty foggy.'

'Jesus, Lissa, you had a chance to help me, and you blew it! You could have told her the whole story!'

She said, 'Didn't you tell me that Hamlin threatened to kill you if you brought the Rehab Center into the picture?'

'That's right. But he wouldn't have known it if *you* had given them the story while I was at work. It was a perfect chance. And you blew it. You blew it.'

'Sorry.' But not very.

'If they phone again, will you do things right?'

'What do you want me to tell them?'

'The straight story. Hamlin coming back. And especially the part about his saying he'll stop my heart if I go near a Rehab Center. Make sure they know he means it. How I set out to go there, how he knocked me down at the Greenwich terminal. You won't forget that part of it?'

'Maybe you better call them yourself.'

'I told you, I can't. Hamlin monitors everything I think or say. The moment I pick up the phone, he'll have his clutches on my –' *Jesus!* Another twinge in the chest. Clammy invisible fingers tweaking the aorta. A cough. A gasp. A slow shivering recovery. Lissa watching, unconcerned. 'There,' Macy said finally. 'He just did it. To let me know he's tuned in.'

'What good is having them know, though, if he'll kill you if they try to help you?'

'At least they'll know. Maybe they have a remote-control way of dealing with situations like this. Maybe they can sneak up on him somehow. They've got their tricks. It can't hurt to have them realize what's happened. Provided they're aware of the risks involved for me. You won't forget that part?'

'If they call,' Lissa said vaguely, 'I'll try to tell them everything. I'll try.' She didn't sound too sure of it.

In the night, fragmentary episodes of not-quite-nightmare, slippery bulletins issued by the psychic underground. Oddly unfrightening moments out of an unremembered past arriving on top deck for the sleeper's inspection and enlightenment. Bucolic scenes: the arrest, the arraignment, the detention center, the courthouse, the trial, the verdict, the sentence. *Keep your fucking hands off me, I told you I'd go peacefully!*

Lights flashing in his eyes. A hovereye camera practically touching his nose. Viewers around the world enjoying the spectacle. See the famed doer of abominations! Watch justice triumph! Death to the enemies of chastity! A jury of twelve honest computers and true.

Sweartotellthetruththewholetruthnothingbutthetruth. IdoIdoIdoIdo. See the sobbing witnesses. Observe their haunted vindictive faces! What memories of obscene violations blaze in their souls? *Yes, that's the man, he's the one! I'd know him anywhere.* The courtroom silent. *Your honor, I ask permission to enter as evidence the taped record of the defendant's intrusion into the home of Maria Alicia Rodriguez on the night of* – Red lights flickering on the lawyerboard. *Objection! Objection!* Commotion. *Denied. Prosecution may proceed.*

On the wallscreen the defendant appears, bent on rape. Had he but known he was performing for a camera, he would have been ever so much more stylish about it. Up onto the windowledge, hup! Pry the window open. Hands cold; this miserable winter weather. Yes. Inside. The trembling victim. And the camera descends to get a good view of the action. If they were so concerned about chastity, why did they let him consummate the rape? A good question for the victim to ask. But of course it was all taped automatically; not till later did anyone realize that the hovereye had caught the mad rapist at his trade. White thighs gleaming in the moonlight. Wiry black bush, almost blue. Push. Push. Wham!

Will the defendant please rise. Nathaniel James Hamlin you have heard the verdict of your peers. This court now declares you guilty on eleven counts of aggravated assault fourteen counts of unsolicited carnal entry five counts of third-degree sodomy seven counts of irremediable psychic injury seventeen counts of violation of marital propriety seven counts of first-degree illicit proximity nine counts of eleven counts of sixteen counts of.

The sleeper becomes restless. Let us perhaps turn our attention to happier times. The artist at work in his splendid studio, cascades of spring sunlight pouring through the grand window. Cleverly constructing the armature for the latest masterpiece. First comes the all-encompassing vision, you understand, the sense of the work as a wholeness, without which it is impossible to begin. This hits you like a bolt of lightning, if it comes any other way, don't trust it. Afterward it's just plonking drudgery, a lot of soldering. I wouldn't bother except that I have to. It's the first moment, the white light falling out of heaven, that makes it all worthwhile.

But of course any shithead phony can say he has inspirations. Can he realize them? I can. You build the armature, see, which means you have to crap around with relays and solenoids and connectors and power-shunts and gate-nexuses and such. You

calculate the atmospherics you want; a computer gives you the
ionization tables, but then you have to make the corrections
yourself, intuitively. You do the lighting. Then you put the
skin on. Throughout the whole business you never lose sight
of the initial impulse, which is, item one, a matter of form,
of the actual goddam shape of the piece, and, item two, a
matter of psychological insight, of the particular movement
of the spirit you mean to express. Now you know as much
about my working methods as I do. You want to know more,
buy one of my pieces and take it apart.

The scene changes. At the gallery now, we are watching the
elite of the art world scrambling to buy his 2002 output; that
was the year of the phallic miniatures, they walk, they talk,
they jerk off, eight grand apiece, every distinguished creator is
entitled to have his little black jest. Sold like hotcakes. Better
than hotcakes: did you ever buy a hotcake in your life? The
hotcake market is extremely depressed these days.

Macy, slumbering, maybe even snoring, makes desperate
mental notes. I must remember all this when I wake up. This
is my genuine past, accept no substitutes. Is Hamlin sending
all this stuff up by way of making friendly overtures to me,
or is he trying to torment me? In any event, more. More, he
cried, give me more! So more. Look at the world through a
madman's eyes. Take the hallucinogenic trip for free. Breathe
in, breathe out, turn on, *tilt!* What are those streaks spanning
the sky? That cockeyed rainbow, black, green, turquoise, gray,
purple, white. And what colors do you see when your eyes are
closed? The same. The very same.

Why is there so much pressure in the groin? You can feel
the pulsations, the throbbings. It's like being sixteen all over
again. You want to plant it fast, you want to pump yourself
dry. Insatiable. But only in strange and reluctant cunts. Why
is that? Can you offer a rational explanation? Ha. Time to
prowl the winter streets. A tightness in the ass, a dryness in
the throat. Your own sweet wifey willing to come across for
you, any time, any place, and the same is true of a myriad of
others, hot available Lissa, so why endanger yourself in this

fashion? But danger defines the man. I climb these peaks because they're here.

Do you realize, though, that you're out of your mind? Naturally I do. *Will the defendant please rise. Nathaniel James Hamlin you have heard the verdict of your peers.* There, you see the risks? You know what those bastards can do to you? Sure I know. I accept the risks. Let them do their worst. *It is the decision of this court that the identity known as Nathaniel James Hamlin having been found guilty of repeated and numerous instances of intolerably antisocial activity and having been declared an incurable and incorrigible sociopathic menace by a properly constituted panel of authorities shall be withdrawn permanently from access to society and shall be at once expunged under the provisions of the Federal Social Rehabilitation Act of 2001 and that in accordance with the terms of that act the physical container as legally defined of the proscribed identity be reconstructed and returned to society at the earliest possible time.*

Let me have your left arm, please, Mr Hamlin. No, this isn't a needle, it's an ultrasonic injector, you won't feel a thing. How long will it be before it takes effect? Oh, you'll sense some effects almost immediately, I'd say, as the short-term memory processes begin to break down. The left arm, now? Thank you. There. See how easy it was? We'll be back in ten hours to begin the next phase. *What is my name? Who am I? Why are they doing this to me?* Now the right arm, please, Mr Hamlin. *Who?* Mr Hamlin. That's you, Nathaniel Hamlin. *Oh.* The right arm, please? No, it's not a needle, it's an ultrasonic injector, just like the last one. You don't remember the last one? Well, of course, I should have realized that. Here we go! *They're washing away my mind! No no no no no no no no no no no no*

At the office the next afternoon Hamlin, who had not been heard from in any overt way for almost two full days, made another attempt at seizing the speech centers of Macy's brain. He chose his moment carefully. Late in the day; Macy trying for the tenth or twelfth time to tape his commentary for the evening news; inner tensions high.

The words weren't flowing and the tones were thorny. He was covering the presumed assassination of the Croatian prime minister, a particularly nasty incident: a gang of monadist radicals had kidnapped the man a week ago and, spiriting him away to an illegal mindpick laboratory thought to be located somewhere in the Caucasus, had subjected him to an intensive three-day personality deconstruct that had wholly obliterated his identity. His soulless shell had been picked up during the night in Istanbul and was now in Zagreb, where platoons of neurologists now were converging in the hope of summoning back his eradicated self. Scarcely any chance of success, according to a British authority on deconstruct techniques. If an identity is taken apart properly, there's no known way of reassembling it. All the king's horses and all the king's men, and so forth. A bad show.

When the story had started to come off the pipe around lunchtime, Macy had instantly volunteered to handle it. He felt he had to prove to his colleagues that he did not need to be sheltered against references to deconstructs and reconstructs, rehabilitation work, and related matters. But it was proving unexpectedly difficult for him to carry out the assignment. The story was full of lumpy Croatian names that refused to cross his tongue in the right order of syllables. Moreover, he was more sensitive to the theme of the incident than he had realized; he burst into uneasy sweats at odd moments while reading his script, usually around the place where he was doing the lead-in to the statement from the London neurologist.

Take it slow, the platform monitor kept calling out to him. You're pressing, Paul. Just go easy and let the words slide out. Everybody was being kind to him, again. A whole taping crew immobilized here for well over an hour while he blundered and staggered his way through an infinity of faulty takes. Take it slow, take it slow.

This time he thought he had it. The polysyllabic names all safely taped. The intricate explication of Balkan politics handled without calamity. For the first time this afternoon, a single usable take covering ninety percent of the script. Now to clinch things: 'This morning in London, we spoke with the celebrated British brain expert Varnum Skillings, who *vdrkh cmpm gzpzp vdrkh* –'

'*Cut!*'

'*Shqkm. Vtpkp. Smss! Grgg!*'

People rushing toward him from all sides of the studio. His skull ablaze. Eyes unfocused. Macy knew precisely what had happened, and after the first instinctive moment of terror he began to take counteroffensive action. Just as he had on Tuesday, he labored to pry Hamlin's mental grip loose. There was a complicating factor here, the public nature of his fit, the disturbed colleagues fluttering around him, asking him things, loosening his collar, otherwise distracting him. And the feeling of calamity that came over him at the realization that he had suffered this upheaval in front of everybody, exposed himself thoroughly as too sick to hold this job. Brushing aside those matters, he worked on Hamlin. The devil had bided his time, collected his strength, made his try when Macy was least prepared for it. All the same, Macy was more powerful. He had the leverage that controlling the body's main neural trunks provided. Back, you fucker! Back! Back! Let go!

Hamlin let go. Foiled again.

Macy's vision returned and he found himself staring into the agitated onyx face of Loftus. Asking him over and over what had happened, was he all right, should they send for a doctor, an ambulance, get him a drink, a gold.

'I'll be fine,' he said. Voice like corroded copper.

'You sounded so weird just then – and your face was so twisted up –'

'I said I'd be all right.' Normal tone returning.

No one must know. No one.

The platform monitor, Smith, Jones, some name like that, coming up to him. 'We got a nearly perfect take, Macy. If you'd like to rest a while, and then you can do the finale for us – no problem to splice it –'

'We'll do it now,' said Macy.

No one must know.

The camera crew returning to places. Confusion defused. Macy, alone under the lights, swaying a little, searched his mind for Hamlin, could not find him, decided that he really had succeeded once again in thwarting a takeover. Nevertheless, he would keep on guard. If it happened again under the cameras he'd be in trouble. No room in this organization for newsmen who throw fits at unpredictable moments.

'Roll it,' said Jones or Smith.

'This morning in London,' Macy said smoothly, 'we spoke with the celebrated British brain expert Varnum Skillings, who gave us this assessment of the situation.'

'Cut,' said Smith or Jones.

Macy smiled. Almost home free, now. The platform monitor gave the signal. Macy delivered the final line. Done. Sighs of relief. People trooping out. Low whispers, everyone no doubt talking about his creepy paroxysm.

Let them talk. I beat him down again, didn't I? He loses every time.

For once Macy thought it might be almost tolerable to have Hamlin alive within him. Hamlin was the perpetual challenge that defined him. Every man needs a nemesis. He arises, I smite him. He arises again, I smite again. And so we go on together through the busy, happy days. He gives me texture and density. With him, I am a man with a unique affliction; I carry tragic *angst*. Without him I would be a shadow. And so we are comfortable with one another. Until the time when the pattern of testing, of thrust and parry, is broken. Until he conquers me. Or I him. When it comes, it will come with one quick sudden triumphant thrust, and one of us will succumb. He? I? We'll see. Home, now. A long wearying day.

NINE

Lissa wasn't there. He looked through the apartment with great care, methodically passing several times from one room to the other and quickly doubling back, as though she might be slipping invisibly through the door just ahead of him; but no, she wasn't anywhere around. He checked the bathroom and the closets. Her things were still hanging helterskelter among his. Not gone permanently, then. A note from her? No, nothing. Might have gone out to take a walk. Or to buy some groceries for dinner. At this hour, though? Knowing he always came home punctually? Briefly alarmed, he searched the place once again, looking now for traces of violence. No. A mystery, then.

She had her own key, and he had reprogrammed the thumbplate safety latch to accept her fingerprint; she could come and go as she pleased. But she should have been on hand when he arrived. He couldn't understand why she wasn't. What now? Notify the police? There was this girl, officer, she's been living with me since Tuesday night, she wasn't home when I returned from work, I wonder if you – No. Hardly. Ask the neighbors if they had seen her? No. Go out and look for her in the local shops? No. Search for her at her own apartment? Maybe. Do nothing, stay here, wait for her to show up? Maybe. For the time being, yes. Give her an hour, two hours. She has her moods. Maybe she went to a show. Feeling tense, just went off by herself. Odd that there's no note, anyway.

He showered, put on his worn dressing gown, poured himself a little cream sherry to blunt the edge of his appetite. Getting later all the time. Half past six, no Lissa. Worry mounting in him. They had not, in the course of constructing him at the Rehab Center, prepared him to handle this sort of situation. He reviewed the possible options. Police. Local shops. Her apartment. Neighbors. Sit and wait. No tactic seemed adequate.

Out of the silence, the voice of the serpent:

– Don't worry about her.

Right now, in his jangled state, even the presence of Hamlin was a comfort. His other self had spoken in a casual, easy way; no challenge, at the moment, merely conversation. Macy was grateful for the muted approach. He wondered how to be properly hospitable. Offer Hamlin some sherry? A gold? Sit down, Nat, make yourself at home. An impulse of lunatic sociability.

I can't help worrying, Macy said.

– She can look after herself.

Can she, though?

– I know her better than you.

You haven't had anything to do with her for almost five years. She's unstable, Hamlin. I don't like the idea of her wandering off by herself this way.

– She probably felt she needed some fresh air. Bad telepathic vibrations bouncing off the walls in here, isn't that what she told you? Getting her down. So she went out.

Without leaving a note?

– Lissa doesn't leave notes much. Lissa's not awfully big on responsibility. Relax, Macy.

That's easy enough to say.

– You know, maybe she walked out for good. Sick of us both, maybe. All the tension and brawling.

Her things are still here, though, Macy pointed out. Grasping at straws. Lissa! Lissa!

– That wouldn't matter to her. Abandoned possessions fall from her like dandruff. Hey, cheer up, will you? The worst that can happen is that you won't ever see her again. Which maybe would be not such a terrible thing.

You'd like it a lot, wouldn't you?

– What's it to me?

You don't want me to have anything to do with her. You're jealous because I'm alive and you're not. Because I have her and you don't.

Robust interior chuckles bubbling in the brain. Derisive guffaws echoing through the involuted corridors.

– You're such a prick, Macy.

Can you deny what I said?

– What you said had more nonsense per square inch than is allowed under present brain-pollution laws.

For example?

– Where you say you 'have' Lissa. Nobody 'has' Lissa, ever. Lissa floats. Lissa drifts in a private orbit. Lissa lives inside a sealed airtight glass cage. She doesn't involve herself with other people. She spends time with them, yes, she talks with them, she fucks them sometimes, but she doesn't surrender anything that's real to her.

She involved herself with you.

– That was different. She loved me. The great exception in her life. But she doesn't love you or anybody else, herself included. You're fooling yourself if you think you mean anything to her.

How can you claim to know so much about her when you haven't seen her in five years?

– I've had all this week to watch her too, haven't I? That girl is very sick. This ESP thing is pulling her apart. She thinks she has to be alone in order to keep the voices out of her head. She can't give herself to anybody for long; she has to retreat, pull back, sink into herself. Otherwise she hurts too much. So you mustn't be surprised that she's walked out. It was inevitable. Believe me, Macy, I'm telling the truth.

A strange note of sincerity in Hamlin's tone. As if he's trying to protect me from a troublesome entanglement, Macy thought. As if he's got my welfare at heart. Curious.

Seven o'clock, now. No Lissa. Another sherry. Feet up on the hassock. Feeling almost relaxed, despite everything. Hardly even hungry. A slight headache. Where is she? She can look after herself. She can look after herself.

– Have you done any further thinking about the proposal I made?

What proposal?

– On Tuesday, in the museum. That you go away and let me have my body back.

You know the answer to that one.

– You're being unreasonable, Macy. I mean, look at it objectively. You may think you exist, but you actually don't. You're a construct. You don't have any more genuine reality as a person, as a human being, than that wall over there.

So you keep telling me. If I don't exist, though, why do I worry about Lissa? Why do I enjoy sipping this sherry? Why do I work so hard at the network?

– Because you've been programmed to. Crap, Macy, can't you see that you're only a clever machine that's been slipped into a vacant human body? Which turned out to be not quite vacant, which still had some bits of its former owner hiding in it. If you were capable of facing your own situation decently and honestly, you'd recognize that –

Right, Macy cut in. *I'd recognize that I'm a nothing and you're a genius, and I'd get the hell out of your head.*

– Yes.

Sorry, Hamlin. You're wasting our time asking me to. Why should I commit suicide just to give you a second chance to mess up your life?

– Suicide! Suicide! You've got to be alive before you can commit suicide!

I'm alive.

– Only in the most narrow technical sense.

Fuck you, Hamlin.

– Let's try to keep the conversation on a friendly basis, okay?

How can I be friendly when you invite me to kill myself? Where's the advantage for me in accepting your deal? What do you have to offer that makes it worth my while to give you this body back?

– Nothing. I can only appeal to your sense of equity. I'm more talented than you. I'm more valuable to society. I deserve to live more than you do.

I'm not so sure of that. Society's verdict was that you had no value at all, in fact that you were dangerous and had to be destroyed. Not even rehabilitated, in the old pre-Rehab sense of the word. Destroyed.

– A miscarriage of justice. I could have been salvaged. I went insane, I don't deny it, I did a lot of harm to a bunch of innocent women. But that's all over. If I came back now, I'd be beyond all that crap. I'd keep to myself and practice my art.

Sure you would. Sure. Look, Hamlin, if you want this body back, take it away from me – if you can. But I'm not giving it to you just for the asking. I don't think as little of myself as you do. Forget it.

– I wish I could make you see my point of view.

Half past seven. Sill no Lissa. Macy switched from sherry to bourbon. Also lit the first gold of the evening. A deep drag; instant response, lightheadedness, a loss of contact with his feet. Just a touch of pot-paranoia, too: suppose Hamlin made a grab for his brain while he was fuddled with liquor and fumes? Could he fight back properly? His skullmate had been quiet for ten or fifteen minutes now. Gathering strength for an assault, maybe. Keep your guard up.

But no assault came. The intoxicants that lulled Macy seemed to lull Hamlin as well.

Eight o'clock.

Hamlin? You still there?

– You rang, milord?

Talk to me.

– Four score and seven years ago, our fathers brought forth upon this continent a new nation conceived in liberty and –

No, be serious. Tell me something. What's it like for you, inside there?

– Crowded and nasty.

How do you visualize yourself?

– As an octopus. A very small octopus, Macy, maybe a millionth of an inch in diameter, sitting smack in the middle of the left side of your head. With long skinny tentacles reaching out to various parts of your brain.

Can you see the outside world?

– When I want to. It uses some energy, but it isn't really hard. I hook into your optic input, is all, and then I see whatever you're seeing.

What about hearing?

– A different kind of hookup. I keep that one patched in nearly all the time.

Sense of touch? Smell? Taste?

– The same. It's no great trick to cut into your sensory receptors and find out what's going on outside.

What about reading my thoughts?

– Easy. A tentacle into the cerebral cortex. I monitor you constantly there, Macy. You think it, I pick it up instantly. And I can sort out your consciously directed mental impulses from the mush of mental noise that you put out steadily, too.

How did you learn these things?

– Trial and error. I woke up, see, not knowing where I was, what had happened to me. Lissa gave me a telepathic nudge, not even realizing she was doing it, and there I was. Locked in a dark room, a coffin, for all I knew. So I started groping around in your head. Accidentally touched something and made a connection. Hey, I can see! Touched something else. I can hear! What's this? Somebody else is wearing my body! But if I make contact here, I can pick up his thoughts. And so on. It took a few days.

And you keep learning things all the time, eh, Hamlin?

– Frankly, I haven't been making much progress lately. I'm finding it hard to override your conscious control, your motor centers, your speech center. To make you walk where I want you to walk, to make you say what I want you to say. I can do a little of that, but it costs me a terrific load of energy, and sooner or later you pull me loose. Maybe there's a secret to overriding you that I haven't found yet.

You manage to mess with my heartbeat pretty easily, though.

– Oh, yes. I've got decent control over most of your autonomic system. I could turn your heart off in five seconds. But what's the use? You die, I'd die too. I could play with your digestive juices and give you an ulcer by morning. Only this is my body as much as yours: I don't gain anything by damaging it.

Nevertheless you can cause me plenty of pain.

– Indeed I can. I could harass you most miserably, Macy.

How would you like the sensation of a toothache, twenty-five hours a day? Not the toothache itself, nothing a dentist could fix, just the sensation of it. How would you like a premature ejaculation, every time? How would you like a feedback loop in your auditory system so that you heard everything twice with a half-second delay? I could make your life hell. But I'm not really a sadist. I don't have any hard feelings toward you. I simply want my body back. I still hope we can work things out in an amiable way, without the need for me to apply real pressure.

Let's not start that routine again. Macy reached for the bourbon. *I want to know more about you. What it's like for you in there. Can you actually see the interior of my brain?*

— See it? The neurons, the synapses, the brain cells? Not really. Only in a metaphorical sense. A visionary sense. I can set up one-to-one percept equivalents, such as my perception of myself as a miniature octopus, do you follow? But I don't actually see. It's hard to explain. I'm aware of things, structures, forms, but I simply can't communicate that awareness to someone who hasn't ever been on the inside himself. You have to remember that I don't have an organic existence. I'm not a lump of something solid under your headbone, a kind of tumor. I'm just a web of electrochemical impulses, Macy, and I perceive things differently.

But aren't we all just webs of electrochemical impulses? What am I if not that?

— True. Except that you're linked with this brain at so many points that you don't have any sense of yourself as something distinct from the bodily organ through which you perceive things. I do. I'm dissociated, disembodied. I sense my own existence as something quite separate from the existence of this brain, here, through which I get various sensory inputs when I ask for them, and through which I can force an output by working at it. It's weird, Macy, and it's lousy, and I don't like it at all. But I can't achieve a real hookup, because you're in the way in so many places, entrenched too deeply for me to dislodge you.

What are we going to do, then?

– Continue annoying each other, I suppose.

Quarter to nine. Really ought to check up on Lissa somehow, go down to her apartment, ask the cops to investigate. Not very ambitious right now, though. Maybe she'll come in soon. A long long walk on a spring night, home after dark.

– You're in love with her, aren't you, Macy?

I don't think so. A certain physical attraction, I don't deny that. And a kind of solidarity of the crippled – she's got troubles, I've got troubles, we really ought to stick together, that kind of feeling. But not love. I don't know her that well. I don't even know myself that well. I have no illusions about that: I'm inexperienced, I'm emotionally immature, I'm brand new in the world.

– And you're in love with her.

Define your terms.

– Don't hand me that sophomoric manure. You know what I mean. Let me tell you a few things about your Lissa, though, that somebody who is as you rightly say emotionally immature might not have noticed.

Go ahead.

– She's completely selfish. She exists only for the benefit of Lissa Moore. A bitch, a witch, a cunt that walks, a life-force eater. She'll try to suck the vitality out of you. She tried it with me, hoping she could drain some of my talent out of me and into her. I was fighting her all the way. I held her off pretty well. Although I think that ESP of hers infected me somehow and caused my breakdown. I didn't realize that at the time it was happening, Macy, but it occurred to me later, that she was fastening onto me, messing up my mind, robbing me of strength, pushing me over some sort of brink. And after a year or so I fell in. She won't need as long with you. She'll bleed you dry in a month.

You make her sound like a monster. She strikes me as being an awfully pathetic monster, Hamlin.

– That's because you've come to know her only when she's in trouble. This ESP of hers, do you think it was an accident?

Something that just sprouted in her, like the measles? It's that hunger of hers. To use people, to devour people, to drain people, to engulf people. Which finally got out of hand, which ran away with her. Now she drains automatically, she pulls in impulses from all sides, more than her mind can stand, and it's killing her. It's burning her out. But she asked for it.

How harsh you are.

– Just realistic. I never knew a woman who wasn't some kind of vampire, and Lissa's the most dangerous one I knew. A cunt is a cunt. A little bundle of ambitions. I fell for it, for a while. And it ruined me, Macy, it used me up.

I think your whole outlook on women is distorted.

– Maybe yes, maybe no. But at least I came by it honestly. Through living. Through experiencing. Through drawing my own conclusions. I didn't pick up my ideas vicariously. I didn't have them pumped into me at a Rehab Center.

Granted. Which still doesn't make your ideas righter than mine.

– Whatever you say. I just wanted to warn you about her.

I'm amazed at the difference in our images of her. You see her as a marauder, a vampire, a drinker of souls. My impression is just the opposite: that she's a weak, passive, dependent girl, terrified by the world. How can they be reconciled?

– They don't need to be. Why shouldn't my image of her be different from yours? I'm different from you. We're two very different persons.

And if an outsider tried to make an assessment of Lissa based on what we told him?

– He'd have to make parallax adjustments to compensate for our differences in perspective.

But which is the real Lissa? Yours or mine?

– Both. She can be passive and weak and still be a monster and a vampire.

You really believe, though, that she deliberately sets out to drain vitality from people?

– Not necessarily deliberately, Macy. She may not even realize what she's doing. I'm sure she didn't realize it until her inputs got too intense to cope with. It was just a thing she had, a telepathic thing, a need, a hunger. Which had the incidental effect of destroying people who came close to her.

I don't feel that she's been destroying me.

– You're welcome to her, pal.

Twenty minutes to ten. Another shot of bourbon. Smo-o-th. Another Acapulco special, long and luscious, in the all-new, improved, negative-ion-filter format. The good haziness happening now. Perhaps Lissa's dismembered body has by this time been scattered throughout the six boroughs of the city. She seems remote and unreal to him. For the past ten minutes he has allowed himself to indulge in a mood of intense nostalgia. A curious species of nostalgia for the life he did not live. Meditating on the fragments of Hamlin's experience that have bled through to him across the boundaries that separate their identities. And yearning for more.

Hamlin?

– Yes.

How hard would it be to merge our memory files entirely?

– I don't follow you. What do you mean?

So that I'd have access to everything you can remember. And you'd have access to all that had happened to me.

– I imagine it wouldn't be hard.

I'm willing if you are.

– It would amount to a merging of identities, you realize. We wouldn't be sure where one of us ends and the other begins. We'd blend, after a while. Frankly, I'd wipe you out.

You think so?

– A pretty good chance of it.

What makes you so sure?

– Because I'd bring to the blending thirty-five years of genuine experience. Your thirty-five years of synthetic memories would overlay that like a film of dirt, and after a time I'd polish it away, leaving my real life blended to your four years in the Rehab Center, with some interplays from your ersatz existence coloring my recollections of the things I actually did. What would emerge would be a Nat Hamlin somewhat

polluted by Paul Macy. Is that what you want? I'm willing if
you are, Macy.

*I didn't mean such a complete joining. Just an exchange of
memory banks.*

– I already have as much access to what the Rehab Center
gave you as I need.

*But I don't have any access to your past, except some stuff that
came floating through the barrier while I was asleep. And I want
more.*

– What for?

*Because I'm starting to recognize it as my own identity. Because I
feel cut off from myself. I want to know what this body did, where
it traveled, what it ate, who it slept with, what it was like to be
a psychosculptor. The need's been growing in me for a couple of
hours now. Or maybe longer. It frustrates me to know that I was
somebody important, somebody vital, and that I'm completely cut off
from his life.*

– But you weren't anybody important, Macy. *I* was. You
weren't anybody at all. A Rehab doctor's wet dream.

Don't rub it in.

– You admit it?

I never denied I was only a construct, Hamlin.

– Then why don't you just step aside and let me have the
body, then?

*I keep telling you. My past may be a fake, but my present is real
as hell, and I'm not giving it up.*

– So you want to add my past to yours, to give you that
extra little dimension of reality. You want to go on being Paul
Macy, but you want to be able to think you used to be Nat
Hamlin, too?

Something like that.

– Up yours, Macy. My memories are my own property.
They're all I've got. Why should I let you muck around in
them? Why should I sweat to make you feel realer?

Ten-fifteen. How quiet it is at this time of night. Somehow went
without dinner and never even noticed. Sleepy. Sleepy. Phone

the police? Tomorrow, maybe. She must have gone back to her own place, I guess. Mmmm. Mmmmmm.

–I have a new proposition for you.

Eh? Huh?

– Wake up, Macy.

What's the matter?

– I want to talk to you. You've been dozing.

Okay. So talk. I'm listening.

– Let's make a deal. Let's share the body on an alternating basis. First you run it, then me, then you again, then me again, and so on indefinitely. Operating it under the Paul Macy identity, naturally, so we don't get into legal difficulties.

You mean we switch every day? Monday Wednesday Friday it's me in charge, Tuesday Thursday Saturday it's you, Sunday we hold dialogs?

– Not exactly like that. You need the body four days a week to do your job, right? Those four days it's yours. Saturdays and Sundays and holidays are mine. Weekday evenings we divide in such a way that you get some, I get some. We can work out ad-hoc arrangements for swapping time back and forth as the occasion demands.

I don't see why I have to give you any time at all, Hamlin. The court awarded your body to me.

– But I'm still in it. And I'm prepared to be a mammoth pain in the ass unless I'm allowed to take charge some of the time.

You want me to yield half my lifespan to you under duress.

– I want you to be sensible and cooperative, that's all. Can you function freely with me playing games inside your nervous system? Do you enjoy being harassed? I can cripple your life, Macy. And what about me? Must I be condemned to be bottled up without any autonomy, with my gifts? Listen, even if you run the body for half the time, that's three and a half days a week more than fate originally intended. By rights you shouldn't be here at all. So why not accept a reasonable compromise? Half the time you'll be you, and you can do any fucking thing you please. The other half you'll surrender autonomy and ride as a passenger while I go about my business. Sculpting, screwing, eating, whatever I feel like doing. We'll both benefit. I'll get to live again, a little, and you'll be free from the annoyance of having me constantly interfering with you.

Well –

– Another incentive. I'll give you the free run of my memory bank. What you were asking for a little while ago. You can find out who you really were, before you became you.

Get thee behind me, Satan!

– Will you tell me what's wrong with the goddam deal?

Nothing wrong with it. It's too damned tempting, that's what.

– Then why not go along with it?

A taut uneasy moment. Considering, weighing, mulling. Blinking his eyes a lot. Aware that his head is really too foggy now for such perilous negotiations. Why surrender a chunk of his life to a condemned criminal? Wouldn't it be better to fight it out, to try to expel Hamlin altogether, to break his grip once and for all? Maybe I can't. Maybe when the showdown comes he'll expel me. Perhaps it makes more sense to accept the half-and-half. But even so – a flood of suspicions, suddenly –

How would we work this switch?

– Easy. I'd penetrate the limbic system. You know what that is? Down underneath, in the depths of the folds. Controls your pituitary, your olfactory system, a lot of other things, blood pressure, digestion, and so forth. Also the seat of the self, so far as I can tell. You have it pretty well guarded, whether you know it or not. A wall of electrical charge sealing it off. But I could come in by way of the thalamus, reverse the charge – if we cooperate, it would be just a matter of a few seconds and we'd have our shift of identity polarity – I've worked out the mechanisms, I know where the levers are –

All right. Let's say I cooperate and you take over. What assurance do I have that you'd let me back on top again when your time was up?

– Why, if I didn't, you could pull all the stuff I've been

pulling on you! The situations would be entirely reversed. You could mess around with my heart, my sex life – you'd learn the right linkups fast, Macy, you aren't dumb –

I'm not convinced what you say is true. Maybe you'd have a natural advantage, because it was your body originally. Maybe when you were in charge again you could evict me altogether.

– What an untrusting bastard you are.

My life's at stake.

– All I can say is you've got to have more faith in my good intentions.

How can I?

– Look, I'll open wide to you for a minute. I'll give you a complete unshielded entry into my personality. Poke around in there, make your own evaluation of my intentions – you'll see them right up front – decide for yourself whether you can trust me. Okay?

Go ahead. But no funny stuff.

– I'm baring my soul to him, and he's still suspicious as hell.

Go ahead, I said. How do we work this?

– First, we make some little electrical adjustments in the corpus callosum –

Odd sensations along the back of the neck. Prickling, tingling, a mild stiffening of the skin. Not entirely unpleasant; a certain agreeable feel to it, in fact. Unseen fingers stroking the lobes of his brain, caressing the prominences and corrugations. A tickling on the underside of the skull. Moss beginning to sprout between the white jagged cranial ridges and the soft cerebral folds below. And the oozing of warm fluids. Pulse. Pulse. A wonderful sleepy feeling. Passivity, yes, how splendid a thing is passivity. We are merging. We are opening the gates. How could one have thought that this admirable human being meant to do one harm? When now his soul is thuswise displayed. Its peaks and valleys. Its exaltations and depressions. Its hungers and fears. See, see, I am as human as thou! And I yearn. And I lament. Come let me enfold you. Come. Put aside these unworthy untrustingnesses. Open. Open. Open. Bathed in the warm river. Lulled on the gentle tide. Tick. Tock. Tick. Tock. This is how we come together. The avoidance of all friction. The total lubrication of the universe. And we dissolve into one another. And we dissolve.

What's that sound?

Buzz saw at work in the forest! Dentist's drill raping a bicuspid! Jackhammers unpeeling the street! Braked wheels squealing! The fury of clawed cats!

Key turning in the lock!

Lissa! Lissa! Lissa!

Standing on the threshold. Fingertips pressed to lips in alarm. Body curved backward, recoiling in shock. Then the scream. And then:

'Leave him alone! Get your filthy hands off him, Nat!'

Followed by a sudden instinctive bombardment of mental force, a single massive jolt out of her that sent Macy crumpling stunned to the floor. Blackout. Internal churning. Clicking of defective gears. Slow return to semiconsciousness. Lissa embracing him, cradling his throbbing head. A coppery taste in his throat. Incredible lancing pain between the eyes. Her face, smudged, strained, close to his. Her faint worried smile. And Hamlin nowhere within reach. There was in Macy's head the strange blessed aloneness that he had experienced so few times since the first awakening of his other self. Alone. Alone. How quiet it is in here.

TEN

'Paul? Can you hear me?'

'From a million miles away.'

'Are you all right?'

'Dazed. Groggy. Jesus, groggy!' Trying to sit up. She tugging him back into his chair. Surprising how strong she is. He looked at his hands. Quivering and twitching. As if a powerful electrical current had passed through his body and was still recycling itself through the peripheral circuits, touching off a muscular spasm here and here and here.

Searching for Hamlin. No, not in evidence. Not at the moment.

'What happened?' he said.

'I was at the door,' said Lissa. 'And from outside, I could feel the waves coming from his mind and yours. Mostly from his. You were – asleep, drugged, drunk, I don't know. Passive, anyway. And he was taking you over, Paul. His mind was wrapped around yours, and he was turning you off switch by switch – that's the only way I can describe it – and you were about half gone already. Submerged, dismantled, switched off, whatever word is best.'

'We made a deal. We were going to share the body, half the time him running the show, and me the rest of the time. He promised me that if I let him take over, he'd turn the body back to me when it was my time to have control.'

'He was tricking you,' she said. 'What were you, drunk? Stoned?'

'Both.'

'Both. It figures. He was just getting you to lower your defenses so that he could get full control. I felt the whole thing from outside. I opened the door. It was much stronger in here. You sitting there with an idiot smile on your face. Eyes open, but you couldn't see. Hamlin swarming all over you. So I – I don't know, I didn't stop to think, I just *hit* him. With my mind.'

'I think you killed him,' Macy said.

'No. I hurt him, but I didn't kill him.'

'I can't feel him any more.'

'I can,' she said. 'He's very weak, but I can sense him down at the bottom of your brain. It's like he fell off a twenty-five-foot wall. I don't know how I did it. I just lashed out.'

'Like you did that time in the restaurant.'

'I suppose,' she said. 'Why did you let him do that to you?'

Macy shrugged. 'We were talking to each other all evening. While I waited for you to come home. Getting chummy with him. We were proposing deals to each other, compromises, arrangements. And then. This talk of sharing came up. I was pretty stoned by then, I suppose. Lucky thing you came in.' He glanced up at her and said, after a moment, 'Where the hell were you, anyway?'

Out, she told him. She just decided to go out, around five o'clock. Back to her apartment to pick up some of her things. He gave her a fishy look. Even in his present shell-shocked condition he was able to see that she had come in emptyhanded. He taxed her with the inconsistency, and she made a stagy attempt to seem innocent, with much shrugging and tossing of the head, telling him that when she reached her place she had decided she didn't need those things after all, and had left them there. And the rest of the evening? From six o'clock till now? Chatting with old friends down at the house, she said. Sure, he thought, remembering the sort of neighbors she had had there, the slummies, the bandits.

Without in so many words accusing her of lying to him, he accused her of lying to him. She was indignant and then at once contrite. Admitting everything. Left here without intending to come back. The strain, too much strain, too much mental noise, the yammering of the double soul within the single brain getting to be more than she can handle. All night long, lying next to him, picking up the blurred shapeless echoes of the conflict going on within his head. You maybe don't even realize it yourself, she told him. How Hamlin hammers all the time, let me out, let me out, let me out. Deep down below the levels of consciousness. That constant agonized cry. And you fighting back, Paul. Suppressing him, squashing him. Don't you know it's going on?

And he shook his head, no, no, I'm only aware when he surfaces and starts talking to me, or when he grabs parts of my nervous system. Tell me more about this. And Lissa told him more. Conveying to him, in short nervous blurts of half-sentences, how much she was suffering from her mere proximity to him, how much it had cost her in extrasensory anguish since she had moved in. It would be bad enough if there was only one of him, but the double identity, no, too much, too fucking much, all that telepathic pressure, her head was splitting.

And it got worse every day. Cumulative. Rebirth of the old overpowering impulse to hide herself away from the whole human race. Not your fault, Paul, I know, not your fault, I asked you to take pity on me and help me, but yet, but yet, this is what happens. Even when you aren't here I feel you and Hamlin hemming me in. Pushing against my temples.

Like a kind of air pollution, it was: he gathered that she felt the sweaty residue of their grappling selves enfogging and enfouling the place, greasy molecules of disembodied consciousness drifting in the rooms, sucked into her lungs with every breath. A daily poisoning. So at last she simply had to get out and clear her head. Setting out at five, a long twilight walk downtown, hour after hour, mechanically moving along, lift foot put foot down lift other foot. Finally reaching the vicinity of West 116th Street by nightfall. A somber prowl in darkness through the ruins of the old university.

He stared at her in alarm. You really went there? Those charred shells of buildings were, they said, a rapist's heaven, a mugger's paradise. Suicidal to stroll there alone after dark. And she gave him an odd masked look, faintly guilty. What had she done this evening? His imagination supplied a possible answer – or was Hamlin planting the thought, or had it come from her, bleeding across the line of mental contact? A dimly perceived figure, say, pursuing her through the shattered campus. But Lissa crazily unafraid, perhaps half eager to court death or mutilation, defiant, turning to the unknown pursuer, winking, pulling up her tunic, waggling her hips. Here, man, bang away, what do I care? Thrust and thrust and thrust on a bed of rubble. Afterward the man giving her a funny look. You must be real weird, lady. And running away from her, leaving her to proceed on her solitary wandering way. Had it happened? Her clothes weren't rumpled or stained or soiled.

Macy told himself that it was all his own ugly fantasy; she had merely been out for a walk, hadn't spread her legs for a stranger, hadn't purged her head of echoes by inviting rape. Go on, he told her. You walked through the ruins. And then? I did a lot of thinking, she said. Wondering if I ought to head back to my old place and stay there. Or go uptown to you. Maybe even to kill myself. The easiest way. Misery no matter what I do, you see, that's no joke. And finally, beginning to tire, to regret her long nocturnal expedition, beginning to worry about worrying him by her disappearance. Getting on the tube, returning. Standing outside the door and becoming aware of the tricky takeover in progress within. The entry. The last-minute rescue. Tarantara!

'Why did you come back here?' he asked.

A shrug. Vague. 'I can't say. Because I was lonely, maybe. Because I had a premonition, maybe, that you were in trouble. I didn't think about it. I just came.'

'Do you want to move out for good?'

'I don't know. I'd like to be able to stay with you, Paul. If only. The pain. Would. Stop.' Drifting away from him again. Her voice dreamy and halting. 'A river of mud flowing through my head,' she murmured. Flopping down on the bed, face in arms. Macy went to her with comfort. Such as he could offer. Stroking her tenderly despite the ache behind his eyes. Again, it seemed, the curious flow of strength had taken place. From her to him. The odd sudden reversal of roles, the comforter becoming the comforted. Ten minutes ago she had been striving to put him back together, now she was crumpled and flaccid. And Hamlin thinks this girl is destructive. A monster, a villainess. Poor pitiful monster.

She said indistinctly, not looking up, 'Your Rehab Center phoned again this morning. A doctor with a Spanish name.'

'Gomez.'

'Gomez, yes, I think so.'

'And?'

Pause. 'I told him the whole thing. He was very upset.'

'What did he say?'

'He wanted to see you right away. I said no, it was impossible, Hamlin would attack you if you went near the Rehab Center. He didn't appear to believe that. I think I convinced him after a while.'

'And then?'

'He said finally he'd have to discuss things with his colleagues, he'd call back in a day or two. Said I should phone him if there were any important new developments.'

Macy considered calling him now. Wake the bastard up. Yank him from his bed of pleasure. He could be at the Rehab Center by one, half past one in the morning; maybe they could give him a shot of something while Hamlin was dormant, knock him out for keeps. Lissa vetoed the idea. Hamlin's not as dormant as you think, she said. He's down, but not out. Sitting there trying to collect some of his power. No telling what he'll do if he feels threatened.

Macy searched his cerebral crannies for Hamlin and could not find him, but left Gomez unphoned anyway. The risks were too great. Lissa probably was right: Hamlin still maintaining surveillance down there, capable of taking severe and possibly mutually fatal defensive action if attempt was made to reach the Center. Paul didn't dare try calling his bluff.

They prepared for bed. Flesh against flesh, but no copulatory gestures. He was carrying too heavy a burden of fatigue to think about mounting the doubtfully willing Lissa just now. Still obsessed by the image of the stranger balling her in the university ruins, too. Tomorrow's another day, heigh-ho! As Macy was falling asleep he heard her say, 'Gomez doesn't want me to stay with you any more. He thinks I'm dangerous for you.'

'Because you awakened Hamlin in me?'

'No, I didn't go into that with him. I didn't say anything to him about my – gift.'

'Then why?'

'Because I'm out of your other life, is why. You aren't supposed to be seeing Nat Hamlin's cast of characters, remember? They conditioned you against it.'

'He knew who you were?'

'I told him I used to model for Nat. Our accidental meeting on the street. He pretty much ordered me to go away from you.'

'Is that why you walked out tonight?'

'How do I know?' she said petulantly. Curling close against him. Tips of her breasts grazing his back. Turn around and do her? No. Not tonight. That lousy meddling fucker Gomez. Like to tell him a thing or two. If only I could. If only. What a bitching mess. But tomorrow's another day. She's snoring already, anyway. Let her rest. Maybe I will too. To sleep. Perchance to dream.

Three days of relative tranquillity. Friday, Saturday, Sunday. His first weekend with Lissa. No news out of Hamlin, save only some irregular psychic belchings and rumblings. Obviously the shot that Lissa had given him had left him pretty feeble. No news out of Gomez, either. A quiet weekend together. Where to go, what to do? The first edge of summer heat lapping the city. We stay in bed late. We screw to Mozart. Dee-dum-dee-dum-dee-*dum*-dum, diddy-dum diddy-dum diddy-*dum*. Her legs up over his shoulders in a nicely wanton way. Her eyes aglow afterward in the shower. Playful, kittenish. Soaping his cock, trying to get him up again and succeeding. For a man of my mature years I'm pretty virile, *hein?* Laughter. Breakfast. The morning news coming out of the slot.

Then out of the house. Her mood already descending; he could sense her turning sullen, starting to withdraw. It just didn't seem possible to keep her happy more than two hours at a stretch. He tried to ignore her darkening outlook, hoping it would go away. Such a beautiful day. The golden sunlight spilling out of the Bronx.

'Where do you want to go, Lissa?' She didn't answer. It seemed almost that she hadn't heard him. He asked again.

'Voices,' she muttered. 'These fucking voices. I'm a crapped-up Joan of Arc.' Lissa? Lissa? Turning toward him, torment in the ocean-colored eyes. 'A river of mud,' she said. 'Thick brown mud piling up in my head. Coming out my ears, soon. A delta on each side.'

'It's such a beautiful day, Lissa. The whole city's ours.'

'Wherever you want to go,' she said.

At his random suggestion they went to the Bronx Zoo. Wandering hand in hand past the cunning habitat groups. Hard to believe that those lions really had no way of jumping the moat. And what kept those birds from flying out of their dome? Wide open on one side, for Christ's sake! But of course they did clever things with air pressure and ion-flows these days. The zoo was crowded. Families, lovers, kids. Most of them funnier-looking than the population behind the moats. The raucousness of the animals. Wet twitching noses, sad eyes.

Every third cage or so was marked with a grim black star, signifying that the species was extinct except in captivity. White rhinoceros. Pygmy hippo. Reticulated giraffe. European bison. Black rhinoceros. South American tapir. Wombat. Arabian oryx. Caspian tiger. Red kangaroo. Bandicoot. Musk-ox. Grizzly bear. So many species gone. Another hundred years, nothing left but dogs and cats and sheep and cattle. But of course the Africans had needed meat in the famine years, before the Population Correction. The South Americans, the Asians. All those babies, all those hungry mouths, and still it hadn't done any good, by the end of it they were eating each other after the animals were gone. Now the zoos were the last refuge. And for some it was too late.

Macy remembered a trip with his father, when he was a boy, ten, twelve years old, the San Diego Zoo, seeing the giant panda they had there. 'That's the last one left in the world, son. Smuggled out of Commie China just before the blowup.' A big two-toned fuzzy toy sitting in the cage. No giant pandas left anywhere, now. Some stuffed ones, as reminders. His father? The San Diego Zoo? Really? Who was his father? Where had he grown up? Had he ever been to the San Diego Zoo? Did they truly have a giant panda there, once? The oscillations of memory. Surely it had never happened. Perhaps there had never been any such animal.

Lissa said, 'I can feel their minds. The animals.'

'Can you?'

'I never realized I could. I never went to the zoo before.'

He was poised, wary, ready to rush her toward the tube if the impact overwhelmed her. It wasn't necessary. She was joyful, ecstatic, standing in the plaza by the seal tank and drinking in the oinks and bleats and honks and nyaaas of a hundred alien species. 'Maybe I can transmit some of what I'm getting to you,' she said, and held both his hands and frowned earnestly at him and peered into his eyes, so that passersby nodded and smiled at the sight of true love being expressed between the seals and the tigers, but he was unable to pick up a shred of what she sent him.

So she described it, in intermittent bursts, whenever she could spare him a moment out of her contemplations. The high piping throaty thoughts of the giraffe. The dull booming ruminations of the rhino. The dense, complex, bleak, and bitter output of the African elephant, he of the big ears, a Kierkegaard of zoology. The sparkling twitter of the chimps. The flippant outbursts of the raccoon. The Galapagos tortoise pondered eternity; the brown bear was surprisingly sensual; the penguins dreamed icy dreams.

'Are you making all this up?' he asked her, and she laughed in his face, like Aquinas accused of inventing the Trinity. Within an hour she was wholly spent. They snacked on algae-burgers and Lenin soda, and took the conveyer to the exit. Lissa giggling, manic, stoned on her beasts. 'The orang-utan,' she said. 'I could tell you exactly how he'd vote in the next election. And if I could only let you hear the gnu! Oh, shit, the gnu!'

But she was brooding again before dark. They went into Manhattan in the afternoon, circling around the burned-out places and drifting through the flamboyant new downtown section, and he tried to interest her in the amusement parlors, the sniffer palaces, the swimming tanks, and such, only she was glassy and distant. They had dinner at a Chinese restaurant on one of the Hudson piers, and she picked idly at her food, leaving most of it, getting clucked at by the waiter. A quiet evening at home. We have no friends, Macy realized. They played Bach and smoked a lot.

Just before bedtime Hamlin seemed to stretch and yawn within him, or was it an illusion? Bad sex that night, Lissa very far down, he not much better, both of them clumsy and halfhearted as they groped each other in bed. He tried to go into her and she was dry. Persevered, God knows why. Finally some lubrication. Not much response from her, though. Like fucking a robot; he was tempted to quit in the middle, but thought it would be impolite, and he chased himself on to a solitary, unrewarding coming. Some nasty dreams later, but nothing he hadn't had before.

Saturday a fizzle. Lissa vacant, absent. An endless day. Sunday much better. Throwing herself on him at sunrise, straddling him, lowering herself until impaled. Good morning, good morning, good morning! Up and down, up and down. Breasts jiggling overhead. His startled fingers encircling the smooth cool globes of her ass. After which she fixed a hearty breakfast. Bouncy, a breathless adolescent giddiness about her, perhaps fake: trying hard to be a good companion, he suspected. After that sulking bitchy day she gave me yesterday. Lose one, win one.

'Where to?' she asked.

'Museum of Modern Art,' he suggested. 'They've got some Hamlins there, don't they?'

'Five or six, yes. But do you really think it's wise to go? I mean, he's been so quiet the last couple of days. The sight of his work might stir him up again.'

'That's exactly what I want to find out,' he told her. They went. The museum, it developed, had *seven* Hamlins, two big pieces almost though not quite as impressive as the *Antigone*, and five minor objects. They all were on display in the same room, four grouped in one corner and three assembled against the opposite wall, which gave Macy the opportunity for a critical test: would the presence of so much of Nat Hamlin's handiwork arouse the submerged artist by some process of psychic leverage?

Boldly Macy planted himself between the two groupings, where he would be exposed to the maximum output of the pieces. Well, Hamlin? Where are you? But though Macy detected some cloudy subliminal squirmings, there was nothing else to indicate Hamlin's existence within him. He studied the sculptures closely. The connoisseur making his lofty observations. Only a few weeks ago, in Harold Griswold's office, the sight of a Hamlin piece had knocked him slappy, and here he was listening critically to the resonances, noting the subtle recurvings of the contours, doing the whole art-appreciation number with great aplomb.

Some kids in the room, researching a report on Hamlin, maybe. Apparently recognizing him. Looking at his face, then at his Rehab badge, then at his face again, then at the sculptures, then at each other. Whispering. Even that didn't bother him, being found out as the walking zombie relict of the great artist. The kids didn't dare approach him. Macy gave them a benevolent smile. I'd give you my autograph if you asked. With these very hands, you know, those masterpieces were created.

He was impressed by his own newfound resilience. To come here, to confront Hamlin's work, to take it all so calmly. Although not entirely calmly. He found the sight of these pieces gradually stirring in him that dismal depressing nostalgia, that yearning to have access to the past in which this body had brought into being those sculptures. His true past. As he was starting to regard it. Implying that his own past was unsatisfactory, insufficient, insubstantial, inadequate. As if he too had come to agree with Hamlin that he was mere fiction, a freakish aberrant unreality that had been appended to Nat Hamlin's authentic life. So he craved knowledge of that other time. Who was I when I was he? How did I bring forth these works? What was it like to be Hamlin? A bad moment. The subtle corrosive influence of Hamlin within me, undermining me even when he's quiescent. So that I have begun to doubt myself. So that I have started to scorn myself. And hunger to be him. This is the road to surrender; let me turn from it.

Lissa seemed troubled by the Hamlin group too. Remembering a jollier past, perhaps. The happy days of first love. The awesome sensation of being chosen by Nathaniel Hamlin for his bed, for his studio. A world of endless sunrises before her. All highways open. And to have come to this. How great the contrast. Macy could see the bleakness spreading across her face. A mistake to inflict Hamlin's art on her? Or maybe she merely felt oppressed by the museum's Sunday throng. We will go now, I think.

Midmorning, Monday, Macy hard at work. Griswold had just assigned him to a new story. Preliminary charisma-level statistics for the 2012 election came out last night, late; let's do a feature on all the candidates, run up a chart of pulse-figures, hormone counts, recognition profile, the whole multivalent works, right? Right. And so to the task. Research assistants scurrying madly. Their pretty pink boobies bobbling. Stacks of documents. Fredericks stopping by to offer bland, useless suggestions. Loftus staggering in with a load of simulations and color overlays for his approval. The hours whisking swiftly by; the mind fully engaged in purposeful activity.

And then an unscheduled interruption. Someone down here to see you, Mr Macy. No appointment. A visitor for me? Who? Image of Lissa, bedraggled, obsessed, freaking out in the reception hall. Please, I must see him, matter of life and death, I'm going to snap, I'm going to blow, let me go upstairs! A messy scene. Only his visitor wasn't Lissa. His visitor turned out to be a Dr Gomez.

Panic. Gomez, here? Hamlin'll kill me!

After the first quick surge of fright, some rethinking. Hamlin had warned him not to go to the Rehab Center, or to telephone his doctors, yes. But the doctor had come to him. Was that covered by the threat? A debatable point. In any case, Hamlin didn't seem to be raising objections. Macy waited a long

troubled moment, expecting a sign from within, a squeeze
of his heart, a pinching of his nerves, some sort of don't-fool-
around signal. Nothing. He sensed Hamlin's presence like a
dull heavy weight in his gut, but he got no specific instructions
about seeing Gomez. *Perhaps Hamlin wants to find out what
Gomez will say. Maybe he's still recovering from the jolt Lissa
gave him. Anyway. Tell Dr Gomez he can come up.*

Gomez, out of context, looked unfamiliar. At the Rehab
Center, surrounded by his phalanxes of computers and his
electronic pharmacopoeia, Gomez was dynamic, formidable,
aggressive, indomitable, confidently vulgar. Entering Macy's
sleek office he was almost meek. *Without his throne and
scepter a king's but a bifurcated radish.* Gomez came slipping
hesitantly through the fancy sliding door. Dressed in excessively contemporary business clothes, greens and reds, much
too young for him, instead of the customary monochrome
lab outfit. Looking shorter and more plump than in his own
domain. His thick drooping mustache seedy and in need of
trimming. The weakness of his chin somehow mattering much
more here. Ten feet apart; eyes meet eyes. Gomez moistening
his lips. *How strange to see him on the defensive.*

Macy said, 'I guess you've decided to believe me after all.'

'We've been discussing your case nonstop for three days,'
said Gomez hoarsely. 'But I had to have firsthand data. And
since you wouldn't come to us –'

'Couldn't.'

'Couldn't.' Gomez nodded. Scowled. Not at Macy but at
himself. His distress was apparent. *Coming here today was
a considerable gesture. The cocky doctor eating crow.* He
said, voice ragged, 'I didn't want to chance phoning you.
In case it might provide too much time for the former ego
to build up negative reactions. Is my presence here causing
any repercussions?'

'Not so far.'

'If it does, tell me and I'll leave. I don't want to endanger you.'

'Don't worry, Gomez, I'll tell you fast if anything begins.'

Checking to see if Hamlin is stirring. All calm. 'Hamlin hasn't been very active since Thursday night.'

'But he's still there?'

'He's there, all right. Despite your loud assurance that it wasn't possible for him to come back.'

'We all make mistakes, Macy.'

'That was a pretty fucking big one. I asked you to run an EEG. You said no, I was merely hallucinating, merely having a fantasy, there was no chance in the world that Hamlin was intact and surfacing. And then you said –'

'All right. Let's not go into that now.' Dabbing at his sweaty forehead. 'I'm concerned with therapy for this, not with placing blame. When did it start?'

'The day I left the Center. When I met the girl, Hamlin's old model, mistress, the one you spoke to a couple of times on the telephone.'

'Miss Moore.'

'Yes. Bumped into her, literally, on the street. I told you all this. She kept calling me Nat, ignoring my badge – you remember?'

'I remember.'

'I saw her again, last Monday. She said she was in trouble and wanted me to help her. I didn't want to get involved and started to leave. She hit me with a two-pronged blast of telepathy. Which woke him up fully, completing the job of arousing him that had started when –'

'Telepathy?'

'ESP. Communication between minds. You know.'

'I know. This girl's a telepath?'

'I'm trying to tell you.'

'You knew she was a telepath, and also that she was a figure out of Hamlin's past who you therefore were under instructions not to see, and nevertheless you arranged to meet her and –'

'I *didn't* know she was a telepath. Until it was too late. Not that I'd have had any particular reason to avoid her because of that. You never said anything about telepaths, Gomez. I didn't even know there were such things as telepaths, not real ones, not walking around in New York City.'

Gomez closed his eyes. 'All right. I get the picture. What we have here is an apparent case of induced identity reestablishment under telepathic stimulus. Of all the shit. A minute theoretical possibility, but who ever expected to run into an actual case of – no fucking literature on the whole subject – no tests, no background, no data –'

'You can write a wonderful paper on me some day,' Macy said bitterly.

'Spare me the crap. You think I'm happy about this?' Indeed genuine agony was visible in Gomez' fleshy features. 'Okay, so she woke Hamlin. Meaning what? Give me the symptomology.'

'He talks to me.'

'Out loud?'

'In my head. A silent voice, but it doesn't seem silent. Twice now he's tried to grab my speech centers. All he can say is gibberish, though, and I knock him away. He also took hold of the muscles of the right side of my face once. I made him let go. Two or three times he's given me a physical shock, a jolt, knocked me down. Last Tuesday, when I set out to the Rehab Center, he staged a little heart attack for me, telling me that he'd give me a niftier one if I persisted in going to the Center. This is no goddam hallucination, Gomez. I've had conversations with him, long rational conversations. He's got very ambitious ideas. He's been inviting me to let him finish me off so he can have his body back.'

'Obviously we can't allow that.'

'Obviously there isn't a fucking thing you can do. If I let you make any hostile moves toward him at all, he'll kill me. It's like I'm carrying a bomb inside me.'

'He's bluffing.'

'You're very sure of that,' Macy said.

'If your body dies, he'll die with it. Whatever he is, he can't survive the decay of your brain cells.'

'He can't survive another round in the Rehab Center, either.

So he'd be willing to take any step to keep me from going there, right up to and including killing us both. If I go to you, he dies. Why shouldn't he kill me anyway and take me along? Or at least threaten to, knowing it'll stop me from going to the Center?'

Gomez considered that. He didn't seem to arrive at any immediate conclusions.

Macy said, 'I'll tell you what's going to happen. One of two things. He'll knock me out and take over the body, or I'll find some way of chopping him up so he can't hurt me.'

'You're playing dangerous games, Macy. Come to the Center, I know Hamlin better than you do: he won't carry out his threat, he won't do anything ultimately to harm you. Killing you would mean the decay and ruin of his own physical self, the last legitimate vestige of Nat Hamlin in the world. He wouldn't do it. He's always been body-proud.'

'Balls. I'm no gambler. He said keep away from you and I'm going to keep away.'

'We can't let you remain at large with the ego of a condemned criminal in partial control of your brain,' Gomez said.

'What will you do, then? Order my arrest? He'll kill me. I believe him when he says that. Do you want to take the chance? It isn't your life on the line, Gomez. You've been wrong in this case once already.'

Twitchings of the mustache tips. The tongue moving restlessly between teeth and lips. Gomez in a pickle. Macy staring across the desk at him. He felt his heart hammering. Was it Hamlin, waking up? Or just the excitement, the adrenalin flow?

Gomez said finally, 'We'll have to put you under surveillance, Macy. The legal problems, the presence of a potentially dangerous criminal in you. But we'll keep our distance. We won't jeopardize you.'

'How will you know whether you're jeopardizing me or not?'

'A signal,' Gomez suggested. 'Wait.' Frowning. 'Let's say that when Hamlin is threatening you, you clap your right hand to your left shoulder. So.'

'So.' Clap.

'That'll tell us to back off, so we don't provoke him. And when you want us to withdraw from the vicinity entirely, that is, when you feel that you're in extreme danger, you also clap your left hand to your right shoulder. So.'

'So.' Clap. Clap. Idiocy. 'How about a secret password, too?'

'I'm trying to help you, Macy. Don't be clever.'

'Is there anything else you want to tell me, or can I get back to my work now?'

'One more signal, if you don't mind.'

'The one that I use in asking for permission to take a crap?'

'The one to tell us that Hamlin is dormant and that it would be safe for us to seize you. Do you agree that it's possible such a situation might arise? All right, then. That would be our opportunity to grab you and try to exorcise him completely, fast. But only when you give the signal.'

'Which is?'

Gomez thought a moment. Deep concentration. All this Boy Scout stuff must really strain his mind. Finally: 'Hands locked together behind neck. Like so.'

'So,' Macy said, imitating. 'You won't let your goons mix up the signals, will you?'

'Just keep them straight in your own head and we'll manage to look after ourselves,' Gomez said. He moved toward the door. Looking back, shaking his head. 'A case of demonic possession, that's what this is. Holy shit. The seventeenth century rides again! But we'll get this corrected, Macy. We owe you an uncrapped-up life, a life without these complications.' Pausing by the exit. 'If you want to know what's good for you, by the way, I recommend you stop screwing around with Miss Moore. You're living with her, aren't you?'

'More or less.'

'You were strongly advised not to get into any entanglements linked to your body's former identity. Specifically including picking up Nat Hamlin's old mistresses, telepaths or not.'

'Should I boot her out on her ass? She's a human being. She's got problems. She needs help.'

'She's the cause of all your problems, too. It's about ten to one you wouldn't be saddled with Hamlin in the first place if you hadn't gotten involved with her.'

'That's easy to tell me now. But I *have* Hamlin, and I feel a responsibility toward her, too. She's a wreck. She needs an anchor, Gomez, somebody to keep her from drifting away.'

'What's the matter with her?'

'The ESP. It's driving her out of her mind. She picks up voices – half the time she doesn't know who she is – she has to hide from people, to shield herself – the telepathy comes and goes, random, not under her conscious control at all. It's like a curse.'

'And this you need?' Gomez asked. 'You're such a solidly established individual yourself that you can keep company with dynamite like this?'

'It wasn't my idea, believe me. But now that I'm involved with her, I'm not going to toss her out. I want to help her.'

'How?'

'Maybe there's some way of disconnecting this ESP of hers. It's burning out her mind. What do you say, Gomez? Could it be done?'

'I don't know item one about ESP. I'm a Rehab specialist.'

'Who does know?'

'I suppose I could find out if there are any hospitals in the metropolitan area with experience in this. Some neuro-psychiatric division must be pissing around with ESP. If she hates it so much, why hasn't she gone in to be examined?'

'She's afraid to let anyone fool with her mind. Afraid that she'll end up losing her whole personality if they try to rip out the telepathy.'

'Shit. You tell me you want to help her, and two seconds

later you tell me she's scared of being helped. This is crazy, man. The girl is poison. Get her into a hospital.'

'Tell me where to send her,' Macy said. 'I'll see if I want to do it. And if she does.' He gave Gomez a sudden savage grin and clapped his right hand to his left shoulder. A moment afterward he put his left hand on his right shoulder. Gomez stared at him, blinking, not moving at all. 'Well, dummy?' Macy asked. 'You forgot your own signals? That's the one for withdrawing from the vicinity.'

'Has Hamlin begun to threaten you?'

'Don't stand there asking stupid questions. You got the signal. Go. Go. I have work to do. Let me be, Gomez.'

'You poor schmuck,' Gomez said. 'What a lousy thing this is. For all of us.' And went. Macy cradled his head in his hands. An ache behind each ear. An ache in his forehead, as though the front of his brain were swollen and pushing against the bone. Practice the signals. Right hand to left shoulder. Left hand to right shoulder. Lock hands behind back of neck. Surveillance. The friendly Rehab Center haunting me too. Jesus. Jesus. Jesus. He thought he could hear Nat Hamlin's ghostly laughter reverberating through the interstices of his frazzled mind. Hey, are you awake, Nat? Did you listen to what Gomez said? Listening now? They're out to get you, Nat. Gomez is after you. To finish the job that he didn't do right the first time. Scared, Nat? I don't mind telling you I am. Because only one of us is going to come out of this whole, at the very best. At the very best only one of us.

ELEVEN

If they really did have him under surveillance, he wasn't aware of it. He went through his daily routines. Finished preparing the script for the charisma story on Monday. Taping on Tuesday. Everything smooth. Back and forth from apartment to the office without trouble. Hamlin, surfacing coherently early Tuesday evening for the first time since Thursday, had a pleasant little chat with him, saying nothing about his conference with Gomez or about the abortive takeover attempt of that stoned Thursday evening. Fair is fair, Macy thought. You try to finesse me, I try to sandbag you, but we don't talk about such sordid things. Hamlin chose to turn on the charm, reminiscing a bit about his life and good times. Selected segments of his autobiography come dancing along the identity interface. With subtitles.

THE ARTIST DISCOVERS HIS GIFT

1984, Orwell's year, the global situation quite thoroughly fucked up on schedule, although not quite as fucked up as the pessimistic old bastard had imagined, and in this small town is twelve-year-old Nat Hamlin, barely pubescent, full of ungrounded wattage and churning unfocused needs. Which small town, where? Mind your own business. The boy is slim and tall for his age. Long sensitive fingers. Father wants him to be a brain surgeon. It's a good living, son, especially now, with all the psychosis flapping in the breeze. You open the skull, you see, and you stick your long sensitive fingers inside and you chop this and you splice that and you amputate this, three thousand dollars, please, and put your money in good growth stocks.

The boy isn't listening. In the attic he models little clay figurines. He has never been to a museum; he has no interest in art. But there is sensual pleasure in squeezing and twisting the clay. He feels a lusty tickle in his crotch and a delicious tension in his jaws when he works with it. Filling the attic with grotesque little images. You sure see the world a funny way, boy. You been looking at some Pee-cas-so, hey? Pee-cas-so, who he? He that old mother from France, he make a million bucks a year turning out this junk. No shit? Where can I see some? And going to the museum, two hours away. Pee-cas-so. That's not how it's spelled. He's pretty good, yeah, yeah. But I'm just as good as he is. And I'm just starting out.

SOLITARY PLEASURES

The first major piece now adorns the attic. Three and a half feet high. Adapted from one of Picasso's paintings: woman with two faces, body twisted weirdly on its perpendicular axis, a veritable bitch of a challenge for a fourteen-year-old boy no matter how good he is. The creator lies naked before it. Straggly mustache. Pimples on his ass. Act of homage to the muse. Seizes rising organ in left hand. Back and forth, back and forth, back and forth. Oooh and ahhh. Sixty seconds: close to his record for speed. And accuracy of aim. He baptizes the masterpiece with jets of salty fluid. Ah. Ah. Ah.

AN END TO SUBLIMATION

She has long straight silken golden hair in the out-of-date style favored by girls of this town. Rimless glasses, fuzzy green cashmere sweater, short skirt. They are fifteen. He has lured her to the attic after telling her, shyly, anesthetized by pot, that he is a sculptor. She is a poet whose work appears regularly in the town newspaper. Appreciates the arts. This village of philistines; the two of us against them all. Look, this I took from Picasso, and these are my early works, and here's what I'm doing now. How strange, Nat, what brilliant work. You mean nobody knows about this? Hardly anybody. Who would understand? *I* understand, Nat. I knew you would, Helene.

You know what? Never worked from a live model. An important step forward in my career. Oh, no, I couldn't, I just couldn't. I mean, I'd be embarrassed to death! But why? God gave you the body. Look, all through history girls have been posing for famous artists. And I have to. How else will I grow as an artist? She hesitates. Well, maybe. Let's smoke first. He brings out stash. She takes two puffs for every one of his. Giggling. He is deadly serious. Reminds her. Yes, yes, yes. You're sure your mother won't come upstairs? Not a chance, she doesn't give a crap what I do up here.

And then. The clothes coming off. Her incandescent body. He can barely look. Fifteen and he's never seen it. Backward for his age, too much time spent alone in the attic. Sweater, bra. Her breasts are heavy; they don't stick out straight when they're bare, they dangle a little. The nipples very tiny, not much bigger than his. Dimples in her ass. The hair down there darker than on her head, and woolier. She looks so incomplete without a prick. His cheeks are blazing. Here, stand like this. Doesn't dare to touch her. Poses her by waving his hands in air. Wishes she'd stand with her legs apart: he isn't sure what it looks like, and he can't see. But she doesn't. She's so stoned, though.

He attacks the clay. Yes. Yes. Works furiously. Meanwhile this posing is turning her on. The artist ought to be naked too, she says. It's only fair. He just laughs. An absurd idea. Couldn't concentrate if. Half an hour. Sweat running down. Tired of posing, she says. Can I stop? They stop. She comes over to him. Leads him on. Put your hand here. And here. Oh. Oh. Oh. Unzipping him. His dong will explode. Quick, on top of me. Oh. Oh, God!

THE BIG CITY

A small apartment. Dozens of his favorite works crammed around everywhere. The famous art critic visiting him. Tall, serious, silver-haired. The artist is tall and serious too. Nineteen. Why should you go to art school, the critic asks? My boy, you are already a master! Paternal hand fondling Hamlin's shoulder. What you need now is a dealer. With the right sponsorship you could go places. And how young you are. Cheeks still downy. So saying the famous art critic rubs the downy cheek. Staring intently into young artist's eyes. You could make me the happiest man in the world tonight, says famous art critic in tender tones.

AT THE GALLERY

Little red circles pasted on every label. Sold. Sold. Sold. Sold. An auspicious debut. All the best people buying. The dealer, fat, glorying in flesh, slapping his back. Twenty-two years old. An instant success. Now scene follows scene helterskelter,

one blurring into the next, sometimes two running at once,
split-screen.

THE ADVENT OF PSYCHOSCULPTURE
UNREQUITED LOVE
THE SEDUCTIONS OF WEALTH
THE CELEBRATED ACTRESS
ALONE ON THE PINNACLE
THE TORMENTS OF FAME
THE DAY THE MUSEUM BOUGHT EVERYTHING
MEETING HELENE AGAIN, FIFTEEN YEARS LATER
THE WORLD TRAVELER
KICKING THE HABIT
FOUR'S COMPANY, FIVE'S A CROWD
MY NAME IS LISSA

And the camera speeding up, running wild.

THE ANTIGONE
THE HEADACHE
THE BREAKDOWN
THE FIRST RAPE
FREAKING OUT ON TERROR
THE QUARREL WITH HIS WIFE
FINISHING ANTIGONE
KNOCKING LISSA DOWNSTAIRS
OUT OF HIS MIND
RAPE UPON RAPE
CAUGHT
CONVICTED
OBLITERATED
AWAKENED

And the sequences jumbled.

ALONE ON THE PINNACLE
AN END TO SUBLIMATION
THE BIG CITY
KICKING THE HABIT

OUT OF HIS MIND
AT THE GALLERY
SOLITARY PLEASURES
THE ARTIST DISCOVERS HIS GIFT

Faster and faster. Names, dates, events, aspirations, swirling
in a thick soup of memory, everything merging, all detail lost.
Perhaps none of it had ever happened.
– Good night, old buddy.

Lissa was crying softly to herself when he got into bed Tuesday
night. He touched her arm and she pulled away from him.
Afterward she told him she was sorry for being so unfriendly.

On Wednesday morning, setting out for work, Macy thought
he saw one of the Rehab Center minions who Gomez had said
would be keeping watch over him. A squat, potbellied man
standing at the entrance to the building across the street, holding a newspaper. An awkward exchange of guarded glances.
From Macy a flicker of a smile. Me and my shadow. Right
hand to left shoulder, hup! Left hand to right shoulder, hup!
Hands clasped at back of neck, hup, hup, hup!

That night he suggested that they go downtown to a sniffer
palace, but Lissa didn't want to. A quiet evening at home
with Brahms and Shostakovich. Near bedtime Lissa said that
she had figured out one way for him to get rid of Hamlin.
  'How?'
  'You could rape somebody and arrange to get caught. And
blame it on him. The authorities would see to it that he was
completely erased.'
  'He'd kill me if we were taken into custody,' Macy said. A
crazy idea. A crazy girl. You could rape somebody and arrange
to get caught. Within him Hamlin laughed. Lissa cried again
that night, and when Macy asked her if he could help her in
any way she made no reply.

*   *   *

There wasn't much for him to do at the network on Thursday –
just a half-hour patch-job on a story he had taped the week
before. He consumed the rest of the day in trying to look busy.
Mainly, with another weekend coming up, he tried to think
of things that would divert Lissa and perhaps yank her from
the mood of withdrawal that was so frequently enveloping
her lately.

He sensed that he was losing her. That she was losing
herself. Slipping away into some tepid shoreless sea blanketed
by thick blue fog. She hadn't left his apartment in three
days. He suspected that she stayed in bed until noon, one
in the afternoon, then sat around smoking, playing music,
turning pages, daydreaming. Drifting. Floating. She seldom
spoke anymore. Or even answered his questions: just a grunt
or two. Last week Macy had felt hemmed in by other people,
what with Lissa sharing his apartment and Hamlin sharing
his brain; but now Lissa was spinning this cocoon about
herself, and Hamlin too was withdrawn and remote. Macy
was experienced in solitude but didn't necessarily like it.

This weekend, he decided, we will explore the wonders
of the world beyond my door. Rent a car, drive up into
the country, two hundred miles, three hundred, however
far one must go to find uncluttered pastures. Picnic on the
grass. A bosky dell. Romantic fornications beneath the boughs
of murmuring fragrant pine trees. If there are any left. And
we'll go to fine restaurants. I'll ask Hamlin to suggest a
few. Hello, hello, are you there? And Saturday night at a
Times Square sniffer palace, all glowlight and tinsel, we will
inhale the most modern hallucinogens and enjoy two hours
of earthy fantasy. Perhaps we will visit the aquarium so
that Lissa can eavesdrop on the ponderous leathery reveries
of the walruses and the whales. Oh, a fine zealous weekend! Recreation and invigoration and the restoration of our
depleted souls!

But when Macy reached his apartment that evening Lissa
wasn't there. A feeling of *déja vu*: she did this last Thursday
too, didn't she? A week gone by and nothing altered. But

there is a difference this time, as his quick search of the closets reveals. She has taken her belongings with her. Cleared out for good.

The easiest thing now was also the hardest. To sit tight, to forget her, to make a life without her. Nothing but trouble and turmoil, wasn't she? The steamy feminine complexities, compounded and exponentialized by the inexplicabilities of telepathy. Let her go. Let her go. A high probability that she'll come back, even as last time. But he couldn't. Damnation. Must go looking for her. The most logical place. Her apartment.

A sweet soft spring night.

Stars on display beyond the towers' tips. Peddlers of blurry dreams sauntering in the streets. Down we go into the tube. Whoosh whoosh whoosh. Transfer to East Side line. Double back on tracks. Her exit. The narrow streets, the decaying buildings, survivors of all the cultural upheavals. Scaly erections protruding from the corpus of the abolished past. Which of these houses is hers? They all look alike. Mysterious figures flitting in alleyways. A visit here is like a journey backward in time. A district of shady deeds and unfathomable espionage; an Istanbul, a Lisbon of the mind, embedded in the quivering fabric of New York. This looks like the right place. I'll go in.

Directory of residents? Don't make me laugh!

Macy squinted through the Jurassic dimness of the cavernous lobby. He caught sight of a figure far away, bent and distorted, which hobbled toward him as he proceeded warily inward. And then the shock of recognition: himself approaching. What he sees is the image of Paul Macy, reflected in a cracked and warped mirror occupying the nether wall. Laughter. Applause. On six levels of this hostelry holovision sets give forth their offerings with numbing simultaneity. Lissa? Lissa? She lived on the fifth floor, didn't she? I'll go up. Knock on her door, if I can find it. Or else ask the neighbors. Miss Moore, the red-haired girl, been away for a week or so? You seen her around here tonight? Not me, man, haven't seen a thing. Up the stairs. Where else could she have fled but here? Her nest. Her hermitage.

On the fourth landing he paused. Had the hirelings of Gomez followed him here? No doubt. Keeping close watch. Maybe creeping up the stairs behind him, not wanting to let him get out of sight. It was entirely possible that some orderly of the Rehab Center was at this moment a flight or two below him, frozen, waiting for him to resume his climb. And when I take a step he takes a step. And when I stop he stops. And so up and up and up. Gripping the banister, Macy swung his body halfway out over it and peered down the stairwell. In this darkness impossible to tell. Did somebody pull his head in fast, down there? Let's check it. Wait a minute, then pop my head out again. There. Still not sure, though. Well, fuck it. I don't care if they follow me or not. Up we go. Step. Step. *Stop.* Listen. That time I was sure I heard someone behind me. Comforting to know that they look after me where'er I go. Up.

He halted again on the fifth-floor landing. Double row of doors receding into infinity. Lissa behind one of them, maybe. Perhaps it would be best to give her some warning that he had come for her. Perhaps then she'll come out into the hall, I won't have to go knocking on doors. A deep breath. Sending forth the most intense mental signal he could manage, hoping that it would be on her wavelength. *Lissa. Lissa. It's me, Paul, out by the stairs. I came to get you, baby. You hear me, Lissa?*

No response from anywhere.

Okay. Now we look. He began strolling down the corridor, studying the faceless doors. In a hole like this you don't put nameplates out. He couldn't remember where her room was. At the far end of the hall, somewhere, away from the stairs, but there were dozens of doors down there. Here's one that looks like it might be right. He started to knock, but held back. Shyness? Fear? These strange savage slum people here. Maybe they don't even speak English. And me intruding on their shabby dinnertime. But yet if I don't I'll never find her.

Again he started to knock. No. Holovision blasting away

in there. Couldn't be her. I'll move on. Here? But they're cooking something in this one. Curried squid. Spider patties. *Lissa? Lissa? Where are you?*

Footsteps in the hall behind him.

Someone running toward him.

Mugger. Slasher. The shadowy pursuer on the stairs. Macy tried to swing around to face his attacker, but before he had completed half a turn the other was upon him, seizing his arms, pulling them up, pinioning him. A big man, as big as he was. They struggled silently in the dark, grunting. A knee rose and jammed itself into the small of Macy's back. He ripped one arm free, clawed at the assailant, tried to get an ear, an eye, any kind of grip. Before the knife flashes. Before the stungun.

Lurching, Macy managed to push the other up against the hallway wall, hard, ramming him with his shoulder, but then he felt his arm, the captive one, being bent back beyond its limits. Wild burst of pain. Desperately Macy banged the other again with his shoulder. Tried to knock his head against the other, hoping to drop him with a single stony smash. No use. No use. The fierce combat raged. Pointless even to call for help; who would open a door in a place like this? Slam and slam and slam. He was fully engaged in the task of defense. Such total concentration. Both of them breathing hard. Putting up more of a fight than he expected, I am! Stalemate. Lucky thing for me there's only one of them. If I could just get my hand free, and bash his head against the hallway wall –

And then. In the most frantic moment of the struggle. An inner convulsion.

Hamlin.

Making his move.

Time fell to stasis, so that Macy could perceive each phase of the conquest in a leisurely, detached way. Hamlin, having collected his strength for some days now, was taking advantage of the hallway battle, of Macy's full absorption in his difficulties, to seize the motor centers of their shared brain. Ripping out connections with both hands, replugging them under his own administration. Macy was tumbling through a timeless abyss. And Hamlin steadily and efficiently consummating what must have been a carefully planned takeover. Right leg. Left leg. Right arm. Left arm. Paralysis setting in, an unexpected summer freeze. Macy sinking and sinking and sinking. No way to defend himself; he had left his flank unguarded, and the enemy was pouring over the palisade. Down. Down. Down. Very cold now, very still. Where was Gomez' surveillance? Right hand to left shoulder. Left hand to right shoulder. Extreme danger. Hah. Much good that would be. Macy realized that he and Gomez had completely forgotten to devise one important signal, the one that said, *Help, he's taking me over!* Not that anybody was here to help him. Right hand to left shoulder. Left hand to right shoulder. Extreme danger. Down. Down. He has me.

TWELVE

He was submerged in a sea of smooth green glass. Wholly engulfed, unable to break through to the surface: above his head a solid sheet, impermeable, infrangible, sealing him away from the air. Choking, lungs bursting, head throbbing. A dull pounding sensation in both his calves; swelling of the toes. Below his dangling feet a fathomless abyss, dark, dense. From far overhead came faint greenish-gold strands of light. Blurred, indistinct images of the upper world. All perceptions refracted and distorted and transformed. His hands pushing desperately at the glassy layer above him. Which would not yield. Oh, God, I must be in hell! How can I breathe? How did he do this to me? How will I get out of here? I must be sinking. Slowly down and down. Toothy fish to pick my bones. He could feel the surging of the currents, rivers in the sea buffeting him as they swept past. He shivered. Terror invaded him. So this is it. He has me. He has me. I am within him.

Macy felt a sharp pang of loss, of displacement. It had been so good living in the world. The sunlight, the people, laughter, even the uncertainties, the tensions. To be alive, at least. And then to be overthrown, cast down, evicted, disinherited. He took it all away from me when I wasn't ready to go. It wasn't fair. And now? The pain of this place. The gasping. The choking. The fear.

But he survived the first lurch of terror and discovered that there was no second one. He grew calm. Gradually Macy refined and clarified his awareness of his new condition. He realized that although he could not reach the air, neither would he sink any deeper, nor was the feeling that he was about to drown to be taken literally. In fact this was no sea. All the marine imagery, he understood now, was purely metaphorical. He was indeed submerged, he did indeed dangle between somewhere and somewhere, but he had become a mere electrochemical network spread thinly through the recesses of what he was forced at this stage to regard as the brain of Nat Hamlin. Hamlin was in charge, on top. Macy occupied some indefinable cranny or series of crannies. He could not see. He could not feel. He could not speak. He could not hear. He could not move. He was nothing but an abstraction, a disembodied identity. Whether he could properly be said to exist at all was questionable.

Now that the first shock was past, he was startled that the loss of his independence brought no despair. Surprise, yes. Irritation and annoyance, yes. (How slickly Hamlin had outmaneuvered him!) Dismay, yes. (How strange it is to be trapped in here. How claustrophobic. Will I ever be able to get out again?) But not despair. Not even fear. Hamlin had once been in this very predicament himself, had he not, and he had endured it and mastered it and escaped. Then why not I? There was of course a great temptation to accept the situation complacently and passively. Telling oneself that one had never been entitled to a real existence anyway. That it would be best for everyone concerned, now that the upheaval of selves had come about, if he sat tight in this womblike place. Placidly letting Hamlin have the body to which he held the original birthright. But the temptation did not tempt Macy greatly. Easy though it might be to take up a vegetable existence, he preferred a more active life. A body of his own. The brief taste of living that he had had left him hungry for more.

I never really began, after all. Just a few weeks on my own away from the Center. With *him* bothering me most of that. And now this. I'll fight back. I'll push him out as he pushed me. I may not have been born, but I was real and I wish to return to existence.

Patiently he sought to examine his available options. Was it possible to establish sensory input? Let us see. Let us muster our powers of concentration. If we gather our energy – so – and direct it purposefully in a single direction – so – do we make contact with anything? No. No. Glassy darkness is all. And yet. Now. What do we have here? A node, a handle. Which we can seize. To which we can apply a subtle interior pressure. Yes! And we perceive. The inward-rushing flood of sensation. But what do we perceive? Our surroundings.

Yes, just as Hamlin said, you arrive at a kind of percept-surrogate image of the brain you're in. If only you had paid more attention, at the Center, when they were trying to teach you a little structural anatomy so that they could explain what they'd been doing to your head. The synaptic vesicles. The synaptic cleft. Dendritic spine. Axon terminal. Organelles, filaments, and tubules. Neural mitochondria. Corpus callosum. Anterior commissure. Limbic cortex. Centrencephlic system. Words. Words. This baffling torrent of referentless nouns. But somehow a little comprehension slides through. You poke around, you insinuate yourself, you learn a thing or two. And the darkness clears.

Macy sent a tendril of himself down a narrow moist corridor and found, at the end of it, a pulsing pink wall on which a golden honeycomb-textured plate was mounted. The tip of the tendril went into one of the apertures of the honeycomb and a tiny explosion of light resulted. Progress, no? Now we subdivide the tendril, and poke one end of it in here, and one in here, and one in here. Flash flash and flash. Presto jingo, we get an input! A bright cluster of sensory data. As yet what comes in is undifferentiated; it might be sight, sound, touch, smell, anything. But at least there is an input. We will continue. Macy tirelessly probing. Seeking out new avenues of exploration. More honeycombs; more subdividing tendrils slipping into slots; more bursts of light.

Will any sense ever come out of this? You are trying to tap a television image, and you can succeed in making contact only with widely scattered phosphors, a dot here and a dot there. Little spiky blurts of information, not enough for comprehension. Not yet. But no one is rushing you. You have no sense of the passage of time. Take an hour, a minute, a century, a year. Sooner or later you'll have a good hookup. It's just a matter of – what was that? A flash of coherence! Here and gone, but it was a total image. Audio? Visual? You still can't tell, but you know that you had all the information, even if you weren't able to interpret it. It was, say, a complete sentence, subject predicate adverbs adjectives expletives articles punctuation dependent clauses, which Hamlin read or heard or spoke out loud. It was, say, a full sweep of Hamlin's optical reservoir taking in the entire visual input of a fiftieth of a second. It was, say, a spear of abstract thought crossing Hamlin's consciousness from northwest to southeast. Let us now relate such random rootless inputs to our own bank of data. So that we may evaluate. So that we may interpret. So that we can tell sight from sound from cognition. Thus. And thus. We string our telegraph wire across miles and miles of desert and at last it brings us messages.

Such as:

A sense of motion. Jolt jolt jolt, stride stride stride, Hamlin is going somewhere.

A sense of position. Hamlin is standing upright.

A sense of muscular activity. Hips and thighs in action, soles of feet hitting pavement. Hamlin is walking.

A sense of environment. Bright light. Sunlight? General warmth and humidity. Morning? A summer morning? Street noises. He is walking along a street.

A sense of vision, coming jerkily into focus, now clear. Office buildings, pedestrians, vehicles. A street in Old Manhattan?

Riding along as though seated on Hamlin's back, legs around his neck, Macy felt a sharp pang of discontinuity at the absence of proper transitions. At the moment of loss of consciousness this body had been grappling in a slum-building corridor with an unknown assailant, late at night. Now it was walking down a busy daytime street. How much time had passed? What was the outcome of that struggle? What injuries, if any, did the body sustain? Where is Hamlin heading now? None of these things could readily be determined with the resources presently at Macy's command. One can try to improve one's resources, though.

The logical next step, Macy told himself, is to hook into Hamlin's consciousness. So I can read him and maybe hamper him if not entirely control him. A tentacle into the cerebral cortex. But where is the cerebral cortex? Macy could only repeat his previous trial-and-error tactics, groping here, groping there. No luck, though. Impossible to grasp the handles of Hamlin's cerebration. Macy's efforts succeeded only in giving Hamlin's memory-storage regions a high colonic, stirring turbid strata of ancient events. Across the screen of Macy's awareness floated a cloud of mucky particles of experience, miscellaneous rapes, seductions, artistic triumphs, investment decisions, childhood traumas, and indignations, drifting murkily about. While the sensory inputs continued to show Hamlin swinging jauntily along down the sunny street.

Now for the first time came desolate moments for Macy. A feeling of hopelessness. A realization of the reality of this unreal captivity. Admissions of defeat, the inevitability and finality of. It was to be expected that he'd catch me and lock me up in here. A stronger ego than mine. Wilier. He lived thirty-five years and I lived only four. A criminal mentality, too. He knows how to defend himself. I'll never be able to meddle with him as he did with me. I'll never get out of here.

But as he mourned for himself Macy automatically went

on searching for the right place to plug in, trying this and that and this, marching into one blind alley after another, battering himself against dead ends and withdrawing to try again. And abruptly he made his connection, tapping into the line he sought and drawing a staggering numbing dizzying but ultimately satisfying current, the pure juice, the unimpeded flow, the hefty amperage of Hamlin's unfettered soul.

Go to see Gargantua first almost there ten minutes more find out what's been going on the business the buying and selling my price these days it must have gone up plenty I bet they figure I'm dead the cocksuckers no more Hamlins so double the price every week well why not why not why not and then out to the studio all boarded up I bet just take a little look of course I'll have to pose as Macy that will present some problems won't even be able to let Gargan know the truth outright although I'll drop him some hints that fucking mass of meat he's clever he's clever he'll figure it out won't say a word a buck or two in it for him you bet your fat ass there is so then to the studio a sentimental journey I mean I need to go there like a shrine like my own shrine like like all dusty I bet the Goths and the Vandals fuck fuck fuck they bust everything up maybe I wasn't so pleasant a guy but I had a decent respect for property except of course all those cunts if you consider a cunt property and anyway I was crazy then much better now purified by adversity my head clear at last rid of Macy stuck him where he belongs the poor dumb shit no personality at all just a construct a plastic man well it wasn't his fault but it wasn't mine either the survival of the fittest don't you see Darwin was no dope and then I'll visit Noreen old time's sake I'll have to play it very cagy with her that bitch is perfectly capable of turning me in but maybe not after all nobody ever gave it to her in her life the way I did even if toward the end we were somewhat estranged nevertheless that's part of the normal risks of marriage especially when you marry an officially accredited genius a member of the international elite of artistic achievement high intensity sometimes boils over

I'm almost at Gargantua's now I think unless he's moved the
gallery four years shit the whole shitting universe changes in
four years every cell in the body turns over doesn't it or is it
seven years anyway we aren't the same and Gargan probably
sells his schlock out of Philadelphia now Chicago Karachi who
knows but we'll find out fast enough God it's good just to walk
the streets again breathe the air throw my shoulders back and
tonight we'll find some friendly hole for dicky dunking yes
indeed four years without a piece that's quite a long time for
a man of my ability artistic and physical well maybe out in
Darien I'll find Noreen willing to come across or one of the
others God that creepy Lissa I guess she'd do it she'd do it for
anyone even Macy thinking she's really fucking me of course
but I don't want her I don't want to go within a million miles
of her too dangerous what a shot in the head she gave me
that time I don't want her ever again ever ever I wonder
what kind of work I'll turn out as soon as I'm back in the
swing of things it better be good if I can't maintain quality
might as well give the body back to Macy but I think I'll pick
up fast enough do some small pieces first recover my grasp of
perspective my perspective of grasp and then we'll see anyway
the important thing is that I'm back

— But you still have me, Hamlin.
*Macy. Oh, shit! Macy. I didn't think I'd be hearing from you
so soon.*
— Sorry to disappoint you.
*Why don't you just erode away? Dissolve. Let yourself be absorbed
by the cranial phagocytes,* Hamlin suggested. *You're over and done
with, anyway. Your nebulous existence has ceased to be, Macy. Admit
it and go.*
— The Rehab Center failed to program me for autodestruct.
I don't need you, though.
— But I do, Macy said.
*What good are you? What imaginable value do you have to the
world? To anyone?*
— I have immense value to me. I'm the only me I have. And

I want to survive. I'm going to beat you, Hamlin. I'm going to throw you out again and this time I'll abolish you. Just watch and see.

Please. Your buzzing is giving me a headache and it's such a beautiful day.

– I'll give you a lot more than a headache.

Noisy threats were pointless. Macy wanted to make some dramatic demonstration of his ability to harass Hamlin. Give him as good as he got when the tables were turned. Clutch his heart, grab a bundle of muscles in his cheek, shut his eyes, make him piss in his pants. Jolt him, but without, naturally, doing real harm to the body they shared. Only he couldn't. Macy's harassment quotient was close to zero. All he could do was ride gain on Hamlin's sensory input and pipe messages directly into his conscious brain. Buzzing. But no control of the motor sectors whatever. No grip on the autonomic system. Merely a passenger who hasn't the foggiest where the throttle might be, or the brakes, or even the switch for the headlights. Meanwhile Hamlin, untroubled, turned a corner and entered the vestibule of a glossy-fronted shop on the smoked-glass window of which danced the words OMNIMUM GALLERIES, LTD. In free-floating globules of green capillary light. Inside, a battery of safety mechanisms bathed him in scanner-glow. An inner door finally rolled aside, and he entered the gallery, pausing not at all to inspect the treasures of contemporary art it displayed. He said to the girl at the desk, 'Is Mr Gargan here?'

'Is he expecting you, sir?'

'I don't think so. But he'll see me.'

'Your name?'

Hamlin faltered at that. Macy picked up the scathing tides of chagrin. A dilemma, yes. After a moment Hamlin said, 'My name is Macy, Paul Macy.' With a meaningful glance at the Rehab badge in his lapel. 'Tell him I used to be Nat Hamlin, though.'

'Oh.' A little gasp. A flutter of confusion; a pretty spasm

of embarrassment that turned the girl scarlet down to her fashionably exposed breasts. A quick recovery. Jeweled finger to the intercom. 'Mr Macy to see you, Mr Gargan. Paul Macy. Formerly Mr Nat Hamlin.'

From some inner office, a bellow of surprise that needed no amplification. Hamlin was speedily ushered in. A spherical room, dense mossy black carpet installed 360°-wise everywhere, a man of implausible corpulence lolling along the curved left wall with a meaty hand held languidly over a control panel bristling with jeweled switches. Not rising when Hamlin entered. An ocean of blubber; flesh hanging in folds over folds of flesh. The features barely discernible within that mass: piggy little eyes, puggy little nose, narrow pinched puritan lips. Out of the vastness a thin man's piping voice: 'God's own cock, what are *you* doing here? You aren't supposed to be coming here, Nat!'

'Do you mind?'

'Do I mind? Do I mind? You know I love you. Only I don't follow this at all. They took you in for Rehab; I thought that was the end of you. When did you get out, anyway?'

'Early in May. I would have seen you before this but there were problems.'

'You look okay. You sound okay. Just like your old self. But you've got the badge. You're somebody else now, right? What's your new name?'

'Macy. Paul Macy.'

'Don't like it. It's a name without any balls.'

'I didn't pick it, Gargantua.'

The fat man tugged at his dewlaps. 'Am I supposed to call you Nat or Paul?'

'You better call me Paul.'

'Paul. Paul. Well, I'll try. Sit down, Paul. Jesus, what a fruity name! Sit down, anyway.' Hamlin sat. Macy, a helpless spectator within him, sat also. Listening to every word of the conversation but unable to speak. As though watching it on a screen. He had seen this fat man, this gallery owner, before, drifting around in the debris of Hamlin's memory; but he seemed much fatter now. This man and Hamlin had grown rich together on the proceeds of Hamlin's genius. Now Hamlin stretched out voluptuously. In full command of his recaptured body. The black carpeting seemed to be a foot thick: bouncy, lush. Gargan touched one of the switches on the panel in front of him and the room silently revolved, changing its axis by some 15°. Hamlin's side of the sphere went up and Gargan's descended. Macy experienced some vertigo. The fat man lay pleasantly sprawled, kneading his belly. Shortly he belched and said, 'How do you like the setup here? Or don't you remember the old one?'

'I remember. This is tremendous, Gargantua. Like a fucking Babylonian palace. A gallery for sybarites, eh?'

'We get a good clientele here.'

'You're prospering. And you've gained some weight, haven't you? Unless I'm mistaken, quite a lot of weight.'

'Quite. Two or three hundred pounds since you last saw me.'

'You're beautiful.'

'I think so.'

'How the crap do you have the patience to eat so much, though?'

'Oh, I don't waste time overeating,' Gargan said. 'I've had my lipostat surgically adjusted. My whole body-fat-and-glucose equation has been changed. I burn slowly, my friend, I burn very slowly. The eating it takes to give you an ounce gives me a pound. And I grow lovely, eh, more lovely every day. I want to weigh a thousand pounds, Nat! Paul. I must call you Paul.'

'Paul, yes.'

'But none of this makes any sense.' Gargan stirred ever so slightly, craning his neck. 'How can you remember me? Why didn't Rehab wipe you out?'

'It did.'

'But you sound just like –'

'I'm a special case. Don't ask too many questions.'

'I follow you, Nat.'

'Paul.'

'Paul.'

'Be more careful about my name, will you? I'm a brand-new man. The loathsome countersocial rapist who did such grievous damage to so many innocent women has been humanely destroyed, Gargantua, and will never walk the earth again.'

'I follow. Where are you living?'

'Way uptown. A temporary place. You can have the address if you want.'

'Please. And the phone.'

'I won't be there long. As soon as I've got some cash together I'll find something a little more suitable.'

'Are you working yet?'

'As a holovision commentator,' Hamlin said. 'Maybe you've seen me. The late news.'

'I mean *working*.'

'No. I have no equipment, no studio. I haven't even had a chance to think about work in a serious way.'

'But soon?'

'Soon, yes.' Macy felt Hamlin's lips curve into a sly, malicious smile. 'Would you like to represent me when I get started again, Gargantua?'

'Why ask? You know we have a contract.'

'We don't,' said Hamlin.

'I could show it to you. Wait, let me punch the retrieve.' Gargan's meaty fingers hovered over the console buttons. As he started to stab a stud Hamlin reached out and stopped him.

'You had a contract with Nat Hamlin,' Hamlin said. 'Hamlin's dead. You can't represent his ghost. My name is Paul Macy, and I'm looking for a dealer. You interested?'

Gargan's face looked puffier. 'You know I am.'

'Fifteen percent.'

'The old contract said thirty.'

'The old contract was signed twenty years ago. The situation then doesn't apply now. Fifteen.'

Lengthy tugging at dewlaps. 'I never take less than thirty.'

'You will if you want me to come back to you.' The voice
very flat now. 'All Hamlin's contracts were legally dissolved
when his personality underwent deconstruct. I'm not bound
by anything. Also I'm without assets and I need to rebuild my
capital in a hurry. Fifteen. Take it or leave it.'

In Gargan's eyes a countervailing slyness. 'Nat Hamlin was
an established master with a line of museum credits longer
than my cock. Paul – what is it, Macy? – Paul Macy is a
nobody. I had a waiting list for Hamlins, for anything he'd
turn out. Why should people buy you?'

'Because I'm as good as Hamlin.'

'How do I know that?'

'Because I tell you so. Business may be slow at first until
the word-of-mouth starts, but when the public realizes that
Macy is as good as Hamlin, even better than Hamlin because
he's been through an extra hell and knows how to make use
of it, the public will come around and clean you out. You'll
cover your nut with plenty to spare. Do we have a deal at
fifteen or don't we?'

'I want to see some of Paul Macy's work,' Gargan said slowly,
'before I offer a contract.'

'Contract first or you don't see a thing.'

A tut and a tut from the narrow lips. 'Artists aren't supposed
to be rapacious. That's why they need dealers, to be sons of
bitches on their behalf.'

'I can be my own son of a bitch,' Hamlin said. 'Look,
Gargantua, don't waltz around with me. You know who I
am and you know how good I am. I've had a rough time
and I need money, and anyway at this stage of my career
it's crazy for me to be cutting my dealer in for thirty. Give
me a contract and advance me ten thousand so I can set up
a studio, and let's not crap around any more.'

'And if I don't?'

'There are two dozen dealers within five blocks of here.'

'Who would jump at the chance of taking on somebody
named Paul Macy, I suppose?'

'They'd know who I really was.'

'Would they? The Rehab process is supposed to be foolproof. Suppose this is all a clever hoax? Suppose you *are* Paul Macy, and somebody's coached you on how to sound like Nat Hamlin, and you're just trying to sweat some quick cash out of me?'

'Test me. Ask me anything about Hamlin's life.' Macy sensed Hamlin's distress now. Adrenalin flooding. Pores opening. Genitals contracting.

'I don't play guessing games,' said Gargan. Idly he punched a button; the room tilted the other way. Hamlin's intestine lolled. The dealer said, 'You've got no leverage, friend. No reputable dealer would trust a Rehab reconstruct who says he's still got the skills of his old self. So the take-it-or-leave-it is on my side. I'll sign you, Paul, because I'm sentimental and I love you, loved you in the old days, anyway, and I'll give you some money to start you up again. But I won't be blackjacked. Twenty-five percent and nothing lower.'

'Twenty.'

'Twenty-five.' A gargantuan yawn. 'You're starting to bore me, Paul.'

'Don't get snotty. Remember who you're talking to, what kind of talent you've got sitting next to you here. A year from now you'll regret having muscled me. Twenty percent, Gargantua.'

'Twenty-five.'

Now Hamlin was plainly upset. The swagger was gone; his ductless glands were working overtime. Macy, who had not ceased to probe avenues of neural connections, thought he had found a good one and that this might be a suitable moment for making a try at retaking the body. He pressed hard. Lunged. Claws outstretched, attacking the cerebral switchboard. But no go. Hamlin brushed him away as though he were a mosquito and said aloud, 'Let's split the difference. Twenty-two and a half and I'm yours.'

An hour's smooth drive in a rented car brought Hamlin to his old Connecticut estate. The car did its best to cope with

Hamlin's surprising ineptness as a driver. He handled the steering-stick crudely, overpushing it, frequently trying to override the car's gyroscopic mind, constantly messing up the delicate homeostasis that kept the vehicle in its proper lane. Macy, from his vantage-point within, monitored Hamlin's performance with mixed feelings. Obviously Hamlin, four or five years away from driving, had lost whatever skill at it he once had had, and that was worrying him, for it had occurred to him that in his absence he might have lost other skills also. Therefore he was working himself into a singleminded frenzy of concentration, gripping the stick in sweaty palm and trying to psych himself into complete mastery over the car. Macy knew he could play on Hamlin's fears, intensifying his distress. *You think you've come back to life, Nat, but nothing came back except your ego and your dirty mouth. You've lost your manual skills. You couldn't cut paper dolls now, let alone turn out museum masterpieces.* And so on. Undermining Hamlin's self-confidence, attacking his main justification for having expelled his reconstruct. Weakening his grip on the body's central nervous system, setting him up for a push. *You think you're still a great artist? Jesus, you don't even know how to drive! The Rehab Center smashed you to bits, Nat, and you won't ever be whole again.* And then, getting Hamlin fuddled and panicky, he could make a try for a takeover.

The process was already well under way. The fumes of Hamlin's tensions drifted through Macy's interior holdfast. The oily smell of fear and doubt. Go on, give him a shove, he's vulnerable now. But the scheme was futile, Macy knew. He hadn't yet found the handles with which he could flip Hamlin out of his dominant position. Even if he had, he wouldn't dare attempt a takeover at 120 miles an hour; no matter how good this car's homeostasis was supposed to be, it wasn't programmed for self-drive, and while he and Hamlin struggled for control the auto might go over the edge of the embankment, or up a wall, or into the oncoming flow, in some wild uncorrected orgy of positive feedback.

So Macy sat passive while Hamlin shakily negotiated the

highway and more capably guided the car up the winding leafy country lanes to the place where he once had lived. Parking the car perhaps a quarter of a mile away. Leaving the road, walking cautiously through the woods. Heartbreaking summeriness here. The foliage so green and new. Bright yellow and white flowers. Chipmunks and squirrels. Clumps of frondy ferns. They had held back the urban tide here, the surging sea of concrete and pollution, the onslaught of extinctions. An outpost of natural life, maintained for the very rich.

And there, beyond that blinding white stand of stunning birches, the house. Lofty walls of high-piled gray-brown boulders set in ancient gray mortar. Leaded-glass windows agleam in the moonlight. Hamlin's heart leaping and bouncing. Old memories in an agitated dance. Look, look there. The pond, the creek, the pool. Exactly as Lissa had described it, exactly as Macy had seen it through the lens of Hamlin's reminiscing mind. And the studio annex. Where so many miracles were worked.

– Why did you come here?

A pilgrimage. A sentimental journey.

– It's somebody else's house now.

Why don't you go fuck yourself, Macy?

– I have your welfare at heart. You can't just prowl around here. It may be patrolled by dogs. Scanners everywhere. You know what'll happen to you if you're caught?

Hamlin didn't reply. He edged toward the studio, and Macy picked up an inchoate scheme for forcing a window and getting inside. Hamlin seemed to expect to find his workshop intact, all the elaborate psychosculpting apparatus still sitting where he had left it. Folly. The studio was probably some blithery suburbanite matron's greenhouse now. Hamlin continued to slink through the copse bordering the creek. Let him try, let him just try. The alarm will go off and the place will be full of cops in ten minutes. A frantic chase through the woods. Snub-nosed shiny cyber-hounds snuffing on silent treads over last year's fallen leaves, homing in on the fleeing man's telltale thermals. The fugitive encircled, entrapped, seized. Identified

as Paul Macy, Rehab reconstruct, but the police, checking
with Gomez & Co., would swiftly discover that Macy had
been plagued by a resurgence of his prior identity. And then.
Swift action. Wham! Needles in his arm. Hamlin reamed out
a second time.

What about his threat to destroy their shared body in case
of trouble? No, Macy thought, he can't do it, not while he's up
there running the conscious brain. A man can't simply shut off
his own heartbeat by willing it. He could when he was down
here where I am, plugged into all the neural connections, but
he can't do it now. So Hamlin will die a second time, and the
body will survive. For me to have. Go on, Nat, creep and creep
and creep, bust into your studio, trip the alarm, summon the
hounds, start me on the road back to independent life. Yes.
I'll be so very grateful.

What's this rising from the pool, though? Blithery suburban
matron herself! Venus on the half shell. Woman in her middle
forties, tall, not exactly plump but well endowed, dark hair,
long arching waist, thickish thighs, amiable vacuous face. Her
snatch chastely shielded by a skimpy cache-sexe; breasts bare,
full, probably not as high as they used to be. Staring in surprise
at Hamlin advancing toward her.

Quick adrenal response from Hamlin, too. Pupils dilated,
heartbeat accelerated, prick stiffening. No wonder he's excited.
The quintessential rape situation. Daytime, suburbs, woman
alone, scantily clad, man emerges out of woods. Fling her
down, hand over mouth, spread the thighs, give her the ram.
Ooom. Load the box and prance away. Another notch carved
in your cock.

– Ahaha! Still at it. Your old tricks.

Don't bother me, Hamlin snapped. Making an effort, recovering his sexual equilibrium, his social poise. Giving her a
sexosocial smile and a little genteel nod. Everything under control. 'I hope I didn't startle you, ma'am.' The voice unctuous.

'Not fatally.' Her eyes fluttering from his face to the Rehab
badge and back to face. A little confused but not alarmed.
She didn't try to cover her breasts despite the potential

provocativeness of the situation. The cheerful poise of the upper crust. 'Forgive me if I'm making a terrible mistake, but aren't you – weren't you –'

'Nat Hamlin, yes. Who used to live here. But my name is Paul Macy now.'

– Liar!

'I recognized you at once. How pleasant of you to visit us!' Obviously unaware of the impropriety of a reconstruct's visiting his earlier self's old haunts. Or not caring. 'Lynn Bryson, by the way. We've been here two years now. My husband is a helix surgeon. Shall I get you a drink, Mr ah Macy? Or something to smoke?'

'No, thank you, Mrs Bryson. You bought the place from Hamlin's ah widow?'

'From Mrs Hamlin, yes. Such a fascinating woman! Naturally she didn't care to stay here any longer, with such terrible memories on all sides. We struck up a wonderful friendship during the time when the house was changing hands.'

'I've heard many fine things about her,' Hamlin said. 'Of course I have no recollection of her. You understand.'

'Of course.'

'Hamlin's past is a closed book to me. But you understand I have a certain natural curiosity about the people and places of his life. As if he were, in a sense, a famous ancestor of mine, and I felt I should know more about him.'

'Of course.'

'Does Mrs Hamlin still live in this area?'

'Oh, no, she's in Westchester now. Bedford City, I believe.'

'Remarried?'

'Yes, of course.'

The knife turning in Hamlin's gut.

'You happen to know her new husband's name?' Very carefully, concealing all traces of tension.

'I could find it,' the woman said. 'A Jewish name. Klein, Schmidt, Katz, something like that, a short word, Germanic. A person in the theater, a producer maybe, a very fine man.' Her smile grew broader. Her eyes appraised Hamlin's body with complacent sensuality. As if she wouldn't mind some pronging. Her vicarious way of attaining intimacy with the departed great artist. She should only know. Off with that bit of plastic about her waist, down on the grass, the white fleshy thighs parting. *Ooom.* 'Won't you come with me?' she said airily. 'I have it in the house. And you'll want to see the house, anyway. The studio. Do you know, we've kept Mr Hamlin's studio exactly as it was when he – before he – when his troubles started –'

'You have?' A wild interior leap. Excited. 'Everything still intact?'

'Mrs Hamlin didn't want any of his things, so they came to us with the house. And we thought, well, the way they have Rembrandt's house on display in Amsterdam, or the house of Rubens in what is it Antwerp, so we would keep Nathaniel Hamlin's studio intact here, not for public display of course, but simply as a kind of shrine, a memorial, and in case some scholar wished to see it, some great admirer of Hamlin, well, we would make it accessible. And then of course future generations. Won't you come with me?' Smiling, turning, striding across the barbered lawn. Meaty buttocks waggle waggle waggle. Hamlin, sweating, adrenalized, following. The familiar old stone house. The squat spacious annex. A cheery wave of her hand. 'There's an entrance to the studio on the far side of –' Hamlin was already on his way around there. 'Oh, I see you know that.' But how is it that he knows it? No indication that she suspects anything. 'I'll look for Mrs Hamlin's new name, and her address too, I suppose, and I'll meet you in a couple of minutes in the –'

Studio. Exactly as he had left it. To the left of the door, the big rectangular window. Floods of light. Facing the window, the posing dais with the microphones and scanners and sensors still in place and even his last chalk-marks still on the floor. On the right-hand wall his command console, levers and knobs and studs and dials that would surely have perplexed Rembrandt or Rubens or for that matter Leonardo da Vinci.

The headphones. The ionization controller. The unjacked connectors. The data-screen. The light-pen. The sonic generator. Such a tangle of apparatus. In back, the other little room, the annex of the annex, more things visible, coils of wire, metal struts, mounds of modeling clay, the big electropantograph, the photomultiplier, the image intensifier, and other things which Hamlin did not seem to recognize. Hamlin wandered numbly among it all. Macy picked up his somber thoughts. The artist was frightened, even appalled, by the complexity of the studio. Trying to adjust to the idea that he had once used all this stuff by second nature. What was this thing for? And this? And this? Shit, how does it all work? I can't remember a thing.

– Rehab wrecked you, Nat, more than you realize.

Shut your hole. I could pick all this up again in three hours. A note of false bravado, though. Powerful currents of uncertainty coming from him. Hamlin broke off a chunk of modeling clay and began to knead it. Stiff, after all this time. The clay. And he was too. The fingers unresponsive. Let's sculpt Mrs Bryson. Here, we roll a long tube of clay like so, and we. No. Instantly the proportions were awry. Hamlin nibbled his lip. Correcting his intuitive beginning. She's tall, yes, and wide through the hips, and we'll need some clay here for the boobs.

– Give up, Nat, you don't have it any more.

Piss off, Macy. What do you know?

Yet Hamlin was unable to conceal the extent of his uneasiness from his passenger. He was fumbling with the clay, mangling it, blundering at this elementary task of modeling, straining to get the image in his mind transferred to the lump in his hands. In that tense moment Macy made new connections and for the first time gained some control over Hamlin's central nervous system. *Plink.* Strumming the neurons. Hamlin's elbow jerked. The tube of clay bent double at the sudden accidental convulsion. *Plink.* Another twitch. Hamlin shouting silently at him now, bellowing in rage. Macy was enjoying this. He continued to tug at Hamlin's synapses while the artist trembled and shivered in mounting wrath and frustration. The half-shaped model of Mrs Bryson a ruin. Hamlin glancing around nervously at his own equipment, so alien to him, so terrifying. Telling himself that in four, four and a half years it was possible for a person to forget all sorts of superficial mechanical things, but that you never lost the real talent, the basic underlying inborn gift, the set of perceptions and insights that is the real material to which the artist applies his learned craftsmanship.

– Go on, Nat, keep saying it, you may even start to believe it soon.

Let me alone. Let me alone. I could learn all this machinery again in half a day!

– Sure you could, sweetheart. Who ever doubted it?

Giving Hamlin another twong in the medulla, a blork in the autonomic, a whonk in the limbic. Yes! Really learning my way around in here, now! Just as he did in me. The shoe on the other cortex, though. I'll get him. I'll get him good. Hamlin was doing a manic dance, twitching around the room as Macy toyed with him. He couldn't seem to get himself together enough to deliver a retaliatory shot; it was as if the vibrations emanated by all the psychosculpting apparatus kept him dizzy and off balance. Keep hammering away, Macy told himself. This may be your chance to get back on top. Twong and twong and twong! Arms whipping about wildly. Knees jerking. I think I could make him crap in his undies now. A nice psychological point to score, but why shit things up for myself in case I take over?

And then Hamlin began to fight back. Coldly, furiously, ramming Macy down into subservience once more. Sweeping from his mind the distractions of this dismaying studio in order to regain inner discipline. There. There. There. Macy saw that he did not yet have the power to vanquish the other, although he was constantly learning and gaining strength. Later. Another time. He has me now.

'Isn't the studio *absolutely fascinating*, Mr Macy?'

An idiot warble, a gay contralto trill. Enter Mrs Bryson. A slip of paper in her hand. By no accident, she has rid herself of her loincloth, and she comes jollying in, starkers, with flat-footed buoyancy. Eyes sparkling, breasts heaving expectantly. Thick curling deep-piled black triangle. Her nipples turning to turrets. The hot scent of a rutting bitch spreading in the warm air. We're very casual about nudity out here, you see, Mr Macy. Clothes are so primitive, don't you think! And then maybe making a quick grab for his crotch, getting the pole out in the open, down on the floor amid the paraphernalia of the great artist. To be had by his simulacrum. *Ooom.* But not this time, lady. 'I had some trouble finding Mrs Hamlin's new name and address,' she said. 'It was with our papers on the house, you know, tucked away, but I dug everything out, and now –'

'Yes,' Hamlin said. Blurted. A frantic need to get out of here. Throat dry; face flushed; eyes unfocused. Defending himself simultaneously against Macy's assaults from within and the mockeries of this equipment from without. Her black bush and hot slot of no interest to him now. The unexpectedly overbearing atmosphere of his studio had unmanned him utterly. To escape, fast. Snatching the slip of paper from her startled hand. 'Thankyouverymuchgottogonow.' Moving rapidly past her toward the door. Her face suddenly a rigid mask of surprise and anger: she knows she will be denied. Hell hath no fury.

She looks ten years older. Deep lines from cheeks to chin. The nipples going soft; the shoulders slumping. All her naked-ness wasted on him. Her arm outstretched, the fingers working eagerly as if to pull him back. No chance. Hamlin had reached the exit. Out into the midday brightness. Pursued by phantom tendrils of feminine libido. 'You needn't leave so soon!' she calls to him. Hamlin made no reply. Glanced back once, saw her outside the studio door, naked well-endowed idle-rich lass on the threshold of middle age, bewildered by his panic, astounded by his rejection of her body. His panic bewildered him too. Head awhirl. Macy did his best to make things worse, yanking on all the neural lines at once. Hamlin yelped, but stayed in control, and went on running. Running. Run. Ning.

*   *   *

In the car again, jouncing helter-skelter westward across several counties, Macy wondered if they were going to survive this trip. These back roads didn't have any protective strips, and thus the auto's homeostasis mechanisms were essentially cancelled out; if the car started to slide off the road, nothing would keep it from smashing into the bulky oaks that awaited it.

And Hamlin was in a ghastly state. Madly gripping the stick. Eyes glazed in Dostoevskian fixity. Jaws clenched. He was driving on reflex alone, employing one tiny plaque of cerebral tissue to operate the vehicle while the rest of his mind wildly revolved the events of the past half hour. The car teetered from side to side on the narrow road, now and then crossing the center line or running onto the shoulder.

Most of Hamlin's defenses were relaxed, but as before Macy feared to make a takeover attempt in a moving car. He hunkered down inside Hamlin's brain as though it were a storm-shelter and temporarily disconnected his optical hookup, for the view of the madly slewing road through Hamlin's eyes was making him seasick. Better, this way. To sit in solemn silence in a dull dark dock. About him still flashed the lightnings and eruptions of Hamlin's distress. The studio visit had really shaken him. Moving among his implements, his elaborate sculpting apparatus, Hamlin had seemed not to know what from which or up from down. Macy wondered why. Had the Rehab process done irreversible damage to the Hamlin persona? Was there actually nothing left of the original Nat Hamlin except a clutch of old memories, a cluster of attitudes and phrases, some tics and twitches of the spirit? The sculptor, the man of genius, had he been irretrievably demolished, and was this comeback merely a delusion?

On the other hand, Macy thought, it might have been the strain of maintaining control of their shared body that had so severely drained Hamlin's psychic energy. There had been definite signs all day that Hamlin's grip was none too strong and was slipping from hour to hour. In the morning, striding jauntily down the street to Gargan's gallery, presenting the

contract ultimatum to the fat dealer, all that hard bargaining –
Hamlin had appeared to be in full command then, but by the
end of the encounter with Gargan he had started to show some
fatigue, and the troubles he had had in driving from the city
to his Connecticut studio had revealed a further weakening
of control.

And then the disastrous studio visit. Continued slippage.
The battery running down and no time for recharging. It
must take a constant terrific effort for Hamlin to operate
this body, injured as he had been by the Rehab obliteration
experts. Macy knew that he himself was nowhere near the
point where he could regain the body, but the way things
were going that moment couldn't be very far away. It was
coming. It was coming. Or was he fooling himself?

He reconnected the visuals. The car still careening along
the suburban back roads. Hamlin sitting rigidly, lost in contemplation, paying minimal attention. Horrifying. The body
wouldn't be worth shit to them if Hamlin smashed up the
car. Certainly fatal to both of them. But there was nothing
Macy could do about that right now. He blanked the scene
again, escaping. Diving down deep, burrowing into Hamlin's
memory bank. Everything there was accessible to him, all
the stored scenes of his prior self's active life. Failures and
triumphs, mostly triumphs. The women. The critics. The press
clippings. The one-man shows. The money. The accumulation
of possessions. All the surface glamor. Yet beneath the shiny
shallow business of career-making Macy could see in Hamlin
the authentic artistic impulse, the hunger to make his visions
real. Give Hamlin credit for that. He had been a bastard,
sure, still was, but he pursued a vision, he realized it, he
gave it to the world. There are those who make and give,
and those who take and consume, and Hamlin had been a
maker and giver.

Macy envied that. Who are the real ones among us, anyway,
if not those who create, who give, who enrich those about
them? Regardless of their motives. Doing it for the money,
for the ego trip, for whatever unworthy reason, but *doing* it.

Having something worth doing and doing it. Hamlin was one of those.

I'm one of the consumers thought Macy. Blame Gomez & Co., I guess: they could have made me someone worthwhile. Their own artistic achievement, their creative self-justification. But of course they aren't paid to do that. Just to fill up vacant bodies with reasonably functional human beings. Gomez isn't an artist, he's a doctor, and he can't transcend himself when he does a reconstruct. If I am second-rate, it's because my makers were second-raters too.

Unlike this bastard Hamlin. Whose darker side was also visible: the inner collapse, the breaking free from moorings. Roaming the quiet streets. The artist as predator. Each rape neatly labeled and cataloged in the archives. And not just mere rape, either. Not just the shoving of Blunt Object X into Unwilling Orifice Y, but also the associated stuff, the peripherals, the leering, the mocking, the capering, the perversions, the garbage. Even in a permissive age there still are such things as abominations. Hamlin must have been out of his mind. The big-eyed twelve-year-old forced to watch her pretty young blonde mother blowing the famous artist: what kind of scars does that leave on an unformed psyche? And all this buggery. A trail of torn sphincters across four states. Not even greasing it first. That's sadism, Hamlin. Out of your fucking mind.

But how crazy were you, really? Didn't you have a clear conscious awareness of what was going on, and didn't you enjoy it? Yes. And wasn't all this crap latent in you all along? Yes. Okay, something brought you out. Suddenly it was Monster Time in your head, and you went forth to fulfill all the steamy dreams you had nurtured since your cramped lonely adolescence. Right? Right. And filed everything away for subsequent gloating. No wonder they sentenced you to deconstruct. Jesus, I feel filthy just rummaging through this stuff. Maker of masterpieces. Giver of unique visions. And your demonic laughter underneath. Telling the court you were insane, that you were in the grip of an irresistible impulse, an obsessive compulsion, but were you? Perhaps you thought you were creating a new kind of work of art, made not out of paint or clay or plastic or bronze but out of bleeding invaded female bodies, an abstract sculpture composed of dozens of victims, forming a pattern you alone could have designed. Jesus. What a case for obliteration you were!

Macy noticed that the car no longer was moving. Hastily he plugged in the visuals again.

They were parked in the central shopping plaza of a medium-sized suburban city, with two- and three-story Westchester Tudor half-timbered shops, freshly whitewashed and their brown beams newly painted, glistening in the amber light of late afternoon. Hamlin had his head out the side door; he was asking a policeman – a *policeman!* – how to find Lotus Lane. A rapid-fire stream of instructions. Turn left at the computer stanchion, follow Colonial Avenue to Route 4480, turn right at the yellow blinker, go about ten blocks, no, twelve, you'll come to the industrial park, you turn right there past the tall building and you drive on to the sniffer palace – a grin, we've even got that stuff up here! – and make a left and that puts you on Route 519, all the cross streets there are marked, you won't miss Lotus. On the left.

Thank you, officer. And off we go. Left, right, right, left. Quiet country lanes again. Hamlin tense. No difficulty following the instructions, though. Left, right, right, left, the sniffer palace, the residential area, Cypress Walk, Redbud Drive, Oak Pond Road, Lotus Lane. Lotus. Number 55. A trim stucco house twenty or thirty years old, with a perspex sundome and glossy oval opaquer-windows. A sign out front: THE KRAFFTS. Hamlin presented himself to the doorscanner. From within, via intercom, a warm firm sweetly modulated mezzo voice: 'Who is it?'

'Paul Macy.'

'Paul. Macy.' Doubtfully. 'Paul Macy? Oh, my God! My God, you shouldn't have come here!'

'Please,' Hamlin said. 'Just a few minutes. To talk.'

A moment of empty humming from the intercom. Then,

hesitantly, 'Well, I suppose. All right. Although this is probably a big mistake.' Two moments more; then the door began to open. In the same instant Hamlin's left hand rose toward his throat. For the purpose, Macy sensed, of ripping the tell-tale Rehab badge from his clothing. Macy blocked the attempt with a fierce neural jab, the accuracy of which surprised him; Hamlin, his arm arrested in midclimb, stiffened and let the arm sag to his side, while simultaneously snapping a furious silent curse at Macy. The door was open. Framed in the vaulted entranceway stood a woman of extraordinary poise and beauty. Tall, nearly to his shoulder, but slender, fine-boned, a delicate tiny-featured face, alert ironic eyes, sleek glossy black hair in tumbling cascades, full sardonic lips, strong chin, long columnar neck. An aristocrat. Paul guessed her age at thirty-one or thirty-two. She held herself well.

'Why did you come here?' she asked.

'To see you, Noreen.'

'Noreen?' The lips quirking with distaste. 'Are we so intimate, then, that we use first names?'

'Formality's foolish. We were married once,' Hamlin said.

'I was married to Nathaniel Hamlin, God help me.' She conspicously eyed the Rehab badge. 'Your name is Paul Macy, and I have a stack of data cubes inside containing the documents that indicate that Paul Macy is in no way an heir or assign of the former Nat Hamlin. I don't know you. I never did.'

'Don't be too sure of that. Won't you ask me in?'

'My husband isn't home.'

'What of it? Am I some kind of wild beast? I'm housebroken, Noreen. You can let me in.'

Her invisible shrug was unmistakable. A quick grudging nod. 'All right. For a few moments.'

The house was small but handsomely and expensively furnished. Hamlin's gaze traveled quickly along the walls, taking in a pair of nightmarish masks from New Guinea, an African figurine, a baffling shaped painting in the form of a tesseract, and three magnificent little crystallines. Macy would have liked to linger and study the tesseract, but he was the prisoner of Hamlin's eyes, and Hamlin continued turning until he came to rest on one of his works, an exquisite porcelain-finish image of Noreen, half life size, nude. Small high breasts, flaring waist, and, coming from the cloud of airborne speakers mounted in the dark hair, an ominously sensual viewer-responsive hundred-cycle rumble. Hamlin turned from Noreen to Noreen. 'I wondered whether you'd kept it,' he said.

'Why wouldn't I? It's superb.' Clouds crossing her face. 'You remember it?'

'I remember plenty.'

'But the Rehab –'

'Let's not talk about that. Who's your new husband?'

'Sy Krafft. I don't think you knew him.' Pausing. As if to run the tape of her conversation back a bit for a correction. 'I don't think *Hamlin* knew him. He does floating spectaculars. A charming and cultivated person.' Pausing again. 'How did you find me?'

'I went to the old house. The woman who owned it gave me your name and address.'

'The Rehab Center assured me that I'd never be troubled by you.'

'Am I making trouble?'

'You're here,' she said. 'That's enough. What is it you want with me, Mr Macy?'

'Don't call me Macy. You know who I am.'

She stepped back from him, doing it artfully, so that she seemed merely to be moving about the room and not retreating. She looked like a bird thinking of taking wing. In a low voice she said, 'I never expected this. They assured me you were gone forever.'

'They made a mistake.'

'Rehab doesn't make mistakes. I saw your body after they burned you out of it. No, you aren't Nat. You're Macy, the new one, and you're trying to play a joke on me, and I assure you it's not in the least funny.'

'I'm Nat Hamlin. His ghost walks the earth.'

'You're Paul Macy.'

'Hamlin.'

'It can't be.'

'You're so fucking beautiful, Noreen. What is it, five years, and you haven't changed at all. I get hard just standing in the same room with you. Are you making any films these days?'

'I think it's time you left.'

'You still love me, don't you? I know, I know, you feel uncomfortable having me here, you're edgy and tense because you think Mr Sy Krafft is going to walk in on us, but you want me as much as ever. I could prove it. I could put my hand between your legs and it would come away wet. It was always easy for me to smell a woman in heat, Noreen.'

'You're crazy, whoever you are. I want you to go.'

'And I love you too, even more than before. Listen, don't play-act with me, don't give me that icy I-want-you-to-go crap. I'm *back*, Noreen. Don't ask me how I managed it. I'm back. I'll be going under the name of Macy, but it's me, the real me here, and I'm going to start working again soon. I've already seen Gargantua. He's signing me, he's giving me money to open a studio. Very quietly I'll reestablish myself. No rapes any more. None of that. I'll be sedate and bourgeois, Mr Paul Macy, Mr Nobody, only underneath it'll be Nat Hamlin. And you'll come visit me, won't you?'

'I'll visit you in jail, yes.'

'You'll visit me in my studio. We'll sit and talk about how good it was before I crapped everything up. Remember, '02, '03, when we were just starting out? Lying on the beach in Antigua, and we couldn't leave each other alone, we did it right out there. Sand in your snatch, eh, Noreen? You didn't like that so much, but even so, you loved it. And then. The other times. I've got them all up here in my head. They banged me around at Rehab, but they didn't destroy me. They tried hard enough, but they didn't destroy me.' He took a step toward her. Throat dry, fingertips cold. Getting harder and harder down below. 'Don't be afraid of me. I love you. *I love you*. I wouldn't hurt you for anything. Stop backing away. Listen, it'll be our secret, you and me, the world will think I'm Macy, you can go on being Mrs Sy Krafft, this cute little house, kids – do you have kids? – whatever you want, only on the side it'll be you and me again, Nat and Noreen, at my studio.

'I'll do another nude of you. Life-size. It'll be better than the *Antigone*. Remember how sore you were, because I used Lissa for the *Antigone* instead of you? But we were drifting apart then. I didn't know what was good for me. I had to go through hell to find out. But now. You'll pose. Shit, I can see it now. You standing over there. Those sweet little tits of yours. Ten electrodes on you. And I'm at the machine, sweating like a bastard. Getting you down, immortalizing your body and your soul. An hour for work, an hour for screwing, an hour for work, an hour for screwing. Oh, Jesus, Noreen, stop staring at me like that!'

'I'll call the police. When they catch you, Nat, they'll finish you for good. They won't even put you through Rehab. They'll chop you up and flush you away.'

'No. A silver bullet in my head. A stake through the heart.'

'I'll call them, Nat.'

'Wait. Please, no. Look, I don't mean to frighten you. I came here to tell you how much I love you. I've been in hell, Noreen, literally in hell, and now I'm coming out, I'm going to live again. And I had to come to you. Why be afraid? Tell me you love me.'

'I don't love you, Nat. You disgust me.'

Hamlin began to shake.

'Brava!' he cried. 'Brava! Bravissima!' He started to applaud. 'What an actress! What fire in your reading! What steel in your voice!' Imitating her: ' "I don't love you, Nat. You disgust me." ' Wildly applauding. 'Curtain. End of Act Two. Now tell me the real stuff, Noreen. How much you want me. You're scared, yes, you remember me when I was crazy, when I was doing all that hideous crap, but you've got to remember the other me, too, the one you loved, the one you married, everything we did together, the places we saw, the people, the stuff in bed, remember, even the weird stuff, you and me and Donna in the same bed, and then you and me and Alex, eh, Noreen? Love. Trust. Passion.' He reached toward her. 'Come on. Now. Where's the bedroom? Or right here on the floor. Let me prove it to you, that you still turn on for me. Okay? Why the hell not? You opened your gate for me five hundred times. Eight hundred. So one more won't cost you anything.'

He was shouting now. Her cool poise was deserting her. She look terrified, moving away from him, stumbling over things. He lunged at her. Seizing her wrist, pulling her close. The sweet fragrance of her body mixed with fear-sweat. Her eyes glazed with fright. 'Noreen,' he muttered. 'Noreen. Noreen. Noreen.' The syllables losing meaning and becoming hollow sounds. His skull aflame. His jaws aching. His hands clutching at her clothing. Ripping. The little round breasts popping into view. Oh, Christ, how tender they are! His hands on them. Squeezing. She flailed at him with her fists, clubbing him on the mouth, the nose, the ears. He had one arm locked around her waist; the other, having laid bare her bosom, went for her crotch. To see if she was wet there. To prove to her how wrong she was to refuse him. He was snorting. Like the old days, the bad old days. Hamlin the animal. Hamlin the horny Minotaur. Fragile woman struggling in his arms. A red haze before his eyes. Sweat running down his sides. Noreen kicking, screaming, clawing.

Now, Macy thought, and shoved with all his might. Hamlin toppled from his perch. Fell moaning into the abyss. A moment of total disorientation, infinite in duration. Who am I? What am I? Where am I? He let go of the woman he held. She slumped to the floor; he lurched backward and slammed against the wall, and stood there, gasping, exhausted. Blood draining from his skull.

But it was all right. He was in charge again. He was Paul Macy, and he was back in charge.

THIRTEEN

To get away from there, fast, that was the important thing now. But first some peace making. Gestures of reassurance. Noreen Hamlin Krafft lay looking up dazedly at him, a dribble of bright red on her swelling lower lip, hair in disarray, angry blotches on her exposed white breasts where Hamlin had clutched her. They would be dark bruises tomorrow. She didn't move. Waiting numbly for the next onslaught. Resigned to her fate. He said, his voice coming out oddly furry and unfocused, 'It's okay now. I've taken control away from him. I'm Macy. I won't hurt you.'

'Macy.'

'Paul Macy. The Rehab reconstruct. They did a bad deconstruct job on Hamlin and he's still loose in my head. He grabbed the body's motor and speech centers last night.' Last night? Last week, last month? How long had Hamlin been running things, anyway? 'But he's down underneath again, where he can't make trouble. While he was fighting with you I was able to take over.' Gently helping her to her feet. He wondered if she had gone into shock. Making no attempt to cover herself. Tip of her tongue licking at the cut on her lip. He said, 'I'm sorry you had to go through all this. Are you badly injured?'

'No. No.' Staring at him. Trying to come to terms with his abrupt transformation. Dr Jekyll, Mr Hyde. 'Just shaken up.' With trembling fingers she concealed her bosom, tidied her hair. Staring at him. Was his face different now? The lunatic glare of Hamlin gone from his eyes? He knew it wasn't easy for her to understand any of what had taken place. These shifts of identity: he had come to accept them as part of the human condition, but to her they must be alien, incredible, bizarre. Maybe she thought he had been Macy all along, playing insane pranks on her. Or that he was still Hamlin.

He said, 'It would be best if you didn't tell anyone about this. The police, your husband, anyone. I'm trying to have Hamlin permanently eradicated before he can do some real harm, but there are problems, and getting the police into things would only make it worse for me. You see, I'm in constant danger from him, and if I went to the authorities he might force the destruction of this body, so –' He stopped. She didn't seem to be comprehending. 'Just don't say anything, yes? If it's at all in my power I'll see to it you never go through a scene like this again. Do you follow me?'

She nodded distantly. Pacing about, now, working off her fright. Time for him to go. At the front door he turned and said, 'One last thing, though. Can you tell me today's date?'

'Today's date.' She repeated it in a flat empty tone. As if he had asked her the name of the planet they were currently on.

'Yes, please. The date. It's important.'

She shrugged. 'The fourth of June, I think.'

'Friday?'

'Friday, yes.'

He thanked her gravely and went out. His body was stiff and he moved gracelessly toward the car, arms flailing spastically, shoulders ramming the air. He and Hamlin evidently had different notions of physical coordination, and his muscles, having taken orders from another mind for eighteen hours or so, were reluctant to go back to the mode he preferred. Not surprising: Hamlin's way was this body's normal way, and his own was something imposed from without. He concentrated on reimposing it. Damned good thing Hamlin had only been running the show since last night, since that takeover during the mugging in the hallway of Lissa's house. Macy had been afraid he might have been unconscious for a week or more before surfacing this morning. In which case he'd have an endless trail of Hamlin's deeds and misdeeds to trace and follow.

But no. It seemed that he had been awake for most of the period of Hamlin's dominance, missing only the first eight hours or so after the takeover. Some comfort in that. Where had Hamlin been in those eight hours? Most likely at my place, getting some rest. And the mugging? It couldn't have been too serious. Macy patted his pocket. Wallet gone. Okay, so he must have collapsed at the moment of takeover, the mugger cleaned him out, then Hamlin picked himself up and left unharmed. The wallet was no big loss. Identity papers, credit cards – all replaceable, all useless to the assailant. Macy didn't even need them himself, so long as he had a thumb with a fingerprint on it. Why, Hamlin had even managed to rent this car using only his thumbprint, not even his, *my* thumbprint. Ours, I guess. But the charge is debited to me. Macy felt vaguely sorry for the mugger, living a squalid lower-class life on a level of society where cash still called the tune. Fine lot of good it must have been for him to lift an executive's wallet, the wallet of a thumb-tripper, five or six dollars in it at most. Oh, well.

Moving more easily now, Macy reached the car and thumbed the doorplate. The door slid open. He got behind the controls and tentatively grasped the steering-stick. The prospect of having to drive scared him suddenly. They had taught him how to drive at the Rehab Center, a couple of years ago, but he hadn't had much chance to practice lately; and just now there was the special risk that Hamlin might surface and screw him up on the highway. I hit him pretty hard when I grabbed control, but even so.

Hamlin? You awake?

No reply from the depths. Macy felt his other self's presence, though: a tinny faint reverberation out of the far-below, like the cries of an angry djinn who has been conjured back into his bottle.

Good. Stay like that. I don't need any static from you while I'm driving.

If only I can keep the goddam stopper in place on the bottle this time.

He put his thumb to the ignition panel, and the car, scanning the print and finding it to be that of its duly licensed present master, came to life. Warily Macy let out the brake. Cautiously he rolled forward. The car responded well, great snorting beast under harness. Which way New York, now? Long afternoon shadows. The sun halfway down the sky on his right. Pick a direction, any direction. He found his way out of the residential area, cut off two drivers as he blurted into the business road, was rudely but deservedly screeched at, and discovered a green-on-white sign directing him to the city. Onward. Homeward. A ticklish trip. He survived it.

He hoped to find Lissa waiting for him at his apartment, slouched in bed in her pleasant wanton way, music playing, her hair a tangle, the aroma of pot in the air. Throw himself wearily down on top of her, bury his aching head between her bouncy boobs. Some chance. The apartment, empty, deserted for a mere twenty-odd hours, had the forlorn and abandoned look of a fifth-rate catacomb. Off with the sweaty crumpled clothing. Shower. Shave. Vague thoughts of dinner. The last meal he remembered having eaten was lunch on Thursday. Now it was dinnertime on Friday. Had Hamlin bothered to refuel their body at all during his eighteen hours on top? Macy wasn't particularly hungry. All this shuttling about of identities. It must have wrecked my appetite. Odd. You'd think that much mental exertion would have burned up a lot of energy. A drink might be in order, though.

He poured himself a hefty bourbon and, naked, flopped down in a chair. A little of the liquor went sloshing out onto his thigh. Cold brown drops on the golden hairs. He felt not at all triumphant at having ousted Hamlin from control. What good was it, being in charge again? Who was he, anyway, that he needed so badly to live? An oppressive sense of having come to the end of the line grew in him. Paul Macy, born 1972 Idaho Falls, Idaho, father a propulsion engineer mother a schoolteacher, no brothers no sisters.

False. False. False shit. I wasn't born anywhere. I am a thing out of a test tube. I am a golem, a dybbuk, a construct. Without friends, without family, without purpose. At least *he* was real.

He'd fuck his kid sister, he'd steal toys from a baby, but he had an identity, a personality that he had earned by living. An artistic gift.

What about it, Hamlin? You want to have it all back? Why do I insist on getting in your way? Maybe you're right: maybe I should let you win.

Hamlin respondeth not. Only the tinny echoes, *ex profundis*. He must be dormant, worn out by everything he was doing. Well, fuck him. He's no good. His soul is full of poison. Damned if I'll step aside for him, genius or no genius. The world has enough great artists. It's only got one Paul Macy, for what that's worth. This would be a good moment to go to the Rehab Center, while Hamlin's groggy. Get him carved out of me for once and all. And if he surfaces? And if he gives me that coronary he's been threatening? Fuck him. If he wants to, he can. So go ahead, coronary. So we'll both be dead. *Pax vobiscum.* We shall sleep the eternal sleep, he and I. Anything would be better than this. Nodding solemnly, Macy reached for the phone to call Gomez.

The phone rang with his arm still in midstretch.

Lissa, he thought. Calling to find out where I've been, asking if she can come back!

Joy. Excitement. That startled him: the intensity of his wish that it be Lissa calling. What was all this crap about dying? He wanted to live. He had someone to look after. And to look after him. They needed each other.

'Hello?' he said eagerly.

On the green screen bloomed the swarthy face of Dr Gomez. The angel of death himself. Speak of the devil.

'I've been phoning all day,' Gomez said. 'Where the fuck have you been?'

'Driving around the suburbs. Weren't you supposed to be keeping me under surveillance?'

'We lost track of you.'

'Is that a fact?' Macy said harshly. 'Well, let me be the first to tell you, then. Hamlin got me last night and kept control until late this afternoon.'

Gomez made elaborate facial gestures of exasperation. 'And did what?'

'Visited his dealer, his old studio, and his former wife. Who he was in the process of raping when I got control again.'

'He's still a psychopath, you mean?'

'He still gets a kick out of manhandling women, anyway.'

'All right. All right. Too fucking much, Macy. Taking you over, running around the countryside. I'm having the van sent for you. Sit tight and if Hamlin makes another try at you, fight him off somehow. We'll have you safely inside the Center under sedation in an hour and a half, and then –'

'No.'

'What, no?'

'Keep away from me if you want me to go on living. I tell you, Gomez, he's a wild man. If he thinks you're seriously after him he'll shut off my heart.'

'That isn't a realistic fear.'

'It's realistic enough for me.'

'I assure you, Macy, he wouldn't do any such thing. We've let this situation drag on too long as it is. We'll come and get you, and we'll do a proper job of deconstructing Hamlin, and I assure you –'

'Shove your assurances, Gomez. We're talking about *my survival* that's being gambled with. *My survival*. I refuse to let you have me. Where's your authority for picking me up without my consent? Where's your court order? No, Gomez. No. Keep away.'

Gomez was silent a moment. A crafty look flickered into his eyes; he immediately tried to hide it, but not before Macy had picked it up. At length Gomez said in his heaviest I-know-this-will-hurt-but-it's-for-the-general-welfare manner, 'You realize, Macy, that your safety isn't the only thing we have to consider here. A court has ruled that society must be protected against Nat Hamlin. The moment you notified me that Hamlin wasn't entirely gone, it became my obligation to take him into custody and carry out the court's sentence the right way. Okay, so you said you felt you were in jeopardy, you asked me to leave you alone until we worked out some sure-thing way of coping, and I let you have your way. It was against every rule, but I gave in. Out of friendship for you, Macy. Will you buy that? Out of friendship. Out of concern. And we've been trying since Monday to figure out a way of handling the situation without endangering you. But now you tell me that Hamlin actually regained command of his body for a little while, for long enough to commit an assault against a human being. Okay. Friendship can go only so far. Can you guarantee Hamlin won't take you over again half an hour from now? Can you guarantee he won't be out banging housewives tomorrow? We *have* to seize him now, Macy, we *have* to finish him off.'

'Even if it entails danger for me?'

'Even if it entails danger for you.'

'I see,' Macy said. 'You figure what the hell, I'm only a construct anyway and if I get wiped out, tough shit on me. The important thing is catching Hamlin. Nothing doing, doctor. I'm not going to be the innocent bystander who gets zapped while you and Hamlin shoot it out. Keep away from me.'

'Macy –'

Macy hung up. Gomez' image shrank and vanished like a photo being sucked into a whirlpool. Macy gulped the last of his drink, dropped the glass, and looked around for some clothing. He understood that his conversation with Gomez had worked a significant and perilous change in his status. The Rehab man had served notice that they were going to come after Hamlin, no matter what risks were in it for anyone else who happened to be inhabiting Hamlin's body. He could wait here meekly for the van, of course. Let himself be hauled off to the Rehab Center. Taking his chances that Gomez would be able to get Hamlin before Hamlin got *him*. But how chancy a chance that was! He knew Hamlin. They hadn't shared a brain all these weeks for nothing. And he knew that if Hamlin surfaced and found himself at the Center, being readied for a new deconstruct job, he'd explode with destructive fury. Samson pulling the pillars down around his ears. If Hamlin

couldn't have the body, he'd see to it that no one would have
it. So it didn't make sense to surrender to Gomez, not now.
His fatalism of half an hour ago had gone from him. He didn't
want to die or even to risk dying. He wasn't sure what it was
he had to live for, but even so. He would have to run. He was
going to have to become a fugitive.

Night had come. Everything was washed in a peculiar faded
gray light. Out the side way, down the alley. Macy looked in all
directions as he left the building. Feeling faintly absurd about
it. This silly skulking, so melodramatic, so unreal. But what
if Gomez had a man watching the main entrance? More than
a touch of paranoia. They'll have hovereyes searching for me,
a ten-state alarm, all the airports being watched. And where
can I go? Jesus, where can I go? Macy wanted to laugh. Some
fugitive. What am I going to do, camp out in Central Park?
Eat squirrels and acorns?

He thought of going to the crumbling roominghouse where
Lissa had lived. A double advantage to that: he might find
her there, his only friend, his only ally, and in any case
the place was such an armpit, such a ghastly hole, that
he'd be beyond the reach of the slick computerized search
processes of the contemporary age. Hiding deep down in a
rotting pretechnological subterranea. But there was one huge
disadvantage, too. Gomez, knowing about Lissa, knowing that
her place was where he'd be most likely to go, would certainly
set up a stakeout there. Waiting for him. Too risky. So where,
then? He didn't know.

He walked north. Keeping close to the darkened buildings,
trying to attract no attention. One shoulder higher than the
other as if he might shield his face that way. Randomly
north as night closed in. Or not so randomly. He realized
that his feet were taking him up Broadway, across the bridge,
into Manhattan North. Toward the only other point on his
compass, the vicinity of the network office.

Landmarks of his slender tattered past. Here he had walked

that uneasy hopeful Maytime day. One-and-two-and-*one*-and-
two. Step. Step. Feeling clumsy and uncertain within his own
body. Trying to be natural about it. This is how Paul Macy
walks. Proudly down the goddam street. Shoulders square.
Belly sucked in. Opportunity beckons you. A second trip, a
second start. The bad dream is over; now you're awake. Step.
Step. Coming to an abrupt stop, he turned to his left and picked
his reflection off the mirror-bright pilaster beside an office
building's entrance. Wide-cheeked, thin-lipped, standard sort
of Anglo-Saxon face. And the girl, coming up behind him,
caught short by his sudden halt, crashing into him. Nat,
she said. Nat Hamlin, for God's sake! The long cold needle
slipping into his eye. Telling her politely but firmly, I'm sorry,
but you're mistaken. My name's Paul Macy. People flowing
smoothly around them. She was tall and slender, with long
straight hair, troubled green eyes, fine features. Attractive in
a tired, frayed way. Telling him not to play around with her:
I know you're Nat Hamlin, she said. Leaning toward him,
fingertips clutching hard into the bones of his right wrist. A
baffling sensation in the top of his skull. A sort of intrusion.
A tickling. A mild glow of heat. Along with it a disturbing
blurring of identity, a doubling of self. The first surfacing of
Hamlin, only he hadn't known that then. Clinging to the side
of the building with one hand and making a little shooing
gesture at her with the other. Go on. Away. Out of my life.
Whoever you were, there's no room now.

And he hurried on toward the network office. Block after
block, and there it was. Grim black tower. Windowless walls.
He didn't go in, not now, certainly not now. Fredericks.
Griswold. Loftus. My colleagues. Smith or Jones. The Hamlin
over there. One of my favorites, Griswold said. A gift from my
first wife, ten years back, when Hamlin was still an unknown.
Coughing. If you don't mind – some cold water. Forgive me.
You know, it's only my first day on the outside. The strain,
the tension. No, we'll keep away from the network office
tonight.

And here, the corner of Broadway and 227th, northeast

side. Where he met her on a Monday evening. Pacing in a taut little circle. A self-contained zone of tension on the busy street. Looking at him in mingled amazement and delight. Color stippling her cheeks. Eyes fluttering: she's scared of me, he realized. Oh, Nat, thank God you came! No, he said, let's get this established once and for all. My name's Paul Macy. What do you want? We can't talk here, she said. Not in the middle of a crowd. Where, then? Your place? He shook his head. Absolutely not. Mine, then. We can be there in fifteen minutes. But everything's filthy, she said, and he said, What about a restaurant? There's a people's restaurant two blocks from here, she said. I've been having lunch at it a lot. You know it? He didn't. We could go there, she said. Yes.

I could go there again, too. Now. Now. The sudden call of hunger. Two blocks. Macy walked quickly. One shoulder higher than the other. Reaching the restaurant. A spartan socialist front, a plain glass window. Within, a deep narrow room with tarnishing brass walls and a bunch of sputtering defective light-loops threaded through the thatchwork ceiling. All right. Let's get some dinner. In here he had dinner with Lissa that night. Standing up, turning, walking away from her. And her scream. No! Come back! Paul! Paul! *Nat!* Her words leaping across the gulf between them like a flight of arrows. Six direct hits. St Sebastian stumbling in the restaurant aisle. His brain on fire. And Hamlin's voice, quite distinct, from a point just above his left shoulder. – How could you walk out on her like that, you snotty creep.

So here is where he first manifested himself. Very well. Let's go in.

He thought he was hungry, and loaded his tray accordingly, stacking it with meat and vegetables and rolls and more. But when he had taken a seat at one of the long tables he found he had no desire for food. He nibbled a little. He let his eyes drift out of focus and disconnected himself from reality. How restful this is. I could sit here forever. But someone was touching his shoulder. A quick impertinent prod, a withdrawal, another prod. Why can't people leave me alone? One of Gomez' flunkies, maybe. If I pay no attention perhaps he'll go away. He tried to sink deeper into disconnection. Another prod, more insistent. A hoarse harsh voice. 'You. Hey, you, will you look at me a second? You stoned or something?' Reluctantly Macy let himself slip back into focus. A fat, stale-smelling girl in a gray dress stood beside him. Her face was as flat as a Mongol's, but her skin was pasty white, her eyes did not slant. She said, 'There's a girl upstairs needs some help from you. You're the one.'

'Upstairs? Girl?'

'You, yes. I know you. You were in here two, three weeks ago with that girl, that redhead, that Lisa. You're the one who collapsed, fell flat on your sniffer, we had to carry you out, me and the redhead and the cabdriver. Lisa, her name is.'

'Lissa,' Macy corrected, blinking.

'Lisa, Lissa, I don't know. Look, she helped you, now you help her.'

A floating film of memory. Standing by the restaurant's credit console at the end of the counter that other time, authorizing it to charge his account ten dollars for his dinner. And a fat flat-faced girl waiting behind him in line snorting contemptuously. Was he paying too much? Too little? This girl.

'Where is she?' Macy asked.

'I told you. Upstairs. She came in yesterday, she was crying a lot, a big fuss. Passed out, finally. We got her a room and she's still there. Won't eat. Won't talk. You must know her, so you go look after her.'

'But where? Upstairs, you said.'

'The people's co-op, moron,' the fat girl said. 'Where else? Where else do you think?' And strode away.

FOURTEEN

The people's co-op, moron. Where else? Leaving his laden
tray, he went outside and looked around. Of course: there
was a hotel associated with the restaurant. Or vice-versa.
They shared the building. Stark green-tiled facade; a separate
entrance for the hotel, escalator going up, the office on the
second floor. In a wide low empty lobby, much too brightly
lit, a directory screen offered sketchy information about the
present residents of the building. Macy, frowning, checked
the *M* column first. Moore, Lissa? Not there. He glanced at
L and, yes, there was an entry for 'Lisa,' nothing else, no
surname, checked in June 3, eleven p.m., room 1114. There's
a girl upstairs needs some help from you. And how to get
upstairs?

A door to his left opened and a blind man came in, moving
confidently and swiftly around table and chairs and other
obstacles. The sonar mounted in his headband going boing
boing boing. Tan jacket, yellow pants, fleshy face, eyes half-
closed showing only the whites. 'Excuse me,' Macy said,
'can you tell me where the liftshaft is?' The blind man,
without stopping, pointed over his right shoulder and said,
'Elevator's back there,' and disappeared through a door to
Macy's right. Macy went through the other door. Elevator.
Eleventh floor. Up.

Room 1114.

No fancy communication or scanning devices here, just a
plain wooden door. He knocked and got no response from
within. He knocked again. 'Lissa? It's me, Paul.' Knock knock.
Silence. As he stood there, puzzled, a girl stepped out of the
room across the hall, a thin bony girl, naked and casual about
it, towel draped over one shoulder, ribs prominent, hipbones
sharp, small pointed breasts. 'Looking for Lisa?' she asked, and
when Macy nodded the girl said, 'She's in there. Go on in.'

'I knocked. She didn't answer.'

'No, she won't answer. Just go on in.'

'The door –'

'No locks *here*, brother.' The girl winked and sauntered down the hall. Her backbone standing sharply out against her skin. Pushing open another door; sound of water running, from within; the showerroom, Macy guessed. No locks here, brother. Okay. He tried the door of room 1114 and found that it was indeed open.

'Lissa?' he said.

This was what he imagined a jail cell would be like. His room at the Rehab Center had been palatial by comparison. A low narrow bed – a cot, really. A flimsy green plastic chair. A small squat brown dresser. A chipped yellow-white washstand. A grimy sliver of window. Bare flooring; cruel naked lights. Lissa was naked too, slouched on the bed, knees up, arms locked across them. She looked gaunt, almost frail, as if she had dropped eight or ten pounds in the thirty-six hours since he last had seen her. Her hair was a knotted mess and her eyes were red and raw. The room reeked of sweat. Her clothes lay in a heap near the window; the closet, its door ajar, was empty; near the washstand stood the big dilapidated green suitcase that she had used in bringing her things from her apartment to his, and from his place to here. Its sides bulged: she hadn't bothered to unpack. As he entered, her head moved slowly in his direction, and she looked at him and did not look. And her head moved back so that she stared again at the brown dresser.

Macy walked past the foot of the bed and tried to open the window, but there was no way of doing it. He spoke her name again; she gave no sign of hearing him. Crouching beside her, he took one of her feet in his hand, lifted it six inches, watched it drop heavily back, and slid the hand upward to the meaty part of her calf. Her skin blazed. Fever was consuming her. His hand went to her thigh. His fingertips dug in high, just below the curling auburn thatch, but she took no notice. He shook her thigh. Nothing. He stroked her breasts, he cupped one. Nothing. He rubbed the tip of his thumb back and forth over the nipple. Zero. He fanned his fingers in front of her eyes. She blinked once, absently. 'Lissa?' he said a third time. She was gone, lost, cocooned in introspection. Beyond his reach. Anyone could do anything to her now and probably she wouldn't react. How to break through? No way. No way.

He stood by the window with his back to her.

A long time later she said, voice thin and distant, 'The talking in my head was driving me crazy. Bouncing off the walls. I couldn't stay.'

He swung around to face her. She was wholly expressionless. Still staring at the dresser. Her words might have been those of a ventriloquist. 'You didn't need to run away,' he said. 'I was trying to help you.'

'You had no help to give. And I couldn't help you either. We were destroying each other.'

'No.'

'I opened you to Hamlin.'

'It doesn't matter. We needed each other.'

'I needed to go,' she said. 'I was choking there, I had to get out. So I went. So I came here.'

'Why?'

'To hide. To rest.' Murmured words, windsounds. 'Go away, now. I have the voices again. The pressure building up. Can't you feel it? The pressure. The pressure building up.'

He caught her hand in his. The fever raging. The muscles of her arm entirely limp. Like holding a length of rope. 'You're ill, Lissa, physically ill. Let me get a doctor for you.' He wasn't sure she heard him. Floating away from him again. 'I'll call a doctor,' he said. 'All right.'

Her eyes like glass spheres. She was adrift, heading out on the tide. He shook her, he fondled her, he talked to her. Zero. Talked *at* her. An urgent torrent. Flooding her with words, trying to talk her back into some sort of contact with him. Come on, snap out of it. Telling her of love, of need, of second starts, of new tomorrows, of shared anguishes, of an end to self-pity and vulnerability. Anything. Inspirational words. The old sunny platitudes. Why not tell her such things? To reach her. We'll go far away and try again, you and me, me and you. A whole world of happiness. Come, Lissa. Come.

Knowing that he is losing her, moment by moment. Has lost her. A million million miles away on her planetoid of ice. Yet he continued. Striving to pour his frantic energy into her, to fill her with enough stamina to return and rise. Visions of hope, daydreams of health and joy. A shimmering rainbow curving across the room from door to window. On and on and on, his voice growing rasping and edgy and desperate, Lissa paying no attention; the ice now entombed her, she could only dimly be seen within the sparkling wall of the glacier. He was tiring. Why go on? She didn't want to hear this.

He became angry with her, hostile, irritated, begrudging her the resources of strength she was draining from him. And for what, this tremendous effort of his? What good? Everything he gave her the fever ate. She was the conduit through which his energies rushed uselessly into a shoreless sea. Now there was loud in him the voice of temptation, telling him to leave her while he still could, to forget her, to make his own difficult way through the world without dragging her on his back.

You owe her nothing. You have troubles of your own, many of them caused by her. Why this quixotic desire to rescue and repair her? Let her sink. Let her fry. Let her freeze. Let her stew. Go. She told you to go: therefore go. This shabby burned-out girl with her implausible affliction, her ESP. Her chattering angry voices. The necklace of grime on her chest. Vacant glassy eyes. Go.

To this Macy answered, not releasing Lissa's sweating palm, that he would hear no counsel of defeat, nor would he abandon her now. He went on urging her to come out of her trance; he pleaded with her not to give up. Here I am: take strength from me. Let me be your shield and your support. He conceived the notion of hauling her from the bed and carrying her out of the room, to that shower in the hall, where he would let the cool cleansing water sluice her from her lethargy. He naked beside her as the purifying deluge descended.

Up, then. To the shower. Grunting, he seized her by the

shoulders, but her body was a dead weight and there was suddenly a terrific fiery bolus in his chest and a band of hot steel across his forehead, and he realized that she had already drained too much from him, that he was no longer strong enough to lift her. He let her fall back and collapsed across her, panting. His eyes were wet, he knew not whether from pain or despair or frustration or rage. Saving her was beyond him. He was too weak. He was too weary. He was too empty. He had given all he could give, and it had not been enough, and now he could give no more. *Perhaps if I rest. Perhaps in a little while.*

But he knew he was being foolish. He was drained. He would not soon recover. And now, too, he knew who it was who had tempted him to turn back before reaching this point, for he felt the presence hot within him, rising, expanding, glowing, the dark presence of his other self coming forth from his hidden lair, whispering wordlessly to him, crooning, inviting him to yield.

Shall I fight him? Can I fight him? I must. I must. Macy readied himself to resist. Searching the corridors of his soul for forgotten reservoirs of strength. But he feared it was too late, that the takeover was already beginning. Already he felt a familiar sensation, a prickling at the back of his neck, a tingling, a mild stiffening of the skin. The unseen fingers were at work, stroking the lobes of his brain, caressing the prominences and corrugations. Inviting him to yield. *Yes. Yes.* Temptation. An end to turmoil and torment. *No*, Macy said, *I will not let you have me*.

He attempted to get to his feet, but the best he could manage was to roll heavily free of Lissa and lie beside her. She seemed to be unconscious. A sleep beyond all dreams. *How peaceful she looks. And I could sleep that sleep.* Come, said the voiceless voice in wordless words, let me enfold you, let me supplant you. Let there no longer be struggle between us. Give way to me. *No! You will not have me!*

And Macy reached out toward Lissa, seeking her, asking alliance. *The two of us against him. We can strike at him, we*

can destroy him. Lissa was a million million miles away. Her
planetoid of ice. The cold light of the distant sun dancing on
the walls of the glacier. The tempter said, You see, there is no
help to be had from her. Now is the time. Step aside for me.
Be realistic, Macy, be realistic! Macy attempted to be realistic.
Where shall I go? How shall I fight? Who shall I be? And saw
how little hope there was. He could not save himself. He had
not been designed for this sort of stress. They had sent him
on this second trip laden with an impossible burden, and was
it then any surprise that the trip was a bummer? Let us end
it. Let us fight no more. He would rest, he would close himself
to struggling and hoping, he would surrender. The odds were
too high against him. Outside waited Gomez, the van, the long
cold needles, the drugs, all the machinery of deconstruction.
Inside lurked Hamlin. Beside him lay this shattered girl. All
right. I yield. I will fight no more.

  – Then get out of the way, Hamlin said, and let me become
you.

The mixing of selves was beginning. The dissolving, the
blending. Paul Hamlin. Nat Macy, I am he. He is I. Mael-
strom. Blinded by churning debris raining upon them out of
their entangled pasts. A holocaust of dislocated events. As we
dissolve into one another. Jeanie Grossman beneath the snows
of Mount Rainier. And the girl with the long straight silken
golden hair. Look, all through history girls have been posing
for famous artists. Let me show you these charts, ma'am,
explaining the special advantages of our encyclopedia. Why
should you go to art school? My boy, you are already a
master! Members of the class of '93, welcome to the UCLA
campus. Hey, no, officer! Put that stunner down! I surrender,
damn you, I surrender! I'll go peacefully! It isn't a matter
of opinion, it's a matter of voltage thresholds. A voltage
doesn't lie. Amperes don't have opinions. Resistances don't
fuck around with you for sly tactical reasons. We're dealing
in objective facts, and the objective facts tell me that Nat
Hamlin has been wiped out. One-and-two-and-*one*-and-two.
Proudly down the goddam street. Your new career. Your new

life. *Shqkm. Vtpkp.* Smss! Grgg! Will the defendant please rise. Nathaniel James Hamlin you have heard the verdict of your peers. Don't play around with me. I know you're Nat Hamlin. You're looking good, Nat. THE TORMENTS OF FAME. THE DAY THE MUSEUM BOUGHT EVERYTHING. MY NAME IS LISSA. No! Come back! Paul! Paul! *Nat!* Paul Hamlin. Nat Macy. We are becoming one. We are dissolving each into each. I will be you and you will be nothing.

And there will be peace at last.

Lissa! *LISSA!*

Abruptly the sky darkened and without warning bolts of lightning flashed and terrible thunder came and a sword swept down, trailing streamers of fire, to cleave the hemispheres of his brain one from the other. Between the two there loomed an unbridgeable gap, and on the far side of it Macy beheld Hamlin, stunned, dazed, wandering through a charred and blasted meadow as lightning struck all about him. That sudden fierce blow had severed all connection between them just at the instant of merger. I am Paul Macy. He is Nat Hamlin. And the crashing of the lightning. Blinding white streaks splitting the sky. Is that Lissa up there? Yes. Yes. Yes. Yes. She hurls the bolts. Crash! Crash! Hamlin tries to dodge. Across the great gulf drifts the scent of burning flesh. He is wounded. He moves more slowly. Crash! She has hemmed him in by a zone of fire on every side. Now Hamlin offers resistance. He shakes his fist; he shouts; he seizes her bolts and hurls them back at her. But each act of defiance brings redoubled furies out of the heavens. Her aim is deadly. Lightning spears his toes. Lightning licks at his heels. He hops. He dances. He screams in rage and then in pain. His arm is blackened by a bolt; he can no longer return her shafts. Now he writhes on the smouldering earth; now he shrieks for mercy. But there will be no mercy. Lissa is the avenging goddess. Hamlin will be destroyed.

But what's this? In the moment of triumph she tires. She weakens. The bolts lose intensity, and Hamlin still lives! He

regains strength. She cries out for help. *Paul, Paul, Paul,* Paul.
Yes, he replies, from his place beyond the zone of combat.
Hamlin has risen. He is hideously disfigured, he is maimed
and ruined, but yet there is demonic power in him, and now
he lashes back at her, trying to bring her tumbling down to his
own level. Crackling energies climb the sky. Help me, Paul!

And Macy opens himself to her, letting her take from him
whatever she must have, and he arms her so that she can
return to the attack. Again her lightnings flash. Again Hamlin
howls. His thrusts are beaten back. He cannot fight on. He
falls. A bolt pierces his back. He twists and coils in frightful
convulsions. Lissa transfixes him again. Again. He is burning.
He is dying. The odor of charred flesh on the wind. The sky is
a sheet of white fire. She is spending herself, emptying herself,
to eradicate him. She is cutting him to pieces.

Hamlin still moves, but now only in the random galvanic
twitches of the dead. The meadow is a blazing pyre. He burns.
He burns. He dwindles. He is gone. The sky grows still. Lissa
can no longer be seen. A strange silence has come; a gentle
cooling rain begins to fall. The air is sweet. The clouds part; the
rain ends; the soft sunlight returns. There is no gulf between
the regions of the brain. Macy crosses over. He sees no trace
of Hamlin but only a dark place on the ground, a blackened
scar in the grass, and quickly the grass grows to hide it, tall
green blades moving swiftly in, sprouting tender new shoots
that rise and meet, and soon there is no sign of destruction
anywhere, although Macy knows that beneath the graceful
grassy carpet one might find a layer of ash, if one chose to
excavate. He walks away from that place. He is utterly alone.
Lissa? he calls. Lissa? But there is no reply. Silence governs.
He is utterly alone.

After a time he sat up and got carefully to his feet. The
sense of being alone remained with him. There was a faint
throbbing in his head, of the sort one might feel if one were
transported suddenly from the heart of some great city to the
eerie soundless wastelands of the polar plateau, but otherwise

he was aware of no aftereffects of the battle. Except one. Hamlin was gone from him. That much was certain: Hamlin was gone.

He looked at Lissa. She lay as before, limp, glassy-eyed, self-isolated. Her bare skin glistened with sweat. The feverish look had left her, and, touching her side, he found that she was indeed cooler. Not only the fever had departed from her, though. For the first time since he had known her, Macy was unable to detect that look of terrible strain in her features, that expression of barely suppressed despair. She was calm. Her inner storms, as well as his, were over. But her calmness was of a frightening sort. She seemed vacant, almost entirely absent.

'Lissa?' he said. 'Can you hear me?'

'Lis – Lis –'

'Lissa.'

'Lissa,' he said. 'Lissa is you.'

'Lissa is you.' Her voice was high, childish, fluting, toneless.

'No. No. I'm Paul. You're Lissa.'

'I'm Paul. You're Lissa.'

He sat beside her. He took her hands in his. Her fingers were very cold. Her eyes closed a moment; then the lids fluttered and she opened them and looked at him in a sunny, uncomprehending way, and she smiled. He said, 'You've burned yourself out, haven't you? You just used up everything you had. To save me. And now there's nothing left but a husk.'

'Husk.'

'Is the ESP gone too, I wonder? Can you still hear the voices? Do you hear them, Lissa?'

'Voices? Do you. Hear them. Lissa.'

'You don't, do you? Not any more.'

'No,' she said unexpectedly. 'I don't hear. Anything.'

Her response startled him. 'You can understand me now? The voices are really gone?'

A smile. A fluttering of the eyelids. A babyish giggle. 'The.

Voices. Are. Really. Gone.' She had slipped away from him once more.

He searched the room for a telephone. None. He went to the door and looked into the hall. A phone out there, yes. Someone using it. Chattering away. All right, I'll wait. A few minutes. And then phone Gomez. Send your van, I'll tell him. Manhattan North People's Co-op, and hurry. Not for me. For her, for Lissa. Yes. Burned out, hardly knows her own name. But there's something still intact down deep inside her. Not much, but enough, maybe, for you to work with, Gomez. No, you don't have to bother with me. I'm okay. It's over. Hamlin's gone, obliterated for keeps, gone, really gone. A total deconstruct. But the girl. Can you fix her, Gomez? Can you put her back together? It won't be like a reconstruct, exactly. You won't have to pour a new identity into an old body, just put an old identity back where it belongs. Okay, Gomez? You'll do it? Good. Good. And how long will it take? Five months, six, a year? Whatever. Just do it.

Five months. Six. November. December. Macy saw himself waiting at the main building of the Rehab Center. Snow on the ground, the branches of the trees heavy with whiteness, the sky a wintry blue. And Lissa, renewed, repaired, coming toward him out of the inner wing. No longer a telepath. A brand-new Lissa, stripped of her gift and of her torment. Uncertain of herself as she goes forth to face the world. Hello, he'll say. Hello, she'll say. An awkward little kiss. Button up, he'll tell her, it's cold. I've got a car. She'll look worried. Are we going into the city? she'll ask. My first day out. I'm nervous. You know what it's like, Paul, coming out. Sure, he'll say, I know just what it's like. But you'll be all right. New people, new lives. The second trip. Paul and Lissa, Lissa and Paul. Minus our old friend Nat. A great artist has gone from the world. How quiet it is inside my head. Five months. Six. November. December. Lissa?

She was giggling softly, and her hands were exploring her body, discovering this and that as a baby might. Lightly he touched her cheek. She wriggled in pleasure. You wait, he

said. Gomez will fix you better than you were before. Macy
peered into the hall again. The phone still busy. Come on, get
off the line, get off, get off! He didn't say it. He stood in the
doorway, waiting to make his call, half expecting Hamlin to
rise from somewhere, but Hamlin did not arise. Gone. Gone.
My other self, my dark twin. He has left the world, and I have
his place. Macy almost felt guilty about it. The merest flicker
of regret. Farewell to you, Nat, a long farewell to Mr Hyde.
And I will go on through life without you. Wearing your skin,
wearing your face. I am you, Nat, and you are nothing.

   Macy looked back at Lissa. She was drooling. As I must have
drooled, he thought. Four years ago when I was very new. He
went to her and mopped her chin. It's all right, he said to her
without bothering to speak aloud. December isn't so far away.
And then hello, and then we start again. Two ordinary people.
Trip two, yours, mine. The second trip. The good one, maybe.
From the hall came the click of the receiver. The phone was
free at last. He went out to call Gomez.

Dying Inside

For B and T and C and me –
we sweated it out

ONE

So, then, I have to go downtown to the University and forage for dollars again. It doesn't take much cash to keep me going – $200 a month will do nicely – but I'm running low, and I don't dare try to borrow from my sister again. The students will shortly be needing their first term papers of the semester; that's always a steady business. The weary, eroding brain of David Selig is once more for hire. I should be able to pick up $75 worth of work on this lovely golden October morning. The air is crisp and clear. A high-pressure system covers New York City, banishing humidity and haze. In such weather my fading powers still flourish. Let us go then, you and I, when the morning is spread out against the sky. To the Broadway-IRT subway. Have your tokens ready, please.

You and I. To whom do I refer? I'm heading downtown alone, after all. *You and I.*

Why, of course I refer to myself and to that creature which lives within me, skulking in its spongy lair and spying on unsuspecting mortals. That sneaky monster within me, that ailing monster, dying even more swiftly than I. Yeats once wrote a dialog of self and soul; why then shouldn't Selig, who is divided against himself in a way poor goofy Yeats could never have understood, speak of his unique and perishable gift as though it were some encapsulated intruder lodged in his skull? Why not? Let us go then, you and I. Down the hall. Push the button. Into the elevator. There is a stink of garlic in it. These peasants, these swarming Puerto Ricans, they leave their emphatic smells everywhere. My neighbors. I love them. Down. Down.

It is 10.43 a.m., Eastern Daylight Savings Time. The current temperature reading in Central Park is 57°. The humidity

stands at 29% and the barometer is 30.30 and falling, with
the wind northeast at 11 miles per hour. The forecast is for
fair skies and sunny weather today, tonight, and tomorrow,
with the highs in the low to middle 60's. The chance of
precipitation is zero today and 10% tomorrow. Air quality
level is rated good. David Selig is 41 and counting. Slightly
above medium height, he has the lean figure of a bachelor
accustomed to his own meager cooking, and his customary
facial expression is a mild, puzzled frown. He blinks a lot. In his
faded blue denim jacket, heavy-duty boots, and 1969-vintage
striped bells he presents a superficially youthful appearance,
at least from the neck down; but in fact he looks like some
sort of refugee from an illicit research laboratory where the
balding, furrowed heads of anguished middle-aged men are
grafted to the reluctant bodies of adolescent boys. How did
this happen to him? At what point did his face and scalp begin
to grow old? The dangling cables of the elevator hurl shrieks
of mocking laughter at him as he descends from his two-room
refuge on the twelfth floor. He wonders if those rusty cables
might be even older than he is. He is of the 1935 vintage. This
housing project, he suspects, might date from 1933 or 1934.
The Hon. Fiorello H. LaGuardia, Mayor. Though perhaps it's
younger – just immediately pre-war, say. (Do you remember
1940, Duvid? That was the year we took you to the World's
Fair. This is the trylon, that's the perisphere.) Anyway the
buildings are getting old. What isn't?

The elevator halts grindingly at the 7th floor. Even before
the scarred door opens I detect a quick mental flutter of female
Hispanic vitality dancing through the girders. Of course, the
odds are overwhelming that the summoner of the elevator is
a young Puerto Rican wife – the house is full of them, the husbands are away at work at this time of day – but all the same I'm
pretty certain that I'm reading her psychic emanations and not
just playing the hunches. Sure enough. She is short, swarthy,
maybe about 23 years old, and very pregnant. I can pick up
the double neural output clearly: the quicksilver darting of her
shallow, sensual mind and the furry, blurry thumpings of the

fetus, about six months old, sealed within her hard bulging body. She is flat-faced and broad-hipped, with little glossy eyes and a thin, pinched mouth. A second child, a dirty girl of about two, clutches her mother's thumb. The babe giggles up at me and the woman favors me with a brief, suspicious smile as they enter the elevator.

They stand with their backs toward me. Dense silence. *Buenos dias, señora.* Nice day, isn't it, ma'am? What a lovely little child. But I remain mute. I don't know her; she looks just like all the others who live in this project, and even her cerebral output is standard stuff, unindividuated, indistinguishable: vague thoughts of plantains and rice, this week's lottery results, and tonight's television highlights. She is a dull bitch but she is human and I love her. What's her name? Maybe it's Mrs Altagracia Morales. Mrs Amantina Figueroa. Mrs Filomena Mercado. I love their names. Pure poetry. I grew up with plump clumping girls named Sondra Wiener, Beverly Schwartz, Sheila Weisbard. Ma'am, can you possibly be Mrs Inocencia Fernandez? Mrs Clodomira Espinosa? Mrs Bonifacia Colon? Perhaps Mrs Esperanza Dominguez. Esperanza. Esperanza. I love you, Esperanza springs eternal in the human breast. (I was there last Christmas for the bullfights. Esperanza Springs, New Mexico; I stayed at the Holiday Inn. No, I'm kidding.) Ground floor. Nimbly I step forward to hold the door open. The lovely stolid pregnant chiquita doesn't smile at me as she exits.

To the subway now, hippity-hop, one long block away. This far uptown the tracks are still elevated. I sprint up the cracking, peeling staircase and arrive at the station level hardly winded at all. The results of clean living, I guess. Simple diet, no smoking, not much drinking, no acid or mesc, no speed. The station, at this hour, is practically deserted. But in a moment I hear the wailing of onrushing wheels, metal on metal, and simultaneously I pick up the blasting impact of a sudden phalanx of minds all rushing toward me at once out of the north, packed aboard the five or six cars of the oncoming train. The compressed souls of those passengers from a single inchoate mass, pressing insistently against me. They quiver like trembling jellylike bites of plankton squeezed brutally together in some oceanographer's net, creating one complex organism in which the separate identities of all are lost. As the train glides into the station I am able to pick up isolated blurts and squeaks of discrete selfhood: a fierce jab of desire, a squawk of hatred, a pang of regret, a sudden purposeful inner mumbling, rising from the confusing totality the way odd little scraps and stabs of melody rise from the murky orchestral smear of a Mahler symphony. The power is deceptively strong in me today. I'm picking up plenty. This is the strongest it's been in weeks. Surely the low humidity is a factor. But I'm not deceived into thinking that the decline in my ability has been checked. When I first began to lose my hair, there was a happy period when the process of erosion seemed to halt and reverse itself, when new patches of fine dark floss began to sprout on my denuded forehead. But after an initial freshet of hope I took a more realistic view: this was no miraculous reforestation but only a twitch of the hormones, a temporary cessation of decay, not to be relied upon. And in time my hairline resumed its retreat. So too in this instance. When one knows that something is dying inside one, one learns not to put much trust in the random vitalities of the fleeting moment. Today the power is strong yet tomorrow I may hear nothing but distant tantalizing murmurs.

I find a seat in the corner of the second car, open my book, and wait out the ride downtown. I am reading Beckett again, *Malone Dies*; it plays nicely to my prevailing mood, which as you have noticed is one of self-pity. *My time is limited. It is thence that one fine day, when all nature smiles and shines, the rack lets loose its black unforgettable cohorts and sweeps away the blue for ever. My situation is truly delicate. What fine things, what momentous things, I am going to miss through fear, fear of falling back into the old error, fear of not finishing in time, fear of revelling, for the last time, in a last outpouring of misery, impotence and hate. The forms are many in which the unchanging seeks relief from its formlessness.* Ah yes, the good Samuel, always ready with a word or two of bleak comfort.

Somewhere about 180th Street I look up and see a girl sitting diagonally opposite me and apparently studying me. She is in her very early twenties, attractive in a sallow way, with long legs, decent breasts, a bush of auburn hair. She has a book too – the paperback of *Ulysses*, I recognize the cover – but it lies neglected on her lap. Is she interested in me? I am not reading her mind; when I entered the train I automatically stopped my inputs down to the minimum, a trick I learned when I was a child. If I don't insulate myself against scatter-shot crowd-noises on trains or in other enclosed public places I can't concentrate at all. Without attempting to detect her signals, I speculate on what she's thinking about me, playing a game I often play. *How intelligent he looks . . . He must have suffered a good deal, his face is so much older than his body . . . tenderness in his eyes . . . so sad they look . . . a poet, a scholar . . . I bet he's very passionate . . . pouring all his pent-up love into the physical act, into screwing. . . . What's he reading? Beckett? Yes, a poet, a novelist, he must be . . . maybe somebody famous . . . I mustn't be too aggressive, though. He'll be turned off by pushiness. A shy smile, that'll catch him . . . One thing leads to another . . . I'll invite him up for lunch . . .* Then, to check on the accuracy of my intuitive perceptions, I tune in on her mind. At first there is no signal. My damnable waning powers betraying me again! But then it comes – static, first, as I get the low-level muzzy ruminations of all the passengers around me, and then the clear sweet tone of her soul. She is thinking about a karate class she will attend later this morning on 96th Street. She is in love with her instructor, a brawny pockmarked Japanese. She will see him tonight. Dimly through her mind swims the memory of the taste of sake and the image of his powerful naked body rearing above her. There is nothing in her mind about me. I am simply part of the scenery, like the map of the subway system on the wall above my head. Selig, your egocentricity kills you every time. I note that she does indeed wear a shy smile now, but it is not for me, and when she sees me staring at her the smile vanishes abruptly. I return my attention to my book.

The train treats me to a long sweaty unscheduled halt in the tunnel between stations north of 137th Street; eventually it gets going again and deposits me at 116th Street, Columbia University. I climbed toward the sunlight. I first climbed these stairs a full quarter of a century ago, October '51, a terrified high-school senior with acne and a crew-cut, coming out of Brooklyn for my college entrance interview. Under the bright lights in University Hall. The interviewer terribly poised, mature – why, he must have been 24, 25 years old. They let me into their college, anyway. And then this was my subway station every day, beginning in September '52 and continuing until I finally got away from home and moved up close to the campus. In those days there was an old cast-iron kiosk at street level marking the entrance to the depths; it was positioned between two lanes of traffic, and students, their absent minds full of Kierkegaard and Sophocles and Fitzgerald, were forever stepping in front of cars and getting killed. Now the kiosk is gone and the subway entrances are placed more rationally, on the sidewalks.

I walk along 116th Street. To my right, the broad greensward of South Field; to my left, the shallow steps rising to Low Library. I remember South Field when it was an athletic field in the middle of the campus: brown dirt, basepaths, fence. My freshman year I played softball there. We'd go to the lockers in University Hall to change, and then, wearing sneakers, polo shirts, dingy gray shorts, feeling naked amidst the other students in business suits or ROTC uniforms, we'd sprint down the endless steps to South Field for an hour of outdoor activity. I was good at softball. Not much muscle, but quick reflexes and a good eye, and I had the advantage of knowing what was on the pitcher's mind. He'd stand there thinking, *This guy's too skinny to hit, I'll give him a high fast one*, and I'd be ready for it and bust it out into left field, circling the bases before anyone knew what was happening. Or the other side would try some clumsy bit of strategy like hit-and-run, and I'd move effortlessly over to gather up the grounder and start the double play. Of course it was only softball and my classmates were mostly pudgy dubs who couldn't even run, let alone read minds, but I enjoyed the unfamiliar sensation of being an outstanding athlete and indulged in fantasies of playing shortstop for the Dodgers. The *Brooklyn* Dodgers, remember? In my sophomore year they ripped up South Field and turned it into a fine grassy showplace divided by a paved promenade, in honor of the University's 200th birthday. Which happened in 1954, Christ, so very long ago. I grow old . . . I grow old . . . I shall wear the bottoms of my trousers rolled. The mermaids singing, each to each. I do not think that they will sing to me.

I go up the steps and take a seat about fifteen feet to the left of the bronze statue of Alma Mater. This is my office in fair weather or foul. The students know where to look for me, and when I'm there the word quickly spreads. There are five or six other people who provide the service I provide – impecunious graduate students, mostly, down on their luck – but I'm the quickest and most reliable, and I have an enthusiastic following. Today, though, business gets off to a slow start. I sit for twenty minutes, fidgeting, peering into Beckett, staring at Alma Mater. Some years ago a radical bomber blew a hole in her side, but there's no sign of the damage now. I remember being shocked at the news, and then shocked at being shocked – why should I give a damn about a dumb statue symbolic of a dumb school? That was about 1969, I guess. Back in the Neolithic.

'Mr Selig?'

Big brawny jock looming above me. Colossal shoulders, chubby innocent face. He's deeply embarrassed. He's taking Comp Lit 18 and needs a paper fast, on the novels of Kafka, which he hasn't read. (This is the football season; he's the starting halfback and he's very very busy.) I tell him the terms and he hastily agrees. While he stands there I covertly take a reading of him, getting the measure of his intelligence, his probable vocabulary, his style. He's smarter than he appears. Most of them are. They could write their own papers well enough if they only had the time. I make notes, setting down my quick impressions of him, and he goes away happy. After that, trade is brisk: he sends a fraternity brother, the brother sends a friend, the friend sends one of *his* fraternity brothers, a different fraternity, and the daisy-chain lengthens until by early afternoon I find I've taken on all the work I can handle. I know my capacity. So all is well. I'll eat regularly for two or three weeks, without having to tap my sister's grudging generosity. Judith will be pleased not to hear from me. Home, now, to begin my ghostly tasks. I'm good – glib, earnest, profound in a convincingly sophomoric way – and I can vary my styles. I know my way around literature, psychology, anthropology, philosophy, all the soft subjects. Thank God I kept my own term papers; even after twenty-odd years they can still be mined. I charge $3.50 a typed page, sometimes more if my probing reveals that the client has money. A minimum grade of B+ guaranteed or there's no fee. I've never had to make a refund.

TWO

When he was seven and a half years old and causing a great deal of trouble for his third-grade teacher, they sent little David to the school psychiatrist, Dr Hittner, for an examination. The school was an expensive private one on a quiet leafy street in the Park Slope section of Brooklyn; its orientation was socialist-progressive, with a smarmy pedagogical underpinning of warmed-over Marxism and Freudianism and John Deweyism, and the psychiatrist, a specialist in the disturbances of middle-class children, paid a call every Wednesday afternoon to peer into the soul of the current problem child. Now it was David's turn. His parents gave their consent, of course. They were deeply concerned about his behavior. Everyone agreed that he was a brilliant child: he was extraordinarily precocious, with a reading-comprehension score on the twelve-year-old level, and adults found him almost frighteningly bright. But he was uncontrollable in class, raucous, disrespectful; the schoolwork, hopelessly elementary for him, bored him to desperation; his only friends were the class misfits, whom he persecuted cruelly; most of the children hated him and the teachers feared his unpredictability. One day he had up-ended a hallway fire extinguisher simply to see if it would spray foam as promised. It did. He brought garter snakes to school and let them loose in the auditorium. He mimed classmates and even teachers with vicious accuracy. 'Dr Hittner would just like to have a little chat with you,' his mother told him. 'He's heard you're a very special boy and he'd like to get to know you better.' David resisted, kicking up a great fuss over the psychiatrist's name. 'Hitler? Hitler? I don't want to talk to Hitler!' It was the fall of 1942 and the childish pun was an inevitable one, but he clung to it with irritating stubbornness. Dr Hitler wants to see me. Dr Hitler wants to get to know me.' And his mother said, 'No, Duvid, it's *Hittner, Hittner*, with an *n*.' He went anyway. He strutted into the psychiatrist's office, and when Hittner smiled benignly and said, 'Hello, there, David,' David shot forth a stiff arm and snapped: '*Heil!*'

Dr Hittner chuckled. 'You've got the wrong man,' he said. 'I'm *Hittner*, with an *n*.' Perhaps he had heard such jokes before. He was a huge man with a long horsey face, a wide fleshy mouth, a high curving forehead. Watery blue eyes twinkled behind rimless glasses. His skin was soft and pink and he had a good tangy smell, and he was trying hard to seem friendly and amused and big-brotherly, but David couldn't help picking up the impression that Dr Hittner's brotherliness was just an act. It was something he felt with most adults: they smiled a lot, but inside themselves they were thinking things like, *What a scary brat, what a creepy little kid.* Even his mother and father sometimes thought things like that. He didn't understand why adults said one thing with their faces and another with their minds, but he was accustomed to it. It was something he had come to expect and accept.

'Let's play some games, shall we?' Dr Hittner said.

Out of the vest pocket of his tweed suit he produced a little plastic globe on a metal chain. He showed it to David; then he pulled on the chain and the globe came apart into eight or nine pieces of different colors. 'Watch closely, now, while I put it back together,' said Dr Hittner. His thick fingers expertly reassembled the globe. Then he pulled it apart again and shoved it across the desk toward David. 'Your turn. Can you put it back together too?'

David remembered that the doctor had started by taking the E-shaped white piece and fitting the D-shaped blue piece, but David didn't recall what to do with it; he sat there a moment, puzzled, until Dr Hittner obligingly flashed him a mental image of the proper manipulation. David did it and the rest was easy. A couple of times he got stuck, but he was always able to pull the answer out of the doctor's mind. Why does he think he's testing me, David wondered, if he keeps giving me so many hints? What's he proving? When the globe was intact David handed it back. 'Would you like to keep it?' Dr Hittner asked.

'I don't need it,' David said. But he pocketed it anyway.

They played a few more games. There was one with little cards about the size of playing cards, with drawings of animals and birds and trees and houses on them; David was supposed to arrange them so that they told a story, and then tell the doctor what the story was. He scattered them at random on the desk and made up a story as he went along. 'The duck goes into the forest, you see, and he meets a wolf, so he turns into a frog and jumps over the wolf right into the elephant's mouth, only he escapes out of the elephant's tushie and falls into a lake, and when he comes out he sees the pretty princess here, who says come home and I'll give you gingerbread, but he can read her mind and he sees that she's really a wicked witch, who –' Another game involved slips of paper that had big blue ink-blots on them. 'Do any of these shapes remind you of real things?' the doctor asked. 'Yes,' David said, 'this is an elephant, see, his tail is here and here all crumpled up, and this is his tushie, and this is where he makes pee-pee.' He had already discovered that Dr Hittner became very interested when he talked about tushies or pee-pee, so he gave the doctor plenty to be interested about, finding such things in every ink-blot picture. This seemed a very silly game to David, but apparently it was important to Dr Hittner, who scribbled notes on everything David was saying. David studied Dr Hittner's mind while the psychiatrist wrote things down. Most of the words he picked up were incomprehensible, but he did recognize a few, the grown-up terms for the parts of the body that David's mother had taught him: *penis, vulva, buttocks, rectum*, things like that. Obviously Dr Hittner liked those words a great deal, so David began to use them. 'This is a picture of an eagle that's picking up a little sheep and flying away with it. This is the eagle's penis, down here, and over here is the sheep's rectum. And in the next one there's a man and a woman, and they're both naked, and the man is trying to put his penis inside the woman's vulva only it won't fit, and –' David watched the fountain pen flying over the paper. He grinned at Dr Hittner and turned to the next ink-blot.

Next they played word games. The doctor spoke a word and asked David to say the first word that came into his head. David found it more amusing to say the first word that came into Dr Hittner's head. It took only a fraction of a second to pick it up, and Dr Hittner didn't seem to notice what was going on. The game went like this:

'Father.'
'Penis.'
'Mother.'
'Bed.'
'Baby.'
'Dead.'
'Water.'
'Belly.'
'Tunnel.'
'Shovel.'
'Coffin.'
'Mother.'

Were those the right words to say? Who was the winner in this game? Why did Dr Hittner seem so upset?

Finally they stopped playing games and simply talked.

'You're a very bright little boy,' Dr Hittner said. 'I don't have to worry about spoiling you by telling you that, because you know it already. What do you want to be when you grow up?'

'Nothing.'

'Nothing?'

'I just want to play and read a lot of books and swim.'

'But how will you earn a living?'

'I'll get money from people when I need it.'

'If you find out how, I hope you'll tell me the secret,' the doctor said. 'Are you happy here in school?'

'No.'

'Why not?'

'The teachers are too strict. The work is too dumb. The children don't like me.'

'Do you ever wonder why they don't like you?'

'Because I'm smarter than they are,' David said. 'Because I –' Ooops. Almost said it. *Because I can see what they're thinking.* Mustn't ever tell anyone that. Dr Hittner was waiting for him to finish the sentence. 'Because I make a lot of trouble in class.'

'And why do you do that, David?'

'I don't know. It gives me something to do, I guess.'

'Maybe if you didn't make so much trouble, people would like you more. Don't you want people to like you?'

'I don't care. I don't need it.'

'Everybody needs friends, David.'

'I've got friends.'

'Mrs Fleischer says you don't have many, and that you hit them a lot and make them unhappy. Why do you hit your friends?'

'Because I don't like them. Because they're dumb.'

'Then they aren't really friends, if that's how you feel about them.'

Shrugging, David said, 'I can get along without them. I have fun just being by myself.'

'Are you happy at home?'

'I guess so.'

'You love your mommy and daddy?'

A pause. A feeling of great tension coming out of the doctor's mind. This is an important question. Give the right answer, David. Give him the answer he wants.

'Yes,' David said.

'Do you ever wish you had a baby brother or sister?'

No hesitation now. 'No.'

'Really, no? You like being all alone?'

David nodded. 'The afternoons are the best time. When I'm home from school and there's nobody around. Am I going to have a baby brother or sister?'

Chuckles from the doctor. 'I'm sure I don't know. That would be up to your mommy and daddy, wouldn't it?'

'You won't tell them to get one for me, will you? I mean, you might say to them that it would be good for me to have one, and then they'd go and get one, but I really don't want –' I'm in trouble, David realized suddenly.

'What makes you think I'd tell your parents it would be good for you to have a baby brother or sister?' the doctor asked quietly, not smiling now at all.

'I don't know. It was just an idea.' Which I found inside your head, doctor. And now I want to get out of here. I don't want to talk to you any more. 'Hey, your name isn't really Hittner, is it? With an *n*? I bet I know your real name. *Heil!*'

THREE

I never could send my thoughts into anybody else's head. Even when the power was strongest in me, I couldn't transmit. I could only receive. Maybe there are people around who do have that power, who can transmit thoughts even to those who don't have any special receiving gift, but I wasn't ever one of them. So right there I was condemned to be society's ugliest toad, the eavesdropper, the voyeur. Old English proverb: *He who peeps through a hole may see what will vex him.* Yes. In those years when I was particularly eager to communicate with people, I'd work up fearful sweats trying to plant my thoughts in them. I'd sit in a classroom staring at the back of some girl's head, and think hard at her: *Hello, Annie, this is David Selig calling, do you read me? Do you read me? I love you, Annie. Over. Over and out.* But Annie never read me, and the currents of her mind would roll on like a placid river, undisturbed by the existence of David Selig.

No way, then, for me to speak to other minds, only to spy on them. The way the power manifests itself in me has always been highly variable. I never had much conscious control over it, other than being able to stop down the intensity of input and to do a certain amount of fine tuning; basically I had to take whatever came drifting in. Most often I would pick up a person's surface thoughts, his subvocalizations of the things he's just about to say. These would come to me in a clear conversational manner, exactly as though he *had* said them, except the tone of voice was different, it was plainly not a tone produced by the vocal apparatus. I don't remember any period even in my childhood when I confused spoken communication with mental communication. This ability to read surface thoughts has been fairly consistent throughout: I still can anticipate verbal statements more often than not, especially when I'm with someone who has the habit of rehearsing what he intends to say.

I could also and to some extent still can anticipate immediate intentions, such as the decision to throw a short right jab to the jaw. My way of knowing such things varies. I might pick up a coherent inner verbal statement – *I'm now going to throw a short right jab to his jaw* – or, if the power happens to be working on deeper levels that day, I may simply pick up a series of non-verbal instructions to the muscles, which add up in a fraction of a second to the process of bringing the right arm up for a short jab to the jaw. Call it body language on the telepathic wavelength.

Another thing I've been able to do, though never consist-ently, is tune in to the deepest layers of the mind – where the soul lives, if you will. Where the consciousness lies bathed in a murky soup of indistinct unconscious phenomena. Here lurk hopes, fears, perceptions, purposes, passions, memories, philosophical positions, moral policies, hungers, sorrows, the whole ragbag accumulation of events and attitudes that defines the private self. Ordinarily some of this bleeds through to me even when the most superficial mental contact is established: I can't help getting a certain amount of information about the coloration of the soul. But occasionally – hardly ever, now – I fasten my hooks into the real stuff, the whole person. There's ecstasy in that. There's an electrifying sense of contact. Coupled, of course, with a stabbing, numbing sense of guilt, because of the totality of my voyeurism: how much more of a peeping tom can a person be? Incidentally, the soul speaks a universal language. When I look into the mind of Mrs Esperanza Dominguez, say, and I get a gabble of Spanish out of it, I don't really know what she's thinking, because I don't understand very much Spanish. But if I were to get into the depths of her soul I'd have complete comprehension of anything I picked up. The mind may think in Spanish or Basque or Hungarian or Finnish, but the soul thinks in a languageless language accessible to any prying sneaking freak who comes along to peer at its mysteries.

No matter. It's all going from me now.

FOUR

Paul F. Bruno
Comp Lit 18, Prof. Schmitz
October 15, 1976

THE NOVELS OF KAFKA

In the nightmare world of *The Trial* and *The Castle*, only one thing is certain: that the central figure, significantly known by the initial

K, is doomed to frustration. All else is dreamlike and unsure; courtrooms spring up in tenements, mysterious warders devour one's breakfast, a man thought to be Sordini is actually Sortini. The central fact is certain, though: K will fail in his attempt to attain grace.

The two novels have the same theme and approximately the same basic structure. In both, K seeks for grace and is led to the final realization that it is to be withheld from him. (*The Castle* is unfinished, but its conclusion seems plain.) Kafka brings his heroes into involvement with their situations in opposite ways: in *The Trial*, Joseph K. is passive until he is jolted into the action of the book by the unexpected arrival of the two warders; in *The Castle*, K is first shown as an active character making efforts on his own behalf to reach the mysterious Castle. To be sure, though, he has originally been summoned by the Castle; the action did not originate in himself, and thus he began as passive a character as Joseph K. The distinction is that *The Trial* opens at a point earlier in the time-stream of the action – at the earliest possible point, in fact. *The Castle* follows more closely the ancient rule of beginning *in medias res*, with K already summoned and trying to reach the Castle.

Both books get off to rapid starts. Joseph K. is arrested in the very first sentence of *The Trial*, and his counterpart K arrives at what he thinks is going to be the last stop before the Castle on the first page of that novel. From there, both K's struggle futilely toward their goals (in *The Castle*, simply to get to the top of the hill; in *The Trial*, first to understand the nature of his guilt, and then, despairing of this, to achieve acquittal without understanding). Both actually get farther from their goals with each succeeding action. *The Trial* reaches its peak in the wonderful Cathedral scene, quite likely the most terrifying single sequence in any of Kafka's work, in which K is given to realize that he is guilty and can never be acquitted; the chapter that follows, describing K's execution, is little more than an anticlimactic appendage. *The Castle*, less complete than *The Trial*, lacks the counterpart of the Cathedral scene (perhaps Kafka was unable to devise one?) and thus is artistically less satisfying than the shorter, more intense, more tightly constructed *Trial*.

Despite their surface artlessness, both novels appear to be built on the fundamental threepart structure of the tragic rhythm, labeled by the critic Kenneth Burke as 'purpose, passion, perception'. *The Trial* follows this scheme with greater success than does the incomplete *Castle*; the purpose, to achieve acquittal, is demonstrated through as harrowing a passion as any fictional hero has undergone. Finally, when Joseph K. has been reduced from his original defiant, self-confident attitude to a fearful, timid state of mind, and he is obviously ready to capitulate to the forces of the Court, the time is at hand for the final moment of perception.

The agent used to bring him to the scene of the climax is a classically Kafkaesque figure – the mysterious 'italian colleague who was on his first visit to the town and had influential connexions that made him important to the Bank'. The theme that runs through all of Kafka's work, the impossibility of human communication, is repeated here: though Joseph has spent half the night studying Italian in preparation for the visit, and is half asleep in consequence, the stranger speaks an unknown southern dialect which Joseph cannot understand. Then – a crowning comic touch – the stranger shifts to French, but his French is just as difficult to follow, and his bushy mustache foils Joseph's attempts at lip-reading.

Once he reaches the Cathedral, which he has been asked to show to the Italian (who, as we are not surprised to find, never keeps the date), the tension mounts, Joseph wanders through the building, which is empty, dark, cold, lit only by candles flickering far in the distance, while night inexplicably begins fast to fall outside. Then the priest calls to him, and relates the allegory of the Doorkeeper. It is only when the story is ended that we realize we did not at all understand it; far from being the simple tale it had originally seemed to be, it reveals itself as complex and difficult. Joseph and the priest discuss the story at great length, in the manner of a pair of rabbinical scholars disputing a point in the Talmud. Slowly its implications sink in, and we and Joseph see that the light streaming from the door to the Law will not be visible for him until it is too late.

Structurally the novel is over right here. Joseph has received the final perception that acquittal is impossible; his guilt is established, and he is not yet to receive grace. His quest is ended. The final element of the tragic rhythm, the perception that ends the passion, has been reached.

We know that Kafka planned further chapters showing the progress of Joseph's trial through various later stages, ending in his execution. Kafka's biographer Max Brod says the book could have been prolonged infinitely. This is true, of course; it is inherent in the nature of Joseph K.'s guilt that he could never get to the highest Court, just as the other K could wander for all time without ever reaching the Castle. But structurally the novel ends in the Cathedral; the rest of what Kafka intended would not have added anything essential to Joseph's self-knowledge. The Cathedral scene shows us what we have known since page one: that there is no acquittal. The action concludes with that perception.

The Castle, a much longer and more loosely constructed book, lacks the power of *The Trial*. It rambles. The passion of K is much less clearly defined, and K is a less consistent character, not as interesting psychologically as he is in *The Trial*. Whereas in the earlier book he takes active charge of his case as soon as he realizes his danger, in *The Castle* he quickly becomes the victim of the bureaucracy. The transit of character in *The Trial* is from early passivity to activity back to passive resignation after the epiphany in the Cathedral. In *The Castle* K undergoes no such clearcut changes; he is an active character as the novel opens, but soon is lost in the nightmare maze of the village below the Castle, and sinks deeper and deeper into degradation. Joseph K. is almost an heroic character, while K of *The Castle* is merely a pathetic one.

The two books represent varying attempts at telling the same story, that of the existentially disengaged man who is suddenly involved in a situation from which there is no escape, and who, after making attempts to achieve the grace that will release him from his predicament, succumbs. As they exist today, *The Trial* is unquestionably the greater artistic success, firmly constructed and at all times under the author's technical control. *The Castle*, or rather the fragment of it we have, is potentially the greater novel, however. Everything that was in *The Trial* would have been in *The Castle*, and a great deal more. But, one feels, Kafka abandoned work on *The Castle* because he saw he lacked the resources to carry it through. He could not handle the world of the Castle, with its sweeping background of Brueghelesque country life, with the same assurance as he did the urban world of *The Trial*. And there is a lack of urgency in *The Castle*; we are never too concerned over K's doom because it is inevitable; Joseph K., though, is fighting more tangible forces, and until the end we have the illusion that victory is possible for him. *The Castle*, also, is too ponderous. Like a Mahler symphony, it collapses of its own weight. One wonders if Kafka had in mind some structure enabling him to end *The Castle*. Perhaps he never intended to close the novel at all, but meant to have K wander in ever-widening circles, never arriving at the tragic perception that he can never reach the Castle. Perhaps this is the reason for the comparative formlessness of the later work; Kafka's discovery that the true tragedy of K, his archetypical hero-as-victim figure, lies not in his final perception of the impossibility of attaining grace, but in the fact that he will never reach even as much as that final perception. Here we have the tragic rhythm, a structure found throughout literature, truncated to depict more pointedly the contemporary human condition – a condition so abhorrent to Kafka. Joseph K., who actually reaches a form of grace, thereby attains true tragic stature; K, who simply sinks lower and lower, might symbolize for Kafka the contemporary individual, so crushed by the general tragedy of the times that he is incapable of any tragedy on an individual level. K is a pathetic figure, Joseph K. a tragic one. Joseph K. is a more interesting character, but perhaps it was K whom Kafka understood more deeply. And for K's story no ending is possible, perhaps, save the pointless one of death.

That's not so bad. Six double-spaced typed pages. At $3.50

per, it earns me a cool $21 for less than two hours' work, and it'll earn the brawny halfback, Mr Paul F. Bruno, a sure B+ from Prof. Schmitz. I'm confident of that because the very same paper, differing only in a few minor stylistic flourishes, got me a B from the very demanding Prof. Dupee in May, 1955. Standards are lower today, after two decades of academic inflation. Bruno may even rack up an A – for the Kafka job. It's got just the right quality of earnest intelligence, with the proper undergraduate mixture of sophisticated insight and naïve dogmatism, and Dupee found the writing 'clear and forceful' in '55, according to his note in the margin. All right, now. Time out for a little chow mein, with maybe a side order of eggroll. Then I'll tackle *Odysseus as a Symbol of Society* or perhaps *Aeschylus and the Aristotelian Tragedy*. I can't work from my own old term papers for those, but they shouldn't be too tough to do. Old typewriter, old humbugger, stand me now and ever in good stead.

FIVE

Aldous Huxley thought that evolution has designed our brains to serve as filters, screening out a lot of stuff that's of no real value to us in our daily struggle for bread. Visions, mystical experiences, psi phenomena such as telepathic messages from other brains – all sorts of things along these lines would forever be flooding into us were it not for the action of what Huxley called, in a little book entitled *Heaven and Hell*, 'the cerebral reducing valve.' Thank God for the cerebral reducing valve! If we hadn't evolved it, we'd be distracted all the time by scenes of incredible beauty, by spiritual insights of overwhelming grandeur, and by searing, utterly honest mind-to-mind contact with our fellow human beings. Luckily, the workings of the valve protect us – most of us – from such things, and we are free to go about our daily lives, buying cheap and selling dear.

Of course, some of us seem to be born with defective valves. I mean the artists like Bosch or El Greco, whose eyes did not see the world as it appears to thee and me; I mean the visionary philosophers, the ecstatics and the nirvana-attainers; I mean the miserable freakish flukes who can read the thoughts of others. Mutants, all of us. Genetic sports.

However, Huxley believed that the efficiency of the cerebral reducing valve could be impaired by various artificial means, thus giving ordinary mortals access to the extrasensory data customarily seen only by the chosen few. The psychedelic drugs, he thought, have this effect. Mescaline, he suggested, interferes with the enzyme system that regulates cerebral function, and by so doing 'lowers the efficiency of the brain as an instrument for focusing mind on the problems of life on the surface of our planet. This . . . seems to permit the entry into consciousness of certain classes of mental events, which are normally excluded, because they possess no survival value. Similar intrusions of biologically useless, but aesthetically and sometimes spiritually valuable, material may occur as the result of illness or fatigue; or they may be induced by fasting, or a period of confinement in a place of darkness and complete silence.'

Speaking for himself, David Selig can say very little about the psychedelic drugs. He had only one experience with them, and it wasn't a happy one. That was in the summer of 1968, when he was living with Toni.

Though Huxley thought highly of the psychedelics, he didn't see them as the only gateway to visionary experience. Fasting and physical mortification could get you there also. He wrote of mystics who 'regularly used upon themselves the whip of knotted leather or even of iron wire. These beatings were the equivalent of fairly extensive surgery without anaesthetics, and their effects on the body chemistry of the penitent were considerable. Large quantities of histamine and adrenalin were released while the whip was actually being plied; and when the resulting wounds began to fester (as wounds practically always did before the age of soap), various toxic substances, produced by the decomposition of protein, found their way into the bloodstream. But histamine produces shock, and shock affects the mind no less profoundly than the body. Moreover, large quantities of adrenalin may cause hallucinations, and some of the products of its decomposition are known to induce symptoms resembling those of schizophrenia. As for toxins from wounds – these upset the enzyme systems regulating the brain, and lower its efficiency as an instrument for getting on in a world where the biologically fittest survive. This may explain why the Curé d'Ars used to say that, in the days when he was free to flagellate himself without mercy, God would refuse him nothing. In other words, when remorse, self-loathing, and the fear of hell release adrenalin, when self-inflicted surgery releases adrenalin and histamine, and when infected wounds release decomposed protein into the blood, the efficiency of the cerebral reducing valve is lowered and unfamiliar aspects of Mind-at-Large (including psi phenomena, visions, and, if he is philosophically and ethically prepared for it, mystical experiences) will flow into the ascetic's consciousness.'

Remorse, self-loathing, and the fear of hell. Fasting and prayer, Whips and chains. Festering wounds. Everybody to his own trip, I suppose, and welcome to it. As the power fades in me, as the sacred gift dies, I toy with the idea of trying to revive it by artificial means. Acid, mescaline, psilocybin? I don't think I'd care to go there again. Mortification of the flesh? That seems obsolete to me, like marching off to the Crusades or wearing spats: something that simply isn't appropriate for 1976. I doubt that I could get very deep into flagellation, anyway. What does that leave? Fasting and prayer? I could fast, I suppose. Prayer? To whom? To what? I'd feel like a fool. Dear God, give me my power again. Dear Moses, please help me. Crap on that. Jews don't pray for favors, because they know nobody will answer. What's left, then? Remorse, self-loathing, and the fear of hell? I have those three already, and they do me no good. We must try some other way of goading the power back to life. Invent something new. Flagellation of the mind, perhaps? Yes. I'll try that. I'll get out the metaphorical cudgels and let myself have it. Flagellation of the aching, weakening, throbbing, dissolving mind. The treacherous, hateful mind.

SIX

But why does David Selig want his power to come back? Why not let it fade? It's always been a curse to him, hasn't it? It's cut him off from his fellow men and doomed him to a loveless life. Leave well enough alone, Duvid. Let it fade. Let it fade. On the other hand, without the power, what are you? Without that one faltering unpredictable unsatisfactory means of contact with them, how will you be able to touch them at all? Your power joins you to mankind, for better or for worse, in the only joining you have: you can't bear to surrender it. Admit it. You love it and you despise it, this gift of yours. You dread losing it despite all it's done to you. You'll fight to cling to the last shreds of it, even though you know the struggle's hopeless. Fight on, then. Read Huxley again. Try acid, if you dare. Try flagellation. Try fasting, at least. All right, fasting. I'll skip the chow mein. I'll skip the eggroll. Let's slide a fresh sheet into the typewriter and think about Odysseus as a symbol of society.

SEVEN

Hark to the silvery jangle of the telephone. The hour is late. Who calls? Is it Aldous Huxley from beyond the grave, urging me to have courage? Dr Hittner, with some important questions about making pee-pee? Toni, to tell me she's in the neighborhood with a thousand mikes of dynamite acid and is it okay to come up? Sure. Sure. I stare at the telephone, clueless.

My power even at its height was never equal to the task of penetrating the consciousness of the American Telephone & Telegraph Company. Sighing, I pick up the receiver on the fifth ring and hear the sweet contralto voice of my sister Judith.

'Am I interrupting something?' Typical Judith opening.

'A quiet night at home. I'm ghosting a term paper on *The Odyssey*. Got any bright ideas for me, Jude?'

'You haven't called in two weeks.'

'I was broke. After that scene the last time I didn't want to bring up the subject of money, and lately it's been the only subject I can think of talking about, so I didn't call.'

'Shit,' she says, 'I wasn't angry at you.'

'You sounded mad as hell.'

'I didn't mean any of that stuff. Why did you think I was serious? Just because I was yelling? Do you really believe that I regard you as – as – what did I call you?'

'A shiftless sponger, I think.'

'A shiftless sponger. Shit. I was tense that night, Duv; I had personal problems, and my period was coming on besides. I lost control. I was just shouting the first dumb crap that came into my head, but why did you believe I meant it? You of all people shouldn't have thought I was serious. Since when do you take what people say with their mouths at face value?'

'You were saying it with your head too, Jude.'

'I was?' Her voice is suddenly small and contrite. 'Are you sure?'

'It came through loud and clear.'

'Oh, Jesus, Duv, have a heart! In the heat of the moment I could have been thinking anything. But underneath the anger – *underneath*, Duv – you must have seen that I didn't mean it. That I love you, that I don't want to drive you away from me. You're all I've got, Duv, you and the baby.'

Her love is unpalatable to me, and her sentimentalism is even less to my taste. I say, 'I don't read much of what's underneath any more, Jude. Not much comes through these days. Anyway, look, it isn't worth hassling over. I *am* a shiftless sponger, and I *have* borrowed more from you than you can afford to give.

The black sheep brother feels enough guilt as it is. I'm damned if I'm ever going to ask for money from you again.'

'Guilt? You talk about guilt, when I –'

'No,' I warn her, 'don't you go on a guilt trip now, Jude. Not now.' Her remorse for her past coldness toward me has a flavor even more stinking than her newfound love. 'I don't feel up to assigning the ratio of blames and guilts tonight.'

'All right. All right. Are you okay now for money, though?'

'I told you, I'm ghosting term papers. I'm getting by.'

'Do you want to come over here for dinner tomorrow night?'

'I think I'd better work instead. I've got a lot of papers to write, Jude. It's the busy season.'

'It would be just the two of us. And the kid, of course, but I'll put him to sleep early. Just you and me. We could talk. We've got so much to talk about. Why don't you come over, Duv? You don't need to work all day and all night. I'll cook up something you like. I'll do the spaghetti and hot sauce. Anything. You name it.' She is pleading with me, this icy sister who gave me nothing but hatred for twenty-five years. Come over and I'll be a mama for you, Duv. Come let me be loving, brother.

'Maybe the night after next. I'll call you.'

'No chance for tomorrow?'

'I don't think so,' I say. There is silence. She doesn't want to beg me. Into the sudden screeching silence I say, 'What have you been doing with yourself, Judith? Seeing anyone interesting?'

'Not seeing anyone at all.' A flinty edge to her voice. She is two and a half years into her divorce; she sleeps around a good deal; juices are souring in her soul. She is 31 years old. 'I'm between men right now. Maybe I'm off men altogether. I don't care if I never do any screwing again ever.'

I throttle a somber laugh. 'What happened to that travel agent you were seeing? Mickey?'

'Marty. That was just a gimmick. He got me all over Europe for 10% of the fare. Otherwise I couldn't have afforded to go. I was using him.'

'So?'

'I felt shitty about it. Last month I broke off. I wasn't in love with him. I don't think I even liked him.'

'But you played around with him long enough to get a trip to Europe, first.'

'It didn't cost *him* anything, Duv. I had to go to bed with him; all he had to do was fill out a form. What are you saying, anyway? That I'm a whore?'

'Jude –'

'Okay, I'm a whore. At least I'm trying to go straight for a while. Lots of fresh orange juice and plenty of serious reading. I'm reading Proust now, would you believe that? I just finished *Swann's Way* and tomorrow –'

'I've still got some work to do tonight, Jude.'

'I'm sorry. I didn't mean to intrude. Will you come for dinner this week?'

'I'll think about it. I'll let you know.'

'Why do you hate me so much, Duv?'

'I don't hate you. And we were about to get off the phone, I think.'

'Don't forget to call,' she says. Clutching at straws.

EIGHT

Toni. I should tell you about Toni now.

I lived with Toni for seven weeks, one summer eight years ago. That's as long as I've ever lived with anybody, except my parents and my sister, whom I got away from as soon as I decently could, and myself, whom I can't get away from at all. Toni was one of the two great loves of my life, the other being Kitty. I'll tell you about Kitty some other time.

Can I reconstruct Toni? Let's try it in a few swift strokes. She was 24 that year. A tall coltish girl, five feet six, five feet seven. Slender. Agile and awkward, both at once. Long legs, long arms, thin wrists, thin ankles. Glossy black hair, very straight, cascading to her shoulders. Warm, quick brown eyes, alert and quizzical. A witty, shrewd girl, not really well educated but extraordinarily wise. The face by no means conventionally pretty – too much mouth, too much nose, the cheekbones too high – but yet producing a sexy and highly attractive effect, sufficient to make a lot of heads turn when she enters a room. Full, heavy breasts. I dig busty women. I often need a soft place to rest my tired head. So often so tired. My mother was built 32-A, no cozy pillows there. She couldn't have nursed me if she'd wanted to, which she didn't. (Will I ever forgive her for letting me escape from the womb? Ah, now, Selig, show some filial piety, for God's sake!)

I never looked into Toni's mind except twice, once on the day I met her and once a couple of weeks after that, plus a third time on the day we broke up. The third time was a sheer disastrous accident. The second was more or less an accident too, not quite. Only the first was a deliberate probe. After I realized I loved her I took care never to spy on her head. *He who peeps through a hole may see what will vex him.* A lesson I learned very young. Besides, I didn't want Toni to suspect anything about my power. My curse. I was afraid it might frighten her away.

That summer I was working as an $85-a-week researcher, latest in my infinite series of odd jobs, for a well-known professional writer who was doing an immense book on the political machinations involved in the founding of the State of Israel. Eight hours a day I went through old newspaper files for him in the bowels of Columbia library. Toni was a junior editor for the publishing house that was bringing out his book. I met her one afternoon in late spring at his posh apartment on East End Avenue. I went over there to deliver a bundle of notes on Harry Truman's 1948 campaign speeches and she happened to be there, discussing some cuts to be made in the early chapters. Her beauty stung me. I hadn't been with a woman in months. I automatically assumed she was the writer's mistress – screwing editors, I'm told, is standard practice on certain high levels of the literary profession – but my old peeping-tom instincts quickly gave me the true scoop. I tossed a fast probe at him and found that his mind was a cesspool of frustrated longings for her. He ached for her and she had no yen for him at all, evidently. Next I poked into *her* mind. I sank in, deep, finding myself in warm, rich loam. Quickly got oriented. Stray fragments of autobiography bombarded me, incoherent, non-linear: a divorce, some good sex and some bad sex, college days, a trip to the Caribbean, all swimming around in the usual chaotic way. I got past that fast and checked out what I was after. No, she wasn't sleeping with the writer. Physically he registered absolute zero for her. (Odd. To me he seemed attractive, a romantic and appealing figure, so far as a drearily heterosexual soul like me is able to judge such things.) She didn't even like his writing, I learned. Then, still rummaging around, I learned something else, much more surprising: *I* seemed to be turning her on. Forth from her came the explicit line: *I wonder if he's free tonight.* She looked upon the aging researcher, a venerable 33 and already going thin on top, and did not find him repellent. I was so shaken by that – her dark-eyed glamor, her leggy sexiness, aimed at *me* – that I got the hell out of her head, fast. 'Here's the Truman stuff,' I said to my employer. 'There's more coming in from the Truman Library in Missouri.' We talked a few minutes about the next assignment he had for me, and then I made as though to leave. A quick guarded look at her.

'Wait,' she said. 'We can ride down together. I'm just about done here.'

The man of letters shot me a poisonous envious glance. Oh, God, fired again. But he bade us both civil goodbyes. In the elevator going down we stood apart, Toni in this corner, I in that one, with a quivering wall of tension and yearning separating and uniting us. I had to struggle to keep from reading her; I was afraid, terrified, not of getting the wrong answer but of getting the right one. In the street we stood apart also, dithering a moment. Finally I said I was getting a cab to take me to the Upper West Side – me, a cab, on $85 a week! – and could I drop her off anywhere? She said she lived on 105th and West End. Close enough. When the cab stopped outside her place she invited me up for a drink. Three rooms, indifferently furnished: mostly books, records, scatter-rugs, posters. She went to pour some wine for us and I caught her and pulled her around and kissed her. She trembled against me, or was I the one who was trembling?

Over a bowl of hot-and-sour soup at the Great Shanghai, a little later that evening, she said she'd be moving in a couple of days. The apartment belonged to her current roommate – male – with whom she'd split up just three days before. She had no place to stay. 'I've got only one lousy room,' I said, 'but it has a double bed.' Shy grins, hers, mine. So she moved in. I didn't think she was in love with me, not at all, but I wasn't going to ask. If what she felt for me wasn't love, it was good enough, the best I could hope for; and in the privacy of my own head I could feel love for her. She had needed a port in a storm. I had happened to offer one. If that was all I meant to her now, so be it. So be it. There was time for things to ripen.

We slept very little, our first two weeks. Not that we were screwing all the time, though there was a lot of that; but we *talked*. We were new to each other, which is the best time of any relationship, when there are whole pasts to share, when everything pours out and there's no need to search for things to say. (Not quite everything poured out. The only thing I concealed from her was the central fact of my life, the fact that had shaped my every aspect.) She talked of her marriage – young, at 20, and brief, and empty – and of how she had lived in the three years since its ending – a succession of men, a dip into occultism and Reichian therapy, a newfound dedication to her editing career. Giddy weeks.

Then, our third week. My second peep into her mind. A sweltering June night, with a full moon sending cold illumination through the slatted blinds into our room. She was sitting astride me – her favorite position – and her body, very pale, wore a white glow in the eerie darkness. Her long lean form rearing far above me. Her face half hidden in her own dangling unruly hair. Her eyes closed. Her lips slack. Her breasts, viewed from below, seeming even bigger than they really were. Cleopatra by moonlight. She was rocking and jouncing her way to a private ecstasy, and her beauty and the strangeness of her so overwhelmed me that I could not resist watching her at the moment of climax, watching on all levels, and so I opened the barrier that I had so scrupulously erected, and, just as she was coming, my mind touched a curious finger to her soul and received the full uprushing volcanic intensity of her pleasure. I found no thought of me in her mind. Only sheer animal frenzy, bursting from every nerve. I've seen that in other women, before and after Toni, as they come: they are islands, alone in the void of space, aware only of their bodies and perhaps of that intrusive rigid rod against which they thrust. When pleasure takes them it is a curiously impersonal phenomenon, no matter how titanic its impact. So it was then with Toni. I didn't object; I knew what to expect and I didn't feel cheated or rejected. In fact my joining of souls with her at that awesome moment served to trigger my own coming and to treble its intensity. I lost contact with her then. The upheavals of orgasm shatter the fragile telepathic link. Afterwards I felt a little sleazy at having spied, but not overly guilty about it. How magical a thing it was, after all, to have been with her at that moment. To be aware of her joy not just as mindless spasms of her loins but as jolts of brilliant light flaring across the dark terrain of her soul. An instant of beauty and wonder, an illumination never to be forgotten. But never to be repeated, either. I resolved, once more, to keep our relationship clean and honest. To take no unfair advantage of her. To stay out of her head forever after.

Despite which, I found myself some weeks later entertaining Toni's consciousness a third time. By accident. By damnable abominable accident. Oy, that third time!

That bummer – that disaster –
That catastrophe –

NINE

In the early spring of 1945, when he was ten years old, his
loving mother and father got him a little sister. That was exactly
how they phrased it: his mother, smiling her warmest phony
smile, hugging him, telling him in her best this-is-how-we-talk-
to-bright-children tone, 'Dad and I have a wonderful surprise for
you, Duvid. We're going to get a little sister for you.'

It was no surprise, of course. They had been discussing
it among themselves for months, maybe for years, always
making the fallacious assumption that their son, clever as
he was, didn't understand what they were talking about.
Thinking that he was unable to associate one fragment of
conversation with another, that he was incapable of putting the
proper antecedents to their deliberately vague pronouns, their
torrent of 'it' and 'him'. And, naturally, he had been reading
their minds. In those days the power was sharp and clear;
lying in his bedroom, surrounded by his dog-eared books and
his stamp albums, he could effortlessly tune in on everything
that went on behind the closed doors of theirs, fifty feet away.
It was like an endless radio broadcast without commercials.
He could listen to WJZ, WHN, WEAF, WOR, all the stations
on the dial, but the one he listened to most was WPMS,
Paul-and-Martha-Selig. They had no secrets from him. He had
no shame about spying. Preternaturally adult, privy to all the
privities, he meditated daily on the raw torrid stuff of married
life: the financial anxieties, the moments of sweet undifferentiated lovingness, the moments of guiltily suppressed hatred
for the wearisome eternal spouse, the copulatory joys and
anguishes, the comings together and the fallings apart, the
mysteries of failed orgasms and wilted erections, the intense

and terrifyingly singleminded concentration on the growth
and proper development of The Child. Their minds poured
forth a steady stream of rich yeasty foam and he lapped it all
up. Reading their souls was his game, his toy, his religion, his
revenge. They never suspected he was doing it. That was one
point on which he constantly sought reassurance, anxiously
prying for it, and constantly he was reassured: they didn't
dream his gift existed. They merely thought he was abnormally
intelligent, and never questioned the means by which he
learned so much about so many improbable things. Perhaps
if they had realized the truth, they would have choked him
in his crib. But they had no inkling. He went on comfortably
spying, year after year, his perceptions deepening as he came
to comprehend more and more of the material his parents
unwittingly offered.

He knew that Dr Hittner – baffled, wholly out of his depth
with the strange Selig child – believed it would be better for
everyone if David had a sibling. That was the word he used,
sibling, and David had to fish out the meaning out of Hittner's
head as though out of a dictionary. Sibling: a brother or a
sister. Oh, the treacherous horse-faced bastard! The one thing
young David had asked Hittner not to suggest, and naturally
he had suggested it. But what else could he have expected?
The desirability of siblings had been in Hittner's mind all along,
lying there like a grenade. David, picking his mother's mind
one night, had found the text of a letter from Hittner. *The only
child is an emotionally deprived child. Without the rough-and-tumble
interplay with siblings he has no way of learning the best techniques
of relating to his peers, and he develops a dangerously burdensome
relation with his parents, for whom he becomes a companion instead
of a dependent.* Hittner's universal panacea: lots of siblings. As
though there are no neurotics in big families.

David was aware of his parents' frantic attempts at filling
Hittner's prescription. No time to waste; the boy grows older
all the time, siblingless, lacking each day the means of learning
the best techniques of relating to his peers. And so, night after
night, the poor aging bodies of Paul and Martha Selig grapple

with the problem. They force themselves sweatily onward to self-defeating prodigies of lustfulness, and each month the bad news comes in a rush of blood: there will be no sibling this time. But at last the seed takes root. They said nothing about that to him, ashamed, perhaps, to admit to an eight-year-old that such things as sexual intercourse occurred in their lives. But he knew. He knew why his mother's belly was beginning to bulge and why they still hesitated to explain it to him. He knew, too, that his mother's mysterious 'appendicitis' attack of July, 1944, was actually a miscarriage. He knew why they both wore tragic faces for months afterward. He knew that Martha's doctor had told her that autumn that it really wasn't wise for her to be having babies at the age of 35, that if they were going to insist on a second child the best course was to adopt one. He knew his father's traumatic response to that suggestion: *What, bring into the household a bastard that some shiksa threw away?* Poor old Paul lay tossing awake every night for weeks, not even confessing to his wife why he was so upset, but unknowingly spilling the whole thing to his nosy son. The insecurities, the irrational hostilities. *Why do I have to raise a stranger's brat, just because this psychiatrist says it'll do David some good? What kind of garbage will I be taking into the house? How can I love this child that isn't mine? How can I tell it that it's a Jew when – who knows? – it may have been made by some Irish mick, some Italian bootblack, some carpenter?* All this the all-perceiving David perceives. Finally the elder Selig voices his misgivings, carefully edited, to his wife, saying, Maybe Hittner's wrong, maybe this is just a phase David's going through and another child isn't the right answer at all. Telling her to consider the expense, the changes they'd have to make in their way of life – they're not young, they've grown settled in their ways, a child at this time of their lives, the getting up at four in the morning, the crying, the diapers. And David silently cheering his father on, because who needs this intruder, this sibling, this enemy of the peace? But Martha tearfully fights back, quoting Hittner's letter, reading key passages out of her extensive library on child psychology, offering damning statistics on the incidence of neurosis, maladjustment, bed-wetting, and homosexuality among only children. The old man yields by Christmas. *Okay, okay, we'll adopt, but let's not take just anything, hear? It's got to be Jewish.* Wintry weeks of touring the adoption agencies, pretending all the while to David that these trips to Manhattan are mere innocuous shopping excursions. He wasn't fooled. How could anyone fool this omniscient child? He had only to look behind their foreheads to know that they were shopping for a sibling. His one comfort was the hope that they would fail to find one. This was still wartime: if you couldn't buy a new car, maybe you couldn't get siblings either. For many weeks that appeared to be the case. Not many babies were available, and those that were seemed to have some grave defect: insufficiently Jewish, or too fragile-looking, or too cranky, or of the wrong sex. Some boys were available but Paul and Martha had decided to get David a little sister. Already that limited things considerably, since people tended not to give girls up for adoption as readily as they did boys, but one snowy night in March David detected an ominous note of satisfaction in the mind of his mother, newly returned from yet another shopping trip, and, looking more closely, he realized that the quest was over. She had found a lovely little girl, four months old. The mother, aged 19, was not only certifiably Jewish but even a college girl, described by the agency as 'extremely intelligent'. Not so intelligent, evidently, as to avoid being fertilized by a handsome, young air force captain, also Jewish, while he was home on leave in February, 1944. Though he felt remorse over his carelessness he was unwilling to marry the victim of his lusts, and was now on active duty in the Pacific, where, so far as the girl's parents were concerned, he should only be shot down ten times over. They had forced her to give the child out for adoption. David wondered why Martha hadn't brought the baby home with her that very afternoon, but soon he discovered that several weeks of legal formalities lay ahead, and April was well along before his mother finally announced, 'Dad and I have a wonderful surprise for you, Duvid.'

They named her Judith Hannah Selig, after her adoptive

father's recently deceased mother. David hated her instantly. He had been afraid they were going to move her into his bedroom, but no, they set up her crib in their own room; nevertheless, her crying filled the whole apartment night after night, unending raucous wails. It was incredible how much noise she could emit. Paul and Martha spent practically all their time feeding her or playing with her or changing her diapers, and David didn't mind that very much, for it kept them busy and took some of the pressure off him. But he loathed having Judith around. He saw nothing cute about her pudgy limbs and curly hair and dimpled cheeks. Watching her while she was being changed, he found some academic interest in observing her little pink slit, so alien to his experience; but once he had seen it his curiosity was assuaged. *So they have a slit instead of a thing. Okay, but so what?* In general she was an irritating distraction. He couldn't read properly because of the noise she made, and reading was his one pleasure. The apartment was always full of relatives or friends, paying ceremonial visits to the new baby, and their stupid conventional minds flooded the place with blunt thoughts that impinged like mallets on David's vulnerable consciousness. Now and then he tried to read the baby's mind, but there was nothing in it except vague blurry formless globs of cloudy sensation; he had had more rewarding insights reading the minds of dogs and cats. She didn't appear to have any thoughts. All he could pick up were feelings of hunger, of drowsiness, and of dim orgasmic release as she wet her diaper. About ten days after she arrived, he decided to try to kill her telepathically. While his parents were busy elsewhere he went to their room, peered into his sister's bassinet, and concentrated as hard as he could on draining her unformed mind out of her skull. If only he could manage somehow to suck the spark of intellect from her, to draw her consciousness into himself, to transform her into an empty mindless shell, she would surely die. He sought to sink his hooks into her soul. He stared into her eyes and opened his power wide, taking her entire feeble output and pulling for more. *Come . . . come. . . . your mind is sliding toward me . . . I'm getting it, I'm getting all of it*

. . . zam! I have your whole mind! Unmoved by his conjurations, she continued to gurgle and wave her arms about. He stared more intensely, redoubling the vigor of his concentration. Her smile wavered and vanished. Her brows puckered into a frown. Did she know he was attacking her, or was she merely bothered by the faces he was making? *Come . . . come . . . your mind is sliding toward me . . .*

For a moment he thought he might actually succeed. But then she shot him a look of frosty malevolence, incredibly fierce, truly terrifying coming from an infant, and he backed away, frightened, fearing some sudden counterattack. An instant later she was gurgling again. She had defeated him. He went on hating her, but he never again tried to harm her. She, by the time she was old enough to know what the concept of hatred meant, was well aware of how her brother felt about her. And she hated back. She proved to be a far more efficient hater than he was. Oh, was she ever an expert at hating.

TEN

The subject of this composition is My Very First Acid Trip.

My first and my last, eight years ago. Actually it wasn't my trip at all, but Toni's. D-lysergic acid diethlyamide has never passed through my digestive tract, if truth be told. What I did was hitchhike on Toni's trip. In a sense I'm still a hitchhiker on that trip, that very bad trip. Let me tell you.

This happened in the summer of '68. That summer was a bad trip all in itself. Do you remember '68 at all? That was the year we all woke up to the fact that the whole business was coming apart. I mean American society. That pervasive feeling of decay and imminent collapse, so familiar to us all – it really dates from '68, I think. When the world around us became a metaphor for the process of violent entropic increase that had been going on inside our souls – inside my soul, at any rate – for some time.

That summer Lyndon Baines MacBird was in the White House, just barely, serving out his time after his abdication in March. Bobby Kennedy had finally met the bullet with his name on it, and so had Martin Luther King. Neither killing was any surprise; the only surprise was that they had been so long in coming. The blacks were burning down the cities – back then, it was their *own* neighborhoods they burned, remember? Ordinary everyday people were starting to wear freaky clothes to work, bells and body shirts and mini-miniskirts, and hair was getting longer even for those over 25. It was the year of sideburns and Buffalo Bill mustachios. Gene McCarthy, a Senator from – where? Minnesota? Wisconsin? – was quoting poetry at news conferences as part of his attempt to gain the Democratic presidential nomination, but it was a sure bet that the Democrats would give it to Hubert Horatio Humphrey when they got together for their convention in Chicago. (And wasn't that convention a lovely festival of American patriotism?) Over in the other camp Rockefeller was running hard to catch up with Tricky Dick, but everybody knew where that was going to get him. Babies were dying of malnutrition in a place called Biafra, which you don't remember, and the Russians were moving troops into Czechoslovakia in yet another demonstration of socialist brotherhood. In a place called Vietnam, which you probably wish you didn't remember either, we were dumping napalm on everything in sight for the sake of promoting peace and democracy, and a lieutenant named William Calley had recently coordinated the liquidation of 100-odd sinister and dangerous old men, women, and children at the town of Mylai, only we didn't know anything about that yet. The books everybody was reading were *Couples*, *Myra Breckinridge*, *The Confessions of Nat Turner*, and *The Money Game*. I forget that year's movies. *Easy Rider* hadn't happened yet and *The Graduate* was the year before. Maybe it was the year of *Rosemary's Baby*. Yes, that sounds right: 1968 was the devil's year for sure. It was also the year when a lot of middle-class middle-aged people started using, self-consciously, terms like 'pot' and 'grass' when they

meant 'marijuana'. Some of them were smoking it as well as
talking it. (Me. Finally turning on at the age of 33.) Let's see,
what else? President Johnson nominated Abe Fortas to replace
Earl Warren as Chief Justice of the Supreme Court. Where are
you now, Chief Justice Fortas, when we need you? The Paris
peace talks, believe it or not, had just begun that summer. In
later years it came to seem that the talks had been going on
since the beginning of time, as eternal and everlasting as the
Grand Canyon and the Republican Party, but no, they were
invented in 1968. Denny McLain was on his way toward
winning 31 games that season. I guess McLain was the only
human being who found 1968 a worthwhile experience. His
team lost the World Series, though. (No. What am I saying?
The Tigers *won*, 4 games to 3. But Mickey Lolich was the star,
not McLain.) That was the sort of year it was. Oh, Christ, I've
forgotten one significant chunk of history. In the spring of '68
we had the riots at Columbia, with radical students occupying
the campus (*'Kirk Must Go!'*) and classes being suspended (*'Shut
It Down!'*) and final exams called off and nightly confrontations
with the police, in the course of which a good many undergraduate skulls were laid open and much high-quality blood
leaked into the gutters. How funny it is that I pushed that
event out of my mind, when of all the things I've listed here it
was the only one I actually experienced at first hand. Standing
at Broadway and 116th Street watching platoons of cold-eyed
fuzz go racing toward Butler Library. ('Fuzz' is what we called
policemen before we started calling them 'pigs', which happened a little later that same year.) Holding my hand aloft in
the forked V-for-Peace gesture and screaming idiotic slogans
with the best of them. Cowering in the lobby of Furnald Hall as
the blue-clad nightstick brigade went on its rampage. Debating
tactics with a ragged-bearded SDS gauleiter who finally spat in
my face and called me a stinking liberal fink. Watching sweet
Barnard girls ripping open their blouses and waving their
bare breasts at horny, exasperated cops, while simultaneously
shrieking ferocious Anglo-Saxonisms that the Barnard girls of
my own remote era hadn't ever heard. Watching a group of

young shaggy Columbia men ritualistically pissing on a pile of research documents that had been liberated from the filing cabinet of some hapless instructor going for his doctorate. It was then that I knew there could be no hope for mankind, when even the best of us were capable of going berserk in the cause of love and peace and human equality. On those dark nights I looked into many minds and found only hysteria and madness, and once, in despair, realizing I was living in a world where two factions of lunatics were battling for control of the asylum, I went off to vomit in Riverside Park after a particularly bloody riot and was caught unawares (me, caught unawares!) by a lithe 14-year-old black mugger who smilingly relieved me of $22.

I was living near Columbia in '68, in a seedy residence hotel on 114th Street, where I had one medium-big room plus kitchen and bathroom privileges, cockroaches at no extra charge. It was the very same place where I had lived as an undergraduate in my junior and senior years, 1955–56. The building had been going downhill even then and was an abominable hellhole when I came back to it twelve years later – the courtyard was littered with broken hypodermic needles the way another building's courtyard might be littered with cigarette butts – but I have an odd way, maybe masochistic, of not letting go of bits of my past however ugly they may be, and when I needed a place to live I picked that one. Besides, it was cheap – $14.50 a week – and I had to be close to the University because of the work I was doing, researching that Israel book. Are you still following me? I was telling you about my first acid trip, which was really Toni's trip.

We had shared our shabby room nearly seven weeks – a bit of May, all of June, some of July – through thick and thin, heat waves and rainstorms, misunderstandings and reconciliations, and it had been a happy time, perhaps the happiest of my life. I loved her and I think she loved me. I haven't had much love in my life. That isn't intended as a grab for your pity, just as a simple statement of fact, objective and cool. The nature of my condition diminishes my capacity to love and be loved. A man in my circumstances, wide open to everyone's innermost thoughts, really isn't going to experience a great deal of love. He is poor at giving love because he doesn't much trust his fellow human beings: he knows too many of their dirty little secrets, and that kills his feelings for them. Unable to give, he cannot get. His soul, hardened by isolation and unforgivingness, becomes inaccessible, and so it is not easy for others to love him. The loop closes upon itself and he is trapped within. Nevertheless I loved Toni, having taken special care not to see too deeply into her, and I didn't doubt my love was returned. What defines love, anyway? We preferred each other's company to the company of anyone else. We excited one another in every imaginable way. We never bored each other. Our bodies mirrored our souls' closeness: I never failed of erection, she never lacked for lubrication, our couplings carried us both to ecstasy. I'd call these things the parameters of love.

On the Friday of our seventh week Toni came home from her office with two small squares of white blotting paper in her purse. In the center of each square was a faint blue-green stain. I studied them a moment or two, without comprehending.

'Acid,' she said finally.

'Acid?'

'You know. LSD. Teddy gave them to me.'

Teddy was her boss, the editor-in-chief. LSD, yes. I knew. I had read Huxley on mescaline in 1957. I was fascinated and tempted. For years I had flirted with the psychedelic experience, even once attempting to volunteer for an LSD research program at the Columbia Medical Center. I was too late signing up, though; and then, as the drug became a fad, came all the horror stories of suicides, psychoses, bad trips. Knowing my vulnerabilities, I decided it was the part of wisdom to leave acid to others. Though still I was curious about it. And now these squares of blotting paper sitting in the palm of Toni's hand.

'It's supposed to be dynamite stuff,' she said. 'Absolutely pure, laboratory quality. Teddy's already tripped on a tab from this batch and he says it's very smooth, very clean, no speed in it or any crap like that. I thought we could spend tomorrow tripping, and sleep it off on Sunday.'

'Both of us?'

'Why not?'

'Do you think it's safe for both of us to be out of our minds at the same time?'

She gave me a peculiar look. 'Do you think acid drives you out of your mind?'

'I don't know. I've heard a lot of scary stories.'

'You've never tripped?'

'No,' I said. 'Have you?'

'Well, no. But I've watched friends of mine while they were tripping.' I felt a pang at this reminder of the life she had led before I met her. 'They don't go out of their minds, David. There's a kind of wild high for an hour or so when things sometimes get jumbled up, but basically somebody who's tripping sits there as lucid and as calm as – well, Aldous Huxley. Can you imagine Huxley out of his mind? Gibbering and drooling and smashing furniture?'

'What about the fellow who killed his mother-in-law while he was on acid, though? And the girl who jumped out of a window?'

Toni shrugged. 'They were unstable,' she said loftily. 'Perhaps murder or suicide was where they were really at, and the acid just gave them the push they needed to go and do it. But that doesn't mean you would, or me. Or maybe the doses were too strong, or the stuff was cut with some other drug. Who knows? Those are one-in-a-million cases. I have friends who've tripped fifty, sixty times, and they've never had any trouble.' She sounded impatient with me. There was a patronizing, lecturing tone in her voice. Her esteem for me seemed clearly diminished by these old-maid hesitations of mine; we were on the threshold of a real rift. 'What's the matter, David? Are you afraid to trip?'

'I think it's unwise for both of us to trip at once, that's all. When we aren't sure where the stuff is going to take us.'

'Tripping together is the most loving thing two people can do,' she said.

'But it's a risky thing. We just don't know. Look, you can get more acid if you want it, can't you?'

'I suppose so.'

'Okay, then. Let's do this thing in an orderly way, one step at a time. There's no hurry. You trip tomorrow and I'll watch. I'll trip on Sunday and you'll watch. If we both like what the acid does to our heads, we can trip together next time. All right, Toni? All right?'

It wasn't all right. I saw her begin to speak, begin to frame some argument, some objection; but also I saw her catch herself, back up, rethink her position, and decide not to make an issue of it. Although I at no time entered her mind, her facial expressions made her sequence of thoughts wholly evident to me. 'All right,' she said softly. 'It isn't worth a hassle.'

Saturday morning she skipped breakfast – she'd been told to trip on an empty stomach – and, after I had eaten, we sat for a time in the kitchen with one of the squares of blotting paper lying innocently on the table between us. We pretended it wasn't there. Toni seemed a little clutched; I didn't know whether she was bothered about my insisting that she trip without me or just troubled, here at the brink of it, by the whole idea of tripping. There wasn't much conversation. She filled an ashtray with a great dismal mound of half-smoked cigarettes. From time to time she grinned nervously. From time to time I took her hand and smiled encouragingly. During this touching scene various of the tenants with whom we shared the kitchen on this floor of the hotel drifted in and out. First Eloise, the sleek black hooker. Then Miss Theotokis, the grim-faced nurse who worked at St Luke's. Mr Wong, the mysterious little roly-poly Chinese who always walked around in his underwear. Aitken, the scholarly fag from Toledo, and his cadaverous mainlining roommate, Donaldson. A couple of them nodded to us but no one actually said anything, not even 'Good morning.' In this place it was proper to behave as though your neighbors were invisible. The fine old New York tradition.

About half past ten in the morning Toni said, 'Get me some orange juice, will you?' I poured a glass from the container in the refrigerator that was labeled with my name. Giving me a wink and a broad toothy smile, all false bravado, she wadded up the blotting paper and pushed it into her mouth, bolting it and gulping the orange juice as a chaser.

'How long will it take to hit?' I asked.

'About an hour and a half,' she said.

In fact it was more like fifty minutes. We were back in our own room, the door locked, faint scratchy sounds of Bach coming from the portable phonograph. I was trying to read, and so was Toni; the pages weren't turning very fast. She looked up suddenly and said, 'I'm starting to feel a little funny.'

'Funny how?'

'Dizzy. A slight touch of nausea. There's a prickling at the back of my neck.'

'Can I get you anything? Glass of water? Juice?'

'Nothing, thanks. I'm fine. Really I am.' A smile, timid but genuine. She seemed a little apprehensive but not at all frightened. Eager for the voyage. I put down my book and watched her vigilantly, feeling protective, almost wishing that I'd have some occasion to be of service to her. I didn't want her to have a bad trip but I wanted her to need me.

She gave me bulletins on the progress of the acid through her nervous system. I took notes until she indicated that the scratching of pencil against paper was distracting her. Visual effects were beginning. The walls looked a trifle concave to her, and the flaws in the plaster were taking on extraordinary texture and complexity. The color of everything was unnaturally bright. The shafts of sunlight coming through the dirty window were prismatic, shattering and spewing pieces of the spectrum over the floor. The music – I had a stack of her favorite records on the changer – had acquired a curious new intensity; she was having difficulty following melodic lines, and it seemed to her that the turntable kept stopping and starting, but the sound itself, as sound, had some indescribable quality of density and tangibility that fascinated her. There was a whistling sound

in her ears, too, as of air rushing past her cheeks. She spoke
of a pervading sense of strangeness – 'I'm on some other
planet,' she said twice. She looked flushed, excited, happy.
Remembering the terrible tales I had heard of acid-induced
descents into hell, harrowing accounts of grueling bummers
lovingly recounted for the delight of the millions by the diligent
anonymous journalists of *Time* and *Life*, I nearly wept in relief at
this evidence that my Toni would come through her journey
unscathed. I had feared the worst. But she was making out all
right. Her eyes were closed, her face was serene and exultant,
her breathing was deep and relaxed. Lost in transcendental
realms of mystery was my Toni. She was barely speaking
to me now, breaking her silences only every few minutes
to murmur something indistinct and oblique. Half an hour
had passed since she first had reported strange sensations.
As she drifted deeper into her trip, my love for her grew
deeper also. Her ability to cope with acid was proof of the
basic toughness of her personality, and that delighted me.
I admire capable women. Already I was planning my own
trip for the next day – selecting the musical accompaniment,
trying to imagine the sort of interesting distortions of reality
I'd experience, looking forward to comparing notes with Toni
afterward. I was regretting the cowardice that had deprived me
of the pleasure of tripping with Toni this day.

But what is this, now? What's happening to my head? Why
this sudden feeling of suffocation? The pounding in my chest?
The dryness in my throat? The walls are flexing; the air seems
close and heavy; my right arm is suddenly a foot longer than
the left one. These are effects Toni had noticed and described
a little while ago. Why do I feel them now? I tremble. Muscles
leap about of their own accord in my thighs. Is this what they
call a contact high? Merely being so close to Toni while she
trips – did she breathe particles of LSD at me, have I inadvertently turned on through some contagion of the atmosphere?

'My dear Selig,' says my armchair smugly, 'how can you be
so foolish? Obviously you're picking these phenomena right
out of her mind!'

Obviously? Is it so obvious? I consider the possibility. Am I reading Toni without knowing it? Apparently I am. In the past some effort of concentration, however slight, has always been necessary in order for me to manage a fine-focus peep into another head. But it seems that the acid must intensify her outputs and bring them to me unsolicited. What other explanation can there be? She is broadcasting her trip; and somehow I have tuned to her wavelength, despite all my noble resolutions about respecting her privacy. And now the acid's strangenesses, spreading across the gap between us, infect me as well.

Shall I get out of her mind?

The acid effects distract me. I look at Toni and she seems tranformed. A small dark mole on her lower cheek, near the corner of her mouth, flashes a vortex of blazing color: red, blue, violet, green. Her lips are too full, her mouth too wide. All those teeth. Row upon row upon row, like a shark. Why have I never noticed that predatory mouth before? She frightens me. Her neck elongates; her body compresses; her breasts move about like restless cats beneath her familiar red sweater, which itself has taken on an ominous, threatening purplish tinge. To escape her I glance toward the window. A pattern of cracks that I have never been aware of before runs through the soiled panes. In a moment, surely, the shattered window will implode and shower us with fiery fragments of glass. The building across the street is unnaturally squat today. There is menace in its altered form. The ceiling is coming toward me, too. I hear muffled drumbeats overhead – the footsteps of my upstairs neighbor, I tell myself – and I imagine cannibals preparing their dinner. Is this what tripping is like? Is this what the young of our nation have been doing to themselves, voluntarily, even eagerly, for the sake of amusement?

I should turn this off, before it freaks me altogether. I want out.

Well, easily done. I have my ways of stopping down the inputs, of blocking the flow. Only they don't work this time. I am helpless before the power of the acid. I try to shut myself away from these unfamiliar and unsettling sensations, and they march onward into me all the same. I am wide open to everything emanating from Toni. I am caught up in it. I go deeper and deeper. This is a trip. This is a bad trip. This is a very bad trip. How odd: Toni was having a good trip, wasn't she? So it seemed to one outside observer. Then why do I, accidentally hitchhiking on her trip, find myself having a bad one?

Whatever is in Toni's mind floods into mine. Receiving another's soul is no new experience for me, but this is a transfer such as I have never had before, for the information, modulated by the drug, comes to me in ghastly distortions. I am an unwilling spectator in Toni's soul, and what I see is a feast of demons. Can such darkness really live within her? I saw nothing like this those other two times: has the acid released some level of nightmare not accessible to me before? Her past is on parade. Gaudy images, bathed in a lurid light. Lovers. Copulations. Abominations. A torrent of menstrual blood, or is that scarlet river something more sinister? Here is a clot of pain: what is that, cruelty to others, cruelty to self? And look how she gives herself to that army of monstrous men! They advance mechanically, a thundering legion. Their rigid cocks blaze with a terrible red light. One by one they plunge into her, and I see the light streaming from her loins as they plow her. Their faces are masks. I know none of them. Why am I not on line too? Where am I? Where am I? Ah, there: off to one side, insignificant, irrelevant. Is that thing me? Is that how she really sees me? A hairy vampire bat, a crouching huddled bloodsucker? Or is that merely David Selig's own image of David Selig, bouncing between us like the reflections in a barber shop's parallel mirrors? God help me, am I laying my own bad trip on her, then reading it back from her and blaming her for harboring nightmares not of her own making?

How can I break this link?

I stumble to my feet. Staggering, splay-footed, nauseated. The room whirls. Where is the door? The doorknob retreats from me. I lunge for it.

'David?' Her voice reverberates unendingly. 'David David David David David David –'

'Some fresh air,' I mutter. 'Just stepping outside a minute –'

It does no good. The nightmare images pursue me through the door. I lean against the sweating wall, clinging to a flickering sconce. The Chinaman drifts by me as though a ghost. Far away I hear the telephone ringing. The refrigerator door slams, and slams again, and slams again, and the Chinaman goes by me a second time from the same direction, and the doorknob retreats from me, as the universe folds back upon itself, locking me into a looped moment. Entropy decreases. The green wall sweats green blood. A voice like thistles says, 'Selig? Is something wrong?' It's Donaldson, the junkie. His face is a skull's face. His hand on my shoulder is all bones. 'Are you sick?' he asks. I shake my head. He leans toward me until his empty eye-sockets are inches from my face, and studies me a long moment. He says, 'You're *tripping*, man! Isn't that right? Listen, if you're freaking out, come on down the hall, we've got some stuff that might help you.'

'No. No problem.'

I go lurching into my room. The door, suddenly flexible, will not close; I push it with both hands, holding it in place until the latch clicks. Toni is sitting where I left her. She looks baffled. Her face is a monstrous thing, pure Picasso; I turn away from her, dismayed.

'David?'

Her voice is cracked and harsh, and seems to be pitched in two octaves at once, with a filling of scratchy wool between the top tone and the bottom. I wave my hands frantically, trying to get her to stop talking, but she goes on, expressing concern for me, wanting to know what's happening, why I've been running in and out of the room. Every sound she makes is torment for me. Nor do the images cease to flow from her mind to mine. That shaggy toothy bat, wearing my face, still glowers in a corner of her skull. Toni, I thought you loved me. Toni, I thought I made you happy. I drop to my knees and explore the dirt-encrusted carpet, a million years old, a faded

thinning threadbare piece of the Pleistocene. She comes to me,
bending down solicitously, she who is tripping looking after
the welfare of her untripping companion, who mysteriously
is tripping also. 'I don't understand,' she whispers. 'You're
crying, David. Your face is all blotchy. Did I say something
wrong? Please don't carry on, David. I was having such a good
trip, and now – I just don't understand –'

The bat. The bat. Spreading its rubbery wings. Baring its
yellow fangs.

Biting. Sucking. Drinking.

I choke a few words out: 'I'm – tripping – too –'

My face pushed against the carpet. The smell of dust in my
dry nostrils. Trilobites crawling through my brain. A bat crawling through hers. Shrill laughter in the hallway. The telephone.
The refrigerator door: slam, slam, slam! The cannibals dancing
upstairs. The ceiling pressing against my back. My hungry mind
looting Toni's soul. He who peeps through a hole may see what
will vex him. Toni says, 'You took the other acid? When?'

'I didn't.'

'Then how can you be tripping?'

I make no reply. I crouch, I huddle, I sweat, I moan. This is
the descent into hell. Huxley warned me. I didn't want Toni's
trip. I didn't ask to see any of this. My defenses are destroyed
now. She overwhelms me. She engulfs me.

Toni says, 'Are you reading my mind, David?'

'Yes.' The miserable ultimate confession. 'I'm reading your
mind.'

'What did you say?'

'I said I'm reading your mind. I can see every thought. Every
experience. I see myself the way you see me. Oh, Christ, Toni,
Toni, Toni, it's so awful!'

She tugs at me and tries to pull me up to look at her. Finally
I rise. Her face is horribly pale; her eyes are rigid. She asks for
clarifications. What's this about reading minds? Did I really say
it, or is it something her acid-blurred mind invented? I really
said it, I tell her. You asked me if I was reading your mind and
I said yes, I was.

'I never asked any such thing,' she says.

'I heard you ask it.'

'But I didn't –' Trembling, now. Both of us. Her voice is bleak. 'You're trying to bum-trip me, aren't you, David? I don't understand. Why would you want to hurt me? Why are you messing me up? It was a good trip. *It was a good trip.*'

'Not for me,' I say.

'You weren't tripping.'

'But I was.'

She gives me a look of total incomprehension and pulls away from me and throws herself on the bed, sobbing. Out of her mind, cutting through the grotesqueries of the acid images, comes a blast of raw emotion: fear, resentment, pain, anger. She thinks I've deliberately tried to injure her. Nothing I can say now will repair things. Nothing can ever repair things. She despises me. I am a vampire to her, a bloodsucker, a leech; she knows my gift for what it is. We have crossed some fatal threshold and she will never again think of me without anguish and shame. Nor I her. I rush from the room, down the hall to the room shared by Donaldson and Aitken. 'Bad trip,' I mutter. 'Sorry to trouble you, but –'

I stayed with them the rest of the afternoon. They gave me a tranquilizer and brought me gently through the downslope of the trip. The psychedelic images still came to me out of Toni for half an hour or so, as though an inexorable umbilical chain linked us across all the length of the hallway; but then to my relief the sense of contact began to slip and fade, and suddenly, with a kind of audible click at the moment of severance, it was gone altogether. The flamboyant phantoms ceased to vex my soul. Color and dimension and texture returned to their proper states. And at last I was free from that merciless reflected self-image. Once I was fully alone in my own skull again I felt like weeping to celebrate my deliverance, but no tears would come, and I sat passively, sipping a Bromo-Seltzer. Time trickled away. Donaldson and Aitken and I talked in a peaceful, civilized, burned-out way about Bach, medieval art, Richard M. Nixon, pot, and a great many other things. I hardly knew these two, yet they were willing to surrender their time to ease a stranger's pain. Eventually I felt better. Shortly before six o'clock, thanking them gravely, I went back to my room. Toni was not there. The place seemed oddly altered. Books were gone from the shelves, prints from the walls; the closet door stood open and half the things in it were missing. In my befuddled, fatigued state it took me a moment or two to grasp what had happened. At first I imagined burglary, abduction, but then I saw the truth. She had moved out.

ELEVEN

Today there is a hint of encroaching winter in the air: it takes tentative nips at the cheeks. October is dying too quickly. The sky is mottled and unhealthy-looking, cluttered by sad, heavy, low-hanging clouds. Yesterday it rained, skinning yellow leaves from the trees, and now they lie pasted to the pavement of College Walk, their tips fluttering raggedly in the harsh breeze. There are puddles everywhere. As I settled down beside Alma Mater's massive green form I primly spread newspaper sheets, selected portions of today's issue of *The Columbia Daily Spectator*, over the cold damp stone steps. Twenty-odd years ago, when I was a foolishly ambitious sophomore dreaming of a career in journalism – how sly, a reporter who reads minds! – *Spec* seemed central to my life; now it serves only for keeping my rump dry.

Here I sit. Office hours. On my knees rests a thick manila folder, held closed by a ballsy big rubber band. Within, neatly typed, each with its own coppery paperclip, are five term papers, the products of my busy week. *The Novels of Kafka. Shaw as Tragedian. The Concept of Synthetic A Priori Statements. Odysseus as a Symbol of Society. Aeschylus and the Aristotelian Tragedy.* The old academic bullshit, confirmed in its hopeless fecality by the cheerful willingness of these bright young men to let an old grad turn the stuff out for them. This is the day appointed for delivering the goods and, perhaps, picking up some new assignments. Five minutes to eleven. My clients will be arriving soon. Meanwhile I scan the passing parade. Students hurrying by, clutching mounds of books. Hair rippling in the wind, breasts bobbling. They all look frighteningly young to me, even the bearded ones. Especially the bearded ones. Do you realize that each year there are more and more young people in the world? Their tribe ever increases as the old farts drop off the nether end of the curve and I shuttle graveward. Even the professors look young to me these days. There are people with doctorates who are fifteen years younger than I am. Isn't that a killer? Imagine a kid born in 1950 who has a doctorate already. In 1950 I was shaving three times a week, and masturbating every Wednesday and Saturday; I was a hearty pubescent *bulyak* five feet nine inches tall, with ambitions and griefs and knowledge, with an identity. In 1950 today's newly fledged Ph.D.'s were toothless infants just squirting from the womb, their faces puckered, their skins sticky with amniotic juices. How can those infants have doctorates so soon? Those infants have lapped me as I plod along the track.

I find my own company wearisome when I descend into self-pity. To divert myself I try to touch the minds of passers-by and learn what I can learn. Playing my old game, my only game. Selig the voyeur, the soul-vampire, ripping off the intimacies of innocent strangers to cheer his chilly heart. But no: my head is full of cotton today. Only muffled murmurs come to me, indistinct, content-free. No discrete words, no flashes of identity, no visions of soul's essence. This is one of the bad days. All inputs converge into unintelligibility; each bit of information is identical to all others. It is the triumph of entropy. I am reminded of Forster's Mrs Moor, listening tensely for revelation in the echoing Marabar caves, and hearing only the same monotonous noise, the same meaningless all-dissolving sound: *Boum*. The sum and essence of mankind's

earnest strivings: *Boum*. The minds flashing past me on College
Walk now give me only: *Boum*. Perhaps it is all I deserve. Love,
fear, faith, churlishness, hunger, self-satisfaction, every species
of interior monolog, all come to me with identical content.
Boum. I must work to correct this. It is not too late to wage war
against entropy. Gradually, sweating, struggling, scrabbling for
solid purchase, I widen the aperture, coaxing my perceptions
to function. Yes. Yes. Come back to life. Get it up, you miserable
spy! Give me my fix! Within me the power stirs. The inner
murk clears a bit; stray scraps of isolated but coherent thought
find their way into me. *Neurotic but not altogether psycho yet. Going
to see the department head and tell him to shove it up. Tickets for the
opera, but I have to. Fucking is fun, fucking is very important, but
there's more. Like standing on a very high diving board about to take
a plunge.* This scratchy chaotic chatter tells me nothing except
that the power is not yet dead, and I take comfort enough in
that. I visualized the power as a sort of worm wrapped around
my cerebrum, a poor tired worm, wrinkled and shrunken, its
once-glossy skin now ulcerous with shabby, flaking patches.
That is a relatively recent image, but even in happier days I
always thought of the gift as something apart from myself,
something intrusive. An inhabitant. It and me, me and it. I
used to discuss such things with Nyquist. (Has he entered
these exhalations yet? Perhaps not. A person I once knew,
a certain Tom Nyquist, a former friend of mine. Who carried
a somewhat similar intruder within his skull.) Nyquist didn't
like my outlook. 'That's schizoid, man, setting up a duality
like that. Your power is you. You are your power. Why try
to alienate yourself from your own brain?' Probably Nyquist
was right, but it's much too late. It and me is how it will be,
till death do us part.

  Here is my client, the bulky halfback, Paul F. Bruno. His face
is swollen and purple, and he is unsmiling, as though Saturday's heroics have cost him some teeth. I flip the rubber band
down, extract *The Novels of Kafka*, and offer the paper to him.
'Six pages,' I say. He has given me a ten-dollar advance. 'You
owe me another eleven bucks. Do you want to read it first?'

'How good is it?'

'You won't be sorry.'

'I'll take your word for it.' He manages a painful, close-mouthed grin. Pulling forth his thick wallet, he crosses my palm with greenbacks. I slip quickly into his mind, just for the hell of it now that my power is working again, a fast psychic rip-off, and pick up the surface levels: loose teeth at the football game, a sweet compensatory blow-job at the frat house Saturday night, vague plans for getting laid after next Saturday's game, etc., etc. Concerning the present transaction I detect guilt, embarrassment, even some annoyance with me for having helped him. Oh, well: the gratitude of the *goy*. I pocket the money. He favors me with a curt nod and tucks *The Novels of Kafka* under his immense forearm. Hastily, in shame, he goes hustling down the steps and off in the direction of Hamilton Hall. I watch his broad retreating back. A sudden gust of malevolent wind, rising off the Hudson, comes knifing eastward and cuts me bone-deep.

Bruno has paused at the sundial, where a slender black student close to seven feet tall has intercepted him. A basketball player, obviously. The black wears a blue varsity jacket, green sneakers, and tight tubular yellow slacks. His legs alone seem five feet long. He and Bruno talk for a moment. Bruno points toward me. The black nods. I am about to gain a new client, I realize. Bruno vanishes and the black trots springlegged across the walk, up the steps. He is very dark, almost purple-skinned, yet his features have a Caucasian sharpness, fierce cheekbones, proud aquiline nose, thin frosty lips. He is formidably hand-some, some kind of walking statuary, some sort of idol. Perhaps his genes are not Negroid at all: an Ethiopian, maybe, some tribesman of the Nile bulrushes? Yet he wears his midnight mass of kinky hair in a vast aggressive Afro halo a foot in diameter or more, fastidiously trimmed. I would not have been surprised by scarified cheeks, a bone through the nostrils. As he nears me, my mind, barely slitwide, picks up peripheral gener-alized emanations of his personality. Everything is predictable, even stereotyped: I expect him to be touchy, cocky, defensive, hostile, and what comes to me is a bouillabaisse of ferocious racial pride, overwhelming physical self-satisfaction, explosive mistrust of others, especially whites. All right. Familiar patterns.

His elongated shadow falls suddenly upon me as the sun momentarily pierces the clouds. He sways bouncily on the balls of his feet. 'Your name Selig?' he asks. I nod. 'Yahya Lumumba,' he says.

'Pardon me?'

'*Yahya Lumumba*.' His eyes, glossy white against glossy purple, blaze with fury. From the impatience of his tone I realize that he is telling me his name, or at least the name he prefers to use. His tone indicates also that he assumes it's a name everyone on this campus will recognize. Well, what would I know of college basketball stars? He could throw the ball through the hoop fifty times a game and I'd still not have heard of him. He says, 'I hear you do term papers, man.'

'That's right.'

'You got a good recommend from my pal Bruno there. How much you charge?'

'$3.50 a page. Typed, double-spaced.'

He considers it. He shows many teeth and says, 'What kind of fucking rip-off is that?'

'It's how I earn my living, Mr Lumumba.' I hate myself for that toadying, cowardly *mister*. 'That's about $20 for an average-length paper. A decent job takes a fair amount of time, right?'

'Yeah. Yeah.' An elaborate shrug. 'Okay, I'm not hassling you, man. I got need for your work. You know anything about Europydes?'

'Euripides?'

'That's what I said.' He's baiting me, coming on with exaggerated black mannerisms, talking watermelon-nigger at me with his *Europydes*. 'That Greek cat who wrote plays.'

'I know who you mean. What sort of paper do you need, Mr Lumumba?'

He pulls a scrap of a notebook sheet from a breast pocket

and makes a great show of consulting it. 'The prof he want us to compare the "Electra" theme in Europydes, Sophocles, and Eesk – Aysk –'

'Aeschylus?'

'Him, yeah. Five to ten pages. It due by November 10. Can you swing it?'

'I think so,' I say, reaching for my pen. 'It shouldn't be any trouble at all,' especially since there resides in my files a paper of my own, vintage 1952, covering this very same hoary old humanities theme. 'I'll need some information about you for the heading. Exact spelling of your name, the name of your professor, the course number –' He starts to tell me these things. As I jot them down, I simultaneously open the aperture of my mind for my customary scan of the client's interior, to give me some idea of the proper tone to use in the paper. Will I be able to do a convincing job of faking the kind of essay Yahya Lumumba is likely to turn in? It will be a taxing technical challenge if I have to write in black hipster jargon, coming on all cool and jazzy and snotty, every line laughing in the ofay prof's fat face. I imagine I could do it: but does Lumumba want me to? Will he think I'm mocking *him* if I adopt the jiveass style and seem to be putting him on as he might put on the prof? I must know these things. So I slip my snaky tendrils past his woolly scalp into the hidden gray jelly. Hello, big black man. Entering, I pick up a somewhat more immediate and vivid version of the generalized persona he constantly projects: the hyped-up black pride, the mistrust of the paleface stranger, the chuckling enjoyment of his own lean long-legged muscular frame. But these are mere residual attitudes, the standard furniture of his mind. I have not yet reached the level of this-minute thought. I have not penetrated to the essential Yahya Lumumba, the unique individual whose style I must assume. I push deeper. As I sink in, I sense a distinct warming of the psychic temperature, an outflow of heat, comparable perhaps to what a miner might experience five miles down, tunneling toward the magmatic fires at the earth's core. This man Lumumba is constantly boiling within, I realize. The glow from his tumultuous soul warns me to be careful, but I have not yet gained the information I seek, and so I go onward, until abruptly the molten frenzy of his stream of consciousness hits me with terrible force. *Fucking Jew bigbrain shithead Christ how I hate the little bald mother conning me three-fifty a page I ought to jew him down I ought to bust his teeth the exploiter the oppressor he wouldn't charge a Jew that much I bet special price for niggers sure well I ought to jew him down that's a good one jew him down I ought to bust his teeth pick him up throw him into the trash what if I wrote the fucking paper myself show him but I can't shit I can't that's the whole fucking trouble mom I can't Europydes Sophocles Eeskilus who knows shit about them I got other stuff on my mind the Rutgers game one-on-one down the court gimme the ball you dumb prick that's it and it's up and in for Lumumba! and wait folks he was fouled in the act of shooting now he goes to the line big confident easy six feet ten inches tall holder of every Columbia scoring record bounces the ball one twice up, swish! Lumumba on his way to another big evening tonight folks Europydes Sophocles Eeskilus why the fuck do I have to know anything about them write anything about them what good is it to a black man those old dead Greek fuckers how are they relevant to the black experience relevant relevant relevant not to me just to the Jews shit what do any of them know four hundred years of slavery we got other stuff on our minds what do any of them know especially this shithead mother here I got to pay him twenty bucks to do something I'm not good enough to do for myself who says I have to what good is any of it why why why why*

A roaring furnace. The heat is overwhelming. I've been in contact with intense minds before, far more intense than this one, but that was when I was younger, stronger, more resilient. I can't handle this volcanic blast. The force of his contempt for me is magnified factorially by the force of the self-contempt that needing my services makes him feel. He is a pillar of hatred. And my poor enfeebled power can't take it. Some sort of automatic safety device cuts in to protect me from an overload: the mental receptors shut themselves down. This is a new experience for me, a strange one, this load-shedding phenomenon. It is as though limbs are dropping off, ears, balls, anything disposable, leaving nothing but a smooth torso. The inputs fall away, the mind of Yahya Lumumba retreats and is inaccessible to me, and I find myself involuntarily reversing the process of penetration until I can feel only his most superficial emanations, then not even those, only a gray furry exudation marking the mere presence of him alongside me. All is indistinct. All is muffled. *Boum.* We are back to that again. There is a ringing in my ears: it is an artifact of the sudden silence, a silence loud as thunder. A new stage on my downward path. Never have I lost my grip and slipped from a mind like this. I look up, dazed, shattered. Yahya Lumumba's thin lips are tightly compressed; he stares down at me in distaste, having no inkling of what has occurred. I say faintly, 'I'd like ten dollars now in advance. The rest you pay when I deliver the paper.' He tells me coldly that he has no money to give me today. His next check from the scholarship fund isn't due until the beginning of the coming month. I'll just have to do the job on faith, he says. Take it or leave it, man. 'Can you manage five?' I ask. 'As a binder. Faith isn't enough. I have expenses.' He glares. He draws himself to his full height; he seems nine or ten feet tall. Without a word he takes a five-dollar bill from his wallet, crumples it, scornfully tosses it into my lap. 'I'll see you here the morning of November 9,' I call after him, as he stalks away. Europydes, Sophocles, Eeskilus. I sit stunned, shivering, listening to the bellowing silence. *Boum. Boum. Boum.*

TWELVE

In his more flamboyantly Dostoevskian moments, David Selig liked to think of his power as a curse, a savage penalty for some unimaginable sin. The mark of Cain, perhaps. Certainly his special ability had caused a lot of trouble for him, but in his saner moments he knew that calling it a curse was sheer self-indulgent melodramatic bullshit. The power was a divine gift. The power brought ecstasy. Without the power he was nothing, a schmendrick; with it he was a god. Is that a curse? Is that so terrible? Something funny happens when gamete meets gamete, and destiny cries, Here, Selig-baby: be a god! This you would spurn? Sophocles, age 88 or so, was heard to express his great relief at having outlived the pressures of the physical passions. I am freed at last from a tyrannical master, said the wise and happy Sophocles. Can we then assume that Sophocles, had Zeus given him a chance retroactively to alter the entire course of his days, would have opted for lifelong impotence? Don't kid yourself, Duvid: no matter how badly the telepathy stuff fucked you up, and it fucked you up pretty badly, you wouldn't have done without it for a minute. Because the power brought ecstasy.

The power brought ecstasy. That's the whole megillah in a single crisp phrase. Mortals are born into a vale of tears and they get their kicks wherever they can. Some, seeking pleasure, are compelled to turn to sex, drugs, booze, television, movies, pinochle, the stock market, the racetrack, the roulette wheel, whips and chains, collecting first editions, Caribbean cruises, Chinese snuff bottles, Anglo-Saxon poetry, rubber garments, professional football games, whatever. Not him, not the accursed David Selig. All he had to do was sit quietly with his apparatus wide open and drink in the thought-waves drifting on the telepathic breeze. With the greatest of ease he lived a hundred vicarious lives. He heaped his treasurehouse with the plunder of a thousand souls. Ecstasy. Of course, the ecstatic part was all quite some time ago.

The best years were those between the ages of fourteen and twenty-five. Younger, and he was still too naïve, too unformed, to wring much appreciation from the data he took in. Older, and his growing bitterness, his sour sense of isolation, damped his capacity for joy. Fourteen to twenty-five, though. The golden years. Ah!

It was so very much more vivid then. Life was like a waking dream. There were no walls in his world; he could go anywhere and see anything. The intense flavor of existence. Steeped in the rich juices of perception. Not until Selig was past forty did he realize how much he had lost, over the years, in the way of fine focus and depth of field. The power had not begun detectably to dim until he was well along in his thirties, but it obviously must have been fading by easy stages all through his manhood, dwindling so gradually that he remained unaware of the cumulative loss. The change had been absolute, qualitative rather than quantitative. Even on a good day, now, the inputs did not begin to approach the intensity of those he remembered from his adolescence. In those remote years the power had brought him not only bits of subcranial conversation and scattered snatches of soul, as now, but also a gaudy universe of colors, textures, scents, densities: the world through an infinity of other sensory intakes, the world captured and played out for his delight on the glassy radiant spherical screen within his mind.

For instance. He lies propped against an itchy August haystack in a hot Bruegelesque landscape, shortly past noon. This is 1950 and he hangs becalmed midway between his fifteenth birthday and his sixteenth. Some sound effects, Maestro: Beethoven's Sixth, bubbling up gently, sweet flutes and playful piccolos. The sun dangles in a cloudless sky. A gentle wind stirs the willows bordering the cornfield. The young corn trembles. The brook burbles. A starling circles overhead. He hears crickets. He hears the drone of a mosquito, and watches calmly as it zeroes in on his bare, hairless, sweat-shiny chest. His feet are bare too; he wears only tight, faded blue jeans. City boy, digging the country.

The farm is in the Catskills, twelve miles north of Ellenville. It is owned by the Schieles, a tribe of tawny Teutons, who produce eggs and an assortment of vegetable crops and who supplement their earnings every summer by renting out their guest house to some family of urban Yids looking for rural solace. This year the tenants are Sam and Annette Stein of Brooklyn, New York, and their daughter Barbara. The Steins have invited their close friends, Paul and Martha Selig, to spend a week on the farm with their son David and their daughter Judith. (Sam Stein and Paul Selig are hatching a scheme, destined ultimately to empty their bank accounts and destroy the friendship between the two families, to enter into a partnership and act as jobbers for replacement parts for television sets. Paul Selig is forever attempting unwise business ventures.) Today is the third day of the visit, and this afternoon, mysteriously, David finds himself utterly alone. His father has gone on an all-day hike with Sam Stein: in the serenity of the nearby hills they will plot the details of their commercial coup. Their wives have driven off, taking five-year-old Judith with them, to explore the antique shops of Ellenville. No one remains on the premises except the tightlipped Schieles, going somberly about their unending chores, and sixteen-year-old Barbara Stein, who has been David's classmate from the third grade on through high school. Willy-nilly, David and Barbara are thrown together for the day. The Steins and the Seligs evidently have some unvoiced hope that romance will blossom between their offspring. This is naïve of them. Barbara, a lush and reasonably beautiful dark-haired girl, sleek-skinned and long-legged, sophisticated and smooth of manner, is six months older than David chronologically and three or four years ahead of him in social development. She does not actually dislike him, but she regards him as strange, disturbing, alien, and repellent. She has no knowledge of his special gift – no one does; he's seen to that – but she's had seven years to observe him at close range, and she knows there's something fishy about him. She is a conventional girl, plainly destined to marry early (a doctor, a lawyer, an insurance broker) and have lots of babies, and the chances of romance flowering between her and anyone as dark-souled and odd as David Selig are slight. David knows this very well and he is not at all surprised, or even dismayed, when Barbara slips away in mid-morning. 'If anyone asks,' she says, 'tell them I went for a stroll in the woods.' She carries a paperback poetry anthology. David is not deceived by it. He knows she goes off to screw 19-year-old Hans Schiele at every chance she gets.

So he is left to his own resources. No matter. He has ways of entertaining himself. He wanders the farm for a while, peering at the hen-coop and the combine, and then settles down in a quiet corner of the fields. Time for mind-movies. Lazily he casts his net. The power rises and goes forth, looking for emanations. What shall I read, what shall I read? Ah. A sense of contact. His questing mind has snared another mind, a buzzing one, small, dim, intense. It is a bee's mind, in fact: David is not limited only to contact with humans. Of course there are no verbal outputs from the bee, nor any conceptual ones. If the bee thinks at all, David is incapable of detecting those thoughts. But he does get into the bee's head. He experiences a strong sense of what it is like to be tiny and compact and winged and fuzzy. How *dry* the universe of a bee is: bloodless, desiccated, arid. He soars. He swoops. He evades a passing bird, as monstrous as a winged elephant. He burrows deep into a steamy, pollen-laden blossom. He goes aloft again. He sees the world through the bee's faceted eyes. Everything breaks into a thousand fragments, as though seen through a cracked glass; the essential color of everything is gray, but odd hues lurk at the corners of things, peripheral blues and scarlets that do not correspond in any way to the colors he knows. The effect, he might have said twenty years later, is an extremely trippy one. But the mind of a bee is a limited one. David bores easily. He abandons the insect abruptly and, zooming his perceptions barnward, clicks into the soul of a hen. She is laying an egg! Rhythmic internal contractions, pleasurable and painful, like the voiding of a mighty turd. Frenzied squawks. The smarmy hen-coop odor, sharp and biting. A sense of too much straw all about. The world looks dark and dull to this bird. *Heave. Heave.* Oooh! Orgasmic excitement! The egg slides through the hatch and lands safely. The hen subsides, fulfilled, exhausted. David departs from her in this moment of rapture. He plunges deep into the adjoining woods, finds a human mind, enters it. How much richer and more intense it is to make communion with his own species. His identity blurs into that of his communicant, who is Barbara Stein, who is getting laid by Hans

Schiele. She is naked and lying on a carpet of last year's fallen leaves. Her legs are spread and her eyes are closed. Her skin is damp with sweat. Hans' fingers dig into the soft flesh of her shoulders and his cheek, rough with blond stubble, abrades her cheek. His weight presses down on her chest, flattening her breasts and emptying her lungs. With steady thrusts and unvarying tempo he penetrates her, and as his long stiff member slowly and patiently rams into her again and again, throbbing sensation spreads in eddying ripples outward from her loins, growing less intense with distance. Through her mind David observes the impact of the hard penis against the tender, slippery internal membranes. He picks up her clamorous heartbeat. He notices her hammering her heels against the calves of Hans' legs. He is aware of the slickness of her own fluids on her buttocks and thighs. And now he senses the first dizzying spasms of orgasm. David struggles to remain with her, but he knows he won't succeed; clinging to the consciousness of someone who's coming is like trying to ride a wild horse. Her pelvis bucks and heaves, her fingernails desperately rake her lover's back, her head twists to one side, she gulps for air, and, as she erupts with pleasure, she catapults David from her unsaddled mind. He travels only a short way, into the stolid soul of Hans Schiele, who unknowingly grants the virgin voyeur a few instants of knowledge of what it is like to be stoking the furnace of Barbara Stein, thrust and thrust and thrust and thrust, her inner muscles clamping fiercely against the swollen prod, and then, almost immediately, comes the tickle of Hans' onrushing climax. Hungry for information, David holds on with all his strength, hoping to keep contact right through the tumult of fulfillment, but no, he is flipped free, he tumbles uncontrollably, the world goes swinging past him in giddy streaks of color, until – click! – he finds a new sanctuary. All is calm here. He glides through a dark cold environment. He has no weight; his body is long and slender and agile; his mind is nearly a void, but through it run faint chilly flickering perceptions of a low order. He has entered the consciousness of a fish, perhaps a brook trout.

Downstream he moves in the swiftly rushing creek, taking delight in the smoothness of his motions and the delicious texture of the pure icy water flowing past his fins. He can see very little and smell even less; information comes to him in the form of minute impacts on his scales, tiny deflections and interferences. Easily he responds to each incoming news item, now twisting to avoid a fang of rock, now fluttering his fins to seize some speedy subcurrent. The process is fascinating, but the trout itself is a dull companion, and David, having extracted the troutness of the experience in two or three minutes, leaps gladly to a more complex mind the moment he approaches one. It is the mind of gnarled old George Schiele, Hans' father, who is at work in a remote corner of the cornfield. David has never entered the elder Schiele's mind before. The old man is a grim and forbidding character, well past sixty, who says little and stalks dourly through his day-long round of chores with his heavy-jowled face perpetually locked in a frosty scowl. David occasionally wonders whether he once might have been a concentration-camp attendant, though he knows the Schieles came to America in 1935. The farmer gives off so unpleasant a psychic aura that David has steered clear of him, but so bored is he with the trout that he slips into Schiele now, slides down through dense layers of unintelligible Deutsch ruminations, and strikes bottom in the basement of the farmer's soul, the place where his essence lives. Astonishment: old Schiele is a mystic, an ecstatic! No dourness here. No dark Lutheran vindictiveness. This is pure Buddhism: Schiele stands in the rich soil of his fields, leaning on his hoe, feet firmly planted, communing with the universe. God floods his soul. He touches the unity of all things. Sky, trees, earth, sun, plants, brook, insects, birds – everything is one, part of a seamless whole, and Schiele resonates in perfect harmony with it. How can this be? How can such a bleak, inaccessible man entertain such raptures in his depths? Feel his joy! Sensations drench him! Birdsong, sunlight, the scent of flowers and clods of upturned earth, the rustling of the sharp-bladed green cornstalks, the trickle of sweat down the reddened deep-channeled

neck, the curve of the planet, the fleecy premature outline of
the full moon – a thousand delights enfold this man. David
shares his pleasure. He kneels in his mind, reverent, awed. The
world is a mighty hymn. Schiele breaks from his stasis, raises
his hoe, brings it down; heavy muscles go taut and metal digs
into earth, and everything is as it should be, all conforms to the
divine plan. Is this how Schiele goes through his days? Is such
happiness possible? David is surprised to find tears bulging in
his eyes. This simple man, this narrow man, lives in daily
grace. Suddenly sullen, bitterly envious, David rips his mind
free, whirls, projects it toward the woods, drops down into
Barbara Stein again. She lies back, sweat-sticky, exhausted.
Through her nostrils David receives the stink of semen already
going sour. She rubs her hands over her skin, plucking stray
bits of leaf and grass from herself. Idly she touches her softening nipples. Her mind is slow, dull, almost as empty as
the trout's, just now: sex seems to have drained her of personality. David shifts to Hans and finds him no better. Lying
by Barbara's side, still breathing hard after his exertions, he
is torpid and depressed. His wad is shot and all desire is gone
from him; peering sleepily at the girl he has just possessed, he
is conscious mainly of body odors and the untidiness of her
hair. Through the upper levels of his mind wanders a wistful
thought, in English punctuated by clumsy German, of a girl
from an adjoining farm who will do something to him with
her mouth that Barbara refuses to do. Hans will be seeing her
on Saturday night. Poor Barbara, David thinks, and wonders
what she would say if she knew what Hans is thinking. Idly
he tries to bridge their two minds, entering both in the mischievous hope that thoughts may flow from one to the other,
but he miscalculates his span and finds himself returning to old
Schiele, deep in his ecstasy, while holding contact with Hans
as well. Father and son, old and young, priest and profaner.
David sustains the twin contact a moment. He shivers. He is
filled with a thundering sense of the wholeness of life.

*   *   *

It was like that all the time, in those years: an endless trip, a gaudy voyage. But powers decay. Time leaches the colors from the best of visions. The world becomes grayer. Entropy beats us down. Everything fades. Everything goes. Everything dies.

THIRTEEN

Judith's dark, rambling apartment fills with pungent smells. I hear her in the kitchen, bustling, dumping spices into the pot: hot chili, oregano, tarragon, cloves, garlic, powdered mustard, sesame oil, curry powder, God knows what else. Fire burn and cauldron bubble. Her famous fiery spaghetti sauce is in the making, a compound product of mysterious antecedents, part Mexican in inspiration, part Szechuan, part Madras, part pure Judith. My unhappy sister is not really much of a domestic type, but the few dishes she can cook she does extraordinarily well, and her spaghetti is celebrated on three continents; I'm convinced there are men who go to bed with her just to have dining-in privileges here.

I have arrived unexpectedly early, half an hour before the appointed time, catching Judith unprepared, not even dressed; so I am on my own while she readies dinner. 'Fix yourself a drink,' she calls to me. I go to the sideboard and pour a shot of dark rum, then into the kitchen for ice cubes. Judith, flustered, wearing housecoat and headband, flies madly about, breathlessly selecting spices. She does everything at top speed. 'Be with you in another ten minutes,' she gasps, reaching for the pepper mill. 'Is the kid making a lot of trouble for you?'

My nephew, she means. His name is Paul, in honor of our father which art in heaven, but she never calls him that, only 'the baby', 'the kid'. Four years old. Child of divorce, destined to be as taut-strung as his mother. 'He's not bothering me at all,' I assure her, and go back to the livingroom.

The apartment is one of those old, immense West Side jobs, roomy and high-ceilinged, which carries with it some sort of aura of intellectual distinction simply because so many critics, poets, playwrights, and choreographers have lived in similar apartments in this very neighborhood. Giant livingroom with many windows looking out over West End Avenue; formal dining room; big kitchen; master bedroom; child's room; maid's room; two bathrooms. All for Judith and her cub. The rent is cosmic but Judith can manage it. She gets well over a thousand a month from her ex, and earns a modest but decent living of her own as an editor and translator; aside from that she has a small income from a portfolio of stocks, shrewdly chosen for her a few years ago by a lover from Wall Street, which she purchased with her inherited share of our parents' surprisingly robust savings. (My share went to clean up accumulated debts; the whole thing melted like June snow.) The place is furnished half in 1960 Greenwich Village and half in 1970 Urban Elegance – black pole-lamps, gray string chairs, red brick bookcases, cheap prints, and wax-encrusted Chianti bottles on the one hand; leather couches, Hopi pottery, psychedelic silkscreens, glass-topped coffee-tables, and giant potted cacti on the other. Bach harpsichord sonatas tinkle from the thousand-dollar speaker system. The floor, ebony-dark and mirror-bright, gleams between the lush, thick area rugs. A pile of broken-backed paperbacks clutters one wall. Opposite it stand two rough unopened wooden crates, wine newly arrived from her vintner. A good life my sister leads here. Good and miserable.

The kid eyes me untrustingly. He sits twenty feet away, by the window, fiddling with some intricate plastic toy but keeping close watch on me. A dark child, slender and tense like his mother, aloof, cool. No love is lost between us: I've been inside his head and I know what he thinks of me. To him I'm one of the many men in his mother's life, a real uncle being not very different from the unnumerable uncle-surrogates forever sleeping over; I suppose he thinks I'm just one of her lovers who shows up more often than most. An understandable error. But while he resents the others merely because they compete with him for her affection, he looks coldly upon me because he thinks I've caused his mother pain; he dislikes me for her sake. How shrewdly he's discerned the decades-old network of hostilities and tensions that shapes and defines my relationship with Judith! So I'm an enemy. He'd gut me if he could.

I sip my drink, listen to Bach, smile insincerely at the kid, and inhale the aroma of spaghetti sauce. My power is practically quiescent; I try not to use it much here, and in any case its intake is feeble today. After some time Judith emerges from the kitchen and, flashing across the livingroom, says, 'Come talk to me while I get dressed, Duv.' I follow her to her bedroom and sit down on the bed; she takes her clothes into the adjoining bathroom, leaving the door open only an inch or two. The last time I saw her naked she was seven years old. She says, 'I'm glad you decided to come.'

'So am I.'

'You look awfully peaked though.'

'Just hungry, Jude.'

'I'll fix that in five minutes.' Sounds of water running. She says something else; the sink drowns her out. I look idly around the bedroom. A man's white shirt, much too big for Judith, hangs casually from the doorknob of the closet. On the night-table sit two fat textbooky-looking books, *Analytical Neuro-endocrinology* and *Studies in the Physiology of Thermoregulation*. Unlikely reading for Judith. Maybe she's been hired to translate them into French. I observe that they're brand new copies, though one book was published in 1964 and the other in 1969. Both by the same author: K. F. Silvestri, M.D., Ph.D.

'You going to medical school these days?' I ask.

'The books, you mean? They're Karl's.'

Karl? A new name. Dr Karl F. Silvestri. I touch her mind lightly and extract his image: a tall hefty sober-faced man, broad shoulders, strong dimpled chin, flowing mane of graying hair. About fifty, I'd guess. Judith digs older men. While I raid her consciousness she tells me about him. Her current 'friend', the kid's latest 'uncle'. He's someone very big at Columbia Medical Center, a real authority on the human body. Including her body, I assume. Newly divorced after a 25-year marriage. Uh-huh: she likes getting them on the rebound. He met her three weeks ago through a mutual friend, a psychoanalyst. They've only seen each other four or five times; he's always busy, committee meetings at this hospital or that, seminars, consultations. It wasn't very long ago that Judith told me she was between men, maybe off men altogether. Evidently not. It must be a serious affair if she's trying to read his books. They look absolutely opaque to me, all charts and statistical tables and heavy Latinate terminology.

She comes out of the bathroom wearing a sleek purple pants-suit and the crystal earrings I gave her for her 29th birthday. When I visit she always tries to register some little sentimental touch to tie us together; tonight it's the earrings. There is a convalescent quality to our friendship nowadays, as we tiptoe gently through the garden where our old hatred lies buried. We embrace, a brother-sister hug. A pleasant perfume. 'Hello,' she says. 'I'm sorry I was such a mess when you walked in.'

'It's my fault. I was too early. Anyway, you weren't a mess at all.'

She leads me to the livingroom. She carries herself well. Judith is a handsome woman, tall and extremely slender, exotic-looking, with dark hair, dark complexion, sharp cheekbones. The slim sultry type. I suppose she'd be considered very sexy, except that there is something cruel about her thin lips and her quick glistening brown eyes, and that cruelty, which grows more intense in these years of divorce and discontent, turns people off. She's had lovers by the dozen, by the gross, but not much love. You and me, sis, you and me. Chips off the old block.

She sets the table while I fix a drink for her, the usual, Pernod on the rocks. The kid, thank God, has already eaten; I hate having him at the table. He plays with his plastic thingy and favors me with occasional sour glares. Judith and I clink our cocktail glasses together, a stagy gesture. She produces a wintry smile. 'Cheers,' we say. Cheers.

'Why don't you move back downtown?' she asks. 'We could see more of each other.'

'It's cheap up there. Do we want to see more of each other?'

'Who else do we have?'

'You have Karl.'

'I don't *have* him or anybody. Just my kid and my brother.'

I think of the time when I tried to murder her in her bassinet. She doesn't know about that. 'Are we really friends, Jude?'

'Now we are. At last.'

'We haven't exactly been fond of each other all these years.'

'People change, Duv. They grow up. I was dumb, a real shithead, so wrapped up in myself that I couldn't give anything but hate to anybody around me. That's over now. If you don't believe me, look into my head and see.'

'You don't want me poking around in there.'

'Go ahead,' she says. 'Take a good look and see if I haven't changed toward you.'

'No. I'd rather not.' I deal myself another two ounces of rum. The hand shakes a little. 'Shouldn't you check the spaghetti sauce? Maybe it's boiling over.'

'Let it boil. I haven't finished my drink. Duv, are you still having trouble? With your power, I mean.'

'Yes. Still. Worse than ever.'

'What do you think is happening?'

I shrug. Insouciant old me. 'I'm losing it, that's all. It's like hair, I suppose. A lot of it when you're young, then less and less, and finally none. Fuck it. It never did me any good anyway.'

'You don't mean that.'

'Show me any good it did me, Jude.'

'It made you someone special. It made you unique. When everything else went wrong for you, you could always fall back on that, the knowledge that you could go into minds, that you

could see the unseeable, that you could get close to people's
souls. A gift from God.'

'A useless gift. Except if I'd gone into the sideshow business.'

'It made you a richer person. More complex, more interesting. Without it you might have been someone quite ordinary.'

'With it I turned out to be someone quite ordinary. A
nobody, a zero. Without it I might have been a happy nobody
instead of a dismal one.'

'You pity yourself a lot, Duv.'

'I've got a lot to pity myself for. More Pernod, Jude?'

'Thanks, no. I ought to look after dinner. Will you pour
the wine?'

She goes into the kitchen. I do the wine thing; then I carry
the salad bowl to the table. Behind me the kid begins to chant
derisive nonsense syllables in his weirdly mature baritone.
Even in my current state of dulled deceptivity I feel the
pressure of the kid's cold hatred against the back of my
skull. Judith returns, toting a well-laden tray: spaghetti, garlic
bread, cheese. She flashes a warm smile, evidently sincere, as
we sit down. We clink wine-glasses. We eat in silence a few
minutes. I praise the spaghetti. She says, finally, 'Can I do some
mindreading on you, Duv?'

'Be my guest.'

'You say you're glad the power's going. Is that snow-job
directed at me or at yourself? Because you're snowing somebody. You hate the idea of losing it, don't you?'

'A little.'

'A lot, Duv.'

'All right, a lot. I'm of two minds. I'd like it to vanish
completely. Christ, I wish I'd never had it. But on the other
hand, if I lose it, who am I? Where's my identity? I'm Selig
the Mind-reader, right? The Amazing Mental Man. So if I stop
being him – you see, Jude?'

'I see. The pain's all over your face. I'm so sorry, Duv.'

'For what?'

'That you're losing it.'

'You despised my guts for using it on you, didn't you?'

'That's different. That was a long time ago. I know what you must be going through, now. Do you have any idea why you're losing it?'

'No. A function of aging, I guess.'

'Is there anything that might be done to stop it from going?'

'I doubt it, Jude. I don't even know why I have the gift in the first place, let alone how to nurture it now. I don't know how it works. It's just something in my head, a genetic fluke, a thing I was born with, like freckles. If your freckles start to fade, can you figure out a way of making them stay, if you want them to stay?'

'You've never let yourself be studied, have you?'

'No.'

'Why not?'

'I don't like people poking in my head any more than you do,' I say softly. 'I don't want to be a case history. I've always kept a low profile. If the world ever found out about me, I'd become a pariah. I'd probably be lynched. Do you know how many people there are to whom I've openly admitted the truth about myself? In my whole life, how many?'

'A dozen?'

'Three,' I say. 'And I wouldn't willingly have told any of them.'

'Three?'

'You. I suppose you suspected it all along, but you didn't find out for sure till you were sixteen, remember? Then there's Tom Nyquist, who I don't see any more. And a girl named Kitty, who I don't see any more either.'

'What about the tall brunette?'

'Toni? I never explicitly told her. I tried to hide it from her. She found out indirectly. A lot of people may have found out indirectly. But I've only told three. I don't want to be known as a freak. So let it fade. Let it die. Good riddance.'

'You want to keep it, though.'

'To keep it and lose it both.'

'That's a contradiction.'

'Do I contradict myself? Very well, then I contradict myself. I am large, I contain multitudes. What can I say, Jude? What can I tell you that's true?'

'Are you in pain?'

'Who isn't in pain?'

She says, 'Losing it is almost like becoming impotent, isn't it, Duv? To reach into a mind and find out that you can't connect? You said there was ecstasy in it for you, once. That flood of information, that vicarious experience. And now you can't get it as much, or at all. Your mind can't get it up. Do you see it that way, as a sexual metaphor?'

'Sometimes.' I give her more wine. For a few minutes we sit silently, shoveling down the spaghetti, exchanging tentative grins. I almost feel warmth toward her. Forgiveness for all the years when she treated me like a circus attraction. *You sneaky fucker, Duv, stay out of my head or I'll kill you! You voyeur. You peeper. Keep away, man, keep away.* She didn't want me to meet her fiancé. Afraid I'd tell him about her other men, I guess. *I'd like to find you dead in the gutter some day, Duv, with all my secrets rotting inside you.* So long ago. Maybe we love each other a little now, Jude. Just a little, but you love me more than I love you.

'I don't come any more,' she says abruptly. 'You know, I used to come, practically every time. The original Hot Pants Kid, me. But around five years ago something happened, around the time my marriage was first breaking up. A short circuit down below. I started coming every fifth time, every tenth time. Feeling the ability to respond slip away from me. Lying there waiting for it to happen, and of course that doused it every time. Finally I couldn't come at all. I still can't. Not in three years. I've laid maybe a hundred men since the divorce, give or take five or ten, and not one brought me off, and some of them were studs, real bulls. It's one of the things Karl's going to work on with me. So I know what it's like, Duv. What you must be going through. To lose your best way of making contact with others. To lose contact gradually with yourself. To become a stranger in your own head.' She smiles.

'Did you know that about me? About the troubles I've been having in bed?'

I hesitate briefly. The icy glare in her eyes gives her away. The aggressiveness. The resentment she feels. Even when she tries to be loving she can't help hating. How fragile our relationship is! We're locked in a kind of marriage, Judith and I, an old burned-out marriage held together with skewers. What the hell, though. 'Yes,' I tell her. 'I know about it.'

'I thought so. You've never stopped probing me.' Her smile is all hateful glee now. She's glad I'm losing it. She's relieved. 'I'm always wide open to you, Duv.'

'Don't worry, you won't be much longer.' Oh, you sadist bitch! Oh, you beautiful ball-buster! And you're all I've got. 'How about some more spaghetti, Jude?' Sister. Sister. Sister.

FOURTEEN

Yahya Lumumba
Humanities 2A, Dr Katz
November 10, 1976

THE 'ELECTRA' THEME IN AESCHYLUS, SOPHOCLES, AND EURIPIDES

The use of the 'Electra' motif by Aeschylus, Sophocles, and Euripides is a study in varying dramatic methods and modes of attack. The plot is basically the same in Aeschylus' *Choephori* and the *Electras* of Sophocles and Euripides: Orestes, exiled son of murdered Agamemnon, returns to his native Mycenae, where he discovers his sister Electra. She persuades him to avenge Agamemnon's murder by killing Clytemnestra and Aegisthus, who had slain Agamemnon on his return from Troy. The treatment of the plot varies greatly at the hands of each dramatist.

Aeschylus, unlike his later rivals, held as prime consideration

the ethical and religious aspects of Orestes' crime. Characterization and motivation in *The Cheophori* are simple to the point of
inviting ridicule – as, indeed, can we see when the more wordly-
minded Euripides ridicules Aeschylus in the recognition scene of
his *Electra*. In Aeschylus' play Orestes appears accompanied by
his friend Pylades and places an offering on Agamemnon's tomb:
a lock of his hair. They withdraw, and lamenting Electra comes
to the tomb. Noticing the lock of hair, she recognizes it as being
'like unto those my father's children wear,' and decides Orestes
has sent it to the tomb as a token of mourning. Orestes then
reappears, and identifies himself to Electra. It is this implausible
means of identification which was parodied by Euripides.

Orestes reveals that Apollo's oracle had commanded him to
avenge Agamemnon's murder. In a long poetic passage, Electra
steels Orestes' courage, and he goes forth to kill Clytemnestra
and Aegisthus. He obtains entrance to the palace by deception,
pretending to his mother Clytemnestra that he is a messenger
from far-off Phocis, bearing news of Orestes' death. Once inside,
he slays Aegisthus, and then, confronting his mother, he accuses
her of the murder and kills her.

The play ends with Orestes, maddened by his crime, seeing
the Furies coming to pursue him. He takes refuge in the temple
of Apollo. The mystic and allegorical sequel, *The Eumenides*, sees
Orestes absolved of blame.

Aeschylus, in short, was not overly concerned with the credibility of his play's action. His purpose in the *Oresteia* trilogy was
a theological one: to examine the actions of the gods in placing a
curse upon a house, a curse stemming from murder and leading
to further murder. The keynote of his philosophy is perhaps the
line, ''Tis Zeus alone who shows the perfect way of knowledge:
He hath ruled, men shall learn wisdom by affliction schooled.'
Aeschylus sacrifices dramatic technique, or at least holds it in
secondary importance, in order to focus attention on the religious
and psychological aspects of the matricide.

The *Electra* of Euripides is virtually at an opposite pole from
the concept of Aeschylus; though he uses the same plot, he
elaborates and innovates to provide far richer texture. Electra

and Orestes stand out in relief in Euripides: Electra a near-mad woman, banished from the court, married to a peasant, craving vengeance; Orestes a coward, sneaking into Mycenae the back way, abjectly stabbing Aegisthus from behind, luring Clytemnestra to her doom by a ruse. Euripides is concerned with dramatic credibility, whereas Aeschylus is not. After the famous parody of the Aeschylean recognition scene, Orestes makes himself known to Electra not by his hair or the size of his foot, but rather by

Oh God. Oh shit shit shit. This is deadly. This is no fucking good at all. Could Yahya Lumumba have written any of this crap? Phony from Word One. Why should Yahya Lumumba give a shit about Greek tragedy? Why should I? What's Hecuba to him or he to Hecuba, that he should weep for her? I'll tear this up and start again. I'll write it jivey, man. I'll give it dat ole water-melon rhythm. God help me to think black. But I can't. But I can't. But I can't. Christ, I'd like to throw up. I think I'm getting a fever. Wait. Maybe a joint would help some. Yeah. Let's get high and try again. A lil ole stick of mootah. Get some soul into it, man. Smartass white Jew-bastard, get some soul into it, you hear? Okay, now. There was this cat Agamemnon, he was one big important fucker, you hear, he was The Man, but he got fucked all the same. His old lady Clytemnestra, she was makin' it with this chickenshit muthafuck Aegisthus, and one day she say, Baby, let's waste old Aggie, you and me, and then you gonna be king – gwine be king? – gonna – and we have a high ole time. Aggie, he off in the Nam runin' the show, but he come home for some R & R and before he know what happenin' they stick him good, right, they really cut him, and that all for *him*. Now there this crazy cunt Electra, dig, she the daughter of ole Aggie, and she get real uptight when they use him up, so she say to her brother, his name Orestes, she say, listen, Orestes, I want you to *get* them two muthafucks, I want you to get them real good. Now, this cat Orestes he been out of town for a while, he don't know the score, but –

Yeah, that's it man! You're digging it! Now go on to explain about Euripides' use of the *deus ex machina* and the cathartic virtues of Sophocles' realistic dramatic technique. Sure. What a dumb schmuck you are, Selig. What a dumb schmuck.

FIFTEEN

I tried to be good to Judith, I tried to be kind and loving, but our hatred kept coming between us. I said to myself, She's my kid sister, my only sibling, I must love her more. But you can't will love. You can't conjure it into existence on nothing more than good intentions. Besides, my intentions had never been that good. I saw her as a rival from the word go. I was the first-born, I was the difficult one, the maladjusted one. I was supposed to be the center of everything. Those were the terms of my contract with God: I must suffer because I am different, but by way of compensation the entire universe will revolve about me. The girl-baby who was brought into the household was intended to be nothing more than a therapeutic aid designed to help me relate better to the human race. That was the deal: she wasn't supposed to have independent reality as a person, she wasn't supposed to have her own needs or make demands or drain away their love. Just a thing, an item of furniture. But I knew better than to believe that. I was ten years old, remember, when they adopted her. Your ten-year-old, he's no fool. I knew that my parents, no longer feeling obliged now to direct all their concern exclusively toward their mysteriously intense and troubled son, would rapidly and with great relief transfer their attention and their love – yes, particularly their love – to the cuddly, uncomplicated infant. She would take my place at the center; I'd become a quirky obsolescent artifact. I couldn't help resenting that. Do you blame me for trying to kill her in her bassinet? On the other hand you can understand the origin of her lifelong coldness toward me. I offer no defense at this late date. The cycle of hatred began with me. With me,

Jude, with me, with me, with me. You could have broken it with love, though, if you wanted to. You didn't want to.

On a Saturday afternoon in May, 1961, I went out to my parents' house. In those years I didn't go there often, though I lived twenty minutes away by subway. I was outside the family circle, autonomous and remote, and I felt powerful resistance to any kind of reattachment. For one thing I had free-floating hostilities toward my parents: it was their fluky genes, after all, that had sent me into the world this way. And then too there was Judith, shriveling me with her disdain: did I need more of that? So I stayed away from the three of them for weeks, months, at a time, until the melancholy maternal phonecalls became too much for me, until the weight of my guilt overcame my resistances.

I was happy to discover, when I got there, that Judith was still in her bedroom, asleep. At three in the afternoon? Well, my mother said, she was out very late last night on a date. Judith was sixteen, I imagined her going to a high school basketball game with some skinny pimply kid and sipping milkshakes afterwards. Sleep well, sister, sleep on and on. But of course her absence put me into direct and unshielded confrontation with my sad depleted parents. My mother, mild and dim; my father, weary and bitter. All my life they had steadily grown smaller. They seemed very small now. They seemed close to the vanishing point.

I had never lived in this apartment. For years Paul and Martha had struggled with the upkeep of a three-bedroom place they couldn't afford, simply because it had become impossible for Judith and me to share the same bedroom once she was past her infancy. The moment I left for college, taking a room near campus, they found a smaller and far less expensive one. Their bedroom was to the right of the entry foyer, and Judith's, down a long hall and past the kitchen, was to the left; straight ahead was the livingroom, in which my father sat dreamily leafing through the *Times*. He read nothing but the newspaper these days, though once his mind had been more active. From him came a dull sludgy emanation of fatigue. He was making some decent money for the first time in his life, actually would end up quite prosperous, yet he had conditioned himself to the poor-man psychology: poor Paul, you're a pitiful failure, you deserved so much better from life. I looked at the newspaper through his mind as he turned the pages. Yesterday Alan Shepard had made his epochal sub-orbital flight, the first manned venture into space by the United States. U.S. HURLS MAN 115 MILES INTO SPACE, cried the banner headline. SHEPARD WORKS CONTROLS IN CAPSULE, REPORTS BY RADIO IN 15-MINUTE FLIGHT. I groped for some way to connect with my father. 'What did you think of the space voyage?' I asked. 'Did you listen to the broadcast?' He shrugged. 'Who gives a damn? It's all crazy. A mishigos. A waste of everybody's time and money.' ELIZABETH VISITS POPE IN VATICAN. Fat Pope John, looking like a well-fed rabbi. JOHNSON TO MEET LEADERS IN ASIA ON U.S. TROOP USE. He skimmed onward, skipping pages. HELP OF GOLDBERG ASKED ON ROCKETS. KENNEDY SIGNS WAGE-FLOOR BILL. Nothing registered on him, not even KENNEDY TO SEEK INCOME TAX CUTS. He lingered at the sports pages. A faint flicker of interest. MUD MAKES CARRY BACK STRONGER FAVORITE FOR 87th KENTUCKY DERBY TODAY. YANKS OPPOSE ANGELS IN OPENER OF 3-GAME SERIES BEFORE 21,000 ON COAST. 'Who do you like in the Derby?' I asked. He shook his head. 'What do I know about horses?' he said. He was, I realized, already dead, although in fact his heart would beat for another decade. He had stopped responding. The world had defeated him.

I left him to his brooding and made polite talk with my mother: her Hadassah reading group was discussing *To Kill a Mockingbird* next Thursday and she wanted to know if I had read it. I hadn't. What was I doing with myself? Had I seen any good movies? *L'Avventura*, I said. Is that a French film? She asked. Italian, I said. She wanted me to describe the plot. She listened patiently, looking troubled, not following anything. 'Who did you go with?' she asked. 'Are you seeing any nice girls?' My son the bachelor. Already 26 and not even engaged.

I deflected the tiresome question with patient skill born of long experience. Sorry, Martha. I won't give you the grandchildren you're waiting for. You'll have to get them from Judith; it won't be all that long.

'I have to baste the chicken now,' she said, and disappeared. I sat with my father for a while, until I couldn't stand that and went down the hall to the john, next to Judith's room. Her door was ajar. I glanced in. Lights off, blinds drawn, but I touched her mind and found that she was awake and thinking of getting up. All right, make a gesture, be friendly, Duvid. It won't cost you anything. I knocked lightly. 'Hi, it's me,' I said. 'Okay if I come in?'

She was sitting up, wearing a frilly white bathrobe over dark-blue pajamas. Yawning, stretching. Her face, usually so taut, was puffy from too much sleep. Out of force of habit I went into her mind, and saw something new and surprising there. My sister's erotic inauguration. The night before. The whole thing: the scurry in the parked car, the rise of excitement, the sudden realization that this was going to be more than an interlude of petting, the panties coming down, the awkward shiftings of position, the fumble with the condom, the moment of ultimate hesitation giving way to total willingness, the hasty inexpert fingers coaxing lubrication out of the virgin crevice, the cautious clumsy poking, the thrust, the surprise of discovering that penetration was accomplished without pain, the pistoning of body against body, the boy's quick explosion, the messy aftermath, the guilt and confusion and disappointment as it ended with Judith still unsatisfied. The drive home, silent, shamefaced. Into the house, tiptoe, hoarsely greeting the vigilant, unsleeping parents. The late-night shower. Inspection and cleansing of the deflowered and slightly swollen vulva. Uneasy sleep, frequently punctured. A long stretch of wakefulness, in which the night's event is considered: she is pleased and relieved to have entered womanhood, but also frightened. Unwillingness to rise and face the world the next day, especially to face Paul and Martha. Judith, your secret is no secret to me.

'How are you?' I asked.

Stagily casual, she drawled, 'Sleepy. I was out very late. How come you're here?'

'I drop in to see the family now and then.'

'Nice to have seen you.'

'That isn't friendly, Jude. Am I that loathsome to you?'

'Why are you bothering me, Duv?'

'I told you, I'm trying to be sociable. You're my only sister, the only one I'll ever have. I thought I'd stick my head in the door and say hello.'

'You've done that. So?'

'You might tell me what you've been doing with yourself since the last time I saw you.'

'Do you care?'

'If I didn't care, would I ask?'

'Sure,' she said. 'You don't give a crap about what I've been doing. You don't give a crap about anybody but David Selig, and why pretend otherwise? You don't need to ask me polite questions. It isn't natural coming from you.'

'Hey, hold on!' Let's not be dueling so fast, sister. 'What gives you the idea that –'

'Do you think of me from one week to the next? I'm just furniture to you. The drippy little sister. The brat. The inconvenience. Have you ever talked to me? About anything? Do you even know the name of the school I go to? I'm a total stranger to you.'

'No, you're not.'

'What the hell *do* you know about me?'

'Plenty.'

'For example.'

'Quit it, Jude.'

'One example. Just one. One thing about me. For example –'

'For example. All right. For example, I know that you got laid last night.'

We were both amazed by that. I stood in shocked silence, not believing that I had allowed those words to pass my lips; and Judith jerked as though electrified, her body stiffening and

rearing, her eyes blazing with astonishment. I don't know how
long we remained frozen, unable to speak.

'What?' she said finally. 'What did you say, Duv?'

'You heard it.'

'I heard it but I think I must have dreamed it. Say it again.'

'No.'

'Why not?'

'Leave me alone, Jude.'

'Who told you?'

'Please, Jude –'

'*Who told you?*'

'Nobody,' I muttered.

Her smile was terrifying triumphant. 'You know something?
I believe you. I honestly believe you. Nobody told you. You
pulled it right out of my mind, didn't you Duv?'

'I wish I had never come in here.'

'Admit it. Why won't you admit it? You see into people's
minds, don't you. Duvid? You're some kind of circus freak. I've
suspected that a long time. All those little hunches you have,
and they always turn out to be right, and the embarrassed
phony way you cover up for yourself when you're right.
Talking about your "luck" at guessing things. Sure! Sure,
luck! I knew the real scoop. I said to myself, This fucker is
reading my mind. But I told myself it was crazy, there aren't
any such people, it has to be impossible. Only it's true, isn't it?
You don't guess. You look. We're wide open to you and you
read us like books. Spying on us. Isn't that so?'

I heard a sound behind me. I jumped, frightened. But it
was only Martha, poking her head into Judith's bedroom. A
vague, dreamy grin. 'Good morning, Judith. Or good afternoon, I should say. Having a nice chat, children? I'm so glad.
Don't forget to have breakfast, Judith.' And she drifted on
her way.

Judith said sharply, 'Why didn't you tell her? Describe the
whole thing. Who I was with last night, what I did with him,
how it felt –'

'Stop it, Jude.'

'You didn't answer my other question. You've got this weird power, don't you? *Don't you?*'

'Yes.'

'And you've been secretly spying on people all your life.'

'Yes. Yes.'

'I knew it. I didn't know, but I really did, all along. And it explains so much. Why I always felt dirty when I was a kid and you were around. Why I felt as if anything I did was likely to show up in tomorrow's newspapers. I never had any privacy, even when I was locked in the bathroom. I didn't *feel* private.' She shuddered. 'I hope I never see you again, Duv. Now that I know what you are. I wish I never *had* seen you. If I ever catch you poking around in my head after this, I'll cut your balls off. Got that? I'll cut your balls off. Now clear out of here so I can get dressed.'

I stumbled away. In the bathroom I gripped the cold edge of the sink and leaned close to the mirror to study my flushed, flustered face. I looked stunned and dazed, my features as rigid as though I had had a stroke. *I know that you got laid last night.* Why had I told her that? An accident? The words spilling out of me because she had goaded me past the point of prudence? But I had never let anyone push me into a revelation like that before. There are no accidents, Freud said. There are never any slips of the tongue. Everything's deliberate, on one level or another. I must have said what I did to Judith because I wanted her at last to know the truth about me. But why? Why her? I had already told Nyquist, yes; there could be no risk in that; but I had never admitted it to anyone else. Always taken such great pains to conceal it, eh, Miss Mueller? And now Judith knew. I had given her a weapon with which she could destroy me.

I had given her a weapon. How strange that she never chose to use it.

SIXTEEN

Nyquist said, 'The real trouble with you, Selig, is that you're a deeply religious man who doesn't happen to believe in God.' Nyquist was always saying things like that, and Selig never could be sure whether he meant them or was just playing verbal games. No matter how deeply Selig penetrated the other man's soul, he never could be sure of anything. Nyquist was too wily, too elusive.

Playing it safe, Selig said nothing. He stood with his back to Nyquist, looking out the window. Snow was falling. The narrow streets below were choked with it; not even the municipal snowplows could get through, and a strange serenity prevailed. High winds whipped the drifts about. Parked cars were disappearing under the white blanket. A few janitors from the apartment houses on the block were out, digging manfully. It had been snowing on and off for three days. Snow was general all over the Northeast. It was falling on every filthy city, on the arid suburbs, falling softly upon the Appalachians and, farther eastward, softly falling into the dark mutinous Atlantic waves. Nothing was moving in New York City. Everything was shut down: office buildings, schools, the concert halls, the theaters. The railroads were out of commission and the highways were blocked. There was no action at the airports. Basketball games were being canceled at Madison Square Garden. Unable to get to work, Selig had waited out most of the blizzard in Nyquist's apartment, spending so much time with him that by now he had come to find his friend's company stifling and oppressive. What earlier had seemed amusing and charming in Nyquist had become abrasive and tricksy. Nyquist's bland self-assurance conveyed itself now as smugness; his casual forays into Selig's mind were no longer affectionate gestures of intimacy, but rather, conscious acts of aggression. His habit of repeating aloud what Selig was thinking was increasingly irritating, and there seemed to be no deterring him from that.

Here he was doing it again, plucking a quotation from Selig's head and declaiming it in half-mocking tones: 'Ah. How pretty. 'His soul swooned slowly as he heard the snow falling faintly through the universe and faintly falling, like the descent of their last end, upon all the living and the dead.' I like that. What is it, David?'

'James Joyce,' said Selig sourly. '"The Dead", from *Dubliners*, I asked you yesterday not to do that.'

'I envy the breadth and depth of your culture. I like to borrow fancy quotations from you.'

'Fine. Do you always have to play them back at me?'

Nyquist, gesturing broadly as Selig stepped away from the window, humbly turned his palms outward. 'I'm sorry. I forget you didn't like it.'

'You never forget a thing, Tom. You never do anything accidentally.' Then, guilty over his peevishness: 'Christ, I've had about enough snow!'

'Snow is general,' said Nyquist. 'It isn't ever going to stop. What are we going to do today?'

'The same as yesterday and the day before, I imagine. Sitting around watching the snowflakes fall and listening to records and getting sloshed.'

'How about getting laid?'

'I don't think you're my type,' Selig said.

Nyquist flashed an empty smile. 'Funny man. I mean finding a couple of ladies marooned somewhere in this building and inviting them to a little party. You don't think there are two available ladies under this roof?'

'We could look, I suppose,' Selig said, shrugging. 'Is there any more bourbon?'

'I'll get it,' Nyquist said.

He brought the bottle over. Nyquist moved with a strange slowness, like a man moving through a dense reluctant atmosphere of mercury or some other viscous fluid. Selig had never seen him hurry. He was heavy without being fat, a thick-shouldered, thick-necked man with a square head, close-cropped yellow hair, a flat wide-flanged nose, and an easy, innocent grin. Very, very Aryan: he was Scandinavian, a Swede perhaps, raised in Finland and transplanted to the United States at the age of 10. He still had the elusive traces of an accent. He said he was 28 and looked a few years older than that to Selig, who had just turned 23. This was February, 1958, in an era when Selig still had the delusion that he was going to make it in the adult world. Eisenhower was President, the stock market had gone to hell, the post-Sputnik emotional slump was troubling everybody even though the first American space satellite had just been orbited, and the latest feminine fashion was the gunny-sack chemise. Selig was living in Brooklyn Heights, on Pierrepont Street, commuting several days a week to the lower Fifth Avenue office of a publishing company for which he was doing freelance copy-editing at $3 an hour. Nyquist lived in the same building, four floors higher.

He was the only other person Selig knew who had the power. Not only that, having it hadn't crippled him at all. Nyquist used his gift as simply and naturally as he did his eyes or his legs, for his own advantage, without apologies and without guilt. Perhaps he was the least neurotic person Selig had ever met. By occupation he was a predator, skimming an income by raiding the minds of others; but, like any jungle cat, he pounced only when hungry, never for sheer love of pouncing. He took what he needed, never questioning the providence that had made him so superbly fitted for taking, yet he did not take more than he needed, and his needs were moderate. He held no job and apparently never had. Whenever he wanted money he made the ten-minute subway ride to Wall Street, sauntered through the gloomy canyons of the financial district, and rummaged about freely in the minds of the moneymen cloistered in the lofty boardrooms. On any given day there was always some major development hatching that would have an impact on the market – a merger, a stock split, an ore discovery, a favorable earnings report – Nyquist had no difficulty learning the essential details. This information he swiftly sold at handsome but reasonable fees to some twelve or fifteen private investors who had learned in the happiest possible way that Nyquist was a reliable tout. Many of the unaccountable leaks on which quick fortunes had been made in the bull market of the '50's were his doing. He earned a comfortable living this way, enough to support himself in a congenial style. His apartment was small and agreeable – black Naugahyde upholstery, Tiffany lamps, Picasso wallpaper, a well-stocked liquor closet, a superb music system that emitted a seamless flow of Monteverdi and Palestrina, Bartok and Stravinsky. He lived a gracious bachelor life, going out often, making the rounds of his favorite restaurants, all of them obscure and ethnic – Japanese, Pakistani, Syrian, Greek. His circle of friends was limited but distinguished: painters, writers, musicians, poets, mainly. He slept with many women, but Selig rarely saw him with the same one twice.

Like Selig, Nyquist could receive but was unable to send; he was, however, able to tell when his own mind was being probed. That was how they had happened to meet. Selig, newly arrived in the building, had indulged himself in his hobby, letting his consciousness rove freely from floor to floor by way of getting acquainted with his neighbors. Bouncing about, surveying this head and that, finding nothing of any special interest, and then suddenly:

– Tell me where you are.

A crystalline string of words glimmering at the periphery of a sturdy, complacent mind. The statement came through with the immediacy of an explicit message. Yet Selig realized that no act of active transmission had taken place; he had simply found the words lying passively in wait. He made quick reply:

– 35 Pierrepont Street.

– No, I know that. I mean, where are you in the building?

– Fourth floor.

– I'm on the eighth. What's your name?

– Selig.

– Nyquist.

The mental contact was stunningly intimate. It was almost a sexual thing, as though he were slicing into a body, not a mind, and he was abashed by the resonant masculinity of the soul he had entered; he felt that there was something not quite permissible about such closeness with another man. But he did not draw back. That rapid interplay of verbal communication across the gap of darkness was a delicious experience, too rewarding to reject. Selig had the momentary illusion of having expanded his powers, of having learned how to send as well as to draw forth the contents of other minds. It was, he knew only an illusion. He was sending nothing, nor was Nyquist. He and Nyquist were merely picking information out of each other's minds. Each planted phrases for the other to find, which was not quite the same thing, in terms of the situational dynamics, as sending messages to one another. It was a fine and possibly pointless distinction, though; the net effect of the juxtaposition of two wide-open receivers was an efficient send/receive circuit as reliable as a telephone. The marriage of true minds, to which let no impediments be admitted. Tentatively, self-consciously, Selig reached into the lower levels of Nyquist's consciousness, seeking the man as well as the messages, and as he did so he was vaguely aware of disquiet in the depths of his own mind, probably indicating that Nyquist was doing the same to him. For long minutes they explored each other like lovers entwined in the first discovering caresses, although there was nothing loving about Nyquist's touch, which was cool and impersonal. Nevertheless Selig quivered; he felt as if he stood at the edge of an abyss. At last he gently withdrew as did Nyquist. Then, from the other:

– Come upstairs. I'll meet you by the elevator.

He was bigger than Selig expected, a fullback of a man, his blue eyes uninviting, his smile a purely formal one. He was remote without actually being cold. They went into his apartment: soft lights, unfamiliar music playing, an atmosphere of unostentatious elegance. Nyquist offered him a drink and they talked, keeping out of one another's mind as much as possible. It was a subdued visit, unsentimental, no tears of joy at having come together at last. Nyquist was affable, accessible, pleased that Selig had appeared, but not at all delirious with excitement at the discovery of a fellow freak. Possibly it was because he had discovered fellow freaks before. 'There are others,' he said. 'You're the third, fourth, fifth I've met since I came to the States. Let's see: one in Chicago, one in San Francisco, one in Miami, one in Minneapolis. You're the fifth. Two women, three men.'

'Are you still in touch with the others?'

'No.'

'What happened?'

'We drifted apart.' Nyquist said. 'What did you expect? That we'd be clannish? Look, we talked, we played games with our minds, we got to know each other, and after a while we got bored. I think two of them are dead now. I don't mind being isolated from the rest of my kind. I don't think of myself as one of a tribe.'

'I never met another one,' said Selig. 'Until today.'

'It isn't important. What's important is living your own life. How old were you when you found out you could do it?'

'I don't know. Five, six years old, maybe. And you?'

'I didn't realize I had anything special until I was eleven. I thought everybody could do it. It was only after I came to the States and heard people thinking in a different language that I knew there was something out of the ordinary about my mind.'

'What kind of work do you do?' Selig asked.

'As little as I can,' said Nyquist. He grinned and thrust his perceptors brusquely into Selig's mind. It seemed like an invitation of sorts; Selig accepted it and pushed forth his own antennae. Roaming the other man's consciousness, he quickly grasped the picture of Nyquist's Wall Street sorties. He saw the entire balanced, rhythmic, unobsessive life of the man. He was amazed by Nyquist's coolness, his wholeness, his clarity of spirit. How limpid Nyquist's soul was! How unmarred by life! Where did he keep his anguish? Where did he hide his loneliness, his fear, his insecurity? Nyquist, withdrawing, said, 'Why do you feel so sorry for yourself?'

'Do I?'

'It's all over your head. What's the problem, Selig? I've looked into you and I don't see the problem, only the pain.'

'The problem is that I feel isolated from other human beings.'

'Isolated? You? You can get right inside people's heads. You can do something that 99.999% of the human race can't do. They've got to struggle along using words, approximations, semaphore signals, and you go straight to the core of meaning. How can you pretend you're isolated?'

'The information I get is useless,' Selig said. 'I can't act on it. I might just as well not be reading it in.'

'Why?'

'Because it's just voyeurism. I'm spying on them.'

'You feel guilty about that?'

'Don't you?'

'I didn't ask for my gift,' Nyquist said. 'I just happen to have it. Since I have it, I use it. I like it. I like the life I lead. I like myself. Why don't you like yourself, Selig?'

'You tell me.'

But Nyquist had nothing to tell him, and when he finished his drink he went back downstairs. His own apartment seemed so strange to him as he re-entered it that he spent a few minutes handling familiar artifacts: his parents' photograph, his little collection of adolescent love-letters, the plastic toy that the psychiatrist had given him years ago. The presence of Nyquist continued to buzz in his mind – a residue of the visit, nothing more, for Selig was certain that Nyquist was not now probing him. He felt so jarred by their meeting, so intruded upon, that he resolved never to see him again, in fact to move somewhere else as soon as possible, to Manhattan, to Philadelphia, to Los Angeles, anywhere that might be beyond Nyquist's reach. All his life he had yearned to meet someone who shared his gift, and now that he had, he felt threatened by it. Nyquist was so much in control of his life that it was terrifying. He'll humiliate me, Selig thought. He'll devour me. But that panic faded. Two days later Nyquist came around to ask him out to dinner. They ate in a nearby Mexican restaurant and got smashed on Carta Blanca. It still appeared to Selig that Nyquist was toying with him, teasing him, holding him at arm's length and tickling him; but it was all done so amiably that Selig felt no resentment. Nyquist's charm was irresistible, and his strength was worth taking as a model of behavior. Nyquist was like an older brother who had preceded him through this same vale of traumas and had emerged unscathed long ago; now he was jollying Selig into an acceptance of the terms of his existence. The superhuman condition, Nyquist called it.

They became close friends. Two or three times a week they went out together, ate together, drank together. Selig had always imagined that a friendship with someone else of his kind would be uniquely intense, but this was not; after the first week they took their specialness for granted and rarely discussed the gift they shared, nor did they ever congratulate each other on having formed an alliance against the ungifted world around them. They communicated sometimes by words, sometimes by the direct contact of minds; it became an easy, cheerful relationship, strained only when Selig slipped into his habitual brooding mood and Nyquist mocked him for such self-indulgence. Even that was no difficulty between them until the days of the blizzard, when all tensions became exaggerated because they were spending so much time together.

'Hold out your glass,' Nyquist said.

He poured an amber splash of bourbon. Selig settled back to drink while Nyqist set about finding girls for them. The project took him five minutes. He scanned the building and turned up a pair of roommates on the fifth floor. 'Take a look,' he said to Selig. Selig entered Nyquist's mind. Nyquist had attuned himself to the consciousness of one of the girls – sensual, sleepy kittenish – and was looking through her eyes at the other, a tall gaunt blonde. The doubly refracted mental image nevertheless was quite clear: the blonde had a leggy voluptuousness and fashion-model poise. 'That one's mine.' Nyquist said. 'Now tell me if you like yours.' He jumped, Selig following along, to the mind of the blonde. Yes, a fashion model, more intelligent than the other girl, cold, selfish, passionate. From her mind, via Nyquist, came the image of her roommate, sprawled out on a sofa in a pink housecoat: a short plump redhead, breasty, fullfaced. 'Sure,' Selig said. 'Why not?' Nyquist, rummaging through minds, found the girls' phone number, called, worked his charm. They came up for drinks. 'This awful snowstorm,' the blonde said, shuddering. 'It can drive you crazy!' The four of them went through a lot of liquor to a tinkling jazz accompaniment: Mingus, MJQ, Chico Hamilton. The redhead was better-looking than Selig expected, not quite so plump or course – the double refraction must have introduced some distortions – but she giggled too much, and he found himself disliking her to some degree. Still, there was no backing out now. Eventually, very late in the evening, they coupled off, Nyquist and the blonde in the bedroom, Selig and the redhead in the livingroom. Selig grinned selfconsciously at her when they were finally alone. He had never learned how to suppress that infantile grin, which he knew must reveal a mingling of gawky anticipation and plummeting terror. 'Hello,' he said. They kissed and his hands went to her breasts, and she pushed herself up against him in an unashamedly hungry way. She seemed a few years older than he was, but most women seemed that way to him. Their clothes dropped away. 'I like lean men,' she said, and giggled as she pinched his sparse flesh. Her breasts rose to him like pink birds. He caressed her with a virgin's timid intensity. During the months of their friendship Nyquist had occasionally supplied him with his own discarded women, but it was weeks since he had been to bed with anyone, and he was afraid that his abstinence would rush him into an embarrassing calamity. No: the liquor cooled his ardor just enough, and he held himself in check, ploughing her solemnly and energetically with no fears of going off too fast.

About the time he realized the redhead was too drunk to come, Selig felt a tickle in his skull: Nyquist was probing him! This show of curiosity, this voyeurism, seemed an odd diversion for the usually self-contained Nyquist. Spying's *my* trick, Selig thought, and for a moment he was so disturbed by being observed in the act of love that he began to soften. Through conscious effort he reconstituted himself. This has no

deep significance, he told himself. Nyquist is wholly amoral
and does what he pleases, peeks here and peeks there without
regard for property, and why should I let his scanning bother
me? Recovering, he reached toward Nyquist and reciprocated
the probe. Nyquist welcomed him:
- How you doing, Davey?
- Fine. Just fine.
- I got me a hot one here. Take a look.
Selig envied Nyquist's cool detachment. No Shame, no guilt,
no hangups of any kind. No trace of exhibitionistic pride nor
voyeuristic panting, either: it seemed altogether natural to him
to exchange such contacts now. Selig, though, could not help
feeling queasy as he watched, through closed eyes, Nyquist
busily working over the blonde, and watched Nyquist similarly
watching him, echoing images of their parallel copulations
reverberating dizzily from mind to mind. Nyquist, pausing
a moment to detect and isolate Selig's sense of uneasiness,
mocked it gently. You're worried that there's some kind of
latent gayness in this thing, Nyquist told him. But I think what
really scares you is contact, any sort of contact. Right? Wrong,
Selig said, but he had felt the point hit home. For five minutes
more they monitored each other's minds, until Nyquist decided
the time had come to come, and the tempestuous tremors of his
nervous system flung Selig, as usual, from his consciousness.
Soon after, growing bored with humping the jiggling, sweaty
redhead, Selig let his own climax overwhelm him and slumped
down, shivering, weary.

Nyquist came into the livingroom half an hour later, the
blonde with him, both of them naked. He didn't bother to
knock, which surprised the redhead a little; Selig had no way
of telling her that Nyquist had known they were finished.
Nyquist put some music on and they all sat quietly, Selig
and the redhead working on the bourbon, Nyquist and the
blonde nipping into the Scotch, and toward dawn, as the snow
began to slacken, Selig tentatively suggested a second round of
lovemaking with a change of partners. 'No,' the redhead said.
'I'm all fucked out. I want to go to sleep. Some other time,

okay?' She fumbled for her clothes. At the door, wobbling and staggering, making a boozy farewell, she let something slip. 'I can't help thinking there's something peculiar about you two guys,' she said. *In vino veritas*. 'You aren't a couple of queers, by any chance, are you?'

SEVENTEEN

I remain on dead center. Becalmed, static, anchored. No, that's a lie, or if not a lie then at the very least a benign misstatement, a faulty cluster of metaphors. I am ebbing. Ebbing all the time. My tide is going out. I am revealed as a bare rocky shore, ironhard, with trailing streamers of dirty brown seaweed dangling toward the absenting surf. Green crab scuttling about. Yes, I ebb, which is to say I diminish, I attenuate. Do you know, I feel quite calm about it now? Of course my moods fluctuate but

I feel

Quite calm

About it now.

This is the third year since first I began to recede from myself. I think it started in the spring of 1974. Up till then it worked faultlessly, I mean the power, always there when I had occasion to call upon it, always dependable, doing all its customary tricks, serving me in all my dirty needs; and then without warning, without reason, it began dying. Little failures of input. Tiny episodes of psychic impotence. I associate these events with early spring, blackened wisps of late snow still clinging to the streets, and it could not have been '75 nor was it '73, which leads me to place the onset of outgo in the intermediate year. I would be snug and smug inside someone's head, scanning scandals thought to be safely hidden, and suddenly everything would blur and become uncertain. Rather like reading the *Times* and having the text abruptly turn to Joycean dream-gabble between one line and the next, so that a straightforward dreary account of the latest Presidential fact-finding commission's finding of futile facts has metamorphosed into a foggy impenetrable report on old Earwicker's borborygmi. At such times I would falter and pull out in fear. What would you do if you believed you were in bed with your heart's desire and awakened to find yourself screwing a starfish? But these unclarities and distortions were not the worst part: I think the inversions were, the total reversal of signal. Such as picking up a flash of love when what is really being radiated is frosty hatred. Or vice versa. When that happens I want to pound on walls to test reality. From Judith one day I got strong waves of sexual desire, an overpowering incestuous yearning, which cost me a fine dinner as I ran nauseated and retching to the bowl. All an error, all a deception; she was aiming spears at me and I took them for Cupid's arrows, more fool I. Well, after that I got blank spaces, tiny deaths of perception in mid-contact, and after that came mingled inputs, crossed wires, two minds coming in at once and me unable to tell the which from the which. For a time the color appercept dropped out, though that has come back, one of the many false returns. And there were other losses, barely discernible ones but cumulative in their effect. I make lists now of the things I once could do that I can no longer. Inventories of the shrinking. Like a dying man confined to his bed, paralyzed but observant, watching his relatives pilfer his goods. This day the television set has gone, and this day the Thackeray first editions, and this day the spoons, and now they have made off with my Piranesis, and tomorrow it will be the pots and pans, the Venetian blinds, my neckties, and my trousers, and by next week they will be taking toes, intestines, corneas, testicles, lungs, and nostrils. What will they use my nostrils for? I used to fight back with long walks, cold showers, tennis, massive doses of Vitamin A, and other hopeful, implausible remedies, and more recently I experimented with fasting and pure thoughts, but such struggling now seems to me inappropriate and even blasphemous; these days I strive toward cheerful acceptance of loss, with such success as you may have already perceived. Aeschylus warns me not to kick against the pricks, also Euripides and I believe Pindar, and if I were to check the New Testament I think I would find the injunction there as well, and so I obey, I kick not, even when the pricks are fiercest. I accept, I accept. Do you see that quality of acceptance growing in me? Make no mistake, I am sincere. This morning, at least, I am well on my way to acceptance, as golden autumn sunlight floods my room and expands my tattered soul. I lie here practicing the techniques that will make me invulnerable to the knowledge that it's all fleeing from me. I search for the joy that I know lies buried in the awareness of decline. Grow old along with me! The best is yet to be. The last of life, for which the first was made. Do you believe that? I believe that. I'm getting better at believing all sorts of things. Why, sometimes I've believed as many as six impossible things before breakfast. Good old Browning! How comforting he is:

> Then welcome each rebuff
> That turns earth's smoothness rough,
> Each sting that bids nor sit nor stand, but go!
> Be our joys three parts pain!
> Strive, and hold cheap the strain.

Yes. Of course. And be our pains three parts joy, he might have added. Such joy this morning. And it's all fleeing from me, all ebbing. Going out of me from every pore.

Silence is coming over me. I will speak to no one after it's gone. And no one will speak to me.

I stand here over the bowl patiently pissing my power away. Naturally I feel some sorrow over what's happening, I feel regret, I feel – why crap around? – I feel anger and frustration and despair, but also, strangely, I feel shame. My cheeks burn, my eyes will not meet other eyes, I can hardly face my fellow

mortals for the shame of it, as if something precious has been
entrusted to me and I have failed in my trusteeship. I must
say to the world, I've wasted my assets, I've squandered my
patrimony, I've let it slip away, going, going, I'm a bankrupt
now, a bankrupt. Perhaps this is a family trait, this embarrassment when disaster comes. We Seligs like to tell the world we
are orderly people, captains of our souls, and when something
external downs us we are abashed. I remember when my
parents briefly owned a car, a dark-green 1948 Chevrolet
purchased at some absurdly low price in 1950, and we were
driving somewhere deep in Queens, perhaps on our way to my
grandmother's grave, the annual pilgrimage, and a car emerged
from a blind alley and hit us. A schvartze at the wheel, drunk,
giddy. Nobody hurt, but our fender badly crumpled and our
grille broken, the distinctive T-bar that identified the 1948
model hanging loose. Though the accident was in no way his
fault my father reddened and reddened, transmitting feverish
embarrassment, as though he were apologizing to the universe
for having done anything so thoughtless as allowing his car to
be hit. How he apologized to the other driver, too, my grim
bitter father! It's all right, it's all right, accidents can happen,
you mustn't feel upset about it, see, we're all okay! Looka
mah car, man, looka mah car, the other driver kept saying,
evidently aware that he was on to a soft touch, and I feared
my father was going to give him money for the repairs, but
my mother, fearing the same thing, headed him off at the
pass. A week later he was still embarrassed; I popped into
his mind while he was talking with a friend and heard him
trying to pretend my mother had been driving, which was
absurd – she never had a license – and then I felt embarrassed
for him. Judith, too, when her marriage broke up, when she
walked out on an impossible situation, registered enormous
grief over the shameful fact that someone so purposeful and
effective in life as Judith Hannah Selig should have entered
into a lousy, murderous marriage which had to be terminated
vulgarly in the divorce courts. Ego, ego, ego. I the miraculous
mindreader, entering upon a mysterious decline, apologizing

for my carelessness. I have misplaced my gift somewhere. Will you forgive me?

> Good, to forgive;
> Best, to forget!
> Living, we fret;
> Dying, we live.

Take an imaginary letter, Mr Selig. Harrumph. Miss Kitty Holstein, Something West Sixty-something Street, New York City. Check the address later. Don't bother about the zipcode.

Dear Kitty:

I know you haven't heard from me in ages but I think now it's appropriate to try to get in touch with you again. Thirteen years have passed and a certain maturity must have come over both of us, I think, healing old wounds and making communication possible. Despite all hard feelings that may once have existed between us I never lost my fondness for you, and you remain bright in my mind.

Speaking of my mind, there's something I ought to tell you. I no longer do things very well with it. By 'things' I mean the mental thing, the mindreading trick, which of course I couldn't do on you on any case, but which defined and shaped my relationship to everybody else in the world. This power seems to be slipping away from me now. It caused us so much grief, remember? It was what ultimately split us up, as I tried to explain in my last letter to you, the one you never answered. In another year or so – who knows, six months, a month, a week? – it will be totally gone and I will be just an ordinary human being, like yourself. I will be a freak no longer. Perhaps then there will be an opportunity for us to resume the relationship that was interrupted in 1963 and to reestablish it on a more realistic footing.

I know I did dumb things then. I pushed you mercilessly. I refused

*to accept you for yourself, and tried to make something else out of you,
something freakish, in fact, something just like myself. I had good
reasons in theory for attempting that, I thought then, but of course
they were wrong, they had to be wrong, and I never saw that until it
was too late. To you I seemed domineering, overpowering, dictatorial –
me, mild self-effacing me! Because I was trying to transform you.
And eventually I bored you. Of course you were very young then,
you were – shall I say it? – shallow, unformed, and you resisted
me. But now that we're both adults we might be able to make a
go of it.*

*I hardly know what my life will be like as an ordinary human
being unable to enter minds. Right now I'm floundering, looking for
definitions of myself, looking for structures. I'm thinking seriously of
entering the Roman Catholic Church.* (Good Christ, am I? That's
the first I've heard of that! The stink of incense, the mumble
of priests, is that what I want?) *Or perhaps the Episcopalians, I
don't know. It's a matter of affiliating myself with the human race.
And also I want to fall in love again. I want to be part of someone
else. I've already begun tentatively, timidly getting in touch with my
sister Judith again, after a whole lifetime of warfare; we're starting
to relate to each other for the first time, and that's encouraging to me.
But I need more: a woman to love, not just sexually but in all ways.
I've really had that only twice in my life, once with you, once about
five years later with a girl named Toni who wasn't very much like
you, and both times this power of mine ruined things, once because
I got too close with it, once because I couldn't get close enough. As
the power slips away from me, as it dies, perhaps there's a chance
for an ordinary human relationship between us at last, of the kind
that ordinary human beings have all the time. For I will be ordinary.
For I will be very ordinary.*

*I wonder about you. You're 35 years old now, I think. That sounds
very old to me, even though I'm 41. (41 doesn't sound old, somehow!)
I still think of you as being 22. You seemed even younger than that:
sunny, open, naïve. Of course that was my fantasy-image of you; I had
nothing to go by but externals, I couldn't do my usual number on your
psyche, and so I made up a Kitty who probably wasn't the real Kitty at
all. Anyway, so you're 35. I imagine you look younger than that today.*

Did you marry? Of course you did. A happy marriage? Lots of kids? Are you still married? What's your married name, then, and where do you live, and how can I find you? If you're married, will you be able to see me anyway? Somehow I don't think you'd be a completely faithful wife – does that insult you? – and so there ought to be room in your life for me, as a friend, as a lover. Do you ever see Tom Nyquist? Did you go on seeing him for long, after you and I broke up? Were you bitter toward me for the things I told you about him in that letter? If your marriage has broken up, or if somehow you never married, would you live with me now? Not as a wife, not yet, just as a companion. To help me get through the last phases of what's happening to me? I need help so much. I need love. I know that's a lousy way to go about making a proposition, let alone a proposal, that is, saying, Help me, comfort me, stay with me. I'd rather reach to you in strength than in weakness. But right now I'm weak. There's this globe of silence growing in my head, expanding, expanding, filling my whole skull, creating this big empty place. I'm suffering a slow reality leakage. I can only see the edges of things, not their substance, and now the edges are getting indistinct too. Oh, Christ. Kitty I need you. Kitty how will I find you? Kitty I hardly knew you. Kitty Kitty Kitty

Twang. The plangent chord. *Twing*. The breaking string. *Twong*. The lyre untuned. Twang. Twing. Twong.

Dear children of God, my sermon this morning will be a very short one. I wish only that you should ponder and meditate the deep meaning and mystery of a few lines I intend to rip off the saintly Tom Eliot, a thoughtful guide for troubled times. Beloved, I direct you to his *Four Quartets*, to his paradoxical line, 'In my beginning is my end,' which he amplifies some pages later with the comment, 'What we call the beginning is often the end/ And to make an end is to make a beginning.' Some of us are ending right now, dear children; that is to say, aspects of their lives that once were central to them are drawing to a close. Is this an end or is it a beginning? Can the end of one thing not be the beginning of another? I think so, beloved. I think that the closing of a door does not preclude the opening of a different door. Of course, it takes courage to walk through that new door when we do not know what may lie beyond it, but one who has faith in Our Lord who died for us, who trusts fully in Him who came for the salvation of man, need have no fears. Our lives are pilgrimages toward Him. We may die small deaths every day, but we are reborn from death to death, until at last we go into the dark, into the vacant interstellar spaces where He awaits us, and why should we fear that, if He is there? And until that time comes let us live our lives without giving way to the temptation to grieve for ourselves. Remember always that the world still is full of wonders, that there are always new quests, that seeming ends are not ends in truth, but only transitions, stations of the way. Why should we mourn? Why should we give ourselves over to sorrow, though our lives be daily subtractions? If we lose *this*, do we also lose *that*? If sight goes, does love go also? If feeling grows faint, may we not return to old feelings and draw comfort from them? Much of our pain is mere confusion.

Be then of good cheer on this Our Lord's day, beloved, and spin no snares in which to catch yourselves, nor allow yourselves the self-indulgent sin of misery, and make no false distinctions between ends and beginnings, but go onward, ever searching, to new ecstasies, to new communions, to new worlds, and give no space in your soul to fear, but yield yourself up to the Peace of Christ and await that which must come. In the Name of the Father, and of the Son, and of the Holy Ghost, Amen.

Now comes a dark equinox out of its proper moment. The bleached moon glimmers like a wretched old skull. The leaves shrivel and fall. The fires die down. The dove, wearying, flutters to earth. Darkness spreads. Everything blows away. The purple blood falters in the narrowing veins; the chill impinges on the straining heart; the soul dwindles; even the feet become untrustworthy. Words fail. Our guides admit they are lost.

That which has been solid grows transparent. Things pass away. Colors fade. This is a gray time, and I fear it will be grayer still, one of these days. Tenants of the house, thoughts of a dry brain in a dry season.

EIGHTEEN

When Toni moved out of my place on 114th Street I waited two days before I did anything. I assumed she would come back when she calmed down; I figured she'd call, contrite, from some friend's house and say she was sorry she panicked and would I come get her in a cab. Also, in those two days I was in no shape to take any sort of action, because I was still suffering the after-effects of my vicarious trip; I felt as though someone had seized my head and pulled on it, stretching my neck like a rubber band, letting it finally snap back into place with a sharp *thwock!* that addled my brains. I spent those two days in bed, dozing mostly, occasionally reading, and rushing madly out into the hall every time the telephone rang.

But she didn't come back and she didn't call, and on the Tuesday after the acid trip I started searching for her. I phoned her office first. Teddy, her boss, a bland sweet scholarly man, very gentle, very gay. No, she hadn't been to work this week. No, she hadn't been in touch at all. Was it urgent? Would I like to have her home number? 'I'm *calling* from her home number,' I said. 'She isn't here and I don't know where she's gone. This is David Selig, Teddy.' 'Oh,' he said. Very faintly, with great compassion. 'Oh.' And I said, 'If she happens to call in, will you tell her to get in touch with me?' Next I started to phone her friends, those whose numbers I could find: Alice, Doris, Helen, Pam, Grace. Most of them, I knew, didn't like me. I didn't have to be telepathic to realize that. They thought she was throwing herself away on me, wasting her life with a man without career, prospects, money, ambition, talent, or looks.

All five of them told me they hadn't heard from her. Doris, Helen, and Pam sounded sincere. The other two, it seemed to me, were lying. I took a taxi over to Alice's place in the Village and shot a probe upward, *zam!* nine stories into her head, and I learned a lot of things about Alice that I hadn't really wanted to know, but I didn't find out where Toni was. I felt dirty about spying and didn't probe Grace. Instead I called my employer, the writer, whose book Toni was editing, and asked if he'd seen her. Not in weeks, he told me, all ice. Dead end. The trail had run out.

I dithered on Wednesday, wondering what to do, and finally, melodramatically, called the police. Gave a bored desk sergeant her description: tall, thin, long dark hair, brown eyes. No bodies found in Central Park lately? In subway trash cans? The basements of Amsterdam Avenue tenements? No. No. No. Look, buddy, if we hear anything we'll let you know, but it don't sound serious to me. So much for the police. Restless, hopelessly strung out, I walked down to the Great Shanghai for a miserable half-eaten dinner, good food gone to waste. (Children are starving in Europe, Duv. Eat. Eat.) Afterwards, sitting around over the sad scattered remnants of my shrimp with sizzling rice and feeling myself drop deep into bereavement, I scored a cheap pickup in a manner I've always despised: I scanned the various single girls in the big restaurant, of whom there were numerous, looking for one who was lonely, thwarted, vulnerable, sexually permissive, and in generally urgent need of ego reinforcement. It's no trick getting laid if you have a sure way of knowing who's available, but there's not much sport in the chase. She was, this fish in the barrel, a passably attractive married lady in her mid-20's, childless, whose husband, a Columbia instructor, evidently had more interest in his doctoral thesis than in her. He spent every night immured in the stacks of Butler Library doing research, creeping home late, exhausted, irritable, and generally impotent. I took her to my room, couldn't get it up either – that bothered her; she assumed it was a sign of rejection – and spent two tense hours listening to her life story.

Ultimately I managed to screw her, and I came almost instantly. Not my finest hour. When I returned from walking her home – 110th and Riverside Drive – the phone was ringing. Pam. 'I've heard from Toni,' she said, and suddenly I was slimy with guilt over my sleazy consolatory infidelity. 'She's staying with Bob Larkin at his place over on East 83rd Street.'

Jealousy, despair, humiliation, agony.

'Bob who?'

'Larkin. He's that high-bracket interior decorator she always talks about.'

'Not to me.'

'One of Toni's oldest friends. They're very close. I think he used to date her when she was in high school.' A long pause. Then Pam chuckled warmly into my numb silence. 'Oh, relax, relax, David! He's *gay!* He's just a kind of father-confessor for her. She goes to him when there's trouble.'

'I see.'

'You two have broken up, haven't you?'

'I'm not sure. I suppose we have. I don't know.'

'Is there anything I can do to help?' This from Pam, who I had always thought regarded me as a destructive influence of whom Toni was well advised to be quit.

'Just give me his phone number,' I said.

I phoned. It rang and rang and rang. At last Bob Larkin picked up. Gay, all right, a sweet tenor voice complete with lisp, not very different from the voice of Teddy-at-work. Who teaches them to speak with the homo accent? I asked, 'Is Toni there?' A guarded response: 'Who's calling, please?' I told him. He asked me to wait, and a minute or so passed while he conferred with her, hand over the mouthpiece. At last he came back and said Toni was there, yes, but she was very tired and resting and didn't want to talk to me right now. 'It's urgent,' I said. 'Please tell her it's urgent.' Another muffled conference. Same reply. He suggested vaguely that I call back in two or three days. I started to wheedle, to whine, to beg. In the middle of that unheroic performance the phone abruptly changed hands and Toni said to me, 'Why did you call?'

'That ought to be obvious. I want you to come back.'

'I can't.'

She didn't say *I won't*. She said *I can't*.

I said, 'Would you like to tell me why?'

'Not really.'

'You didn't even leave a note. Not a word of explanation. You ran out so fast.'

'I'm sorry, David.'

'It was something you saw in me while you were tripping, wasn't it?'

'Let's not talk about it,' she said. 'It's over.'

'I don't want it to be over.'

'I do.'

I do. That was like the sound of a great gate clanging shut in my face. But I wasn't going to let her throw home the bolts just yet. I told her she had left some of her things in my room, some books, some clothing. A lie: she had made a clean sweep. But I can be persuasive when I'm cornered, and she began to think it might be true. I offered to bring the stuff over right now. She didn't want me to come. She preferred never to see me again, she told me. Less painful all around, that way. But her voice lacked conviction; it was higher in pitch and much more nasal than it was when she spoke with sincerity. I knew she still loved me, more or less; even after a forest fire, some of the burned snags live on, and green new shoots spring from them. So I told myself. Fool that I was. In any case she couldn't entirely turn me away. Just as she had been unable to refrain from picking up the telephone, now she found it impossible to refuse me access to her. Talking very fast, I bludgeoned her into yielding. All right, she said. Come over. Come over. But you're wasting your time.

It was close to midnight. The summer air was clinging and clammy, with a hint of rain on the way. No stars visible. I hurried crosstown, choked with the vapors of the humid city and the bile of my shattered love. Larkin's apartment was on the nineteenth floor of an immense new terraced white-brick tower, far over on York Avenue. Admitting me, he gave me a tender, compassionate smile, as if to say. You poor bastard, you've been hurt and you're bleeding and now you're going to get ripped open again. He was about 30, a stocky, boyish-faced man with long unruly brown hair and large uneven teeth. He radiated warmth and sympathy and kindness. I could understand why Toni ran to him at times like this. 'She's in the livingroom,' he said. 'To the left.'

It was a big, impeccable place, somewhat freaky in decor, with jagged blurts of color dancing over the walls, pre-Columbian artifacts in spotlighted showcases, bizarre African masks, chrome-steel furniture – the kind of implausible apart-ment you see photographed in the Sunday *Times'* magazine section. The livingroom was the core of the spectacle, a vast white-walled room with a long curving window that revealed all the splendors of Queens across the East River. Toni sat at the far end, near the window, on an angular couch, dark blue flecked with gold. She wore old, dowdy clothes that clashed furiously with the splendor around her: a motheaten red sweater that I detested, a short frumpy black skirt, dark hose – and she was slumped down sullenly on her spine, leaning on one elbow, her legs jutting awkwardly forward. It was a posture that made her look bony and ungraceful. A cigarette drooped in her hand and there was a huge pile of butts in the ashtray beside her. Her eyes were bleak. Her long hair was tangled. She didn't move as I walked toward her. Such an aura of hostility came from her that I halted twenty feet away.

'Where's the stuff you were bringing?' she asked.

'There wasn't any. I just said that to have an excuse to see you.'

'I figured that.'

'What went wrong, Toni?'

'Don't ask. Just don't ask.' Her voice had dropped into its lowest register, a bitter husky contralto. 'You shouldn't have come here at all.'

'If you'd tell me what I did –'

'You tried to hurt me,' she said. 'You tried to bumtrip me.'

She stubbed out her cigarette and immediately lit another. Her eyes, somber and hooded, refused to meet mine. 'I realized finally that you were my enemy, that I had to escape from you. So I packed and got out.'

'Your enemy? You know that isn't true.'

'It was strange,' she said. 'I didn't understand what was happening, and I've talked to some people who've dropped a lot of acid and they can't understand it either. It was like our minds were linked, David. Like a telepathic channel had opened between us. And all sorts of stuff was pouring from you into me. Hateful stuff. Poisonous stuff. I was thinking your thoughts. Seeing myself as you saw me. Remember, when you said you were tripping too, even though you hadn't had any acid? And then you told me you were, like, reading my mind. That was what scared me. The way our minds seemed to blur together, to overlap. To become one. I never knew acid could do that to people.'

This was my cue to tell her that it wasn't only the acid, that it hadn't been some druggy delusion, that what she had felt was the impingement of a special power granted me at birth, a gift, a curse, a freak of nature. But the words congealed in my mouth. They sounded insane to me. How could I confess such stuff? I let the moment pass. Instead I said lamely, 'Okay, it was a strange moment for both of us. We were a little out of our heads. But the trip's over. You don't have to hide from me now. Come back, Toni.'

'No.'

'In a few days, then?'

'No.'

'I don't understand this.'

'Everything's changed,' she said. 'I couldn't ever live with you now. You scare me too much. The trip's over, but I look at you and I see demons. I see some kind of thing that's half-bat, half-man, with big rubbery wings and long yellow fangs and – oh, Jesus, David, I can't help any of this! I *still* feel as if our minds are linked. Stuff creeping out of you into my head. I should never have touched the acid.' Carelessly she crushed her cigarette and found another. 'You make me uncomfortable now. I wish you'd go. It gives me a headache just being this close to you. Please. Please. I'm sorry, David.'

I didn't dare look into her mind. I was afraid that what I'd find there would blast and shrivel me. But in those days my power was still so strong that I couldn't help picking up, whether I sought it or not, a generalized low-level mental radiation from everyone I came close to, and what I picked up now from Toni confirmed what she was saying. She hadn't stopped loving me. But the acid, though lysergic and not sulfuric, had scarred and corroded our relationship by opening that terrible gateway between us. It was torment for her to be in the same room with me. No resources of mine could deal with that. I considered strategies, looked for angles of approach, ways to reason with her, to heal her through soft earnest words. No way. No way at all. I ran a dozen trial dialogs in my head and they all ended with Toni begging me to get out of her life. So. The end. She sat there all but motionless, downcast, dark-faced, her wide mouth clamped in pain, her brilliant smile extinguished. She seemed to have aged twenty years. Her odd, exotic desert-princess beauty had wholly fled from her. Suddenly she was more real to me, in her shroud of pain, than ever before. Ablaze with suffering, alive with anguish. And no way for me to reach her. 'All right,' I said quietly. 'I'm sorry too.' Over, done with, swiftly, suddenly, no warning, the bullet singing through the air, the grenade rolling treacherously into the tent, the anvil falling from the placid sky. Done with. Alone again. Not even any tears. Cry? What shall I cry?

Bob Larkin had tactfully remained outside, in his long foyer papered with dazzling black and white optical illusions, during our brief muffled conversation. Again the gentle sorrowing smile from him as I emerged.

'Thanks for letting me bother you this late,' I said.

'No trouble at all. Too bad about you and Toni.'

I nodded. 'Yes. Too bad.'

We faced each other uncertainly, and he moved toward me,

digging his fingers momentarily into the muscle of my arm, telling me without words to shape up, to ride out the storm, to get myself together. He was so open that my mind sank unexpectedly into his, and I saw him plain, his goodness, his kindness, his sorrow. Out of him an image rose to me, a sharp encapsulated memory: himself and a sobbing, demolished Toni, the night before last, lying naked together on his modish round bed, her head cradled against his muscular hairy chest, his hands fondling the pale heavy globes of her breasts. Her body trembling with need. His unwilling drooping manhood struggling to offer her the consolation of sex. His gentle spirit at war with itself, flooded with pity and love for her but dismayed by her disturbing femaleness, those breasts, that cleft, her softness. You don't have to, Bob, she keeps saying, you don't have to, you really don't have to, but he tells her he wants to, it's about time we made it after knowing each other all these years, it'll cheer you up, Toni, and anyway a man needs a little variety, right? His heart goes out to her but his body resists, and their lovemaking, when it happens, is a hurried, pathetic, fumbled thing, a butting of troubled reluctant bodies, ending in tears, tremors, shared distress, and, finally, laughter, a triumph over pain. He kisses her tears away. She thanks him gravely for his efforts. They fall into childlike sleep, side by side. How civilized, how tender. My poor Toni. Goodbye. Goodbye. 'I'm glad she went to you,' I said. He walked me to the elevator. What shall I cry? 'If she snaps out of it I'll make sure she calls you,' he told me. I put my hand to his arm as he had to mine, and gave him the best smile in my repertoire. Goodbye.

NINETEEN

This is my cave. Twelve floors high in the Marble Hill Houses, Broadway and 228th Street, formerly a middle-income munici-pal housing project, now a catchall for classless and deracinated urban detritus. Two rooms plus bathroom, kitchenette, hallway. Once upon a time you couldn't get into this project unless you were married and had kids. Nowadays a few singles have slipped in, on the grounds that they're destitute. Things change as the city decays; regulations break down. Most of the building's population is Puerto Rican, with a sprinkling of Irish and Italian. In this den of papists a David Selig is a great anomaly. Sometimes he thinks he owes his neighbors a daily lusty rendition of the *Shma Yisroel*, but he doesn't know the words. *Kol Nidre*, perhaps. Or the *Kaddish*. This is the bread of affliction which our forefathers ate in the land of Egypt. He is lucky to have been led out of Egypt into the Promised Land.

Would you like the guided tour of David Selig's cave? Very well. Please come this way. No touching anything, please, and don't park your chewing gum on the furniture. The sensitive, intelligent, amiable, neurotic man who will be your guide is none other than David Selig himself. No tipping allowed. Welcome, folks, welcome to my humble abode. We'll begin our tour in the bathroom. See, this is the tub – that yellow stain in the porcelain was already there when he moved in – this is the crapper, this is the medicine chest. Selig spends a great deal of time in here; it's a room significant to any in-depth understanding of his existence. For example, he sometimes takes two or three showers a day. What is it, do you think, that he's trying to wash away? Leave that toothbrush alone, sonny. All right, come with me. Do you see those posters in the hallway? They are artifacts of the 1960's. This one shows the poet Allen Ginsberg in the costume of Uncle Sam. This one is a crude vulgarization of a subtle topological paradox by the Dutch printmaker M. G. Escher. This one shows a nude young couple making love in the Pacific surf. Eight to ten years ago, hundreds of thousands of young people decorated their rooms with such posters. Selig, although he was not exactly young even then, did the same. He often has followed current fads and modes in an attempt to affiliate himself more firmly with the structures of contemporary existence. I suppose these posters are quite valuable now; he takes them with him from one cheap rooming house to the next.

This room is the bedroom. Dark and narrow, with the low ceiling typical of municipal construction a generation ago. I keep the window closed at all times so that the elevated train, roaring through the adjacent sky late at night, doesn't awaken me. It's hard enough to get some sleep even when things are quiet around you. This is his bed, in which he dreams uneasy dreams, occasionally, even now, involuntarily reading the minds of his neighbors and incorporating their thoughts in his fantasies. On this bed he had fornicated perhaps fifteen women, one or two or occasionally three times each, during the two and a half years of his residence here. Don't look so abashed, young lady! Sex is a healthy human endeavor and it remains an essential aspect of Selig's life, even now in middle age! It may become even more important to him in the years ahead, for sex is, after all, a way of establishing communication with other human beings, and certain other channels of communication appear to be closing for him. Who are these girls? Some of them are not girls; some are women well along in life. He charms them in his diffident way and persuades them to share an hour of joy with him. He rarely invites any of them back, and those whom he does invite back often refuse the invitation, but that's all right. His needs are met. What's that? Fifteen girls in two and a half years isn't very many for a bachelor? Who are you to judge? He finds it sufficient. I assure you, he finds it sufficient. Please don't sit on his bed. It's an old one, bought secondhand at an upstairs bargain basement that the Salvation Army runs in Harlem. I picked it up for a few bucks when I moved out of my last place, a furnished room on St Nicholas Avenue, and needed some furniture of my own. Some years before that, around 1971, 1972, I had a waterbed, another example of my following of transient fads, but I couldn't ever get used to the swooshing and gurgling and I gave it, finally, to a hip young lady who dug it the most. What else is in the bedroom? Very little of interest, I'm afraid. A chest of drawers containing commonplace clothing. A pair of worn slippers. A cracked mirror: are you superstitious? A lopsided bookcase packed tight with old magazines that he will never look at again – *Partisan Review, Evergreen, Paris Review, New York Review of Books, Encounter*, a mound of trendy literary stuff, plus a few journals of psychoanalysis and psychiatry, which Selig reads sporadically in the hope of increasing his self-knowledge; he always tosses them aside in boredom and disappointment. Let's get out of here. This room must be depressing you. We go past the kitchenette – four-burner stove, half-size refrigerator, formica-topped table – where he assembles very modest breakfasts and lunches (dinner he usually eats out) and enter the main focus of the apartment, the L-shaped blue-walled jam-packed livingroom/study.

Here you can observe the full range of David Selig's intellectual development. This is his record collection, about a hundred well-worn disks, some of them purchased as far back as 1951. (Archaic monophonic records!) Almost entirely classical music, although you will note two intrusive deposits: five or six jazz records dating from 1959 and five or six rock records dating from 1969, both groups acquired in vague, abortive efforts at expanding the horizons of his taste. Otherwise, what you will find here, in the main, is pretty austere stuff, thorny, inaccessible: Schoenberg, late Beethoven, Mahler, Berg, the Bartok quartets, Bach passacaglias. Nothing that you'd be likely to whistle after one hearing. He doesn't know a lot about music, but he knows what he likes; you wouldn't much care for it.

And these are his books, accumulated since the age of ten and hauled lovingly about him from place to place. The archaeological strata of his reading can readily be isolated and examined. Jules Verne, H. G. Wells, Mark Twain, Dashiell Hammett at the bottom. Sabatini. Kipling. Sir Walter Scott. Van Loon, *The Story of Mankind*. Verrill, *Great Conquerors of South and Central America*. The books of a sober, earnest, alienated little boy. Suddenly, with adolescence, a quantum leap: Orwell, Fitzgerald, Hemingway, Hardy, the easier Faulkner. Look at these rare paperbacks of the 1940's and early 1950's, in old off-sized formats, with laminated plastic covers! See what you could buy then for only 25¢! Look at the prurient paintings, the garish lettering! These science-fiction books date from that era too. I gobbled the stuff whole, hoping to find some clues to my own dislocated self's nature in the fantasies of Bradbury, Heinlein, Asimov, Sturgeon, Clarke. Look, here's Stapledon's *Odd John*, here's Beresford's *Hampdenshire Wonder*, here's a whole book called *Outsiders: Children of Wonder*, full of stories of little superbrats with freaky powers. I've underlined a lot of passages in that last one, usually places where I quarreled with the writers. *Outsiders?* Those writers, gifted as they were, were the outsiders, trying to imagine powers they'd never had; and I, who was on the inside, I the youthful mind-prowler (the book is dated 1954), had bones to pick with them. They stressed the angst of being supernormal, forgot about the ecstasy. Although, thinking about angst vs. ecstasy now, I have to admit they knew whereof they writ. Fellows, I have fewer bones to pick these days. This is rats' alley, where the dead men lost their bones.

Observe how Selig's reading becomes more rarefied as we reach the college years. Joyce, Proust, Mann, Eliot, Pound, the old avant-garde hierarchy. The French period: Zola, Balzac, Montaigne, Celine, Rimbaud, Baudelaire. This thick slug of Dostoevsky occupying half a shelf, Lawrence. Woolf. The mystical era: Augustine, Aquinas, the *Tao Te Ching*, the *Upanishads*, the *Bhagavad-Gita*. The psychological era. Freud, Jung, Adler, Reich, Reik. The philosophical era. The Marxist era. All that Koestler. Back to literature: Conrad, Forster, Beckett. Moving onward toward the fractured '60's. Bellow, Pynchon, Malamud, Mailer, Burroughs, Barth. *Catch-22* and *The Politics of Experience*. Oh, yes, ladies and gentlemen, you are in the presence of a well-read man!

Here we have his files. A treasure-trove of personalia, awaiting a biographer yet unknown. Report cards, always with low marks for conduct. ('David shows little interest in his work and frequently disrupts the class.') Crudely crayoned birthday cards for his mother and father. Old photographs: can this fat freckled boy be the gaunt individual who stands before you now? This man with the high forehead and the forced rigid smile is the late Paul Selig, father of our subject, deceased (*olav hasholom!*) 11 August 1971 of complications following surgery for a perforated ulcer. This gray-haired woman with the hyperthyroid eyes is the late Martha Selig, wife of Paul, mother of David, deceased (*oy, veh, mama!*) 15 March 1973 of mysterious rot of internal organs, probably cancerous. This grim young lady with cold knifeblade face is Judith Hannah Selig, adopted child of P. and M., unloving sister of D. Date on back of photo: July 1963. Judith is therefore 18 years old and in the summertime of her hate for me. How much she looks like Toni in this picture! I never noticed the resemblance before, but they've got the same dusky Yemenite look, the same long black hair. But Toni's eyes were always warm and loving, except right at the very end, and Jude's eyes never held anything for me other than ice, ice, Plutonian ice. Let us continue with the examination of David Selig's private effects. This is his collection of essays and term papers, written during his college years ('Carew is a courtly and elegant poet, whose work reflects influences both of Jonson's precise classicism and Donne's grotesque fancy – an interesting synthesis. His poems are neatly constructed and sharp of diction; in a poem such as "Ask me no more where Jove bestows", he captures Jonson's harmonious austerity perfectly, while in others, such as "Mediocrity in Love Rejected" or "Ingrateful Beauty Threatened", his wit is akin to that of Donne.') How fortunate for D. Selig that he kept all this literary twaddle: here in his later years these papers have become the capital on which he lives, for you know, of course, how the central figure of our investigations earns his livelihood nowadays. What else do we find in these archives? The carbon copies of innumerable letters. Some of them are quite impersonal missives. *Dear President Eisenhower. Dear Pope John. Dear Secretary-General Hammarskjold.* Quite often, once, though rarely in recent years, he launched these letters to far corners of the globe. His fitful unilateral efforts at making contact with a deaf world. His troubled futile attempts at restoring order in a universe plainly tumbling toward the ultimate thermodynamic doom. Shall we look at a few of these documents? *You say, Governor Rockefeller, that 'with nuclear weapons multiplying, our security is dependent on the credibility of our willingness to resort to our deterrent. It is our heavy responsibility as public officials and as citizens to save the lives and to protect the health of our people. A lagging civil-defense effort cannot be excused by our conviction that nuclear war is a tragedy and that we must strive by all honorable means to assure peace.' Permit me to disagree. Your bomb-shelter program, Governor, is the project of a morally impoverished mind. To divert energy and resources from the search for a lasting peace to this ostrich-in-the-sand scheme is, I think, a foolish and dangerous policy that* ... The Governor, by way of replying, sent his thanks and an offprint of the very speech which Selig was protesting. Can one expect more? *Mr Nixon, your entire campaign is pitched to the theory that America never had it so good under President Eisenhower, and so let's have four more years of the same. To me you sound like Faust, crying out to the passing moment, Verweile doch, du bist so schoen! (Am I too literate for you, Mr Vice-President?) Please bear in mind that when Faust utters those words, Mephistopheles arrives to collect his soul. Does it honestly seem to you that this instant in history is so sweet that you would stop the clocks forever? Listen to the anguish in the land. Listen to the voices of Mississippi's Negroes, listen to the cries of the hungry children of factory workers thrown out of work by a Republican recession, listen to* ... *Dear Mrs Hemingway: Please allow me to add my words to the thousands expressing sorrow at the death of your husband. The bravery he showed in the face of a life-situation that had become unendurable and intolerable is indeed an example for those of us who* ... *Dear Dr Buber* ... *Dear Professor Toynbee* ... *Dear President Nehru* ... *Dear Mr Pound: The whole civilized world rejoices with you upon your liberation from the cruel and unnatural confinement which* ... *Dear Lord Russell* ... *Dear Chairman Khrushchev* ... *Dear M. Malraux* ... *dear* ... *dear* ... *dear* ... A remarkable collection of correspondence, you must agree. With equally remarkable replies. See, this answer says, *You may be right*, and this one says, *I am grateful for your interest*, and this one says, *Of course time does not permit individual replies to all letters received, but nevertheless please be assured that your thoughts will receive careful consideration,* and this one says, *Send this bastard the bedbug letter.*

Unfortunately we do not have the imaginary letters which he dictates constantly to himself but never sends. *Dear Mr Kierkegaard: I agree entirely with your celebrated dictum equating 'the absurd' with 'the fact that with God all things are possible', and declaring, 'The absurd is not one of the factors which can be discriminated within the proper compass of the understanding: it is not identical with the improbable, the unexpected, the unforeseen.' In my own experiences with the absurd . . . Dear Mr Shakespeare: How aptly you put it when you say, 'Love is not love Which alters when it alteration finds, Or bends with the remover to remove.' Your sonnet, however, begs the question: If love is not love, what then is it, that feeling of closeness which can be so absurdly and unexpectedly destroyed by a trifle? If you could suggest some alternate existential mode of relating to others that . . .* Since they are transient, the produce of vagrant impulses, and often incomprehensible, we have no satisfactory access to such communications, which Selig sometimes produces at a rate of hundreds per hour. *Dear Mr Justice Holmes: In Southern Pacific Co. v. Jensen, 244 U.S. 205, 221 [1917], you ruled, 'I recognize without hesitation that judges do and must legislate, but they can do so only interstitially; they are confined from molar to molecular motions.' This splendid metaphor is not entirely clear to me, I must confess, and . . .*

Dear Mr Selig:

   The present state of the world and the whole of life is diseased. If I were a doctor and were asked for my advice, I should reply, 'Create silence.'

                                        Yours very sincerely,
                                        Sören Kierkegaard
                                        (1813 –1855)

And then there are these three folders here, thick beige cardboard. They are not available for public inspection, since they contain letters of a rather more personal kind. Under the terms of our agreement with the David Selig Foundation, I am forbidden to quote, though I may paraphrase. These are his letters to and occasionally from the girls he has loved or has wanted to love. The earliest is dated 1950 and bears the notation at the top in large red letters, NEVER SENT. *Dear Beverly*, it begins, and it is full of embarrassingly graphic sexual imagery. What can you tell us about this Beverly, Selig? Well, she was short and cute and freckled, with big headlights and a sunny disposition, and sat in front of me in my biology class, and had a creepy twin sister, Estelle, who scowled a lot and through some fluke of genetics was as flat as Beverly was bosomy. Maybe that was why she scowled so much. Estelle liked me in her bitter murky way and I think might eventually have slept with me, which would have done my 15-year-old ego a lot of good, but I despised her. She seemed like a blotchy, badly done imitation of Beverly, whom I loved. I used to wander barefoot in Beverly's mind while the teacher, Miss Mueller, droned on about mitosis and chromosomes. She had just yielded her cherry to Victor Schlitz, the big rawboned green-eyed red-haired boy who sat next to her, and I learned a lot about sex from her at one remove, with a 12-hour time-lag, as she radiated every morning her adventure of the night before with Victor. I wasn't jealous of him. He was handsome and self-confident and deserved her, and I was too shy and insecure to lay anybody anyway, then. So I rode secretly piggyback on their romance and fantasized doing with Beverly the gaudy things Victor was doing with her, until I desperately wanted to get into her myself, but my explorations of her head told me that to her I was just an amusing gnomish child, an oddity, a jester. How then to score? I wrote her this letter describing in vivid sweaty detail everything that she and Victor had been up to, and said, Don't you wonder how I know all this, heh heh heh? The implication being that I'm some kind of superman with the power to penetrate the intimacies of a woman's mind. I figured that would topple her right into my arms in a swoon of awe, but some second thoughts led me to see that she'd either think I was crazy or a peeping tom, and would in either case be wholly turned off me, so I filed the letter away undelivered. My mother found it one night but she didn't dare say anything about it to me, hopelessly blocked as she was on the entire subject of sexuality; she just put it back in my notebook. I picked her thoughts that night and discovered she'd sneaked a look. Was she shocked and disturbed? Yes, she was, but also she felt very proud that her boy was a man at last, writing smutty stuff to pretty girls. My son the pornographer.

Most of the letters in this file date between 1954 and 1968. The most recent was written in the autumn of 1974, after which time Selig began to feel less and less in touch with the rest of the human race and stopped writing letters, except in his head. I don't know how many girls are represented here, but there must have been quite a few. Generally these were all superficial affairs, for Selig, as you know, never married or even had many serious involvements with women. As in the case of Beverly, the ones he loved most deeply he usually never had actual relationships with, though he was capable of pretending he felt love for someone who was in fact a casual pickup. At times he made use of his special gifts knowingly to exploit women sexually, especially about the age of 25. He is not proud of that period. Wouldn't you like to read these letters, you stinking voyeurs? But you won't. You won't get your paws on them. Why have I invited you in here, anyway? Why do I let you peer at my books and my photographs and my unwashed dishes and my stained bathtub? It must be that my sense of self is slipping. Isolation is choking me; the windows are closed but at least I've opened the door. I need you to bolster my grip on reality by looking into my life, by incorporating parts of it into your own experience, by discovering that I'm real, I exist, I suffer, I have a past if not a future. So that you can go away from here saying, Yes, I know David Selig, actually I know him quite well. But that doesn't mean I have to show you everything. Hey, here's a letter to Amy! Amy who relieved me of my festering virginity in the spring of 1953. Wouldn't you like to know the story of how that happened? Anybody's first time as an irresistible fascination. Well, fuck you: I don't feel like discussing it. It isn't much of a story anyway. I put it in her and I came and she didn't, that's how it was, and if you want to know the rest, who she was, how I seduced her, make up the details yourself. Where's Amy now? Amy's dead. How do you like that? His first lay, and he's outlived her already. She died in an auto accident at the age of 23 and her husband, who knew me vaguely, phoned me to tell me, since I had once been a friend of hers. He was still in trauma because the police had made him come down to identify the body, and she had really been destroyed, mangled, mutilated. Like something from another planet, that's how she looked, he told me. Catapulted through the windshield and into a tree. And I told him, 'Amy was the first girl I ever slept with', and he started consoling me. He, consoling me, and I had only been trying to be sadistic.

Time passes. Amy's dead and Beverly's a pudgy middle-aged housewife, I bet. Here's a letter to Jackie Newhouse, telling her I can't sleep for thinking about her. Jackie Newhouse? Who that? Oh, yes. Five feet two and a pair of boobs that would have made Marilyn Monroe feel topheavy. Sweet. Dumb. Puckered lips, baby-blue eyes. Jackie had nothing going for her at all except her bosom, but that was enough for me, 17 years old and hung up on breasts, God knows why. I loved her for her mammaries, so globular and conspicuous in the tight white polo shirts she liked to wear. Summer of 1952. She loved Frank Sinatra and Perry Como, and had FRANKIE written in lipstick down the left thigh of her jeans and PERRY on the right. She also loved her history teacher, whose name, I think, was Leon Sissinger or Zippinger or something like that, and she had LEON on her jeans too, from hip to hip. I kissed her twice but that was all, not even my tongue in her mouth; she was even more shy than I, terrified that some hideous male hand would violate the purity of those mighty knockers. I followed her around, trying not to get into her head because it depressed me to see how empty it was. How did it end? Oh, yes: her kid brother Arnie was telling me how he sees her naked at home all the time, and I, desperate for a vicarious glimpse of her bare breasts, plunged into his skull and stole a second-hand peek. I hadn't realized until then how important a bra can be. Unbound, they hung to her plump little belly, two mounds of dangling meat crisscrossed by bulging blue veins. Cured me of my fixation. So long ago, so unreal to me now, Jackie.

Here. Look. Spy on me. My fervid frenzied outpourings of love. Read them all, what do I care? Donna, Elsie, Magda, Mona, Sue, Lois, Karen. Did you think I was sexually deprived? Did you think my lame adolescence sent me stumbling into manhood incapable of finding women? I quarried for my life between their thighs. Dear Connie, what a wild night that was! Dear Chiquita, your perfume still lingers in the air. Dear Elaine, when I woke this morning the taste of you was on my lips. Dear Kitty, I –

Oh, God. Kitty. *Dear Kitty, I have so much to explain to you that I don't know where to begin. You never understood me, and I never understood you, and so the love I had for you was fated to bring us to a bad pass sooner or later. Which it now has. The failures of communication extended all up and down our relationship, but because you were different from any person I had ever known, truly and qualitatively different, I made you the center of my fantasies and could not accept you as you were, but had to keep hammering and hammering and hammering away at you, until* – Oh, God. This one's too painful. What the hell are you doing reading someone else's mail? Don't you have any decency? I can't show you this. The tour's over. Out! Out! Everybody out! For Christ's sake, get *out!*

TWENTY

There was always the danger of being found out. He knew he had to be on his guard. This was an era of witch-hunters, when anyone who departed from community norms was ferreted out and burned at the stake. Spies were everywhere, probing for young Selig's secret, fishing for the awful truth about him. Even Miss Mueller, his biology teacher. She was a pudgy little poodle of a woman, about 40, with a glum face and dark arcs under her eyes; like a cryptodyke of some sort she wore her hair cut brutally short, and the back of her neck always showing the stubble of a recent shave, and came to class every day in a gray laboratory smock. Miss Mueller was very deep into the realm of extrasensory and occult phenomena. Of course they didn't use phrases like 'very deep into' in 1949, when David Selig was in her class, but let the anachronism stand: she was ahead of her time, a hippie born too soon. She really grooved behind the irrational, the unknown. She knew her way around the high-school bio curriculum in her sleep, which was more or less the way she taught it. What turned her on, really, were things like telepathy, clairvoyance, telekinesis, astrology, the whole parapsychological bag. The most slender provocation was enough to nudge her away from the day's assignment, the study of metabolism or the circulatory system or whatever, and onto one of her hobbyhorses. She was the first on her block to own the *I Ching*. She had done time inside orgone boxes. She believed that the Great Pyramid of Gizeh held divine relevations for mankind. She had sought deeper truths by way of Zen, General Semantics, the Bates eyesight exercises, and the readings of Edgar Cayce. (How easily I can extend her quest past the year of my own exposure of her! She must have gone on to dianetics, Velikovsky, Bridey Murphy, and Timothy Leary, and ended up, in her old age, as a lady guru in some Los Angeles eyrie, heavy into psilocybin and peyote. Poor silly gullible pitiful old bitch.)

Naturally she kept up with the research into extrasensory perception that J. B. Rhine was doing down at Duke University. It terrified David whenever she spoke of this. He constantly feared that she was going to give way to the temptation to run some Rhine experiments in class, and would thereby flush him out of hiding. He had read Rhine himself, of course, *The Reach of the Mind* and *New Frontiers of the Mind*, had even peered into the opacities of *The Journal of Parapsychology*, hoping to find something that would explain him to himself, but there was nothing there except statistics and foggy conjecture. Okay, Rhine was no threat to him so long as he went on piddling around in North Carolina. But muddled Miss Mueller might just strip him naked and deliver him to the pyre.

Inevitable, the progression toward disaster. The topic for the week, suddenly, was the human brain, its functions and capabilities. See, this is the cerebrum, this is the cerebellum, this is the medulla oblongata. A child's garden of synapses. Fat-cheeked Norman Heimlich, gunning for a 99, knowing precisely which button to push, put up his hand: 'Miss Mueller, do you think it'll ever be possible for people really to read minds, I mean not by tricks or anything but actual mental telepathy?' Oh, the joy of Miss Mueller! Her lumpy face glowing. This was her cue to launch into an animated discussion of ESP, parapsychology, inexplicable phenomena, supernormal modes of communication and perception, the Rhine researches, et cetera, et cetera, a torrent of metaphysical irrelevance. David wanted to hide under his desk. The word 'telepathy' made him wince. He already suspected that half the class realized what he was. Now a flash of wild paranoia. Are they looking at me, are they staring and pointing and tapping their heads and nodding? Certainly these were irrational fears. He had surveyed every mind in the class again and again, desperately trying to amuse himself during the arid stretches of boredom, and he knew that his secret was safe. His classmates, plodding young Brooklynites all, would never cotton to the veiled presence of a superman in their midst. They thought he was strange, yes, but had no notion of *how* strange. Would Miss Mueller now blow his cover, though? She was talking about conducting parapsychology experiments in class to demonstrate the potential reach of the human brain. Oh where can I hide?

No escape. She had her cards with her the next day. 'These are known as Zener cards,' she explained solemnly, holding them up, fanning them out like Wild Bill Hickok about to deal himself a straight flush. David had never actually seen a set of the cards before, yet they were as familiar to him as the deck his parents used in their interminable canasta games. 'They were devised about twenty-five years ago at Duke University by Dr Karl E. Zener and Dr J. B. Rhine. Another name for them is "ESP cards". Who can tell me what "ESP" means?'

Norman Heimlich's stubby hand waving in the air. 'Extrasensory perception, Miss Mueller!'

'Very good, Norman.' Absentmindedly she began to shuffle the cards. Her eyes, normally inexpressive, gleamed with a Las Vegas intensity. She said, 'The deck consists of 25 cards, divided into five "suits" or symbols. There are five cards marked with a star, five with a circle, five with a square, five with a pattern of wavy lines, and five with a cross or plus sign. Otherwise they look just like ordinary playing cards.' She handed the pack to Barbara Stein, another of her favorites, and told her to copy the five symbols on the blackboard. 'The idea is for the subject being examined to look at each card in turn, face down, and try to name the symbol on the other side. The test can be run in many different ways. Sometimes the examiner looks briefly at each card first; that gives the subject a chance to pick the right answer out of the examiner's mind, if he can. Sometimes neither the subject nor the examiner sees the card in advance. Sometimes the subject is allowed to touch the card before he makes his guess. Sometimes he may be blindfolded, and other times he may be permitted to stare at the back of each card. No matter how it's done, though, the basic aim is always the same: for the subject to determine, using extrasensory powers, the design on a card that he can't see. Estelle, suppose the subject has no extrasensory powers at all, but is simply operating on pure guesswork. How many right guesses could we expect him to make, out of the 25 cards?'

Estelle, caught by surprise, reddened and blurted, 'Uh – twelve and a half?'

A sour smirk from Miss Mueller, who turned to the brighter, happier twin. 'Beverly?'

'Five, Miss Mueller?'

'Correct. You always have one chance out of five of guessing the right suit, so five right calls out of 25 is what luck alone ought to bring. Of course, the results are never that neat. On one run through the deck you might have four correct hits, and then next time six, and then five, and then maybe seven, and then perhaps only three – but the *average*, over a long series of trials, ought to be about five. That is, if pure chance is the only factor operating. Actually, in the Rhine experiments some groups of subjects have averaged 6½ or 7 hits out of 25 over many tests. Rhine believes that this above-average performance can only be explained as ESP. And certain subjects have done much better. There was a man once who called nine straight cards right, two days in a row. Then a few days later he hit 15 straight cards, 21 out of 25. The odds against that are fantastic. How many of you think it could have been nothing but luck?'

About a third of the hands in the class went up. Some of them belonged to dullards who failed to realize that it was shrewd politics to show sympathy for the teacher's pet enthusiasms. Some of them belonged to incorrigible skeptics who disdained such cynical manipulations. One of the hands belonged to David Selig. He was merely trying to don protective coloration.

Miss Mueller said, 'Let's run a few tests today. Victor, will you be our first guinea pig? Come to the front of the room.'

Grinning nervously, Victor Schlitz shambled forward. He stood stiffly beside Miss Mueller's desk as she cut the cards and cut them again. Then, peering quickly at the top card, she slid it toward him. 'Which symbol?' she asked.

'Circle?'

'We'll see. Class, don't say anything.' She handed the card to Barbara Stein, telling her to place a checkmark under the proper symbol on the blackboard. Barbara checked the square. Miss Mueller glanced at the next card. *Star*, David thought.

'Waves,' Victor said. Barbara checked the star.

'Plus,' *Square dummy!* Square.

'Circle.' *Circle*. Circle. A sudden ripple of excitement in the classroom at Victor's hit. Miss Mueller, glaring, called for silence.

'Star.' *Waves*. Waves was what Barbara checked.

'Square.' *Square*, David agreed. Square. Another ripple, more subdued.

Victor went through the deck. Miss Mueller had kept score: four correct hits. Not even as good as chance. She put him through a second round. Five, All right, Victor: you may be sexy, but a telepath you aren't. Miss Mueller's eyes roved the room. Another subject? Let it not be me, David prayed. God, let it not be me. It wasn't. She summoned Sheldon Feinberg. He hit five the first time, six the second. Respectable, unspectacular. Then Alice Cohen. Four and four, Stony soil, Miss Mueller. David, following each turn of the cards, had hit 25 out of 25 every time, but he was the only one who knew that.

'Next?' Miss Mueller said, David shrank into his seat. How much longer until the dismissal bell? 'Norman Heimlich.' Norman waddled toward the teacher's desk. She glanced at a card. David, scanning her, picked up the image of a star. Bouncing then to Norman's mind, David was amazed to detect a flicker of an image there, a star perversely rounding its points to form a circle, then reverting to beign a star. What was this? Did the odious Heimlich have a shred of the power? 'Circle,' Norman murmured. But he hit the next one – the waves – and the one after that, the square. He did indeed seem to be picking up emanations, fuzzy and indistinct but emanations all the same, from Miss Mueller's mind. Fat Heimlich had the vestiges of the gift. But only the vestiges; David, scanning his mind and the teacher's, watched the images grow ever more cloudy and vanish altogether by the tenth card, fatigue scattering Norman's feeble strength. He scored a seven, though, the best so far. *The bell,* David prayed. *The bell, the bell, the bell!* Twenty minutes away.

A small mercy. Miss Mueller briskly distributed test paper. She would run the whole class at once. 'I'll call numbers from 1 to 25,' she said. 'As I call each number, write down the symbol you think you see. Ready? *One.*'

David saw a circle. *Waves*, he wrote.

Star. *Square*.

Waves. *Circle*.

Star. *Waves*.

As the test neared its close, it occurred to him that he might be making a tactical error by muffling every call. He told himself to put down two or three right ones, just for camouflage. But it was too late for that. There were only four numbers left; it would look too conspicuous if he hit several of them correctly after missing all the others. He went on missing.

Miss Mueller said, 'Now exchange papers with your neighbor and mark his answers. Ready? Number one: circle. Number two: star. Number three: waves. Number four . . .'

Tensely she called for results. Had anyone scored ten hits or more? No, teacher. Nine? Eight? Seven? Norman Heimlich had seven again. He preened himself: Heimlich the mind-reader. David felt disgust at the knowledge that Heimlich had even a crumb of power. Six? Four students had six. Five? Four? Miss Mueller dilligently jotting down the results. Any other figures? Sidney Goldblatt began to snicker. 'Miss Mueller, how about zero?'

She looked startled. '*Zero?* Was there someone who got all 25 cards *wrong*?'

'David Selig did!'

David Selig wanted to drop through the floor. All eyes were on him. Cruel laughter assailed him. *David Selig got them all wrong*. It was like saying, David Selig wet his pants, David Selig cheated on the exam, David Selig went into the girls' toilet. By trying to conceal himself, he had made himself terribly conspicuous. Miss Mueller, looking stern and oracular, said, 'A null score can be quite significant too, class. It might mean extremely strong ESP abilities, rather than the total absence of such powers, as you might think.' Oh. God. Extremely strong ESP abilities. She went on, 'Rhine talks of phenomena such as 'forward displacement' and 'backward displacement', in which an unusually powerful ESP force might accidentally focus on one card ahead of the right one, or one card behind it, or even two or three cards away. So the subject would appear to get a below-average result when actually he's hitting perfectly, just off the target! David, let me see your answers.'

'I wasn't getting anything, Miss Mueller. I was just putting down my guesses, and I suppose they were all wrong.'

'Let me see.'

As though marching to the scaffold, he brought her the sheet. She placed it beside her own list and tried to realign it, searching for some correlation, some displacement sequence. But the randomness of his deliberately wrong answers protected him. A forward displacement of one card gave him two hits; a backward displacement of one card gave him three. Nothing significant there. Nevertheless, Miss Mueller would not let go. 'I'd like to test you again,' she said. 'We'll run several kinds of trials. A null score is fascinating.' She began to shuffle the deck. God, God, God, where are you? Ah. The bell! Saved by the bell! 'Can you stay after class?' she asked. In agony, he shook his head. 'Got to go to geometry next, Miss Mueller.' She relented. Tomorrow, then. We'll run the tests tomorrow. God! He was up all the night in a turmoil of fear, sweating, shivering; about four in the morning he vomited. He hoped his mother would make him stay home from school, but no luck: at half past seven he was aboard the bus. Would Miss Mueller forget about the test? Miss Mueller had not forgotten. The fateful cards were on the desk. There would be no escape. He found himself the center of all attention. All right, Duv, be cleverer this time. 'Are you ready to begin?' she asked, tipping up the first card. He saw a plus sign in her mind.

'Square,' he said.

He saw a circle. 'Waves,' he said.

He saw another circle. 'Plus,' he said.

He saw a star. 'Circle,' he said.

He saw a square. 'Square,' he said. *That's one*.

He kept careful count. Four wrong answers, then a right one. Three wrong answers, another right one. Spacing them with false randomness, he allowed himself five hits on the first test. On the second he had four. On the third, six. On the fourth, four. Am I being too average, he wondered? Should I give her a one-hit run, now? But she was losing interest. 'I still can't understand your null score, David,' she told him. 'But it does seem to me as if you have no ESP ability whatever.' He tried to look disappointed. Apologetic, even. Sorry, teach, I ain't got no ESP. Humbly the deficient boy made his way to his seat.

In one blazing instant of revelation and communion, Miss Mueller, I could have justified your whole lifelong quest for the improbable, the inexplicable, the unknowable, the irrational. The miraculous. But I didn't have the guts to do it. I had to look after my own skin, Miss Mueller. I had to keep a low profile. Will you forgive me? Instead of giving you truth, I faked you out, Miss Mueller, and sent you spinning blindly onward to the tarot, to the signs of the zodiac, to the flying-saucer people, to a thousand surreal vibrations, to a million apocalyptic astral antiworlds, when the touch of my mind against yours might have been enough to heal your madness. One touch from me. In a moment. In the twinkling of an eye.

TWENTY-ONE

These are the days of David's passion, when he writhes a lot on his bed of nails. Let's do it in short takes. It hurts less that way.

Tuesday. Election Day. For months the clamor of the campaign has fouled the air. The free world is choosing its new maximum leader. The sound-trucks rumble along Broadway, belching slogans. Our next President! The man for all America! Vote! Vote! Vote! Vote for X! Vote for Y! The hollow words merge and blur and flow. Republocrat. Demican. *Boum*. Why should I vote? I will not vote. I do not vote. I am not plugged in. I am not part of the circuit. Voting is for *them*. Once, in the late autumn of 1968, I think it was, I was standing outside Carnegie Hall, thinking of going over to the paperback bookshop on the other side of the street, when suddenly all traffic halted on 57th and scores of policemen sprang up from the pavement like the dragon's-teeth warriors sown by Cadmus, and a motorcade came rumbling out of the east, and lo! in a dark black limousine rode Richard M. Nixon, President-Elect of the United States of America, waving jovially to the assembled populace. My big chance at last, I thought. I will look into his mind and make myself privy to great secrets of state; I will discover what it is about our leaders that sets them apart from ordinary mortals. And I looked into his mind, and what I found in there I will not tell you, except to say that it was more or less what I should have expected to find. And since that day I have had nothing to do with politics or politicians. Today I stay home from the polls. Let them elect the next President without my help.

Wednesday. I doodle with Yahya Lumumba's half-finished term paper and other such projects, a few futile lines on each. Getting nowhere. Judith calls. 'A party,' she says. 'You're invited. Everybody'll be there.'

'A party? Who? Where? Why? When?'

'Saturday night. Near Columbia. The host is Claude Guermantes. Do you know him? Professor of French Literature.'

No, the name is not Guermantes. I have changed the name to protect the guilty. 'He's one of those charismatic new professors. Young, dynamic, handsome, a friend of Simone de Beauvoir, of Genet. Karl and I are coming. And a lot of others. He always invites the most interesting people.'

'Genet? Simone de Beauvoir? Will they be there?'

'No, silly, not them. But it'll be worth your time. Claude gives the best parties of anybody I know. Brilliant combinations of people.'

'Sounds like a vampire to me.'

'He gives as well as takes, Duv. He specifically asked me to invite you.'

'How does he know me at all?'

'Through me,' she says. 'I've talked of you. He's dying to meet you.'

'I don't like parties.'

'*Duv —*'

I know that warning tone of voice. I have no stomach for a hassle just now. 'All right,' I say, sighing. 'Saturday night. Give me the address.' Why am I so pliable? Why do I let Judith manipulate me? Is this how I build my love for her, through these surrenders?

Thursday. I do two paragraphs, a.m., for Yahya Lumumba. Very apprehensive about his reaction to the thing I'm writing for him. He might just loathe it. If I ever finish it. I *must* finish it. Never missed a deadline yet. Don't dare to. In the p.m. I walk up to the 230th St bookstore, needing fresh air and wanting, as usual, to see if anything interesting has come out since my last visit, three days before. Compulsively buy a few paperbacks – an anthology of minor metaphysical poets, Updike's *Rabbit Redux*, and a heavy Levi-Straussian anthropological study, folkways of some Amazonian tribe, that I know I'll *never* get round to reading. A new clerk at the cash register: a girl, 19, 20, pale, blonde, white silk blouse, short plaid skirt, impersonal smile. Attractive in a vacant-eyed way. She isn't at all interesting to me, sexually or otherwise, and as I think that I chide myself for putting her down – let nothing human be alien to me – and on a whim I invade her mind as I pay for my books, so that I won't be judging her by superficials, I burrow in easily, deep, down through layer after layer of trivia, mining her without hindrance, getting right to the real stuff. Oh! What a sudden blazing communion, soul to soul! She glows. She streams fire. She comes to me with a vividness and a completeness that stun me, so rare has this sort of experience become for me. No dumb pallid mannequin now. I see her full and entire, her dreams, her fantasies, her ambitions, her loves, her soaring ecstasies (last night's gasping copulation and the shame and guilt afterward), a whole churning steaming sizzling human soul. Only once in the last six months have I hit this quality of total contact, only once, that awful day with Yahya Lumumba on the steps of Low Library. And as I remember that searing, numbing experience, something is triggered in me and the same thing happens. A dark curtain falls. I am disconnected. My grip on her consciousness is severed. Silence, that terrible mental silence, rushes to enfold me. I stand there, gaping, stunned, alone again and frightened, and I start to shake and drop my change, and she says to me, worried, 'Sir? *Sir?*' in that sweet fluting little-girl voice.

Friday. Wake up with aches, high fever. Undoubtedly an attack of psychosomatic ague. The angry, embittered mind mercilessly flagellating the defenseless body. Chills followed by hot sweats followed by chills. Empty-gut puking. I feel hollow. Headpiece filled with straw. Alas! Can't work. I scribble a few pseudo-Lumumbesque lines and toss the sheet away. Sick as a dog. Well, a good excuse not to go to that dumb party, anyhow. I read my minor metaphysicals. Some of them not so minor. Traherne, Crashak, William Cartwright. As for instance, Traherne:

> Pure native Powers that Corruption loathe,
>   Did, like the fairest Glass
>   Or, spotless polished Brass,
> Themselves soon in their Object's Image clothe:
>   Divine Impressions, when they came,
>   Did quickly enter and my Soul enflame.
>   'Tis not the Object, but the Light,
>   That maketh Heav'n: 'Tis a clearer Sight.
>   Felicity
>   Appears to none but them that purely see.

Threw up again after that. Not to be interpreted as an

expression of criticism. Felt better for a while. I should call
Judith. Have her make some chicken soup for me. Oy, veh.
Veh is mir.

Saturday. Without help of chicken soup I recover and decide
to go to the party. Veh is mir, in spades. Remember, remember,
the sixth of November. Why has David allowed Judith to drag
him from his cave? An endless subway ride downtown; spades
full of weekend wine add a special *frisson* to the ordinary
adventure of Manhattan transportation. At last the familiar
Columbia station. I must walk a few blocks, shivering, not
dressed properly for the wintry weather, to the huge old
apartment house at Riverside Drive and 112th St where Claude
Guermantes is reputed to live. I stand hesitantly outside. A
cold, sour breeze ripping malevolently across the Hudson at
me, bearing the windborne detritus of New Jersey. Dead
leaves swirling in the park. Inside, a mahogany doorman
eyes me fishily. 'Professor Guermantes?' I say. He jerks a
thumb. 'Seventh floor, 7-G.' Waving me toward the elevator.
I'm late; it's almost ten o'clock. Upstairs in the weary Otis, creak
creak creak creak, elevator door rolls back, silkscreen poster in
the hallway proclaims the route to Guermantes' lair. Not that
posters are necessary. A high-decibel roar from the left tells
me where the action is. I ring the bell. Wait. Nothing. Ring
again. Too loud for them to hear me. Oh, to be able to transmit
thoughts instead of just to receive them! I'd announce myself in
tones of thunder. Ring again, more aggressively. Ah! Yes! Door
opens. Short dark-haired girl, undergraduate-looking, wearing
a sort of orange sari that leaves her right breast – small – bare.
Nudity a la mode. Flashes her teeth gaily. 'Come in, come in,
come in!'
   A mob scene. Eighty, ninety, a hundred people, everyone
dressed in Seventies Flamboyant, gathered in groups of eight
to ten, shouting profundities at one another. Those who hold
no highballs are busily passing joints, ritualistic hissing intake
of breath, much coughing, passionate exhaling. Before I have

my coat off someone pops an elaborate ivory-headed pipe in
my mouth. 'Super hash,' he explains. 'Just in from Damascus.
Come on, man, toke up!' I suck smoke willy-nilly and feel
an immediate effect. I blink. 'Yeah,' my benefactor shouts.
'It's got the power to cloud men's minds, don't it?' In this
mob my mind is already pretty well clouded, however, sans
cannabis, solely from input overload. My power seems to be
functioning at reasonably high intensity tonight, only without
much differentiation of persons, and I am involuntarily taking
in a thick soup of overlapping transmissions, a chaos of merging
thoughts. Murky stuff. Pipe and passer vanish and I stumble
stonedly forward into a cluttered room lined from floor to
ceiling with crammed bookcases. I catch sight of Judith just
as she catches sight of me, and from her on a direct line of
contact comes her outflow, fiercely vivid at first, trailing off in
moments into mush: *brother, pain, love, fear, shared memories,
forgiveness, forgetting, hatred, hostility, murmphness, froomz, zzzhhh,
mmm. Brother. Love. Hate. Zzzhhh.*

'Duv!' she cries. 'Oh, here I am, Duvid!'

Judith looks sexy tonight. Her long lithe body is sheathed in
a purple satiny wrap, skin-tight, throat-high, plainly showing
her breasts and the little bumps of her nipples and the cleft
between her buttocks. On her bosom nestles a glittering slab
of gold-rimmed jade, intricately carved; her hair, unbound,
tumbles gloriously. I feel pride in her beauty. She is flanked
by two impressive-looking men. On one side is Dr Karl F.
Silvestri, author of *Studies in the Physiology of Thermoregulation.*
He corresponds fairly closely to the image of him that I had
plucked from Judith's mind at her apartment a week or two
ago, though he is older than I had guessed, as least 55,
maybe closer to 60. Bigger, too – perhaps six feet five. I try
to envision his huge burly body atop Jude's wiry slender self,
pressing down. I can't. He has florid cheeks, a stolid self-satisfied
facial expression, tender intelligent eyes. He radiates something
avuncular or even paternal toward her. I see why Jude is

attracted to him: he is the powerful father-figure that poor beaten Paul Selig never could have been for her. On Judith's other side is a man whom I suspect to be Professor Claude Guermantes; I bounce a quick probe into him and confirm that guess. His mind is quicksilver. A glittering, shimmering pool. He thinks in three or four languages at once. His rampaging energy exhausts me at a single touch. He is about 40, just under six feet tall, muscular, athletic; he wears his elegant sandy hair done in swirling baroque waves, and his short goatee is impeccably clipped. His clothing is so advanced in style that I lack the vocabulary to describe it, being unaware of fashions myself: a kind of mantle of course green and gold fabric (linen? muslin?), a scarlet sash, flaring satin trousers, turned-up pointed-toed medieval boots. His dandyish appearance and mannered posture suggest that he might be gay, but he gives off a powerful aura of heterosexuality, and from Judith's stance and fond way of looking at him I begin to realize that he and she must once have been lovers. May still be. I am shy about probing that. My raids on Judith's privacy are too sore a point between us.

'I'd like you to meet my brother David,' Judith says.

Silvestri beams. 'I've heard so much about you, Mr Selig.'

'Have you really?' (*I've got this freak of a brother, Karl. Would you believe it, he can actually read minds? Your thoughts are as clear as a radio broadcast to him.*) How much has Judith actually revealed about me? I'll try to probe him and see. 'And call me David. You're Dr Silvestri, right?'

'That's right. Karl. I'd prefer Karl.'

'I've heard a lot about you from Jude,' I say. No go on the probe. My abominable waning gifts; I get only sputtering bits of static, misty scraps of unintelligible thought. His mind is opaque to me. My head starts to throb. 'She showed me two of your books. I wish I could understand things like that.'

A pleased chuckle from lofty Silvestri. Judith meanwhile has begun to introduce me to Guermantes. He murmurs his delight at making my acquaintance. I half expect him to kiss my cheeks, or maybe my hand. His voice is soft, purring; it carries an accent, but not a French one. Something strange, a mixture, Franco-Italic, maybe, or Franco-Hispanic. Him at least I can probe, even now; somehow his mind, more volatile than Silvestri's, remains within my reach. I slither in and take a look, even while exchanging platitudes about the weather and the recent election. Christ! Casanova Redivivus! He's slept with everything that walks or crawls, masculine feminine neuter, including of course my accessible sister Judith, whom – according to a neatly filed surface memory – he last penetrated just five hours ago, in this very room. His semen now curdles within her. He is obscurely restless over the fact that she never has come with him; he takes it as a failure of his flawless technique. The professor is speculating in a civilized way on the possibilities of nailing me before the night is out. No hope, professor. I will not be added to your Selig collection. He asks me pleasantly about my degrees. 'Just one,' I say. 'A B.A. in '56. I thought about doing graduate work in English literature but never got around to it.' He teaches Rimbaud, Verlain, Mallarmé, Baudelaire, Lautréamont, the whole sick crew, and identifies with them spiritually; his classes are full of adoring Barnard girls whose thighs open gladly for him, although in his Rimbaud facet he is not averse to romping with hearty Columbia men on occasions. As he talks to me he fondles Judith's shoulderblades affectionately, proprietorially. Dr Silvestri appears not to notice, or else not to care. 'Your sister,' Guermantes murmurs, 'she is a marvel, she is an original, a splendor – a *type*, M'sieu Selig, a *type*.' A compliment, in the froggish sense. I poke his mind again and learn that he is writing a novel about a bitter, voluptuous young divorcee and a French intellectual who is an incarnation of the life-force, and expects to make millions from it. He fascinates me: so blatant, so phony, so manipulative, and yet so attractive despite all his transparent failings. He offers me cocktails, highballs, liqueurs, brandies, pot, hash, cocaine, anything I crave. I feel engulfed and escape from him, in some relief, slipping away to pour a little rum.

A girl accosts me at the liquor table. One of Guermantes' students, no more than 20. Coarse black hair tumbling into ringlets; pug nose; fierce perceptive eyes; full fleshy lips. Not beautiful but somehow interesting. Evidently I interest her, too, for she grins at me and says, 'Would you like to go home with me?'

'I just got here.'

'Later. Later. No hurry. You look like you're fun to fuck.'

'Do you say that to everybody you've just met?'

'We haven't even met,' she points out. 'And no, I don't say it to everybody. To lots, though. What's wrong? Girls can take the initiative these days. Besides, it's leap year. Are you a poet?'

'Not really.'

'You look like one. I bet you're sensitive and you suffer a lot.' My familiar dopy fantasy, coming to life before my eyes. *Her* eyes are red-rimmed. She's stoned. An acrid smell of sweat rising from her black sweater. Her legs are too short for her torso, her hips too wide, her breasts too heavy. Probably she's got the clap. Is she putting me on? *I bet you're sensitive and you suffer a lot. Are you a poet?* I try to explore her, but it's useless; fatigue is blanking my mind, and the collective shriek of the massed mob of partygoers is drowning out all individual outputs now. 'What's your name?' she asks.

'David Selig.'

'Lisa Holstein. I'm a senior at Barn –'

'*Holstein?*' The name triggers me. Kitty, Kitty, Kitty! 'Is that what you said? Holstein?'

'Holstein, yes, and spare me the cow jokes.'

'Do you have a sister named Kitty? Catherine, I guess. Kitty Holstein. About 35 years old. Your sister, maybe your cousin –'

'No. Never heard of her. Someone you know?'

'Used to know,' I say. 'Kitty Holstein.' I pick up my drink and turn away.

'Hey,' she calls after me. 'Did you think I was kidding? Do you want to go home with me tonight or don't you?'

A black colossus confronts me. Immense Afro nimbus, terrifying jungle face. His clothing a sunburst of clashing colors. *Him,*

here? Oh, God. Just who I most need to see. I think guiltily
of the unfinished term paper, lame, humpbacked, a no-ass
monstrosity, sitting on my desk. What is he doing here? How
has Claude Guermantes managed to draw Yahya Lumumba
into his orbit? The evening's token black, perhaps. Or the
delegate from the world of high-powered sports, summoned
here by way of demonstrating our host's intellectual versatility,
his eclectic ballsiness. Lumumba stands over me, glowering,
coldly examining me from his implausible height like an ebony
Zeus. A spectacular black woman has her arm through his, a
goddess, a titan, well over six feet tall, skin like polished onyx,
eyes like beacons. A stunning couple. They shame us all with
their beauty. Lumumba says, finally, 'I *know* you, man. I know
you from someplace.'

'Selig. David Selig.'

'Sounds familiar. Where do I know you?'

'Euripides, Sophocles, and Aeschylus.'

'What the fuck?' Baffled. Pausing, then. Grinning. 'Oh, yeah.
Yeah, baby. That fucking term paper. How you coming along
on that, man?'

'Coming along.'

'You gonna have it Wednesday? Wednesday when it due.'

'I'll have it, Mr Lumumba.' *Doin' my best, massa.*

'You better, boy. I counting on you.'

'– Tom Nyquist –'

The name leaps suddenly, startlingly, out of the whitenoise
background hum of party chatter. For an instant it hangs in
the smoky air like a dead leaf caught by a lazy October breeze.
Who said 'Tom Nyquist' just then? Who was it who spoke his
name? A pleasant baritone voice, no more than a dozen feet
from me. I look for likely owners of that voice. Men all around.
You? You? You? No way of telling. Yes, one way. When words
are spoken aloud, they reverberate in the mind of the speaker
for a short while. (Also in the minds of his hearers, but the
reverberations are different in tonality.) I summon my slippery
skill and, straining, force needles of inquiry into the nearby
consciousnesses, hunting for echoes. The effort is murderously

great. The skulls I enter are solid bony domes through whose few crevices I struggle to ram my limp, feeble probes. But I enter. I seek the proper reverberations. *Tom Nyquist? Tom Nyquist?* Who spoke his name? You? You? Ah. There. The echo is almost gone, just a dim hollow clangor at the far end of a cavern. A tall plump man with a comic fringe of blond beard.

'Excuse me,' I say. 'I didn't mean to eavesdrop, but I heard you mention the name of a very old friend of mine –'

'Oh?'

'– and I couldn't help coming over to ask you about him. Tom Nyquist. He and I were once very close. If you know where he is now, what he's doing –'

'Tom Nyquist?'

'Yes. I'm sure I heard you mention him.'

A blank smile. 'I'm afraid there's been a mistake. I don't know anyone by that name. Jim? Fred? Can you help?'

'But I'm positive I heard –' The echo. *Boum* in the cave. Was I mistaken? At close range I try to get inside his head, to hunt in his filing system for any knowledge of Nyquist. But I can't function at all, now. They are conferring earnestly. Nyquist? Nyquist? Did anybody hear a Nyquist mentioned? Does anyone know a Nyquist?

One of them suddenly cries: 'John Leibnitz!'

'Yes,' says the plump one happily. 'Maybe that's who you heard me mention. I was talking about John Leibnitz a few moments ago. A mutual friend. In this racket that might very well have sounded like Nyquist to you.'

Leibnitz. Nyquist. Leibnitz. Nyquist. *Boum. Boum.* 'Quite possibly,' I agree. 'No doubt that's what happened. Silly of me.' John Leibnitz. 'Sorry to have bothered you.'

Guermantes says, mincing and prancing at my elbow, 'You really must audit my class one of these days. This Wednesday afternoon I start Rimbaud and Verlaine, the first of six lectures on them. Do come around. You'll be on campus Wednesday, won't you?'

Wednesday is the day I must deliver Yahya Lumumba's term paper on the Greek tragedians. I'll be on campus, yes. I'd better be. But how does Guermantes know that? Is he getting into my head somehow? What if he has the gift too? And I'm wide open to him, he knows everything, my poor pathetic secret, my daily increment of loss, and there he stands, patronizing me because I'm failing and he's as sharp as ever I was. Then a quick paranoiac flash: not only does he have the gift but perhaps he's some kind of telepathic leech, draining me, bleeding the power right out of my mind and into his. Perhaps he's been tapping me on the sly ever since '74.

I shake these useless idiocies away. 'I expect to be around on Wednesday, yes. Perhaps I will drop in.'

There is no chance whatever that I will go to hear Claude Guermantes lecture on Rimbaud or Verlaine. If he's got the power, let him put *that* in his pipe and smoke it!

'I'd love it if you came,' he tells me. He leans close to me. His androgynous Mediterranean smoothness permits him casually to breach the established American code of male-to-male distancing customs. I smell hair tonic, shaving lotion, deodorant, and other perfumes. A small blessing: not all my senses are dwindling at once. 'Your sister,' he murmurs. 'Marvelous woman! How I love her! She speaks often of you.'

'Does she?'

'With great love. Also with great guilt. It seems you and she were estranged for many years.'

'That's over now. We're finally becoming friends.'

'How wonderful for you both.' He gestures with a flick of his eyes. 'That doctor. No good for her. Too old, too static. After fifty most men lose the capacity to grow. He'll bore her to death in six months.'

'Maybe boredom is what she needs,' I reply. 'She's had an exciting life. It hasn't made her happy.'

'No one ever needs boredom,' Guermantes says, and winks.

'Karl and I would love to have you come for dinner next week, Duv. There's so much we three need to talk about.'

'I'll see, Jude, I'm not sure about anything next week yet. I'll call you.'

Lisa Holstein. John Leibnitz. I think I need another drink.

Sunday. Greatly overhung. Hash, rum, wine, pot, God knows what else. And somebody popping amyl nitrite under my nose about two in the morning. That filthy fucking party. I should never have gone. My head, my head, my head. Where's the typewriter? I've got to get some work done. Let's go, then:

We see, thus, the difference in method of approach of these three tragedians to the same story. Aeschylus' primary concern is theological implications of the crime and the inexorable workings of the gods: Orestes is torn between the command of Apollo to slay his mother and his own fear of matricide, and goes mad as a result. Euripides dwells on the characterization, and takes a less allegorical

No damned good. Save it for later.

Silence between my ears. The echoing black void. I have nothing going for me at all today, nothing. I think it may be completely gone. I can't even pick up the clamor of the spics next door. November is the cruelest month, breeding onions out of the dead mind. I'm living an Eliot poem. I'm turning into words on a page. Shall I sit here feeling sorry for myself? No. No. No. No. I'll fight back. Spiritual exercises designed to restore my power. On your knees, Selig. Bow the head. Concentrate. Transform yourself into a fine needle of thought, a slim telepathic laser-beam, stretching from this room to the vicinity of the lovely star Betelgeuse. Got it? Good. That sharp pure mental beam piercing the universe. Hold it. Hold it firm. No spreading at the edges allowed, man. Good. Now ascend. We are climbing Jacob's ladder. This will be an out-of-the-body experience, Duvid. Up, up and away! Rise through the ceiling, through the roof, through the atmosphere, through the ionosphere, through the stratosphere, through the

whatisphere. Outward. Into the vacant interstellar spaces. O
dark dark dark. Cold the sense and lost the motive of action.
No, stop that stuff! Only positive thinking is allowed on this
trip. Soar! Soar! Toward the little green men of Betelgeuse
IX. Reach their minds, Selig. Make contact. Make . . . contact.
Soar, you lazy yid-bastard! Why aren't you soaring? *Soar!*

Well?

Nothing. *Nada. Niente.* Nowhere. *Nulla. Nicht.*

Tumbling back to earth. Into the silent funeral. All right, give
up, if that's what you want. All right. Rest, for a little while.
Rest and then pray, Selig. Pray.

Monday. The hangover gone. The brain once again receptive.
In a glorious burst of creative frenzy I rewrite *The 'Electra' Theme
in Aeschylus, Sophocles, and Euripides* from gunwale to fetlock,
completely recasting it, revoicing it, clarifying and strengthen-
ing the ideas while simultaneously catching what I think is just
the perfect tone of offhand niggerish hipness. As I hammer out
the final words the telephone rings. Nicely timed; I feel sociable
now. Who calls? Judith? No. It is Lisa Holstein who calls. 'You
promised to take me home after the party,' she says mourn-
fully, accusingly. 'What the hell did you do, sneak away?'

'How did you get my number?'

'From Claude. Professor Guermantes.' That sleek devil. He
knows everything. 'Look, what are you doing right now?'

'Thinking about having a shower. I've been working all
morning and I stink like a goat.'

'What kind of work do you do?'

'I ghostwrite term papers for Columbia men.'

She ponders that a moment. 'You sure have a weird head,
man. I mean really: what do you do?'

'I just told you.'

A long digestive silence. Then: 'Okay. I can dig it. You
ghostwrite term papers. Look, Dave, go take your shower.
How long is it on the subway from 110th Street and Broadway
to your place?'

'Maybe forty minutes, if you get a train right away.'

'Swell. See you in an hour, then.' *Click*.

I shrug. A crazy broad. Dave, she calls me. Nobody calls me Dave. Stripping, I head for the shower, a long leisurely soaping. Afterward, sprawling out in a rare interlude of relaxation, Dave Selig re-reads this morning's labors and finds pleasure in what he has wrought. Let's hope Lumumba does too. Then I pick up the Updike book. I get to page four and the phone rings again. Lisa: she's on the train platform at 225th, wants to know how to get to my apartment. This is more than a joke, now. Why is she pursuing me so singlemindedly? But okay. I can play her game. I give her the instructions. Ten minutes later, a knock on the door. Lisa in thick black sweater, the same sweaty one as Saturday night, and tight blue jeans. A shy grin, strangely out of character for her. 'Hi,' she says. Making herself comfortable. 'When I first saw you, I had this intuitive flash on you: *This guy's got something special. Make it with him*. If there's one thing I've learned, it's that you've got to trust your intuition. I go with the flow, Dave, I go with the flow.' Her sweater is off by now. Her breasts are heavy and round, with tiny, almost imperceptible nipples. A Jewish star nestles in the deep valley between them. She wanders the room, examining my books, my records, my photographs. 'So tell me,' she says. 'Now that I'm here. Was I right? *Is* there anything special about you?'

'There once was.'

'What?'

'That's for me to know and you to find out,' I say, and gathering my strength, I ram my mind into hers. It's a brutal frontal assault, a rape, a true mindfuck. Of course she doesn't feel a thing. I say, 'I used to have a really extraordinary gift. It's mostly worn off by now, but some of the time I still have it, and as a matter of fact I'm using it on you right now.'

'Far out,' she says, and drops her jeans. No underpants. She will be fat before she's 30. Her thighs are thick, her belly protrudes. Her pubic hair is oddly dense and widespread, less a triangle than a sort of diamond, a black diamond reaching past her loins to her hips, almost. Her buttocks are deeply dimpled.

While I inspect her flesh I savagely ransack her mind, sparing her no areas of privacy, enjoying my access while it lasts. I don't need to be polite. I owe her nothing: she forced herself on me. I check, first, to see if she had been lying when she said she'd never heard of Kitty. The truth: Kitty is no kin to her. A meaningless coincidence of surnames, is all. 'I'm sure you're a poet, Dave,' she says as we entwine and drop onto the unmade bed. 'That's an intuition flash too. Even if you're doing this term paper thing now, poetry is where you're really at, right?' I run my hands over her breasts and belly. A sharp odor comes from her skin. She hasn't washed in three or four days, I bet. No matter. Her nipples mysteriously emerge, tiny rigid pink nubs. She wriggles. I continue to loot her mind like a Goth plundering the Forum. She is fully open to me; I delight in this unexpected return of vigor. Her autobiography assembles itself for me. Born in Cambridge. Twenty years old. Father a professor, Mother a professor. One younger brother. Tomboy childhood. Measles, chicken pox, scarlet fever. Puberty at eleven, lost her virginity at twelve. Abortion at sixteen. Several Lesbian adventures. Passionate interest in French decadent poets. Acid, mescaline, psilocybin, cocaine, even a sniff of smack. Guermantes gave her that. Guermantes also took her to bed five or six times. Vivid memories of that. Her mind shows me more of Guermantes than I want to see. He's hung very impressively. Lisa comes through with a tough, aggressive self-image, captain of her soul, master of her fate, etc. Underneath that it's just the opposite, of course; she's scared as hell. Not a bad kid. I feel a little guilty about the casual way I slammed into her head, no regard for her privacy at all. But I have my needs. I continue to prowl her, and meanwhile she goes down on me. I can hardly remember the last time anyone did that. I can hardly remember my last lay, it's been so bad lately. She's an expert fellatrice. I'd like to reciprocate but I can't bring myself to do it; sometimes I'm fastidious and she's not the douching type. Oh, well, leave that stuff for the Guermanteses of this world. I lie there picking her brain and accepting the gift of her mouth. I feel virile, bouncy, cocksure, and why not, getting my kicks from two inputs at once, head and crotch? Without withdrawing from her mind I withdraw, at last, from her lips, turn around, part her thighs, slide deep into her tight narrow-mouthed harbor. Selig the stallion. Selig the stud. 'Ooh,' she says, flexing her knees. '*Oooh*.' And we begin to play the beast with two backs. Covertly I feed on feedback, tapping into her pleasure-responses and thereby doubling my own; each thrust brings me a factored and deliciously exponential delight. But then a funny thing happens. Although she is nowhere close to coming – an event that I know will disrupt our mental contact when it occurs – the broadcast from her mind is already becoming erratic and indistinct, more noise than signal. The images break up in a pounding of static. What comes through is garbled and distant; I scramble to maintain my hold on her consciousness, but no use, no use, she slips away, moment by moment receding from me, until there is no communion at all. And in that moment of severance my cock suddenly softens and slips out of her. She is jolted by that, caught by surprise. 'What brought you down?' she asks. I find it impossible to tell her. I remember Judith asking me, some weeks back, whether I had ever regarded my loss of mental powers as a kind of metaphor of impotence. Sometimes yes, I told her. And now here, for the first time, metaphor blends with reality; the two failures are integrated. He is impotent here and he is impotent there. Poor David. 'I guess I got distracted,' I tell her. Well, she has her skills; for half an hour she works me over, fingers, lips, tongue, hair, breasts, not getting a rise out of me with anything, in fact turning me off more than ever by her grim purposefulness. 'I don't understand it,' she says. 'You were doing so well. Was there something about me that brought you down?' I reassure her. You were great, baby. Stuff like this sometimes just happens, no one knows why. I tell her, 'Let's just rest and maybe I'll come back to life.' We rest. Side by side, stroking her skin in an abstract way, I run a few tentative probing efforts. Not a flicker on the telepathic level. Not a flicker. The silence of the tomb. Is this it, the end, right here and now? Is this where it finally burns out? And I am like all the rest of you now. I am condemned to make do with mere words. 'I have an idea,' she says. 'Let's take a shower together. That sometimes peps a guy up.' To this I make no objection; it might just work, and in any case she'll smell better afterward. We head for the bathroom. Torrents of brisk cool water.

Success. The ministrations of her soapy hand revive me.

We spring toward the bed. Still stiff, I top her and take her. Gasp gasp gasp, moan moan moan. I can get nothing on the mental band. Suddenly she goes into a funny little spasm, intense but quick, and my own spurt swiftly follows. So much for sex. We curl up together, cuddly in the afterglow. I try again to probe her. Zero. Zee-ro. Is it gone? I think it's really gone. You have been present today at an historic event, young lady. The perishing of a remarkable extrasensory power. Leaving behind this merely mortal husk of mine. Alas.

'I'd love to read some of your poetry, Dave,' she says.

Monday night, about seven-thirty. Lisa has left, finally. I go out for dinner, to a nearby pizzeria. I am quite calm. The impact of what has befallen me hasn't really registered yet. How strange that I can be so accepting. At any moment, I know, it's bound to come rushing in on me, crushing me, shattering me; I'll weep, I'll scream, I'll bang my head against walls. But for now I'm surprisingly cool. An oddly posthumous feeling, as of having outlived myself. And a feeling of relief: the suspense is over, the process has completed itself, the dying is done, and I've survived it. Of course I don't expect this mood to last. I've lost something central to my being, and now I await the anguish and the grief and the despair that must surely be due to erupt shortly.

But it seems that my mourning must be postponed. What I thought was all over isn't over yet. I walk into the pizzeria and the counterman gives me his flat cold New York smile of welcome, and I get this, unsolicited, from behind his greasy face: *Hey, here's the fag who always wants extra anchovies.*

Reading him clearly. So it's not dead yet! Not quite dead! Only resting a while. Only hiding.

Tuesday. Bitter cold; one of those terrible late-autumn days when every drop of moisture has been squeezed from the air and the sunlight is like knives. I finish two more term papers for delivery tomorrow. I read Updike. Judith calls after lunch. The usual dinner invitation. My usual oblique reply.

'What did you think of Karl?' she asks.

'A very substantial man.'

'He wants me to marry him.'

'Well?'

'It's too soon. I don't really know him, Duv. I like him, I admire him tremendously, but I don't know whether I love him.'

'Then don't rush into anything with him,' I say. Her soap-opera hesitations bore me. I don't understand why anybody old enough to know the score ever gets married, anyway. Why should love require a contract? Why put yourself into the clutches of the state and give it power over you? Why invite lawyers to fuck around with your assets? Marriage is for the immature and the insecure and the ignorant. We who see through such institutions should be content to live together without legal coercion, eh, Toni? Eh? I say, 'Besides, if you marry him, he'd probably want you to give up Guermantes. I don't think he could dig it.'

'You know about me and Claude?'

'Of course.'

'You always know everything.'

'This was pretty obvious, Jude.'

'I thought your power was waning.'

'It is, it is, it's waning faster than ever. But this was still pretty obvious. To the naked eye.'

'All right. What did you think of him?'

'He's death. He's a killer.'

'You misjudged him, Duv.'

'I was in his head. I *saw* him, Jude. He isn't human. People are toys to him.'

'If you could hear the sound of your own voice now, Duv. The hostility, the outright jealousy –'

'*Jealousy?* Am I that incestuous?'

'You always were,' she says. 'But let that pass. I really thought you'd enjoy meeting Claude.'

'I did. He's fascinating. I think cobras are fascinating too.'

'Oh, fuck you, Duv.'

'You want me to pretend I liked him?'

'Don't do me any favors.' The old icy Judith.

'What's Karl's reaction to Guermantes?'

She pauses. Finally: 'Pretty negative. Karl's very conventional, you know. Just as you are.'

'Me?'

'Oh, you're so fucking straight, Duv! You're such a puritan! You've been lecturing me on morality all my goddamned life. The very first time I got laid there you were, wagging your finger at me –'

'Why doesn't Karl like him?'

'I don't know. He thinks Claude's sinister. Exploitive.' Her voice is suddenly flat and dull. 'Maybe he's just jealous. He knows I'm still sleeping with Claude. Oh, Jesus, Duv, why are we fighting again? Why can't we just *talk*?'

'I'm not the one who's fighting. I'm not the one who raised his voice.'

'You're challenging me. That's what you always do. You spy on me and then you challenge me and try to put me down.'

'Old habits are hard to break, Jude. Really, though: I'm not angry with you.'

'You sound so smug!'

'I'm *not* angry. You are. You got angry when you saw that Karl and I agree about your friend Claude. People always get angry when they're told something they don't want to hear. Listen, Jude, do whatever you want. If Guermantes is your trip, go ahead.'

'I don't know. I just don't know.' An unexpected concession:

'Maybe there *is* something sick about my relationship with him.' Her flinty self-assurance vanishes abruptly. That's the wonderful thing about her: you get a different Judith every two minutes. Now, softening, thawing, she sounds uncertain of herself. In a moment she'll turn her concern outward, away from her own troubles, toward me. 'Will you come to dinner next week? We very much do want to get together with you.'

'I'll try.'

'I'm worried about you, Duv.' Yes, here it comes. 'You looked so strung out on Saturday night.'

'It's been a pretty rough time for me. But I'll manage.' I don't feel like talking about myself. I don't want her pity, because after I get hers, I'll start giving myself mine. 'Listen, I'll call you soon, okay?'

'Are you still in so much pain, Duv?'

'I'm adapting. I'm accepting the whole thing. I mean, I'll be okay. Keep in touch, Jude. My best to Karl.' And Claude, I add, as I put down the receiver.

Wednesday morning. Downtown to deliver my latest batch of masterpieces. It's colder even than yesterday, the air clearer, the sun brighter, more remote. How dry the world seems. The humidity is minus sixteen percent, I think. The sort of weather in which I used to function with overwhelming clarity of perception. But I was picking up hardly anything at all on the subway ride down to Columbia, just muzzy little blurts and squeaks, nothing coherent. I can no longer be certain of having the power on any given day, apparently, and this is one of the days off. Unpredictable. That's what you are, you who live in my head: unpredictable. Thrashing about randomly in your death-throes. I go to the usual place and await my clients. They come, they get from me what they have come for, they cross my palm with greenbacks. David Selig, benefactor of undergraduate mankind. I see Yahya Lumumba like a black sequoia making his way across from Butler Library. Why am

I trembling? It's the chill in the air, isn't it, the hint of winter, the death of the year. As the basketball star approaches he waves, nods, grins; everyone knows him, everyone calls out to him. I feel a sense of participation in his glory. When the season starts maybe I'll go watch him play.

'You got the paper, man?'

'Right here.' I deal it off the stack. 'Aeschylus, Sophocles, Euripides. Six pages. That's $21, minus the five you already gave me is $16 you owe me.'

'Wait, man.' He sits down beside me on the steps. 'I got to read this fucker first, right? How I know you did a righteous job if I don't read it?'

I watch him as he reads. Somehow I expect him to be moving his lips, to be stumbling over the unfamiliar words, but no, his eyes flicker rapidly over the lines. He gnaws his lip. He reads faster and faster, impatiently turning the pages. At length he looks at me and there is death in his eyes.

'This is shit, man,' he says. 'I mean, this here is just shit. What kind of con you trying to pull?'

'I guarantee you'll get a B+. You don't have to pay me until you get the grade. Anything less than B+ and –'

'No, listen to me. Who talking about grades? I can't turn this fucking thing in *at all*. Look, half of this thing is jive-talk, the other half it copied straight out of some book. Crazy shit, that's what. The Prof he going to read it, he going to look at me, he going to say, Lumumba, who you think I am? You think I a dummy, Lumumba? You didn't write this crap, he going to say to me. You don't believe Word One of this.' Angrily he rises. 'Here, I going to read you some of this, man. I show you what you give me.' Leafing through the pages, he scowls, spits, shakes his head. 'No. Why the hell should I? You know what you up to here, man? You making fun of me, that's what. You playing games with the dumb nigger, man.'

'I was trying to make it look plausible that you had written –'

'Crap. You pulling a mindfuck, man. You making up a pile of stinking Jew shit about Europydes and you hoping I get in trouble trying to pass it off as my own stuff.'

'That's a lie. I did the best possible job for you, and don't think I didn't sweat plenty. When you hire another man to write a term paper for you, I think you have to be prepared to expect a certain –'

'How long this take you? Fifteen minutes?'

'Eight hours, maybe ten,' I say. 'You know what I think you're trying to do, Lumumba? You're pulling reverse racism on me. Jew this and Jew that – if you don't like Jews so much, why didn't you get a black to write your paper for you? Why didn't you write it yourself? I did an honest job for you. I don't like hearing it put down as stinking Jew shit. And I tell you that if you turn it in, you'll get a passing grade for sure, you'll probably get a B+ at the very least.'

'I gonna get flunked, is what.'

'No. No. Maybe you just don't see what I was driving at. Let me try to explain it to you. If you'll give it to me for a minute so I can read you a couple of things – maybe it'll be clearer if I –' Getting to my feet, I extend a hand toward the paper, but he grins and holds it high above my head. I'd need a ladder to reach it. No use jumping. 'Come on, damn it, don't play games with me! Let me have it!' I snap, and he flicks his wrist and the six sheets of paper soar into the wind and go sailing eastward along College Walk. Dying, I watch them go. I clench my fists; an astonishing burst of rage explodes in me. I want to smash in his mocking face. 'You shouldn't have done that,' I say. 'You shouldn't have just thrown it away.'

'You owe me my five bucks back, man.'

'Hold on, now. I did the work you hired me to do, and –'

'You said you don't charge if the paper's no good. Okay, the paper was shit. No charge. Give me the five.'

'You aren't playing fair, Lumumba. You're trying to rip me off.'

'Who's ripping who off? Who set up that money-back deal anyhow? Me? *You*. What I gonna do for a term paper now? I got to take an incomplete and it your fault. Suppose they make me ineligible for the team because of that. Huh? Huh?

What then? Look, man, you make me want to puke. Give me the five.'

Is he serious about the refund? I can't tell. The idea of paying him back disgusts me, and it isn't just on account of losing the money. I wish I could read him, but I can't get anything out of him on that level; I'm completely blocked now. I'll bluff. I say, 'What is this, slavery turned upside down? I did the work. I don't give a damn what kind of crazy irrational reasons you've got for rejecting it. I'm going to keep the five. At least the five.'

'Give me the money, man.'

'Go to hell.'

I start to walk away. He grabs me – his arm, fully outspread toward me, must be as long as one of my legs – and hauls me toward him. He starts to shake me. My teeth are rattling. His grin is broader than ever, but his eyes are demonic. I wave my fists at him, but, held at arm's length, I can't even touch him. I start to yell. A crowd is gathering. Suddenly there are three or four other men in varsity jackets surrounding us, all black, all gigantic, though not as big as he is. His teammates. Laughing, whooping, cavorting. I am a toy to them. 'Hey, man, he bothering you?' one of them asks. 'You need help, Yahya?' yells another. 'What's the mothafuck honkie doing to you, man?' calls a third. They form a ring and Lumumba thrusts me toward the man on his left, who catches me and flings me onward around the circle. I spin; I stumble; I reel; they never let me fall. Around and around and around. An elbow explodes against my lip. I taste blood. Someone slaps me, and my head rockets backward. Fingers jabbing my ribs. I realize that I'm going to get very badly hurt, that in fact these giants are going to beat me up. A voice I barely recognize as my own offers Lumumba his refund, but no one notices. They continue to whirl me from one to the next. Not slapping now, not jabbing, but punching. Where are the campus police? Help! Help! Pigs to the rescue! But no one comes. I can't catch my breath. I'd like to drop to my knees and huddle against the ground. They're yelling at me, racial epithets, words I barely comprehend, soul-brother jargon that must have been invented last week; I don't know what they're calling me, but I can feel the hatred in every syllable. Help? Help? The world spins wildly. I know now how a basketball would feel, if a basketball could feel. The steady pounding, the blur of unending motion. Please, someone, anyone, help me, stop them. Pain in my chest: a lump of white-hot metal back of my breastbone. I can't see. I can only feel. Where are my feet? I'm falling at last. Look how fast the steps rush toward me. The cold kiss of the stone bruises my cheek. I may already have lost consciousness; how can I tell? There's one comfort, at least. I can't get any further down than this.

TWENTY-TWO

He was ready to fall in love when he met Kitty, over-ripe and eager for an emotional entanglement. Perhaps that was the whole trouble; what he felt for her was not so much love as simply satisfaction at the idea of being in love. Or perhaps not. He never understood his feelings for Kitty in any orderly way. They had their romance in the summer of 1963, which he remembers as the last summer of hope and good cheer before the long autumn of entropic chaos and philosophical despair descended on western society. Jack Kennedy was running things then, and while things weren't going especially well for him politically, he still managed to give the impression that he was going to get it all together, if not right away then in his inevitable second term. Atmospheric nuclear tests had just been banned. The Washington-to-Moscow hot line was being set up. Secretary of State Rusk announced in August that the South Vietnamese government was rapidly taking control of additional areas of the countryside. The number of Americans killed fighting in Vietnam had not yet reached 100.

Selig, who was 28 years old, had just moved from his

Brooklyn Heights apartment to a small place in the West Seventies. He was working as a stockbroker then, of all unlikely things. This was Tom Nyquist's idea. After six years, Nyquist was still his closest and possibly only friend, although the friendship had waned considerably in the last year or two. Nyquist's almost arrogant self-assurance made Selig increasingly more uncomfortable, and he found it desirable to put some distance, psychological and geographical, between himself and the older man. One day Selig had said wistfully that if he could only manage to get a bundle of money together – say, $25,000 or so – he'd go off to a remote island and spend a couple of years writing a novel, a major statement about alienation in contemporary life, something like that. He had never written anything serious and wasn't sure he was sincere about wanting to. He was secretly hoping that Nyquist would simply hand him the money – Nyquist could pick up $25,000 in one afternoon's work, if he felt like it – and say, 'Here, chum, go and be creative.' But Nyquist didn't do things that way. Instead he said that the easiest way for someone without capital to make a lot of money in a hurry was to take a job as a customer's man with a brokerage firm. The commissions would be decent, enough to live on and something left over, but the real money would come from riding along on all the in-shop maneuvers of the experienced brokers – the short sales, the new-issue purchases, the arbitrage ploys. If you're dedicated enough, Nyquist told him, you can make just about as much as you like. Selig protested that he knew nothing about Wall Street. 'I could teach you everything in three days,' said Nyquist.

Actually it took less than that. Selig slipped into Nyquist's mind for a quick cram course in financial terminology. Nyquist had all the definitions beautifully arranged: common stocks and preferred, shorts and longs, puts and calls, debentures, convertibles, capital gains, special situations, closed-end versus open-end funds, secondary offerings, specialists and what they do, the over-the-counter market, the Dow-Jones averages, point-and-figure charts, and everything else. Selig memorized

all of it. There was a vivid quality about mind-to-mind trans-
ferences with Nyquist that made memorizing things easy. The
next step was to enroll as a trainee. Every big brokerage firm
was looking for beginners – Merrill Lynch, Goodbody, Hayden
Stone, Clark Dodge, scads of them. Selig picked one at random
and applied. They gave him a stock-market quiz by way of
preliminary screening; he knew most of the answers, and those
he didn't know he picked up out of the minds of his fellow
testees, most of whom had been following the market since
childhood. He got a perfect score and was hired. After a brief
training period he passed the licensing test, and before long he
was a registered representative operating out of a fairly new
brokerage office on Broadway near 72nd Street.

He was one of five brokers, all of them fairly young. The
clientele was predominantly Jewish and generally geriatric: 75-
year-old widows from the huge apartment houses along 72nd
Street, and cigar-chomping retired garment manufacturers who
lived on West End Avenue and Riverside Drive. Some of them
had quite a lot of money, which they invested in the most
cautious way possible. Some were practically penniless, but
insisted on buying four shares of Con Edison or three shares
of Telephone just to have the illusion of prosperity. Since most
of the clients were elderly and didn't work, the bulk of dealings
at the office were transacted in person rather than by phone;
there were always ten or twelve senior citizens schmoozing
in front of the stock ticker, and now and then one of them
would dodder to the desk of his pet broker and place an
order. On Selig's fourth day at work one venerable client
suffered a fatal heart attack during a nine-point rally. Nobody
seemed surprised or even dismayed, neither the brokers nor
the friends of the victim: customers died in the shop about
once a month, Selig learned. Kismet. You come to expect
your friends to drop dead, once you reach a certain age. He
quickly became a favorite, especially among the old ladies;
they liked him because he was a nice Jewish boy, and several
offered to introduce him to comely granddaughters. These
offers he always refused, but politely; he made a point of being

courteous and patient with them, of playing grandson. Most of them were ignorant, practically illiterate women, kept in a state of lifelong innocence by their hard-driving, acquisitive, coronary-prone husbands; now, having inherited more money than they could possibly spend, they had no real idea of how to manage it, and were wholly dependent on the nice young broker. Probing their minds, Selig found them almost always to be dim and sadly unformed – how could you live to the age of 75 without ever having had an idea? – but a few of the livelier ladies showed vigorous, passionate peasant rapacity, charming in its way. The men were less agreeable – loaded with dough, yet always on the lookout for more. The vulgarity and ferocity of their ambitions repelled him, and he glanced into their minds no more often than necessary, merely probing to have a better idea of their investment goals so he could serve them as they would be served. A month among such people, he decided, would be sufficient to turn a Rockefeller into a socialist.

Business was steady but unspectacular; once he had acquired his own nucleus of regulars, Selig's commissions ran to about $160 a week, which was more money than he had ever made before, but hardly the kind of income he imagined brokers pulled down. 'You're lucky you came here in the spring,' one of the other customer's men told him. 'In the winter months all the clients go to Florida and we can choke before anybody gives us any business here.' As Nyquist had predicted, he was able to turn some pleasant profits by trading for his own account; there were always nice little deals circulating in the office, hot tips with substance behind them. He started with savings of $350 and quickly pyramided his wad to a high four-figure sum, making money on Chrysler and Control Data and RCA and Sunray DX Oil, nimbly trading in and out on rumors of mergers, stock splits, or dynamic earnings gains; but he discovered that Wall Street runs in two directions, and much of his winnings melted away through badly timed trades in Brunswick, Beckman Instruments, and Martin Marietta. He came to see that he was never going to have enough of a stake to go off and write that novel. Possibly just as well:

did the world need another amateur novelist? He wondered what he would do next. After three months as a broker he had some money in the bank, but not much, and he was hideously bored.

Luck delivered Kitty to him. She came in one muggy July morning at half past nine. The market hadn't opened yet, most of the customers had fled to the Catskills for the summer, and the only people in the office were Martinson, the manager, Nadel, one of the other customer's men, and Selig. Martinson was going over his totals, Nadel was on the phone to somebody downtown trying to work a complicated finagle in American Photocopy, and Selig, idle, was daydreaming of falling in love with somebody's beautiful granddaughter. Then the door opened and somebody's beautiful granddaughter came in. Not exactly beautiful, maybe, but certainly attractive: a girl in her early twenties, slim and well proportioned, perhaps five feet three or four, with fluffy light-brown hair, blue-green eyes, finely outlined features, a graceful slender figure. She seemed shy, intelligent, somehow innocent, a curious mixture of knowledge and naiveté. She wore a white silk blouse – gold chain lying on the smallish breasts – and an ankle-length brown skirt, offering a hint of excellent legs beneath. No, not a beautiful girl, but certainly pretty. Refreshing to look at. What the hell, Selig wondered, does she want in this temple of Mammon at her age? She's here fifty years too early. Curiosity led him to send a probe drilling into her forehead as she walked toward him. Seeking only surface stuff: name, age, marital status, address, telephone number, purpose of visit – what else?

He got nothing.

That shocked him. It was an incredible experience. Unique. To reach toward a mind and find it absolutely inaccessible, opaque, hidden as if behind an impenetrable wall – he had never had that happen to him before. He got no aura from her at all. She might as well have been a department store's plaster window mannequin, or a mindless robot from another planet. He sat there blinking, trying to account for his failure to make contact. He was so astounded by her total blankness that he forgot to listen to what she was saying to him, and had to ask her to repeat.

'I said, I'd like to open a brokerage account. Are you a broker?'

Sheepish, fumbling, stricken with sudden adolescent clumsiness, he gave her the new-account forms. By this time the other brokers had arrived, but too late: by the rules of the house she was his client. Sitting beside his cluttered desk, she told him of her investment needs while he studied the elegant tapered structure of her high-bridged nose, fought without success against her perplexing and enigmatic mental inaccessibility, and, despite or perhaps because of that inaccessibility, felt himself helplessly falling in love with her.

She was 22, one year out of Radcliffe, came from Long Island, and shared a West End Avenue apartment with two other girls. Unmarried – there had been a long futile love affair ending in a broken engagement not long before, he would discover later. (How strange it was for him not to be discovering everything at once, taking the information as he desired it.) Her background was in mathematics and she worked as a computer programmer, a term which, in 1963, meant very little to him; he wasn't sure whether she designed computers, operated them, or repaired them. Recently she had inherited $6500 from an aunt in Arizona, and her parents, who evidently were stern and formidable advocates of sink-or-swim education, had told her to invest the money on her own, by way of assuming adult responsibilities. So she had gone to her friendly neighborhood brokerage office, a lamb for the shearing, to invest her money. 'What do you want?' Selig asked her. 'To stash it away in safe blue chips, or to go for a little action, a chance for capital gains?'

'I don't know. I don't know the first thing about the market. I just don't want to do anything silly.'

Another broker – Nadel, say – would have given her the Nothing Ventured, Nothing Gained speech, and, advising her to forget about such old and tired concepts as dividends, would have steered her into an action portfolio – Texas Instruments, Collins Radio, Polaroid, stuff like that. Then he would churn her account every few months, switch Polaroid into Xerox, Texas Instruments into Fairchild Camera, Collins into American Motors, American Motors back into Polaroid, running up fancy commissions for himself and, perhaps, making some money for her, or perhaps losing some. Selig had no stomach for such maneuvers. 'This is going to sound stodgy,' he said, 'but let's play it very safe. I'll recommend some decent things that won't ever make you rich but that you won't get hurt on, either. And then you can just put them away and watch them grow, without having to check the market quotations every day to find out if you ought to sell. Because you don't really want to bother worrying about the short-term fluctuations, do you?' This was absolutely not what Martinson had instructed him to tell new clients, but to hell with that. He got her some Jersey Standard, some Telephone, a little IBM, two good electric utilities, and 30 shares of a closed-end fund called Lehman Corporation that a lot of his elderly customers owned. She didn't ask questions, didn't even want to know what a closed-end fund was. 'There,' he said. 'Now you have a portfolio. You're a capitalist.' She smiled. It was a shy, half-forced smile, but he thought he detected flirtatiousness in her eyes. It was agony for him not to be able to read her, to be compelled to depend on external signals alone in order to know where he stood with her. But he took the chance. 'What are you doing this evening?' he asked. 'I get out of here at four o'clock.'

She was free, she said. Except that she worked from eleven to six. He arranged to pick her up at her apartment around seven. There was no mistaking the warmth of her smile as she left the office. 'You lucky bastard,' Nadel said. 'What did you do, make a date with her? It violates the SEC rules for customer's men to go around laying the customers.'

Selig only laughed. Twenty minutes after the market opened he shorted 200 Molybdenum on the Amex, and covered his sale a point and a half lower at lunchtime. That ought to take care of the cost of dinner, he figured, with some to spare. Nyquist had given him the tip yesterday: Moly's a good short, she's sure to fall out of bed. During the mid-afternoon lull, feeling satisfied with himself, he phoned Nyquist to report on his maneuver. 'You covered too soon,' Nyquist said immediately. 'She'll drop five or six more points this week. The smart money's waiting for that.'

'I'm not that greedy. I'll settle for the quick three bills.'

'That's no way to get rich.'

'I guess I lack the gambling instinct,' Selig said. He hesitated. He hadn't really called Nyquist to talk about shorting Molybdenum. I met a girl, he wanted to say, and I have this funny problem with her: I met a girl, I met a girl. Sudden fears held him back. Nyquist's silent passive presence at the other end of the telephone line seemed somehow threatening. He'll laugh at me, Selig thought. He's always laughing at me, quietly, thinking I don't see it. But this is foolishness. He said, 'Tom, something strange happened today. A girl came into the office, a very attractive girl. I'm seeing her tonight.'

'Congratulations.'

'Wait. The thing is, I was entirely unable to read her, I mean, I couldn't even pick up an aura. Blank, absolutely blank. I've never had that with anybody before. Have you?'

'I don't think so.'

'A complete blank. I can't understand it. What could account for her having such a strong screen?'

'Maybe you're tired today,' Nyquist suggested.

'No. No. I can read everybody else, same as always. Just not her.'

'Does that irritate you?'

'Of course it does.'

'Why do you say of course?'

It seemed obvious to Selig. He could tell that Nyquist was baiting him: the voice calm, uninflected, neutral. A game. A way of passing time. He wished he hadn't phoned. Something important seemed to be coming across on the ticker, and the other phone was lighting up. Nadel, grabbing it, shot a fierce look at him: *Come on, man, there's work to do!* Brusquely Selig said, 'I'm – well, very interested in her. And it bothers me that I have no way of getting through to her real self.'

Nyquist said, 'You mean you're annoyed that you can't spy on her.'

'I don't like that phrase.'

'Whose phrase is it? Not mine. That's how you regard what we do, isn't it? As spying. You feel guilty about spying on people, right? But it seems you also feel upset when you can't spy.'

'I suppose,' Selig admitted sullenly.

'With this girl you find yourself forced back on the same old clumsy guesswork techniques for dealing with people that the rest of the world is condemned to use all the time, and you don't like that. Yes?'

'You make it sound so evil, Tom.'

'What do you want me to say?'

'I don't want you to say anything. I'm just telling you that there's this girl I can't read, that I've never been up against this situation before, that I wonder if you have any theories to account for why she's the way she is.'

'I don't,' Nyquist said. 'Not off the top of my head.'

'All right, then. I –'

But Nyquist wasn't finished. 'You realize that I have no way of telling whether she's opaque to the telepathic process in general or just opaque to you, David.' That possibility had occurred to Selig a moment earlier. He found it deeply disturbing. Nyquist went on smoothly, 'Suppose you bring her around one of these days and let me take a look at her. Maybe I'll be able to learn something useful about her that way.'

'I'll do that,' Selig said without enthusiasm. He knew such a meeting was necessary and inevitable, but the idea of exposing Kitty to Nyquist produced agitation in him. He had no clear understanding of why that should be happening. 'One of these days soon,' he said. 'Look, all the phones are lighting up. I'll be in touch, Tom.'

'Give her one for me,' said Nyquist.

TWENTY-THREE

David Selig
Selig Studies 101, Prof. Selig
November 10, 1976

ENTROPY AS A FACTOR IN EVERYDAY LIFE

Entropy is defined in physics as a mathematical expression of the degree to which the energy of a thermodynamic system is so distributed as to be unavailable for conversion into work. In more general metaphorical terms, entropy may be seen as the irreversible tendency of a system, including the universe, toward increasing disorder and inertness. That is to say, things have a way of getting worse and worse all the time, until in the end they get so bad that we lack even the means of knowing how bad they really are.

The great American physicist Josiah Willard Gibbs (1839–1903) was the first to apply the second law of thermodynamics – the law that defines the increasing disorder of energy moving at random within a closed system – to chemistry. It was Gibbs who most firmly enunciated the principle that disorder spontaneously increases as the universe grows older. Among those who extended Gibbs' insights into the realm of philosophy was the brilliant mathematician Norbert Wiener (1894–1964), who declared, in his book *The Human Use of Human Beings*, 'As entropy increases, the universe, and all closed systems in the universe, tend naturally to deteriorate and lose their distinctiveness, to move from the least to the most probable state, from a state of organization and differentiation in which distinctions and forms exist, to a state of chaos and sameness. In Gibbs' universe order is least probable, chaos most probable. But while the universe as a whole, if indeed there is a whole universe, tends to run down, there are local enclaves whose direction seems opposed to that of the universe at large and in which there is a limited and temporary tendency for organization to increase. Life finds its home in some of these enclaves.'

Thus Wiener hails living things in general and human beings in particular as heroes in the war against entropy – which he equates in another passage with the war against evil: 'This random element, this organic incompleteness (that is, the fundamental element of chance in the texture of the universe), is one which without too violent a figure of speech we may consider evil.' Human beings, says Wiener, carry on anti-entropic processes. We have sensory receptors. We communicate with one another. We make use of what we learn from one another. Therefore we are something more than mere passive victims of the spontaneous spread of universal chaos. 'We, as human beings, are not isolated systems. We take in food, which generates energy, from the outside, and are, as a result, parts of that larger world which contains those sources of our vitality. But even more important is the fact that we take in information through our sense organs, and we act on information received.' There is feedback, in other words. Through communication we learn to control our environment, and, he says, 'In control and communication we are always fighting nature's tendency to degrade the organized and to destroy the meaningful; the tendency . . . for entropy to increase.' In the very long run entropy must inevitably nail us all; in the short run we can fight back. 'We are not yet spectators at the last stages of the world's death.'

But what if a human being *turns* himself, inadvertently or by choice, into an isolated system?

A hermit, say. He lives in a dark cave. No information penetrates. He eats mushrooms. They give him just enough energy to keep going, but otherwise he lacks inputs. He's forced back on his own spiritual and mental resources, which he eventually exhausts. Gradually the chaos expands in him, gradually the forces of entropy seize possession of this ganglion, that synapse. He takes in a decreasing amount of sensory data until his surrender to entropy is complete. He ceases to move, to grow, to respire, to function in any way. This condition is known as death.

One doesn't have to hide in a cave. One can make an interior migration, locking oneself away from the life-giving energy sources. Often this is done because it appears that the energy sources are threats to the stability of the self. Indeed, inputs do threaten the self: a push usually will upset equilibrium. However, equilibrium itself is a threat to the self, though this is frequently overlooked. There are married people who strive fiercely to reach equilibrium. They seal themselves off, clinging to one another and shutting out the rest of the universe, making themselves into a two-person closed system from which all vitality is steadily and inexorably expelled by the deadly equilibrium they have established. Two can perish as well as one, if they are sufficiently isolated from everything else. I call this the monogamous fallacy. My sister Judith said she left her husband because she felt herself dying, day by day, while she was living with him. Of course, Judith's a slut.

The sensory shutdown is not always a willed event, naturally. It happens to us whether we like it or not. If we don't climb into the box ourselves, we'll get shoved in anyway. That's what I mean about entropy inevitably nailing us all in the long run. No matter how vital, how vigorous, how world-devouring we are, the inputs dwindle as time goes by. Sight, hearing, touch, smell – everything goes, as good old Will S. said, and we end up sans teeth, sans eyes, sans taste, sans everything. Sans everything. Or, as the same clever man also put it, from hour to hour we ripe and ripe, and then from hour to hour we rot and rot, and thereby hangs a tale.

I offer myself as a case in point. What does this man's sad history reveal? An inexplicable diminution of once-remarkable powers. A shrinkage of the inputs. A small death, endured while he still lives. Am I not a casualty of the entropic wars? Do I not now dwindle into stasis and silence before your very eyes? Is my distress not evident and poignant? Who will I be, when I have ceased to be myself? I am dying the heat death. A spontaneous decay. A random twitch of probability undoes me. And I am made into nothingness. I am becoming cinders and ash. I will wait here for the broom to gather me up.

That's very eloquent, Selig. Take an A. Your writing is clear and forceful and you show an excellent grasp of the underlying philosophical issues. You may go to the head of the class. Do you feel better now?

TWENTY-FOUR

It was a crazy idea, Kitty, a dumb fantasy. It could never have worked. I was asking the impossible from you. There was only one conceivable outcome, really: that is, that I would annoy you and bore you and drive you away from me. Well, blame Tom Nyquist. It was his idea. No, blame me. I didn't have to listen to his crazy ideas, did I? Blame me. Blame me.

Axiom: It's a sin against love to try to remake the soul of someone you love, even if you think you'll love her more after you've transformed her into something else.

Nyquist said, 'Maybe she's a mindreader too, and the blockage is a matter of interference, of a clash between your transmissions and hers, canceling out the waves in one direction or in both. So that there's no transmission from her to you and probably none from you to her.'

'I doubt that very much,' I told him. This was August of 1963, two or three weeks after you and I had met. We weren't living together yet but we had already been to bed a couple of times. 'She doesn't have a shred of telepathic ability,' I insisted. 'She's completely normal. That's the essential thing about her, Tom: she's a completely normal girl.'

'Don't be so sure,' Nyquist said.

He hadn't met you yet. He wanted to meet you, but I hadn't set anything up. You had never heard his name.

I said, 'If there's one thing I know about her, it's that she's a sane, healthy, well-balanced, absolutely normal girl. Therefore she's no mindreader.'

'Because mindreaders are insane, unhealthy, and unbalanced. Like you and like me. Q.E.D., eh? Speak for yourself, man.'

'The gift tips the spirit,' I said. 'It darkens the soul.'

'Yours, maybe. Not mine.'

He was right about that. Telepathy hadn't injured him. Maybe I'd have had the problems I have even if I hadn't been born with the gift. I can't credit all my maladjustments to the presence of one unusual ability, can I? And God knows there are plenty of neurotics around who have never read a mind in their lives.

Syllogism:

Some telepaths are not neurotic.

Some neurotics are not telepaths.

Therefore telepathy and neurosis aren't necessarily related.
Corollary:

You can seem cherry-pie normal and still have the power.

I remained skeptical of this. Nyquist agreed, under pressure, that if you did have the power, you would have probably revealed it to me by now through certain unconscious mannerisms that any telepath would readily recognize; I had detected no such mannerisms. He suggested, though, that you might be a latent telepath – that the gift was there, undeveloped, unfunctional, lurking at the core of your mind and serving somehow to screen your mind from my probing. Just a hypothesis, he said. But it tickled me with temptation. 'Suppose she's got this latent power,' I said. 'Could it be awakened, do you think?'

'Why not?' Nyquist asked.

I was willing to believe it. I had this vision of you awakened to full receptive capacity, able to pick up transmissions as easily and as sharply as Nyquist and I. How intense our love would be, then! We would be wholly open to one another, shorn of all the little pretenses and defenses that keep even the closest of lovers from truly achieving a union of souls. I had already tasted a limited form of that sort of closeness with Tom Nyquist, but of course I had no love for him, I didn't even really *like* him, and so it was a waste, a brutal irony, that our minds could have such intimate contact. But you? If I could only awaken you, Kitty! And why not? I asked Nyquist if he thought it might be possible. Try it and find out, he said. Make experiments. Hold hands, sit together in the dark, put some energy into trying to get across to her. It's worth trying, isn't it? Yes, I said, of course it's worth trying.

You seemed latent in so many other ways, Kitty: a potential human being rather than an actual one. An air of adolescence surrounded you. You seemed much younger than you actually were; if I hadn't known you were a college graduate I would have guessed you were 18 or 19. You hadn't read much outside your fields of interest – mathematics, computers, technology – and, since those weren't my fields of interest, I thought of you as not having read anything at all. You hadn't traveled; your world was limited by the Atlantic and the Mississippi, and the big trip of your life was a summer in Illinois. You hadn't even had much sexual experience: three men, wasn't it, in your 22 years, and only one of those a serious affair? So I saw you as raw material awaiting the sculptor's hand. I would be your Pygmalion.

In September of 1963 you moved in with me. You were spending so much time at my place anyway that you agreed it didn't make sense to keep going back and forth. I felt very married: wet stockings hanging over the shower-curtain rod, an extra toothbrush on the shelf, long brown hairs in the sink. The warmth of you beside me in bed every night. My belly against your smooth cool butt, yang and yin. I gave you books to read: poetry, novels, essays. How diligently you devoured them! You read Trilling on the bus going to work and Conrad in the quiet after-dinner hours and Yeats on a Sunday morning while I was out hunting for the *Times*. But nothing really seemed to stick with you; you had no natural bent for literature; I think you had trouble distinguishing Lord Jim from Lucky Jim, Malcolm Lowry from Malcolm Cowley, James Joyce from Joyce Kilmer. Your fine mind, so easily able to master COBOL and FORTRAN, could not decipher the language of poetry, and you would look up from *The Waste Land*, baffled, to ask some naïve high-school-girl question that would leave me irritated for hours. A hopeless case, I sometimes thought. Although on a day when the stock market was closed you took me down to the computer center where you worked and I listened to your explanations of the equipment and your functions as though you were talking so much Sanskrit to me. Different worlds, different kinds of mind. Yet I always had hope of creating a bridge.

At strategically timed moments I spoke elliptically of my interest in extrasensory phenomena.

I made it out to be a hobby of mine, a cool dispassionate study. I was fascinated, I said, by the possibility of attaining true mind-to-mind communication between human beings. I took care not to come on like a fanatic, not to oversell my case; I kept my desperation out of sight. Because I genuinely couldn't read you, it was easier for me to pretend to a scholarly objectivity than it would have been with anyone else. And I had to pretend. My strategy didn't allow for any true confessions. I didn't want to frighten you, Kitty, I didn't want to turn you off by giving you reason to think I was a freak, or, as I probably would have seemed to you, a lunatic. Just a hobby, then. A hobby.

You couldn't bring yourself to believe in ESP. If it can't be measured with a voltmeter or recorded on an electro-encephalograph, you said, it isn't real. Be tolerant, I pleaded. There *are* such things as telepathic powers. I know there are. (Be careful, Duv!) I couldn't cite EEG readings – I've never been near an EEG in my life, have no idea whether my power would register. And I had barred myself from conquering your skepticism by calling in some outsider and doing some party-game mindreading on him. But I could offer other arguments. Look at Rhine's results, look at all these series of correct readings of the Zener cards. How can you explain them, if not by ESP? And the evidence for telekinesis, teleportation, clairvoyance –

You remained skeptical, coolly putting down most of the

data I cited. Your reasoning was keen and close; there was nothing fuzzy about your mind when it was on its own home territory, the scientific method. Rhine, you said, fudges his results by testing heterogeneous groups, then selecting for further testing only those subjects who show unusual runs of luck, dropping the others from his surveys. And he publishes only the scores that seem to prove his thesis. It's a statistical anomaly, not an extrasensory one, that turns up all those correct guesses of the Zener cards, you insisted. Besides, the experimenter is prejudiced in favor of belief in ESP, and that surely leads to all sorts of unconscious errors of procedure, tiny accesses of unintentional bias that inevitably skew the outcome. Cautiously I invited you to try some experiments with me, letting you set up the procedures to suit yourself. You said okay, mainly, I think, because it was something we could do together, and – this was early October – we were already searching selfconsciously for areas of closeness, your literary education having become a strain for both of us.

We agreed – how subtly I made it seem like your own idea! – to concentrate on transmitting images or ideas to one another. And right at the outset we had a cruelly deceptive success. We assembled some packets of pictures and tried to relay them mentally. I still have, here in the archives, our notes on those experiments:

Pictures Seen By Me	Your Guess
1. A rowboat	1. Oak Trees
2. Marigolds in a field	2. Bouquet of roses
3. A kangaroo	3. President Kennedy
4. Twin baby girls	4. A statue
5. The Empire State Building	5. The Pentagon
6. A snow-capped mountain	6. ?image unclear
7. Profile of old man's face	7. A pair of scissors
8. Baseball player at bat	8. A carving knife

9.	An elephant	9.	A tractor
10.	A locomotive	10.	An airplane

You had no direct hits. But four out of ten could be considered close associations: marigolds and roses, the Empire State and the Pentagon, elephant and tractor, locomotive and airplane. (Flowers, buildings, heavy-duty equipment, means of transportation.) Enough to give us false hopes of true transmission. Followed by this:

Pictures Seen By You	*My Guess*
1. A butterfly	1. A railway train
2. An octopus	2. Mountains
3. Tropical beach scene	3. Landscape, bright sunlight
4. Young Negro boy	4. An automobile
5. Map of South America	5. Grapevines
6. George Washington Bridge	6. The Washington Monument
7. Bowl of apples and bananas	7. Stock market quotations
8. El Greco's *Toledo*	8. A shelf of books
9. A highway at rush hour	9. A beehive
10. An ICBM	10. Cary Grant

No direct hits for me either. But three close associations, of sorts, out of ten: tropical beach and sunny landscape, George Washington Bridge and Washington Monument, highway at rush hour and beehive, the common denominators being sunlight, George Washington, and intense tight-packed activity. At least we deceived ourselves into seeing them as close associations rather than coincidences. I confess I was stabbing in the dark at all times, guessing rather than receiving, and I had little faith even then in the quality of our responses. Nevertheless those probably random collisions of images aroused your curiosity: there's something in this stuff, maybe, you began to say. And we went onward.

We varied the conditions for thought transmission. We tried doing it in absolute darkness, one room apart. We tried it with the lights on, holding hands. We tried it during sex: I entered you and held you in my arms and thought hard at you, and you thought hard at me. We tried it drunk. We tried it fasting. We tried it under conditions of sleep-deprivation, forcing ourselves to stay up around the clock in the random hope that minds groggy with fatigue might permit mental impulses to slip through the barriers separating us. We would have tried it under the influence of pot or acid, but no one thought much about pot or acid in '63. We sought in a dozen other ways to open the telepathic conduit. Perhaps you recall the details of them even now; embarrassment drives them from my mind. I know we wrestled with our futile project night after night for more than a month, while your involvement with it swelled and peaked and dwindled again, carrying you through a series of phases from skepticism to cool neutral interest to unmistakable fascination and enthusiasm, then to an awareness of inevitable failure, a sense of the impossibility of our goal, leading then to weariness, to boredom, and to irritation. I realized none of this: I thought you were as dedicated to the work as I was. But it had ceased to be either an experiment or a game; it was, you saw, plainly an obsessive quest, and you asked several times in November if we could quit. All this mindreading, you said, left you with woeful headaches. But I couldn't give up, Kitty. I overrode your objections and insisted we go on. I was hooked, I was impaled, I browbeat you mercilessly into cooperating, I tyrannized you in the name of love, seeing always that telepathic Kitty I would ultimately produce. Every ten days, maybe, some delusive flicker of seeming contact buoyed my idiotic optimism. We *would* break through; we *would* touch each other's minds. How could I quit now, when we were so close? But we were never close.

Early in November Nyquist gave one of his occasional dinner parties, catered by a Chinatown restaurant he favored. His parties were always brilliant events; to refuse the invitation would have been absurd. So at last I would have to expose you to him. For more than three months I had been more or less deliberately concealing you from him, avoiding the moment of confrontation, out of a cowardice I didn't fully understand. We came late: you were slow getting ready. The party was well under way, fifteen people, many of them celebrities, although not to you, for what did you know of poets, composers, novelists? I introduced you to Nyquist. He smiled and murmured a sleek compliment and gave you a bland, impersonal kiss. You seemed shy, almost afraid of him, of his confidence and smoothness. After a moment of patter he went spinning away to answer the doorbell. A little later, as we were handed our first drinks, I planted a thought for him:

– Well? What do you think of her.

But he was too busy with his other guests to probe me, and didn't pick up on my question. I had to seek my own answers in his skull. I inserted myself – he glanced at me across the room, realizing what I was doing – and rummaged for information. Layers of hostly trivia masked his surface levels; he was simultaneously offering drinks, steering a conversation, signaling for the eggrolls to be brought from the kitchen, and inwardly going over the guest list to see who was yet to arrive. But I cut swiftly through that stuff and in a moment found his locus of Kitty-thoughts. At once I acquired the knowledge I wanted and dreaded. He could read you. Yes. To him you were as transparent as anyone else. Only to me were you opaque, for reasons none of us knew. Nyquist had instantly penetrated you, had assessed you, had formed his judgment of you, there for me to examine: he saw you as awkward, immature, naïve, but yet also attractive and charming. (That's how he really saw you. I'm not trying, for ulterior reasons of my own, to make him seem more critical of you than he really was. You were very young, you were unsophisticated, and he saw that.) The discovery numbed me. Jealousy curdled me. That I should work so ponderously for so many weeks to reach you, getting nowhere, and he could knife so easily to your depths, Kitty! I was instantly suspicious. Nyquist and his malicious games: was this yet one more? *Could* he read you?

How could I be sure he hadn't planted a fiction for me? He picked up on that:

- You don't trust me? Of course I'm reading her.
- Maybe yes, maybe no.
- Do you want me to prove it?
- How?
- Watch.

Without interrupting for a moment his role of host, he entered your mind, while mine remained locked on his. And so, through him, I had my first and only glimpse of your inwardness, Kitty, reflected by way of Tom Nyquist. Oh! It was no glimpse I ever wanted. I saw myself through your eyes through his mind. Physically I looked, if anything, better than I imagined I would, my shoulders broader than they really are, my face leaner, the features more regular. No doubt that you responded to my body. But the emotional associations! You saw me as stern father, as grim schoolmaster, as grumbling tyrant. Read this, read that, improve your mind, girl! Study hard to be worthy of me! Oh! Oh! And that flaming core of resentment over our ESP experiments: worse than useless to you, a monumental bore, an excursion into insanity, a wearying, grinding drag. Night after night to be bugged by monomaniacal me. Even our screwing invaded by the foolish quest for mind-to-mind contact. How sick you were of me, Kitty! How monstrously dull you thought me!

An instant of such revelation was more than enough. Stung, I retreated, pulling away quickly from Nyquist. You looked at me in a startled way, I recall, as if you knew on some subliminal level that mental energies were flashing around the room, revealing the privacies of your soul. You blinked and your cheeks reddened and you took a hasty diving gulp of your drink. Nyquist shot me a sardonic smile. I couldn't meet his eyes. But even then I resisted what he had showed me. Had I not seen odd refraction effects before in such relays? Should I not mistrust the accuracy of his picture of your image of me? Was he not shading and coloring it? Introducing sly distortions and magnifications? Did I truly bug you all that much, Kitty, or was he not playfully exaggerating mild annoyance into vivid distaste? I chose not to believe I bored you quite so much. We tend to interpret events according to the way we prefer to see them. But I vowed to go easier on you in the future.

Later, after we had eaten, I saw you talking animatedly to Nyquist at the far side of the room. You were flirtatious and giddy, as you had been with me that first day at the brokerage office. I imagined you were discussing me and not being complimentary. I tried to pick up the conversation by way of Nyquist, but at my first tentative probe he glared at me.

– Get out of my head, will you?

I obeyed. I heard your laughter, too loud, rising above the hum of conversation. I drifted off to talk to a lithe little Japanese sculptress whose flat tawny chest sprouted untemptingly from a low-cut black sheath, and found her thinking, in French, that she would like me to ask her to go home with me. But I went home with you, Kitty, sitting sullen and graceless beside you on the empty subway train, and when I asked you what you and Nyquist had been discussing you said, 'Oh, we were just kidding around. Just having a little fun.'

About two weeks later, on a clear crisp autumn afternoon, President Kennedy was shot in Dallas. The stock market closed early after a calamitous slide and Martinson shut the office down, turning out, dazed, into the street. I couldn't easily accept the reality of the progression of events. *Someone shot at the President . . . Someone shot the President . . . Someone shot the President in the head . . . The President has been critically wounded . . . The President has been rushed to Parkland Hospital . . . The President has received the last rites . . . The President is dead.* I was never a particularly political person, but this rupture of the commonwealth devastated me. Kennedy was the only presidential candidate I ever voted for who won, and they killed him: the story of my life in one compressed bloody parable. And now there would be a President Johnson. Could I adapt? I cling to zones of stability. When I was 10 years old and Roosevelt died, Roosevelt who had been President all my life, I tested the unfamiliar syllables of *President Truman* on my tongue and rejected them at once, telling myself that I would call him President Roosevelt too, for that was what I was accustomed to calling the President.

That November afternoon I picked up emanations of fear on all sides as I walked fearfully home. Paranoia was general everywhere. People sidled warily, one shoulder in front of the other, ready to bolt. Pale female faces peered between parted curtains in the windows of the towering apartment houses, high above the silent streets. The drivers of cars looked in all directions at intersections, as if expecting the tanks of the storm troopers to come rumbling down Broadway. (At this time of day it was generally believed that the assassination was the first blow in a right-wing putsch.) No one lingered in the open; everyone hurried toward shelter. Anything might happen now. Packs of wolves might burst out of Riverside Drive. Maddened patriots might launch a pogrom. From my apartment – door bolted, windows locked – I tried to phone you at the computer center, thinking you might somehow not have heard the news, or perhaps I just wanted to hear your voice in this traumatic time. The telephone lines were choked. I gave up the attempt after twenty minutes. Then, wandering aimlessly from bedroom to livingroom and back, clutching my transistor, twisting the dial trying to find the one radio station whose newscaster would tell me that he was still alive after all, I detoured into the kitchen and found your note on the table, telling me that you were leaving, that you couldn't stay with me any more. The note was dated 10.30 a.m., before the assassination, in another era. I rushed to the bedroom closet and saw what I had not seen before, that your things were gone. When women leave me, Kitty, they leave suddenly and stealthily, giving no warning.

Toward evening I telephoned Nyquist. This time the lines were open. 'Is Kitty there?' I asked. 'Yes,' he said. 'Just a minute.' And put you on. You explained that you were going to live with him for a while, until you got yourself sorted out. He had been very helpful. No, you had no hard feelings towards me, no bitterness at all. It was just that I seemed, well, insensitive, whereas he – he had this instinctive, intuitive grasp of your emotional needs – he was able to get onto your trip, Kitty, and I couldn't manage that. So you had gone to him for comfort and love. Goodbye, you said, and thanks for everything, and I muttered a goodbye and put down the phone. During the night the weather changed, and a weekend of black skies and cold rain saw JFK to his grave. I missed everything – the casket in the rotunda, the brave widow and the gallant children, the murder of Oswald, the funeral procession, all that instant history. Saturday and Sunday I slept late, got drunk, read six books without absorbing a word. On Monday, the day of national mourning, I wrote you that incoherent letter, Kitty, explaining everything, telling you what I had tried to make out of you and why, confessing my power to you and describing the effects it had had on my life, telling you also about Nyquist, warning you of what he was, that he had the power too, that he could read you and you would have no secrets from him, telling you not to mistake him for a real human being, telling you that he was a machine, self-programmed for maximum self-realization, telling you that the power had made him cold and cruelly strong whereas it had made me weak and jittery, insisting that essentially he was as sick as I, a manipulative man, incapable of giving love, capable only of using. I told you that he would hurt you if you made yourself vulnerable to him. You didn't answer. I never heard from you again, never saw you again, never heard from or saw him again either. Thirteen years. I have no idea what became of either of you. Probably I'll never know. But listen. I loved you, lady, in my clumsy way. I love you now. And you are lost to me forever.

TWENTY-FIVE

He wakes, feeling stiff and sore and numb, in a bleak, dreary hospital ward. Evidently this is St Luke's, perhaps the emergency room. His lower lip is swollen, his left eye opens only reluctantly, and his nose makes an unfamiliar whistling sound at every intake of air. Did they bring him here on a stretcher after the basketball players finished with him? When he succeeds in looking down – his neck, oddly rigid, does not want to obey him – he sees only the dingy whiteness of a hospital gown. Each time he breathes, he imagines he can feel the ragged edges of broken ribs scraping together; slipping a hand under the gown, he touches his bare chest and finds that it has not been taped. He does not know whether to be relieved or apprehensive about that.

Carefully he sits up. A tumult of impressions strikes him. The room is crowded and noisy, with beds pushed close together. The beds have curtains but no curtains are drawn. Most of his fellow patients are black, and many of them are in serious condition, surrounded by festoons of equipment. Mutilated by knives? Lacerated by windshields? Friends and relatives, clustering around each bed, gesticulate and argue and berate; the normal tone of voice is a yelping shout. Impassive nurses drift through the room, showing much the same distant concern for the patients as museum guards do for mummies in display cases. No one is paying any attention to Selig except Selig, who returns to the examination of himself. His fingertips explore his cheeks. Without a mirror he cannot tell how battered his face is, but there are many tender places. His left clavicle aches as from a light, glancing karate chop. His right knee radiates throbbings and twinges, as though he twisted it in falling. Still, he feels less pain than might have been anticipated; perhaps they have given him some sort of shot.

His mind is foggy. He is receiving some mental input from those about him in the ward, but everything is garbled, nothing is distinct; he picks up auras but no intelligible verbalizations. Trying to get his bearings, he asks passing nurses three times to tell him the time, for his wristwatch is gone; they go by, ignoring him. Finally a bulky, smiling black woman in a frilly pink dress looks over at him and says, 'It's quarter to four, love.' In the morning? In the afternoon? Probably the afternoon, he decides. Diagonally across from him, two nurses have begun to erect what perhaps is an intravenous feeding system, with a plastic tube snaking into the nostril of a huge unconscious bandage-swathed black. Selig's own stomach sends him no hunger signals. The chemical smell in the hospital air gives him nausea; he can barely salivate. Will they feed him this evening? How long will he be kept here? Who pays? Should he ask that Judith be notified? How badly has he been injured?

An intern enters the ward: a short dark man, concise and fineboned of body, a Pakistani by the looks of him, moving with bouncy precision. A rumpled and soiled handkerchief jutting from his breast-pocket spoils, though, the trig, smart effect of his tight white uniform. Surprisingly, he comes right to Selig. 'The X-rays show no breakages,' he says without preamble in a firm, unresonant voice. 'Therefore your only injuries are minor abrasions, bruises, cuts, and an unimportant concussion. We are ready to authorize your release. Please get up.'

'Wait,' Selig says feebly. 'I just came to. I don't know what's been going on. Who brought me here? How long have I been unconscious? What –'

'I know none of these things. Your discharge has been approved and the hospital has need of this bed. Please. On your feet, now. I have much to do.'

'A concussion? Shouldn't I spend the night here, at least, if I had a concussion? Or *did* I spend the night here? What day is today?'

'You were brought in about noon today,' says the intern, growing more fretful. 'You were treated in the emergency room and given a thorough examination after having been beaten on the steps of Low Library.' Once more the command to rise, given wordlessly this time, an imperious glare and a pointing forefinger. Selig probes the intern's mind and finds it accessible, but there is nothing apparent in it except impatience and irritation. Ponderously Selig climbs from the bed. His body seems to be held together with wire. His bones grind and scrape. There is still the sensation of broken rib-ends rubbing in his chest; can the X-ray have been in error? He starts to ask, but too late. The intern, making his rounds, has whirled off to another bed.

They bring him his clothing. He pulls the curtain around his bed and dresses. Yes, bloodstains on his shirt, as he had feared; also on his trousers. A mess. He checks his belongings: everything here, wallet, wristwatch, pocket-comb. What now? Just walk out? Nothing to sign? Selig edges uncertainly toward the door. He actually gets into the corridor unperceived. Then the intern materializes as if from ectoplasm and points to another room across the hall, saying, 'You wait in there until the security man comes.' Security man? *What* security man?

There are, as he had feared, papers to sign before he is free of the hospital's grasp. Just as he finishes with the red tape, a plump, gray-faced, sixtyish man in the uniform of the campus security force enters the room, puffing slightly, and says, 'You Selig?'

He acknowledges that he is.

'The dean wants to see you. You able to walk by yourself or you want me to get you a wheelchair?'

'I'll walk,' Selig says.

They go out of the hospital together, up Amsterdam Avenue to the 115th Street campus gate, and into Van Am Quad. The security man stays close beside him, saying nothing. Shortly Selig finds himself waiting outside the office of the Dean of Columbia College. The security man waits with him, arms folded placidly, wrapped in a cocoon of boredom. Selig begins to feel almost as though he is under some sort of arrest. Why is that? An odd thought. What does he have to fear from the dean? He probes the security man's dull mind but can't find nothing in it but drifting, wispy masses of fog. He wonders who the dean is, these days. He remembers the deans of his own college era well enough: Lawrence Chamberlain, with the bow ties and the warm smile, was Dean of the College, and Dean McKnight, Nicholas McD. McKnight, a fraternity enthusiast (Sigma Chi?) with a formal, distinctly nineteenth-century manner, was Dean of Students. But that was twenty years ago. Chamberlain and McKnight must have had several successors by now, but he knows nothing about them; he has never been one for reading alumni newsletters.

A voice from within says, 'Dean Cushing will see him now.'

'Go on in,' the security man says.

Cushing? A fine deanly name. Who is he? Selig limps in, awkward from his injuries, bothered by his sore knee. Facing him behind a glistening uncluttered desk sits a wide-shouldered, smooth-cheeked, youthful-looking man, junior-executive model, wearing a conservative dark suit. Selig's first thought is of the mutations worked by the passage of time: he had always looked upon deans as lofty symbols of authority, necessarily elderly or at least of middle years, but here is the Dean of the College and he seems to be a man of Selig's own age. Then he realizes that this dean is not merely an anonymous contemporary of his but actually a classmate, Ted Cushing '56, a campus figure of some repute back then, class president and football star and A-level scholar, whom Selig had known at least in a passing way. It always surprises Selig to be reminded that he is no longer young, that he has lived into a time when his generation has control of the mechanisms of power. 'Ted?' he blurts. 'Are you dean now, Ted? Christ, I wouldn't have guessed that. When –'

'Sit down, Dave,' Cushing says, politely but with no great show of friendliness. 'Did you get badly hurt?'

'The hospital says nothing's broken. I feel half ruined, though.' As he eases into a chair he indicates the bloodstains on his clothing, the bruises on his face. Talking is an effort; his jaws creak at their hinges. 'Hey, Ted, it's been a long time! Must be twenty years since I last saw you. Did you remember my name, or did they identify me from my wallet?'

'We've arranged to pay the hospital costs,' Cushing says, not seeming to hear Selig's words. 'If there are any further medical expenses, we'll take care of those too. You can have that in writing if you'd like.'

'The verbal commitment is fine. And in case you're worrying that I'll press charges, or sue the University, well, I wouldn't do anything like that. Boys will be boys, they let their feelings run away with themselves a little bit, but –'

'We weren't greatly concerned about your pressing charges, Dave,' Cushing says quietly. 'The real question is whether we're going to press charges against *you*.'

'Me? For what? For getting mauled by your basketball players? For damaging their expensive hands with my face?' He essays a painful grin. Cushing's face remains grave. There is a little moment of silence. Selig struggles to interpret Cushing's joke. Finding no rationale for it, he decides to venture a probe. But he runs into a wall. He is suddenly too timid to push, fearful that he will be unable to break through. 'I don't understand what you mean,' he says finally. 'Press charges for what?'

'For these, Dave.' For the first time Selig notices the stack of typewritten pages on the dean's desk. Cushing nudges them forward. 'Do you recognize them? Here: take a look.'

Selig leafs unhappily through them. They are term papers, all of them his manufacture. *Odysseus as a Symbol of Society. The Novels of Kafka. Aeschylus and the Aristotelian Tragedy. Resignation and Acceptance in the Philosophy of Montaigne. Virgil as Dante's Mentor.* Some of them bear marks: A–, B+, A–, A and marginal comments, mainly favorable. Some are untouched except by smudges and smears; these are the ones he had been about to deliver when he was set upon by Lumumba. With immense care he tidies the stack, aligning the edges of the sheets precisely, and pushes them back toward Cushing. 'All right,' he says. 'You've got me.'

'Did you write those?'

'Yes.'

'For a fee?'

'Yes.'

'That's sad, Dave. That's awfully sad.'

'I needed to earn a living. They don't give scholarships to alumni.'

'What were you getting paid for these things?'

'Three or four bucks a typed page.'

Cushing shakes his head. 'You were good, I'll give you credit for that. There must be eight or ten guys working your racket here, but you're easily the best.'

'Thank you.'

'But you had one dissatisfied customer, at least. We asked Lumumba why he beat you up. He said he hired you to write a term paper for him and you did a lousy job, you ripped him off, and then you wouldn't refund his money. All right, we're dealing with him in our own way, but we have to deal with you, too. We've been trying to find you for a long time, Dave.'

'Have you?'

'We've circulated xeroxes of your work through a dozen departments the last couple of semesters, warning people to be on the lookout for your typewriter and your style. There wasn't a great deal of co-operation. A lot of faculty members didn't seem to care whether the term papers they received were phony or not. But we cared, Dave. We cared very much.' Cushing leans forward. His eyes, terribly earnest, seek Selig's. Selig looks away. He cannot abide the searching warmth of those eyes. 'We started closing in a few weeks ago,' Cushing continues. 'We rounded up a couple of your clients and threatened them with expulsion. They gave us your name, but they didn't know where you lived, and we had no way of finding you. So we waited. We knew you'd show up again to deliver and solicit. Then we got this report of a disturbance on the steps of Low, basketball players beating somebody up, and we found you with a pile of undelivered papers clutched in your arm, and that was it. You're out of business, Dave.'

'I should ask for a lawyer,' Selig says. 'I shouldn't admit anything more to you. I should have denied everything when you showed me those papers.'

'No need to be so technical about your rights.'

'I'll need to be when you take me to court, Ted.'

'No,' Cushing says. 'We aren't going to prosecute, not unless we catch you ghosting more papers. We have no interest in putting you in jail, and in any case I'm not sure that what you've done is a criminal offense. What we really want to do is help you. You're sick, Dave. For a man of your intelligence, of your potential, to have fallen so low, to have ended up faking term papers for college kids – that's sad, Dave, that's awfully sad. We've discussed your case here, Dean Bellini and Dean Tompkins and I, and we've come up with a rehabilitation plan for you. We can find you work on campus, as a research assistant, maybe. There are always doctoral candidates who need assistants, and we have a small fund we could dip into to provide a salary for you, nothing much, but at least as much as you were making on these papers. And we'd admit you to the psychological counseling service here. It wasn't set up for alumni, but I don't see why we need to be inflexible about it, Dave. For myself I have to say that I find it embarrassing that a man of the Class of '56 is in the kind of trouble you're in, and if only out of a spirit of loyalty to our class I want to do everything possible to help you put yourself back together and begin to fulfill the promise that you showed when –'

Cushing rambles on, restating and embellishing his themes, offering pity without censure, promising aid to his suffering classmate. Selig, listening inattentively, discovers that Cushing's mind is beginning to open to him. The wall that earlier had separated their consciousnesses, a product perhaps of Selig's fear and fatigue, has started to dissolve, and Selig is able now to perceive a general image of Cushing's mind, which is energetic, strong, capable, but also conventional and limited, a stolid Republican mind, a prosaic Ivy League mind. Foremost in it is not his concern for Selig but rather his complacent satisfaction with himself: the brightest glow emanates from Cushing's awareness of his happy station in life, ornamented by a suburban split-level, a strapping blonde wife, three handsome children, a shaggy dog, a shining new

Lincoln Continental. Pushing a bit deeper, Selig sees that Cushing's show of concern for him is fraudulent. Behind the earnest eyes and the sincere, heartfelt, sympathetic smile lies fierce contempt. Cushing despises him. Cushing thinks he is corrupt, useless, worthless, a disgrace to mankind in general and the Columbia College Class of '56 in particular. Cushing finds him physically as well as morally repugnant, seeing him as unwashed and unclean, possibly syphilitic. Cushing suspects him of being homosexual. Cushing has for him the scorn of the Rotarian for the junkie. It is impossible for Cushing to understand why anyone who has had the benefit of a Columbia education would let himself slide into the degradations Selig has accepted. Selig shrinks from Cushing's disgust. Am I so despicable, he wonders, am I such trash?

His hold on Cushing's mind strengthens and deepens. It ceases to trouble him that Cushing has such contempt for him. Selig drifts into a mode of abstraction in which he no longer identifies himself with the miserable churl Cushing sees. What does Cushing know? Can Cushing penetrate the mind of another? Can Cushing feel the ecstasy of real contact with a fellow human being? And there is ecstasy in it. God-like he rides passenger in Cushing's mind, sinking past the external defenses, past the petty prides and snobberies, past the self-congratulatory smugness, into the realm of absolute values, into the kingdom of authentic self. Contact! Ecstasy! That stolid Cushing is the outer husk. Here is a Cushing that even Cushing does not know: but Selig does.

Selig has not been so happy in years. Light, golden and serene, floods his soul. An irresistible gaiety possesses him. He runs through misty groves at dawn, feeling the gentle lashing of moist green fern-fronds against his shins. Sunlight pierces the canopy of high foliage, and droplets of dew glitter with a cool inner fire. The birds awaken. Their song is tender and sweet, a distant cheebling, sleepy and soft. He runs through the forest, and he is not alone, for a hand grasps his hand; and he knows that he has never been alone and never will be alone. The forest floor is damp and spongy beneath his bare feet. He runs. He runs. An invisible choir strikes a harmonious note and holds it, holds it, holds it, swelling it in perfect crescendo, until, just as he breaks from the grove and sprints into a sun-bright meadow, that swell of tone fills all the cosmos, reverberating in magical fullness. He throws himself face-forward to the ground, hugging the earth, writhing against the fragrant grassy carpet, flattening his hands against the curve of the planet, and he is aware of the world's inner throbbing. This is ecstasy! This is contact! Other minds surround his. In whatever direction he moves, he feels their presence, welcoming him, supporting him, reaching toward him. Come, they say, join us, join us, be one with us, give up those tattered shreds of self, let go of all that holds you apart from us. Yes, Selig replies. Yes. I affirm the ecstasy of life. I affirm the joy of contact. I give myself to you. They touch him. He touches them. It was for this, he knows, that I received my gift, my blessing, my power. For this moment of affirmation and fulfillment. Join us. Join us. Yes! The birds! The invisible choir! The dew! The meadow! The sun! He laughs; he rises and breaks into an ecstatic dance; he throws back his head to sing, he who has never in his life dared to sing, and the tones that come from him are rich and full, pure, squarely striking the center of the pitch. Yes! Oh, the joining, the touching, the union, the oneness! No longer is he David Selig. He is a part of them, and they are a part of him, and in that joyous blending he experiences loss of self, he gives up all that is tired and worn and sour in him, he gives up his fears and uncertainties, he gives up everything that has separated himself from himself for so many years. He breaks through. He is fully open and the immense signal of the universe rushes freely into him. He receives. He transmits. He absorbs. He radiates. Yes. Yes. Yes. Yes.

He knows this ecstasy will last forever.

But in the moment of that knowledge, he feels it slipping from him. The choir's glad note diminishes. The sun drops toward the horizon. The distant sea, retreating, sucks at the shore. He struggles to hold to the joy, but the more he struggles the more of it he loses. Hold back the tide? How?

Delay the fall of night? How? How? The birdsongs are faint now. The air has turned cold. Everything rushes away from him. He stands alone in the gathering darkness, remembering that ecstasy, recapturing it momentarily, reliving it – for it is already gone, and must be summoned back through an act of the will. Gone, yes. It is very quiet, suddenly. He hears one last sound, a stringed instrument in the distance, a cello, perhaps, being plucked, pizzicato, a beautiful melancholy sound. *Twang*. The plangent chord. *Twing*. The breaking string. *Twong*. The lyre untuned. Twang. Twing. Twong. And nothing more. Silence envelops him. A terminal silence, it is, that booms through the caverns of his skull, the silence that follows the shattering of the cello's strings, the silence that comes with the death of music. He can hear nothing. He can feel nothing. He is alone. He is alone.

He is alone.

'So quiet,' he murmurs. 'So private. It's – so – private – here.'

'Selig?' A deep voice asks. 'What's the matter with you, Selig?'

'I'm all right,' Selig says. He tries to stand, but nothing has any solidity. He is tumbling through Cushing's desk, through the floor of the office, falling through the planet itself, seeking and not finding a stable platform. 'So quiet. The silence, Ted, the silence!' Strong arms seize him. He is aware of several figures bustling about him. Someone is calling for a doctor. Selig shakes his head, protesting that nothing is wrong with him, nothing at all, except for the silence in his head, except for the silence, except for the silence.

Except for the silence.

TWENTY-SIX

Winter is here. Sky and pavement form a seamless, inexorable band of gray. There will be snow soon. For some reason this neighborhood has gone without refuse pickups for three or four days, and bulging plastic sacks of trash are heaped in front of every building, yet there is no odor of garbage in the air. Not even smells can flourish in these temperatures: the cold drains away every stink, every sign of organic reality. Only concrete triumphs here. Silence reigns. Scrawny black and gray cats, motionless, statues of themselves, peer out of alleys. Traffic is light. Walking quickly through the streets from the subway station to Judith's place, I avert my eyes from the faces of the few people I pass. I feel shy and selfconscious among them, like a war veteran who has just been discharged from the rehabilitation center and is still embarrassed about his mutilations. Naturally I'm unable to tell what anybody is thinking; their minds are closed to me now and they go by me wearing shields of impenetrable ice; but, ironically, I have the illusion that they all have access to *me*. They can look right into me and see me for what I've become. There's David Selig, they must be thinking. How careless he was! What a poor custodian of his gift! He messed up and let it all slip away from him, the dope. I feel guilty for causing them this disappointment. Yet I don't feel as guilty as I thought I might. On some ultimate level I just don't give a damn at all. This is what I am, I tell myself. This is what I now shall be. If you don't like it, tough crap. Try to accept me. If you can't do that, just ignore me.

'As the truest society approaches always nearer to solitude, so the most excellent speech finally falls into silence. Silence is audible to all men, at all times, and in all places.' So said Thoreau, in 1849, in *A Week on the Concord and Merrimack Rivers*. Of course, Thoreau was a misfit and an outsider with very serious neurotic problems. When he was a young man just out of college he fell in love with a girl named Ellen Sewall, but she turned him down, and he never married. I wonder if he ever made it with anybody. Probably not. I can't imagine Thoreau actually balling, can you? Oh, maybe he didn't die a virgin, but I bet his sex life was lousy. Perhaps he didn't even masturbate. Can you visualize him sitting next to that pond and whacking off? I can't. Poor Thoreau. Silence is audible, Henry.

I imagine, as I near Judith's building, that I meet Toni in the street. I seem to see a tall figure walking toward me from Riverside Drive, hatless, bundled up in a bulky orange coat. When we are half a block apart I recognize her. Strangely, I feel neither excitement nor apprehension over this unexpected reunion; I am quite calm, almost unmoved. At another time I might have crossed the street to avoid a possibly disturbing encounter, but not now: coolly I halt in her path, smile, hold up my hands in greeting. 'Toni?' I say. 'Don't you know me?'

She studies me, frowns, seems puzzled for a moment. But only a moment.

'David. Hello.'

Her face looks more lean, the cheekbones higher and sharper. There are some strands of gray in her hair. In the days when I knew her she had one curious gray lock at her temple, very unusual; now the gray is scattered more randomly through the black. Well, of course she's in her middle thirties now. Not exactly a girl. As old now, in fact, as I was when I first met her. But in fact I know she has hardly changed at all, only matured a little. She seems as beautiful as ever. Yet desire is absent from me. All passion spent, Selig. All passion spent. And she too is mysteriously free of turbulence. I remember our last meeting, the look of pain on her face, her obsessive heap of cigarette butts. Now her expression is amiable and casual. We both have passed through the realm of storms.

'You're looking good,' I say. 'What is it, eight years, nine?'

I know the answer to that. I'm merely testing her. And she passes the test, saying, 'The summer of '68.' I'm relieved to see that she hasn't forgotten. I'm still a chapter of her autobiography, then. 'How have you been, David?'

'Not bad.' The conversational inanities. 'What are you doing these days?'

'I'm with Random House now. And you?'

'Freelancing,' I say. 'Here and there.' Is she married? Her gloved hands offer no data. I don't dare ask. I'm incapable of probing. I force a smile and shift my weight from foot to foot. The silence that has come between us suddenly seems unbridgeable. Have we exhausted all feasible topics so soon? Are there no areas of contact left except those too pain-filled to reopen?'

She says, 'You've changed.'

'I'm older. Tireder. Balder.'

'It isn't that. You've changed somewhere inside.'

'I suppose I have.'

'You used to make me feel uncomfortable. I'd get a sort of queasy feeling. I don't any more.'

'You mean, after the trip?'

'Before and after both,' she says.

'You were always uncomfortable with me?'

'Always. I never knew why. Even when we were really close, I felt – I don't know, on guard, off balance, ill at ease, when I was with you. And that's gone now. It's entirely gone. I wonder why.'

'Time heals all wounds,' I say. Oracular wisdom.

'I suppose you're right. God, it's cold! Do you think it'll snow?'

'It's bound to, before long.'

'I hate the cold weather.' She huddles into her coat. I never knew her in cold weather. Spring and summer, then goodbye, get out, goodbye, goodbye. Odd how little I feel for her now. If she invited me up to her apartment I'd probably say, No, thank you, I'm on my way to visit my sister. Of course she's imaginary; that may have something to do with it. But also

I'm not getting an aura from her. She's not broadcasting, or
rather I'm not receiving. She's only a statue of herself, like the
cats in the alleys. Will I be incapable of feeling, now that I'm
incapable of receiving? She says, 'It's been good to see you,
David. Let's get together some time, shall we?'

'By all means. We'll have a drink and talk about old times.'

'I'd like that.'

'So should I. Very much.'

'Take care of yourself, David.'

'You too, Toni.'

We smile. I give her a little mock-salute of farewell. We
move apart; I continue walking west, she hurries up the
windy street toward Broadway. I feel a little warmer for having
met her. Everything cool, friendly, unemotional between us.
Everything dead, in fact. All passion spent. It's been good to
see you, David. Let's get together some time, shall we? When I
reach the corner I realize I have forgotten to ask for her phone
number. Toni? Toni? But she is out of sight. As though she
never was there at all.

> It is the little rift within the lute,
> That by and by will make the music mute,
> And ever widening slowly silence all.

That's Tennyson: *Merlin and Vivien*. You've heard that line
about the rift within the lute before, haven't you? But you
never knew it was Tennyson. Neither did I. My lute is riven.
Twang. Twing. Twong.

Here's another little literary gem:

Every sound shall end in silence, but the silence never dies.

Samuel Miller Hageman wrote that, in 1876, in a poem called
Silence. Have you ever heard of Samuel Miller Hageman before?
I haven't. You were a wise old cat, Sam, whoever you were.

*   *   *

One summer when I was eight or nine – it was before they adopted Judith, anyway – I went with my parents to a resort in the Catskills for a few weeks. There was a daycamp for the kiddies, in which we received instruction in swimming, tennis, softball, arts & crafts, and other activities, thus leaving the older folks free for gin rummy and creative drinking. One afternoon the daycamp staged some boxing matches. I had never worn boxing gloves, and in the free-for-alls of boyhood I had found myself to be an incompetent fighter, so I was unenthusiastic. I watched the first five matches in much dismay. All that hitting! All those bloody noses!

Then it was my turn. My opponent was a boy named Jimmy, a few months younger than I but taller and heavier and much more athletic. I think the counselors matched us deliberately, hoping Jimmy would kill me: I was not their favorite child. I started to shake even before they put the gloves on me. 'Round One!' called a counselor, and we approached each other. I distinctly heard Jimmy thinking about hitting me on the chin, and as his glove came toward my face I ducked and hit him in the belly. That made him furious. He proposed now to clobber me on the back of the head, but I saw that coming too and stepped aside and hit him on the neck close to his adam's-apple. He gagged and turned away, half in tears. After a moment he returned to the attack, but I continued to anticipate his moves and he never touched me. For the first time in my life I felt tough, competent, aggressive. As I battered him I looked past the improvised ring and saw my father flushed with pride, and Jimmy's father next to him looking angry and perplexed. End of round one. I was sweating, bouncy, grinning.

Round two: Jimmy came forth determined to knock me to pieces. Swinging wildly, frantically, still going for my head. I kept my head where he couldn't reach it and danced around to his side and hit him in the belly again, very hard, and when he folded up I hit him on the nose and he fell down, crying. The counselor in charge very quickly counted to ten and raised my hand. 'Hey, Joe Louis!' my father yelled. 'Hey, Willie Pep!' The counselor suggested I go over to Jimmy and help him up and

shake his hand. As he got to his feet I very clearly detected him
deciding to butt me in the teeth with his head, and I pretended
to be paying no attention, except when he charged I stepped
coolly to one side and banged my fists down on his lowered
back. That shattered him. 'David cheats!' he moaned. 'David
cheats!'

How they all hated me for my cleverness! What they interpreted as my cleverness, that is. My sly knack of always
guessing what was going to happen. Well, that wouldn't be
a problem now. They'd all love me. Loving me, they'd beat
me to a pulp.

Judith answers the door. She wears an old gray sweater and
blue slacks with a hole in the knee. She holds her arms out
to me and I embrace her warmly, pulling her tight against my
body for perhaps half a minute. I hear music from within: the
Siegfried Idyll, I think. Sweet, loving, accepting music.

'Is it snowing yet?' she asks.

'Not yet. Gray and cold, that's all.'

'I'll get you a drink. Go into the livingroom.'

I stand by the window. A few snowflakes blow by. My
nephew appears and studies me at a distance of thirty feet. To
my amazement he smiles. He says warmly, 'Hi, Uncle David!'

Judith must have put him up to it. Be nice to Uncle David,
she must have said. He isn't feeling well, he's had a lot of
trouble lately. So there the kid stands, being nice to Uncle
David. I don't think he's ever smiled at me before. He didn't
even gurgle and coo at me out of his cradle. Hi, Uncle David.
All right, kid. I can dig it.

'Hello, Pauly. How have you been?'

'Fine,' he says. With that his social graces are exhausted; he
does not inquire in return about the state of my health, but
picks up one of his toys and absorbs himself in its intricacies.
Yet his large dark glossy eyes continue to examine me every
few moments, and there does not seem to be any hostility in
his glance.

Wagner ends. I prowl through the record racks, select one, put it on the turntable. Schoenberg, *Verklaerte Nacht*. Music of tempestuous anguish followed by calmness and resignation. The theme of acceptance again. Fine. Fine. The swirling strings enfold me. Rich, lush chords. Judith appears, bringing me a glass of rum. She has something mild for herself, sherry or vermouth. She looks a little peaked but very friendly, very open.

'Cheers,' she says.

'Cheers.'

'That's good music you put on. A lot of people won't believe Schoenberg could be sensuous and tender. Of course, it's very early Schoenberg.'

'Yes,' I say. 'The romantic juices tend to dry up as you get older, eh? What have you been up to lately, Jude?'

'Nothing much. A lot of the same old.'

'How's Karl?'

'I don't see Karl any more.'

'Oh.'

'Didn't I tell you that?'

'No,' I say. 'It's the first I've heard of it.'

'I'm not accustomed to needing to *tell* you things, Duv.'

'You'd better get accustomed to it. You and Karl —'

'He became very insistent about marrying me. I told him it was too soon, that I didn't know him well enough, that I was afraid of structuring my life again when it might possibly be the wrong structure for me. He was hurt. He began lecturing me about retreats from involvement and commitment, about self-destructiveness, a lot of stuff like that. I looked right at him in the middle of it and I flashed on him as a kind of father-figure; you know, big and pompous and stern, not a lover but a mentor, a professor, and I didn't want that. And I started thinking about what he'd be like in another ten or twelve years. He'd be in his sixties and I'd still be young. And I realized there was no future for us together. I told him that as gently as I could. He hasn't called in ten days or so. I suppose he won't.'

'I'm sorry.'

'No need to be, Duv. I did the smart thing. I'm sure of it. Karl was good for me, but it couldn't have been permanent. My Karl phase. A very healthy phase. The thing is not to let a phase go on too long after you know it's really over.'

'Yes,' I say. 'Certainly.'

'Would you like some more rum?'

'In a little while.'

'What about you?' she asks. 'Tell me about yourself. How you're making out, now that – now that –'

'Now that my superman phase is over?'

'Yes,' she says. 'It's really gone, eh?'

'Really. All gone. No doubt.'

'And so, Duv? How has it been for you since it happened?'

Justice. You hear a lot about justice, God's justice. He looketh after the righteous. He doeth dirt to the ungodly. Justice? Where's justice? Where's God, for that matter? Is He really dead, or merely on vacation, or only absent-minded? Look at His justice. He sends a flood to Pakistan. Zap, a million people dead, the adulterer and the virgin both. Justice? Maybe. Maybe the supposedly innocent victims weren't so innocent after all. Zap, the dedicated nun at the leprosarium gets leprosy and her lips fall off overnight. Justice. Zap, the cathedral that the congregation has been building for the past two hundred years is reduced to rubble by an earthquake the day before Easter. Zap. Zap. God laughs in our faces. This is justice? Where? How? I mean, consider my case. I'm not trying to wring some pity from you now; I'm being purely objective. Listen, I didn't *ask* to be a superman. It was handed to me at the moment of my conception. God's incomprehensible whim. A whim that defined me, shaped me, malformed me, dislocated me, and it was unearned, unasked for, entirely undesired, unless you want to think of my genetic heritage in terms of somebody else's bad karma, and crap on that. It was a random twitch. God said, Let this kid be a superman, and Lo! young Selig was a superman, in one limited sense of the word. For a time, anyhow. God set me up for everything that happened: the isolation, the suffering, the loneliness, even the self-pity. Justice? Where? The Lord giveth, who the hell knoweth why, and the Lord taketh away. Which He has now done. The power's gone. I'm just plain folks, even as you and you and you. Don't misunderstand: I accept my fate, I'm completely reconciled to it, I am NOT asking you to feel sorry for me. I simply want to make a little sense out of this. Now that the power's gone, who am I? How do I define myself now? I've lost my special thing, my power, my wound, my reason for apartness. All I have left now is the memory of having been different. The scars of it. What am I supposed to do now? How do I relate to mankind, now that the difference is gone and I'm still here? *It* died. I live on. What a strange thing you did to me, God. I'm not protesting, you understand. I'm just asking things, in a quiet, reasonable tone of voice. I'm inquiring into the nature of divine justice. I think Boethe's old harpist had the right slant on you, God. You lead us forth into life, you let the poor man fall into guilt, and then you leave him to his misery. For all guilt is revenged on earth. That's a reasonable complaint. You have ultimate power, God, but you refuse to take ultimate responsibility. Is that fair? I think I have a reasonable complaint too. If there's justice, why does so much of life seem unjust? If you're really on our side, God, why do you hand us a life of pain? Where's justice for the baby born without eyes? The baby born with two heads? The baby born with a power men weren't meant to have? Just asking, God. I accept your decree, believe me, I bow to your will, because I might as well – what choice do I have, after all? – but I'm still entitled to ask. Right?

Hey, God? God? Are you listening, God?

I don't think you are. I don't think you give a crap. God, I think you've been fucking me.

Dee-dah-de-doo-dah-dee-da. The music is ending. Celestial harmonies filling the room. Everything merging into one-ness. Snowflakes swirling beyond the windowpane. Right on,

Schoenberg. You understood, at least when you were young.
You caught truth and put it on paper. I hear what you're saying,
man. Don't ask questions, you say. Accept. Only accept, that's
the motto. Accept. Accept. Whatever comes to you, accept.

Judith says, 'Claude Guermantes has invited me to go skiing
with him in Switzerland over Christmas. I can leave the baby
with a friend in Connecticut. But I won't go if you need me,
Duv. Are you okay? Can you manage?'

'Sure I can. I'm not paralyzed, Jude. I haven't lost my sight.
Go to Switzerland, if that's what you want.'

'I'll only be gone eight days.'

'I'll survive.'

'When I come back, I hope you'll move out of that housing
project. You ought to live down here close to me. We should
see more of each other.'

'Maybe.'

'I might even introduce you to some girlfriends of mine. If
you're interested.'

'Wonderful, Jude.'

'You don't sound enthusiastic about it.'

'Go easy with me,' I tell her. 'Don't rush me with a million
things. I need time to sort things out.'

'All right. It's like a new life, isn't it, Duv?'

'A new life. Yes, A new life, that's what it is, Jude.'

The storm is intense, now. Cars are vanishing under the
first layers of whiteness. At dinner time the radio weather
forecaster talked of an accumulation of eight to ten inches
before morning. Judith has invited me to spend the night
here, in the maid's room. Well, why not? Now of all times,
why should I spurn her? I'll stay. In the morning we'll take
Pauly out to the park, with his sled, into the new snow. It's
really coming down, now. The snow is so beautiful. Covering
everything, cleansing everything, briefly purifying this tired

eroded city and its tired eroded people. I can't take my eyes from it. My face is close to the window. I hold a brandy snifter in one hand, but I don't remember to drink from it, because the snow has caught me in its hypnotic spell.

'*Boo!*' someone cries behind me.

I jump so violently that the cognac leaps from the snifter and splashes the window. In terror I whirl, crouching, ready to defend myself; then the instinctive fear subsides and I laugh. Judith laughs too.

'That's the first time I've ever surprised you,' she says. 'In thirty-one years, the first time!'

'You gave me one hell of a jolt.'

'I've been standing here for three or four minutes *thinking* things at you. Trying to get a rise out of you, but no, no, you didn't react, you just went on staring at the snow. So I sneaked up and yelled in your ear. You were really startled, Duv. You weren't faking at all.'

'Did you think I was lying to you about what had happened to me?'

'No, of course not.'

'Then why'd you think I'd be faking?'

'I don't know. I guess I doubted you just a little. I don't any more. Oh, Duv, Duv, I feel so sad for you!'

'Don't,' I say. 'Please, Jude.'

She is crying softly. How strange that is, to watch Judith cry. For love of me, no less. For love of me.

It's very quiet now.

The world is white outside and gray within. I accept that. I think life will be more peaceful. Silence will become my mother tongue. There will be discoveries and revelations, but no upheavals. Perhaps some color will come back into the world for me, later on. Perhaps.

Living, we fret. Dying, we live. I'll keep that in mind. I'll be of good cheer. Twang. Twing. Twong. Until I die again, hello, hello, hello, hello.

Nightwings

For Harlan,
to remind him of open windows,
the currents of the Delaware River,
quarters with two heads,
and other pitfalls.

PART I

Nightwings

ONE

Roum is a city built on seven hills. They say it was a capital of man in one of the earlier cycles. I did not know of that, for my guild was Watching, not Remembering; but yet as I had my first glimpse of Roum, coming upon it from the south at twilight, I could see that in former days it must have been of great significance. Even now it was a mighty city of many thousands of souls.

Its bony towers stood out sharply against the dusk. Lights glimmered appealingly. On my left hand the sky was ablaze with splendor as the sun relinquished possession; streaming bands of azure and violet and crimson folded and writhed about one another in the nightly dance that brings the darkness. To my right, blackness had already come. I attempted to find the seven hills, and failed, and still I knew that this was that Roum of majesty toward which all roads are bent, and I felt awe and deep respect for the works of our bygone fathers.

We rested by the long straight road, looking up at Roum. I said, 'It is a goodly city. We will find employment there.'

Beside me, Avluela fluttered her lacy wings. 'And food?' she asked in her high, fluty voice. 'And shelter? And wine?'

'Those too,' I said. 'All of those.'

'How long have we been walking, Watcher?' she asked.

'Two days. Three nights.'

'If I had been flying, it would have been more swift.'

'For you,' I said. 'You would have left us far behind and never seen us again. Is that your desire?'

She came close to me and rubbed the rough fabric of my sleeve, and then she pressed herself at me the way a flirting cat might do. Her wings unfolded into two broad sheets of gossamer through which I could still see the sunset and the evening lights, blurred, distorted, magical. I sensed the fragrance of her midnight hair. I put my arms to her and embraced her slender, boyish body.

She said, 'You know it is my desire to remain with you always, Watcher. Always!'

'Yes, Avluela.'

'Will we be happy in Roum?'

'We will be happy,' I said, and released her.

'Shall we go into Roum now?'

'I think we should wait for Gormon,' I said, shaking my head. 'He'll be back soon from his explorations.' I did not want to tell her of my weariness. She was only a child, seventeen summers old; what did she know of weariness or of age? And I was old. Not as old as Roum, but old enough.

'While we wait,' she said, 'may I fly?'

'Fly, yes.'

I squatted beside our cart and warmed my hands at the throbbing generator while Avluela prepared to fly. First she removed her garments, for her wings have little strength and she cannot lift such extra baggage. Lithely, deftly, she peeled the glassy bubbles from her tiny feet and wriggled free of her crimson jacket and of her soft furry leggings. The vanishing light in the west sparkled over her slim form. Like all Fliers, she carried no surplus body tissue: her breasts were mere bumps, her buttocks flat, her thighs so spindly that there was a span of inches between them when she stood. Could she have weighed more than a quintal? I doubt it. Looking at her, I felt, as always, gross and earthbound, a thing of loathsome flesh, and yet I am not a heavy man.

By the roadside she genuflected knuckles to the ground, head bowed to knees, as she said whatever ritual it is that the Fliers say. Her back was to me. Her delicate wings fluttered, filled with life, rose about her like a cloak whipped up by the breeze. I could not comprehend how such wings could possibly lift even so slight a form as Avluela's. They were not hawk-like but butterfly-wings, veined and transparent, marked here and there with blotches of pigment, ebony and turquoise and scarlet. A sturdy ligament joined them to the two flat pads of muscle beneath her sharp shoulderblades; but what she did not have was the massive breastbone of a flying creature, the bands of corded muscle needed for flight. Oh, I know that Fliers use more than muscle to get aloft, that there are mystical disciplines in their mystery. Even so, I, who was of the Watchers, remained skeptical of the more fantastic guilds.

Avluela finished her words. She rose; she caught the breeze with her wings; she ascended several feet. There she remained, suspended between earth and sky, while her wings beat frantically. It was not yet night, and Avluela's wings were merely nightwings. By day she could not fly, for the terrible pressure of the solar wind would hurl her to the ground. Now, midway between dusk and dark, it was still not the best time for her to go up. I saw her thrust toward the east by the remnant of light in the sky. Her arms as well as her wings thrashed; her small pointed face was grim with concentration; on her thin lips were the words of her guild. She doubled her body and shot it out, head going one way, rump the other; and abruptly she hovered horizontally, looking groundward, her wings thrashing against the air. *Up, Avluela! Up!*

Up it was, as by will alone she conquered the vestige of light that still glowed.

With pleasure I surveyed her naked form against the darkness. I could see her clearly, for a Watcher's eyes are keen. She was five times her own height in the air, now, and her wings spread to their full expanse, so that the towers of Roum were in partial eclipse for me. She waved. I threw her a kiss and offered words of love. Watchers do not marry, nor do they engender children, but yet Avluela was as a daughter to me, and I took pride in her flight. We had traveled together a year, now, since we had first met in Agupt, and it was as though I had known her all my life. From her I drew a renewal of strength. I do not know what it was she drew from me: security, knowledge, a continuity with the days before her birth. I hoped only that she loved me as I loved her.

Now she was far aloft. She wheeled, soared, dived, pirouetted, danced. Her long black hair streamed from her scalp. Her body seemed only an incidental appendage to those two great wings which glistened and throbbed and gleamed in the night. Up she rose, glorying in her freedom from gravity, making me feel all the more leaden-footed; and like some slender rocket she shot abruptly away in the direction of Roum. I saw the soles of her feet, the tips of her wings; then I saw her no more.

I sighed. I thrust my hands into the pits of my arms to keep them warm. How is it that I felt a winter chill while the girl Avluela could soar joyously bare through the sky?

It was the twelfth of the twenty hours, and time once again for me to do the Watching. I went to the cart, opened my cases, prepared the instruments. Some of the dial covers were yellowed and faded; the indicator needles had lost their luminous coating; sea stains defaced the instrument housings, a relic of the time that pirates had assailed me in Earth Ocean. The worn and cracked levers and nodes responded easily to my touch as I entered the preliminaries. First one prays for a pure and perceptive mind; then one creates the affinity with one's instruments; then one does the actual Watching, searching the starry heavens for the enemies of man. Such was my skill and my craft. I grasped handles and knobs, thrust things from my mind, prepared myself to become an extension of my cabinet of devices.

I was only just past my threshold and into the first phase of Watchfulness when a deep and resonant voice behind me said, 'Well, Watcher, how goes it?'

I sagged against the cart. There is a physical pain in being wrenched so unexpectedly from one's work. For a moment I felt claws clutching at my heart. My face grew hot; my eyes would not focus; the saliva drained from my throat. As soon as I could, I took the proper protective measures to ease the metabolic drain, and severed myself from my instruments. Hiding my trembling as much as possible, I turned round.

Gormon, the other member of our little band, had appeared and stood jauntily beside me. He was grinning, amused at my distress, but I could not feel angry with him. One does not show anger at a guildless person no matter what the provocation.

Tightly, with effort, I said, 'Did you spend your time rewardingly?'

'Very. Where's Avluela?'

I pointed heavenward. Gormon nodded.

'What have you found?' I asked.

'That this city is definitely Roum.'

'There never was doubt of that.'

'For me there was. But now I have proof.'

'Yes?'

'In the overpocket. Look!'

From his tunic he drew his overpocket, set it on the pavement beside me, and expanded it so that he could insert his hands into its mouth. Grunting a little, he began to pull something heavy from the pouch – something of white stone – a long marble column, I now saw, fluted, pocked with age.

'From a temple of Imperial Roum!' Gormon exulted.

'You shouldn't have taken that.'

'Wait!' he cried, and reached into the overpocket once more. He took from it a handful of circular metal plaques and scattered them jingling at my feet. 'Coins! Money! Look at them, Watcher! The faces of the Caesars!'

'Of whom?'

'The ancient rulers. Don't you know your history of past cycles?'

I peered at him curiously. 'You claim to have no guild, Gormon. Could it be you are a Rememberer and are concealing it from me?'

'Look at my face, Watcher. Could I belong to any guild? Would a Changeling be taken?'

'True enough,' I said, eying the golden hue of him, the thick waxen skin, the red-pupiled eyes, the jagged mouth. Gormon had been weaned on teratogenetic drugs; he was a monster, handsome in his way, but a monster nevertheless, a Changeling, outside the laws and customs of man as they are practiced in the Third Cycle of civilization. And there is no guild of Changelings.

'There's more,' Gormon said. The overpocket was infinitely capacious, the contents of a world, if need be, could be stuffed into its shriveled gray maw, and still it would be no longer than a man's hand. Gormon took from it bits of machinery, reading spools, an angular thing of brown metal that might have been an ancient tool, three squares of shining glass, five slips of paper – *paper!* – and a host of other relics of antiquity. 'See?' he said. 'A fruitful stroll, Watcher! And not just random booty. Everything recorded, everything labeled, stratum, estimated age, position when *in situ*. Here we have many thousands of years of Roum.'

'Should you have taken these things?' I asked doubtfully.

'Why not? Who is to miss them? Who of this cycle cares for the past?'

'The Rememberers.'

'They don't need solid objects to help them do their work.'

'Why do you want these things, though?'

'The past interests me, Watcher. In my guildless way I have my scholarly pursuits. Is that wrong? May not even a monstrosity seek knowledge?'

'Certainly, certainly. Seek what you wish. Fulfill yourself in your own way. This is Roum. At dawn we enter. I hope to find employment here.'

'You may have difficulties.'

'How so?'

'There are many Watchers already in Roum, no doubt. There will be little need for your services.'

'I'll seek the favor of the Prince of Roum,' I said.

'The Prince of Roum is a hard and cold and cruel man.'

'You know of him?'

Gormon shrugged. 'Somewhat.' He began to stuff his artifacts back in the overpocket. 'Take your chances with him, Watcher. What other choice do you have?'

'None,' I said, and Gormon laughed, and I did not.

He busied himself with his ransacked loot of the past. I found myself deeply depressed by his words. He seemed so sure of himself in an uncertain world, this guildless one, this mutated monster, this man of inhuman look; how could he be so cool, so casual? He lived without concern for calamity and mocked those who admitted to fear. Gormon had been traveling with us for nine days, now, since we had met him in the ancient city beneath the volcano to the south by the edge of the sea. I had not suggested that he join us; he had invited himself along, and at Avluela's bidding I accepted. The roads are dark and cold at this time of year, and dangerous beasts of many species abound, and an old man journeying with a girl might well consider taking with him a brawny one like Gormon. Yet there were times I wished he had not come with us, and this was one.

Slowly I walked back to my equipment.

Gormon said, as though first realizing it, 'Did I interrupt you at your Watching?'

I said mildly, 'You did.'

'Sorry. Go and start again. I'll leave you in peace.' And he gave me his dazzling lopsided smile, so full of charm that it took the curse off the easy arrogance of his words.

I touched the knobs, made contact with the nodes, monitored the dials. But I did not enter Watchfulness, for I remained aware of Gormon's presence and fearful that he would break into my concentration once again at a painful moment, despite his promise. At length I looked away from the apparatus. Gormon stood at the far side of the road, craning his neck for some sight of Avluela. The moment I turned to him he became aware of me.

'Something wrong, Watcher?'

'No. The moment's not propitious for my work. I'll wait.'

'Tell me,' he said. 'When Earth's enemies really do come from the stars, will your machines let you know it?'

'I trust they will.'

'And then?'

'Then I notify the Defenders.'

'After which your life's work is over?'

'Perhaps,' I said.

'Why a whole guild of you, though? Why not one master center where the Watch is kept? Why a bunch of itinerant Watchers drifting from place to place?'

'The more vectors of detection,' I said, 'the greater the chance of early awareness of the invasion.'

'Then an individual Watcher might well turn his machines on and not see anything, with an invader already here.'

'It could happen. And so we practice redundancy.'

'You carry it to an extreme, I sometimes think.' Gormon laughed. 'Do you actually believe an invasion is coming?'

'I do,' I said stiffly. 'Else my life was a waste.'

'And why should the star people want Earth? What do we have besides the remnants of old empires? What would they do with miserable Roum? With Perris? With Jorslem? Rotting cities! Idiot princes! Come, Watcher, admit it: the invasion's a myth, and you go through meaningless motions four times a day. Eh?'

'It is my craft and my science to Watch. It is yours to jeer. Each of us to our speciality, Gormon.'

'Forgive me,' he said with mock humility. 'Go, then, and Watch.'

'I shall.'

Angrily I turned back to my cabinet of instruments, determined now to ignore any interruption, no matter how brutal. The stars were out; I gazed at the glowing constellations, and automatically my mind registered the many worlds. Let us Watch, I thought. Let us keep our vigil despite the mockers.

I entered full Watchfulness.

I clung to the grips and permitted the surge of power to rush through me. I cast my mind to the heavens and searched for hostile entities. What ecstasy! What incredible splendor! I who had never left this small planet roved the black spaces of the void, glided from star to burning star, saw the planets spinning like tops. Faces stared back at me as I journeyed, some without eyes, some with many eyes, all the complexity of the many-peopled galaxy accessible to me. I spied out possible concentrations of inimicable force. I inspected drilling grounds and military encampments. I sought four times daily for all my adult life, for the invaders who had been promised us, the conquerors who at the end of days were destined to seize our tattered world.

I found nothing, and when I came up from my trance, sweaty and drained, I saw Avluela descending.

Feather-light she landed. Gormon called to her, and she ran, bare, her little breasts quivering, and he enfolded her smallness in his powerful arms, and they embraced, not passionately but joyously. When he released her she turned to me.

'Roum,' she gasped. '*Roum!*'

'You saw it?'

'Everything! Thousands of people! Lights! Boulevards! A market! Broken buildings many cycles old! Oh, Watcher, how wonderful Roum is!'

'Your flight was a good one, then,' I said.

'A miracle!'

'Tomorrow we go to dwell in Roum.'

'No, Watcher, tonight, tonight!' She was girlishly eager, her face bright with excitement. 'It's just a short journey more! Look, it's just over there!'

'We should rest first,' I said. 'We do not want to arrive weary in Roum.'

'We can rest when we get there,' Avluela answered. 'Come! Pack everything! You've done your Watching, haven't you?'

'Yes. Yes.'

'Then let's go. To Roum! To Roum!'

I looked in appeal at Gormon. Night had come; it was time to make camp, to have our few hours of sleep.

For once Gormon sided with me. He said to Avluela. 'The Watcher's right. We can all use some rest. We'll go on into Roum at dawn.'

Avluela pouted. She looked more like a child than ever. Her wings drooped, her underdeveloped body slumped. Petulantly she closed her wings until they were mere fistsized humps on her back, and picked up the garments she had scattered on the road. She dressed while we made camp. I distributed food tablets; we entered our receptacles; I fell into troubled sleep and dreamed of Avluela limned against the crumbling moon, and Gormon flying beside her. Two hours before dawn I arose and performed my first watch of the new day, while they still slept. Then I aroused them, and we went onward toward the fabled imperial city, onward toward Roum.

TWO

The morning's light was bright and harsh, as though this were some young world newly created. The road was all but empty; people do not travel much in these latter days unless, like me, they are wanderers by habit and profession. Occasionally we stepped aside to let a chariot of some member of the guild of Masters go by, drawn by a dozen expressionless neuters harnessed in series. Four such vehicles went by in the first two hours of the day, each shuttered and sealed to hide the Master's proud features from the gaze of such common folk as we. Several rollerwagons laden with produce passed us, and a number of floaters soared overhead. Generally we had the road to ourselves, however.

The environs of Roum showed vestiges of antiquity: isolated columns, the fragments of an aqueduct transporting nothing from nowhere to nowhere, the portals of a vanished temple. That was the oldest Roum we saw, but there were accretions of the later Roums of subsequent cycles: the huts of peasants, the domes of power drains, the hulls of dwelling-towers. Infrequently we met with the burned-out shell of some ancient airship. Gormon examined everything, taking samples from time to time. Avluela looked, wide-eyed, saying nothing. We walked on, until the walls of the city loomed before us.

They were of a blue glossy stone, neatly joined, rising to a height of perhaps eight men. Our road pierced the wall through a corbeled arch; the gate stood open. As we approached the gate a figure came toward us; he was hooded, masked, a man of extraordinary height wearing the somber garb of the guild of Pilgrims. One does not approach such a person oneself, but one heeds him if he beckons. The Pilgrim beckoned.

Through his speaking grille he said, 'Where from?'

'The south. I lived in Agupt awhile, then crossed Land Bridge to Talya,' I replied.

'Where bound?'

'Roum, awhile.'

'How goes the Watch?'

'As customary.'

'You have a place to stay in Roum?' the Pilgrim asked.

I shook my head. 'We trust to the kindness of the Will.'

'The Will is not always kind,' said the Pilgrim absently. 'Nor is there much need of Watchers in Roum. Why do you travel with a Flier?'

'For company's sake. And because she is young and needs protection.'

'Who is the other one?'

'He is guildless, a Changeling.'

'So I can see. But why is he with you?'

'He is strong and I am old, and so we travel together. Where are you bound, Pilgrim?'

'Jorslem. Is there another destination for my guild?'

I conceded the point with a shrug.

The Pilgrim said, 'Why do you not come to Jorslem with me?'

'My road lies north now. Jorslem is in the south, close by Agrup.'

'You have been to Agrup and not to Jorslem?' he said, puzzled.

'Yes. The time was not ready for me to see Jorslem.'

'Come now. We will walk together on the road, Watcher, and we will talk of the old times and of the times to come, and I will assist you in your Watching, and you will assist me in my communions with the Will. Is it agreed?'

It was a temptation. Before my eyes flashed the image of Jorslem the Golden, its holy building and shrines, its places of renewal where the old are made young, its spires, its tabernacles. Even though I am a man set in his ways, I was willing at the moment to abandon Roum and go with the Pilgrim to Jorslem.

I said, 'And my companions –'

'Leave them. It is forbidden for me to travel with the guildless, and I do not wish to travel with a female. You and I, Watcher, will go to Jorslem together.'

Avluela, who had been standing to one side frowning through all this colloquy, shot me a look of sudden terror.

'I will not abandon them,' I said.

'Then I go to Jorslem alone,' said the Pilgrim. Out of his robe stretched a bony hand, the fingers long and white and steady. I touched my fingers reverently to the tips of his, and the Pilgrim said, 'Let the Will give you mercy, friend Watcher. And when you reach Jorslem, search for me.'

He moved on down the road without further conversation.

Gormon said to me, 'You would have gone with him, wouldn't you?'

'I considered it.'

'What could you find in Jorslem that isn't here? That's a holy city and so is this. Here you can rest awhile. You're in no shape for more walking now.'

'You may be right,' I conceded, and with the last of my energy I strode toward the gate of Roum.

Watchful eyes scanned us from slots in the wall. When we were at midpoint in the gate, a fat, pockmarked Sentinel with sagging jowls halted us and asked our business in Roum. I stated my guild and purpose, and he gave a snort of disgust.

'Go elsewhere, Watcher! We need only useful men here!'

'Watching has its uses,' I said mildly.

'No doubt. No doubt.' He squinted at Avluela. 'Who's this? Watchers are celibates, no?'

'She is nothing more than a traveling companion.'

The Sentinel guffawed coarsely. 'It's a route you travel often, I wager! Not that there's much to her. What is she, thirteen, fourteen? Come here, child. Let me check you for contraband.' He ran his hands quickly over her, scowling as he felt her breasts, then raising an eyebrow as he encountered the mounds of her wings below her shoulders. 'What's this? What's this? More in back than in front! A Flier, are you? Very dirty business, Fliers consorting with foul old Watchers.' He chuckled and put his hand on Avluela's body in a way that sent Gormon starting forward in fury, murder in his fire-circled eyes. I caught him in time and grasped his wrist with all my strength, holding him back lest he ruin the three of us by an attack on the Sentinel. He tugged at me, nearly pulling me over; then he grew calm and subsided, icily watching as the fat one finished checking Avluela for 'contraband.'

At length the Sentinel turned in distaste to Gormon and said, 'What kind of thing are you?'

'Guildless, your mercy,' Gormon said in sharp tones. 'The humble and worthless product of teratogenesis, and yet nevertheless a free man who desires entry to Roum.'

'Do we need more monsters here?'

'I eat little and work hard.'

'You'd work harder still if you were neutered,' said the Sentinel.

Gormon glowered. I said, 'May we have entry?'

'A moment.' The Sentinel donned his thinking cap and narrowed his eyes as he transmitted a message to the memory tanks. His face tensed with the effort; then it went slack, and moments later came the reply. We could not hear the transaction at all; but from his disappointed look, it appeared evident that no reason had been found to refuse us admission to Roum.

'Go on in,' he said. 'The three of you. Quickly!'

We passed beyond the gate.

Gormon said, 'I could have split him open with a blow.'

'And be neutered by nightfall. A little patience, and we've come into Roum.'

'The way he handled her –!'

'You have a very possessive attitude toward Avluela,' I said. 'Remember that she's a Flier, and not sexually available to the guildless.'

Gormon ignored my thrust. 'She arouses me no more than you do, Watcher. But it pains me to see her treated that way. I would have killed him if you hadn't held me back.'

Avluela said, 'Where shall we stay, now that we're in Roum?'

'First let me find the headquarters of my guild,' I said. 'I'll register at the Watchers' Inn. After that, perhaps we'll hunt up the Fliers' Lodge for a meal.'

'And then,' said Gormon drily, 'we'll go to the Guildless Gutter and beg for coppers.'

'I pity you because you are a Changeling,' I told him, 'but I find it ungraceful of you to pity yourself. Come.'

We walked up a cobbled, winding street away from the gate and into Roum itself. We were in the outer ring of the city, a residential section of low, squat houses topped by the unwielding bulk of defense installations. Within lay the shining towers we had seen from the fields the night before; the remnant of ancient Roum carefully preserved across ten thousand years or more; the market, the factory zone, the communications hump, the temples of the Will, the memory tanks, the sleepers' refuges, the outworlders' brothels, the government buildings, the headquarters of the various guilds.

At the corner, beside a Second Cycle building with walls of rubbery texture, I found a public thinking cap and slipped it on my forehead. At once my thoughts raced down the conduit until they came to the interface that gave them access to one of the storage brains of a memory tank. I pierced the interface and saw the wrinkled brain itself, a pale gray against the deep green of its housing. A Rememberer once told me that, in cycles past, men built machines to do their thinking for them, although these machines were hellishly expensive and required vast amounts of space and drank power gluttonously. That was not the worst of our forefathers' follies; but why build artificial brains when death each day liberates scores of splendid natural ones to hook into the memory tanks? Was it that they lacked the knowledge to use them? I find that hard to believe.

I gave the brain my guild identification and asked the co-ordinates of our inn. Instantly I received them, and we set out, Avluela on one side of me, Gormon on the other, myself wheeling as always, the cart in which my instruments resided.

The city was crowded. I had not seen such throngs in sleepy, heat-fevered Agupt, nor at any other point on my northward journey. The streets were full of Pilgrims, secretive and masked. Jostling through them went busy Rememberers and glum Merchants and now and then the litter of a Master. Avluela saw a number of Fliers, but was barred by the tenets of her guild from greeting them until she had undergone her ritual purification. I regret to say that I spied many Watchers, all of whom looked upon me disdainfully and without welcome. I noted a good many Defenders and ample representation of such lesser guilds as Vendors, Servitors, Manufactories, Scribes, Communicants, and Transporters. Naturally, a host of neuters went silently about their humble business, and numerous outworlders of all descriptions flocked the streets, most of them probably tourists, some here to do what business could be done with the sullen, poverty-blighted people of Earth. I noticed many Changelings limping furtively through the crowd, not one of them as proud of bearing as Gormon beside me. He was unique among his kind; the others, dappled and piebald and asymmetrical, limbless or overlimbed, deformed in a thousand imaginative and artistic ways, were slinkers, squinters, shufflers, hissers, creepers; they were cut-purses, brain-drainers, organ-peddlers, repentance-mongers, gleam-buyers, but none held himself upright as though he thought he were a man.

The guidance of the brain was exact, and in less than an hour of walking we arrived at the Watchers' Inn. I left Gormon and Avluela outside and wheeled my cart within.

Perhaps a dozen members of my guild lounged in the main hall. I gave them the customary sign, and they returned it languidly. Were these the guardians on whom Earth's safety depended? Simpletons and weaklings!

'Where may I register?' I asked.

'New? Where from?'

'Agupt was my last place of registry.'

'Should have stayed there. No need of Watchers here.'

'Where may I register?' I asked again.

A foppish youngster indicated a screen in the rear of the great room. I went to it, pressed my fingertips against it, was interrogated, and gave my name, which a Watcher must utter only to another Watcher and only within the precincts of an inn. A panel shot open, and a puffy-eyed man who wore the Watcher emblem on his right cheek and not on the left, signifying his high rank in the guild, spoke my name and said, 'You should have known better than to come to Roum. We're over our quota.'

'I claim lodging and employment nonetheless.'

'A man with your sense of humor should have been born into the guild of Clowns,' he said.

'I see no joke.'

'Under laws promulgated by our guild in the most recent session, an inn is under no obligation to take new lodgers once it has reached its assigned capacity. We are at our assigned capacity. Farewell, my friend.'

I was aghast. 'I know of no such regulation! This is incredible! For a guild to turn away a member from its own inn – when he arrives footsore and numb! A man of my age, having crossed Land Bridge out of Agupt, here as a stranger and hungry in Roum –'

'Why did you not check with us first?'

'I had no idea it would be necessary.'

'The new regulations –'

'May the Will shrivel the new regulations!' I shouted. 'I demand lodging! To turn away one who has Watched since before you were born –'

'Easy, brother, easy.'

'Surely you have some corner where I can sleep – some crumbs to let me eat –'

Even as my tone had changed from bluster to supplication, his expression softened from indifference to mere disdain. 'We have no room. We have no food. These are hard times for our guild, you know. There is talk that we will be disbanded altogether, as a useless luxury, a drain upon the Will's resources. We are very limited in our abilities. Because Roum has a surplus of Watchers, we are all on short rations as it is, and if we admit you our rations will be all the shorter.'

'But where will I go? What shall I do?'

'I advise you,' he said blandly, 'to throw yourself upon the mercy of the Prince of Roum.'

THREE

Outside, I told that to Gormon, and he doubled with laughter, guffawing so furiously that the striations on his lean cheeks blazed like bloody stripes. 'The mercy of the Prince of Roum!' he repeated. 'The mercy – of the Prince of Roum –'

'It is customary for the unfortunate to seek the aid of the local ruler,' I said coldly.

'The Prince of Roum knows no mercy,' Gormon told me. 'The Prince of Roum will feed you your own limbs to ease your hunger!'

'Perhaps,' Avluela put in, 'we should try to find the Fliers' Lodge. They'll feed us there.'

'Not Gormon,' I observed. 'We have obligations to one another.'

'We could bring food out to him,' she said.

'I prefer to visit the court first,' I insisted. 'Let us make sure of our status. Afterwards we can improvise living arrangements, if we must.'

She yielded, and we made our way to the palace of the Prince of Roum, a massive building fronted by a colossal column-ringed plaza, on the far side of the river that splits the city. In the plaza we were accosted by mendicants of many sorts, some not even Earthborn; something with ropy tendrils and a corrugated, noseless face thrust itself at me and jabbered for alms until Gormon pushed it away, and moments later a second creature, equally strange, its skin pocked with luminescent craters and its limbs studded with eyes, embraced my knees and pleaded in the name of the Will for my mercy. 'I am only a poor Watcher,' I said, indicating my cart, 'and am here to gain mercy myself.' But the being persisted, sobbing out its misfortunes in a blurred, feathery voice, and in the end, to Gormon's immense disgust, I dropped a few food tablets into the shelf-like pouch on its chest. Then we muscled on toward the doors of the palace. At the portico a more horrid sight presented itself: a maimed Flier, fragile limbs bent and twisted, one wing half-unfolded and severely cropped, the other missing altogether. The Flier rushed upon Avluela, called her by a name not hers, moistened her leggings with tears so copious that the fur of them matted and stained. 'Sponsor me to the lodge,' he appealed. 'They have turned me away because I am crippled, but if you sponsor me –' Avluela explained that she could do nothing, that she was a stranger to this lodge. The broken Flier would not release her, and Gormon with great delicacy lifted him like the bundle of dry bones that he was and set him aside. We stepped up onto the portico and at once were confronted by a trio of soft-faced neuters, who asked our business and admitted us quickly to the next line of barrier, which was manned by a pair of wizened Indexers. Speaking in unison, they queried us.

'We seek audience,' I said. 'A matter of mercy.'

'The day of audience is four days hence,' said the Indexer on the right. 'We will enter your request on the rolls.'

'We have no place to sleep!' Avluela burst out. 'We are hungry! We –'

I hushed her. Gormon, meanwhile, was groping in the mouth of his overpocket. Bright things glimmered in his hand; pieces of gold, the eternal metal, stamped with hawk-nosed, bearded faces. He had found them grubbing in the ruins. He tossed one coin to the Indexer who had refused us. The man snapped it from the air, rubbed his thumb roughly across its shining obverse, and dropped it instantly into a fold of his garment. The second Indexer waited expectantly. Smiling, Gormon gave him his coin.

'Perhaps,' I said, 'we can arrange for a special audience within.'

'Perhaps you can,' said one of the Indexers. 'Go through.'

And so we passed into the nave of the palace itself and stood in the great, echoing space, looking down the central aisle toward the shielded throne-chamber at the apse. There were more beggars in here – licensed ones holding hereditary concessions – and also throngs of Pilgrims, Communicants, Rememberers, Musicians, Scribes, and Indexers. I heard muttered prayers; I smelled the scent of spicy incense; I felt the vibration of subterranean gongs. In cycles past, this building had been a shrine of one of the old religions – the Christers, Gormon told me, making me suspect once more that he was a Rememberer masquerading as a Changeling – and it still maintained something of its holy character even though it served as Roum's seat of secular government. But how were we to get to see the Prince? To my left I saw a small ornate chapel which a line of prosperous-looking Merchants and Landholders was slowly entering. Peering past them, I noted three skulls mounted on an interrogation fixture – a memory-tank input – and beside them, a burly Scribe. Telling Gormon and Avluela to wait for me in the aisle, I joined the line.

It moved infrequently, and nearly an hour passed before I reached the interrogation fixture. The skulls glared sightlessly at me; within their sealed crania, nutrient fluids bubbled and gurgled, caring for the dead, yet still functional, brains whose billion billion synaptic units now served as incomparable mnemonic devices. The Scribe seemed aghast to find a Watcher in this line, but before he could challenge me I blurted, 'I come as a stranger to claim the Prince's mercy. I and my companions are without lodging. My own guild has turned me away. What shall I do? How may I gain an audience?'

'Come back in four days.'

'I've slept on the road for more days than that. Now I must rest more easily.'

'A public inn –'

'But I am guilded!' I protested. 'The public inns would not admit me while my guild maintains an inn here, and my guild refuses me because of some new regulation, and – you see my predicament?'

In a wearied voice the Scribe said, 'You may have application for a special audience. It will be denied, but you may apply.'

'Where?'

'Here. State your purpose.'

I identified myself to the skulls by my public designation, listed the names and status of my two companions, and explained my case. All this was absorbed and transmitted to the ranks of brains mounted somewhere in the depths of the city, and when I was done the Scribe said, 'If the application is approved, you will be notified.'

'Meanwhile where shall I stay?'

'Close to the palace, I would suggest.'

I understood. I could join that legion of unfortunates packing the plaza. How many of them had requested some special favor of the Prince and were still there, months or years later, waiting to be summoned to the Presence? Sleeping on stone, begging for crusts, living in foolish hope!

But I had exhausted my avenues. I returned to Gormon and Avluela, told them of the situation, and suggested that we now attempt to hunt whatever accommodations we could. Gormon, guildless, was welcome at any of the squalid public inns maintained for his kind; Avluela could probably find residence at her own guild's lodge; only I would have to sleep in the streets – and not for the first time. But I hoped that we would not have to separate. I had come to think of us as a family, strange thought though that was for a Watcher.

As we moved toward the exit, my timepiece told me softly that the hour of Watching had come round again. It was my obligation and my privilege to tend to my Watching wherever I might be, regardless of the circumstances, whenever my hour came round; and so I halted, opened the cart, activated the equipment. Gormon and Avluela stood beside me. I saw smirks and open mockery on the faces of those who passed in and out of the palace; Watching was not held in very high repute, for we had Watched so long, and the promised enemy had never come. Yet one has one's duties, comic though they may seem to others. What is a hollow ritual to some is a life's work to others. Doggedly I forced myself into a state of Watchfulness. The world melted away from me, and I plunged into the heavens. The familiar joy engulfed me; and I searched the familiar places, and some that were not so familiar, my amplified mind leaping through the galaxies in wild swoops. Was an armada massing? Were troops drilling for the conquest of Earth? Four times a day I Watched, and the other members of my guild did the same, each at slightly different hours, so that no moment went by without some vigilant mind on guard. I do not believe that that was a foolish calling.

When I came up from my trance, a brazen voice was crying, ' – for the Prince of Roum! Make way for the Prince of Roum!'

I blinked and caught my breath and fought to shake off the last strands of my concentration. A gilded palanquin borne by a phalanx of neuters had emerged from the rear of the palace and was proceeding down the nave toward me. Four men in the elegant costumes and brilliant masks of the guild of Masters flanked the litter, and it was preceded by a trio of Changelings, squat and broad, whose throats were so modified to imitate the sounding-boxes of bullfrogs; they emitted a trumpetlike boom of majestic sound as they advanced. It struck me as most strange that a prince would admit Changelings to his service, even ones as gifted as these.

My cart was blocking the progress of this magnificent procession, and hastily I struggled to close it and move it aside before the parade swept down upon me. Age and fear made my fingers tremble, and I could not make the sealings properly; while I fumbled in increasing clumsiness, the strutting Changelings drew so close that the blare of their throats was deafening, and Gormon attempted to aid me, forcing me to hiss at him that it is forbidden for anyone not of my guild to touch the equipment. I pushed him away; and an instant later a vanguard of neuters descended on me and prepared to scourge me from the spot with sparkling whips. 'In the Will's name,' I cried, 'I am a Watcher.'

And in antiphonal response came the deep, calm, enormous reply, 'Let him be. He is a Watcher.'

All motion ceased. The Prince of Roum had spoken.

The neuters drew back. The Changelings halted their music. The bearers of the palanquin eased it to the floor. All those in the nave of the palace had pulled back, save only Gormon and Avluela and myself. The shimmering chain-curtains of the palanquin parted. Two of the Masters hurried forward and thrust their hands through the sonic barrier within, offering aid to their monarch. The barrier died away with a whimpering buzz.

The Prince of Roum appeared.

He was so young! He was nothing more than a boy, his hair full and dark, his face unlined. But he had been born to rule, and for all his youth he was as commanding as anyone I had ever seen. His lips were thin and tightly compressed; his aquiline nose was sharp and aggressive; his eyes, deep and cold, were infinite pools. He wore the jeweled garments of the guild of Dominators, but incised on his cheek was the double-barred cross of the Defenders, and around his neck he carried the dark shawl of the Rememberers. A Dominator may enrol in as many guilds as he pleases, and it would be a strange thing for a Dominator not also to be a Defender; but it startled me to find this prince a Rememberer as well. That is not normally a guild for the fierce.

He looked at me with little interest and said, 'You choose an odd place to do your Watching, old man.'

'The hour chose the place, sire,' I replied. 'I was here, and my duty compelled me. I had no way of knowing that you were about to come forth.'

'Your Watching found no enemies?'

'None, sire.'

I was about to press my luck, to take advantage of the unexpected appearance of the Prince to beg for his aid; but his interest in me died like a guttering candle as I stood there, and I did not dare call to him when his head had turned. He eyed Gormon a long moment, frowning and tugging at his chin. Then his gaze fell on Avluela. His eyes brightened. His jaw muscles flickered. His delicate nostrils widened. 'Come up here, little Flier,' he said, beckoning. 'Are you this Watcher's friend?'

She nodded, terrified.

The Prince held out a hand to her and grasped; she floated up onto the palanquin, and with a grin so evil it seemed a parody of wickedness, the young Dominator drew her through the curtain. Instantly a pair of Masters restored the sonic barrier, but the procession did not move on. I stood mute. Gormon beside me was frozen, his powerful body rigid as a rod. I wheeled my cart to a less conspicuous place. Long moments passed. The courtiers remained silent, discreetly looking away from the palanquin.

At length the curtain parted once more. Avluela came stumbling out, her face pale, her eyes blinking rapidly. She seemed dazed. Streaks of sweat gleamed on her cheeks. She nearly fell, and a neuter caught her and swung her down to floor level. Beneath her jacket her wings were partly erect, giving her a hunchbacked look and telling me that she was in great emotional distress. In ragged sliding steps she came to us, quivering, wordless; she darted a glance at me and flung herself against Gormon's broad chest.

The bearers lifted the palanquin. The Prince of Roum went out from his palace.

When he was gone, Avluela stammered hoarsely, 'The Prince has granted us lodging in the royal hostelry!'

FOUR

The hostelkeepers, of course, would not believe us.

Guests of the Prince were housed in the royal hostelry, which was to the rear of the palace in a small garden of frostflowers and blossoming ferns. The usual inhabitants of such a hostelry were Masters and an occasional Dominator; sometimes a particularly important Rememberer on an errand of research would win a niche there, or some highly placed Defender visiting for purposes of strategic planning. To house a Flier in a royal hostelry was distinctly odd; to admit a Watcher was unlikely; to take in a Changeling or some other guildless person was improbable beyond comprehension. When we presented ourselves, therefore, we were met by Servitors whose attitude was at first one of high humor at our joke, then of irritation, finally of scorn. 'Get away,' they told us ultimately. 'Scum! Rabble!'

Avluela said in a grave voice, 'The Prince has granted us lodging here, and you may not refuse us.'

'Away! Away!'

One snaggle-toothed Servitor produced a neural truncheon and brandished it in Gormon's face, passing a foul remark about his guildlessness. Gormon slapped the truncheon from the man's grasp, oblivious to the painful sting, and kicked him in the gut, so that he coiled and fell over, puking. Instantly a throng of neuters came rushing from within the hostelry. Gormon seized another of the Servitors and hurled him into the midst of them, turning them into a muddled mob. Wild shouts and angry cursing cries attracted the attention of a venerable Scribe who waddled to the door, bellowed for silence, and interrogated us. 'That's easily checked,' he said, when Avluela had told the story. To a Servitor he said contemptuously, 'Send a think to the Indexers, fast!'

In time the confusion was untangled and we were admitted. We were given separate but adjoining rooms. I had never known such luxury before, and perhaps never shall again. The rooms were long, high and deep. One entered them through telescopic pits keyed to one's own thermal output, to assure privacy. Lights glowed at the resident's merest nod, for hanging from ceiling globes and nestling in cupolas on the walls were spicules of slave-light from one of the Brightstar worlds, trained through suffering to obey such commands. The windows came and went at the dweller's whim; when not in use, they were concealed by streamers of quasi-sentient outworld gauzes, which not only were decorative in their own right, but which functioned as monitors to produce delightful scents according to requisitioned patterns. The rooms were equipped with individual thinking caps connected to the main memory banks. They likewise had conduits that summoned Servitors, Scribes, Indexers, or Musicians as required. Of course, a man of my own humble guild would not deign to make use of other human beings that way, out of fear of their glowering resentment; but in any case I had little need of them.

I did not ask of Avluela what had occurred in the Prince's palanquin to bring us such bounty. I could well imagine, as could Gormon, whose barely suppressed inner rage was eloquent of his never-admitted love for my pale, slender little Flier.

We settled in. I placed my cart beside the window, draped it with gauzes, and left it in readiness for my next period of Watching. I cleaned my body of grime while entities mounted in the wall sang me to peace. Later I ate. Afterwards Avluela came to me, refreshed and relaxed, and sat beside me in my room as we talked of our experiences. Gormon did not appear for hours. I thought that perhaps he had left this hostelry altogether, finding the atmosphere too rarefied for him, and had sought company among his own guildless kind. But at twilight, Avluela and I walked in the cloistered courtyard of the hostelry and mounted a ramp to watch the stars emerge in Roum's sky, and Gormon was there. With him was a lanky and emaciated man in a Rememberer's shawl; they were talking in low tones.

Gormon nodded to me and said, 'Watcher, meet my new friend.'

The emaciated one fingered his shawl. 'I am the Rememberer Basil,' he intoned, in a voice as thin as a fresco that has been peeled from its wall. 'I have come from Perris to delve into the mysteries of Roum. I shall be here many years.'

'The Rememberer has fine stories to tell,' said Gormon. 'He is among the foremost of his guild. As you approached, he was describing to me the techniques by which the past is revealed. They drive a trench through the strata of Third Cycle deposits, you see, and with vacuum cores they lift the molecules of earth to lay bare the ancient layers.'

'We have found,' Basil said, 'the catacombs of Imperial Roum, and the rubble of the Time of Sweeping, the books inscribed on slivers of white metal, written toward the close of the Second Cycle. All these go to Perris for examination and classification and decipherment; then they return. Does the past interest you, Watcher?'

'To some extent.' I smiled. 'This Changeling here shows much more fascination for it. I sometimes suspect his authenticity. Would you recognize a Rememberer in disguise?'

Basil scrutinized Gormon; he lingered over the bizarre features, the excessively muscular frame. 'He is no Rememberer,' he said at length. 'But I agree that he has antiquarian interests. He has asked me many profound questions.'

'Such as?'

'He wishes to know the origin of Guilds. He asks the name of the genetic surgeon who crafted the first true-breeding Fliers.

He wonders why there are Changelings, and if they are truly under the curse of the Will.'

'And do you have answers for these?' I asked.

'For some,' said Basil. 'For some.'

'The origin of guilds?'

'To give structure and meaning to a society that has suffered defeat and destruction,' said the Rememberer. 'At the end of the Second Cycle all was in flux. No man knew his rank nor his purpose. Through our world strode haughty outworlders who looked upon us all as worthless. It was necessary to establish fixed frames of reference by which one man might know his value beside another. So the first guilds appeared: Dominators, Masters, Merchants, Landholders, Vendors and Servitors. Then came Scribes, Musicians, Clowns and Transporters. Afterwards Indexers became necessary, and then Watchers and Defenders. When the Years of Magic gave us Fliers and Changelings, those guilds were added, and then the guildless ones, the neuters, were produced, so that —'

'But surely the Changelings are guildless too!' said Avluela.

The Rememberer looked at her for the first time. 'Who are you, child?'

'Avluela of the Fliers. I travel with this Watcher and this Changeling.'

Basil said, 'As I have been telling the Changeling here, in the early days his kind was guilded. The guild was dissolved a thousand years ago by the order of the Council of Dominators after an attempt by a disreputable Changeling faction to seize control of the holy places of Jorslem, and since that time Changelings have been guildless, ranking only above neuters.'

'I never knew that,' I said.

'You are no Rememberer,' said Basil smugly. 'It is our craft to uncover the past.'

'True. True.'

Gormon said, 'And today, how many guilds are there?'

Discomfited, Basil replied vaguely, 'At least a hundred, my friend. Some quite small; some are local. I am concerned only

with the original guilds and their immediate successors; what
has happened in the past few hundred years is in the province
of others. Shall I requisition an information for you?'

'Never mind,' Gormon said. 'It was only an idle question.'

'Your curiosity is well developed,' said the Rememberer.

'I find the world and all it contains extremely fascinating.
Is this sinful?'

'It is strange,' said Basil. 'The guildless rarely look beyond
their own horizons.'

A Servitor appeared. With a mixture of awe and contempt he
genuflected before Avluela and said, 'The Prince has returned.
He desires your company in the palace at this time.'

Terror glimmered in Avluela's eyes. But to refuse was inconceivable. 'Shall I come with you?' she asked.

'Please. You must be robed and perfumed. He wishes you
to come to him with your wings open, as well.'

Avluela nodded. The Servitor led her away.

We remained on the ramp a while longer; the Rememberer Basil talked of the old days of Roum, and I listened,
and Gormon peered into the gathering darkness. Eventually,
his throat dry, the Rememberer excused himself and moved
solemnly away. A few moments later, in the courtyard below
us, a door opened and Avluela emerged, walking as though
she were of the guild of Somnambulists, not of Fliers. She
was nude under transparent draperies, and her fragile body
gleamed ghostly in the starbeams. Her wings were spread and
fluttered slowly in a somber systole and diastole. One Servitor
grasped each of her elbows: they seemed to be propelling her
toward the palace as though she were but a dreamed facsimile
of herself and not a real woman.

'Fly, Avluela, fly,' Gormon growled. 'Escape while you
can!'

She disappeared into a side entrance of the palace.

The Changeling looked at me. 'She has sold herself to the
Prince to provide lodging for us.'

'So it seems.'

'I could smash down that palace!'

'You love her?'

'It should be obvious.'

'Cure yourself,' I advised. 'You are an unusual man, but still a Flier is not for you. Particularly a Flier who has shared the bed of the Prince of Roum.'

'She goes from my arms to his.'

I was staggered. 'You've known her?'

'More than once,' he said, smiling sadly. 'At the moment of ecstasy her wings thrash like leaves in a storm.'

I gripped the railing of the ramp so that I would not tumble into the courtyard. The stars whirled overhead; the old moon and its two blank-faced consorts leaped and bobbed. I was shaken without fully understanding the cause of my emotion. Was it wrath that Gormon had dared to violate a canon of the law? Was it a manifestation of those pseudo-parental feelings I had toward Avluela? Or was it mere envy of Gormon for daring to commit a sin beyond my capacity, though not beyond my desires?

I said, 'They could burn your brain for that. They could mince your soul. And now you make me an accessory.'

'What of it? That Prince commands, and he gets – but others have been there before him. I had to tell someone.'

'Enough. Enough.'

'Will we see her again?'

'Princes tire quickly of their women. A few days, perhaps a single night – then he will throw her back to us. And perhaps then we shall have to leave this hostelry.' I sighed. 'At least we'll have known it a few nights more than we deserved.'

'Where will you go then?' Gormon asked.

'I will stay in Roum a while.'

'Even if you sleep in the streets? There does not seem to be much demand for Watchers here.'

'I'll manage,' I said. 'Then I may go toward Perris.'

'To learn from the Rememberers?'

'To see Perris. What of you? What do you want in Roum?'

'Avluela.'

'Stop that talk!'

'Very well,' he said, and his smile was bitter. 'But I will stay here until the Prince is through with her. Then she will be mine, and we'll find ways to survive. The guildless are resourceful. They have to be. Maybe we'll scrounge lodgings in Roum awhile, and then follow you to Perris. If you're willing to travel with monsters and faithless Fliers.'

I shrugged. 'We'll see about that when the time comes.'

'Have you ever been in the company of a Changeling before?'

'Not often. Not for long.'

'I'm honored.' He drummed on the parapet. 'Don't cast me off, Watcher. I have a reason for wanting to stay with you.'

'Which is?'

'To see your face on the day your machines tell you that the invasion of Earth has begun.'

I let myself sag forward, shoulders drooping. 'You'll stay with me a long time, then.'

'Don't you believe the invasion is coming?'

'Some day. Not soon.'

Gormon chuckled. 'You're wrong. It's almost here.'

'You don't amuse me.'

'What is it, Watcher? Have you lost your faith? It's been known for a thousand years: another race covets Earth and owns it by treaty, and will some day come to collect. That much was decided at the end of the Second Cycle.'

'I know all that, and I am no Rememberer.' Then I turned to him and spoke words I never thought I would say aloud. 'For twice your lifetime, Changeling, I've listened to the stars and done my Watching. Something done that often loses meaning. Say your own name ten thousand times and it will be an empty sound. I have Watched, and Watched well, and in the dark hours of the night I sometimes think I Watch for nothing, that I have wasted my life. There is a pleasure in Watching, but perhaps there is no real purpose.'

His hand encircled my wrist. 'Your confession is as shocking as mine. Keep your faith, Watcher. The invasion comes!'

'How could you possibly know?'

'The guildless also have their skills.'

The conversation troubled me. I said, 'Is it painful to be guildless?'

'One grows reconciled. And there are certain freedoms to compensate for the lack of status. I may speak freely to all.'

'I notice.'

'I move freely. I am always sure of food and lodging, though the food may be rotten and the lodging poor. Women are attracted to me despite all prohibitions. Because of them, perhaps. I am untroubled by ambitions.'

'Never desire to rise above your rank?'

'Never.'

'You might have been happier as a Rememberer.'

'I am happy now. I can have a Rememberer's pleasures without his responsibility.'

'How smug you are!' I cried. 'To make a virtue of guild-lessness!'

'How else does one endure the weight of the Will?' He looked towards the palace. 'The humble rise. The mighty fall. Take this as prophecy, Watcher: that lusty Prince in there will know more of life before summer comes. I'll rip out his eyes for taking Avluela!'

'Strong words. You bubble with treason tonight.'

'Take it as prophecy.'

'You can't get close to him,' I said. Then, irritated for taking his foolishness seriously, I added, 'And why blame him? He only does as princes do. Blame the girl for going to him. She might have refused.'

'And lost her wings. Or died. No, she had no choice. I do!' In a sudden, terrible gesture the Changeling held out thumb and forefinger, double-jointed, long-nailed, and plunged them into imagined eyes. 'Wait,' he said. 'You'll see!'

In the courtyard two Chronomancers appeared, set up the apparatus of their guild, and lit tapers by which to read the shape of tomorrow. A sickly odor of pallid smoke rose to my nostrils. I had now lost further desire to speak with the Changeling.

'It grows late,' I said. 'I need rest, and soon I must do my Watching.'

'Watch carefully,' Gormon told me.

FIVE

At night in my chamber I performed my fourth and last Watch of that long day, and for the first time in my life I detected an anomaly. I could not interpret it. It was an obscure sensation, a mingling of tastes and sounds, a feeling of being in contact with some colossal mass. Worried, I clung to my instruments far longer than usual, but perceived no more clearly at the end of my seance than at its commencement.

Afterward I wondered about my obligations.

Watchers are trained from childhood to be swift to sound the alarm; and the alarm must be sounded when the Watcher judges the world in peril. Was I now obliged to notify the Defenders? Four times in my life the alarm had been given, on each occasion in error; and each Watcher who had thus touched off a false mobilization had suffered a fearful loss of status. One had contributed his brain to the memory banks; one had become a neuter out of shame; one had smashed his instruments and gone to live among the guildless; and one, vainly attempting to continue in his profession, had discovered himself mocked by all his comrades. I saw no virtue in scorning one who had delivered a false alarm, for was it not preferable for a Watcher to cry out too soon than not at all? But those were the customs of our guild, and I was constrained by them.

I evaluated my position and decided that I did not have valid grounds for an alarm.

I reflected that Gormon had placed suggestive ideas in my mind that evening. I might possibly be reacting only to his jeering talk of imminent invasions.

I could not act. I dared not jeopardize my standing by hasty outcry. I mistrusted my own emotional state.

I gave no alarm.

Seething, confused, my soul boiling, I closed my cart and let myself sink into a drugged sleep.

At dawn I woke and rushed to the window, expecting to find invaders in the streets. But all was still; a winter grayness hung over the courtyard, and sleepy Servitors pushed passive neuters about. Uneasily I did my first Watching of the day, and to my relief the strangeness of the night before did not return, although I had it in mind that my sensitivity is always greater at night than upon arising.

I ate and went to the courtyard. Gormon and Avluela were already there. She looked fatigued and downcast, depleted by her night with the Prince of Roum, but I said nothing to her about it. Gormon, slouching disdainfully against a wall embellished with the shells of radiant mollusks, said to me, 'Did your Watching go well?'

'Well enough.'

'What of the day?'

'Out to roam Roum,' I said. 'Will you come? Avluela? Gormon?'

'Surely,' he said, and she gave a faint nod; and, like the tourists we were, we set off to inspect the splendid city of Roum.

Gormon acted as our guide to the jumbled pasts of Roum, belying his claim never to have been here before. As well as any Rememberer he described the things we saw as we walked the winding streets. All the scattered levels of thousands of years were exposed. We saw the power domes of the Second Cycle, and the Colosseum where at an unimaginably early date man and beast contended like jungle creatures. In the broken hull of that building of horrors Gormon told us of the savagery of that unimaginably ancient time. 'They fought,' he said, 'naked before huge throngs. With bare hands men challenged beasts called lions, great hairy cats with swollen heads; and when the lion lay in its gore, the victor turned to the Prince of Roum and asked to be pardoned for whatever crime it was that had cast him into the arena. And if he had fought well, the Prince made a gesture with his hand, and the man was freed.' Gormon made the gesture for us: a thumb upraised and jerked backward over the right shoulder several times. 'But if the man had shown cowardice, or if the lion had distinguished itself in the manner of its dying, the Prince made another gesture, and the man was condemned to be slain by a second beast.' Gormon showed us that gesture too: the middle finger jutting upward from a clenched fist and lifted in a short sharp thrust.

'How are these things known?' Avluela asked, but Gormon pretended not to hear her.

We saw the line of fusion-pylons built early in the Third Cycle to draw energy from the world's core; they were still functioning, although stained and corroded. We saw the shattered stump of a Second Cycle weather machine, still a mighty column at least twenty men high. We saw a hill on which white marble relics of First Cycle Roum sprouted like pale clumps of winter deathflowers. Penetrating toward the inner part of the city, we came upon the embankment of defensive amplifiers waiting in readiness to hurl the full impact of the Will against invaders. We viewed a market where visitors from the stars haggled with peasants for excavated fragments of antiquity. Gormon strode into the crowd and made several purchases. We came to a flesh-house for travelers from afar, where one could buy anything from quasi-life to mounds of passion-ice. We ate at a small restaurant by the edge of the River Tver, where guildless ones were served without ceremony, and at Gormon's insistence we dined on mounds of a soft doughy substance and drank a tart yellow wine, local specialities.

Afterward we passed through a covered arcade in whose many aisles plump Vendors peddled star-goods, costly trinkets from Afreek, and the flimsy constructs of the local Manufactories. Just beyond we emerged in a plaza that contained a fountain in the shape of a boat, and to the rear of this rose a flight of cracked and battered stone-stairs ascending to a zone of rubble and weeds. Gormon beckoned, and we scrambled into this dismal area, then passed rapidly through it to a place where a sumptuous palace, by its looks early Second Cycle or even First, brooded over a sloping vegetated hill.

'They say this is the center of the world,' Gormon declared. 'In Jorslem one finds another place that also claims the honor. They mark the spot here by a map.'

'How can the world have one center,' Avluela asked, 'when it is round?'

Gormon laughed. We went in. Within, in wintry darkness, there stood a colossal jeweled globe lit by some inner glow.

'Here is your world,' said Gormon, gesturing grandly.

'Oh!' Avluela gasped. 'Everything! Everything is here!'

The map was a masterpiece of craftsmanship. It showed natural contours and elevations, its seas seemed deep liquid pools, its deserts were so parched as to make thirst spring in one's mouth, its cities swirled with vigor and life. I beheld the continents, Eyrop, Afreek, Ais, Stralya. I saw the vastness of Earth Ocean. I traversed the golden span of Land Bridge, which I had crossed so toilfully on foot not long before. Avluela rushed forward and pointed to Roum, to Agupt, to Jorslem, to Perris. She tapped the globe at the high mountains north of Hind and said softly, 'This is where I was born, where the ice lives, where the mountains touch the moons. Here is where the Fliers have their kingdom.' She ran a finger westward toward Fars and beyond it into the terrible Arban Desert, and on to Agupt. 'This is where I flew. By night, when I left my girlhood. We all must fly, and I flew here. A hundred times I thought I would die. Here, here in the desert, sand in my throat as I flew, sand beating against my wings – I was forced down, I lay naked on the hot sand for days, and another Flier saw me, he came down to me and pitied me, and lifted me up, and when I was aloft my strength returned, and we flew on toward Agupt. And he died over the sea, his life stopped though he was young and strong, and he fell down into the sea, and I flew down to be with him, and the water was hot

even at night. I drifted and morning came, and I saw the living
stones growing like trees in the water, and the fish of many
colors, and they came to him and pecked at his flesh as he
floated with his wings outspread on the water, and I left him,
I thrust him down to rest there, and I rose, and I flew on
to Agupt, alone, frightened, and there I met you, Watcher.'
Timidly she smiled at me. 'Show us the place where you were
young, Watcher.'

Painfully, for I was suddenly stiff at the knees, I hobbled
to the far side of the globe. Avluela followed me; Gormon
hung back, as though not interested at all. I pointed to the
scattered islands rising in two long strips from Earth Ocean –
the remnants of the Lost Continents.

'Here,' I said, indicating my native island in the west. 'I was
born here.'

'So far away!' Avluela cried.

'And so long ago,' I said. 'In the middle of the Second Cycle,
it sometimes seems to me.'

'No! That is not possible!' But she looked at me as though
it might have been true that I was thousands of years old.

I smiled and touched her satiny cheek. 'It only seems that
way to me,' I said.

'When did you leave home?'

'When I was twice your age,' I said. 'I came first to here –' I
indicated the eastern group of islands. 'I spent a dozen years as
a Watcher on Palash. Then the Will moved me to cross Earth
Ocean to Afreek. I came. I lived awhile in the hot countries.
I went on to Agupt. I met a certain small Flier.' Falling silent,
I looked a long while at the islands that had been my home,
and within my mind my image changed from the gaunt and
eroded thing I now had become, and I saw myself young and
well-fleshed, climbing the green mountains and swimming in
the chill sea, doing my Watching at the rim of a white beach
hammered by surf.

While I brooded Avluela turned away from me to Gormon
and said, 'Now you. Show us where you came from, Changeling!'

Gormon shrugged. 'The place does not appear to be on this globe.'

'But that's *impossible!*'

'Is it?' he asked.

She pressed him, but he evaded her, and we passed through a side exit and into the streets of Roum.

I was growing tired, but Avluela hungered for this city and wished to devour it all in an afternoon, and so we went on through a maze of interlocking streets, through a zone of sparkling mansions of Masters and Merchants, and through a foul den of Servitors and Vendors that extended into subterranean catacombs, and to a place where Clowns and Musicians resorted, and to another where the guild of Somnambulists offered its doubtful wares. A bloated female Somnambulist begged us to come inside and buy the truth that comes with trances, and Avluela urged us to go, but Gormon shook his head and I smiled, and we moved on. Now we were at the edge of a park close to the city's core. Here the citizens of Roum promenaded with an energy rarely seen in hot Agupt, and we joined the parade.

'Look there!' Avluela said. 'How bright it is!'

She pointed toward the shining arc of a dimensional sphere enclosing some relic of the ancient city; shading my eyes, I could make out a weathered stone wall within, and a knot of people. Gormon said, 'It is the Mouth of Truth.'

'What is that?' Avluela asked.

'Come. See.'

A line progressed into the sphere. We joined it and soon were at the tip of the interior, peering at the timeless region just across the threshold. Why this relic and so few others had been accorded such special protection I did not know, and I asked Gormon, whose knowledge was so unaccountably as profound as any Rememberer's, and he replied, 'Because this is the realm of certainty, where what one says is absolutely congruent with what actually is the case.'

'I don't understand,' said Avluela.

'It is impossible to lie in this place,' Gormon told her. 'Can you imagine any relic more worthy of protection?' He stepped across the entry duct, blurring as he did so, and I followed him quickly within. Avluela hesitated. It was a long moment before she entered; pausing a moment on the very threshold, she seemed buffeted by the wind that blew along the line of demarcation between the outer world and the pocket universe in which we stood.

An inner compartment held the Mouth of Truth itself. The line extended toward it, and a solemn Indexer was controlling the flow of entry to the tabernacle. It was a while before we three were permitted to go in. We found ourselves before the ferocious head of a monster in high relief, affixed to an ancient wall pockmarked by time. The monster's jaws gaped; the open mouth was a dark and sinister hole. Gormon nodded, inspecting it, as though he seemed pleased to find it exactly as he had thought it would be.

'What do we do?' Avluela asked.

Gormon said, 'Watcher, put your right hand into the Mouth of Truth.'

Frowning, I complied.

'Now,' said Gormon, 'one of us asks a question. You must answer it. If you speak anything but the truth, the mouth will close and sever your hand.'

'No!' Avluela cried.

I stared uneasily at the stone jaws rimming my wrist. A Watcher without both his hands is a man without a craft; in Second Cycle days one might have obtained a prosthesis more artful than one's original hand, but the Second Cycle had long ago been concluded, and such niceties were not to be purchased on Earth nowadays.

'How is such a thing possible?' I asked.

'The Will is unusually strong in these precincts,' Gormon replied. 'It distinguishes sternly between truth and untruth. To the rear of this wall sleeps a trio of Somnambulists through whom the Will speaks, and they control the Mouth. Do you fear the Will, Watcher?'

'I fear my own tongue.'

'Be brave. Never has a lie been told before this wall. Never has a hand been lost.'

'Go ahead, then,' I said. 'Who will ask me a question?'

'I,' said Gormon. 'Tell me, Watcher: all pretense aside, would you say that a life spent in Watching has been a life spent wisely?'

I was silent a long moment, rotating my thoughts, eyeing the jaws.

At length I said, 'To devote oneself to vigilance on behalf of one's fellow man is perhaps the noblest purpose one can serve.'

'Careful!' Gormon cried in alarm.

'I am not finished,' I said.

'Go on.'

'But to devote oneself to vigilance when the enemy is an imaginary one is idle, and to congratulate oneself for looking long and well for a foe that is not coming is foolish and sinful. My life has been a waste.'

The jaws of the Mouth of Truth did not quiver.

I removed my hand. I stared at it as though it had newly sprouted from my wrist. I felt suddenly several cycles old. Avluela, her eyes wide, her hands to her lips, seemed shocked by what I had said. My own words appeared to hang congealed in the air before the hideous idol.

'Spoken honestly,' said Gormon, 'although without much mercy for yourself. You judge yourself too harshly, Watcher.'

'I spoke to save my hand,' I said. 'Would you have had me lie?'

He smiled. To Avluela the Changeling said, 'Now it's your turn.'

Visibly frightened, the little Flier approached the Mouth. Her dainty hand trembled as she inserted it between the slabs of cold stone. I fought back an urge to rush toward her and pull her free of that devilish grimacing head.

'Who will question her? I asked.

'I,' said Gormon.

Avluela's wings stirred faintly beneath her garments. Her

face grew pale; her nostrils flickered; her upper lip slid over
the lower one. She stood slouched against the wall and stared
in horror at the termination of her arm. Outside the chamber
vague faces peered at us; lips moved in what no doubt were
expressions of impatience over our lengthy visit to the Mouth;
but we heard nothing. The atmosphere around us was warm
and clammy, with a musty tang like that which would come
from a well that was driven through the structure of Time.

Gormon said slowly, 'This night past you allowed your
body to be possessed by the Prince of Roum. Before that,
you granted yourself to the Changeling Gormon, although
such liaisons are forbidden by custom and law. Much prior
to that you were the mate of a Flier, now deceased. You may
have had other men, but I know nothing of them, and for the
purposes of my question they are not relevant. Tell me this,
Avluela: which of the three gave you the most intense physical
pleasure, which of the three aroused your deepest emotions,
and which of the three would you choose as a mate?'

I wanted to protest that the Changeling had asked her three
questions, not one, and so had taken unfair advantage. But I
had no chance to speak, because Avluela replied unfalteringly,
hand wedged deep into the Mouth of Truth, 'The Prince of
Roum gave me greater pleasure of the body than I had
ever known before, but he is cold and cruel, and I despise
him. My dead Flier I loved more deeply than any person
before or since, but he was weak, and I would not have
wanted a weakling as a mate. You, Gormon, seem almost a
stranger to me even now, and I feel that I know neither
your body nor your soul, and yet, though the gulf between
us is wide, it is you with whom I would spend my days
to come.'

She drew her hand from the Mouth of Truth.

'Well spoken!' said Gormon, though the accuracy of her
words had clearly wounded as well as pleased him. 'Suddenly
you find eloquence, eh, when the circumstances demand it.
And now the turn is mine to risk my hand.'

He neared the Mouth. I said, 'You have asked the first two

questions. Do you wish to finish the job and ask the third as well?'

'Hardly,' he said. He made a negligent gesture with his free hand. 'Put your heads together and agree on a joint question.'

Avluela and I conferred. With uncharacteristic forwardness she proposed a question; and since it was the one I would have asked, I accepted it and told her to ask it.

She said, 'When we stood before the globe of the world, Gormon, I asked you to show me the place where you were born, and you said you were unable to find it on the map. That seemed most strange. Tell me now: are you what you say you are, a Changeling who wanders the world?'

He replied. 'I am not.'

In a sense he had satisfied the question as Avluela had phrased it; but it went without saying that his reply was inadequate, and he kept his hand in the Mouth of Truth as he continued, 'I did not show my birthplace to you on the globe because I was born nowhere on this globe, but on a world of a star I must not name. I am no Changeling in your meaning of the word, though by some definitions I am, for my body is somewhat disguised, and on my own world I wear a different flesh. I have lived here ten years.'

'What was your purpose in coming to Earth?' I asked.

'I am obliged only to answer one question,' said Gormon. Then he smiled. 'But I give you the answer anyway: I was sent to Earth in the capacity of a military observer, to prepare the way for the invasion for which you have Watched so long and in which you have ceased to believe, and which will be upon you in a matter now of some hours.'

'Lies!' I bellowed. '*Lies!*'

Gormon laughed. And drew his hand from the Mouth of Truth, intact, unharmed.

SIX

Numb with confusion, I fled with my cart of instruments from that gleaming sphere and emerged into a street suddenly cold and dark. Night had come with winter's swiftness; it was almost the ninth hour, and almost the time for me to Watch once more.

Gormon's mockery thundered in my brain. He had arranged everything: he had maneuvered us in to the Mouth of Truth; he had wrung a confession of lost faith from me and a confession of a different sort from Avluela; he had mercilessly volunteered information he need not have revealed, spoken words calculated to split me to the core.

Was the Mouth of Truth a fraud? Could Gormon lie and emerge unscathed?

Never since I first took up my tasks had I Watched at anything but the appointed hours. This was a time of crumbling realities; I could not wait for the ninth hour to come round; crouching in the windy street, I opened my cart, readied my equipment, and sank like a diver into Watchfulness.

My amplified consciousness roared toward the stars.

Godlike I roamed infinity. I felt the rush of the solar wind, but I was no Flier to be hurled to destruction by that pressure, and I soared past it, beyond the reach of those angry particles of light, into the blackness at the edge of the sun's dominion. Down upon me there beat a different pressure.

Starships coming near.

Not the tourist lines bringing sightseers to gape at our diminished world. Not the registered mercantile transport vessels, nor the scoopships that collect the interstellar vapors, nor the resort craft on their hyperbolic orbits.

These were military craft, dark, alien, menacing. I could not tell their number; I knew only that they sped Earthward at many lights, nudging a cone of deflected energies before them; and it was that cone that I had sensed, that I had felt also the night before, booming into my mind through my instruments, engulfing me like a cube of crystal through which stress patterns play and shine.

All my life I had watched for this.

I had been trained to sense it. I had prayed that I never would sense it, and then in my emptiness I had prayed that I *would* sense it, and then I had ceased to believe in it. And then by grace of the Changeling Gormon, I had sensed it after all, Watching ahead of my hour, crouching in a cold Roumish street just outside the Mouth of Truth.

In his training, a Watcher is instructed to break from his Watchfulness as soon as his observations are confirmed by a careful check, so that he can sound the alarm. Obediently I made my check by shifting from one channel to another to another, traingulating and still picking up that foreboding sensation of titanic force rushing upon Earth at unimaginable speed.

Either I was deceived, or the invasion was come. But I could not shake from my trance to give the alarm.

Lingeringly, lovingly, I drank in the sensory data for what seemed like hours. I fondled my equipment; I drained from it the total affirmation of faith that my readings gave me. Dimly I warned myself that I was wasting vital time, that it was my duty to leave this lewd caressing of destiny to summon the Defenders.

And at last I burst free from Watchfulness and returned to the world I was guarding.

Avluela was beside me; she was dazed, terrified, her knuckles to her teeth, her eyes blank.

'Watcher! Watcher, do you hear me? What's happening? What's going to happen?'

'The invasion,' I said. 'How long was I under?'

'About half a minute. I don't know. Your eyes were closed. I thought you were dead.'

'Gormon was speaking the truth! The *invasion* is almost here. Where is he? Where did he go?'

'He vanished as we came away from that place with the

Mouth,' Avluela whispered. 'Watcher, I'm frightened. I feel everything collapsing. I have to fly – I can't stay down here now!'

'Wait,' I said, clutching at her and missing her arm. 'Don't go now. First I have to give the alarm, and then –'

But she was already stripping off her clothing. Bare to the waist, her pale body gleamed in the evening light, while about us people were rushing to and fro in ignorance of all that was about to occur. I wanted to keep Avluela beside me, but I could delay no longer in giving the alarm, and I turned away from her, back to my care.

As though caught up in a dream born of overripe longings I reached for the node that I had never used, the one that would send forth a planetwide alert to the Defenders.

Had the alarm already been given? Had some other Watcher sensed what I had sensed, and less paralyzed by bewilderment and doubt, performed a Watcher's final task?

No. No. For then I would be hearing the sirens' shriek reverberating from the orbiting loudspeakers above the city.

I touched the node. From the corner of my eye I saw Avluela, free of her encumbrances now, kneeling to say her words, filling her tender wings with strength. In a moment she would be in the air, beyond my grasp.

With a single swift tug I activated the alarm.

In that instant I became aware of a burly figure striding toward us. Gormon, I thought: and as I rose from my equipment I reached out to him; I wanted to seize him and hold him fast. But he who approached was not Gormon but some officious dough-faced Servitor who said to Avluela, 'Go easy, Flier, let your wings drop. The Prince of Roum sends me to bring you to his presence.'

He grappled with her. Her little breasts heaved; her eyes flashed anger at him.

'Let go of me! I'm going to fly!'

'The Prince of Roum summons you,' the Servitor said, enclosing her in his heavy arms.

'The Prince of Roum will have other distractions tonight,' I said. 'He'll have no need of her.'

As I spoke the sirens began to sing from the skies.

The Servitor released her. His mouth worked noiselessly for an instant; he made one of the protective gestures of the Will; he looked skyward and grunted, 'The alarm! Who gave the alarm? You, old Watcher?'

Figures rushed about insanely in the streets.

Avluela, freed, sped past me – on foot, her wings but half-furled – and was swallowed up in the surging throng. Over the terrifying sound of the sirens came booming messages from the public annunciators, giving instructions for defense and safety. A lanky man with the mark of the guild of Defenders upon his cheek rushed to me, shouted words too incoherent to be understood, and sped on down the street. The world seemed to have gone mad.

Only I remained calm. I looked to the skies, half-expecting to see the invaders' black ships already hovering above the towers of Roum. But I saw nothing except the hovering nightlights and the other objects one might expect overhead.

'Gormon?' I called. 'Avluela?'

I was alone.

A strange emptiness swept over me. I had given the alarm; the invaders were on their way; I had lost my occupation. There was no need of Watchers now. Almost lovingly I touched the worn cart that had been my companion for so many years. I ran my fingers over its stained and pitted instruments; and then I looked away, abandoning it, and went down the dark streets cartless, burdenless, a man whose life had found and lost meaning in the same instant. And about me raged chaos.

SEVEN

It was understood that when the moment of Earth's final battle arrived, all guilds would be mobilized, the Watchers alone exempted. We who had manned the perimeter of defense for so long had no part in the strategy of combat; we were discharged by the giving of a true alarm. Now it was the time of the guild of Defenders to show its capabilities. They had planned for half a cycle what they would do in time of war. What plans would they call forth now? What deeds would they direct?

My only concern was to return to the royal hostelry and wait out the crisis. It was hopeless to think of finding Avluela, and I pummeled myself savagely for having let her slip away, naked and without a protector, in that confused moment. Where would she go? Who would shield her?

A fellow Watcher, pulling his cart madly along, nearly collided with me. 'Careful!' I snapped. He looked up, breathless, stunned. 'Is it true?' he asked. 'The alarm?'

'Can't you hear?'

'But is it real?'

I pointed to his cart. 'You know how to find that out.'

'They say the man who gave the alarm was drunk, an old fool who was turned away from the inn yesterday.'

'It could be so,' I admitted.

'But if the alarm is real –!'

Smiling, I said, 'If it is, now we all may rest. Good day to you, Watcher.'

'Your cart! Where's your cart?' he shouted at me.

But I had moved past him, toward the mighty carven stone pillar of some relic of Imperial Roum.

Ancient images were carved on that pillar; battles and victories, foreign monarchs marched in the chains of disgrace through the streets of Roum, triumphant eagles celebrating imperial grandeur. In my strange new calmness I stood awhile before the column of stone and admired its elegant engravings. Toward me rushed a frenzied figure whom I recognized as the Rememberer Basil; I hailed him, saying, 'How timely you come! Do me the kindness of explaining these images, Rememberer. They fascinate me, and my curiosity is aroused.'

'Are you insane? Can't you hear the alarm?'

'I gave the alarm, Rememberer.'

'Flee, then! Invaders come! We must fight!'

'Not I. Basil. Now my time is over. Tell me of these images. These beaten kings, these broken emperors. Surely a man of your years will not be doing battle.'

'All are mobilized now!'

'All but Watchers,' I said. 'Take a moment. Yearning for the past is born in me. Gormon has vanished; be my guide to these lost cycles.'

The Rememberer shook his head wildly, circled around me, and tried to get away. Hoping to seize his skinny arm and pin him to the spot, I made a lunge at him, but he eluded me and I caught only his dark shawl, which pulled free and came loose in my hands. Then he was gone, his spindly limbs pumping madly as he fled down the street and left my view. I shrugged and examined the shawl I had so unexpectedly acquired. It was shot through with glimmering threads of metal arranged in intricate patterns that teased the eye: it seemed to me that each strand disappeared into the weave of the fabric, only to appear at some improbable point, like the lineage of dynasties unexpectedly revived in distant cities. The workmanship was superb. Idly I draped the shawl about my shoulders.

I walked on.

My legs, which had been on the verge of failing me earlier in the day, now served me well. With renewed youthfulness I made my way through the chaotic city, finding no difficulties in choosing my route. I headed for the river, then crossed it and, on the Tver's far side, sought the palace of the Prince. The night had deepened, for most lights were extinguished under the mobilization orders; and from time to time a dull boom signaled the explosion of a screening bomb overhead, liberating clouds of murk that shielded the city from most forms of long-range scrutiny. There were fewer pedestrians in the streets. The sirens still cried out. Atop the buildings the defense installations were going into action; I heard the bleeping sounds of repellors warming up, and I saw long spidery arms of amplification booms swinging from tower to tower as they linked for maximum output. I had no doubt now that the invasion actually was coming. My own instruments might have been fouled by inner confusion, but they would not have proceeded thus far with the mobilization if the initial report had not been confirmed by the findings of hundreds of other members of my guild.

As I neared the palace a pair of breathless Rememberers sped toward me, their shawls flapping behind them. They called to me in words I did not comprehend – some code of their guild, I realized, recollecting that I wore Basil's shawl. I could not reply, and they rushed upon me, still gabbling; and switching to the language of ordinary men they said, 'What is the matter with you? To your post! We must record! We must comment! We must observe!'

'You mistake me,' I said mildly. 'I keep this shawl only for your brother Basil, who left it in my care. I have no post to guard at this time.'

'A Watcher,' they cried in unison, and cursed me separately, and ran on. I laughed and went to the palace.

Its gates stood open. The neuters who had guarded the outer portals had gone, as were the two Indexers who had stood just within the door. The beggars that had thronged the vast plaza had jostled their way into the building itself to seek shelter; this had awakened the anger of the licensed hereditary mendicants whose customary stations were in that part of the building, and they had fallen upon the inflowing refugees with fury and unexpected strength. I saw cripples lashing out with their crutches held as clubs; I saw blind men landing blows with suspicious accuracy; meek penitents were wielding a variety of weapons ranging from stilettos to sonic pistols. Holding myself aloof from this shameless spectacle, I penetrated to the inner recesses of the palace and peered into chapels where I saw Pilgrims beseeching the blessings of the Will, and Communicants desperately seeking spiritual guidance as to the outcome of the coming conflict.

Abruptly I heard the blare of trumpets and cries of, 'Make way! Make way!'

A file of sturdy Servitors marched into the palace, striding toward the Prince's chambers in the apse. Several of them held a struggling, kicking, frantic figure with half-unfolded wings: Avluela! I called out to her, but my voice died in the din, nor could I reach her. The Servitors shoved me aside. The procession vanished into the princely chambers. I caught a final glimpse of the little Flier, pale and small in the grip of her captors, and then she was gone once more.

I seized a bumbling neuter who had been moving uncertainly in the wake of the Servitors.

'That Flier! Why was she brought here?'

'Ha – he – they –'

'Tell me!'

'The Prince – his woman – in his chariot – he – he – they – the invaders –'

I pushed the flabby creature aside and rushed toward the apse. A brazen wall ten times my own height confronted me. I pounded on it. 'Avluela!' I shouted hoarsely. '*Av . . . lu . . . ela . . . !*'

I was neither thrust away nor admitted. I was ignored. The bedlam at the western doors of the palace had extended itself now to the nave and aisles, and as the ragged beggars boiled toward me I executed a quick turn and found myself passing through one of the side doors of the palace.

Suspended and passive, I stood in the courtyard that led to the royal hostelry. A strange electricity crackled in the air. I assumed it was an emanation from one of Roum's defense installations, some kind of beam designed to screen the city from attack. But an instant later I realized that it presaged the actual arrival of the invaders.

Starships blazed in the heavens.

When I had perceived them in my Watching they had appeared black against the infinite blackness, but now they burned with the radiance of suns. A stream of bright, hard, jewel-like globes bedecked the sky; they were ranged side by side, stretching from east to west in a continuous band, filling all the celestial arch, and as they erupted simultaneously into being it seemed to me that I heard the crash and throb of an invisible symphony heralding the arrival of the conquerors of Earth.

I do not know how far above me the starships were, nor how many of them hovered there, not any of the details of their design. I know only that in sudden massive majesty they were there, and that if I had been a Defender my soul would have withered instantly at the sight.

Across the heavens shot light of many hues. The battle had been joined. I could not comprehend the actions of our warriors, and I was equally baffled by the maneuvers of those who had come to take possession of our history-crusted but time-diminished planet. To my shame I felt not only out of the struggle but above the struggle, as though this was no quarrel of mine. I wanted Avluela beside me, and she was somewhere within the depths of the palace of the Prince of Roum. Even Gormon would have been a comfort now, Gormon the Changeling, Gormon the spy, Gormon the monstrous betrayer of our world.

Gigantic amplified voices bellowed, 'Make way for the Prince of Roum! The Prince of Roum leads the Defenders in the battle for the fatherworld!'

From the palace emerged a shining vehicle the shape of a teardrop, in whose bright-metaled roof a transparent sheet had been mounted so that all the populance could see and take heart in the presence of the ruler. At the controls of the vehicle sat the Prince of Roum, proudly erect, his cruel, youthful features fixed in harsh determination; and beside him, robed like an empress, I beheld the slight figure of the Flier Avluela. She seemed in a trance.

The royal chariot soared upward and was lost in the darkness.

It seemed to me that a second vehicle appeared and followed its path, and that the Prince's reappeared, and that the two flew in tight circles, apparently locked in combat. Clouds of blue sparks wrapped both chariots now; and then they swung high and far and were lost to me behind one of the hills of Roum.

Was the battle now raging all over the planet? Was Perris in jeopardy, and holy Jorslem, and even the sleepy isles of the Lost Continents? Did starships hover everywhere? I did not know. I perceived events in only one small segment of the sky over Roum, and even there my awareness of what was taking place was dim, uncertain, and ill-informed. There were momentary flashes of light in which I saw battalions of Fliers streaming across the sky; and then darkness returned as though a velvet shroud had been hurled over the city. I saw the great machines of our defense firing in fitful bursts from the tops of our towers; and yet I saw the starships untouched, unharmed, unmoved above. The courtyard in which I stood was deserted, but in the distance I heard voices, full of fear and foreboding, shouting in tinny tones that might have been the screeching of birds. Occasionally there came a booming sound that rocked all the city. Once a platoon of Somnambulists was driven past where I was; in the plaza fronting the palace I observed what appeared to be an array of Clowns unfolding some sort of sparkling netting of a military look; by one flash of lightning I was able to see a trio of Rememberers making copious notes of all that elapsed as they soared aloft on the gravity plate. It seemed – I was not sure – that the vehicle of the Prince of Roum returned, speeding across the sky with its pursuer clinging close. 'Avluela,' I whispered, as the twin dots of light left my sight. Were the starships disgorging troops? Did colossal pylons of force spiral down from those orbiting brightnesses to touch the surface of the Earth? Why had the Prince seized Avluela? Where was Gormon? What were our

Defenders doing? Why were the enemy ships not blasted from the sky?

Rooted to the ancient cobbles of the courtyard, I observed the cosmic battle in total lack of understanding throughout the long night.

Dawn came. Strands of pale light looped from tower to tower. I touched fingers to my eyes, realizing that I must have slept while standing. Perhaps I should apply for membership in the guild of Somnambulists, I told myself lightly. I put my hands to the Rememberer's shawl about my shoulders and wondered how I managed to acquire it, and the answer came.

I looked toward the sky.

The alien starships were gone. I saw only the ordinary morning sky, gray with pinkness breaking through. I felt the jolt of compulsion and looked about for my cart, and reminded myself that I need do no more Watching, and I felt more empty than one would ordinarily feel at such an hour.

Was the battle over?

Had the enemy been vanquished?

Were the ships of the invaders blasted from the sky and lying in charred ruin outside Roum?

All was silent. I heard no more celestial symphonies. Then out of the eerie stillness there came a new sound, a rumbling noise as of wheeled vehicles passing through the streets of the city. And the invisible Musicians played one final note, deep and resonant, which trailed away jaggedly as though every string had been broken at once.

Over the speakers used for public announcements came quiet words.

'Roum is fallen. Roum is fallen.'

EIGHT

The royal hostelry was untended. Neuters and members of the servant guilds all had fled. Defenders, Masters, and Dominators must have perished honorably in combat. Basil the Rememberer was nowhere about; likewise none of his brethren. I went to my room, cleansed and refreshed and fed myself, gathered my few possessions, and bade farewell to the luxuries I had known so briefly. I regretted that I had had such a short time to visit Roum; but at least Gormon had been a most excellent guide, and I had seen a great deal.

Now I proposed to move on.

It did not seem prudent to remain in a conquered city. My room's thinking cap did not respond to my queries, and so I did not know what the extent of the defeat was, here or in other regions, but it was evident to me that Roum at least had passed from human control, and I wished to depart quickly. I weighed the thought of going to Jorslem, as that tall pilgrim had suggested upon my entry into Roum; but then I reflected and chose a westward route, toward Perris, which not only was closer but held the headquarters of the Rememberers. My own occupation had been destroyed; but on this first morning of Earth's conquest I felt a sudden powerful and strange yearning to offer myself humbly to the Rememberers and seek with them knowledge of our more glittering yesterdays.

At midday I left the hostelry. I walked first to the palace, which still stood open. The beggars lay strewn about, some drugged, some sleeping, most dead; from the crude manner of their death I saw that they must have slain one another in their panic and frenzy. A despondent-looking Indexer squatted beside the three skulls of the interrogation fixture in the chapel. As I entered he said, 'No use. The brains do not reply.'

'How goes it with the Prince of Roum?'

'Dead. The invaders shot him from the sky.'

'A young Flier rode beside him. What do you know of her?'

'Nothing. Dead, I suppose.'

'And the city?'

'Fallen. Invaders are everywhere.'

'Killing?'

'Not even looting,' the Indexer said. 'They are most gentle. They have *collected* us.'

'In Roum alone, or everywhere?'

The man shrugged. He began to rock rhythmically back and forth. I let him be, and walked deeper into the palace. To my surprise, the imperial chambers of the Prince were unsealed. I went within; I was awed by the sumptuous luxury of the hangings, the draperies, the lights, the furnishings. I passed from room to room, coming at last to the royal bed, whose coverlet was the flesh of a colossal bivalve of the planet of another star, and as the shell yawned for me I touched the infinitely soft fabric under which the Prince of Roum had lain, and I recalled that Avluela too had lain here, and if I had been a younger man I would have wept.

I left the palace and slowly crossed the plaza to begin my journey toward Perris.

As I departed I had my first glimpse of our conquerors. A vehicle of alien design drew up at the plaza's rim and perhaps a dozen figures emerged. They might almost have been human. They were tall and broad, deep-chested, as Gormon had been, and only the extreme length of their arms marked them instantly as alien. Their skins were of strange texture, and if I had been closer I suspect I would have seen eyes and lips and nostrils that were not of a human design. Taking no notice of me, they crossed the plaza, walking in a curiously loose-jointed loping way that reminded me irresistibly of Gormon's stride, and entered the Palace. They seemed neither swaggering nor belligerent.

Sightseers. Majestic Roum once more exerted its magnetism upon strangers.

Leaving our new masters to their amusement, I walked off,

toward the outskirts of the city. The bleakness of eternal winter crept into my soul. I wondered: did I feel sorrow that Roum had fallen? Or did I mourn the loss of Avluela? Or was it only that I now had missed three successive Watchings, and like an addict I was experiencing the pangs of withdrawal?

It was all of these that pained me, I decided. But mostly the last.

No one was abroad in the city as I made for the gates. Fear of the new masters kept the Roumish in hiding, I supposed. From time to time one of the alien vehicles hummed past, but I was unmolested. I came to the city's western gate in the late afternoon. It was open, revealing to me a gentle rising hill on whose breast rose trees with dark green crowns. I passed through and saw, a short distance beyond the gate, the figure of a Pilgrim who was shuffling slowly away from the city.

I overtook him easily.

His faltering, uncertain walk seemed strange to me, for not even his thick brown robes could hide the strength and youth of his body; he stood erect, his shoulders square and his back straight, and yet he walked with the hesitating, trembling step of an old man. When I drew abreast of him and peered under his hood I understood, for affixed to the bronze mask all Pilgrims wear was a reverberator, such as is used by blind men to warn them of obstacles and hazards. He became aware of me and said, 'I am a sightless Pilgrim. I pray you do not molest me.'

It was not a Pilgrim's voice. It was a strong and harsh and imperious voice.

I replied, 'I molest no one. I am a Watcher who has lost his occupation this night past.'

'Many occupations were lost this night past, Watcher.'

'Surely not a Pilgrim's.'

'No,' he said. 'Not a Pilgrim's.'

'Where are you bound?'

'Away from Roum.'

'No particular destination?'

'No,' the Pilgrim said. 'None. I will wander.'

'Perhaps we should wander together,' I said, for it is accounted good luck to travel with a Pilgrim, and, shorn of my Flier and my Changeling, I would otherwise have traveled alone. 'My destination is Perris. Will you come?'

'There as well as anywhere else,' he said bitterly. 'Yes. We will go to Perris together. But what business does a Watcher have there?'

'A Watcher has no business anywhere. I go to Perris to offer myself in service to the Rememberers.'

'Ah,' he said. 'I was of that guild too, but it was only honorary.'

'With Earth fallen, I wish to learn more of Earth in its pride.'

'Is all Earth fallen, then, and not only Roum?'

'I think it is so,' I said.

'Ah,' replied the Pilgrim. 'Ah!'

He fell silent and we went onward. I gave him my arm, and now he shuffled no longer, but moved with a young man's brisk stride. From time to time he uttered what might have been a sigh or a smothered sob. When I asked him details of his Pilgrimage, he answered obliquely or not at all. When we were an hour's journey outside Roum, and already amid forests, he said suddenly, 'This mask gives me pain. Will you help me adjust it?'

To my amazement he began to remove it. I gasped, for it is forbidden for a Pilgrim to reveal his face. Had he forgotten that I was not sightless too?

As the mask came away he said, 'You will not welcome this sight.'

The bronze grillwork slipped down from his forehead, and I saw first eyes that had been newly blinded, gaping holes where no surgeon's knife, but possibly thrusting fingers, had penetrated, and then the sharp regal nose, and finally the quirked, taut lips of the Prince of Roum.

'Your Majesty!' I cried.

Trails of dried blood ran down his cheeks. About the raw sockets themselves were smears of ointment. He felt little pain,

I suppose, for he had killed it with those green smears, but the pain that burst through me was real and potent.

'Majesty no longer,' he said. 'Help me with the mask!' His hands trembled as he held it forth. 'These flanges must be widened. They press cruelly at my cheeks. Here – here –'

Quickly I made the adjustments, so that I would not have to see his ruined face for long.

He replaced the mask. 'I am a Pilgrim now,' he said quietly. 'Roum is without its Prince. Betray me if you wish, Watcher; otherwise help me to Perris; and if ever I regain my power you will be well rewarded.'

'I am no betrayer,' I told him.

In silence we continued. I had no way of making small talk with such a man. It would be a somber journey for us to Perris; but I was committed now to be his guide. I thought of Gormon and how well he had kept his vows. I thought too of Avluela, and a hundred times the words leaped to my tongue to ask the fallen Prince how his consort the Flier had fared in the night of defeat, and I did not ask.

Twilight gathered, but the sun still gleamed golden-red before us in the west. And suddenly I halted and made a hoarse sound of surprise deep in my throat, as a shadow passed overhead.

High above me Avluela soared. Her skin was stained by the colors of the sunset, and her wings were spread to their fullest, radiant with every hue of the spectrum. She was already at least the height of a hundred men above the ground, and still climbing, and to her I must have been only a speck among the trees.

'What is it?' the Prince asked. 'What do you see?'

'Nothing.'

'Tell me what you see!'

I could not deceive him. 'I see a Flier, your Majesty. A slim girl far aloft.'

'Then the night must have come.'

'No,' I said. 'The sun is still above the horizon.'

'How can that be? She can only have nightwings. The sun would hurl her to the ground.'

I hesitated. I could not bring myself to explain how it was that Avluela flew by day, though she had only nightwings. I could not tell the Prince of Roum that beside her, wingless, flew the invader Gormon, effortlessly moving through the air, his arms about her thin shoulders, steadying her, supporting her, helping her resist the pressure of the solar wind. I could not tell him that his nemesis flew with the last of his consorts above his head.

'Well?' he demanded. 'How does she fly by day?'

'I do not know,' I said. 'It is a mystery to me. There are many things nowadays I can no longer understand.'

The Prince appeared to accept that. 'Yes, Watcher. Many things none of us can understand.'

He fell once more into silence. I yearned to call out to Avluela, but I knew she could not and would not hear me, and so I walked on toward the sunset, toward Perris, leading the blind Prince. And over us Avluela and Gormon sped onward, limned sharply against the day's last glow, until they climbed so high they were lost to my sight.

PART II

Among the Rememberers

ONE

To journey with a fallen Prince is no easy thing. His eyes were gone, but not his pride; blinding had taught him no humility. He wore the robes and mask of a Pilgrim, but there was no piety in his soul and little grace. Behind his mask he still knew himself to be the Prince of Roum.

I was all his court now, as we walked the road to Perris in early springtime. I led him along the right roads; I amused him at his command with stories of my wanderings; I nursed him through moods of sulky bitterness. In return I got very little except the assurance that I would eat regularly. No one denies food to a Pilgrim, and in each village on our way we stopped in inns, where he was fed and I, as his companion, also was given meals. Once, early in our travels, he erred and haughtily told an innkeeper, 'See that you feed my servant as well!' The blinded Prince could not see that look of shocked disbelief – for what would a Pilgrim be doing with a servant? – but I smiled at the innkeeper, and winked, and tapped my forehead, and the man understood and served us both without discussion. Afterward I explained the error to the Prince, and thereafter he spoke of me as his companion. Yet I knew that to him I was nothing but a servant.

The weather was fair. Eyrop was growing warm as the year turned. Slender willows and poplars were greening beside the road, though much of the way out of Roum was planted with lavish star-trees imported during the gaudy days of the Second Cycle, and their blue-bladed leaves had resisted our puny Eyropan winter. The birds, too, were coming back from their season across the sea in Afreek. They sparkled overhead, singing, discussing among themselves the change of masters in the world. 'They mock me,' said the Prince one dawn. 'They sing to me and defy me to see their brightness!'

Oh, he was bitter, and with good reason. He, who had had so much and lost all, had a good deal to lament. For me, the defeat of Earth meant only an end to habits. Otherwise all was the same: no longer need I keep my Watch, but I still wandered the face of the world, alone even when, as now, I had a companion.

I wondered if the Prince knew why he had been blinded. I wondered if, in the moment of his triumph, Gormon had explained to the Prince that it was as elemental a matter as jealousy over a woman that had cost him his eyes.

'You took Avluela,' Gormon might have said. 'You saw a little Flier, and you thought she'd amuse you. And you said, here, girl, come to my bed. Not thinking of her as a person. Not thinking she might prefer others. Thinking only as a Prince of Roum might think – imperiously. Here, Prince!'

– and the quick, forked thrust of long-tipped fingers –

But I dared not ask. That much awe remained in me for this fallen monarch. To penetrate his privacy, to strike up a conversation with him about his mishaps as though he were an ordinary companion of the road – no, I could not. I spoke when I was spoken to. I offered conversation upon command. Otherwise I kept my silence, like a good commoner in the presence of royalty.

Each day we had our reminders that the Prince of Roum was royalty no longer.

Overhead flew the invaders, sometimes in floaters or other chariots, sometimes under their own power. Traffic was heavy. They were taking inventory of their world. Their shadows passed over us, tiny eclipses, and I looked up to see our new masters and oddly felt no anger at them, only relief that Earth's long vigil was over. For the Prince it was different. He always seemed to know when some invader passed above, and he clenched his fists, and scowled, and whispered black curses.

Did his optic nerves still somehow record the movements of shadows? Or were his remaining senses so sharpened by the loss of one that he could detect the imperceptible humming of a floater and sniff the skins of the soaring invaders? I did not ask. I asked so little.

Sometimes at night, when he thought I slept, he sobbed. I pitied him then. He was so young to lose what he had, after all. I learned in those dark hours that even the sobs of a Prince are not those of ordinary men. He sobbed defiantly, belligerently, angrily. But yet he sobbed.

Much of the time he seemed stoic, resigned to his losses. He put one foot before the other and walked on briskly beside me, every step taking him farther from his great city of Roum, nearer to Perris. At other times, though, it seemed I could look through the bronze grillwork of his mask to see the curdled soul within. His pent-up rage took petty outlets. He mocked me for my age, for my low rank, for the emptiness of my life's purpose now that the invasion for which I had Watched had come. He toyed with me.

'Tell me your name, Watcher!'

'It is forbidden, Majesty.'

'Old laws are now repealed. Come on, man, we have months to travel together. Can I go on calling you Watcher all that time?'

'It is the custom of my guild.'

'The custom of mine,' he said, 'is to give orders and have them obeyed. Your name!'

'Not even the guild of Dominators can have a Watcher's name without due cause and a guildmaster's writ.'

He spat. 'What a jackal you are, to defy me when I'm like this! If we were in my palace now you'd never dare!'

'In your palace, Majesty, you would not make this unjust demand on me before your court. Dominators have obligations too. One of them is to respect the ways of lesser guilds.'

'He lectures me,' said the Prince. Irritably he threw himself down beside the road. Stretching against the grassy slope, he leaned back, touched one of the star-trees, snapped off a row of blades, clenched them in his hand so that they must have pricked his palm painfully. I stood beside him. A heavy land-vehicle rumbled by, the first we had seen on that empty road this morning. Within it were invaders. Some of them waved to us. After a long while the Prince said in a lighter, almost wheedling tone, 'My name is Enric. Now tell me yours.'

'I beg you to let me be, Majesty.'

'But you have my name! It is just as forbidden for me to give mine as you yours!'

'I did not ask yours,' I said firmly.

In the end I did not give him my name. It was a small enough victory, to refuse such information to a powerless Prince, but in a thousand little ways he made me pay for it. He nagged, chivvied, teased, cursed, and berated me. He spoke with contempt of my guild. He demanded menial services of me. I lubricated his metal mask; I sponged ointment into his ruined eyes; I did other things too humiliating to recall. And so we stumbled along the highway to Perris, the empty old man and the emptied young man, full of hatred for one another, and yet bound by the needs and the duties of wayfarers.

It was a difficult time. I had to cope with his changing moods as he soared to cosmic rapture over his plans for redeeming conquered Earth, and as he sank to abysses upon his realization that the conquest was final. I had to protect him from his own rashness in the villages, where he sometimes behaved as though he were still Prince of Roum, ordering folk about, slapping them even, in a way that was unbecoming to a holy man. Worse yet, I had to minister to his lusts, buying him women who came to him in darkness, unaware that they were dealing with one who claimed to be a Pilgrim. As a Pilgrim he was a fraud, for he did not carry the starstone with which Pilgrims make communion with the Will. Somehow I got him past all of these crises, even the time when we encountered on the road another Pilgrim, a genuine one. This was a formidable and disputatious old man full of theological quibbles. 'Come and talk with me of the immanence of the Will,' he said to the Prince, and the Prince, whose patience was frayed that afternoon, replied obscenely. I kicked the princely shin in a surreptitious way, and to the shocked Pilgrim I said, 'Our friend is unwell today. Last night he held communion with the Will and received a revelation that unsettled his mind. I pray you, let us go on, and give him no talk of holiness until he is himself once more.'

With such improvisations I managed our journey.

As the weather warmed, the Prince's attitude mellowed. Perhaps he was growing reconciled to his catastrophe, or possibly, in the prison of his lightless skull, he was teaching himself new tactics for meeting his changed existence. He talked almost idly of himself, his downfall, his humiliation. He spoke of the power that had been his in terms that said unmistakably that he had no illusions about ever recapturing it. He talked of his wealth, his women, his jewels, his strange machines, his Changelings and Musicians and Servitors, the Masters and even fellow Dominators who had knelt to him. I will not say that at any time I liked him, but at least at these times I recognized a suffering human being behind his impassive mask.

He even recognized in me a human being. I know it cost him much.

He said, 'The trouble with power, Watcher, is that it cuts you off from people. People become things. Take yourself. To me, you were nothing but a machine that walked around Watching for invaders. I suppose you had dreams, ambitions, angers, all the rest, but I saw you as a dried-up old man without any independent existence outside of your guild function. Now I see much more by seeing nothing.'

'What do you see?'

'You were young once, Watcher. You had a town you loved. A family. A girl, even. You chose, or had chosen for you, a guild, you went into apprenticeship, you struggled, your head ached you, your belly griped you, there were many dark moments when you wondered what it was all about, what it was for. And you saw us ride by, Masters,

Dominators, and it was like comets going past. Yet here we are together, cast up by the tides on the road to Perris. And which of us is happier now?'

'I am beyond happiness or sorrow,' I said.

'Is that the truth? Is that the truth? Or is it a line you hide behind? Tell me, Watcher: I know your guild forbids you to marry, but have you ever loved?'

'Sometimes.'

'And are you beyond that now?'

'I am old,' I said evasively.

'But you could love. You could love. You're released from your guild vows now, eh? You could take a bride.'

I laughed. 'Who'd have me?'

'Don't speak that way. You're not that old. You have strengths. You've seen the world, you understand it. Why, in Perris you could find yourself some wench who –' He paused. 'Were you ever tempted, while you still were under your vows?'

Just then a Flier passed overhead. She was a woman of middle years, struggling a little in the sky, for some daylight remained to press on her wings. I felt a pang, and I wanted to tell the Prince: yes, yes, I was tempted, there was a little Flier not long ago, a girl, a child, Avluela; and in my way I loved her, though I never touched her; and I love her still.

I said nothing to Prince Enric.

I looked, though, at that Flier, freer than I because she had wings, and in the warmth of that spring evening I felt the chill of desolation enfolding me.

'Is it far to Perris?' the Prince asked.

'We will walk, and one day we will get there.'

'And then?'

'For me an apprenticeship in the guild of Rememberers, and a new life. For you?'

'I hope to find friends there,' he said.

We walked on, long hours each day. There were those who went by and offered us rides, but we refused, for at the checkpoints the invaders would be seeking such wandering nobility as the Prince. We walked a tunnel miles long under sky-storming mountains sheathed in ice, and we entered a flat land of farming peasants, and we paused by awakening rivers to cool our toes. Golden summer burst upon us. We moved through the world but were not of it; we listened to no news of the conquest, although it was obvious that the invaders had taken full possession. In small vehicles they hovered everywhere, seeing our world that now was theirs.

I did the bidding of the Prince in all ways, including the unpleasant ones. I attempted to make his life less bleak. I gave him a sensation of being still a ruler – albeit of only one useless old Watcher. I taught him, too, how best to masquerade as a Pilgrim. From what little I knew I gave him postures, phrases, prayers. It was obvious that he had spent little time in contact with the Will while he reigned. Now he pretended faith, but it was insincere, part of his camouflage.

In a town called Dijon, he said, 'Here I will purchase eyes.'

Not true eyes. The secret of making such replacements perished in the Second Cycle. Out among the more fortunate stars any miracle is available for a price, but our Earth is a neglected world in a backwater of the universe. The Prince might have got out there in the days before conquest to purchase new sight, but now the best that was available to him was a way of distinguishing light from dark. Even that would give him a rudiment of sight; at present he had no other guidance than the reverberator that warned him of obstacles in his path. How did he know, though, that in Dijon he would find a craftsman with the necessary skills? And with what would he meet the cost?

He said, 'The man here is a brother of one of my Scribes. He is of the guild of Artificers, and I often bought his work in Roum. He'll have eyes for me.'

'And the cost?'

'I am not entirely without resources.'

We stopped in a field of gnarled cork-trees, and the Prince undid his robes. Indicating a place in the fleshy part of his thigh, he said, 'I carry a reserve here for emergencies. Give me your blade!' I handed it to him, and he seized the handle and pressed the stud that brought forth the cool, keen beam of light. With his left hand he felt his thigh, surveying for the exact place; then, stretching the flesh between two fingers, he made a surgically precise cut two inches long. He did not bleed, nor was there a sign that he felt pain. I watched in bewilderment as he slipped his fingers into the cut, spread its edges, and seemed to grope as if in a sack. He tossed my blade back to me.

Treasures tumbled from his thigh.

'Watch that nothing is lost,' he ordered me.

To the grass there fell seven sparkling jewels of alien origin, a small and artful celestial globe, five golden coins of Imperial Roum of cycles past, a ring set with a glowing dab of quasi-life, a flask of some unknown perfume, a group of miniature musical instruments done in precious woods and metals, eight statuettes of regal-looking men, and more. I scooped these wonders into a dazzling heap.

'An overpocket,' the Prince said coolly, 'which a skilled Surgeon implanted in my flesh. I anticipated a time of crisis in which I might need to leave the palace hurriedly. Into it I stuffed what I could; there is much more where these came from. Tell me, tell me what I have taken out!'

I gave him the full inventory. He listened tensely to the end, and I knew that he had kept count of all that had poured forth, and was testing my honesty. When I was done, he nodded, pleased. 'Take the globe,' he said, 'and the ring, and the two brightest jewels. Hide them in your pouch. The rest goes back within.' He spread the lips of the incision, and one by one I dropped the glories inside, where they joined who knew what splendid things lying in another dimension, the outlet from which was embedded in the Prince. He might have half the contents of the palace tucked away in his thigh. At the end he pressed the cut together, and it healed without a trace of a mark as I watched. He robed himself.

In town we quickly located the shop of Bordo the Artificer.

He was a squat man with a speckled face, a grizzled beard, a tic in one eye, and a flat coarse nose, but his fingers were as delicate as a woman's. His shop was a dark place with dusty wooden shelves and small windows; it could have been a building ten thousand years old. A few elegant items were on display. Most were not. He looked at us guardedly, obviously baffled that a Watcher and a Pilgrim should come to him.

At the Prince's prodding I said, 'My friend needs eyes.'

'I make a device, yes. But it is expensive, and it takes many months to prepare. Beyond the means of any Pilgrim.' I laid one jewel on the weathered counter. 'We have means.'

Shaken, Bordo snatched up the jewel, turned it this way and that, saw alien fires glowing at its heart.

'If you come back when the leaves are falling –'

'You have no eyes in stock?' I asked.

He smiled. 'I get few calls for such things. We keep a small inventory.'

I put down the celestial globe. Bordo recognized it as the work of a master, and his jaw sagged. He put it in one palm and tugged at his beard with the other hand. I let him look at it long enough to fall in love with it, and then I took it back and said, 'Autumn is too long to wait. We will have to go elsewhere. Perris, perhaps.' I caught the Prince's elbow, and we shuffled toward the door.

'Stop!' Bordo cried. 'At least let me check! Perhaps I have a pair somewhere –' And he began to rummage furiously in overpockets mounted in the rear wall.

He had eyes in stock, of course, and I haggled a bit on the price, and we settled for the globe, the ring, and one jewel. The Prince was silent throughout the transaction. I insisted on immediate installation and Bordo, nodding excitedly, shut his shop, slipped on a thinking cap, and summoned a sallow-faced Surgeon. Shortly the preliminaries of the operation were under way. The Prince lay on a pallet in a sealed and sterile room. He removed his reverberator and then his mask; and as those sharp features came into view, Bordo – who had been to the court of Roum – grunted in amazement and began to say something. My foot descended heavily on his. Bordo swallowed his words; and the Surgeon, unaware, began tranquilly to swab the ruined sockets.

The eyes were pearl-gray spheres, smaller than real eyes and broken by transverse slits. What mechanism was within I do not know, but from their rear projected tiny golden connections to fasten to the nerves. The Prince slept through the early part of the task, while I stood guard and Bordo assisted the Surgeon. Then it was necessary to awaken him. His face convulsed in pain, but it was so quickly mastered that Bordo muttered a prayer at this display of determination.

'Some light here,' said the Surgeon.

Bordo nudged a drifting globe closer. The Prince said, 'Yes, yes, I see the difference.'

'We must test. We must adjust,' the Surgeon said.

Bordo went outside. I followed. The man was trembling, and his face was green with fear.

'Will you kill us now?' he asked.

'Of course not.'

'I recognized —'

'You recognized a poor Pilgrim,' I said, 'who has suffered a terrible misfortune while on his journey. No more. Nothing else.'

I examined Bordo's stock awhile. Then the Surgeon and his patient emerged. The Prince now bore the pearly spheres in his sockets, with a meniscus of false flesh about them to insure a tight fit. He looked more machine than man, with those dead things beneath his brows, and as he moved his head the slits widened, narrowed, widened again, silently, stealthily. 'Look,' he said, and walked across the room, indicating objects, even naming them. I knew that he saw as though through a thick veil, but at least he saw, in a fashion. He masked himself again and by nightfall we were gone from Dijon.

The Prince seemed almost buoyant. But what he had in his skull was a poor substitute for what Gormon had ripped from him, and soon enough he knew it. That night, as we slept on stale cots in a Pilgrim's hostelry, the Prince cried out in wordless sounds of fury, and by the shifting light of the true moon and the two false ones I saw his arms rise, his fingers curl, his nails strike at an imagined enemy, and strike again, and again.

TWO

It was summer's end when we finally reached Perris. We came into the city from the south, walking a broad, resilient highway bordered by ancient trees, amid a fine shower of rain. Gusts of wind blew shriveled leaves about us. That night of terror on which we both had fled conquered Roum now seemed almost a dream; we were toughened by a spring and summer of walking, and the gray towers of Perris seemed to hold out promise of new beginnings. I suspected that we deceived ourselves, for what did the world hold for a shattered Prince who saw only shadows, and a Watcher long past his proper years?

This was a darker city than Roum. Even in late winter, Roum had had clear skies and bright sunlight. Perris seemed perpetually clouded over, buildings and environment both somber. Even the city walls were ash-gray, and they had no sheen. The gate stood wide. Beside it there lounged a small, sullen man in the garb of the guild of Sentinels, who made no move to challenge us as we approached. I looked at him questioningly. He shook his head.

'Go in, Watcher.'

'Without a check?'

'You haven't heard? All cities were declared free six nights ago. Order of the invaders. Gates are never closed now. Half the Sentinels have no work.'

'I thought the invaders were searching for enemies,' I said. 'The former nobility.'

'They have their checkpoints elsewhere, and no Sentinels are used. The city is free. Go in. Go in.'

As we went in, I said, 'Then why are you here?'

'It was my post for forty years,' the Sentinel said. 'Where should I go?'

I made the sign that told him I shared his sorrow, and the Prince and I entered Perris.

'Five times I came to Perris by the southern gate,' said the Prince. 'Always by chariot, with my Changelings walking before me and making music in their throats. We proceeded to the river, past the ancient buildings and monuments, on to the palace of the Comt of Perris. And by night we danced on gravity plates high above the city, and there were ballets of Fliers, and from the Tower of Perris there was performed an aurora for us. And the wine, the red wine of Perris, the women in their saucy gowns, the red-tipped breasts, the sweet thighs! We bathed in wine, Watcher.' He pointed vaguely. 'Is that the Tower of Perris?'

'I think it is the ruin of this city's weather machine,' I said.

'A weather machine would be a vertical column. What I see rises from a wide base to a slender summit, as does the Tower of Perris.'

'What I see,' I said gently, 'is a vertical column, at least thirty men high, ending in a rough break. The Tower would not be this close to the southern gate, would it?'

'No,' said the Prince, and muttered a foulness. 'The weather machine it is, then. These eyes of Bordo's don't see so clearly for me, eh? I deceive myself, Watcher. I deceive myself. Find a thinking cap and see if the Comt has fled.'

I stared a moment longer at the truncated pillar of the weather machine, that fantastic device which had brought such grief upon the world in the Second Cycle. I tried to penetrate its sleek, almost oily marble sides, to see the coiling intestines of mysterious devices that had been capable of sinking whole continents, that long ago had transformed my homeland in the west from a mountainous country to a chain of islands. Then I turned away, donned a public cap, asked for the Comt, got the answer I expected, and demanded to know the locations of places where we might find lodging.

The Prince said, 'Well?'

'The Comt of Perris was slain during the conquest along with all his sons. His dynasty is extinguished, his title is abolished, his palace has been transformed into a museum by the invaders. The rest of the Perrisian nobility is dead or has taken flight. I'll find a place for you at the lodge of Pilgrims.'

'No. Take me with you to the Rememberers.'

'Is that the guild you seek now?'

He gestured impatiently. 'No, fool! But how can I stay alone in a strange city, with all my friends gone? What would I say to true Pilgrims in their hostelry? I'll stay with you. The Rememberers can hardly turn away a blind Pilgrim.'

He gave me no choice. And so he accompanied me to the Hall of Rememberers.

We had to cross half the city, and it took us nearly the whole day. Perris seemed to me to be in disarray. The coming of the invaders had upset the structure of our society, liberating from their tasks great blocs of people, in some cases whole guilds. I saw dozens of my fellow Watchers in the streets, some still dragging about with them their cases of instruments, others, like me, freed of that burden and scarcely knowing what to do with their hands. My guildmates looked glum and hollow; many of them were dull-eyed with carousing, now that all discipline was shattered. Then there were Sentinels, aimless and dispirited because they had nothing to guard, and Defenders, cowed and dazed at the ending of defense. I saw no Masters and of course no Dominators, but many unemployed Clowns, Musicians, Scribes, and other court functionaries drifted randomly. Also there were hordes of dull neuters, their nearly mindless bodies slumped from unfamiliar disuse. Only Vendors and Somnambulists seemed to be carrying on business as usual.

The invaders were very much in evidence. In twos and threes they strolled on every street, long-limbed beings whose hands dangled nearly to their knees; their eyelids were heavy, their nostrils were hidden in filtration pouches, their lips were full and, when not apart, joined almost seamlessly. Most of them were dressed in identical robes of a deep, rich green, perhaps a uniform of military occupation; a few carried weapons of an oddly primitive kind, great heavy things slung across their backs, probably more for display than for self-defense. They seemed generally relaxed as they moved among us – genial conquerors, self-confident and proud, fearing no molestation from the defeated populace. Yet the fact that they never walked alone argued that they felt an inner wariness. I could not find it in me to resent their presence, nor even the implied arrogance of their possessive glances at the ancient monuments of Perris; yet the Prince of Roum, to whom all figures were merely upright bars of dark gray against a field of light gray, instinctively sensed their nearness to him and reacted with quick hostile intakes of breath.

Also there were many more outworld visitors than usual, star-beings of a hundred kinds, some able to breathe our air, others going about in hermetic globes or little pyramid-shaped breathing-boxes or contour suits. It was nothing new to see such strangers on Earth, of course, but the sheer quantity of them was astonishing. They were everywhere, prowling into the houses of Earth's old religion, buying shining models of the Tower of Perris from Vendors at street corners, clambering precariously into the upper levels of the walkways, peering into occupied dwellings, snapping images, exchanging currency with furtive hucksters, flirting with Fliers and Somnambulists, risking their lives at our restaurants, moving in shepherded groups from sight to sight. It was as though our invaders had passed the word through the galaxies: SEE OLD EARTH NOW. UNDER NEW MANAGEMENT.

At least our beggars were flourishing. The outworld ones fared poorly at the hands of the alien almsgivers, but those who were Earthborn did well, except for the Changelings, who could not be recognized as native stock. I saw several of these mutants, disgruntled at being refused, turn on other beggars who had had better luck and beat them to the ground, while image-snappers recorded the scene for the delight of galactic stay-at-homes.

We came in time to the Hall of Rememberers.

It was an imposing building, as well it might be, housing as it did all our planet's past. It rose to an enormous height on the southern bank of the Senn, just opposite the equally massive palace of the Comt. But the dwelling of the deposed Comt was an ancient building, truly ancient, of the First Cycle even, a long, involuted structure of gray stone with a green metal roof in the traditional Perrisian style, while the Hall of Rememberers was a shaft of polished whiteness, its surface unbroken by windows, about which there coiled from summit to base a golden helix of burnished metal that bore inscribed on it the history of mankind. The upper coils of the helix were blank. At a distance I could read nothing, and I wondered whether the Rememberers had taken the trouble to inscribe upon their building the tale of Earth's final defeat. Later I learned that they had not – that the story, in fact, terminated at the end of the Second Cycle, leaving untold much for which little pleasure was felt.

Night was falling now. And Perris, which had looked so dreary in the clouded and drizzly day, came to beauty like a dowager returning from Jorslem with her youth and volup-tuousness restored. The city's lights cast a soft but dazzling radiance that magically illuminated the old gray buildings, turning angles hazy, hiding antiquity's grime, blurring ugliness into poetry. The Comt's palace was transformed from a heavy thing of sprawling bulk into an airy fable. The Tower of Perris, spotlighted against the dusk, loomed above us to the east like a giant gaunt spider, but a spider of grace and charm. The whiteness of the Hall of Rememberers was now intolerably beautiful, and the helical coil of history no longer seemed to wind to the summit, but plunged directly into one's heart. The Fliers of Perris were abroad at this hour, taking their ease above us in a graceful ballet, their filmy wings spread wide

to catch the light from below, their slender bodies trailing at
an angle to the horizon. How they soared, these genetically
altered children of Earth, these fortunate members of a guild
that demands only that its members find pleasure in life!
They shed beauty upon the groundlings like little moons.
They were joined in their airborne dance by invaders, flying
in some method unknown to me, their lengthy limbs drawn
close to their bodies. I noticed that the Fliers showed no
distaste for those who had come to share their sport, but
rather appeared to welcome the outworlders, allowing them
places in the dance.

Higher, on the backdrop of the sky itself, whirled the two
false moons, blank and burnished, skimming from west to
east; and blobs of disciplined light swirled in mid-atmosphere
in what I supposed was a customary Perrisian diversion;
and speakers floating beneath the clouds showered us with
sparkling music. I heard the laughter of girls from somewhere;
I scented bubbling wine. If this is Perris conquered, I wondered,
what must Perris free have been like?

'Are we at the Hall of Rememberers?' asked Prince Enric
testily.

'This is it, yes,' I replied. 'A tower of white.'

'I know what it looks like, idiot! But now – I see less well
after dark – that building there?'

'You point to the palace of the Comt, Majesty.'

'There, then.'

'Yes.'

'Why have we not gone in?'

'I am seeing Perris,' I said. 'I have never known such beauty.
Roum is attractive too, in a different way. Roum is an emperor;
Perris is a courtesan.'

'You talk poetry, you shriveled old man!'

'I feel my age dropping away. I could dance in the streets
now. This city sings to me.'

'Go in. Go in. We are here to see the Rememberers. Let it
sing to you later.'

I sighed and guided him toward the entrance to the great

hall. We passed up a walkway of some black glossy stone, while beams of light played down on us, scanning us and recording us. A monstrous ebon door, five men wide and ten men high, proved to be only a projected illusion, for as we neared it I sensed the depth of it, saw its vaulted interior, and knew it for a deception. I felt a vague warmth and tasted a strange perfume as we passed through it.

Within was a mammoth antechamber nearly as awesome as the grand inner space of the palace of the Prince of Roum. All was white, the stone glowing with an inner radiance that bathed everything in brilliance. To right and left, heavy doorways led to inner wings. Although night had come, many individuals were clustered about access banks mounted on the rear wall of the antechamber, where screens and caps gave them contact with the massive files of the guild of Rememberers. I noticed with interest that many of those who had come here with questions about mankind's past were invaders.

Our footsteps crackled on the tiled floor as we crossed it.

I saw no actual Rememberers, and so I went to an access bank, put on a thinking cap, and notified the embalmed brain to which it was connected that I sought the Rememberer Basil, he whom I had met briefly in Roum.

'What is your business with him?'

'I bring with me his shawl, which he left in my care when he fled Roum.'

'The Rememberer Basil has returned to Roum to complete his research, by permission of the conqueror. I will send to you another member of the guild to receive the shawl.'

We did not have long to wait. We stood together near the rear of the antechamber, and I contemplated the spectacle of the invaders who had so much to learn, and in moments there came to us a thick-set, dour-faced man some years younger than myself, but yet not young, who wore about his broad shoulders the ceremonial shawl of his guild.

'I am the Rememberer Elegro,' he announced portentously.

'I bring you Basil's shawl.'

'Come. Follow.'

He had emerged from an imperceptible place in the wall where a sliding block turned on pivots. Now he slid it once more and rapidly went down a passageway. I called out to him that my companion was blind and could not match his pace, and the Rememberer Elegro halted, looking visibly impatient. His downcurving mouth twitched, and he buried his short fingers in the deep black curls of his beard. When we had caught up with him he moved on less swiftly. We pursued an infinity of passageways and ended in Elegro's domicile, somewhere high in the tower.

The room was dark but amply furnished with screens, caps, scribing equipment, voice-boxes, and other aids to scholarship. The walls were hung with a purple-black fabric, evidently alive, for its marginal folds rippled in pulsating rhythms. Three drifting globes gave less than ample light.

'The shawl,' he said.

I produced it from my pouch. It had amused me to wear it for a while in those first confused days of the conquest – after all, Basil had left it in my hands when he fled down the street, and I had not meant to wrest it from him, but he obviously had cared little for its loss – but shortly I had put it away, since it bred confusion for a man in Watcher's garb to wear a Rememberer's shawl. Elegro took it from me curtly and unfolded it, scrutinizing it as though looking for lice.

'How did you get this?'

'Basil and I encountered one another in the street during the actual moment of the invasion. He was highly agitated. I attempted to restrain him and he ran past me, leaving me still grasping his shawl.'

'He told a different story.'

'I regret if I have compromised him,' I said.

'At any rate, you have returned his shawl. I'll communicate the news to Roum tonight. Are you expecting a reward for delivering it?'

'Yes.'

Displeased, Elegro said, 'Which is?'

'To be allowed to come among the Rememberers as an apprentice.'

He looked startled. 'You have a guild!'

'To be a Watcher in these days is to be guildless. For what should I watch? I am released from my vows.'

'Perhaps. But you are old to be trying a new guild.'

'Not *too* old.'

'Ours is a difficult one.'

'I am willing to work hard. I desire to learn. In my old age curiosity is born in me.'

'Become a Pilgrim like your friend here. See the world.'

'I have seen the world. Now I wish to join the Rememberers and learn of the past.'

'You can dial an information below. Our access banks are open to you, Watcher.'

'It is not the same. Enroll me.'

'Apprentice yourself to the Indexers,' Elegro suggested. 'The work is similar, but not so demanding.'

'I claim apprenticeship here.'

Elegro sighed heavily. He steepled his fingers, bowed his head, quirked his lips. This was plainly unique to him. While he pondered, an inner door opened and a female Rememberer entered the room, carrying a small turquoise music-sphere cradled in both her hands. She took four paces and halted, obviously surprised that Elegro was entertaining visitors.

She made a nod of apology and said, 'I will return later.'

'Stay,' said the Rememberer. To myself and the Prince he said, 'My wife. The Rememberer Olmayne.' To his wife he said, 'These are travelers newly come from Roum. They have delivered Basil's shawl. The Watcher now asks apprenticeship in our guild. What do you advise?'

The Rememberer Olmayne's white brow furrowed. She put down her music-sphere in a dark crystal vase; the sphere was unintentionally activated as she did so, and it offered us a dozen shimmering notes before she switched it off. Then she contemplated us, and I her. She was notably younger than her husband, who was of middle years, while she seemed to be hardly past first bloom. Yet there was a strength about her that argued for greater maturity. Perhaps, I thought, she had been to Jorslem to renew her youth; but in that case it was odd that her husband had not done the same, unless he prized his look of age. She was surely attractive. Her face was broad, with a high forehead, pronounced cheekbones, a wide, sensual mouth, a jutting chin. Her hair was lustrous black, constrasting most vividly with the pallor of her skin. Such white skin is a rarity among us, though now I know that it was more common in ancient times, when the breed was different. Avluela, my lovely little Flier, had displayed that same combination of black and white, but there the resemblance ended, for Avluela was all fragility, and the Rememberer Olmayne was strength itself. Below her long slender neck her body blossomed into well-set shoulders, high breasts, firm legs. Her posture was regal.

She studied us at length, until I could scarcely meet the level gaze of her widely spaced dark eyes. Ultimately she said, 'Does the Watcher regard himself as qualified to become one of us?'

The question appeared aimed at anyone in the chamber who cared to reply. I hesitated; Elegro did likewise; and at length it was the Prince of Roum who replied in his voice of command, 'The Watcher is qualified to enter your guild.'

'And who are you?' Olmayne demanded.

Instantly the Prince adopted a more accommodating tone. 'A miserable blind Pilgrim, milady, who has wandered here on foot from Roum, in this man's company. If I am any judge, you could do worse than admit him as an apprentice.'

Elegro said, 'And yourself? What plans have you?'

'I wish only refuge here,' said the Prince. 'I am tired of roaming and there is much thinking I must do. Perhaps you could allow me to carry out small tasks here. I would not want to be separated from my companion.'

To me Olmayne said, 'We will confer on your case. If there is approval, you will be given the tests. I will be your sponsor.'

'Olmayne!' blurted Elegro in unmistakable amazement.

She smiled serenely at us all.

A family quarrel appeared on the verge; but it was averted, and the Rememberers offered us hospitality, juices, sharper beverages, a night's lodging. We dined apart from them in one section of their suite, while other Rememberers were summoned to consider my irregular application. The Prince seemed in strange agitation; he bolted down his food, spilled a flask of wine, fumbled with his eating utensils, put his fingers again and again to his gray metallic eyeballs as though trying to scratch an itch upon the lobes of his brain.

At length he said in a low, urgent voice, 'Describe her to me!'

I did so, in detail, coloring and shading my words to draw him the most vivid pictures I could.

'She is beautiful, you say?'

'I believe so. You know that at my age one must work from abstract notions, not from the flow of the glands.'

'Her voice arouses me,' said the Prince. 'She has power. She is queenly. She *must* be beautiful; there'd be no justice if her body failed to match the voice.'

'She is,' I said heavily, 'another man's wife, and the giver of hospitality.'

I remembered a day in Roum when the Prince's palanquin had come forth from the palace, and the Prince had spied Avluela, and ordered her to him, drawing her through the curtain to make use of her. A Dominator may command lesser folk that way; but a Pilgrim may not, and I feared Prince Enric's schemes now. He dabbed at his eyes again. His facial muscles worked.

'Promise me you'll not start trouble with her,' I said.

The corner of his mouth jerked in what must have been the beginning of an angry retort, quickly stifled. With effort he said, 'You misjudge me, old man. I'll abide by the laws of hospitality here. Be a good man and get me more wine, eh?'

I thumbed the serving niche and obtained a second flask. It was strong red wine, not the golden stuff of Roum. I poured;

we drank; the flask was swiftly empty. I grasped it along its lines of polarity and gave it the proper twist, and it popped and was gone like a bubble. Moments later the Rememberer Olmayne entered. She had changed her garments; earlier she had worn an afternoon gown of dull hue and coarse fabric, but now she was garbed in a sheer scarlet robe fastened between her breasts. It revealed to me the planes and shadows of her body, and it surprised me to see that she had chosen to retain a navel. It broke the smooth downward sweep of her belly in an effect so carefully calculated to arouse that it nearly incited even me.

She said complacently, 'Your application has been approved under my sponsorship. The tests will be administered tonight. If you succeed, you will be pledged to our division.' Her eyes twinkled in sudden mischief. 'My husband, you should know, is most displeased. But my husband's displeasure is not a thing to be feared. Come with me, both of you.'

She stretched forth her hands, taking mine, taking the Prince's. Her fingers were cool. I throbbed with an inner fever and marveled at this sign of new youth that arose within me – not even by virtue of the waters of the house of renewal in sacred Jorslem.

'Come,' said Olmayne, and led us to the place of test.

THREE

And so I passed into the guild of Rememberers.

The tests were perfunctory. Olmayne brought us to a circular room somewhere near the summit of the great tower. Its curving walls were inlaid with rare woods of many hues, and shining benches rose from the floor, and in the center of all was a helix the height of a man, inscribed with letters too small to be read. Half a dozen Rememberers lounged about, plainly there only by Olmayne's whim, and not in the slightest interested in this old and shabby Watcher whom she had so unaccountably sponsored.

A thinking cap was offered me. A scratchy voice asked me a dozen questions through the cap, probing for my typical responses, querying me on biographical details. I gave my guild identification so that they could contact the local guildmaster, check my *bona fides*, and obtain my release. Ordinarily one could not win release from a Watcher's vows, but these were not ordinary times, and I knew my guild was shattered.

Within an hour all was done. Olmayne herself placed the shawl over my shoulders.

'You'll be given sleeping quarters near our suite,' she said. 'You'll have to surrender your Watcher garb, though your friend may remain in Pilgrim's clothes. Your training will begin after a probationary period. Meanwhile you have full access to any of our memory tanks. You realize, of course, that it will be ten years or more before you can win full admission to the guild.'

'I realize that,' I said.

'Your name now will be Tomis,' Olmayne told me. 'Not yet the Rememberer Tomis, but Tomis of the Rememberers. There is a difference. Your past name no longer matters.'

The Prince and I were conducted to the small room we would share. It was a humble enough place, but yet it had facilities for washing, outlets for thinking caps and other information devices, and a food vent. Prince Enric went about the room, touching things, learning the geography. Cabinets, beds, chairs, storage units, and other furniture popped in and out of the walls as he blundered onto the controls. Eventually he was satisfied; not blundering now, he activated a bed, and a sheaf of brightness glided from a slot. He stretched out.

'Tell me something, Tomis of the Rememberers.'

'Yes?'

'To satisfy curiosity that eats me. What was your name in previous life?'

'It does not matter now.'

'No vows bind you to secrecy. Will you thwart me still?'

'Old habit binds me,' I said. 'For twice your lifetime I was conditioned never to speak my name except lawfully.'

'Speak it now.'

'Wuellig,' I said.

It was strangely liberating to commit that act. My former name seemed to hover in the air before my lips; to dart from the room like a jewelbird released from its captivity; to soar, to turn sharply, to strike a wall and shiver to pieces with a light, tinkling sound. I trembled, 'Wuellig,' I said again. 'My name was Wuellig.'

'Wuellig no more.'

'Tomis of the Rememberers.'

And we both laughed until it hurt, and the blinded Prince swung himself to his feet and slapped his hand against mine in high good fellowship, and we shouted my name and his and mine again and again, like small boys who suddenly have learned the words of power and have discovered at last how little power those words really have.

Thus I took up my new life among the Rememberers.

For some time to come I did not leave the Hall of Rememberers at all. My days and nights were completely occupied, and I remained a stranger to Perris without. The Prince, too, though his time was not as fully taken up, stayed in the building almost always, going out only when boredom or fury overtook him. Occasionally the Rememberer Olmayne went with him, or he with her, so that he would not be alone in his darkness; but I know that on occasion he left the building by himself, defiantly intending to show that, even sightless, he could cope with the challenges of the city.

My waking hours were divided among these activities:

+ Primary orientations.

+ Menial duties of an apprentice.

+ Private researches.

Not unexpectedly, I found myself much older than the other apprentices then in residence. Most were youngsters, the children of Rememberers themselves; they looked upon me in bafflement, unable to comprehend having such an ancient for a schoolmate. There were a few fairly mature apprentices, those who had found a vocation for Remembering midway in life, but none approaching my age. Hence I had little social contact with my fellows in training.

For a part of each day we learned the techniques by which the Rememberers recapture Earth's past. I was shown wide-eyed through the laboratories where analysis of field specimens is performed; I saw the detectors which, by pinpointing the decay of a few atoms, give an age to an artifact; I watched as beams of many-colored light lancing from a ringed outlet turned a sliver of wood to ash and caused it to give up its secrets; I saw the very images of past events peeled from inanimate substance. We leave our imprint where we go: the particles of light rebound from our faces, and the photonic flux nails them to the environment. From which the Rememberers strip them, categorize them, fix them. I entered a room where a phantasmagoria of faces drifted on a greasy blue mist: vanished kings and guild-masters, lost dukes, heroes of ancient days. I beheld cold-eyed technicians prodding history from handfuls of charred matter. I saw damp lumps of trash give up tales of revolutions and assassinations, of cultural change, of the discarding of mores.

Then I was instructed superficially in the techniques of the field. Through cunning simulation I was shown Rememberers at work with vacuum cores digging through the mounds of the great ruined cities of Afreek and Ais. I participated vicariously in the undersea quest for the remnants of the civilizations of the Lost Continents; teams of Rememberers entered translucent, teardrop-shaped vehicles like blobs of green gelatin and sped into the depths of Earth Ocean, down and down to the slime-crusted prairies of the former land and with dancing beams of violet force, they drilled through muck and girders to find buried truths. I watched the gatherers of shards, the diggers of shadows, the collectors of molecular films. One of the best of the orientation experiences they provided was a sequence in which truly heroic Rememberers excavated a weather machine in lower Afreek, baring the base of the titanic thing, lifting it on power pulls from the soil, an extraction so mighty that the earth itself seemed to shriek when it was done. High aloft they floated the ponderous relic of Second Cycle folly, while shawled experts prodded in its root-place to learn how the column had been erected in the first instance. My eyes throbbed at the spectacle.

I emerged from the sessions with an overwhelming awe for this guild I had chosen. Individual Rememberers whom I had known had struck me generally as pompous, disdainful, haughty, or merely aloof; I did not find them charming. Yet is the whole greater than the sum of its parts, and I saw such men as Basil and Elegro, so vacant, so absent from ordinary human concerns, so disinterested, as part of a colossal effort to win back from eternity our brilliant yesterdays. This research into lost time was magnificent, the only proper substitute for mankind's former activities; having lost our present and our future, we had of necessity to bend all our endeavors to the past, which no one could take from us if only we were vigilant enough.

For many days I absorbed the details of this effort, every stage of the work from the collection of specks of dust in the field through their treatment and analysis in the laboratory to the highest endeavor of all, synthesis and interpretation, which was carried out by senior Rememberers on the highest level of this building. I was given but a glimpse of those sages: withered and dry, old enough to be grandfathers to me, white heads bent forward, thin lips droning comments and interpretations, quibbles and corrections. Some of them, I was told in a hushed whisper, had been renewed at Jorslem two and three times apiece, and now were beyond renewal and in their final great age.

Next we were introduced to the memory tanks where the Rememberers store their findings, and from which are dispensed informations for the benefit of the curious.

As a Watcher I had had little curiosity and less interest in visiting memory tanks. Certainly I had never seen anything like this, for the tanks of the Rememberers were no mere

three-brain or five-brain storage units, but mammoth installations with a hundred brains or more hooked in series. The
room to which they took us – one of dozens beneath the
building, I learned – was an oblong chamber, deep but not
high, in which brain cases were arrayed in rows of nine that
faded into shadowed depths. Perspective played odd tricks; I
was not sure if there were ten rows or fifty, and the sight of
those bleached domes was overpoweringly immense.

'Are these the brains of former Rememberers?' I asked.

The guide replied, 'Some of them are. But there's no
necessity to use only Rememberers. Any normal human
brain will do; even a Servitor has more storage capacity
than you'd believe. We have no need for redundancy in our
circuits, and so we can use the full resources of each brain.'

I tried to peer through the heavy block of sleekness that
protected the memory tanks from harm. I said, 'What is
recorded in this particular room?'

'The names of dwellers in Afreek in Second Cycle times,
and as much personal data about each as we have so far
recovered. Also, since these cells are not fully charged, we
have temporarily stored in them certain geographical details
concerning the Lost Continents, and information pertaining
to the creation of Land Bridge.'

'Can such information be easily transferred from temporary
storage to permanent?' I asked.

'Easily, yes. Everything is electromagnetic here. Our facts
are aggregates of charges; we shift them from brain to brain
by reversing polarities.'

'What if there were an electrical failure?' I demanded. 'You
say you have no redundancy here. Is there no possibility of
losing data through some accident?'

'None,' said the guide smoothly. 'We have a series of fallback
devices to insure continuity of power. And by using organic
tissue for our storage cells, we have the best assurance of
safety of all: for the brains themselves will retain their data
in the event of a power interruption. It would be taxing but
not impossible to recapture their contents.'

'During the invasion,' I said, 'were difficulties experienced?'

'We are under the protection of the invaders, who regard our work as vital to their own interests.'

Not long afterward, at a general convocation of the Rememberers, we apprentices were permitted to look on from a balcony of the guildhall; below us, in full majesty, were the guild members, shawls in place, Elegro and Olmayne among them. On a dais that bore the helical symbol was Chancellor Kenishal of the Rememberers, an austere and commanding figure, and beside him was an even more conspicuous personage who was of the species that had conquered Earth. Kenishal spoke briefly. The resonance of his voice did not entirely conceal ths hollowness of his words; like all administrators everywhere, he gushed platitudes, praising himself by implication as he congratulated his guild for its notable work. Then he introduced the invader.

The alien stretched forth his arms until they seemed to touch the walls of the auditorium.

'I am Manrule Seven,' he said quietly. 'I am Procurator of Perris, with particular responsibility for the guild of Rememberers. My purpose here today is to confirm the decree of the provisional occupational government. You Rememberers are to go totally unhampered in your work. You are to have free access to all sites on this planet or on any other planet or on any other world that may have bearing on your mastery of the past of this planet. All files are to remain open to you, except those pertaining to the organization of the conquest itself. Chancellor Kenishal has informed me that the conquest lies outside the scope of your present research in any case, so no hardship will be worked. We of the occupying government are aware of the value of the work of your guild. The history of this planet is of great significance, and we wish your efforts continued.'

'To make Earth a better tourist attraction,' said the Prince of Roum bitterly at my side.

Manrule Seven went on, 'The Chancellor has requested me to inform you of one administrative change that will necessarily follow from the occupied status of your planet. In the past, all disputes among you were settled by the courts of your own guild, with Chancellor Kenishal having the highest right of appeal. For the sake of efficient administration it now becomes mandatory for us to impose our jurisdiction over that of the guild. Therefore the Chancellor will transfer to us those litigations which he feels no longer fall into his sphere of authority.'

The Rememberers gasped. There was a sudden shifting of postures and exchanging of glances on the floor below.

'The Chancellor's abdicating!' blurted an apprentice near me.'

'What choice does he have, fool?' another whispered harshly.

The meeting broke up in some confusion. Rememberers flooded into the hallways, gesticulating, debating, expostulating. One venerable wearer of the shawl was so shaken that he crouched down and began to make the series of stabilizer responses, heedless of the throng. The tide swept over us apprentices, forcing us back. I attempted to protect the Prince, fearing that he would be thrown to the floor and trampled; but we were swept apart and I lost sight of him for minutes. When I saw him again he stood with the Rememberer Olmayne. Her face was flushed, her eyes were bright; she was speaking rapidly, and the Prince was listening. His hand clung to her elbow as if for support.

FOUR

After the conclusion of the early period of orientations, I was given trivial tasks. Chiefly I was asked to do things that in an earlier time would have been performed wholly by machine: for example, to monitor the feed lines that oozed nutrients into the brain-boxes of the memory tanks. For several hours each day I walked through the narrow corridor of the inspection panels, searching for clogged lines. It had been so devised that when a line became blocked, a stress pattern was created the length of the clear tubing that contained it, and beams of a special polarised light illuminated that pattern for benefit of the inspector. I did my humble task, now and again finding a blockage, and I did other little jobs as befitted my status of apprenticeship.

However, I also had the opportunity to pursue my own investigations into the events of my planet's past.

Sometimes one does not learn the value of things until they are lost. For a lifetime I served as a Watcher, striving to give early warning of a promised invasion of Earth, while caring little who might wish to invade us, or why. For a lifetime I realised dimly that Earth had known grander days than those of the Third Cycle into which I had been born, and yet I sought no knowledge of what those days had been like and of the reasons of our present diminished condition. Only when the starships of the invaders blossomed in the sky did I feel a sudden hunger to know of that lost past. Now, as the most elderly of apprentices, I, Tomis of the Rememberers rummaged through the archives of vanished time.

Any citizen has the right to go to a public thinking cap and requisition an information from the Rememberers on any given subject. Nothing is concealed. But the Rememberers volunteer no aid; you must know how to ask, which means you must know what to ask. Item by item you must seek your facts. It is useful for those who must know, say, the long-term patterns of climate in Agupt, or the symbols of the crystallisation disease, or the limitations in the charter of one of the guilds; but it is no help at all to the man who wishes knowledge of the larger questions. One would need to requisition a thousand informations merely to make a beginning. The expense would be great; few would bother.

As an apprentice Rememberer I had full access to all data. More important, I had access to the indexes. The Indexers are a guild subsidiary to the Rememberers, a donkey-guild of drudges who record and classify that which they often do not understand; the end product of their toil serves the greater guild, but the indexes are not open to all. Without them one scarcely is able to cope with the problems of research. I will not summarise the stages by which I came by my knowledge – the hours spent shuffling through interwoven corridors, the rebuffs, the bewilderments, the throbbing of the brain. As a foolish novice I was at the mercy of pranksters, and many a fellow apprentice, even a guild member or two, led me astray for the sheer wicked joy of it. But I learned which routes to follow, how to set up sequences of questions, how to follow a path of references higher and higher until the truth bursts dazzlingly upon one. With persistence rather than with great intellect I wrung from the files of the Rememberers a coherent tale of the downfall of man.

This:

There was a time in ages past when life on Earth was brutal and primitive. We call this time the First Cycle. I do not speak of the period before civilisation, that time of grunting and hairiness, of caves and stone tools. We consider the First Cycle to have commenced when man first learned to record information and to control environment. This occurred in Agupt and Sumir. By our way of reckoning the First Cycle commenced some 40,000 years ago – however, we are uncertain of its true length in its own terms, since the span of the year was altered at the end of the Second Cycle, and we have been unable thus far to determine how long, in previous eras, it took for our world to circle its sun. Somewhat longer than at present, perhaps.

The First Cycle was the time of Imperial Roum and of the first flowering of Jorslem. Eyrop remained savage long after Ais and parts of Afreek were civilised. In the west, two great continents occupied much of Earth Ocean, and these too were held by savages.

It is understood that in this cycle mankind had no contact with other worlds or stars. Such solitude is difficult to comprehend, but yet so it occurred. Mankind had no way of creating light except through fire; he could not cure his ills; life was not susceptible to renewal. It was a time without comforts, a gay time, harsh in its simplicity. Death came early; one barely had time to scatter a few sons about, and one was carried off. One lived with fear, but mostly not fear of real things.

The soul recoils from such an era. But yet it is true that in the First Cycle magnificent cities were founded – Roum, Perris, Atin, Jorslem – and splendid deeds were accomplished. One stands in awe of those ancestors, foul-smelling (no doubt), illiterate, without machines, and still capable of coming to terms with their universe and to some extent of mastering it.

War and grief were constant throughout the First Cycle.

Destruction and creation were nearly simultaneous. Flames ate man's most glorious cities. Chaos threatened always to engulf order. How could men have endured such conditions for thousands of years?

Towards the close of the First Cycle much of the primitivism was outgrown. At last sources of power were accessible to man; there was the beginning of true transportation; communications over distances became possible; many inventions transformed the world in a short time. Methods of making war kept pace with the technological growth in other directions; but total catastrophe was averted, although several times it appeared to have arrived. It was during the final phase of the cycle that the Lost Continents were colonised, also Stralya, and that first contact was made with the adjoining planets of our solar system.

The transition from First Cycle to Second is arbitrarily fixed at the point when man first encountered intelligent beings from distant worlds. This, the Rememberers now believe, took place less than fifty generations after the First Cycle folk had mastered electronic and nuclear energy. Thus we may rightly say that the early people of Earth stumbled headlong from savagery to galactic contact – or, perhaps, that they crossed that gap in a few quick strides.

This too is cause for pride. For if the First Cycle was great despite its handicaps, the Second Cycle knew of no handicaps and achieved miracles.

In this epoch mankind spread out to the stars, and the stars came to mankind. Earth was a market for goods of all worlds. Wonders were commonplace. One might hope to live for hundreds of years; eyes, hearts, lungs, kidneys were replaced as easily as shoes; the air was pure, no man went hungry, war was forgotten. Machines of every sort served man. But the machines were not enough, and so the Second Cycle folk bred men who were machines, or machines who were men: creatures that were genetically human, but were born artificially, and were treated with drugs that prevented the permanent storing of memories. These creatures, analogous to our neuters, were capable of performing an efficient day's work, but were unable to build up that permanent body of experiences, memories, expectations, and abilities that is the mark of a human soul. Millions of such not-quite humans handled the duller tasks of the day, freeing others for lives of glistening fulfillment. After the creation of the subhumans came the creation of the superanimals who, through biochemical manipulation of the brain, were able to carry out tasks once beyond the capacity of their species: dogs, cats, mice, and cattle were enrolled in the labour force, while certain high primates received functions formerly reserved for humans. Through this exploitation of the environment to the fullest, man created a paradise on Earth.

The spirit of man soared to the loftiest peak it had known. Poets, scholars, and scientists made splendid contributions. Shining cities sprawled across the land. The population was enormous, and even so, there was ample room for all, with no shortage of resources. One could indulge one's whims to any extent; there was much experimentation with genetic surgery and with mutagenetic and teratogenetic drugs, so that the human species adopted many new forms. There was, however, nothing yet like the variant forms of our cycle.

Across the sky in stately procession moved space stations serving every imaginable need. It was at this time that the two new moons were built, although the Rememberers have not yet determined whether their purpose was functional or esthetic. The auroras that now appear each night in the sky may have been installed at this time, although some factions of Rememberers argue that the presence of temperate-zone auroras began with the geophysical upheavals that heralded the close of the cycle.

It was, at any rate, the finest of times to be alive.

'See Earth and die,' was the watchword of the outworlders. No one making the galactic grand tour dared pass up this planet of miracles. We welcomed the strangers, accepted their compliments and their money, made them comfortable in the ways they preferred, and proudly displayed our greatnesses.

The Prince of Roum can testify that it is the fate of the mighty eventually to be humbled, and also that the higher one reaches for splendor, the more catastrophic one's downfall is apt to be. After some thousands of years of glories beyond my capacity to comprehend, the fortunate ones of the Second Cycle overreached themselves and committed two misdeeds, one born of foolish arrogance, the other born of excessive confidence. Earth is paying yet for those overreachings.

The effects of the first were slow to be felt. It was a function of Earth's attitude toward the other species of the galaxy, which had shifted during the Second Cycle from awe to matter-of-fact acceptance to contempt. At the beginning of the cycle, brash and naive Earth had erupted into a galaxy already peopled by advanced races that long had been in contact with one another. This could well have produced a soul-crushing trauma, but instead it generated an aggressive urge to excel and surpass. And so it happened that Earthmen quickly came to look upon most of the galactics as equals, and then, as progress continued on Earth, as inferiors. This bred the easy habit of contempt for the backward.

Thus it was proposed to establish 'study compounds' on Earth for specimens of inferior races. These compounds would reproduce the natural habitat of the races and would be accessible to scholars wishing to observe the life-processes of these races. However, the expense of collecting and maintaining the specimens was such that it quickly became necessary to open the compounds to the public at large, for purposes of amusement. These supposedly scientific compounds were, in fact, zoos for other intelligent species.

At the outset only the truly alien beings were collected, those so remote from human biological or psychological norms that there was little danger of regarding them as 'people.' A many-limbed being that dwells in a tank of methane under high pressure does not strike a sympathetic response from those likely to object to the captivity of intelligent creatures. If that methane-dweller happens to have a complex civilization of a sort uniquely fitted to its environment, it can be argued that it is all the more important to duplicate that environment on Earth so that one can study so strange a civilization. Therefore the early compounds contained only the bizarre. The collectors were limited, also, to taking creatures who had not attained the stage of galactic travel themselves. It would not have been good form to kidnap life-forms whose relatives were among the interstellar tourists on whom our world's economy had come so heavily to depend.

The success of the first compounds led to the demand for the formation of others. Less critical standards were imposed; not merely the utterly alien and grotesque were collected, but samplings of any sort of galactic life not in a position to register diplomatic protests. And, as the audacity of our ancestors increased, so did the restrictions on collection loosen, until there were samplings from a thousand worlds on Earth, including some whose civilizations were older and more intricate than our own.

The archives of the Rememberers show that the expansion of our compounds stirred some agitation in many parts of the universe. We were denounced as marauders, kidnappers, and pirates; committees were formed to criticize our wanton disregard for the rights of sentient beings; Earthmen traveling to other planets were occasionally beset by mobs of hostile life-forms demanding that we free the prisoners of the compounds at once. However, these protesters were only a minority – most galactics kept an uncomfortable silence about our compounds. They regretted the barbarity of them, and nevertheless made a point of touring them when they visited Earth. Where else, after all, could one see hundreds of life-forms, culled from every part of the universe, in a few days? Our compounds were a major attraction, one of the wonders of the cosmos. By silent conspiracy our neighbors in the galaxy winked at the amorality of the basic concept in order to share the pleasure of inspecting the prisoners.

There is in the archives of the Rememberers a memory-tank entry of a visit to a compound area. It is one of the oldest visual records possessed by the guild, and I obtained a look at it only with great difficulty and upon the direct intercession of the Rememberer Olmayne. Despite the use of a double filter in the cap, one sees the scene only blurredly; but yet it is clear enough. Behind a curved shield of a transparent material are fifty or more beings of an unnamed world. Their bodies are pyramidial, with dark blue surfaces and pink visual areas at each vertex; they walk upon short, thick legs; they have one pair of grasping limbs on each face. Though it is risky to attempt to interpret the inner feelings of extraterrestrial beings, one can clearly sense a mood of utter despair in these creatures. Through the murky green gases of their environment they move slowly, numbly, without animation. Several have joined tips in what must be communication. One appears newly dead. Two are bowed to the ground like tumbled toys, but their limbs move in what perhaps is prayer. It is a dismal scene. Later, I discovered other such records in neglected corners of the building. They taught me much.

For more than a thousand Second Cycle years the growth of these compounds continued unchecked, until it came to seem logical and natural to all except the victims that Earth should practice these cruelties in the name of science. Then, upon a distant world not previously visited by Earthmen, there were discovered certain beings of a primitive kind, comparable perhaps to Earthmen in early First Cycle days. These beings were roughly humanoid in form, undeniably intelligent, and fiercely savage. At the loss of several Earthborn lives, a collecting team acquired a breeding colony of these people and transported them to Earth to be placed in a compound.

This was the first of the Second Cycle's two fatal errors.

At the time of the kidnapping, the beings of this other world – which is never named in the records, but known only by the code designation H362 – were in no position to protest or to take punitive steps. But shortly they were visited by emissaries from certain other worlds aligned politically against Earth. Under the guidance of these emissaries, the beings of H362 requested the return of their people. Earth refused, citing the long precedent of interstallar condonement of the compounds. Lengthy diplomatic representations followed, in the course of which Earth simply reaffirmed its right to have acted in such a fashion.

The people of H362 responded with threats. 'One day,' they said, 'we will cause you to regret this. We will invade and conquer your planet, set free all the inhabitants of the compounds, and turn Earth itself into a gigantic compound for its own people.'

Under the circumstances this appeared quite amusing.

Little more was heard of the outraged inhabitants of H362 over the next few millennia. They were progressing rapidly, in their distant part of the universe, but since by all calculations it would take them a cosmic period to pose any menace to Earth, they were ignored. How could one fear spear-wielding savages?

Earth addressed itself to a new challenge: full control of the planetary climate.

Weather modification had been practiced on a small scale since late First Cycle. Clouds holding potential rain could be induced to release it; fogs could be dispelled; hail could be made less destructive. Certain steps were taken toward reducing the polar ice packs and toward making deserts more fruitful. However, these measures were strictly local and, with few exceptions, had no lasting effects on environment.

The Second Cycle endeavor involved the erection of enormous columns at more than one hundred locations around the globe. We do not know the heights of these columns, since none has survived intact and the specifications are lost, but it is thought that they equaled or exceeded the highest buildings previously constructed, and perhaps attained altitudes of two miles or more. Within these columns was equipment which was designed, among other things, to effect displacements of the poles of Earth's magnetic field.

As we understand the aim of the weather machines, it was to modify the planet's geography according to a carefully conceived plan arising from the division of what we call Earth Ocean into a number of large bodies. Although interconnected, these suboceans were considered to have individual existences, since along most of their boundary region they were cut off from the rest of Earth Ocean by land masses. In the northern Lost Continent (known as Usa-amrik) in the west and the proximity of Usa-amrik to Eyrop in the east left only narrow straits through which the polar waters could mingle with those of the warmer oceans flanking the Lost Continents.

Manipulation of magnetic forces produced a libration of Earth on its orbit, calculated to break up the north polar ice pack and permit the cold water trapped by this pack to come in contact with warmer water from elsewhere. By removing the northern ice pack and thus exposing the northern ocean to evaporation, precipitation would be greatly increased there. To prevent this precipitation from falling in the north as snow, additional manipulations were to be induced to change the pattern of the prevailing westerly winds which carried precipitation over temperate areas. A natural conduit was to be established that would bring the precipitation of the polar region to areas in lower latitudes lacking in proper moisture.

There was much more to the plan than this. Our knowledge of the details is hazy. We are aware of schemes to shift ocean currents by causing land subsidence or emergence, of proposals to deflect solar heat from the tropics to the poles, and of other rearrangements. The details are unimportant. What is significant to us are the consequences of this grandoise plan.

After a period of preparation lasting centuries and after absorbing more effort and wealth than any other project in human history, the weather machines were put into operation.

The result was devastation.

The disastrous experiment in planetary alteration resulted in a shifting of the geographical poles, a lengthy period of glacial conditions throughout most of the northern hemisphere, the unexpected submergence of Usa-amrik and Sud-amrik, its neighbor, the creation of Land Bridge joining Afreek and Eyrop, and the near destruction of human civilization. These upheavals did not take place with great speed. Evidently the project went smoothly for the first several centuries; the polar ice thawed, and the corresponding rise in sea levels was dealt with by constructing fusion evaporators – small suns, in effect – at selected oceanic points. Only slowly did it become clear that the weather machines were bringing about architectonic changes in the crust of Earth. These, unlike the climatic changes, proved irreversible.

It was a time of furious storms followed by unending droughts; of the loss of hundreds of millions of lives; of the disruption of all communications; of panicky mass migrations out of the doomed continents. Chaos triumphed. The splendid civilization of the Second Cycle was shattered. The compounds of alien life were destroyed.

For the sake of saving what remained of its population, several of the most powerful galactic races took command of our planet. They established energy pylons to stabilize Earth's axial wobble; they dismantled those weather machines that had not been destroyed by the planetary convulsions; they fed the hungry, clothed the naked, and offered reconstruction loans. For us it was a Time of Sweeping, when all the structures and conventions of society were expunged. No longer masters in our own world, we accepted the charity of strangers and crept pitifully about.

Yet, because we were still the same race we had been, we recovered to some extent. We had squandered our planet's capital and so could never again be anything but bankrupts and paupers, but in a humbler way we entered into our Third Cycle. Certain scientific techniques of earlier days still remained to us. Others were devised, working generally on different principles. Our guilds were formed to give order to society: Dominators, Master, Merchants, and the rest. The Rememberers strove to salvage what could be pulled from the wreck of the past.

Our debts to our rescuers were enormous. As bankrupts, we had no way of repaying those debts; we hoped instead for a quitclaim, a statement of absolution. Negotiations to that effect were already under way when an unexpected intervention occurred. The inhabitants of H362 approached the committee of Earth's receivers and offered to reimburse them for their expenses – in return for an assignment of all rights and claims in Earth to H362.

It was done.

H362 now regarded itself the owner by treaty of our world." It served notice to the universe at large that it reserved the right to take possession at any future date. As well it might, since at that time H362 was still incapable of interstellar travel. Thereafter, though, H362 was deemed legal possessor of the assets of Earth, as purchaser in bankruptcy.

No one failed to realize that this was H362's way of fulfilling its threat to 'turn Earth itself into a gigantic compound,' as revenge for the injury inflicted by our collecting team long before.

On Earth, Third Cycle society constituted itself along the lines it now holds, with its rigid stratification of guilds. The threat of H362 was taken seriously, for ours was a chastened world that sneered at no menace, however slight; and a guild of Watchers was devised to scan the skies for attackers. Defenders and all the rest followed. In some small ways we demonstrated our old flair for imagination, particularly in the Years of Magic, when a fanciful impulse created the self-perpetuating mutant guild of Fliers, a parallel guild of Swimmers, of whom little is heard nowadays, and several other varieties, including a troublesome and unpredictable guild of Changelings whose genetic characteristics were highly erratic.

The Watchers watched. The Dominators ruled. The Fliers soared. Life went on, year after year, in Eyrop and in Ais, in Stralya, in Afreek, in the scattered islands that were the only remnants of the Lost Continents of Usa-amrik and Sud-amrik. The vow of H362 receded into mythology, but yet we remained vigilant. And far across the cosmos our enemies gathered strength, attaining some measure of the power that had been ours in our Second Cycle. They never forgot the day when their kinsmen had been held captive in our compounds.

In a night of terror they came to us. Now they are our masters, and their vow is fulfilled, their claim asserted.

All this, and much more, I learned as I burrowed in the accumulated knowledge of the guild of Rememberers.

FIVE

Meanwhile the former Prince of Roum was wantonly abusing the hospitality of our co-sponsorer, the Rememberer Elegro. I should have been aware of what was going on, for I knew the Prince and his ways better than any other man in Perris. But I was too busy in the archives, learning of the past. While I explored the details of the Second Cycle's protoplasm files and regeneration nodules, its time-wind blowers and its photonic-flue fixers, Prince Enric was seducing the Rememberer Olmayne.

Like most seductions, I imagine that this was no great contest of wills. Olmayne was a woman of sensuality, whose attitude toward her husband was affectionate but patronizing.

She regarded Elegro openly as ineffectual, a bumbler; and Elegro, whose haughtiness and stern mien did not conceal his underlying weakness of purpose, seemed to merit her disdain. What kind of marriage they had was not my business to observe, but clearly she was the stronger, and just as clearly he could not meet her demands.

Then, too, why had Olmayne agreed to sponsor us into her guild?

Surely not out of any desire for a tattered old Watcher. It must have been the wish to know more of the strange and oddly commanding blind Pilgrim who was that Watcher's companion. From the very first, then, Olmayne must have been drawn to Prince Enric; and he, naturally, would need little encouragement to accept the gift she offered.

Possibly they were lovers almost from the moment of our arrival in the Hall of Rememberers.

I went my way, and Elegro went his, and Olmayne and Prince Enric went theirs, and summer gave way to autumn and autumn to winter. I excavated the records with passionate impatience. Never before had I known such involvement, such intensity of curiosity. Without benefit of a visit to Jorslem I felt renewed. I saw the Prince infrequently, and our meetings were generally silent; it was not my place to question him about his doings, and he felt no wish to volunteer information to me.

Occasionally I thought of my former life, and of my travels from place to place, and of the Flier Avluela who was now, I supposed, the consort of one of our conquerors. How did the false Changeling Gormon style himself, now that he had emerged from his disguise and owned himself to be one of those from H362? Earthking Nine? Oceanlord Five? Overman Three? Wherever he was, he must feel satisfaction, I thought, at the total success of the conquest of Earth.

Toward winter's end I learned of the affair between the Rememberer Olmayne and Prince Enric of Roum. I picked up whispered gossip in the apprentice quarters first; then I noticed the smiles on the faces of other Rememberers when Elegro and Olmayne were about; lastly, I observed the behavior of the Prince and Olmayne toward one another. It was obvious. Those touchings of hand to hand, those sly exchanges of catchwords and private phrases – what else could they mean?'

Among the Rememberers the marriage vow is regarded solemnly. As with Fliers, mating is for life, and one is not supposed to betray one's partner as Olmayne was doing. When one is married to a fellow Rememberer – a custom in the guild, but not universal – the union is all the more sacred.

What revenge would Elegro take when in time he learned the truth?

It happened that I was present when the situation at last crystallized into conflict. It was a night in earliest spring. I had worked long and hard in the deepest pits of the memory tanks, prying forth data that no one had bothered with since it had first been stored; and, with my head aswim with images of chaos, I walked through the glow of the Perris night, seeking fresh air. I strolled along the Senn and was accosted by an agent for a Somnambulist, who offered to sell me insight into the world of dreams. I came upon a lone Pilgrim at his devotions before a temple of flesh. I watched a pair of young Fliers in passage overhead, and shed a self-pitying tear or two. I was halted by a starborn tourist in breathing mask and jeweled tunic; he put his cratered red face close to mine and vented hallucinations in my nostrils. At length I returned to the Hall of Rememberers and went to the suite of my sponsors to pay my respects before retiring.

Olmayne and Elegro were there. So, too, was Prince Enric. Olmayne admitted me with a quick gesture of one fingertip, but took no further notice of me, nor did the others. Elegro was tensely pacing the floor, stomping about so vehemently that the delicate life-forms of the carpet folded and unfolded their petals in wild agitation. 'A Pilgrim!' Elegro cried. 'If it had been some trash of a Vendor, it would only be humiliating. But a Pilgrim? That makes it monstrous!'

Prince Enric stood with arms folded, body motionless. It

was impossible to detect the expression beneath his mask of Pilgrimage, but he appeared wholly calm.

Elegro said, 'Will you deny that you have been tampering with the sanctity of my pairing?'

'I deny nothing. I assert nothing.'

'And you?' Elegro demanded, whirling on his lady. 'Speak truth, Olmayne! For once, speak truth! What of the stories they tell of you and this Pilgrim?'

'I have heard no stories,' said Olmayne sweetly.

'That he shares your bed! That you taste potions together! That you travel to ecstasy together!'

Olmayne's smile did not waver. Her broad face was tranquil. To me she looked more beautiful than ever.

Elegro tugged in anguish at the strands of his shawl. His dour, bearded face darkened in wrath and exasperation. His hand slipped within his tunic and emerged with the tiny glossy bead of a vision capsule, which he thrust forth toward the guilty pair on the palm of his hand.

'Why should I waste breath?' he asked. 'Everything is here. The full record in the photonic flux. You have been under surveillance. Did either of you think anything could be hidden here, of all places? You, Olmayne, a Rememberer, how could you think so?'

Olmayne examined the capsule from a distance, as though it were a primed implosion bomb. With distaste she said, 'How like you to spy on us, Elegro. Did it give you great pleasure to watch us in our joy?'

'Beast!' he cried.

Pocketing the capsule, he advanced toward the motionless Prince. Elegro's face was now contorted with righteous wrath. Standing at arm's length from the Prince he declared icily, 'You will be punished to the fullest for this impiety. You will be stripped of your Pilgrim's robes and delivered up to the fate reserved for monsters. The Will shall consume your soul!'

Prince Enric replied, 'Curb your tongue.'

'Curb my tongue? Who are you to speak that way? A Pilgrim who lusts for the wife of his host – who doubly violates holiness – who drips lies and sanctimony at the same moment?' Elegro frothed. His iciness was gone. Now he ranted in nearly incoherent frenzy, displaying his interior weakness by his lack of self-control. We three stood frozen, astounded by his torrent of words, and at last the stasis broke when the Rememberer, carried away by the tide of his own indignation, seized the Prince by the shoulders and began violently to shake him.

'Filth,' Enric bellowed, 'you may not put your hands to me!'

With a double thrust of his fists against Elegro's chest he hurled the Rememberer reeling backward across the room. Elegro crashed into a suspension cradle and sent a flank of watery artifacts tumbling; three flasks of scintillating fluids shivered and spilled their contents; the carpet set up a shrill cry of pained protest. Gasping, stunned, Elegro pressed a hand to his breast and looked to us for assistance.

'Physical assault –' Elegro wheezed. 'A shameful crime!'

'The first assault was your doing,' Olmayne reminded her husband.

Pointing trembling fingers, Elegro muttered, 'For this there can be no forgiveness, Pilgrim!'

'Call me Pilgrim no longer,' Enric said. His hands went to the grillwork of his mask. Olmayne cried out, trying to prevent him; but in his anger the Prince knew no check. He hurled the mask to the floor and stood with his harsh face terribly exposed, the cruel features hawk-lean, the gray mechanical spheres in his eyesockets masking the depths of his fury. 'I am the Prince of Roum,' he announced in a voice of thunder. 'Down and abase! Down and abase! Quick, Rememberer, the three prostrations and five abasements!'

Elegro appeared to crumble. He peered in disbelief; then he sagged, and in a kind of reflex of amazement he performed a ritual obeisance before his wife's seducer. It was the first time since the fall of Roum that the Prince had asserted his former status, and the pleasure of it was so evident on his ravaged face that even the blank eyeballs appeared to glow in regal pride.

'Out,' the Prince ordered. 'Leave us.'

Elegro fled.

I remained, astounded, staggered. The Prince nodded cour-
teously to me. 'Would you pardon us, old friend, and grant
us some moments of privacy?'

SIX

A weak man can be put to rout by a surprise attack, but
afterward he pauses, reconsiders, and hatches schemes. So
was it with the Rememberer Elegro. Driven from his own
suite by the unmasking of the Prince of Roum, he grew
calm and crafty once he was out of that terrifying presence.
Later that same night, as I settled into my sleeping cradle and
debated aiding slumber with a drug, Elegro summoned me to
his research cell on a lower level of the building.

There he sat amid the paraphernalia of his guild: reels and
spools, data-flakes, capsules, caps, a quartet of series-linked
skulls, a row of output screens, a small ornamental helix,
all the symbology of the gatherers of information. In his
hands he grasped a tension-draining crystal from one of the
Cloud-worlds; its milky interior was rapidly tingeing with sepia
as it pulled anxieties from his spirit. He pretended a look of
stern authority, as if forgetting that I had seen him exposed
in his spinelessness.

He said, 'Were you aware of this man's identity when you
came with him to Perris?'

'Yes.'

'You said nothing about it.'

'I was never asked.'

'Do you know what a risk you have exposed all of us to,
by causing us unknowingly to harbor a Dominator?'

'We are Earthmen,' I said. 'Do we not still acknowledge the
authority of the Dominators?'

'Not since the conquest. By decree of the invaders all former governments are dissolved and their leaders subject to arrest.'

'But surely we should resist such an order!'

The Rememberer Elegro regarded me quizzically. 'Is it a Rememberer's function to meddle in politics? Tomis, we obey the government in power, whichever it may be and however it may have taken control. We conduct no resistance activities here.'

'I see.'

'Therefore we must rid ourselves at once of this dangerous fugitive. Tomis, I instruct you to go at once to occupation headquarters and inform Manrule Seven that we have captured the Prince of Roum and hold him here for pickup.'

'*I* should go?' I blurted. 'Why send an old man as a messenger in the night? An ordinary thinking-cap transmission would be enough!'

'Too risky. Strangers may intercept cap communications. It would not go well for our guild if this were spread about. This has to be a personal communication.'

'But to choose an unimportant apprentice to carry it – it seems strange.'

'There are only two of us who know,' said Elegro. 'I will not go. Therefore you must.'

'With no introduction to Manrule Seven I will never be admitted.'

'Inform his aides that you have information leading to the apprehension of the Prince of Roum. You'll be heard.

'Am I to mention your name?'

'If necessary. You may say that the Prince is being held prisoner in my quarters with the cooperation of my wife.'

I nearly laughed at that. But I held a straight face before this cowardly Rememberer, who did not even dare to go himself and denounce the man who had cuckolded him.

'Ultimately,' I said, 'the Prince will become aware of what we have done. Is it right of you to ask me to betray a man who was my companion for so many months?'

'It is not a matter of betrayal. It is a matter of obligations to the government.'

'I feel no obligation to this government. My loyalties are to the guild of Dominators. Which is why I gave assistance to the Prince of Roum in his moment of peril.'

'For that,' said Elegro, 'your own life could be forfeit to our conquerors. Your only expiation is to admit your error and cooperate in bringing about his arrest. Go. Now.'

In a long and tolerant life I have never despised anyone so vehemently as I did the Rememberer Elegro at that moment.

Yet I saw that I was faced with few choices, none of them palatable. Elegro wished his undoer punished, but lacked the courage to report him himself; therefore I must give over to the conquering authorities one whom I had sheltered and assisted, and for whom I felt a responsibility. If I refused, Elegro would perhaps hand me to the invaders for punishment myself, as an accessory to the Prince's escape from Roum; or he might take vengeance against me within the machinery of the guild of Rememberers. If I obliged Elegro, though, I would have a stain on my conscience forever, and in the event of a restoration of the power of the Dominators I would have much to answer for.

As I weighed the possibilities, I triply cursed the Rememberer Elegro's faithless wife and her invertebrate husband.

I hesitated a bit. Elegro offered more persuasion, threatening to arraign me before the guild on such charges as unlawfully gaining access to secret files and improperly introducing into guild precincts a proscribed fugitive. He threatened to cut me off forever from the information pool. He spoke vaguely of vengeance.

In the end I told him I would go to the invaders' headquarters and do his bidding. I had by then conceived a betrayal that would – I hoped – cancel the betrayal Elegro was enforcing on me.

Dawn was near when I left the building. The air was mild and sweet; a low mist hung over the streets of Perris, giving them a gentle shimmer. No moons were in sight. In the deserted streets I felt uneasy, although I told myself that no one would care to do harm to an aged Rememberer; but I was armed only with a small blade, and I feared bandits.

My route lay on one of the pedestrian ramps. I panted a bit at the steep incline, but when I had attained the proper level I was more secure, since here there were patrol nodes at frequent intervals, and here, too, were some other late-night strollers. I passed a spectral figure garbed in white satin through which Alien features peered: a revenant, a ghostly inhabitant of a planet of the Bull, where reincarnation is the custom and no man goes about installed in his own original body. I passed three female beings of a Swan planet who giggled at me and asked if I had seen males of their species, since the time of conjugation was upon them. I passed a pair of Changelings who eyed me speculatively, decided I had nothing on me worth robbing, and moved on, their piebald dewlaps jiggling and their radiant skins flashing like beacons.

At last I came to the squat octagonal building occupied by the Procurator of Perris.

It was indifferently guarded. The invaders appeared confident that we were incapable of mounting a counter-assault against them, and quite likely they were right; a planet which can be conquered between darkness and dawn is not going to launch a plausible resistance afterwards. Around the building rose the pale glow of a protective scanner. There was a tinge of ozone in the air. In the wide plaza across the way, Merchants were setting up their market for the morning; I saw barrels of spices being unloaded by brawny Servitors, and dark sausages carried by files of neuters. I stepped through the scanner beam and an invader emerged to challenge me.

I explained that I carried urgent news for Manrule Seven, and in short order, with amazingly little consultation of intermediaries, I was ushered into the Procurator's presence.

The invader had furnished his office simply but in good style. It was decked entirely with Earthmade objects: a drapery from Afreek weave, two alabaster pots from ancient Agupt, a marble statuette that might have been early Roumish, and

a dark Talyan vase in which a few wilting deathflowers
languished. When I entered, he seemed preoccupied with
several message-cubes; as I had heard, the invaders did most of
their work in the dark hours, and it did not surprise me to find
him so busy now. After a moment he looked up and said, 'What
is it, old man? What's this about a fugitive Dominator?'

'The Prince of Roum,' I said. 'I know of his location.'

At once his cold eyes sparkled with interest. He ran his
many-fingered hands across his desk, on which were mounted
the emblems of several of our guilds, Transporters and Rememberers and Defenders and Clowns, among others. 'Go on,'
he said.

'The Prince is in this city. He is in a specific place and has
no way of escaping from it.'

'And you are here to inform me of his location?'

'No,' I said. 'I'm here to buy his liberty.'

Manrule Seven seemed perplexed. 'There are times when
you humans baffle me. You say you've captured this runaway
Dominator, and I assume that you want to sell him to us, but
you say you want to *buy* him. Why bother coming to us? Is
this a joke?'

'Will you permit an explanation?'

He brooded into the mirrored top of his desk while I told
him in a compressed way of my journey from Roum with
the blinded Prince, of our arrival at the Hall of Rememberers,
of Prince Enric's seduction of Olmayne, and of Elegro's petty,
fuming desire for vengeance. I made it clear that I had come
to the invaders only under duress and that it was not my
intention to betray the Prince into their hands. Then I said,
'I realize that all Dominators are forfeit to you. Yet this
one has already paid a high price for his freedom. I ask
you to notify the Rememberers that the Prince of Roum
is under amnesty, and to permit him to continue on as
a Pilgrim to Jorslem. In that way Elegro will lose power
over him.'

'What is it that you offer us,' asked Manrule Seven, 'in
return for this amnesty for your Prince?'

'I have done research in the memory tanks of the Rememberers.'

'And?'

'I have found that for which your people have been seeking.'

Manrule Seven studied me with care. 'How would you have any idea of what we seek?'

'There is in the deepest part of the Hall of Rememberers,' I said quietly, 'an image recording of the compound in which your kidnapped ancestors lived while they were prisoners on Earth. It shows their sufferings in poignant detail. It is a superb justification for the conquest of Earth by H362.'

'Impossible! There's no such document!'

From the intensity of the invader's reaction, I knew that I had stung him in the vulnerable place.

He went on, 'We've searched your files thoroughly. There's only one recording of compound life, and it doesn't show our people. It shows a nonhumanoid pyramid-shaped race, probably from one of the Anchor worlds.'

'I have seen that one,' I told him. 'There are others. I spent many hours searching for them, out of hunger to know of our past injustices.'

'The indexes –'

'– are sometimes incomplete. I found this recording only by accident. The Rememberers themselves have no idea it's there. I'll lead you to it – if you agree to leave the Prince of Roum unmolested.'

The Procurator was silent a moment. At length he said, 'You puzzle me. I am unable to make out if you are a scoundrel or a man of the highest virtue.'

'I know where true loyalty lies.'

'To betray the secrets of your guild, though –'

'I am no Rememberer, only an apprentice, formerly a Watcher. I would not have you harm the Prince at the wish of a cuckolded fool. The Prince is in his hands; only you can obtain his release now. And so I must offer you this document.'

'Which the Rememberers have carefully deleted from their indexes, so it will not fall into our hands.'

'Which the Rememberers have carelessly misplaced and forgotten.'

'I doubt it,' said Manrule Seven. 'They are not careless folk. They hid that recording; and by giving it to us, are you not betraying all your world? Making yourself a collaborator with the hated enemy?'

I shrugged. 'I am interested in having the Prince of Roum made free. Other means and ends are of no concern to me. The location of the document is yours in exchange for the grant of amnesty.'

The invader displayed what might have been his equivalent of a smile. 'It is not in our best interests to allow members of the former guild of Dominators to remain at large. Your position is precarious, do you see? I could extract the document's location from you by force – and still have the Prince as well.'

'So you could,' I agreed. 'I take that risk. I assume a certain basic honor among people who came to avenge an ancient crime. I am in your power, and the whereabouts of the document is in my mind, yours for the picking.'

Now he laughed in an unmistakable show of good humor.

'Wait a moment,' he said. He spoke a few words of his own language into an amber communication device, and shortly a second member of his species entered the office. I recognized him instantly, although he was shorn of some of the flamboyant disguise he had worn when he traveled with me as Gormon, the supposed Changeling. He offered the ambivalent smile of his kind and said, 'I greet you, Watcher.'

'And I greet you, Gormon.'

'My name now is Victorious Thirteen.'

'I now am called Tomis of the Rememberers,' I said.

Manrule Seven remarked, 'When did you two become such fast friends?'

'In the time of the conquest,' said Victorious Thirteen. 'While performing my duties as an advance scout, I encountered this man in Talya and journed with him to Roum. But we were companions, in truth, and not friends.'

I trembled. 'Where is the Flier Avluela?'

'In Pars, I believe,' he said offhandedly. 'She spoke of returning to Hind, to the place of her people.'

'You loved her only a short while, then?'

'We were more companions than lovers,' said the invader. 'It was a passing thing for us.'

'For you, maybe,' I said.

'For us.'

'And for this passing thing you stole a man's eyes?'

He who had been Gormon shrugged. 'I did that to teach a proud creature a lesson in pride.'

'You said at the time that your motive was jealousy,' I reminded him. 'You claimed to act out of love.'

Victorious Thirteen appeared to lose interest in me. To Manrule Seven he said, 'Why is this man here? Why have you summoned me?'

'The Prince of Roum is in Perris,' said Manrule Seven.

Victorious Thirteen registered sudden surprise.

Manrule Seven went on, 'He is a Prisoner of the Rememberers. This man offers a strange bargain. You know the Prince better than any of us; I ask your advice.'

The Procurator sketched the outlines of the situation. He who had been Gormon listened thoughtfully, saying nothing. At the end, Manrule Seven said, 'The problem is this: shall we give amnesty to a proscribed Dominator?'

'He is blind,' said Victorious Thirteen. 'His power is gone. His followers are scattered. His spirit may be unbroken, but he presents no danger to us. I say accept the bargain.'

'There are adminsitrative risks in exempting a Dominator from arrest,' Manrule Seven pointed out. 'Nevertheless, I agree. We undertake the deal.' To me he said, 'Tell us the location of the document we desire.'

'Arrange the liberation of the Prince of Roum first,' I said calmly.

Both invaders displayed amusement. 'Fair enough,' said Manrule Seven. 'But look: how can we be certain that you'll keep your word? Anything might happen to you in the next hour while we're freeing the Prince.'

'A suggestion,' put in Victorious Thirteen. 'This is not so much a matter of mutual mistrust as it is one of timing. Tomis, why not record the document's location on a six-hour delay cube? We'll prime the cube so that it will release its information only if within that six hours the Prince of Roum himself, and no one else, commands it to do so. If we haven't found and freed the Prince in that time, the cube will destruct. If we do release the Prince, the cube will give us the information, even if – ah – something should have happened to you in the interval.'

'You cover all contingencies,' I said.

'Are we agreed?' Manrule Seven asked.

'We are agreed,' I said.

They brought me a cube and placed me under a privacy screen while I inscribed on its glossy surface the rack number and sequence equations of the document I had discovered. Moments passed; the cube everted itself and the information vanished into its opaque depths. I offered it to them.

Thus did I betray my Earthborn heritage and perform a service for our conquerors, out of loyalty to a blinded wife-stealing Prince.

SEVEN

Dawn had come by this time. I did not accompany the invaders to the Hall of Rememberers; it was no business of mine to oversee the intricate events that must ensue, and I preferred to be elsewhere. A fine drizzle was falling as I turned down the gray streets that bordered the dark Senn. The timeless river, its surface stippled by the drops, swept unwearingly against stone arches of First Cycle antiquity, bridges spanning uncountable millennia, survivors from an era when the only problems of mankind were of his own making. Morning engulfed the city. Through an old and ineradicable reflex I searched for my instruments so that I could do my Watching, and had to remind myself that that was far behind me now. The Watchers were disbanded, the enemy had come, and old Wuellig, now Tomis of the Rememberers, had sold himself to mankind's foes.

In the shadow of a twin-steepled religious house of the ancient Christers I let myself be enticed into the booth of a Somnambulist. This guild is not one with which I have often had dealings; in my way I am wary of charlatans, and charlatans are abundant in our time. The Somnambulist, in a state of trance, claims to see what has been, what is, and what will be. I know something of trances myself, for as a Watcher I entered such a state four times each day; but a Watcher with pride in his craft must necessarily despise the tawdry ethics of those who use second sight for gain, as Somnambulists do.

However, while among the Rememberers I had learned, to my surprise, that Somnambulists frequently were consulted to aid in unearthing some site of ancient times, and that they had served the Rememberers well. Though still skeptical, I was willing to be instructed. And, at the moment, I needed a shelter from the storm that was breaking over the Hall of Rememberers.

A dainty, mincing figure garbed in black greeted me with a mocking bow as I entered the low-roofed booth.

'I am Samit of the Somnambulists,' he said in a high, whining voice. 'I offer you welcome and good tidings. Behold my companion, the Somnambulist Murta.'

The Somnambulist Murta was a robust woman in lacy robes. Her face was heavy with flesh, deep rings of darkness

surrounded her eyes, a trace of mustache lined her upper
lip. Somnambulists work their trade in teams, one to do
the huckstering, one to perform; most teams were man and
wife, as was this. My mind rebelled at the thought of the
embrace of the flesh-mountain Murta and the miniature-man
Samit, but it was no concern of mine. I took my seat as
Samit indicated. On a table nearby I saw some food tablets
of several colors; I had interrupted this family's breakfast.
Murta, deep in trance, wandered the room with ponderous
strides, now and again grazing some article of furniture in
a gentle way. Some Somnambulists, it is said, waken only
two or three hours of the twenty, simply to take meals
and relieve bodily needs; there are some who ostensibly
live in continuous trance and are fed and cared for by
acolytes.

I scarcely listened as Samit of the Somnambulists delivered
his sales-talk in rapid, feverish bursts of ritualized word-
clusters. It was pitched to the ignorant; Somnambulists do
much of their trade with Servitors and Clowns and other
menials. At length, seemingly sensing my impatience, he cut
short his extolling of the Somnambulist Murta's abilities and
asked me what it was I wished to know.

'Surely the Somnambulist already is aware of that,' I
said.

'You wish a general analysis?'

'I want to know of the fate of those about me. I wish
particularly for the Somnambulist's concentration to center
on events now occurring in the Hall of Rememberers.'

Samit tapped long fingernails against the smooth table and
shot a glaring look at the cowlike Murta. 'Are you in contact
with the truth?' he asked her.

Her reply was a long feathery sigh wrenched from the core
of all the quivering meat of her.

'What do you see?' he asked her.

She began to mutter thickly. Somnambulists speak in a
language not otherwise used by mankind; it is a harsh thing of
edgy sounds, which some claim is descended from an ancient

tongue of Agupt. I know nothing of that. To me it sounded incoherent, fragmentary, impossible to hold meaning. Samit listened a while, then nodded in satisfaction and extended his palm to me.

'There is a great deal,' he said.

We discussed the fee, bargained briefly, came to a settlement. 'Go on,' I told him. 'Interpret the truth.'

Cautiously he began, 'There are outworlders involved in this, and also several members of the guild of Rememberers.' I was silent, giving him no encouragement. 'They are drawn together in a difficult quarrel. A man without eyes is at the heart of it.'

I sat upright with a jolt.

Samit smiled in cool triumph. 'The man without eyes has fallen from greatness. He is Earth, shall we say, broken by conquerors? Now he is near the end of his time. He seeks to restore his former condition, but he knows it is impossible. He has caused a Rememberer to violate an oath. To their guildhall have come several of the conquerors to – to chastise him? No. No. To free him from captivity. Shall I continue?'

'Quickly!'

'You have received all that you have paid for.'

I scowled. This was extortion; but yet the Somnambulist had clearly seen the truth. I had learned nothing here that I did not already know, but that was sufficient to tell me I might learn more. I added to my fee.

Samit closed his fist on my coins and conferred once more with Murta. She spoke at length, in some agitation, whirling several times, colliding violently with a musty divan.

Samit said, 'The man without eyes has come between a man and his wife. The outraged husband seeks punishment; the outworlders will thwart that. The outworlders seek hidden truths; they will find them, with a traitor's help. The man without eyes seeks freedom and power; he will find peace. The stained wife seeks amusement; she will find hardship.'

'And I?' I said into an obstinate and expensive silence. 'You say nothing of me!'

'You will leave Perris soon, in the same manner as you entered it. You will not leave alone. You will not leave in your present guild.'

What will be my destination?'

'You know that as well as we do, so why waste your money to tell you?'

He fell silent again.

'Tell me what will befall me as I journey to Jorslem,' I said.

'You could not afford such information. Futures become costly. I advise you to settle for what you now know.'

'I have some questions about what has already been said.'

'We do not clarify at any price.'

He grinned. I felt the force of his contempt. The Somnambulist Murta, still bumbling about the room, groaned and belched. The powers with whom she was in contact appeared to impart new information to her; she whimpered, shivered, made a blurred chuckling sound. Samit spoke to her in their language. She replied at length. He peered at me. 'At no cost,' he said, 'a final information. Your life is in no danger, but your spirit is. It would be well if you made your peace with the Will as quickly as possible. Recover your moral orientation. Remember your true loyalties. Atone for well-intentioned sins. I can say no more.'

Indeed Murta stirred and seemed to wake. Great slabs of flesh jiggled in her face and body as the convulsion of leaving the trance came over her. Her eyes opened, but I saw only whites, a terrible sight. Her thick lips twitched to reveal crumbling teeth. Samit beckoned me out with quick brushing gestures of his tiny hands. I fled into a dark, rain-drenched morning.

Hurriedly I returned to the Hall of Rememberers, arriving there out of breath, with a red spike of pain behind my breastbone. I paused a while outside the superb building to recover my strength. Floaters passed overhead, leaving the guildhall from an upper level. My courage nearly failed me. But in the end I entered the hall and ascended to the level of the suite of Elegro and Olmayne.

A knot of agitated Rememberers filled the hall. A buzz of whispered comment drifted toward me. I pressed forward; and a man whom I recognized as high in the councils of the guild held up a hand and said, 'What business do you have here, apprentice?'

'I am Tomis, who was sponsored by the Rememberer Olmayne. My chamber is close to here.'

'Tomis!' a voice cried.

I was seized and thrust ahead into the familiar suite, now a scene of devastation.

A dozen Rememberers stood about, fingering their shawls in distress. I recognized among them the taut and elegant figure of Chancellor Kenishal, his gray eyes now dull with despair. Beneath a coverlet to the left of the entrance lay a crumpled figure in the robes of a Pilgrim: the Prince of Roum, dead in his own pooled blood. His gleaming mask, now stained, lay beside him. At the opposite side of the room, slumped against an ornate credenza containing Second Cycle artifacts of great beauty, was the Rememberer Elegro, seemingly asleep, looking furious and surprised both at once. His throat was transfixed by a single slender dart. To the rear, with burly Rememberers flanking her, stood the Rememberer Olmayne looking wild and disheveled. Her scarlet robe was torn in front and revealed high white breasts; her black hair tumbled in disorder; her satiny skin glistened with perpiration. She appeared lost in a dream, far from these present surroundings.

'What has happened here?' I asked.

'Murder twice over,' said Chancellor Kenishal in a broken voice. He advanced toward me: a tall, haggard man, white-haired, an uncontrollable tic working in the lid of one eye. 'When did you last see these people alive, apprentice?'

'In the night.'

'How did you come to be here?'

'A visit, no more.'

'Was there a disturbance?'

'A quarrel between the Rememberer Elegro and the Pilgrim, yes,' I admitted.

'Over what?' asked the Chancellor thinly.

I looked uneasily at Olmayne, but she saw nothing and heard less.

'Over her,' I said.

I heard snickerings from the other Rememberers. They nudged each other, nodded, even smiled; I had confirmed the scandal. The Chancellor grew more solemn.

He indicated the body of the Prince.

'This was your companion when you entered Perris,' he said. 'Did you know of his true identity?'

I moistened my lips. 'I had suspicions.'

'That he was –'

'The fugitive Prince of Roum,' I said. I did not dare attempt subterfuges now; my status was precarious.

More nods, more nudges. Chancellor Kenishal said, 'This man was subject to arrest. It was not your place to conceal your knowledge of his identity.'

I remained mute.

The Chancellor went on, 'You have been absent from this hall for some hours. Tell us of your activities after leaving the suite of Elegro and Olmayne.'

'I called upon the Procurator Manrule Seven,' I said.

Sensation.

'For what purpose?'

'To inform the Procurator,' I said, 'that the Prince of Roum had been apprehended and was now in the suite of a Rememberer. I did this at the instruction of the Rememberer Elegro. After delivering my information I walked the streets several hours for no particular end, and returned here to find – to find –'

'To find everything in chaos,' said Chancellor Kenishal. 'The Procurator was here at dawn. He visited this suite; both Elegro and the Prince must still have been alive at that time. Then he went into our archives and removed –

and removed – material of the highest sensitivity – the highest sensitivity – removed – material not believed to be accessible to – the highest sensitivity –' The Chancellor faltered. Like some intricate machine smitten with instant rust, he slowed his motions, emitted rasping sounds, appeared to be on the verge of systematic breakdown. Several high Rememberers rushed to his aid; one thrust a drug against his arm. In moments the Chancellor appeared to recover. 'These murders occurred after the Procurator departed from the building,' he said. 'The Rememberer Olmayne has been unable to give us information concerning them. Perhaps you, apprentice, know something of value.'

'I was not present. Two Somnambulists near the Senn will testify that I was with them at the time the crimes were committed.'

Someone guffawed at my mention of Somnambulists. Let them; I was not seeking to retrieve dignity at a time like this. I knew that I was in peril.

The Chancellor said slowly, 'You will go to your chamber, apprentice, and you will remain there to await full interrogation. Afterwards you will leave the building and be gone from Perris within twenty hours. By virtue of my authority I declare you expelled from the guild of Rememberers.'

Forewarned as I had been by Samit, I was nevertheless stunned.

'*Expelled?* Why?'

'We can no longer trust you. Too many mysteries surround you. You bring us a Prince and conceal your suspicions; you are present at murderous quarrels; you visit a Procurator in the middle of the night. You may even have helped to bring about the calamitous loss suffered by our archive this morning. We have no desire for men of enigmas here. We sever our relationship with you.' The Chancellor waved his hand in a grand sweep. 'To your chamber now, to await interrogation, and then go!'

I was rushed from the room. As the entrance pit closed behind me, I looked back and saw the Chancellor, his face ashen, topple into the arms of his associates, while in the same instant the Rememberer Olmayne broke from her freeze and fell to the floor, screaming.

EIGHT

Alone in my chamber, I spent a long while gathering together my possessions, though I owned little. The morning was well along before a Rememberer whom I did not know came to me; he carried interrogation equipment. I eyed it uneasily, thinking that all would be up with me if the Rememberers found proof that it was I who had betrayed the location of that compound record to the invaders. Already they suspected me of it; the Chancellor had hesitated to make the accusation only because it must have seemed odd to him that an apprentice such as myself would have cared to make a private search of the guild archive.

Fortune rode with me. My interrogator was concerned only with the details of the slaying; and once he had determined that I knew nothing on that subject, he let me be, warning me to depart from the hall within the allotted time. I told him I would do so.

But first I needed rest. I had had none that night; and so I drank a three-hour draught and settled into soothing sleep. When I awakened a figure stood beside me: the Rememberer Olmayne.

She appeared to have aged greatly since the previous evening. She was dressed in a single chaste tunic of a somber color, and she wore neither ornament nor decoration. Her features were rigidly set. I mastered my surprise at finding her there, and sat up, mumbling an apology for my delay in acknowledging her presence.

'Be at ease,' she said gently. 'Have I broken your sleep?'

'I had my full hours.'

'I have had none. But there will be time for sleep later. We owe each other explanations, Tomis.'

'Yes.' I rose uncertainly. 'Are you well? I saw you earlier, and you seemed lost in trance.'

'They have given me medicines,' she replied.

'Tell me what you can about last night.'

Her eyelids slid momentarily closed. 'You were there when Elegro challenged us and was cast out by the Prince. Some hours later, Elegro returned. With him were the Procurator of Perris and several other invaders. Elegro appeared to be in a mood of great jubiliation. The Procurator produced a cube and commanded the Prince to put his hand to it. The Prince balked, but Manrule Seven persuaded him finally to cooperate. When he had touched the cube, the Procurator and Elegro departed, leaving the Prince and myself together again, neither of us comprehending what had happened. Guards were posted to prevent the Prince from leaving. Not long afterward the Procurator and Elegro returned. Now Elegro seemed subdued and even confused, while the Procurator was clearly exhilarated. In our room the Procurator announced that amnesty had been granted to the former Prince of Roum, and that no man was to harm him. Thereupon all of the invaders departed.'

'Proceed.'

Olmayne spoke as though a Somnambulist. 'Elegro did not appear to comprehend what had occurred. He cried out that treason had been done; he screamed that he had been betrayed. An angry scene followed. Elegro was womanish in his fury; the Prince grew more haughty; each ordered the other to leave the suite. The quarrel became so violent that the carpet itself began to die. The petals drooped; the little mouths gaped. The climax came swiftly. Elegro seized a weapon and threatened to use it if the Prince did not leave at once. The Prince misjudged Elegro's temper, thought he was bluffing, and came forward as if to throw Elegro out. Elegro slew the Prince. An instant later I grasped a dart from our rack of artifacts and hurled it into Elegro's throat. The dart bore poison; he died at once. I summoned others, and I remember no more.'

'A strange night,' I said.

'Too strange. Tell me now, Tomis: why did the Procurator come, and why did he not take the Prince into custody?'

I said, 'The Procurator came because I asked him to, under the orders of your late husband. The Procurator did not arrest the Prince because the Prince's liberty had been purchased.'

'At what price?'

'The price of a man's shame,' I said.

'You speak a riddle.'

'The truth dishonors me. I beg you not to press me for it.'

'The Chancellor spoke of a document that had been taken by the Procurator –'

'It has to do with that,' I confessed, and Olmayne looked toward the floor and asked no further questions.

I said ultimately, 'You have committed a murder, then. What will your punishment be?'

'The crime was committed in passion and fear,' she replied. 'There will be no penalty of the civil administration. But I am expelled from my guild for my adultery and my act of violence.'

'I offer my regrets.'

'And I am commanded to undertake the Pilgrimage to Jorslem to purify my soul. I must leave within the day, or my life is forfeit to the guild.'

'I too am expelled,' I told her. 'And I too am bound at last for Jorslem, though of my own choosing.'

'May we travel together?'

My hesitation betrayed me. I had journeyed here with a blind Prince; I cared very little to depart with a murderous and guildless woman. Perhaps the time had come to travel alone. Yet the Somnambulist had said I would have a companion.

Olmayne said smoothly, 'You lack enthusiasm. Perhaps I can create some in you.' She opened her tunic. I saw mounted between the snowy hills of her breasts a gray pouch. She was tempting me not with her flesh but with an overpocket. 'In this,' she said, 'is all that the Prince of Roum carried in his thigh. He showed me those treasures, and I removed them from his body as he lay dead in my room. Also there are certain objects of my own. I am not without resources. We will travel comfortably. Well?'

'I find it hard to refuse.'

'Be ready in two hours.'

'I am ready now,' I said.

'Wait, then.'

She left me to myself. Nearly two hours later she returned, clad now in the mask and robes of a Pilgrim. Over her arm she held a second set of Pilgrim's gear, which she offered to me. Yes: I was guildless now, and it was an unsafe way to travel. I would go, then, as a Pilgrim to Jorslem. I donned the unfamiliar gear. We gathered our possessions.

'I have notified the guild of Pilgrims,' she declared as we left the Hall of Rememberers. 'We are fully registered. Later today we may hope to receive our starstones. How does the mask feel, Tomis?'

'Snug.'

'As it should be.'

Our route out of Perris took us across the great plaza before the ancient gray holy building of the old creed. A crowd had gathered; I saw invaders at the center of the group. Beggars made the profitable orbit about it. They ignored us, for no one begs from a Pilgrim; but I collared one rascal with a gouged face and said, 'What ceremony is taking place here?'

'Funeral of the Prince of Roum,' he said. 'By order of the Procurator. State funeral with all the trimmings. They're making a real festival out of it.'

'Why hold such an event in Perris?' I asked. 'How did the Prince die?'

'Look, ask somebody else. I got work to do.'

He wriggled free and scrambled on to work the crowd.

'Shall we attend the funeral?' I asked Olmayne.

'Best not to.'

'As you wish.'

We moved toward the massive stone bridge that spanned the Senn. Behind us, a brilliant blue glow arose as the pyre of the dead Prince was kindled. That pyre lit the way for us as we made our slow way through the night, eastward to Jorslem.

PART III

The Road to Jorslem

ONE

Our world was now truly theirs. All the way across Eyrop I could see that the invaders had taken everything, and we belonged to them as beasts in a barnyard belong to the farmer.

They were everywhere, like fleshy weeds taking root after a strange storm. They walked with cool confidence, as if telling us by the sleekness of their movements that the Will had withdrawn favor from us and conferred it upon them. They were not cruel to us, and yet they drained us of vitality by their mere presence among us. Our sun, our moons, our museums of ancient relics, our ruins of former cycles, our cities, our palaces, our future, our present, and our past had all undergone a transfer of title. Our lives now lacked meaning.

At night the blaze of the stars mocked us. All the universe looked down on our shame.

The cold wind of winter told us that for our sins our freedom had been lost. The bright heat of summer told us that for our pride we had been humbled.

Through a changed world we moved, stripped of our past selves. I, who had roved the stars each day now had lost that pleasure. Now, bound for Jorslem, I found cool comfort in the hope that as a Pilgrim I might gain redemption and renewal in that holy city. Olmayne and I repeated each night the rituals of our Pilgrimage toward that end:

'We yield to the Will.'

'We yield to the Will.'

'In all things great and small.'

'In all things great and small.'
'And ask forgiveness.'
'And ask forgiveness.'
'For sins actual and potential.'
'For sins actual and potential.'
'And pray for understanding and repose.'
'And pray for understanding and repose.'
'Through all our days until redemption comes.'
'Through all our days until redemption comes.'

Thus we spoke the words. Saying them, we clutched the cool polished spheres of starstone, icy as frostflowers, and made communion with the Will. And so we journeyed Jorslemward in this world that no longer was owned by man.

TWO

It was at the Talyan approach to Land Bridge that Olmayne first used her cruelty on me. Olmayne was cruel by first nature; I had had ample proof of that in Perris; and yet we had been Pilgrims together for many months, traveling from Perris eastward over the mountains and down the length of Talya to the Bridge, and she had kept her claws sheathed. Until this place.

The occasion was our halting by a company of invaders coming north from Afreek. There were perhaps twenty of them, tall and harsh-faced, proud of being masters of conquered Earth. They rode in a gleaming covered vehicle of their own manufacture, long and narrow, with thick sand-colored treads and small windows. We could see the vehicle from far away, raising a cloud of dust as it neared us.

This was a hot time of year. The sky itself was the color of sand, and it was streaked with folded sheets of heat-radiation – glowing and terrible energy streams of turquoise and gold.

Perhaps fifty of us stood beside the road, with the land of

Talya at our backs and the continent of Afreek before us. We were a varied group: some Pilgrims, like Olmayne and myself, making the trek toward the holy city of Jorslem, but also a random mix of the rootless, men and women who floated from continent to continent for lack of other purpose. I counted in the band five former Watchers, and also several Indexers, a Sentinel, a pair of Communicants, a Scribe, and even a few Changelings. We gathered into a straggling assembly awarding the road by default to the invaders.

Land Bridge is not wide, and the road will not allow many to use it at any time. Yet in normal times the flow of traffic had always gone in both directions at once. Here, today, we feared to go forward while invaders were this close, and so we remained clustered timidly, watching our conquerors approach.

One of the Changelings detached himself from the others of his kind and moved toward me. He was small of stature for that breed, but wide through the shoulders; his skin seemed much too tight for his frame; his eyes were large and green-rimmed; his hair grew in thick widely spaced pedestal-like clumps, and his nose was barely perceptible, so that his nostrils appeared to sprout from his upper lip. Despite this he was less grotesque than most Changelings appear. His expression was solemn, but had a hint of bizarre playfulness lurking somewhere.

He said in a voice that was little more than a feathery whisper. 'Do you think we'll be delayed long, Pilgrims?'

In former times one did not address a Pilgrim unsolicited – especially if one happened to be a Changeling. Such customs meant nothing to me, but Olmayne drew back with a hiss of distaste.

I said, 'We will wait here until our masters allow us to pass. Is there any choice?'

'None, friend, none.'

At that *friend*, Olmayne hissed again and glowered at the little Changeling. He turned to her, and his anger showed, for suddenly six parallel bands of scarlet pigment blazed brightly beneath the glossy skin of his cheeks. But his only overt response to her was a courteous bow. He said, 'I introduce myself. I am Bernalt, naturally guildless, a native of Nayrub in Deeper Afreek. I do not inquire after your names, Pilgrims. Are you bound for Jorslem?'

'Yes,' I said, as Olmayne swung about to present her back. 'And you? Home to Nayrub after travels?'

'No,' said Bernalt. 'I go to Jorslem also.'

Instantly I felt cold and hostile, my initial response to the Changeling's suave charm fading at once. I had had a Changeling, false though he turned out to be, as a traveling companion before; he too had been charming, but I wanted no more like him. Edgily, distantly, I said, 'May I ask what business a Changeling might have in Jorslem?'

He detected the chill in my tone, and his huge eyes registered sorrow. 'We too are permitted to visit the holy city, I remind you. Even our kind. Do you fear that Changelings will once again seize the shrine of renewal, as we did a thousand years ago before we were cast down into guildlessness?' He laughed harshly. 'I threaten no one, Pilgrim. I am hideous of face, but not dangerous. May the Will grant you what you seek, Pilgrim.' He made a gesture of respect and went back to the other Changelings.

Furious, Olmayne spun round on me.

'Why do you talk to such beastly creatures?'

'The man approached me. He was merely being friendly. We are all cast together here, Olmayne, and –'

'*Man. Man!* You call a Changeling a man?'

'They *are* human, Olmayne.'

'Just barely. Tomis, I loathe such monsters. My flesh creeps to have them near me. If I could, I'd banish them from this world!'

'Where is the serene tolerance a Rememberer must cultivate?'

She flamed at the mockery in my voice. 'We are not required to love Changelings, Tomis. They are one of the curses laid upon our planet – parodies of humanity, enemies of truth and beauty. I despise them!'

It was not a unique attitude. But I had no time to reproach Olmayne for her intolerance; the vehicle of the invaders was drawing near. I hoped we might resume our journey once it went by. It slowed and halted, however, and several of the invaders came out. They walked unhurriedly toward us, their long arms dangling like slack ropes.

'Who is the leader here?' asked one of them.

No one replied, for we were independent of one another in our travel.

The invader said impatiently, after a moment, 'No leader? No leader? Very well, all of you, listen. The road must be cleared. A convoy is coming through. Go back to Palerm and wait until tomorrow.'

'But I must be in Agupt by –' the Scribe began.

'Land Bridge is closed today,' said the invader. 'Go back to Palerm.'

His voice was calm. The invaders are never peremptory, never overbearing. They have the poise and assurance of those who are secure possessors.

The Scribe shivered, his jowls swinging, and said no more.

Several of the others by the side of the road looked as if they wished to protest. The Sentinel turned away and spat. A man who boldly wore the mark of the shattered guild of Defenders in his cheek clenched his fists and plainly fought back a surge of fury. The Changelings whispered to one another. Bernalt smiled bitterly at me and shrugged.

Go back to Palerm? Waste a day's march in this heat? For what? For what?

The invader gestured casually, telling us to disperse.

Now it was that Olmayne was unkind to me. In a low voice she said, 'Explain to them, Tomis, that you are in the pay of the Procurator of Perris, and they will let the two of us pass.'

Her dark eyes glittered with mockery and contempt.

My shoulders sagged as if she had loaded ten years on me. 'Why did you say such a thing?' I asked.

'It's hot. I'm tired. It's idiotic of them to send us back to Palerm.'

'I agree. But I can do nothing. Why do you hurt me?'

'Does the truth hurt that much?'

'I am no collaborator, Olmayne.'

She laughed. 'You say that so well! But you are, Tomis, you are! You sold them the documents.'

'To save the Prince, your lover,' I reminded her.

'You dealt with the invaders, though. No matter what your motive was, that fact remains.'

'Stop it, Olmayne.'

'Now you give me orders?'

'Olmayne —'

'Go up to them, Tomis. Tell them who you are, make them let us go ahead.'

'The convoys would run us down on the road. In any case I have no influence with invaders. I am not the Procurator's man.'

'I'll die before I go back to Palerm!'

'Die, then,' I said wearily, and turned my back on her.

'Traitor! Treacherous old fool! Coward!'

I pretended to ignore her, but I felt the fire of her words. There was no falsehood in them, only malice. I *had* dealt with the conquerors, I *had* betrayed the guild that sheltered me, I *had* violated the code that calls for sullen passivity as our only way of protest for Earth's defeat. All true; yet it was unfair for her to reproach me with it. I had given no thought to higher matters of patriotism when I broke my trust; I was trying only to save a man to whom I felt bound, a man moreover with whom she was in love. It was loathsome of Olmayne to tax me with treason now, to torment my conscience, merely because of a petty rage at the heat and dust of the road.

But this woman had coldly slain her own husband. Why should she not be malicious in trifles as well?

The invaders had their way; we abandoned the road and straggled back to Palerm, a dismal, sizzling, sleepy town. That evening, as if to console us, five Fliers passing in formation overhead took a fancy to the town, and in the moonless night they came again and again through the sky, three men and two women, ghostly and slender and beautiful. I stood watching them for more than an hour, until my soul itself seemed lifted from me and into the air to join them. Their great shimmering wings scarcely hid the starlight; their pale angular bodies moved in graceful arcs, arms held pressed close to sides, legs together, backs gently curved. The sight of these five stirred my memories of Avluela and left me tingling with troublesome emotions.

The Fliers made their last pass and were gone. The false moons entered the sky soon afterward. I went into our hostelry then, and shortly Olmayne asked admittance to my room.

She looked contrite. She carried a squat octagonal flask of green wine, not a Talyan brew but something from an outworld, no doubt purchased at great price.

'Will you forgive me, Tomis?' she asked. 'Here. I know you like these wines.'

'I would rather not have had those words before, and not have the wine now,' I told her.

'My temper grows short in the heat. I'm sorry, Tomis. I said a stupid and tactless thing.'

I forgave her, in hope of a smoother journey thereafter, and we drank most of the wine, and then she went to her own room nearby to sleep. Pilgrims must live chaste lives – not that Olmayne would ever have bedded with such a withered old fossil as I, but the commandments of our adopted guild prevented the question from arising.

For a long while I lay awake beneath a lash of guilt. In her impatience and wrath Olmayne had stung me at my vulnerable place: I was a betrayer of mankind. I wrestled with the issue almost to dawn.

– What had I done?

I had revealed to our conquerors a certain document.

– Did the invaders have a moral right to the document?

It told of the shameful treatment they had had at the hands of our ancestors.

– What, then, was wrong about giving it to them?

One does not aid one's conquerors even when they are morally superior to one.

– Is a small treason a serious thing?

There are no small treasons.

– Perhaps the complexity of the matter should be investigated. I did not act out of love of the enemy, but to aid a friend.

Nevertheless I collaborated with our foes.

– This obstinate self-laceration smacks of sinful pride.

But I feel my guilt. I drown in shame.

In this unprofitable way I consumed the night. When the day brightened, I rose and looked skyward and begged the Will to help me find redemption in the waters of the house of renewal in Jorslem, at the end of my Pilgrimage. Then I went to awaken Olmayne.

THREE

Land Bridge was open on this day, and we joined the throng that was crossing over out of Talya into Afreek. It was the second time I had traveled Land Bridge, for the year before – it seemed so much farther in the past – I had come the other way, out of Agupt and bound for Roum.

There are two main routes for Pilgrims from Eyrop to Jorslem. The northern route involves going through the Dark Lands east of Talya, taking the ferry at Stanbool, and skirting the western coast of the continent of Ais to Jorslem. It was the route I would have preferred since, of all the world's great cities, old Stanbool is the one I have never visited. But Olmayne had been there to do research in the days when she was a Rememberer, and disliked the place; and so we took the southern route – across Land Bridge into Afreek and along the shore of the great Lake Medit, through Agupt and the fringes of the Arban Desert and up to Jorslem.

A true Pilgrim travels only by foot. It was not an idea that had much appeal to Olmayne, and though we walked a great deal, we rode whenever we could. She was shameless in commandeering transportation. On only the second day of our journey she had gotten us a ride from a rich Merchant bound for the coast; the man had no intention of sharing his sumptuous vehicle with anyone, but he could not resist the sensuality of Olmayne's deep, musical voice, even though it issued from the sexless grillwork of a Pilgrim's mask.

The Merchant traveled in style. For him the conquest of Earth might never have happened, nor even all the long centuries of Third Cycle decline. His self-primed landcar was four times the length of a man and wide enough to house five people in comfort; and it shielded its riders against the outer world as effectively as a womb. There was no direct vision, only a series of screens revealing upon command what lay outside. The temperature never varied from a chosen norm. Spigots supplied liquers and stronger things; food tablets were available; pressure couches insulated travelers against the irregularities of the road. For illumination, there was slavelight keyed to the Merchant's whims. Beside the main couch sat a thinking cap, but I never learned whether the Merchant carried a pickled brain for his private use in the depths of the landcar, or enjoyed some sort of remote contact with the memory tanks of the cities through which he passed.

He was a man of pomp and bulk, clearly a savorer of his own flesh. Deep olive skin, with a thick pompadour of well-oiled black hair and somber, scrutinizing eyes, he rejoiced in his solidity and in his control of an uncertain environment. He dealt, we learned, in foodstuffs of other worlds; he bartered our poor manufacturers for the delicacies of the starborn ones. Now he was en route to Marsay to examine a cargo of hallucinatory insects newly come in from one of the Belt planets.

'You like the car?' he asked, seeing our awe. Olmayne, no stranger to ease herself, was peering at the dense inner mantle of diamonded brocade in obvious amazement. 'It was owned by the Comt of Perris,' he went on. 'Yes, I mean it, the Comt himself. They turned his palace into a museum, you know.'

'I know,' Olmayne said softly.

'This was his chariot. It was supposed to be part of the museum, but I bought it off a crooked invader. You didn't know they had crooked ones too, eh?' The Merchant's robust laughter caused the sensitive mantle on the walls of the car to recoil in disdain. 'This one was the Procurator's boy friend. Yes, they've got *those*, too. He was looking for a certain fancy root that grows on a planet of the Fishes, something to give his virility a little boost, you know, and he learned that I controlled the whole supply here, and so we were able to work out a little deal. Of course, I had to have the car adapted, a little. The Comt kept four neuters up front and powered the engine right off their metabolisms, you understand, running the thing on thermal differentials. Well, that's a fine way to power a car, if you're a Comt, but it uses up a lot of neuters through the year, and I felt I'd be overreaching my status if I tried anything like that. It might get me into trouble with the invaders, too. So I had the drive compartment stripped down and replaced with a standard heavy-duty roller-wagon engine – a really subtle job – and there you are. You're lucky to be in here. It's only that you're Pilgrims. Ordinarily I don't let folks come inside, on account of them feeling envy, and envious folks are dangerous to a man who's made something out of his life. Yet the Will brought you two to me. Heading for Jorslem, eh?'

'Yes,' Olmayne said.

'Me too, but not yet! Not just yet, thank you!' He patted his middle. 'I'll be there, you can bet on it, when I feel ready for renewal, but that's a good way off, the Will willing! You two been Pilgriming long?'

'No,' Olmayne said.

'A lot of folks went Pilgriming after the conquest, I guess. Well, I don't blame 'em. We each adapt in our own ways to changing times. Say, you carrying those little stones the Pilgrims carry?'

'Yes,' Olmayne said.

'Mind if I see one? Always been fascinated by the things. There was this trader from one of the Darkstar worlds – little skinny bastard with skin like oozing tar – he offered me ten quintals of the things. Said they were genuine, gave you the real communion, just like the Pilgrims had. I told him no, I wasn't going to fool with the Will. Some things you don't do, even for profit. But afterward I wished I'd kept one as a souvenir. I never even touched one.' He stretched a hand toward Olmayne. 'Can I see?'

'We may not let others handle the starstone,' I said.

'I wouldn't tell anybody you let me!'

'It is forbidden.'

'Look, it's private in here, the most private place on Earth, and –'

'Please. What you ask is impossible.'

His face darkened, and I thought for a moment he would halt the car and order us out, which would have caused me no grief. My hand slipped into my pouch to finger the frigid starstone sphere that I had been given at the outset of my Pilgrimage. The touch of my fingertips brought faint resonances of the communion-trance to me, and I shivered in pleasure. He must not have it, I swore. But the crisis passed without incident. The Merchant, having tested us and found resistance, did not choose to press the matter.

We sped onward toward Marsay.

He was not a likeable man, but he had a certain gross charm, and we were rarely offended by his words. Olmayne, who after all was a fastidious woman and had lived most of her years in the glossy seclusion of the Hall of Rememberers, found him harder to take than I; my intolerances have been well blunted by a lifetime of wandering. But even Olmayne seemed to find him amusing when he boasted of his wealth and influence, when he told of the women who waited for him on many worlds, when he catalogued his homes and his trophies and the guildmasters who sought his counsel, when he bragged of friendships with former Masters and Dominators. He talked almost wholly of himself and rarely of us, for which we were thankful; once he asked how it was that a male Pilgrim and a female Pilgrim were traveling together, implying that we must be lovers; we admitted that the arrangement was slightly irregular and went on to another theme, and I think he remained persuaded of our unchastity. His bawdy guesses mattered not at all to me nor, I believe, to Olmayne. We had more serious guilts as our burdens.

Our Merchant's life seemed enviably undisrupted by the fall of our planet: he was as rich as ever, as comfortable, as free to move about. But even he felt occasionally irked by the presence of the invaders, as we found out by night not far from Marsay, when we were stopped at a checkpoint on the road.

Spy-eye scanners saw us coming, gave a signal to the spin-nerets, and a golden spiderweb spurted into being from one shoulder of the highway to the other. The landcar's sensors detected it and instantly signaled us to a halt. The screens showed a dozen pale human faces clustered outside.

'Bandits?' Olmayne asked.

'Worse,' said the Merchant. 'Traitors.' He scowled and turned to his communicator horn. 'What is it?' he demanded.

'Get out for inspection.'

'By whose writ?'

'The Procurator of Marsay,' came the reply.

It was an ugly thing to behold: human beings acting as road-agents for the invaders. But it was inevitable that we should have begun to drift into their civil service, since work was scarce, especially for those who had been in the defensive guilds. The Merchant began the complicated process of unsealing his car. He was stormy-faced with rage, but he was stymied, unable to pass the checkpoint's web. 'I go armed,' he whispered to us. 'Wait inside and fear nothing.'

He got out and engaged in a lengthy discussion, of which we could hear nothing, with the highway guards. At length some impasse must have forced recourse to higher authority, for three invaders abruptly appeared, waved their hired collaborators away, and surrounded the Merchant. His demeanor changed; his face grew oily and sly, his hands moved rapidly in eloquent gestures, his eyes glistened. He led the three interrogators to the car, opened it, and showed them his two passengers, ourselves. The invaders appeared puzzled by the sight of Pilgrims amid such opulence, but they did not ask us to step out. After some further conversation the Merchant rejoined us and sealed the car; the web was dissolved; we sped onward toward Marsay.

As we gained velocity he muttered curses and said, 'Do you know how I'd handle that long-armed filth? All we need is a coordinated plan. A night of knives: every ten Earthmen make themselves responsible for taking out one invader. We'd get them all.'

'Why has no one organized such a movement?' I asked.

'It's the job of the Defenders, and half of them are dead, and the other half's in the pay of *them*. It's not my place to set up a resistance movement. But that's how it should be done. Guerrilla action: sneak up behind 'em, give 'em the knife. Quick. Good old First Cycle methods; they've never lost their value.'

'More invaders would come,' Olmayne said morosely.

'Treat 'em the same way!'

'They would retaliate with fire. They would destroy our world,' she said.

'These invaders pretend to be civilized, more civilized than ourselves,' the Merchant replied. 'Such barbarity would give them a bad name on a million worlds. No, they wouldn't come with fire. They'd just get tired of having to conquer us over and over, of losing so many men. And they'd go away, and we'd be free again.'

'Without having won redemption for our ancient sins,' I said.

'What's that, old man? What's that?'

'Never mind.'

'I suppose you wouldn't join them, either of you, if we struck back at them?'

I said, 'In former life I was a Watcher, and I devoted myself to the protection of this planet against them. I am no more fond of our masters than you are, and no less eager to see them depart. But your plan is not only impractical: it is also morally valueless. Mere bloody resistance would thwart the scheme the Will has devised for us. We must earn our freedom in a nobler way. We were not given this ordeal simply so that we might have practice in slitting throats.'

He looked at me with contempt and snorted. 'I should have remembered. I'm talking to Pilgrims. All right. Forget it all. I wasn't serious, anyway. Maybe you like the world the way it is, for all I know.'

'I do not,' I said.

He glanced at Olmayne. So did I, for I half-expected her to tell the Merchant that I had already done my bit of collaborating with our conquerors. But Olmayne fortunately was silent on that topic, as she would be for some months more, until that unhappy day by the approach to Land Bridge when, in her impatience, she taunted me with my sole fall from grace.

We left our benefactor in Marsay, spent the night in a Pilgrim hostelry, and set out on foot along the coast the next morning. And so we traveled, Olmayne and I, through pleasant lands swarming with invaders; now we walked, now we rode some peasant's rollerwagon, once even we were the guests of touring conquerors. We gave Roum a wide berth when we entered Talya, and turned south. And so we came to Land Bridge, and met delay, and had our frosty moment of bickering, and then were permitted to go on across that narrow tongue of sandy ground that links the lake-sundered continents. And so we crossed into Afreek, at last.

FOUR

Our first night on the other side, after our long and dusty crossing, we tumbled into a grimy inn near the lake's edge. It was a square whitewashed stone building, practically windowless and arranged around a cool inner courtyard. Most of its clientele appeared to be Pilgrims, but there were some members of other guilds, chiefly Vendors and Transporters. At a room near the turning of the building there stayed a Rememberer, whom Olmayne avoided even though she did not know him; she simply did not wish to be reminded of her former guild.

Among those who took lodging there was the Changeling Bernalt. Under the new laws of the invaders, Changelings might stay at any public inn, not merely those set aside for their special use; yet it seemed a little strange to see him here. We passed in the corridor. Bernalt gave me a tentative smile, as though about to speak again, but the smile died and the glow left his eyes. He appeared to realize I was not ready to accept his friendship. Or perhaps he merely recalled that Pilgrims, by the laws of their guild, were not supposed to have much to do with guildless ones. That law still stood.

Olmayne and I had a greasy meal of soups and stews. Afterward I saw her to her room and began to wish her good night when she said, 'Wait. We'll do our communion together.'

'I've been seen coming into your room,' I pointed out. 'There will be whispering if I stay long.'

'We'll go to yours, then!'

Olmayne peered into the hall. All clear: she seized my wrist, and we rushed toward my chamber, across the way. Closing and sealing the warped door, she said, 'Your starstone, now!'

I took the stone from its hiding place in my robe, and she produced hers, and our hands closed upon them.

During this time of Pilgrimage I had found the starstone a great comfort. Many seasons now had passed since I had last entered a Watcher's trance, but I was not yet reconciled entirely to the breaking of my old habit; the starstone provided a kind of substitute for the swooping ecstasy I had known in Watching.

Starstones come from one of the outer worlds – I could not tell you which – and may be had only by application to the guild. The stone itself determines whether one may be a

Pilgrim, for it will burn the hand of one whom it considers unworthy to don the robe. They say that without exception every person who has enrolled in the guild of Pilgrims has shown uneasiness as the stone was offered to him for the first time.

'When they gave you yours,' Olmayne asked, 'were you worried?'

'Of course.'

'So was I.'

We waited for the stones to overwhelm us. I gripped mine tightly. Dark, shining, more smooth than glass, it glowed in my grasp like a pellet of ice, and I felt myself becoming attuned to the power of the Will.

First came a heightened perception of my surroundings. Every crack in the walls of this ancient inn seemed now a valley. The soft wail of the wind outside rose to a keen pitch. In the dim glow of the room's lamp I saw colors beyond the spectrum.

The quality of the experience the starstone offered was altogether different from that given by my instruments of Watching. That, too, was a transcending of self. When in a state of Watchfulness I was capable of leaving my Earth-bound identity and soaring at infinite speed over infinite range, perceiving all, and this is as close to godhood as a man is likely to come. The starstone provided none of the highly specific data that a Watcher's trance yielded. In the full spell I could see nothing, nor could I identify my sur-roundings. I knew only that when I let myself be drawn into the stone's effect, I was engulfed by something far larger than myself, that I was in direct contact with the matrix of the universe.

Call it communion with the Will.

From a great distance I heard Olmayne say, 'Do you believe what some people say of these stones? That there is no com-munion, that it's all an electrical deception?'

'I have no theory about that,' I said. 'I am less interested in causes than in effects.'

Skeptics say that the starstones are nothing more than amplifying loops which bounce a man's own brain-waves back into his mind; the awesome oceanic entity with which one comes in contact, these scoffers hold, is merely the thunderous recycling oscillation of a single shuttling electrical pulse beneath the roof of the Pilgrim's own skull. Perhaps.

Olmayne extended the hand that gripped her stone. She said, 'When you were among the Rememberers, Tomis, did you study the history of early religion? All through time, man has sought union with the infinite. Many religions – not all! – have held forth the hope of such a divine merging.'

'And there were drugs, too,' I murmured.

'Certain drugs, yes, cherished for their ability to bring the taker momentarily to a sensation of oneness with the universe. These starstones, Tomis, are only the latest in a long sequence of devices for overcoming the greatest of human curses, that, is, the confinement of each individual soul within a single body. Our terrible isolation from one another and from the Will itself is more than most races of the universe would be able to bear. It seems unique to humanity.'

Her voice grew feathery and vague. She said much more, speaking to me out of the wisdom she had learned with the Rememberers, but her meaning eluded me; I was always quicker to enter communion than she, because of my training as a Watcher, and often her final words did not register.

That night as on other nights I seized my stone and felt the chill and closed my eyes, and heard the distant tolling of a mighty gong, the lapping of waves on an unknown beach, the whisper of the wind in an alien forest. And felt a summons. And yielded. And entered the state of communion. And gave myself up to the Will.

And slipped down through the layers of my life, through my youth and middle years, my wanderings, my old loves, my torments, my joys, my troubled later years, my treasons, my insufficiencies, my griefs, my imperfections.

And freed myself of myself. And shed my selfness. And merged. And became one of thousands of Pilgrims, not merely

Olmayne nearby, but others trekking the mountains of Hind
and the sands of Arba, Pilgrims at their devotions in Ais and
Palash and Stralya, Pilgrims moving toward Jorslem on the
journey that some complete in months, some in years, and
some never at all. And shared with all of them the instant
of submergence into the Will. And saw in the darkness a deep
purple glow on the horizon – which grew in intensity until it
became an all-encompassing red brilliance. And went into it,
though unworthy, unclean, flesh-trapped, accepting fully the
communion offered and wishing no other state of being than
this divorce from self.

And was purified.

And wakened alone.

FIVE

I knew Afreek well. When still a young man I had settled in
the continent's dark heart for many years. Out of restlessness I
had left, finally, going as far north as Agupt, where the antique
relics of First Cycle days have survived better than anywhere
else. In those days antiquity held no interest for me, however.
I did my Watching and went about from place to place, since
a Watcher does not need to have a fixed station; and chance
brought me in contact with Avluela just as I was ready to roam
again, and so I left Agupt for Roum and then Perris.

Now I had come back with Olmayne. We kept close to the
coast and avoided the sandy inland wastes. As Pilgrims we
were immune from most of the hazards of travel: we would
never go hungry or without shelter, even in a place where no
lodge for our guild existed, and all owed us respect. Olmayne's
great beauty might have been a hazard to her, traveling as she
was with no escort other than a shriveled old man, but behind
the mask and robe of a Pilgrim she was safe. We unmasked
only rarely, and never where we might be seen.

I had no illusions about my importance to Olmayne. To her I was merely part of the equipment of a journey – someone to help her in her communions and rituals, to arrange for lodgings, to smooth her way for her. That role suited me. She was, I knew, a dangerous woman, given to strange whims and unpredictable fancies. I wanted no entanglements with her.

She lacked a Pilgrim's purity. Even though she had passed the test of the starstone, she had not triumphed – as a Pilgrim must – over her own flesh. She slipped off, sometimes, for half a night or longer, and I pictured her lying maskless in some alley gasping in a Servitor's arms. That was her affair entirely; I never spoke of her absences upon her return.

Within our lodgings, too, she was careless of her virtue. We never shared a room – no Pilgrim hostelry would permit it – but we usually had adjoining ones, and she summoned me to hers or came to mine whenever the mood took her. Often as not she was unclothed; she attained the height of the grotesque one night in Agupt when I found her wearing only her mask, all her gleaming white flesh belying the intent of the bronze grillwork that hid her face. Only once did it seem to occur to her that I might ever have been young enough to feel desire. She looked my scrawny, shrunken body over and said, 'How will you look, I wonder, when you've been renewed in Jorslem? I'm trying to picture you young, Tomis. Will you give me pleasure then?'

'I gave pleasure in my time,' I said obliquely.

Olmayne disliked the heat and dryness of Agupt. We traveled mainly by night and clung to our hostelries by day. The roads were crowded at all hours. The press of Pilgrims towards Jorslem was extraordinarily heavy, it appeared. Olmayne and I speculated on how long it might take us to gain access to the waters at such a time.

'You've never been renewed before?' she asked.

'Never.'

'Nor I. They say they don't admit all who come.'

'Renewal is a privilege, not a right,' I said. 'Many are turned away.'

'I understand also,' said Olmayne, 'that not all who enter the waters are successfully renewed.'

'I know little of this.'

'Some grow older instead of younger. Some grow young too fast, and perish. There are risks.'

'Would you not take those risks?'

She laughed. 'Only a fool would hesitate.'

'You are in no need of renewal at this time,' I pointed out. 'You were sent to Jorslem for the good of your soul, not that of your body, as I recall.'

'I'll tend to my soul as well, when I'm in Jorslem.'

'But you talk as if the house of renewal is the only shrine you mean to visit.'

'It's the important one,' she said. She rose, flexing her supple body voluptuously. 'True, I have atoning to do. But do you think I've come all the way to Jorslem just for the sake of my spirit?'

'I have,' I pointed out.

'*You!* You're old and withered! You'd better look after your spirit – and your flesh as well. I wouldn't mind shedding some age, though. I won't have them take off much. Eight, ten years, that's all. The years I wasted with that fool Elegro. I don't need a full renewal. You're right: I'm still in my prime.' Her face clouded. 'If the city is full of Pilgrims, maybe they won't let me into the house of renewal at all! They'll say I'm too young – tell me to come back in forty or fifty years – Tomis, would they do that to me?'

'It is hard for me to say.'

She trembled. 'They'll let *you* in. You're a walking corpse already – they have to renew you! But me – Tomis, I won't let them turn me away! If I have to pull Jorslem down stone by stone, I'll get in somehow!'

I wondered privately if her soul were in fit condition for one who poses as a candidate for renewal. Humility is recommended when one becomes a Pilgrim. But I had no wish to feel Olmayne's fury, and I kept my silence. Perhaps they would admit her to renewal despite her flaws. I had concerns of my own. It was vanity that drove Olmayne; my goals were different. I had wandered long and done much, not all of it virtuous; I needed a cleansing of my conscience in the holy city more, perhaps, than I did a lessening of my years.

Or was it only vanity for me to think so?

SIX

Several days eastward of that place, as Olmayne and I walked through a parched countryside, village children chattering in fear and excitement rushed upon us.

'Please, come, come!' they cried. 'Pilgrims, come!'

Olmayne looked bewildered and irritated as they plucked at her robes. 'What are they saying, Tomis? I can't get through their damnable Aguptan accents!'

'They want us to help,' I said. I listened to their shouts. 'In their village,' I told Olmayne, 'there is an outbreak of the crystallization disease. They wish us to seek the mercies of the Will upon the sufferers.'

Olmayne drew back. I imagined the disdainful wince behind her mask. She flicked out her hands, trying to keep the children from touching her. To me she said, 'We can't go there!'

'We must.'

'We're in a hurry! Jorslem's crowded; I don't want to waste time in some dreary village.'

'They need us, Olmayne.'

'Are we Surgeons?'

'We are Pilgrims,' I said quietly. 'The benefits we gain from that carry certain obligations. If we are entitled to the hospitality of all we meet, we must also place our souls at the free disposal of the humble. Come.'

'I won't go!'

'How will that sound in Jorslem, when you give an accounting of yourself, Olmayne?'

'It's a hideous disease. What if we get it?'

'Is that what troubles you? Trust in the Will! How can you expect renewal if your soul is so deficient in grace?'

'May you rot, Tomis,' she said in a low voice. 'When did you become so pious? You're doing this deliberately, because of what I said to you by Land Bridge. In a stupid moment I taunted you, and now you're willing to expose us both to a ghastly afflction for your revenge. Don't do it, Tomis!'

I ignored her accusation. 'The children are growing agitated, Olmayne. Will you wait here for me, or will you go to the next village and wait in the hostelry there?'

'Don't leave me alone in the middle of nowhere!'

'I have to go to the sick ones,' I said.

In the end she accompanied me – I think not out of any suddenly conceived desire to be of help, but rather out of fear that her selfish refusal might somehow be held against her in Jorslem. We came shortly to the village, which was small and decayed, for Agupt lies in a terrible hot sleep and changes little with the millennia. The contrast with the busy cities farther to the south in Afreek – cities that prosper on the output of luxuries from their great manufactories – is vast.

Shivering with heat, we followed the children to the houses of sickness.

The crystallization disease is an unlovely gift from the stars. Not many afflictions of outworlders affect the Earthborn; but from the worlds of the Spear came this ailment, carried by alien tourists, and the disease has settled among us. If it had come during the glorious days of the Second Cycle we might have eradicated it in a day; but our skills are dulled now, and no year has been without its outbreak. Olmayne was plainly terrified as we entered the first of the clay huts where the victims were kept.

There is no hope for one who has contracted this disease. One merely hopes that the healthy will be spared; and fortunately it is not a highly contagious disease. It works insidiously, transmitted in an unknown way, often failing to pass from husband to wife and leaping instead to the far side of a city, to another land entirely, perhaps. The first symptom is a scaliness of the skin; itch, flakes upon the clothing, inflammation. There follows a weakness in the bones as the calcium is dissolved. One grows limp and rubbery, but this is still an early phase. Soon the outer tissues harden. Thick, opaque membranes form on the surface of the eyes; the nostrils may close and seal; the skin grows coarse and pebbled. In this phase prophecy is common. The sufferer partakes of the skills of a Somnambulist, and utters oracles. The soul may wander, separating from the body for hours at a time, although the life-processes continue. Next, within twenty days after the onset of the disease, the crystallization ocurrs. While the skeletal structure dissolves, the skin splits and cracks, forming shining crystals in rigid geometrical patterns. The victim is quite beautiful at this time and takes on the appearance of a replica of himself in precious gems. The crystals glow with rich inner lights, violet and green and red; their sharp facets adopt new alignments from hour to hour; the slightest illumination in the room causes the sufferer to give off brilliant glittering reflections that dazzle and delight the eye. All this time the internal body is changing, as if some strange chrysalis is forming. Miraculously the organs sustain life throughout every transformation, although in the crystalline phase the victim is no longer able to communicate with others and possibly is unaware of the changes in himself. Ultimately the metamorphosis reaches the vital organs, and the process fails. The alien infestation is unable to reshape those organs without killing its host. The crisis is swift: a brief convulsion, a final discharge of energy along the nervous system of the crystallized one, and there is a quick arching of the body, accompanied by the delicate tinkling sounds of shivering glass, and then all is over. On the planet to which this is native, crystallization is not a disease but an actual metamorphosis, the result of thousands of years of evolution toward a symbiotic relationship. Unfortunately, among the Earthborn, the evolutionary preparation did not take place, and the agent of change invariably brings its subject to a fatal outcome.

Since the process is irreversible, Olmayne and I could do nothing of real value here except offer consolation to these ignorant and frightened people. I saw at once that the disease had seized this village some time ago. There were people in all stages, from the first rash to the ultimate crystallization. They were arranged in the hut according to the intensity of their infestation. To my left was a somber row of new victims, fully conscious and morbidly scratching their arms as they contemplated the horrors that awaited them. Along the rear wall were five pallets on which lay villagers in the coarse-skinned and prophetic phase. To my right were those in varying degrees of crystallization, and up front, the diadem of the lot, was one who clearly was in his last hours of life. His body, encrusted with false emeralds and rubies and opals, shimmered in almost painful beauty; he scarcely moved; within that shell of wondrous color he was lost in some dream of ecstasy, finding at the end of his days more passion, more delight, than he could ever have known in all his harsh peasant years.

Olmayne shied back from the door.

'It's horrible,' she whispered. 'I won't go in!'

'We must. We are under an obligation.'

'I never wanted to be a Pilgrim!'

'You wanted atonement,' I reminded her. 'It must be earned.'

'We'll catch the disease!'

'The Will can reach us anywhere to infect us with this, Olmayne. It strikes at random. The danger is no greater for us inside this building than it is in Perris.'

'Why, then, are so many in this one village smitten?'

'This village has earned the displeasure of the Will.'

'How neatly you serve up the mysticism, Tomis,' she said bitterly. 'I misjudged you. I thought you were a sensible man. This fatalism of yours is ugly.'

'I watched my world conquered,' I said. 'I beheld the Prince of Roum destroyed. Calamities breed such attitudes as I now have. Let us go in, Olmayne.'

We entered, Olmayne still reluctant. Now fear assailed me, but I concealed it. I had been almost smug in my piety while arguing with the lovely Rememberer woman who was my companion, but I could not deny the sudden seething of fright.

I forced myself to be tranquil.

There are redemptions and redemptions, I told myself. If this disease is to be the source of mine, I will abide by the Will.

Perhaps Olmayne came to some such decision too, as we went in, or maybe her own sense of the dramatic forced her into the unwanted role of the lady of mercy. She made the rounds with me. We passed from pallet to pallet, heads bowed, starstones in our hands. We said words. We smiled when the newly sick begged for reassurance. We offered prayers. Olmayne paused before one girl in the secondary phase, whose eyes already were filming over with horny tissue, and knelt and touched her starstone to the girl's scaly cheek. The girl spoke in oracles, but unhappily not in any language we understood.

At last we came to the terminal case, he who had grown his own superb sarcophagus. Somehow I felt purged of fear, and so too was Olmayne, for we stood a long while before this grotesque sight, silent, and then she whispered, 'How terrible! How wonderful! How beautiful!'

Three more huts similar to this one awaited us.

The villagers clustered at the doorways. As we emerged from each building in turn, the healthy ones fell down about us, clutching at the hems of our robes, stridently demanding that we intercede for them with the Will. We spoke such words as seemed appropriate and not too insincere. Those within the huts received our words blankly, as if they already realized there was no chance for them; those outside, still untouched by the disease, clung to every syllable. The headman of the village – only an acting headman; the true chief lay crystallized – thanked us again and again, as though we had done something real. At least we had given comfort, which is not to be despised.

When we came forth from the last of the sickhouses, we saw

a slight figure watching us from a distance: the Changeling Bernalt. Olmayne nudged me.

'That creature has been following us, Tomis. All the way from Land Bridge!'

'He travels to Jorslem also.'

'Yes, but why should he stop here? Why in this awful place?'

'Hush, Olmayne. Be civil to him now.'

'To a *Changeling?*'

Bernalt approached. The mutated one was clad in a soft white robe that blunted the strangeness of his appearance. He nodded sadly toward the village and said, 'A great tragedy. The Will lies heavily on this place.'

He explained that he had arrived here several days ago and had met a friend from his native city of Nayrub. I assumed he meant a Changeling, but no, Bernalt's friend was a Surgeon, he said, who had halted here to do what he could for the afflicted villagers. The idea of a friendship between a Changeling and a Surgeon seemed a bit odd to me, and positively contemptible to Olmayne, who did not trouble to hide her loathing of Bernalt.

A partly crystallized figure staggered from one of the huts, gnarled hands clutching. Bernalt went forward and gently guided it back within. Returning to us, he said, 'There are times one is actually glad one is a Changeling. That disease does not affect us, you know.' His eyes acquired a sudden glitter. 'Am I forcing myself on you, Pilgrims? You seem like stone behind your masks. I mean no harm; shall I withdraw?'

'Of course not,' I said, meaning the opposite. His company disturbed me; perhaps the ordinary disdain for Changelings was a contagion that had at last reached me. 'Stay awhile. I would ask you to travel with us to Jorslem, but you know it is forbidden for us.'

'Certainly. I quite understand.' He was coolly polite, but the seething bitterness in him was close to the surface. Most Changelings are such degraded bestial things that they are incapable of knowing how detested they are by normal guilded men and women; but Bernalt clearly was gifted with the torment of comprehension. He smiled, and then he pointed. 'My friend is here.'

Three figures approached. One was Bernalt's Surgeon, a slender man, dark-skinned, soft-voiced, with weary eyes and sparse yellow hair. With him were an official of the invaders and another outworlder from a different planet. 'I had heard that two Pilgrims were summoned to this place,' said the invader. 'I am grateful for the comfort you may have brought these sufferers. I am Earthclaim Nineteen; this district is under my administration. Will you be my guests at dinner this night?'

I was doubtful of taking an invader's hospitality, and Olmayne's sudden clenching of her fist over her starstone told me that she also hesitated. Earthclaim Nineteen seemed eager for our acceptance. He was not as tall as most of his kind, and his malproportioned arms reached below his knees. Under the blazing Aguptan sun his thick waxy skin acquired a high gloss, although he did not perspire.

Into a long, tense, and awkward silence the Surgeon inserted: 'No need to hold back. In this village we all are brothers. Join us tonight, will you?'

We did. Earthclaim Nineteen occupied a villa by the shore of Lake Medit; in the clear light of late afternoon I thought I could detect Land Bridge jutting forward to my left, and even Eyrop at the far side of the lake. We were waited upon by members of the guild of Servitors who brought us cool drinks on the patio. The invader had a large staff, all Earthborn; to me it was another sign that our conquest had become institutionalized and was wholly accepted by the bulk of the populace. Until long after dusk we talked, lingering over drinks even as the writhing auroras danced into view to herald the night. Bernalt the Changeling remained apart, though, perhaps ill at ease in our presence. Olmayne too was moody and withdrawn; a mingled depression and exaltation had settled over her in the stricken village, and the presence of Bernalt at the dinner party had reinforced her silence, for she

had no idea how to be polite in the presence of a Changeling.
The invader, our host, was charming and attentive, and tried
to bring her forth from her bleakness. I had seen charming
conquerors before. I had traveled with one who had posed as
the Earthborn Changeling Gormon in the days just before the
conquest. This one, Earthclaim Nineteen, had been a poet on
his native world in those days. I said, 'It seems unlikely that
one of your inclinations would care to be part of a military
occupation.'

'All experiences strengthen the art,' said Earthclaim Nineteen. 'I seek to expand myself. In any case I am not a warrior
but an administrator. Is it so strange that a poet can be
an administrator, or an administrator a poet?' He laughed.
'Among your many guilds, there is no guild of Poets. Why?'

'There are Communicants,' I said. 'They serve your muse.'

'But in a religious way. They are interpreters of the Will, not
of their own souls.'

'The two are indistinguishable. The verses they make are
divinely inspired, but rise from the hearts of their makers,' I
said.

Earthclaim Nineteen looked unconvinced. 'You may argue
that all poetry is at bottom religious, I suppose. But this stuff
of your Communicants is too limited in scope. It deals only
with acquiescence to the Will.'

'A paradox,' said Olmayne. 'The Will encompasses everything, and yet you say that our Communicants' scope is
limited.'

'There are other themes for poetry besides immersion in the
Will, my friends. The love of person for person, the joy of
defending one's home, the wonder of standing naked beneath
the fiery stars –' The invader laughed. 'Can it be that Earth fell
so swiftly because its only poets were poets of acquiescence to
destiny?'

'Earth fell,' said the Surgeon, 'because the Will required
us to atone for the sin our ancestors committed when they
treated your ancestors like beasts. The quality of our poetry
had nothing to do with it.'

'The Will decreed that you would lose to us by way of punishment, eh? But if the Will is omnipotent, it must have decreed the sin of your ancestors that made the punishment necessary. Eh? Eh? The Will playing games with itself. You see the difficulty of believing in a divine force that determines all events? Where is the element of choice that makes suffering meaningful? To force you into a sin, and then to require you to endure as atonement, seems to me an empty exercise. Forgive my blasphemy.'

The Surgeon said, 'You misunderstand. All that has happened on this planet is part of a process of moral instruction. The Will does not shape every event great or small; it provides the raw material of events, and allows us to follow such patterns as we desire.'

'Example?'

'The Will imbued the Earthborn with skills and knowledge. During the First Cycle we rose from savagery in little time; in the Second Cycle we attained greatness. In our moment of greatness we grew swollen with pride, choosing to exceed our limitations. We imprisoned intelligent creatures of other worlds under the pretense of "study," when we acted really out of an arrogant desire for amusement, and we toyed with our world's climate until oceans joined and continents sank and our old civilization was destroyed. Thus the Will instructed us in the boundaries of human ambition.'

'I dislike that dark philosophy even more,' said Earthclaim Nineteen. 'I —'

'Let me finish,' said the Surgeon. 'The collapse of Second Cycle Earth was our punishment. The defeat of Third Cycle Earth by you folk from the stars is a completion of that earlier punishment, but also the beginning of a new phase. You are the instruments of our redemption. By inflicting on us the final humiliation of conquest, you bring us to the bottom of our trough; now we renew our souls, now we begin to rise, tested by adversities.'

I stared in sudden amazement at this Surgeon, who was uttering ideas that been stirring in me all along the road to

Jorslem, ideas of redemption both personal and planetary. I had paid little attention to the Surgeon before.

'Permit me a statement,' Bernalt said suddenly, his first words in hours.

We looked at him. The pigmented bands in his face were ablaze, marking his emotion.

He said, nodding to the Surgeon, 'My friend, you speak of redemption for the Earthborn. Do you mean *all* Earthborn, or only the guilded ones?'

'All Earthborn, of course,' said the Surgeon mildly. 'Are we not all equally conquered?'

'We are not equal in other things, though. Can there be redemption for a planet that keeps millions of its people thrust into guildlessness? I speak of my own folk, of course. We sinned long ago when we thought we were striking out against those who had created us as monsters. We strove to take Jorslem from you; and for this we were punished, and our punishment has lasted for a thousand years. We are still outcasts, are we not? Where has our hope of redemption been? Can you guilded ones consider yourself purified and made virtuous by your recent suffering, when you still step on us?'

The Surgeon looked dismayed. 'You speak rashly, Bernalt. I know that Changelings have a grievance. But you know as well as I that the time of deliverance is at hand. In the days to come no Earthborn one will scorn you, and you will stand beside us when we regain our freedom.'

Bernalt peered at the floor. 'Forgive me, my friend. Of course, of course, you speak the truth. I was carried away. The heat – this splendid wine – how foolishly I spoke!'

Earthclaim Nineteen said, 'Are you telling me that a resistance movement is forming that will shortly drive us from your planet?'

'I speak only in abstract terms,' said the Surgeon.

'I think your resistance movement will be purely abstract too,' the invader replied easily. 'Forgive me, but I see little strength in a planet that could be conquered in a single night.

We expect our occupation of Earth to be a long one and to meet little opposition. In the months that we have been here there has been no sign of increasing hostility to us. Quite the contrary: we are increasingly accepted among you.'

'It is part of a process,' said the Surgeon. 'As a poet, you should understand that words carry meanings of many kinds. We do not need to overthrow our alien masters in order to be free of them. Is that poetic enough for you?'

'Splendid,' said Earthclaim Nineteen, getting to his feet. 'Shall we go to dinner now?'

SEVEN

There was no way to return to the subject. A philosophical discussion at the dinner table is difficult to sustain; and our host did not seem comfortable with this analysis of Earth's destinies. Swiftly he discovered that Olmayne had been a Rememberer before turning Pilgrim, and thereafter directed his words to her, questioning her on our history and our early poetry. Like most invaders he had a fierce curiosity concerning our past. Olmayne gradually came out of the silence that gripped her, and spoke at length about her researches in Perris. She talked with great familiarity of our hidden past, with Earthclaim Nineteen occasionally inserting an intelligent and informed question; meanwhile we dined on delicacies of a number of worlds, perhaps imported by the same fat, insensitive Merchant who had driven us from Perris to Marsay; the villa was cool and the Servitors attentive; that miserable plague-stricken peasant village half an hour's walk away might well have been in some other galaxy, so remote was it from our discourse now.

When we left the villa in the morning, the Surgeon asked permission to join our Pilgrimage. 'There is nothing further I can do here,' he explained. 'At the outbreak of the disease I came up from my home in Nayrub, and I've been here many days, more to console than to cure, of course. Now I am called to Jorslem. However, if it violates your vows to have company on the road –'

'By all means come with us,' I said.

'There will be one other companion,' the Surgeon told us. He meant the third person who had met us at the village: the outworlder, an enigma, yet to say a word in our presence. This being was a flattened spike-shaped creature somewhat taller than a man and mounted on a jointed tripod of angular legs; its place of origin was in the Golden Spiral; its skin was rough and bright red in hue, and vertical rows of glassy oval eyes descended on three sides from the top of its tapered head. I had never seen such a creature before. It had come to Earth, according to the Surgeon, on a data-gathering mission, and had already roamed much of Ais and Stralya. Now it was touring the lands on the margin of Lake Medit; and after seeing Jorslem it would depart for the great cities of Eyrop. Solemn, unsettling in its perpetual watchfulness, never blinking its many eyes nor offering a comment on what those eyes beheld, it seemed more like some odd machine, some information-intake for a memory tank, than a living creature. But it was harmless enough to let it come with us to the holy city.

The Surgeon bade farewell to his Changeling friend, who went on alone ahead of us, and paid a final call on the crystallized village. We stayed back, since there was no point in our going. When he returned, his face was somber. 'Four new cases,' he said. 'This entire village will perish. There has never been an outbreak of this kind before on Earth – so concentrated an epidemic.'

'Something new, then?' I asked. 'Will it spread everywhere?'

'Who knows? No one in the adjoining village has caught it. The pattern is unfamiliar: a single village wholly devastated, and nowhere else besides. These people see it as divine retri-bution for unknown sins.'

'What could peasants have done,' I asked, 'that would bring the wrath of the Will so harshly upon them?'

'They are asking that too,' said the Surgeon.

Olmayne said, 'If there are new cases, our visit yesterday was useless. We risked ourselves and did them no good.'

'Wrong,' the Surgeon told her. 'These cases were already incubating when we arrived. We may hope that the disease will not spread to those who still were in full health.'

He did not seem confident of that.

Olmayne examined herself from day to day for symptoms of the disease, but none appeared. She gave the Surgeon much trouble on that score, bothering him for opinions concerning real or fancied blemishes of her skin, embarrassing him by removing her mask in his presence so that he could determine that some speck on her cheek was not the first trace of crystallization.

The Surgeon took all this in good grace, for, while the outworld being was merely a cipher plodding alongside us, the Surgeon was a man of depth, patience and sophistication. He was native to Afreek, and had been dedicated to his guild at birth by his father, since healing was the family tradition. Traveling widely, he had seen most of our world and had forgotten little of what he had seen. He spoke to us of Roum and Perris, of the frostflower fields of Stralya, of my own birthplace in the western island group of the Lost Continents. He questioned us tactfully about our starstones and the effects they produced – I could see he hungered to try the stone himself, but that of course was forbidden to one who had not declared himself a Pilgrim – and when he learned that in former life I had been a Watcher, he asked me a great deal concerning the instruments by which I had scanned the heavens, wishing to know what it was I perceived and how I imagined the perception was accomplished. I spoke to him as fully as I could on these matters, though in truth I knew little.

Usually we kept on the green strip of fertile land bordering the lake, but once, at the Surgeon's insistence, we detoured into the choking desert to see something that he promised would be of interest. He would not tell us what it was. We were at this point traveling in hired rollerwagons, open on top, and sharp winds blew gusts of sand in our faces. Sand adhered briefly to the outworlder's eyes, I saw; and I saw how efficiently it flushed each eye with a flood of blue tears every few moments. The rest of us huddled in our garments, heads down, whenever the wind arose.

'We are here,' the Surgeon announced finally. 'When I traveled with my father I first visited this place long ago. We will go inside – and then you, the former Rememberer, will tell us where we are.'

It was a building two stories high made of bricks of white glass. The doors appeared sealed, but they gave at the slightest pressure. Lights glowed into life the moment we entered.

In long aisles, lightly strewn with sand, were tables on which instruments were mounted. Nothing was comprehensible to me. There were devices shaped like hands, into which one's own hand could be inserted; conduits led from the strange metal gloves to shining closed cabinets, and arrangements of mirrors transmitted images from the interiors of those cabinets to giant screens overhead. The Surgeon placed his hands in the gloves and moved his fingers; the screens brightened, and I saw images of tiny needles moving through shallow arcs. He went to other machines and released dribbles of unknown fluids; he touched small buttons and produced musical sounds; he moved freely through a laboratory of wonders, clearly ancient, which seemed still in order and awaiting the return of its users.

Olmayne was ecstatic. She followed the Surgeon from aisle to aisle, handling everything.

'Well, Rememberer?' he asked finally. 'What is this?'

'A Surgery,' she said in lowered voice. 'A Surgery of the Years of Magic!'

'Exactly! Splendid!' He seemed in an oddly excited state. 'We could make dazzling monsters here! We could work miracles! Fliers, Swimmers, Changelings, Twiners, Burners, Climbers – invent your own guilds, shape men to your whims! This was the place!'

Olmayne said, 'These Surgeries have been described to me. There are six of them left, are there not, one in northern Eyrop, one on Palash, one here, one far to the south in Deeper Afreek, one in western Ais –' She faltered.

'And one in Hind, the greatest of all!' said the Surgeon.

'Yes, of course, Hind! The home of the Fliers!'

Their awe was contagious. I said, 'This was where the shapes of men were changed? How was it done?'

The Surgeon shrugged. 'The art is lost. The Years of Magic were long ago, old man.'

'Yes, yes, I know. But surely if the equipment survives, we could guess how –'

'With these knives,' said the Surgeon, 'we cut into the fabric of the unborn, editing the human seed. The Surgeon placed his hands here – he manipulated – and within that incubator the knives did their work. Out of this came Fliers and all the rest. The forms bred true. Some are extinct today, but our Fliers and our Changelings owe their heritage to some such building as this. The Changelings, of course, were the Surgeons' mistakes. They should not have been permitted to live.'

'I thought that these monsters were the products of teratogenic drugs given to them when they still were within the womb,' I said. 'You tell me now that Changelings were made by Surgeons. Which is so?'

'Both,' he replied. 'All Changelings today are descended from the flaws and errors committed by the Surgeons of the Years of Magic. Yet mothers in that unhappy group often enhance the monstrousness of their children with drugs, so that they will be more marketable. It is an ugly tribe not merely in looks. Small wonder that their guild was dissolved and they were thrust outside society. We –'

Something bright flew through the air, missing his face by less than a hand's breadth. He dropped to the floor and shouted to us to take cover. As I fell I saw a second missile fly toward us. The outworld being, still observing all phenomena, studied it impassively in the moment of life that remained to it. Then the weapon struck two thirds of the way up the outworlder's body and severed it instantly. Other missiles followed, clattering against the wall behind us. I saw our attackers: a band of

Changelings, fierce, hideous. We were unarmed. They moved toward us. I readied myself to die.

From the doorway a voice cried out: a familiar voice, using the thick and unfamiliar words of the language Changelings speak among themselves. Instantly the assault ceased. Those who menaced us turned toward the door. The Changeling Bernalt entered.

'I saw your vehicle,' he said. 'I thought you might be here, and perhaps in trouble. It seems I came in time.'

'Not altogether,' said the Surgeon. He indicated the fallen outworlder, which was beyond all aid. 'But why this attack?'

Bernalt gestured. '*They* will tell you.'

We looked at the five Changelings who had ambushed us. They were not of the educated, civilized sort such as Bernalt, nor were any two of them of the same styles; each was a twisted, hunched mockery of the human form, one with ropy tendrils descending from his chin, one with a face that was a featureless void, another whose ears were giant cups, and so forth. From the one closest to us, a creature with small platforms jutting from his skin in a thousand places, we learned why we had been assaulted. In a brutal Aguptan dialect he told us that we had profaned a temple sacred to Changelings. 'We keep out of Jorslem,' he told us. 'Why must you come here?'

Of course he was right. We asked forgiveness as sincerely as we could, and the Surgeon explained that he had visited this place long ago and it had not been a temple then. That seemed to soothe the Changeling, who admitted that only in recent years had his kind used it as a shrine. He was soothed even more when Olmayne opened the overpocket fastened between her breasts and offered a few glittering gold coins, part of the treasure she had brought with her from Perris. The bizarre and deformed beings were satisfied at that and allowed us to leave the building. We would have taken the dead outworlder with us, but during our parley with the Changelings the body had nearly vanished, nothing but a faint gray streak remaining on the sandy floor to tell us where it had fallen. 'A mortuary enzyme,' the

Surgeon explained. 'Triggered by interruption of the life processes.'

Others of this community of desert-dwelling Changelings were lurking about outside the building as we came forth. They were a tribe of nightmares, with skin of every texture and color, facial features arranged at random, all kinds of genetic improvisations of organs and bodily accessories. Bernalt himself, although their brother, seemed appalled by their monstrousness. They looked at him with awe. At the sight of us some of them fondled the throwing weapons at their hips, but a sharp command from Bernalt prevented any trouble.

He said, 'I regret the treatment you received and the death of the outworlder. But of course it is risky to enter a place that is sacred to backward and violent people.'

'We had no idea,' the Surgeon said. 'We never would have gone in if we had realized –'

'Of course. Of course.' Was there something patronizing about Bernalt's soft, civilized tones? 'Well, again I bid you farewell.'

I blurted suddenly, 'No. Travel with us to Jorslem! It's ridiculous for us to go separately to the same place.'

Olmayne gasped. Even the Surgeon seemed amazed. Only Bernalt remained calm. He said, 'You forget, friend, that it is improper for Pilgrims to journey with the guildless. Besides, I am here to worship at this shrine, and it will take me a while. I would not wish to delay you.' His hand reached out to mine. Then he moved away, entering the ancient Surgery. Scores of his fellow Changelings rushed in after him. I was grateful to Bernalt for his tact; my impulsive offer of companionship, though sincerely meant, had been impossible for him to accept.

We boarded our rollerwagons. In a moment we heard a dreadful sound: a discordant Changeling hymn in praise of I dare not think what deity, a scraping, grinding, screeching song as misshapen as those who uttered it.

'The beasts,' Olmayne muttered. 'A sacred shrine! A Changeling temple! How loathsome! They might have killed us all, Tomis. How can such monsters have a religion?'

I made no reply. The Surgeon looked at Olmayne sadly and shook his head as though distressed by so little charity on the part of one who claimed to be a Pilgrim.

'They also are human,' he said.

At the next town along our route we reported the starborn being's death to the occupying authorities. Then, saddened and silent, we three survivors continued onward to the place where the coastline trends north rather than east. We were leaving sleepy Agupt behind and entering now into the borders of the land in which holy Jorslem lies.

EIGHT

The city of Jorslem sits some good distance inland from Lake Medit on a cool plateau guarded by a ring of low, barren, rock-strewn mountains. All my life, it seemed, had been but a preparation for my first glimpse of this golden city, whose image I knew so well. Hence when I saw its spires and parapets rising in the east, I felt not so much awe as a sense of homecoming.

A winding road took us down through the encircling hills to the city, whose wall was made of squared blocks of a fine stone, dark pink-gold in color. The houses and shrines, too, were of this stone. Groves of trees bordered the road, nor were they star-trees, but native products of Earth, as was fitting to this, the oldest of man's cities, older than Roum, older than Perris, its roots deep in the First Cycle.

The invaders, shrewdly, had not meddled with Jorslem's administration. The city remained under the governorship of the Guildmaster of Pilgrims, and even an invader was required to seek the Guildmaster's permission to enter. Of course, this was strictly a matter of form; the Pilgrim Guildmaster, like the Chancellor of the Rememberers and other such officials, was in truth a puppet subject to our conqueror's wishes. But that harsh fact was kept concealed. The invaders had left our holy city as a city apart, and we would not see them swaggering in armed teams through Jorslem's streets.

At the outer wall we formally requested entry from the Sentinel guarding the gate. Though elsewhere most Sentinels were now unemployed – since cities stood open by command of our masters – this man was in full guild array and calmly insisted on thorough procedure. Olmayne and I, as Pilgrims, were entitled to automatic access to Jorslem; yet he made us produce our starstones as evidence that we came by our robes and masks honestly, and then donned a thinking cap to check our names with the archives of our guild. In time we met approval. The Surgeon our companion had an easier time; he had applied in advance for entry while in Afreek, and after a moment to check his identity he was admitted.

Within the walls everything had the aspect of great antiquity. Jorslem alone of the world's cities still preserves much of its First Cycle architecture: not merely broken columns and ruined aqueducts, as in Roum, but whole streets, covered arcades, towers, boulevards, that have lasted through every upheaval our world has seen. And so once we passed into the city we wandered in wonder through its strangeness, down streets paved with cobbled stones, into narrow alleys cluttered with children and beggars, across markets fragrant with spices. After an hour of this we felt it was time to seek lodgings, and here it was necessary for us to part company with the Surgeon, since he was ineligible to stay at a Pilgrim hostelry, and it would have been costly and foolish for us to stay anywhere else. We saw him to the inn where he had previously booked a room. I thanked him for his good companionship on our journey, and he thanked us just as gravely and expressed the hope that he would see us again in Jorslem in the days to come. Then Olmayne and I took leave of him and rented quarters in one of the numerous places catering to the Pilgrim trade.

The city exists solely to serve Pilgrims and casual tourists, and so it is really one vast hostelry; robed Pilgrims are as common in Jorslem's streets as Fliers in Hind. We settled and rested awhile; then we dined and afterward walked along a broad street from which we could see, to the east, Jorslem's inner and most sacred district. There is a city within a city here. The most ancient part, so small it can be traversed in less than an hour on foot, is wrapped in a high wall of its own. Therein lie shrines revered by Earth's former religions: the Christers, the Hebers, the Mislams. The place where the god of the Christers died is said to be there, but this may be a distortion wrought by time, since what kind of god is it that dies? On a high place in one corner of the Old City stands a gilded dome sacred to the Mislams, which is carefully tended by the common folk of Jorslem. And to the fore part of that high place are the huge gray blocks of a stone wall worshiped by the Hebers. These things remain, but the ideas behind them are lost; never while I was among the Rememberers did I meet any scholar who could explain the merit of worshiping a wall or a gilded dome. Yet the old records assure us that these three First Cycle creeds were of great depth and richness.

In the Old City, also, is a Second Cycle place that was of much more immediate interest to Olmayne and myself. As we stared through the darkness at the holy precincts Olmayne said, 'We should make application tomorrow at the house of renewal.'

'I agree. I long now to give up some of my years.'

'Will they accept me, Tomis?'

'Speculating on it is idle,' I told her. 'We will go, and we will apply, and your question will be answered.'

She said something further, but I did not hear her words, for at that moment three Fliers passed above me, heading east. One was male, two female; they flew naked, according to the custom of their guild; and the Flier in the center of the group was a slim, fragile girl, mere bones and wings, moving with a grace that was exceptional even for her airy kind.

'*Avluela!*' I gasped.

The trio of Fliers disappeared beyond the parapets of the Old City. Stunned, shaken, I clung to a tree for support and struggled for breath.

'Tomis?' Olmayne said. 'Tomis, are you ill?'

'I know it was Avluela. They said she had gone back to Hind, but no, that was Avluela! How could I mistake her?'

'You've said that about every Flier you've seen since leaving Perris,' said Olmayne coldly.

'But this time I'm certain! Where is a thinking cap? I must check with the Fliers' Lodge at once!'

Olmayne's hand rested on my arm. 'It's late, Tomis. You act feverish. Why this excitement over your skinny Flier, anyway? What did she mean to you?'

'She –'

I halted, unable to put my meaning in words. Olmayne knew the story of my journey up out of Agupt with the girl, how as a celibate old Watcher I had conceived a kind of parental fondness for her, how I had perhaps felt something more powerful than that, how I had lost her to the false Changeling Gormon, and how *he* in turn had lost her to the Prince of Roum. But yet what was Avluela to me? Why did a glimpse of someone who merely might have been Avluela send me into this paroxysm of confusion? I chased symbols in my turbulent mind and found no answers.

'Come back to the inn and rest,' Olmayne said. 'Tomorrow we must seek renewal.'

First, though, I donned a cap and made contact with the Fliers' Lodge. My thoughts slipped through the shielding interface to the storage brain of the guild registry; I asked and received the answer I had sought. Avluela of the Fliers was indeed now a resident in Jorslem. 'Take this message for her,' I said. 'The Watcher she knew in Roum now is here as a Pilgrim, and wishes to meet her outside the house of renewal at midday tomorrow.'

With that done, I accompanied Olmayne to our lodgings. She seemed sullen and aloof; and when she unmasked in my room her face appeared rigid with – jealousy? Yes. To Olmayne all men were vassals, even one so shriveled and worn as I; and she loathed it that another woman could kindle such a flame in me. When I drew forth my starstone, Olmayne at first would not join me in communion. Only when I began the rituals did she submit. But I was so tense that night I was unable to make the merging with the Will, nor could she achieve it; and thus we faced one another glumly for half an hour, and abandoned the attempt, and parted for the night.

NINE

One must go by one's self to the house of renewal. At dawn I awoke, made a brief and more successful communion, and set out unbreakfasted, without Olmayne. In half an hour I stood before the golden wall of the Old City; in half an hour more I had finished my crossing of the inner city's tangled lanes. Passing before that gray wall so dear to the ancient Hebers, I went up onto the high place; I passed near the gilded dome of the vanished Mislams and, turning to the left, followed the stream of Pilgrims which already at this early hour was proceeding to the house of renewal.

This house is a Second Cycle building, for it was then that the renewal process was conceived; and of all that era's science, only renewal has come down to us approximately as it must have been practiced in that time. Like those other few Second Cycle structures that survive, the house of renewal is supple and sleek, architecturally understated, with deft curves and smooth textures; it is without windows; it bears no external ornament whatever. There are many doors. I placed myself before the easternmost entrance, and in an hour's time I was admitted.

Just inside the entrance I was greeted by a green-robed member of the guild of Renewers – the first member of this guild I had ever seen. Renewers are recruited entirely from Pilgrims who are willing to make it their life's work to remain in Jorslem and aid others toward renewal. Their guild is under the same administration as the Pilgrims; a single guildmaster directs the destinies of both; even the garb is the same except for color. In effect Pilgrims and Renewers are of one guild and represent different phases of the same affiliation. But a distinction is always drawn.

The Renewer's voice was light and cheerful. 'Welcome to this house, Pilgrim. Who are you, where are you from?'

'I am the Pilgrim Tomis, formerly Tomis of the Rememberers, and prior to that a Watcher, born to the name Wuellig. I am native to the Lost Continents and have traveled widely both before and after beginning my Pilgrimage.'

'What do you seek here?'

'Renewal. Redemption.'

'May the Will grant your wishes,' said the Renewer. 'Come with me.'

I was led through a close, dimly lit passage into a small stone cell. The Renewer instructed me to remove my mask, enter into a state of communion, and wait. I freed myself from the bronze grillwork and clasped my starstone tightly. The familiar sensations of communion stole over me, but no union with the Will took place; rather, I felt a specific link forming with the mind of another human being. Although mystified, I offered no resistance.

Something probed my soul. Everything was drawn forth and laid out as if for inspection on the floor of the cell: my acts of selfishness and of cowardice, my flaws and failings, my doubts, my despairs, above all the most shameful of my acts, the selling of the Rememberers' document to the invader overlord. I beheld these things and knew that I was unworthy of renewal. In this house one might extend one's lifetime two or three times over; but why should the Renewers offer such benefits to anyone as lacking in merit as I?

I remained a long while in contemplation of my faults. Then the contact broke, and a different Rememberer, a man of remarkable stature, entered the cell.

'The mercy of the Will is upon you, friend,' he said, reaching forth fingers of extraordinary length to touch the tips of mine.

When I heard that deep voice and saw those white fingers,

I knew that I was in the presence of a man I had met briefly before, as I stood outside the gates of Roum in the season before the conquest of Earth. He had been a Pilgrim then, and he had invited me to join him on his journey to Jorslem, but I had declined, for Roum had beckoned to me.

'Was your Pilgrimage an easy one?' I asked.

'It was a valuable one,' he replied. 'And you? You are a Watcher no longer, I see.'

'I am in my third guild this year.'

'With one more yet to come,' he said.

'Am I to join you in the Renewers, then?'

'I did not mean that guild, friend Tomis. But we can talk more of that when your years are fewer. You have been approved for renewal, I rejoice to tell you.'

'Despite my sins?'

'Because of your sins, such that they are. At dawn tomorrow you enter the first of the renewal tanks. I will be your guide through your second birth. I am the Renewer Talmit. Go, now, and ask for me when you return.'

'One question —'

'Yes?'

'I made my Pilgrimage together with a woman, Olmayne, formerly a Rememberer of Perris. Can you tell me if she has been approved for renewal as well?'

'I know nothing of this Olmayne.'

'She's not a good woman,' I said. 'She is vain, imperious, and cruel. But yet I think she is not beyond saving. Can you do anything to help her?'

'I have no influence in such things,' Talmit said. 'She must face interrogation like everyone else. I can tell you this, though: virtue is not the only criterion for renewal.'

He showed me from the building. Cold sunlight illuminated the city. I was drained and depleted, too empty even to feel cheered that I had qualified for renewal. It was midday; I remembered my appointment with Avluela; I circled the house of renewal in rising anxiety. Would she come?

She was waiting by the front of the building, beside a

glittering monument from Second Cycle days. Crimson jacket, furry leggings, glass bubbles on her feet, telltale humps on her back: from afar I could make her out to be a Flier. 'Avluela!' I called.

She whirled. She looked pale, thin, even younger than when I had last seen her. Her eyes searched my face, once again masked, and for a moment she was bewildered.

'Watcher?' she said. 'Watcher, is that you?'

'Call me Tomis now,' I told her. 'But I am the same man you knew in Agupt and Roum.'

'Watcher! Oh, Watcher! *Tomis*.' She clung to me. 'How long it's been! So much has happened!' She sparkled now, and the paleness fled her cheeks. 'Come, let's find an inn, a place to sit and talk! How did you discover me here?'

'Through your guild. I saw you overhead last night.'

'I came here in the winter. I was in Pars for a while, halfway back to Hind, and then I changed my mind. There could be no going home. Now I live near Jorslem and I help with –' She cut her sentence sharply off. 'Have you won renewal, Tomis?'

We descended from the high place into a humbler part of the inner city. 'Yes,' I said, 'I am to be made younger. My guide is the Renewer Talmit – we met him as a Pilgrim outside Roum, do you remember?'

She had forgotten that. We seated ourselves at an open-air patio adjoining an inn, and Servitors brought us food and wine. Her gaiety was infectious; I felt renewed just to be with her. She spoke of those final cataclysmic days in Roum, when she had been taken into the palace of the Prince as a concubine; and she told me of that terrible moment when Gormon the Changeling defeated the Prince of Roum on the evening of the conquest – announcing himself as no Changeling but an invader in disguise, and taking from the Prince at once his throne, his concubine, and his vision.

'Did the Prince die?' she asked.

'Yes, but not of his blinding.' I told her how that proud man had fled Roum disguised as a Pilgrim, and how I had accompanied him to Perris, and how, while we were among the Rememberers, he had involved himself with Olmayne, and had been slain by Olmayne's husband, whose life was thereupon taken by his wife. 'I also saw Gormon in Perris,' I said. 'He goes by the name of Victorious Thirteen now. He is high in the councils of the invaders.'

Avluela smiled. 'Gormon and I were together only a short while after the conquest. He wanted to tour Eyrop; I flew with him to Donsk and Sved, and there he lost interest in me. It was then that I felt I must go home to Hind, but later I changed my mind. When does your renewal begin?'

'At dawn.'

'Oh, Tomis, how will it be when you are a young man? Did you know that I loved you? All the time we traveled, all while I was sharing Gormon's bed and consorting with the Prince, you were the one I wanted! But of course you were a Watcher, and it was impossible. Besides, you were so old. Now you no longer Watch, and soon you will no longer be old, and –' Her hand rested on mine. 'I should never have left your side. We both would have been spared much suffering.'

'We learn, from suffering,' I said.

'Yes. Yes. I see that. How long will your renewal take?'

'The usual time, whatever that may be.'

'After that, what will you do? What guild will you choose? You can't be a Watcher, not now.'

'No, nor a Rememberer either. My guide Talmit spoke of some other guild, which he would not name, and assumed that I would enroll in it when I was done with renewal. I supposed he thought I'd stay here and join the Renewers, but he said it was another guild.'

'Not the Renewers,' said Avluela. She leaned close. 'The Redeemers,' she whispered.

'Redeemers? That is a guild I do not know.'

'It is newly founded.'

'No new guild has been established in more than a –'

'This is the guild Talmit meant. You would be a desirable member. The skills you developed when you were a Watcher make you exceptionally useful.'

'Redeemers,' I said, probing the mystery. '*Redeemers*. What does this guild do?'

Avluela smiled jauntily. 'It rescues troubled souls and saves unhappy worlds. But this is no time to talk of it. Finish your business in Jorslem, and everything will become clear.' We rose. Her lips brushed mine. 'This is the last time I'll see you as an old man. It will be strange, Tomis, when you're renewed!'

She left me then.

Toward evening I returned to my lodging. Olmayne was not in her room. A Servitor told me that she had been out all day. I waited until it was late; then I made my communion and slept, and at dawn I paused outside her door. It was sealed. I hurried to the house of renewal.

TEN

The renewer Talmit met me within the entrance and conducted me down a corridor of green tile to the first renewal tank. 'The Pilgrim Olmayne,' he informed me, 'has been accepted for renewal and will come here later this day.' This was the last reference to the affairs of another human being that I was to hear for some time. Talmit showed me into a small low room, close and humid, lit by dim blobs of slavelight and smelling faintly of crushed deathflower blossoms. My robe and my mask were taken from me, and the Renewer covered my head with a fine golden-green mesh of some flimsy metal, through which he sent a current; and when he removed the mesh, my hair was gone, my head was as glossy as the tiled walls. 'It makes insertion of the electrodes simpler,' Talmit explained. 'You may enter the tank, now.'

A gentle ramp led me down into the tank, which was a tub of no great size. I felt the warm soft slipperiness of mud beneath my feet, and Talmit nodded and told me it irradiated regenerative mud, which would stimulate the increase of cell division that was to bring about my renewal, and I accepted it. I stretched out on the floor of the tank with only my head above the shimmering dark violet fluid that it contained. The mud cradled and caressed my tired body. Talmit loomed above me, holding what seemed to be a mass of entangled copper wires, but as he pressed the wires to my bare scalp they opened as of their own accord and their tips sought my skull and burrowed down through skin and bone into the hidden wrinkled grayness. I felt nothing more than tiny prickling sensations. 'The electrodes,' Talmit explained, 'seek out the centers of aging within your brain; we transmit signals that will induce a reversal of the normal processes of decay, and your brain will lose its perception of the direction of the flow of time. Your body thus will become more receptive to the stimulation it receives from the environment of the renewal tank. Close your eyes.' Over my face he placed a breathing mask. He gave me a gentle shove, and the back of my head slipped from the edge of the tank, so that I floated out into the middle. The warmth increased. I dimly heard bubbling sounds. I imagined black sulfurous bubbles coming up from the mud and through the fluid in which I floated; I imagined that the fluid had turned the color of mud. Adrift in a tideless sea I lay, distantly aware that a current was passing over the electrodes, that something was tickling my brain, that I was engulfed in mud and in what could well have been an amniotic fluid. From far away came the deep voice of the Renewer Talmit summoning me to youth, drawing me back across the decades, unreeling time for me. There was a taste of salt in my mouth. Again I was crossing Earth Ocean, beset by pirates, defending my Watching equipment against their jeers and thrusts. Again I stood beneath the hot Aguptan sun meeting Avluela for the first time. I lived once more on Palash. I returned to the place of my birth in the western isles of the Lost Continents, in what formerly had been Usa-amrik. I watched Roum fall a second time. Fragments of memories swam through my softening brain. There was no sequence, no rational unrolling of events. I was a child. I was a weary ancient. I was among the Rememberers. I visited the

Somnambulists. I saw the Prince of Roum attempt to purchase eyes from an Artificer in Dijon. I bargained with the Procurator of Perris. I gripped the handles of my instruments and entered Watchfulness. I ate sweet things from a far-off world; I drew into my nostrils the perfume of springtime on Palash; I shivered in an old man's private winter; I swam in a surging sea, buoyant and happy; I sang; I wept; I resisted temptation; I yielded to temptations; I quarreled with Olmayne; I embraced Avluela; I experienced a flickering succession of nights and days as my biological clock moved in strange rhythms of reversal and acceleration. Illusions beset me. It rained fire from the sky; time rushed in several directions; I grew small and then enormous. I heard voices speaking in shades of scarlet and turquoise. Jagged music sparkled on the mountains. The sound of my drumming heartbeats was rough and fiery. I was trapped between strokes of my brain-piston, arms pressed to my sides so that I would occupy as little space as possible as it rammed itself home again and again and again. The stars throbbed, contracted, melted. Avluela said gently, 'We earn a second youthtime through the indulgent, benevolent impulses of the Will and through the performance of individual good works.' Olmayne said, 'How sleek I get!' Talmit said, 'These oscillations of perception signify only the dissolution of the wish toward self-destruction that lies at the heart of the aging process.' Gormon said, 'These perceptions of oscillation signify only the self-destruction of the wish toward dissolution that lies at the aging process of the heart.' The Procurator Manrule Seven said, 'We have been sent to this world as the devices of your purgation. We are instruments of the Will.' Earthclaim Nineteen said, 'On the other hand, permit me to disagree. The intersection of Earth's destinies and ours is purely accidental.' My eyelids turned to stone. The small creatures comprising my lungs began to flower. My skin sloughed off, revealing strands of muscle clinging to bone. Olmayne said, 'My pores grow smaller. My flesh grows tight. My breasts grow small.' Avluela said, 'Afterwards you will fly with us, Tomis.' The Prince of Roum covered his eyes with his hands. The towers of Roum swayed in the winds of the sun. I snatched a shawl from a passing Rememberer. Clowns wept in the streets of Perris. Talmit said, 'Awaken, now, Tomis, come up from it, open your eyes.'

'I am young again,' I said.

'Your renewal has only begun,' he said.

I could no longer move. Attendants seized me and swatched me in porous wrappings, and placed me on a rolling car, and took me to a second tank, much larger, in which dozens of people floated, each in a dreamy seclusion from the others. Their naked skulls were festooned with electrodes; their eyes were covered with pink tape; their hands were peacefully joined on their chests. Into this tank I went, and there were no illusions here, only a long slumber unbroken by dreams. This time I awakened to the sounds of a rushing tide, and found myself passing feet first through a constricted conduit into a sealed tank, where I breathed only fluid, and where I remained something more than a minute and something less than a century, while layers of skin were peeling from my soul. It was slow, taxing work. The Surgeons worked at a distance, their hands thrust into gloves that controlled the tiny flaying-knives, and they flensed me of evil with flick after flick after flick of the little blades, cutting out guilt and sorrow, jealousy and rage, greed, lust, and impatience.

When they were done with me they opened the lid of the tank and lifted me out. I was unable to stand unaided. They attached instruments to my limbs that kneaded and massaged my muscles, restoring the tone. I walked again. I looked down at my bare body, strong and taut-fleshed and vigorous. Talmit came to me and threw a handful of mirror-dust into the air so that I could see myself; and as the tiny particles cohered, I peered at my gleaming reflection.

'No,' I said. 'You have the face wrong. I didn't look like that. The nose was sharper – the lips weren't so full – the hair not such a deep black –'

'We have worked from the records of the guild of Watchers,

Tomis. You are more exactly a replica of your early self than your own memory realizes.'

'Can that be?'

'If you prefer, we can shape you to fit your self-conceptions and not reality. But it would be a frivolous thing to do, and it would take much time.'

'No,' I said. 'It hardly matters.'

He agreed. He informed me that I would have to remain in the house of renewal a while longer, until I was fully adapted to my new self. I was given the neutral clothes of a guildless one to wear, for I was without affiliation now; my status as Pilgrim had ended with my renewal, and I might now opt for any guild that would admit me once I left the house. 'How long did my renewal last?' I asked Talmit as I dressed. He replied, 'You came here in summer. Now it is winter. We do not work swiftly.'

'And how fares my companion Olmayne?'

'We failed with her.'

'I don't understand.'

'Would you like to see her?' Talmit asked.

'Yes,' I said, thinking that he would bring me to Olmayne's tank. I stood on a ramp looking down into a sealed container; Talmit indicated a fiber telescope, and I peered into its staring eye and beheld Olmayne. Or rather, what I was asked to believe was Olmayne. A naked girl-child of about eleven, smooth-skinned and breastless, lay curled up in the tank, knees drawn close to the flat chest, thumb thrust in mouth. At first I did not understand. Then the child stirred, and I recognized the embryonic features of the regal Olmayne I had known: the wide mouth, the strong chin, the sharp, strong cheekbones. A dull shock of horror rippled through me, and I said to Talmit, 'What is this?'

'When the soul is too badly stained, Tomis, we must dig deep to cleanse it. Your Olmayne was a difficult case. We should not have attempted her; but she was insistent, and there were some indications that we might succeed with her. Those indications were in error, as you can see.'

'But what happened to her?'

'The renewal entered the irreversible stage before we could achieve a purging of her poisons,' Talmit said.

'You went too far? You made her too young?'

'As you can see. Yes.'

'What will you do? Why don't you get her out of there and let her grow up again?'

'You should listen more carefully, Tomis. I said the renewal is irreversible.'

'*Irreversible?*'

'She is lost in childhood's dreams. Each day she grows years younger. The inner clock whirls uncontrollably. Her body shrinks; her brain grows smooth. She enters babyhood shortly. She will never awaken.'

'And at the end –' I looked away. 'What then? A sperm and an egg, separating in the tank?'

'The retrogression will not go that far. She will die in infancy. Many are lost this way.'

'She spoke of the risks of renewal,' I said.

'Yet she insisted on our taking her. Her soul was dark, Tomis. She lived only for herself. She came to Jorslem to be cleansed, and now she has been cleansed, and she is at peace with the Will. Did you love her?'

'Never. Not for an instant.'

'Then what have you lost?'

'A segment of my past, perhaps.' I put my eye to the telescope again and beheld Olmayne, innocent now, restored to virginity, sexless, cleansed. At peace with the Will. I searched her oddly altered yet familiar face for an insight into her dreams. Had she known what was befalling her, as she tumbled helplessly into youthfulness? Had she cried out in anguish and frustration when she felt her life slipping away? Had there been a final flare of the old imperious Olmayne, before she sank into this unwanted purity? The child in the tank was smiling. The supple little body uncoiled, then drew more tightly into a huddled ball. Olmayne was at peace with the Will. Suddenly, as though Talmit had spread another mirror in the air, I looked into my own new self, and saw what had been done for me, and knew that I had been granted another life with the proviso that I make something more of it than I had of my first one, and I felt humbled, and pledged myself to serve the Will, and I was engulfed in joy that came in mighty waves, like the surging tides of Earth Ocean, and I said farewell to Olmayne, and asked Talmit to take me to another place.

ELEVEN

And Avluela came to me in my room in the house of renewal, and we both were frightened when we met. The jacket she wore left her bunched-up wings bare; they seemed hardly under her control at all, but fluttered nervously, starting to open a short way, their gossamer tips expanding in little quivering flickers. Her eyes were large and solemn; her face looked more lean and pointed than ever. We stared in silence at one another a long while; my skin grew warm, my vision hazy; I felt the churning of inner forces that had not pulled at me in decades, and I feared them even as I welcomed them.

'Tomis?' she said finally, and I nodded.

She touched my shoulders, my arms, my lips. And I put my fingers to her wrists, her flanks, and then, hesitantly, to the shallow bowls of her breasts. Like two who had lost their sight we learned each other by touch. We were strangers. That withered old Watcher she had known and perhaps loved had gone, banished for the next fifty years or more, and in his place stood someone mysteriously transformed, unknown, unmet. The old Watcher had been a sort of father to her; what was this guildless young Tomis supposed to be? And what was she to me, a daughter no longer? I did not know myself of myself. I was alien to my sleek, taut skin. I was perplexed and delighted by the juices that now flowed, by the throbbings and swellings that I had nearly forgotten.

'Your eyes are the same,' she said. 'I would always know you by your eyes.'

'What have you done these many months, Avluela?'

'I have been flying every night. I flew to Agupt and deep into Afreek. Then I returned and flew to Stanbool. When it gets dark, I go aloft. Do you know, Tomis, I feel truly alive only when I'm up there?'

'You are of the Fliers. It is in the nature of your guild to feel that way.'

'One day we'll fly side by side, Tomis.'

I laughed at that. 'The old Surgeries are closed, Avluela. They work wonders here, but they can't transform me into a Flier. One must be born with wings.'

'One doesn't need wings to fly.'

'I know. The invaders lift themselves without the help of wings. I saw you, one day soon after Roum fell – you and Gormon in the sky together –' I shook my head. 'But I am no invader either.'

'You will fly with me, Tomis. We'll go aloft, and not only by night, even though my wings are merely nightwings. In bright sunlight we'll soar together.'

Her fantasy pleased me. I gathered her into my arms, and she was cool and fragile against me, and my own body pulsed with new heat. For a while we talked no more of flying, though I drew back from taking what she offered at that moment, and was content merely to caress her. One does not awaken in a single lunge.

Later we walked through the corridors, passing others who were newly renewed, and we went into the great central room whose ceiling admitted the winter sunlight, and studied each other by that changing pale light, and walked, and talked again. I leaned a bit on her arm, for I did not have all my strength yet, and so in a sense it was as it had been for us in the past, the girl helping the old dodderer along. When she saw me back to my room, I said, 'Before I was renewed, you told me of a new guild of Redeemers. I –'

'There is time for that later,' she said, displeased.

In my room we embraced, and abruptly I felt the full fire of the renewed leap up within me, so that I feared I might consume her cool slim body. But it is a fire that does not consume – it only kindles its counterpart in others. In her ecstasy her wings unfolded until I was wrapped in their silken softness. And as I gave myself to the violence of joy, I knew I would not need again to lean on her arm.

We ceased to be strangers; we ceased to feel fear with one another. She came to me each day at my exercise time, and I walked with her, matching her stride for stride. And the fire burned even higher and more brightly for us.

Talmit was with me frequently too. He showed me the arts of using my renewed body, and helped me successfully grow youthful. I declined his invitation to view Olmayne once more. One day he told me that her retrogression had come to its end. I felt no sorrow over that, just a curious brief emptiness that soon passed.

'You will leave here soon,' the Renewer said. 'Are you ready?'

'I think so.'

'Have you given much thought to your destination after this house?'

'I must seek a new guild, I know.'

'Many guilds would have you, Tomis. But which do you want?'

'The guild in which I would be most useful to mankind,' I said. 'I owe the Will a life.'

Talmit said, 'Has the Flier girl spoken to you of the possibilities before you?'

'She mentioned a newly founded guild.'

'Did she give it a name?'

'The guild of Redeemers.'

'What do you know of it?'

'Very little,' I said.

'Do you wish to know more?'

'If there is more to know.'

'I am of the guild of Redeemers,' Talmit said. 'So is the Flier Avluela.'

'You both are already guilded! How can you belong to more than one guild? Only the Dominators were permitted such freedom; and they –'

'Tomis, the guild of Redeemers accepts members from all other guilds. It is the supreme guild, as the guild of Dominators once was. In its ranks are Rememberers and Scribes, Indexers, Servitors, Fliers, Landholders, Somnambulists, Surgeons, Clowns, Merchants, Vendors. There are Changelings as well, and –'

'Changelings?' I gasped. 'They are outside all guilds, by law! How can a guild embrace Changelings?'

'This is the guild of Redeemers. Even Changelings may win redemption, Tomis.'

Chastened, I said, 'Even Changelings, yes. But how strange it is to think of such a guild!'

'Would you despise a guild that embraces Changelings?'

'I find this guild difficult to comprehend.'

'Understanding will come at the proper time.'

'When is the proper time?'

'The day you leave this place,' said Talmit.

That day arrived shortly. Avluela came to fetch me. I stepped forth uncertainly into Jorslem's springtime to complete the ritual of renewal. Talmit had instructed her on how to guide me. She took me through the city to the holy places, so that I could worship at each of the shrines. I knelt at the wall of the Hebers and at the gilded dome of the Mislams; then I went down into the lower part of the city, through the marketplace, to the gray, dark, ill-fashioned building covering the place where the god of the Christers is said to have died; then I went to the spring of knowledge and the fountain of the Will, and from there to the guildhouse of the guild of Pilgrims to surrender my mask and robes and starstone, and thence to the wall of the Old City. At each of these places I offered myself to the Will with words I had waited long to speak. Pilgrims and ordinary citizens of Jorslem gathered at a respectful distance; they knew that I had been lately renewed and hoped that some emanation from my new youthful body would bring them good fortune. At last my obligations were fulfilled. I was a free man in full health, able now to choose the quality of the life I wished to lead.

Avluela said, 'Will you come with me to the Redeemers now?'

'Where will we find them? In Jorslem?'

'In Jorslem, yes. A meeting will convene in an hour's time for the purpose of welcoming you into membership.'

From her tunic she drew something small and gleaming, which I recognized in bewilderment as a starstone. 'What are you doing with that?' I asked. 'Only Pilgrims —'

'Put your hand over mine,' she said, extending a fist in which the starstone was clenched.

I obeyed. Her small pinched face grew rigid with concentration for a moment. Then she relaxed. She put the starstone away.

'Avluela, what —?'

'A signal to the guild,' she said gently. 'A notice to them to gather now that you are on your way.'

'How did you get that stone?'

'Come with me,' she said. 'Oh, Tomis, if only we could fly there! But it is not far. We meet almost in the shadow of the house of renewal. Come, Tomis. Come!'

TWELVE

There was no light in the room. Avluela led me into the subterranean blackness, and told me that I had reached the guildhall of the Redeemers, and left me standing by myself. 'Don't move,' she cautioned.

I sensed the presence of others in the room about me. But I heard nothing and saw nothing.

Something was thrust toward me.

Avluela said, 'Put out your hands. What do you feel?'

I touched a small square cabinet resting, perhaps, on a metal framework. Along its face were familiar dials and levers. My groping hands found handles rising from the cabinet's upper surface. At once it was as though all my renewal had been undone, and the conquest of Earth canceled as well: I was a Watcher again, for surely this was a Watcher's equipment!

I said, 'It is not the same cabinet I once had. But it is not greatly different.'

'Have you forgotten your skills, Tomis?'

'I think they remain with me even now.'

'Use the machine, then,' said Avluela. 'Do your Watching once more, and tell me what you see.'

Easily and happily I slipped into the old attitudes. I performed the preliminary rituals quickly, clearing my mind of doubts and frictions. It was surprisingly simple to bring myself into a spirit of Watchfulness; I had not attempted it since the night Earth fell, and yet it seemed to me that I was able to enter the state more rapidly than in the old days.

Now I grasped the handles. How strange they were! They did not terminate in the grips to which I was accustomed: rather, something cool and hard was mounted at the tip of each handle. A gem of some kind, perhaps. Possibly even a starstone, I realized. My hands closed over the twin coolnesses. I felt a moment of apprehension, even of raw fear. Then I regained the necessary tranquillity, and my soul flooded into the device before me, and I began to Watch.

In my Watchfulness I did not soar to the stars, as I had in the old days. Although I perceived, my perception was limited to the immediate surroundings of my room. Eyes closed, body hunched in trance, I reached out and came first to Avluela; she was near me, almost upon me. I saw her plainly. She smiled; she nodded; her eyes were aglow.

— I love you.

– Yes, Tomis. And we will be together always.

– I have never felt so close to another person.

– In this guild we are all close, all the time. We are the Redeemers, Tomis. We are new. Nothing like this has been on Earth before.

– How am I speaking to you, Avluela?

– Your mind speaks to mine through the machine. And some day the machine will not be needed.

– And then we will fly together?

– Long before then, Tomis.

The starstones grew warm in my hands. I clearly perceived the instrument, now: a Watcher's cabinet, but with certain modifications, among them the starstones mounted on the handles. And I looked beyond Avluela and saw other faces, ones that I knew. The austere figure of the Renewer Talmit was to my left. Beside him stood the Surgeon with whom I had journeyed to Jorslem, with the Changeling Bernalt at his elbow, and now at last I knew what business it was that had brought these men of Nayrub to the holy city. The others I did not recognize; but there were two Fliers, and a Rememberer grasping his shawl, and a woman Servitor, and others. And I saw them all by an inner light for the room was as dark as it had been when I entered it. Not only did I see them, but I touched them, mind to mind.

The mind I touched first was Bernalt's. I met it easily though fearfully, drew back, met it again. He greeted me and welcomed me. I realized then that only if I could look upon a Changeling as my brother could I, and Earth itself, win the sought-for redemption. For until we were truly one people, how could we earn an end to our punishment?

I tried to enter Bernalt's mind but I was afraid. How could I hide those prejudices, those petty contempts, those conditioned reflexes with which we unavoidably think of Changelings?

'Hide nothing,' he counseled. 'Those things are no secret to me. Give them up now and join me.'

I struggled. I cast out demons. I summoned up the memory

of the moment outside the Changeling shrine, after Bernalt had saved us, when I had invited him to journey with us. How had I felt then toward him? Had I regarded him, at least for a moment, as a brother?

I amplified that moment of gratitude and companionship. I let it swell, and blaze, and it obliterated the encrustations of scorn and empty disdain; and I saw the human soul beneath the strange Changeling surface, and I broke through that surface and found the path to redemption. He drew me toward his mind.

I joined Bernalt, and he enrolled me in his guild. I was of the Redeemers now.

Through my mind rolled a voice, and I did not know whether I heard the resonant boom of Talmit, or the dry ironic tone of the Surgeon, or Bernalt's controlled murmur, or Avluela's soft whisper, for it was all these voices at once, and others, and they said:

'When all mankind is enrolled in our guild, we will be conquered no longer. When each of us is part of every other one of us, our sufferings will end. There is no need for us to struggle against our conquerors, for we will absorb them, once we are all Redeemed. Enter us, Tomis who was the Watcher Wuellig.'

And I entered.

And I became the Surgeon and the Flier and the Renewer and the Changeling and the Servitor and the rest. And they became me. And so long as my hands gripped the starstones we were of one soul and one mind. This was not the merging of communion, in which a Pilgrim sinks anonymously into the Will, but rather a union of self and self, maintaining independence within a larger dependence. It was the keen perception one gets from Watching coupled with the submergence in a larger entity that one gets from communion, and I knew this was something wholly new on Earth, not merely the founding of a new guild but the initiation of a new cycle of human existence, the birth of the Fourth Cycle upon this defeated planet.

The voice said, 'Tomis, we will Redeem those in greatest need first. We will go into Agupt, into the desert where miserable Changelings huddle in an ancient building that they worship, and we will take them into us and make them clean again. We will go on, to the west, to a pitiful village smitten by the crystallization disease, and we will reach the souls of the villagers and free them from taint, and the crystallization will cease and their bodies will be healed. And we will go on beyond Agupt, to all the lands of the world, and find those who are without guilds, and those who are without hope, and those who are without tomorrows, and we will give them life and purpose again. And a time will come when all Earth is Redeemed.'

They put a vision before me of a transformed planet, and of the harsh-faced invaders yielding peacefully to us and begging to be incorporated into that new thing that had germinated in the midst of their conquest. They showed me an Earth that had been purged of its ancient sins.

Then I felt it was time to withdraw my hands from the machine I grasped, and I withdrew my hands.

The vision ebbed. The glow faded. But yet I was no longer alone in my skull, for some contact lingered, and the room ceased to be dark.

'How did this happen?' I asked. 'When did this begin?'

'In the days after the conquest,' said Talmit, 'we asked ourselves why we had fallen so easily, and how we could lift ourselves above what we had been. We saw that our guilds had not provided enough of a structure for our lives, that some closer union was our way to redemption. We had the starstones; we had the instruments of Watching; all that remained was to fuse them.'

The Surgeon said, 'You will be important to us, Tomis, because you understand how to throw your mind forth. We seek former Watchers. They are the nucleus of our guild. Once your soul roved the stars to search out mankind's enemies; now it will roam the Earth to bring mankind together.'

Avluela said, 'You will help me to fly, Tomis, even by day. And you will fly beside me.'

'When do you leave?' I asked.

'Now,' she said. 'I go to Agupt, to the temple of the Change-lings, to offer them what we have to offer. And all of us will join to give me strength, and that strength will be focused through you, Tomis.' Her hands touched mine. Her lips brushed mine. 'The life of Earth begins again, now, this year, this new cycle. Oh, Tomis, we are all reborn!'

THIRTEEN

I remained alone in the room. The others scattered. Avluela went above, into the street. I put my hands to the mounted starstones, and I saw her as clearly as though she stood beside me. She was preparing herself for flight. First she put off her clothing, and her bare body glistened in the afternoon sun. Her little body seemed impossibly delicate; a strong wind would shatter her, I thought. Then she knelt, bowed, made her ritual. She spoke to herself, yet I heard her words, the words Fliers say as they ready themselves to leave the ground. All guilds are one in this new guild; we have no secrets from one another; there are no mysteries. And as she beseeched the favor of the Will and the support of all her kind, my prayers joined with hers.

She rose and let her wings unfold. Some passers-by looked oddly at her, not because there was anything unusual about the sight of a naked Flier in the streets of Jorslem, but because the sunlight was so strong and her transparent wings, so lightly stained with pigment, were evidently nightwings, incapable of withstanding the pressure of the solar wind.

'I love you,' we said to her, and our hands ran lightly over her satiny skin in a brief caress.

Her nostrils flickered in delight. Her small girl-child's breasts became agitated. Her wings now were fully spread, and they gleamed wonderously in the sunlight.

'Now we fly to Agupt,' she murmured, 'to Redeem the

Changelings and make them one with us, Tomis, will you come with me?'

'I will be with you,' we said, and I gripped the starstones tightly and crouched over my cabinet of instruments in the dark room beneath the place where she stood. 'We will fly together, Avluela.'

'Up then,' she said, and we said, 'Up.'

Her wings beat, curving to take the wind, and we felt her struggling in the first moment, and we gave her the strength she needed, and she took it as it poured from us through me to her, and we rose high. The spires and parapets of Jorslem the golden grew small, and the city became a pink dot in the green hills, and Avluela's throbbing wings thrust her swiftly westward, toward the setting sun, toward the land of Agupt. Her ecstasy swept through us all. 'See, Tomis, how wonderful it is, far above everything? Do you feel it?'

'I feel it,' I whispered. 'The cool wind against bare flesh – the wind in my hair – we drift on the currents, we coast, we soar, Avluela, we soar!'

To Agupt. To the sunset.

We looked down at sparkling Lake Medit. In the distance somewhere was Land Bridge. To the north, Eyrop. To the south, Afreek. Far ahead, beyond Earth Ocean, lay my homeland. Later I would return there, flying westward with Avluela, bringing the good news of Earth's transformation.

From this height one could not tell that our world had ever been conquered. One saw only the beauty of the colors of the land and the sea, not the checkpoints of the invaders.

Those checkpoints would not long endure. We would conquer our conquerors, not with weapons but with love; and as the Redemption of Earth became universal we would welcome into our new self even the beings who had seized our planet.

'I knew that some day you would fly beside me, Tomis,' said Avluela.

In my dark room I sent new surges of power through her wings.

She hovered over the desert. The old Surgery, the Change-ling shrine, would soon be in sight. I grieved that we would have to come down. I wished we could stay aloft forever, Avluela and I.

'We will, Tomis, we will!' she told me. 'Nothing can separate us now! You believe that, don't you, Tomis?'

'Yes,' we said, 'I believe that.' And we guided her down through the darkening sky.

ACKNOWLEDGEMENTS

A Time of Changes first published in Great Britain 1973 by Victor
   Gollancz Ltd and in paperback 1986
Downward to the Earth first published in Great Britain 1977 by
   Victor Gollancz Ltd and in paperback 1990
The Second Trip first published in the United States 1981 by
   Avon Books; not previously published in Great Britain
Dying Inside first published in Great Britain 1975 by Sidgwick
   and Jackson Ltd and in paperback by Victor Gollancz Ltd
   1989
Nightwings first published in Great Britain 1972 by Sidgwick
   and Jackson Ltd and in paperback by Futura 1987

Neuromancer

William Gibson

'A masterpiece that moves faster than the speed of thought and is chilling in its implications.' *New York Times*

The Matrix: a graphic representation of data abstracted from the banks of every computer in the human system; a consensual hallucination experienced daily by billions of legitimate users in the Sprawl alone. And by Case, computer cowboy, until his nervous system is grievously maimed by a client he double crossed. Japanese experts in nerve splicing and microbionics have left him broke and close to dead. But at last Case has found a cure. He's going back into the system. Not for the bliss of cyberspace but to steal again, this time from the big boys, the almighty megacorps. In return, should he survive, he will stay cured.

Cyberspace and virtual reality were invented in this book. It stands alongside *1984* and *Brave New World* as one of the twentieth century's most potent novels of the future.

'Case is the Marlowe of the mainframe age' *Vox*

'The pessimistic vision of *Neuromancer* has inspired technologists from Silicon Valley to Wall Street and a global network of computer hackers who have committed countless nefarious deeds in the book's honour . . . *Neuromancer* was a literary Big Bang' *The Sunday Times*

'Set for brainstun . . . one of the most unusual and involving narratives to be read in many an artificially blue moon' *The Times*

'A mindbender of a read . . . fully realized in its technological and psychosexual dimensions' *Village Voice*

ISBN 0 00 6488041-1

The Collected Stories
of Robert Silverberg

VOLUME 3:
BEYOND THE SAFE ZONE

'When one contemplates Robert Silverberg it can only be
with awe. In terms of excellence he has few peers, if any.
Beyond the Safe Zone is not just a desirable thing, it is a
necessary addition to the archives'   *Locus*

Volume 3 of the Collected Stories of Robert Silverberg,
one of the eminencies of science fiction, gathers together
work from a vital and fertile period, the 1970s. Herein: the
Nebula Award-winning story 'Good News from the
Vatican', in which the first robot pope is elected; the
Jupiter Award-winning novella 'The Feast of St Dionysus',
about a burned-out astronaut finding ecstasy in an ancient
cult; more secrets are revealed in 'Capricorn Games', the
sign of the goat and of Christ; in 'Many Mansions' an
exquisite time-travel paradox is made up of many
murders. A total of 26 dazzling stories from the master of
the craft take us on a voyage to a wealth of different
cultures and futures from which no one will return quite
the same.

'Where Silverberg goes today, the rest of science fiction
will follow tomorrow'   ISAAC ASIMOV

ISBN 0 586 21371 6

Voyage

Stephen Baxter

A novel of the right stuff

Voyage takes place in a world that almost existed but never was. John F. Kennedy survived the assassination attempt in Dallas. From his wheelchair in 1969, the former president sets NASA a new, daunting challenge: '*. . . to continue the building of our great ships, and to fly them onward to Mars.*'

His voice carries beyond the clamour of military and industrial lobbies keen to develop the Space Shuttle. Instead, Apollo flights continue, boosted by Wernher von Braun's cherished nuclear rocket. Both are high-risk technologies . . .

When the first Ares mission lifts off for Mars in 1986, it is both a triumphant climax and the end of a long saga of technical and human over-ambition. Ares carries three dedicated people, one of them a woman, who have sacrificed everything to achieve the single goal of reaching another planet: their stories weave through a decade of political drama leading to the transfiguring experience of a year-long journey away from earth.

'Arthur C. Clarke, Isaac Asimov, Robert Heinlein . . . now Stephen Baxter joins their exclusive ranks'   *New Scientist*

ISBN 0 00 648037 3

3001 The Final Odyssey

Arthur C. Clarke

'A one man literary Big Bang, Clarke has originated his own vast and teeming futurist universe'   *Sunday Times*

The body of Frank Poole, lost for a thousand years since the computer HAL caused his death en route to Jupiter, is retrieved, revived – and enhanced. In the most eagerly awaited sequel of all time, the terrifying truth of the Monoliths' mission is a mystery only Poole can resolve.

'Clarke displays his pre-eminent power to imagine the extraordinary and describe it with conviction. He is a true prophet'   *Times Literary Supplement*

'Well-paced and absorbing . . . It is as a flight of fancy by the master of science fiction that *3001* makes its mark'
     The Times

'Clarke reveals the ominous answer about the ultimate purpose of the monoliths in this excellent novel'
     Daily Telegraph

'The writing is sharp, the pace relentless, the descriptions both grand and graceful, the humour tastefully wry'
     Science Fiction Age

'Serene, uplifting, and icy clear'   *Mail on Sunday*

'From the moment I picked it up, I couldn't put it down. *3001 The Final Odyssey* is a tour de force that finally answers the questions that sparked the imaginations of an entire generation'   BUZZ ALDRIN

ISBN 0 586 06624 1